the jewish lover

The Jewish Lover

EDWARD TOPOL

Translated by
CHRISTOPHER BARNES

ST. MARTIN'S PRESS 🞰 NEW YORK

12/98

Design by Michaelann Zimmerman

Library of Congress Cataloging-in-Publication Data

Topol, Edward
    The Jewish lover / Edward Topol. — 1st ed.
      p. cm.
    ISBN 0-312-15557-3
    1. Jews—Soviet Union—Fiction. I. Title.
PS3570.0643J49 1998   98-21113
891.73—dc21   CIP

First Edition: December 1998

10 9 8 7 6 5 4 3 2 1

TO my beloved wife, Julia

foreword

The "midwife" who "delivered" this book was Mr. Albert Zuckerman, and I feel it would be appropriate here to say a few words about him.

Back in 1977 I made one of my regular applications for a Moscow residence permit, and from the Commission of Old Bolsheviks at the Moscow mayor's office I received one of their routine refusals. This meant I was not legally entitled to reside in Moscow, even though my application was endorsed by the Union of Soviet Cinematographers, and despite the fact that some of Russia's best-known movie producers had waxed eloquent about how vitally the country needed me—I was, after all, the scenarist of seven feature films, I had won several movie prizes, and I was also well known as a journalist. But the Bolsheviks didn't like my Jewish-sounding surname, and they refused even to let me spend my own money on acquiring a Moscow apartment. And since in Russia you couldn't stay in a hotel for more than three nights without a residence permit, I was forced for years to lodge with a series of hospitable friends. Then one day, a friend who later became a well-known deputy in the Russian parliament asked me why I bothered to live there like a dog. "If you want to live like that, you ought to try it in America!" he told me. "Go on, get out of here and try your luck in the U.S.!"

So I did just that. And for seventeen years I survived as a literary lone wolf in the U.S. and Canada. I hooked up with a prestigious literary agent in Manhattan. My books were published by Dutton, Book of the Month Club, and important publishers in England, France, Germany, the Netherlands, Japan, and elsewhere. But during all these years I never received any advice or comment, either from my publishers, editors, or my own agent. Apart, that is, from the usual requests to round each book off nicely by tacking on a happy ending.

Ten years ago, at a time when I was almost howling with loneliness, I called up a well-known Russian émigré writer in Washington. His wife answered. "Congratulations, old man!" she said. "We've seen your books on sale in Japan! It turns out you and Vasya have the same translator! But you'll have to excuse him. He can't come to the phone just now. He's writing a book for Random House!"

At about the same time I met another Russian émigré author at the entrance to the Slavic section of the New York Public Library. He was standing by the card catalogue, sifting through one of the box files. Seeing he was there alone, without his wife, I perked up and homed in on him, hoping the two of us might exchange a word and perhaps share a bottle of beer. But he suddenly thrust out an arm as if to fend me off. "Keep away!" he called. "I haven't time! I've got four books coming out in Germany!"

After that I lay low in the literary undergrowth. And though I had five books published in Germany, eleven in the Netherlands, and thirteen in Japan, I still panicked at rubbing shoulders with the literary elite—both Russian and American.

Perhaps you are wondering why I'm telling you all this? It's so you'll appreciate the change that suddenly took place. After all those years of living inside my lonely tortoiseshell, imagine my astonishment when I suddenly met a real human being. Al Zuckerman saw the translation of my still-raw manuscript as much more than just a means of making a quick sale. He invited me to lunch, and within five minutes of our meeting, I realized the miracle had happened: Here was my Editor, my Guide, my Agent, and my Friend—all rolled into one. Fighting his way through my impenetrable phonetics, Al Zuckerman immediately began putting this book together with me. And what he had to say was not at all the usual graphomaniac drivel. What he offered was precise, creative, and constructive professional advice. What a relief it was to know that I was no longer the only player on the field. Now I had a partner to whom I could pass the ball, who would advance my own game, and then pass back to me. After which, and thanks to him, I was eventually ready to strike for a goal!

In fact Al Zuckerman has helped lead several well-known writers to the goalpost—including Ken Follet, Anne Wallach, Eileen Goudge, Paul Wilson, and Olivia Goldsmith. In their dedications and acknowledgments, some have recorded how their books came to life thanks to his artistic and moral support. But all these authors write in English, of course, so dealing with them was easier. But to be the editor and agent for a foreign-language author is, I think, much harder and much more of a risk. For that reason I take responsibility for all the blemishes in this book. But the credit for many of its virtues should go to Al Zuckerman and also, of course, to my old friend and translator of several of my books, Christopher Barnes. I would also like to record my thanks to Jeremy Katz, a young editor with St. Martin's Press who also, incidentally, emerged from under the wing of Al Zuckerman.

Sexual polarity is the basic law of life and, maybe, the foundation of our world. This was best of all understood by the ancients, whereas we have become wretchedly impotent and continue to degenerate.

—Nicholas Berdyaev

Please note that I am not at all suggesting that to be a Jew is such a great achievement. The Jews, after all, do have their problems.

—Romain Gary

p r o l o g u e

Do you know what it means to be a Russian woman?" he asked. "That is, what it means to be a real Russian woman?"

He surveyed the faces of the girls seated around him. There were thirty of them, all teenage members of the Young Communist movement. Together they made up troop number six at the Sputnik pioneer camp. At his question everyone fell silent and the girls looked at him, intrigued and expectant. A glimmer of flame in the evening campfire glowed on the scarlet pioneer neckerchiefs, the blue shirts clinging to their pliant young breasts, and the shorts bleached and laundered to set off the tan of legs that had grown strong after a summer's hiking, swimming, and volleyball. In the darkness behind them there was only a faint suggestion of the broad river with its lights twinkling on the fishermen's buoys, and the timber rafts in midstream drifting by in slow procession.

"And anyway, who is this real Russian woman, do you think?" he asked in a calm and steady voice. "Is it Anna Karenina who betrayed her husband? Or is it Natasha Rostova, who every year gave birth to yet another child? Or is it some courtesan like Nastasia Filippovna in Dostoyevsky's novel *The Idiot*? Or could it be Sonya Marmeladova, the pathetic little prostitute from *Crime and Punishment*? . . . No, don't laugh. It really is a very interesting question. Just look: the French have persuaded the whole world that French women are more fashion conscious and sophisticated than any others. It's true isn't it? And the Spaniards have convinced us that Spanish women are the most fiery and sensuous, haven't they? And we know that English women are supposed to be cold and standoffish. And Jewish and Japanese women supposedly make the best mothers. But what about Russian women? All of you are going to be the Russian women of the future. No, come on, don't just sit there giggling! You are going to be the next generation of Russian women. . . . Who else if not you? But what do you really know about yourselves?"

He broke a dry fir twig across his knee and stirred the charred logs of the campfire with it. The flame spurted up hungrily as it caught the fir needles, and he looked up again at his audience. He was only slightly older than they were—some six or seven years—and he was exhausted by the daily battle for their attention. Their thoughts were forever drifting away from the subject of discussion. And their eyes always had the mocking glint of provocation—as though these young striplings knew some secret that a twenty-year-old like himself could never guess. At last, however, he now seemed to have found a subject that truly riveted their attention. It was natural, after all: at their age they were interested in anything however remotely connected with the word *woman*. But he had no intention of rushing his story. . . .

" 'She'll halt a charger in its tracks,/Into the blazing hut rush back . . .' " he quoted the lines of Russian poetry. "According to our literature, that's what Russian women are apparently capable of. Even the greatest Russian writers, like Tolstoy, have really added nothing to what these lines tell us. But I wonder, is that really your greatest quality—to behave like Hercules in skirts? Or act like a female fire brigade? Well?"

He waited for the laughter to die down, and then continued.

"No. I'm sure it's not. But, you know, it seems to me there must be something else to explain why half the reigning monarchs of Europe used to fall in love with Russian women. Why did they ignore their own princesses, and instead of them why did they set girls from Russia on the thrones of England, France, and Norway? What is it exactly about Russian women? Is it their beauty? I look at all of you now, and of course, you're all very lovely, all very beautiful. . . . Quiet there! No laughing! . . . But are you all that much more beautiful than French or Italian women, for instance? Be honest, are you really? . . . No, I'm not so sure either. So then we look at past history. We try and find an answer somewhere in bygone centuries, in times of old: what was it that distinguished Russian women from all others? And as you think about this, you suddenly realize that there haven't been any real Russians for a long time now. In fact, there haven't been any proper Russians for almost a thousand years! Yes, it's true. Here we are, living in Russia, and the whole world refers to us as Russians. Yet—facts are stubborn things—the only Russian thing about us that survives is our name. All the historians—both in Russia and the West—have lost trace of the Rus back in the tenth century. The Rus, the real Russians, were an enormous tribe, an entire nation, and during the first millenium they were known all over Europe. But they've disappeared! They have vanished in the darkness of the ages, and to the Scythian tribes who came after them they left only their name and the Ryurik dynasty of tsars. And that's all there was left. No language, no culture, no literature, no legends. Just a few names, such as Oleg, Olga, Igor. And a few names of rivers, like the Dnieper and the Dniester. And even these names sound rather more German than Russian, don't they? Yet how did it happen? How could an entire people disappear without trace? And why? And then you wonder, have they really disappeared?"

He hastily rose to his feet. In the campfire flames his wiry figure was projected on the white canvas of the tents as a gigantic twisted shadow. Lit up by the red fire glow, his thin face also suddenly acquired a Mephistophelian yet inspired expression. His dark eyes glowed with an inner light, and the broad flanges of his nose gave a predatory twitch as a fish suddenly splashed in the river close by—as though the secret he was looking for had splashed up for an instant on the surface of the river.

"Take a look around you!" he suddenly said. With his charred fir branch he described a broad semicircle in the darkness, and the sharp movement caused the glowing tip to flare up, turning the whole branch into a fiery spear. "Twenty centuries ago it was just as dark here as it is now, with the same woods and the same mosquitoes. Along the banks of these rivers lived small tribes such as the Ugor, the Burtas, and the Ghuzz. They lived by fishing and hunting and collecting honey in the forests. Then, between the fifth and seventh centuries, heaven knows where from—from the north, the Baltic area—there came hordes of warlike people called the Rus. These people were bandits and conquering invaders. They produced nothing, their only trade was thievery, and they lived off the spoils of their plundering. In the ninth century they conquered the Slavic capital city of Kiev, and after that ruled and bullied everyone around—the Polyanians, the Derevlians, and other northern tribes. They robbed them, exacted heavy tributes from them and sold them into slavery in Byzantium, Greece, and Khazaria. The Rus were coarse, cruel, merciless in battle, and treacherous in daily life, and all the property they acquired through pillage they used to leave to their daughters. To their sons they bequeathed only their weapons, with the words: 'With this sword I acquired my wealth. Take it and continue where I left off!' In other words these people were a nation of marauders and bandits. But! . . ."

He paused for a moment and raised the blazing fir branch like a staff of office. Then he began pacing up and down the darkened river bank, inspired by the listening girls' attention and by the mirage of the past he had conjured up in the gloom of that summer night.

"But," he continued, "the Rus were a handsome people! There was no denying that. The Rus were extremely handsome. As the Persian envoy Akhmed ibn-Fadlan reported to the Caliph in 922 A.D., 'I have seen the Rus when they arrived to do trade and set themselves up by the River Ityl. I never saw folk with more perfect bodies than theirs. They are tall like palm trees, fair-haired, with fine faces and white bodies. They wear neither jackets nor kaftans, but their men wear a *kisa*, or mantle, which envelops one side, and from which one of their arms projects. Each of them carries an ax, a sword, and a knife, and they never part with these weapons. And from their necks down to their toenails their whole bodies are decorated with drawings depicting trees, birds, deities, and so forth.

" 'As for their women, they are all beautiful. Their bodies are all white like ivory, and each of their breasts is enclosed in a small case in the form of a circle made of iron, or of silver, brass, gold, or wood, depending on the wealth of their husband. They wear these breast cases from childhood, so as to prevent their breasts from becoming too enlarged. Round their necks they have necklaces of gold and silver, and a knife that hangs down between their breasts. But the Rus regard green ceramic beads as the very finest decorations. For every such bead they are willing to give a sable skin, and they make necklaces with them for their wives.

" 'They travel from their home country down the broad river Ityl. They moor their vessels laden with merchandise, and then build themselves large houses of wood on the banks of the Ityl. Ten or twenty of them gather together in each house; and each man has his own bench where he sits together with the various beautiful girls he is offering to the traders. . . .

" 'If the head of a family dies, his kinfolk say to his girls, "Which of you will die together with him?" And the one who loved him most announces she is willing. Then they gather together all that the man owned and divide it into three parts—one-third for his family, one-third to make clothing for the dead man, and a third is spent on making the *nabiz* that they drink for ten days while they cut and sew burial garments for the deceased. And for the next ten days, they lay the dead man in his tomb while they drink, couple with the women, and play on an instrument called the *saz*. And the girl who is going to be burnt with her master drinks and makes merry, decorates herself with various ornaments and dresses, and wearing these garments she offers herself to the other men.

" 'I always wanted to get to know this custom,' ibn-Fadlan told his ruler in a letter. 'Then one day I heard news of the death of a well-known man among their number. When the day arrived for them to burn him together with the girl, I came to the river where his vessel was moored. There his ship was, already hauled up onto the shore on a wooden structure resembling a large platform. In the center of it they had erected a wooden shelter and draped it with cloth of scarlet. Then they brought a bench and covered it with quilted mattresses and brocade from Byzantium, and the cushions too were of Byzantine brocade. And an old woman came whom they called the angel of death. She it is who directed the sewing done for the deceased, and who also dispatches the girls. I saw that she was an old warrior woman, powerfully built and of gloomy visage.

" 'And when they approached his tomb, they removed the earth and took out the deceased man, who was still wrapped in the shroud in which he had died. And they had already placed in the tomb with him some of the *nabiz*, some fruit and a lute, and they now removed all these. And I saw that the deceased man had already turned black from the cold in that country, but apart from his color nothing about him had changed. Then they dressed him in the newly sewn broad breeches, gaiters, boots, jacket, brocade kaftan with buttons of gold: and they put on his head a cap of brocade and sable, and carried him onto the ship and laid him on the quilted mattress, and supported him with cushions and brought *nabiz*, fruit, flowers, and aromatic herbs and placed them next to him. Then they brought bread, meat, and onion and laid this before him. Then they brought his weapon and laid it next to him. Then they took two horses, hacked them to pieces with their swords, and threw the meat of them on board the vessel.

" 'Many men and women gathered, there was playing on the *saz*, and each of the deceased man's relatives set up their tents there. And the girl who wished to be burnt with her master decked herself out and went to the tents of the dead man's relatives. In each of the tents, the head of the household lay with her and proclaimed in a loud voice: "Say to your master that truly I have done this thing out of love and friendship for him." And in this manner she made her way round all the tents. . . .

" 'And when the hour of sunset came, she set her feet on the palms of the men's hands, and was raised up and spoke some words in her own language, after which she was lowered to the ground again. Then they raised her a second time, and a third, and I asked an interpreter about these actions. He explained that as they raised her up the first time, she said: "I see my father and my mother." The second time she said: "There are all my departed relatives seated there." And the third time she said: "Now I see my lord and master seated in a garden, and the garden is green and lovely, and now he is calling me—so lead me to him!"

" 'And so they came with her to the vessel. And she she took off two bracelets she had worn and gave them to the old woman they called the angel of death, and who was to kill her. After this, all the men spread out their palms and made a pathway for the girl, so that by stepping on their hands she could make her way to the vessel. But she was not immediately taken to the shelter where her dead master was. The men came bringing shields and sticks, and they offered her a cup of *nabiz*. She sang a song over the cup and drank it. The interpreter told me that in this way she was bidding farewell to her maiden friends. Then she was handed another cup, and the old woman, who carried a huge dagger with a broad blade, went with her into the shelter. Then six men who were kinsmen of her husband entered the shelter, and each of them lay with the girl in the presence of the dead man, until she was filled with a sense of joy and lightness like an angel. After this, having exercised their rights of love, they laid her down next to her master. Two of them seized her by the legs, and two by the arms, and the woman called the angel of death placed a rope around her neck and plunged the dagger in between her ribs. And the men began beating on their shields with the sticks so that her last mortal cry could not be heard. . . .

" 'When she was dead, the closest relative of the deceased, being still naked, took up his stick and lit it in the fire and then set fire to the wood that had been laid beneath the vessel.

" 'And the fire consumed the wood, and then the vessel, then the shelter, and the master and the girl, and everything that was on board the ship. Then a wind blew up, a great and terrible wind, and the flames of the fire increased and blazed up. And not an hour passed before the vessel, the wood, the maiden, and her master were turned first to ashes, and then to nothing more than a fine dust.

" 'Then, upon the place where the vessel was burnt, they erected something resembling a circular mound, and in the center they set up a large beam on which they inscribed the name of the man and of the tsar and ruler of the Rus, and then they went away.'

"And that," he said, "was what ibn-Fadlan wrote about the people known as the Rus. And he saw them with his own eyes right here, on the banks of this very river. Yes, it was actually just here. This was the place where the Rus sat with their merchandise and their beautiful young women, slender and graceful as palm trees, and beautiful in body and countenance. It was here that those Russian girls followed their beloved lords and masters onto the funeral pyre. And all this happened a mere one thousand and forty-three years ago. But after that, in the course of just seventy or eighty years, all the Rus men perished in various unsuccessful campaigns against Byzantium, Persia, and Bulgaria. And what became of their beautiful women is not recorded anywhere. But most likely they became the wives of the Slavs, the Polyanians, and the Derevlians, who took over their name, because they wanted to be as feared and as handsome as the people that used to rule over them. But do you think they achieved their ambition? Ask yourselves that question when you are on your own at night. Could you follow your beloved man onto the funeral pyre? As you faced death, could you drink the cup of *nabiz*, sing a farewell song to your friends and mount your dead husband's blazing ship? Ask yourselves that, and then you'll know whether the women of Rus have survived in modern Russia. Thanks for your attention. And now everyone back to your tents. It's time to turn in!"

"Tell us some more! Come on, tell us something else! Please!" He waited for the shouts of protest to die down, then he scattered the ash of the burnt-out campfire and said quietly, "That's all. That really is all for today. Time to turn in."

But they crowded round him, jumping around and twittering.

"No! There's a lot more you can tell us! Come on, please! Tell us!"

He looked up at them and they fell silent, expecting the tale to continue. But all he said was, "Maybe I know a hundred more interesting stories. But if you ever wish to hear any of them, you'd better get off to bed now immediately. I'm going to count three. One . . ."

And they rushed away to their tents with a yell and a chortle and a flicker of sunburnt ankles in the darkness. He grinned wearily as they ran off, then turned towards the river.

In the dark distance the last light of a raftsman's brazier drifted away and disappeared in the shroud of darkness. But from higher upstream, coming from the north, he suddenly heard some other sounds—either another convoy of timber rafts moving downriver, or else the faint splash of oars. He stepped towards the water's edge, peering into the gloom of the moonless night. An armada of dark silhouettes could be discerned in the center of the stream, but from afar and in such darkness there was no telling what it was. More timber rafts? A convoy of boats? Or were these the vessels of the ancient Rus, sailing once again in search of fresh plunder? . . .

part one

The Twofold Hunt

one

Iosif Rubinchik never conducted any love affairs in Moscow. This was not just because he prized his reputation as a well-known correspondent for the *Labor Gazette*, where he wrote under the pen name of Iosif Rubin. But in Moscow he simply had neither the time nor the inclination for such pursuits. A lean-built thirty-seven-year-old Jew, who had grown up in a provincial orphanage, he devoted himself to the feverish daily hassle of living in Moscow, holding down a job, looking after his wife and two small children, and following the vile routine of an existence that gobbled up all leisure. Relaxation was replaced by standing in endless lines with their squabbles, queuing up for groceries, footwear, children's medications, and for everything else without which daily life was impossible. Exhausted, Rubinchik never had a spare moment to look around him and admire a woman's face, an alluring low-cut dress, or even enjoy the gentle twirl of snowflakes under a streetlamp.

But it only needed the excuse of some out-of-town assignment for him to cast off the nervous wear and tear of Moscow, and then he would feel rousing within him the mysterious, joyful, predatory exhilaration of the hunter. But his was no indiscriminate pursuit. Rubinchik lacked the omnivorous appetite of most men who escape from the bed of a beloved but all too familiar wife. And in any case, he was not actually ravening after sex. The cause lay elsewhere, and Rubinchik himself would have been hard put to define it. However, once he had settled in the airport bus to fly off to Siberian oilfields, Ural mines, or logging areas in the Altai, he could feel a powerful spurt of adrenalin that entered his bloodstream and knocked all his atoms and electrons out of their settled Moscow orbits. His shoulders straightened, he held his head more erect; he sparkled with a new wit, inhibitions fell away, and there was a new and bold self-assurance in his gaze.

From that moment the hunt was on.

In his mind's eye Rubinchik saw the whole country spread out before him—the gigantic Soviet empire stretching from the Baltic to the Pacific Ocean. He could scarcely contain his excitement. In this country there was always something going on—discoveries of natural gas in the Arctic, the arrest of foreign spies, preparations for the next Olympics, irrigation canals laid in the wilderness around the Caspian, the persecution of dissidents, the construction of hydroelectric stations, the launch of rockets into space, and listening to the Voice of America. Rubinchik digested all with a professional appetite, and he filled notepads with impressions of everything going on around him. This was his country. All of it belonged to him—from Moldavia and Estonia to distant Turkmenia and Kamchatka—and with the whole of his little Jewish heart he loved its immensity, its many faces, and its might. Rubinchik did not in fact consider himself a Jew. He was an atheist. He had no knowledge of Hebrew. He had shortened his surname so that it sounded Russian, and he could hold his own with any Russian when it came to downing vodka. And, most important of all, he loved *Russian* women. Indeed, every time he found himself in the outback—whether in Vyatka, Murmansk, or Siberia—his roving glance would light on some woman who caused his huntsman's heart to misstep. And he would find this new discovery shared one quality in common with all his previous conquests: all these were *Russian* women, women with erect figures and with a mysterious sadness in their gray or green eyes. They had slightly elongated visages, arched eyebrows, and fine transparent skin of the kind to be seen in the paintings by Rokotov, Levitsky, or Borovikovsky on exhibit in the Hermitage Museum.

To find and possess this ideal of female beauty was Rubinchik's obsession. He needed only one glance to identify and pick out among hundreds just one whose pristine beauty had not yet been erased by the rigors of provincial life, defiled by local whoring, or worn out by an alcoholic husband. And on such rare occasions, when at last he lighted on what he privately referred to as an "ikon diva," for an instant everything in him faltered— breathing, pulse, and every thought came to a halt. The moment was a brief one, but then his heart picked up again and sent a surge of blood through his enfeebled veins. And the desire to "possess" this beauty seized him in the legs, groin, and stomach, and even electrified the hair on his chest. Everything in him rejoiced and stood bolt upright, like a Mongolian horseman braced in the stirrups.

Surprisingly, too, these choice young women never offered any resistance. Unlike women in Moscow, they also never required any preliminary flirtation, prolonged seduction, or even dinner in a restaurant. The very instant their eyes met, a mysterious channel seemed to open up between Rubinchik and his ikon diva.

That sense of communion without a single word spoken was something he had actually experienced. It happened out in the taiga. He had chanced across a young female deer, which turned in its path to look at him. Both of them stood stock still, no more than five yards apart, and looked one another in the eye, steadily, calmly. And as the doe stood gazing at him with enormous dark eyes, moist as fresh horse chestnuts, Rubinchik was filled with a sense that the animal was comprehending and absorbing his very essence. He mustered all his willpower to return that penetrating gaze and peer into the soul of this gentle, gracious animal as it stood there immobile on its long, slender legs. And it felt as if the two of them had made contact. Behind the dewy cornea of those plumblike orbs he sensed something ample, dark and warm, something thick as blood that was merely waiting for a sign from him to allow him in more deeply, or simply to follow after him along that pathway through the taiga. And if he made the right gesture, the young doe would walk up to him, gently press its lips against his neck and become his obedient servant, bride, or woodland lover.

But out there in the taiga, he did not know the secret sign that this lovely creature awaited, for five whole minutes or more. Then he either sighed, made some tiny hand movement, or else gave a twitch of his Adam's apple. And in that instant the deer dashed off into the fir thickets with a flicker of its slender legs, its short resilient tail raised pertly above its springing rump. Left alone, Rubinchik felt like a clumsy peasant at life's ball—a princess of the taiga had turned him down, because he didn't know how to dance the forest mazurka.

Among humans, though, Rubinchik had no need of passwords or secret gestures. With one glance he could identify a Russian diva, even if she was swaddled in some hideous provincial outfit, with thick-knitted tights and rubber boots. And thanks to some sixth sense or genetic memory, there was instant recognition on her part too: as he looked at her, in her eyes a broad and expansive wisdom, thick and warm as blood, seemed to unfold before Rubinchik's gaze.

Of course he would immediately make the girl's acquaintance and come out with the usual remarks. But he could tell that she was listening only to the sound of his voice; meanwhile, though, along with his voice, she was absorbing the whole of him, drinking him in like some intoxicating nectar.

Rubinchik could never account for this. There could be a thousand and one reasons why he felt so drawn exclusively toward Russian women—maybe his Russian cultural upbringing, or perhaps his plight as a frustrated Jew adrift in a Slavic ocean of state-inspired anti-Semitism. Yet what did all these Polovtsian princesses and fairy-tale beauties see in a lean little Jew with his pronounced Semitic nose, small brown eyes, and a thick mat of black hair springing from the open neck of his shirt? How was it that after only a casual introduction they came directly to his hotel room of their own accord, like the spellbound young fawn? Moreover they came quite openly, in view of people from their town or village and seemingly oblivious of the stares they got from the hotel personnel.

This was something Rubinchik could never understand. Every time, he was sure he had probably made a mistake and had simply picked up the village's easy lay. But then as the new "princess" carried out his bidding, went under the shower and returned barefoot and swaddled in a worn hotel bathtowel (stamped HOTEL PROPERTY to prevent theft), he could see instantly there was nothing remotely whorish about her. In fact he saw nothing to suggest she'd had any sexual experience at all. In her figure and her gait, in her straight neck and eyes he discerned a sense of rapture, fear, and telepathic obedience to his thought, will, word, and gesture. And as he slowly removed the towel that covered her slim white body and her breasts with their tiny pale nipples, Rubinchik could see that again he had made no mistake, this girl was indeed a virgin.

He seduced them of course. Yet it could hardly be said that he merely deflowered them or indulged in a purely physical act. Here there was no vulgar "screwing" or "popping of cherries," and these girls were neither dishonored nor led astray. What Rubinchik did was to lead them across the narrow divide from a virgin ignorance to femininity, and he did so with paternal care and tenderness. And in the process, he initiated these girls into the noble function of becoming a high priestess of the bed chamber rather than a vulgar block of wood beneath the chopper.

Rubinchik's work was like that of buoy keeper: operating in the fog at night, he had to find the dark anchor buoy by pure intuition; then by touch dismantle the lantern, refill the oil, and trim the wick; and when at last he relighted the flame, he himself was suddenly blinded by its light.

The light of true femininity that Rubinchik kindled on dark nights in the remote towns of Igarka, Izhevsk, Vologda, or Kokchetav, was like restoring the beauty of an old ikon painting. After careful and delicate cleaning, its magical eyes suddenly light up and gaze out at you from the depths of a bygone age.

That moment was one that Rubinchik always prepared with special care and even with ceremony. In these regions, whoring flourished on a grand scale and sexual education was acquired in alleyway entrances, through obscene stories, and via graffiti in public toilets. There was not one book on "how to do it," and people were too shy even to say a word like "gynecologist." The result was that millions of young women knew no more about sex than what they learned from watching their domestic animals. All that ninety percent of Russian men demanded of their wives was simply to lie on their back, spread their legs, and give it to them. No wonder most Russian women suffered from frigidity.

And amid that dark ocean of sexual ignorance, Rubinchik went around lighting the bright lamps of sensuality, and he himself was the first to enjoy their tremulous flame.

"Now, my dear, there's no need to hurry or be afraid. Forget everything your girlfriends ever told you. And forget the filthy expressions you've seen scrawled in dark entrances. We're going to do things quite differently, so that you'll remember this forever. You're going to recall this as the most sacred moment in your life, like the feast of Christmas. Here, have a sip of wine . . . And another . . . And one more . . . Now give me your lips. No, not like that."

Damn it, these girls didn't even know how to kiss properly! Their nipples wouldn't respond to the touch of a man's lips. They were afraid to put their hand down and touch a man in the groin, and they locked their legs together in a rigid spasm. Sometimes, it was true, they made a great effort of will and unclasped their legs and lay in the position of readiness they had seen in lewd drawings on the walls of school toilets. Yet even then their bodies exuded no passion, nor even desire, but only fear.

"Wait," Rubinchik, the painstaking laureate of copulation, would say. "Never mind your legs for the moment. Can you see the night sky outside? What you can see are not just stars. What you see is the sifting filter of eternity. Seventeen years of your life have flowed away through that sieve, and they are gone. Forever. Vanished in space. What do you have left from them? Nothing. Because you haven't lived yet. Well, it's true of course, you've been breathing. You've eaten and drunk and learned a thing or two. But all you've done so far is merely exist. Nothing more. But now you're going to start living. After this, not another night in your life will just flow away and disappear. Each one is going to remain with you. Can you feel it? Your body is filling with sunlight and energy. This is the key, the fountain, and the sword of life, and every time I touch you with it, everything in you gets excited—your nipples, your back, and your belly. . . . Look at it. Don't be shy. Take it in your hand. Only not so tightly. Gently. You know why the dome on churches is shaped like that? Because it expresses divine harmony. And now take it yourself and press it against your breast . . . Yes, like that. Can you feel it? Your nipple is coming alive and growing to meet it. . . ."

But Rubinchik would move no lower than that. Even when her back arched toward him, and her belly began pulsing with the first eddies of desire and her breathing grew heavy and her lips parted, he still held back. He then moved the wand of life from her torso and slid it up toward her lips. This was one of the most critical moments. Brought up with squeamish, ignorant, puritanical Soviet attitudes, young women regarded the male organ as something filthy—like Russia's public toilets. To touch it, let alone take it in their lips, would be an abomination. There was no worse insult than to say that some woman was good only for a blow job. And many Russian men felt a similar disgust at a woman's vagina. Rubinchik reckoned that even if in the dim and distant future they started making erotic films in Russia, one could still never imagine a scene in which a man kissed a women between the thighs.

But he had a way of overcoming this mindless prejudice. His wand of life was now taut and wrapped about with swelling veins. Proudly he raised it and slid it across her breast, her chin, and up to her lips. Slowly and solemnly he raised it, like a holy scepter. More often than not, she closed her eyes in horror. In which case he would never insist. Then he would take her face in both hands and softly and gently he would say to her, "Look at me."

She would open her eyes, and in her gaze there was always the same expression. It showed her readiness to admit him into the warm depths of her soul and body, yet it was accompanied by a horror of how this would occur. And there was something else, something rooted in the ancient past—the inchoate dread of a conquered victim.

But Rubinchik was short on time. How could he fathom the mystery of this fear? Instead he gave these young girls a chance to gaze into his own soul.

"There's nothing shameful in this," he said. "Look me in the eyes. There's nothing shameful about our bodies. Neither yours nor mine. God made us all out of the same flesh and blood. And everything has the same splendid taste. Just you see . . ."

With that he began to kiss her body, starting at the shoulder and slowly working his tongue and lips down over her breasts and belly, lower and lower, until he reached the fine downy curls on her mound. Then with a firm but gentle movement of his palms he moved her knees apart. There in that cleft lay the main lure of his life. That silken downy thicket concealed a mystical magnet whose total and unearthly power he had experienced only once in life—long, long ago on the bank of the river Ityl. Ever since, that irresistible attractive force kept drawing him away from Moscow, hauling him through Russia's dirt and snow, across taiga and tundra, in a search for yet another Russian diva.

Cautiously, like a mine layer or a tiger hunter, Rubinchik moved his face closer to that tender bushy growth and parted its tangles with his chin. Before his inquiring gaze, the closed, dry, somnolent lips of a chaste rosebud lay revealed. And there appeared to be nothing mysterious about those pale pink folds, no more than in the closed shell of a pearl-bearing oyster. But Rubinchik was not deceived by nature's simple stratagem. Breathless, fearing, but thirsting for that perilous marvel, he touched the folds first with his lips and then with his tongue.

The mere contact of lips and tongue came as a shock to the girl—not so much sexually as culturally. Trying to rescue him from what seemed an unnecessary defilement, she gripped his head and tried to push him away from her loins. But Rubinchik seized her hands and pressed them together, preventing any further movement. He knew of course that she would yield to him without all this preamble. At any moment, had he wished, he could have forced her knees apart and entered her; with one thrust he could have burst through the dry labia, the cramped muscles of her orifice, and the thin hymen inside. In their ignorance, this was exactly what they expected—which they could have had in any dark alleyway without his help.

But Rubinchik's mission was different, and so was the magic of that night. His role as Teacher, Enlightener, Mentor, and First Man added a further facet of refinement to his own desire. And quite apart . . . he had further expectations of that night. He was waiting and hoping for something more—something incredible, utterly extraordinary, almost satanic—something he had experienced only that one time, on the banks of the ancient river Ityl. And because of that expectation . . .

Squeezing her slender wrists, he continued gently touching and kissing the still dry and dreaming lips of that rosebud. The sight always reminded him of a sleeping child wrapped in warm flannel that, in this case, had to be undressed with the aid of his tongue. And he set about the task with the same relish as his own three-year-old son opening candy wrappers.

He pointed his tongue, and with its moist warm tip gently parted the petals of flesh that were gradually coming alive, as in a sped-up film. He knew that in her consciousness that little bud was beginning to swell and grow, expanding to gigantic proportions. And this new and powerful desire she felt far exceeded any girlish agonies she'd had. Now in her inflamed mind that tiny lagoon of hers had turned into a separate being, a hungry animal, an enormous mouth that craved to be touched yet again and thirsted for more kisses, more saliva and caressing. It was like the desert after years of drought, it writhed with thirst and impatiently opened its desiccated pores to the first rain clouds to come.

Rubinchik was awaiting a miracle. But this wonder could not be rushed or overheated. It must be left to grow of its own accord and he wanted to nurture it like a gardener cultivating some rare exotic bloom. So the moment his tongue sensed the moistening of her labia and felt a tiny knot of pearl at the top of these folds, Rubinchik stopped. By his own example, he had removed the first psychological barrier—the notion of the sexual organ as something dirty, shameful, and never to be kissed. Now again he raised his key of life to the young girl's face. And at this point no girl had ever yet closed her lips, or turned away. On the contrary, she seized it hastily with hands and lips like a Boy Scout's bugle, and proved to Rubinchik that the lesson had been learnt, and now she could continue. . . .

Even now, though, he wouldn't let her take things into her own hands. Next he removed his magic instrument from her lips and commanded in the severe tone of a lord and master: "No teeth! Gentler and deeper!"

Now he no longer chose his words so carefully, and he paid no attention to the frightened eyes that burned in the darkness like those of a small animal.

"Slowly! Don't rush! And let your tongue play around! As though you were playing on the flute . . . Yes, like that."

He sensed that without her realizing it her upper and lower lips had already come together and turned into a single ravening monster capable of swallowing him up body and soul. But on the fringe of her awareness, faint with terror and rejoicing, a last impatient thought still fluttered: "When? Oh when? I'll do anything you say, but please do it soon . . . the thing I want most of all!" And this was no random thought. It was now the aim of her existence: to become a complete woman. It was written into her genetic code, in the cortex of her brain, and in every cell of her body.

Yet Rubinchik still delayed. Maybe this was bad for his health. Now by an effort of the will he had to tame the raging pressure in his genitals. But he undertook the ordeal as a sacrifice on behalf of a loftier goal. He commanded himself to zone out, to contain himself.

Softened by a lust for consummation, her awareness now yielded to the current and was swimming along in the midst of it. She reeled with desire. Everything gave her a thrill—the taste of his flesh, the sense that after years of waiting she now held in her hands this blazing key of life, and that she was breathing in its scent. Though he couldn't see her in the darkness, he could feel her tongue and lips obeying his orders, not under duress or out of fear, but with exultation. Like a young music student who so far had learned only at her parents' insistence, she could now play her first tune and suddenly began to delight in her skill. Full of pride and joy, she played her piece over and over again, faster and louder, and now with greater artistry, using her new abilities to draw out the nuance and color.

The speed of his pupil's tongue and lips as she played, and her fervent, choking intoxication as she engulfed his flesh told Rubinchik that the transformation had taken place: a new sensuality had awakened in this vessel. Within this awkward infant a woman had been born, a female had come alive within a virgin body, a light had been kindled in the lamp.

And now to the main business. . . .

He plunged his hand into the downy fringe of her mound and began preparing a bridgehead. Slowly, and ever more slowly, with just two fingers . . . And as her feet braced against the mattress and her body arched to meet his fingers, her mouth and lips and tongue were no longer licking and sucking but swallowing him whole, choking on her own saliva. At that moment, caught up by his own desire, Rubinchik forced himself to stretch out a hand and switch on the bedside lamp.

She did not even see the light. She no longer dwelt in the conscious outer world.

But now he had to bring her back to the real world. Removing his proud rod from her lips, Rubinchik offered her another glass of wine. She opened her eyes and her pupils stood out, darting about wildly yet seeing nothing. She seemed to peer out at him from another world with a regard that was quizzical, imploring, and impatient.

"In one moment you'll become a woman," he consoled. "Just one moment. But I want you to see it with your own eyes. Here, drink up your wine. . . ."

Her body below was still pulsing. But obediently she took one or two convulsive swigs. Then she laid her head back on the pillow, ready and maybe even irritated that he had still not yet done it while she was beyond the pale of her awareness.

But like a good piece of prose, a woman in bed was not something to be hurried. In the act of sex a man came closest of all to true creativity—the creation of Life itself. And when He created life on earth, God Himself probably experienced orgasm—how else to explain this supreme earthly joy?

Rubinchik drew the pillow from beneath her head and laid it beneath her buttocks. Then he began licking the hollow of her ears, and this plunged the two of them back into a vortex of desire. Above her hot open loins he then raised the spear of his manhood, engorged with blood, taut, and trembling. Then slowly, ever so slowly, by miniscule degrees, he lowered its blazing tip into that narrow, moist pink cleft, parting the tender orifice wider and wider . . . until he ran up against an obscure barrier.

This, for him, was a sacred moment.

He now pulled back his spear to its full length, braced himself up on his hands, and looked at her spread out before him. In much the same way a horseman stands erect in the stirrups to swing his whole power behind a spear thrust.

Beneath him on the squeaking hotel bed flowed a white river of female flesh. And her breasts with the dark beacons of her pointed nipples became two Scythian tumuli above that river. Her two outspread arms flowed to either side like tributaries. Her long Polovtsian neck stretched up to the chin of her thrown-back head. Further off, a cascade of opulent, russet hair fell from the bed.

Rubinchik surveyed her body with tenderness and compassion. This was his homeland, his Russia. Thirty years ago, when a boy, she had beaten him till he bled, called him "kike," chucked him on the ground, twisted his arms, caked his lips in lard, and made him scoff it together with mouthfuls of dirt. Twenty years ago that Russia had betrayed him in the entrance exams for Moscow, Leningrad, and other universities simply because the little word "Jew" appeared under point five in his ID. Instead, she had sent him trailing round military barracks and workers' hostels. But, then, his big break had come. And now this same Russia belonged to him—the whole of her, with her rivers and forests, and her birds singing in bemisted gardens, and with her pliant neck, her dark nipples surmounting white breasts, the tremulous hollow of her belly, and the confiding embrace of her loins.

At that moment he loved her. He loved this Russian land as tenderly as no other Russian could—as only a man can love his homeland after managing to swim ashore from a storm at sea. Or as a child can love its home despite enduring many a beating from an evil stepmother.

He took a deep breath and without roughness, but decisively he entered her lovely welcoming body. The warmth of her, her quiet moan, her tears of pain and ecstasy, the first ineffable languor of his plunge inside her, and the grip of her virgin muscles filled him with joy. Then, an instant later, came the raging convulsions of her body. Finally, after all those youthful years of growth and ripening, her body was ready for the crowning moment, the moment of communion with male flesh, and in its depths this coming together felt greeted by fireworks and fountains of tenderness that had been gathering throughout her earlier life.

Her slender arms clasped him about the neck and squeezed him in a convulsion of gratitude that prevented any movement. Her lips fastened on his own until it hurt. Her legs locked around his own; her trembling mound followed his own movement and refused to let him withdraw from her by even a millimeter.

At such moments Rubinchik envied these young women. What cosmic downpours shivered their flesh! What lightning bolts pierced them! He realized that no man, not even the most sensuous, could feel so much as a tenth of the divine pleasure that racks all women at such moments. Yet he felt pride and joy at being the courier who delivered this sacred gift that he now held within a woman's body and on the spear tip of his own flesh. God visited on women the awful torment, unknown to men, of giving birth. Yet it was through him, Rubinchik, that God rewarded these women with a pleasure such as males were never allowed to experience. And Rubinchik took great pleasure in imparting this pleasure. At such moments he felt as if he were the agent of an all-powerful God.

Left an orphan by bombings in 1941, when just a few months old, he had seen death throughout the war—in trains, in orphanages where children starved, and on burning Volga barges with other children and their screaming female guardians. And these memories had made death into something for him that was not in the remote or abstract future, but was as ever present and real a likelihood as pleasure in bed. Death and pleasure in his mind were almost interlocked—it was not for nothing that almost every living thing, from humans to small creatures of the forest, experienced in orgasm an enrapturing and vertiginous sense of the closeness of death. Such "joy unto death" could come only from God, Rubinchik believed, yet a mortal man could bring a woman almost to the brink of that entrancing precipice.

And Rubinchik invested all his strength and skill in this art. To prolong his role as God's emissary, to maintain the incandescent pleasure, he contrived not to hurry and use himself up at the sweetest, most sacred moment of first entry. By no more than a millimeter he managed to withdraw his key from the lock of female flesh. . . .

Withdraw and re-enter . . .

Exit and return . . .

At first by a mere fraction . . .

And then slightly more . . .

Then stronger and more broadly . . .

At a trot . . .

And then a canter . . .

And finally at full gallop! . . . Gasping for breath! . . . Crying out aloud! . . .

And the bedsprings pounded like a horse's hooves!

And the white body of his Polovtsian captive howled like a wolf. But this was not a howl of pain. She was beyond all pain, for the flame of her desire was like a narcotic or an anaesthetic. In the cyclotron of her pulsing body, Russian-Jewish erotic polarities were discharged in raging torrents altogether unknown to men and women of the same descent.

Rubinchik twisted the body of his captive maiden into a circle and a spiral, pulled her legs wide apart. And she trusted him, obeyed his every order, like a pupil who implored to be called to the blackboard to demonstrate. Crazed with ecstasy, she seized the initiative and accelerated to the gallop, flailing her head from side to side, thrashing the air with her mane of hair. She seized the back of the bed with her hands, ground her teeth, wept tears of rapture, exuded hot fireworks of fluid, fell as if dead, soared up again. And her mouth sought and found his fingers and sucked them, inflicting sharp animal bites, and her legs flew up to encircle his back and shoulders.

Something or other, a subconscious awareness, an intuitive biological pressure gauge told her that it was only with him—a Jew! a Yid!—that such a total union was possible. So much so that their combined dissonant streams of sexual energy had the force of an explosion. Her body recorded every instant of this pleasure with its own form of carnal memory.

After each orgasm, she collapsed quietly against his breast, and Rubinchik felt like Paganini after the brilliant performance of some finger-breaking concerto. In the silence of the Siberian night he even seemed to hear silent applause from Russian Orthodox or Jewish angels and cries of "Encore!" And he did not tantalize or keep them waiting. Gently shifting his loins, he was amazed at the new strength welling up within him, which he had never known with his Jewish wife. And he began an encore piece—at first in the minor mode, but a moment later striking firm chords in the major, and moving toward a crescendo.

Later, just prior to releasing again, Rubinchik used his last ounce of strength to stay in control and braced himself up on his hairy arms to gaze with a tender smile at this newborn woman. He felt proud. Now the fire of sensuality blazed in her hearth without any further help from him, and she radiated heat. Unable now to reach up to Rubinchik's lips, she licked the hair on his chest, nibbled his shoulders with her teeth, and dug her nails into his back.

He looked at her and realized she would do everything he commanded. And she would carry out his bidding not as at first, in a state of mystical enchantment, but with the joy of a newly converted servant of the temple. Lying on her back beneath him, on her side or belly, braced on elbows and knees, or else riding him like a Scythian horsewoman, this Russian diva would now always see him as a divine incarnation. Toward morning, she seemed to have exuded the last drop of fluid from her body, and her whole being seemed transparent, weightless, almost in free fall. And as the cool light of dawn crept in, she would even pray to him in the innermost recesses of her consciousness; she would cherish his image, much as women of the twelfth century maintained an erotic cult of the figure of Christ.

In the lilac glow of dawn he raised her amazingly light head into his lap and gently, ever so gently, caressed her fine flaxen hair. She was exhausted and floated like an angel. Without even opening her eyes, she began licking his now wilting flesh, drifting into oblivion, back into infancy when she used to lick the last drops of milk from her mother's nipple with the same sated lips, before dropping off to sleep. . . .

As he lovingly caressed and cradled this new Russian diva, Rubinchik thought of the miracle for which he kept searching through the length and breadth of this enormous country. And he realized that here, once again, it had eluded him.

After completing his assignment, Rubinchik would return to Moscow. There, in the office that he shared with three other correspondents of the *Labor Gazette*, he walked over to the large wall map of the Soviet Union. He located the place he had just visited, where he had lit one more beacon of femininity, and he marked the spot with a pin and a little red flag. In his ten years as a roving correspondent he had collected more than a hundred of these little flags, pinned across the whole expanse of Russia. But nowhere had there been a repeat of the miracle he had experienced just once, in his youth, at the Sputnik pioneer camp. So in two or three weeks' time he would be hankering to get on the road again. But where would he head next time?

· · ·

Rubinchik was unaware, however, that in a different Moscow office—one looking onto Dzerzhinsky Square—someone else had started plotting the course of his travels around Russia on a similar map.

The person in question was KGB Colonel Oleg Barsky.

TWO

What is your last name?"

"My last name?" Anna snorted. The idiot seated there beneath a portrait of Brezhnev had known her for four years and still couldn't remember her name. "My surname is Sigal. What about yours?"

Kuzyaev, head of personnel at the Moscow Bar of Attorneys, was a bald weasel of a man, with large ears and the red eyes of a secret alcoholic. He sat there reading from her file, but now looked up in astonishment.

"Do you really not know my name?" he asked.

"Of course," she retorted. "And you know mine. It was you who called me." Anna looked round at the other man seated at the far end of the office who had listened to all this with a faint smile. He was about forty and had the trim physique of a former gymnast or army officer. His face was slightly elongated and of a sort seen in royal profile on coins. His hair was cropped short, and he wore a dark blue foreign-cut suit, smartly topstitched, and a perfectly knotted necktie. He held himself with the air of an outsider, but Anna sensed that the weasel had summoned her here for a meeting with this man. But who was he?

Kuzyaev coughed into his nicotine-stained hand.

"Okay, let's just start by going over the details of your file. Anna Evgenyevna Sigal. Maiden name Krylova. Age—thirty-two. Russian. Non-Party member. Degree in law from Moscow State University. First-class honors. In your second marriage . . ."

Kuzyaev spoke louder than necessary, which suggested he was speaking for the other man rather than for her. But she was baffled. Why was Kuzyaev reading out her file to him?

"Occupation—attorney. Member of the Moscow Southwestern District Bar. You've handled a total of sixty-nine cases, and won thirty-two. . . ."

Could this be true, Anna wondered. By now she had stopped keeping any tally of her professional successes, but evidently the weasel was keeping score. Well, winning thirty-two cases in a lawless country was not at all bad.

"Husband—Arkady Grigoryevich Sigal, doctor of science, director of the Institute of Modern Technology, Ministry of Heavy Industry, Party member . . ."

It was at this point that it dawned on her: she was up for sale! This newcomer was probably from the International Law Bureau and wanted to take her on, and Kuzyaev was simply "displaying the goods." And she had put on that stupid show of impudence! But wait: she didn't know a single foreign language, and the International Bureau only did business with Western countries—inheritances, arbitration, and so on. So who was this guy? As she sat there she could feel his eyes boring into the back of her neck.

"Of reliable morals, well disciplined, politically literate. Ten-year old son by first marriage lives abroad with his father. . . ."

At this juncture the stranger began fidgeting. Like all bureaucrats, Kuzyaev was attuned to the body language of his superiors, and he broke off and looked at the other man inquiringly.

"I don't think we need to hear all this, Ivan Petrovich," the man said and stood up. "And you forgot to introduce us. Anna Evgenyevna, my name is Oleg Dmitryevich Barsky, from the security service. Tell me, are you still in touch with Maxim Rappoport?"

Anna's heart missed a beat and dropped into the pit of her stomach. This man was from the KGB, and it would be stupid to try buttering them up. Yet equally, you should never show you were afraid. Anna summoned up some of the haughty mien that she cultivated for her duels in court. With her large gray-green eyes, she was probably one of the most attractive women in Moscow. And she now turned those eyes at Barsky.

"Surely my relations with men are not a threat to our national security?"

Barsky gave a peal of laughter. It was loud and unexpected, especially here in the weasel's office. Kuzyaev was nonplussed and batted his eyelids. Then, to cover himself, he too forced a smile, showing his little weasel teeth that resembled cedar nuts.

Barsky finally stopped laughing, and even made to wipe a tear from his eye. He walked over and sat down in the chair next to Anna.

"Now I get it, Anna Evgenyevna," he said. "Now I know how you managed to win thirty-two out of sixty-nine cases."

Anna remained aloof, controlling every muscle in her face and following Barsky's every move. What was his game? What did he want? Why had he brought up Maxim Rappoport?

"Vanya," said Barsky, addressing Kuzyaev, "Fix us some coffee, would you? That's a good guy."

Barsky's familiarity clearly pointed out his high rank and the weasel's subordinate position. Nobody, not even the Chairman of the Bar, would have dared call Kuzyaev "Vanya." It was no secret that the heads of personnel in every institution were elite members of the security service.

"Sure, just a moment," the weasel said and left, limping on his left leg—a legacy of the war, as everyone knew. Barsky watched him go, and then turned to Anna.

"No," he resumed, "your liaisons with men are no threat to national security. Especially since your Mr. Rappoport is now past history. Although, to be honest, he did our country considerable harm, and not without the help of some of our attorneys. But, as they say, let bygones be bygones. I'm sure you agree?"

His lips still wore a smile, but there was no laughter in his eyes. Now, Anna thought, he's trying to soften me up, and he's probing for my weak spots. But what did he want?

"But really," Barsky suddenly said, as if interrupting himself, "What am I going on about? It's as though I were probing you to find some weakness. You're an attorney after all, and you know all about these things. Incidentally, I also studied at Moscow University, though I graduated earlier than you. You finished four years ago, didn't you?"

"What exactly do you want of me?" Anna asked coldly.

He looked at her as though reassessing her. Then he snorted with a mixture of puzzlement and satisfaction. He took out his spectacles as if to examine her more closely, but then returned them to his pocket.

"Okay, let's get down to business. To be honest, I'd prepared myself for a long conversation with you. But I can see that Rappoport needn't concern us. And in any case there's no point in playing games with you, right?"

Anna said nothing. Barsky clearly wanted to show that they could easily nail her for complicity in Rappoport's affairs.

"And anyway," Barsky continued, "I guess I'm not much good at psychology, especially when it comes to women. I'd hoped that we would get on in a friendly fashion. But now you've clammed up. And that's my stupid fault. Honestly, when I meet so striking a woman as you, I always lose my nerve and strike the wrong tone. Especially when there's nothing on the table. Where in God's name is that *putz*?" Barsky, annoyed, turned toward the door. "Aha, at long last!"

The leatherette-padded door opened and in came Kuzyaev's secretary with a tray: a coffee pot, sugar bowl, cups, and a box of chocolates. Kuzyaev followed her in carrying a second tray with a bottle of six-star Armenian brandy, glasses, and a bowl of apples.

Wow, not bad, Anna thought. Apples in April! Kuzyaev must have made a quick trip to the Bar Chairman's private dining room. That was the only place where you could find apples and brandy. But who the devil was this Barsky? What rank did he hold if even the weasel groveled before him?

"Much better!" Barsky said approvingly and swept Kuzyaev's papers from the desk to make room for the trays. Then he looked at Kuzyaev. "Thanks, old boy. Now, I know you're a smoker, and I'm allergic to smoke. So why don't you go and have a smoke out there in reception. . . ."

"Certainly. Of course," Kuzyaev answered and hurriedly left, this time limping less than before.

Only then did Anna recall that Barsky had called the weasel by the Yiddish word *putz*. She was surprised. Did the KGB go in for Jewish name-calling? Hard to believe.

"Would you like your brandy in the coffee or separately, Anna Evgen-yevna?" Barsky asked, holding the open bottle poised over one of the glasses.

"Who are you, and what do you want?" she asked coldly, looking him straight in the eye.

"My name is Barsky, Oleg Dmitryevich . . ."

"I've already heard that. And you're from the KGB. And you want to get to know me. Why?"

He withstood her stare and smiled back calmly.

"So, would you like it in your coffee or in a glass?" he asked

Hmm, thought Anna. In principle, he was the sort of man she liked, calm and collected, not easily put out. Men like that presented a challenge that usually roused some response in her. She shot him a mocking reply:

"Well, if you've really done your homework, you'll have studied my habits. So you tell me: do I like brandy in my coffee, or do I prefer it in a glass?"

"Well, I haven't been quite so thorough as all that. . . ." Barsky smiled, still in control, and poured out two glassfuls. "Unfortunately, our weasel has brought us the wrong kind of glasses. Anyway, help yourself."

The sense of danger emanating from Barsky together with the whiff of good brandy and fresh coffee made Anna so desperate for a cigarette that she caught her fingers straying toward her purse. As if reading her thoughts, Barsky produced a pack of Dunhill and offered her one.

"Here you are."

She smirked to herself. He had evicted the weasel because of a supposed allergy to smoke, and he was a smoker himself! She took the glass and quickly downed a large swig—to bolster her courage and also to avoid any friendly toasting with him. After all what did this scoundrel want of her? Then she felt in her purse, produced her Marlboros, and lit up from the gold lighter that he obligingly proffered. She leaned back in her chair.

"Very well, Comrade Barsky," she said. "I'm listening. What are you, incidentally? *Captain* Barsky? Or Major?"

Her tone conveyed that she was trying to assert some advantage. But this only amused Barsky. He lit up one of his Dunhills and sipped his brandy.

"Anna Evgenyevna, have you ever wondered why all your *friends* are Jews?"

He so emphasized the word "friends" that he might as well have said "lovers" straight out. She was incensed, but her professional cool again kept her in control. She narrowed her eyes and inhaled before replying. Of course, she knew why all her men had been Jews, and probably always would be. Because the man she'd fallen for at fifteen, was a Jew. And from that day on all the men in her life had been Jews and only Jews. Nor had she ever been short of attention either. In any crowd, Jewish men always singled her out, looked her in the eye, and immediately tried to get to know her. There was nothing mysterious about this: when she became a woman at fifteen, Anna had thrived and blossomed in an almost botanical sense. Her breasts filled out like ripe fruit, with nipples pressing brazenly inside her dress. Her eyes turned a shade of emerald, her skin acquired the tint of peach juice and sunlight, and even her flaxen hair seemed to become softer and finer. She also acquired a regal bearing and became so lovely that not only passersby turned to look at her, but several film directors invited her to audition. Once, though, she was walking along with her first husband and they were overtaken by two drunks. One said to the other: "Son of a bitch! Every time you see a decent-looking Russian girl, she's always with a kike!" And now here was Barsky, an officer in the KGB, all but repeating those two.

Anna drew on her cigarette again.

"So what?" she said. "Am I supposed to ask the KGB who I should be . . . *friends* with?" She too emphasized the word so as to leave no doubt as to what she meant.

Barsky looked puzzled and scratched his cheek with carefully groomed nails.

"Well now," he began. "I think that makes it thirty–love in your favor. But remember, really, all we're doing is having a friendly chat. All I wanted was simply to caution you."

"About what?"

"Making mistakes. You're well aware that various folk of Jewish nationality are emigrating from this country. Some to their *historic* homeland," he pronounced the word "historic" with exaggerated irony, "and some—simply to America."

Anna's heart missed a beat and again crashed to the pit of her stomach. Now everything was clear. This was about the Israeli invitation that her husband Arkady had found in their mailbox a month ago. "The Ministry of Foreign Affairs of the State of Israel hereby confirms an invitation to Arkady Grigoryevich SIGAL (born 1934) and his wife Anna Evgenyevna SIGAL (born 1946) to take up permanent residence in Israel to reunite the family of Ms. Zvi SIGAL, resident at 12 HaGanet Street, Tel Aviv." But they'd never requested such an invitation. They didn't know any Zvi Sigal, and had no intention of leaving the Soviet Union. Yet here was this invitation. . . . True, when they left the USSR, many Jews wanted to get their friends out too, and they passed their addresses on to the Israeli authorities so that official invitations could be sent to them. The Soviet authorities however regarded even receipt of such an invitation as tantamount to an intention to emigrate. Arkady Sigal knew this and therefore intended to immediately hand this invitation over to the Party committee at his institute. As he told Anna, the KGB itself sometimes abetted the dispatch of these invitations to Jewish scientists to test how they reacted—to see whether they handed the invitation in or kept it for a rainy day. That way the authorities could check on the loyalty of their Jewish scientists.

"But this is a disgrace, Arkady!" Anna had said at the time. "It's like kindergarten! There you are, a State Prize winner and a doctor of science, and you have to go running to the Party with this paper like a little boy! Surely they realize that with all the secret information you have access to, you couldn't dream of leaving! And if you were thinking about it, you'd certainly never get an invitation through the mail. Any fool knows that all foreign mail is censored!"

Now, though, it was turning out that Arkady had been right. They really were idiots in the KGB! That invitation was theirs. And Arkady *should* have handed it in.

"Of course, your husband isn't under suspicion," Barsky said, as though reading her thoughts. "We know he received an Israeli invitation, but he didn't turn it in. And between you and me, he was quite right: I've always been against this humiliating way we have of checking up on our major scientists. On the other hand, though, what if you were in our shoes? More than two hundred thousand citizens of Jewish nationality now hold invitations to leave for Israel. Furthermore, some of them, like your husband and his friends, occupy important positions. And any of them, at any moment, could pull this emigration stunt on us. And before we know it, because one engineer suddenly takes it into his head to emigrate, we might have to halt production on an entire secret project! The state has already wasted millions this way. There was a scandalous case quite recently. A sculptor—you probably heard his name, or you may even know him personally. He went and won a competition to design a Lenin memorial. A sixty-foot granite statue erected in the main square of Tselinograd, all to his design. You get the picture? Sixty feet of granite! But that's not the worst of it—the statue went into multiple production. Forty-seven of those Lenin monuments are being put up all over Siberia. And now he goes and applies to emigrate! So what are we supposed to do? Take them all down again? It's a real case of *gevalt!*"

Anna said nothing. She knew that *gevalt* in Yiddish meant a scandal. But she didn't know the sculptor, and she didn't care a damn for those silly monuments getting stuck up all over the country like Matryoshka dolls. And whatever Barsky said, however much he tried to sweeten things by bandying a few Yiddish words—this whole business was to do with Arkady's failure to report that Israeli invitation. Her bad advice had put him on the spot.

"So you understand the situation we're in, Anna?" Barsky said, interpreting her silence as sympathy for his position and now addressing her familiarly by her first name. "Two hundred thousand potential . . . I don't even know how to put it—let's say potential deserters. Or even worse. Because today some Jew might develop a new missile guidance system, and we spend millions on research. Then—wham!—the man's in the West and handing all this work to the Americans. On the other hand, we can't fire every Jew just because he gets an invitation from Israel. That's just what the CIA would like. We'd have to remove our best scientists from their projects. Like your husband, for instance. That way they could send a shoal of Israeli invitations to all our leading scientists—including the Russian ones, so as to paralyze our whole economy. That's the situation we're facing, you see?"

Anna laughed to herself. What a great idea! With their suspicion of everyone, the KGB had landed in their own trap. So why didn't Israel send out about twenty million invitations? What would the KGB do if this Barsky guy, and Andropov, and Suslov, and Brezhnev all received invitations to join their Israeli relatives in Tel Aviv?

Her answer, however, was as cool as before:

"No," she said, "I don't see. What has this all got to do with me? My husband and I have no intention of going anywhere. Furthermore, I'm not Jewish, as you full well know. So what are you going on about?"

"That's exactly the point!" Barsky said hastily, delighted that at least he had gotten her to respond. He downed the rest of his brandy. "That's exactly why we're turning to you, because we have no doubt about your patriotism, nor that of your husband. You are friendly with a lot of talented Jews— scientists, engineers, lawyers, writers. You could be of serious help to your country. Like your father. Wait!" He fended off her protest with a wave of the hand. "Nobody is saying that you have to be an informer or, as they say, 'squeal.' That's not what we're talking about, Anna. And in fact there'd be nothing to fear in that anyway. But we are counting on you with exactly the opposite aim in mind. We need to know who is *not* intending to leave. Who can we completely rely on, if only for two or three years? You understand? Why aren't you drinking anything?"

Anna observed her own nervous movement as she stubbed her cigarette in the ashtray. Her posing was all in vain. Her gesture revealed the visceral terror that had gripped her as soon as Barsky mentioned the security services. What swine they were, recruiting her to spy for them! And blackmailing her because of Rappoport!

"You know, Anna," Barsky smiled confidingly, "they tell me your friends even call you not Anna Evgenyevna, but Evreyevna—as though your father was a Jew. Which means that they trust you as one of their own. And probably they discuss in front of you and your husband such things as whether to leave for Israel or not. No, wait!" He again raised a hand, fending off her objection. "We aren't asking you to canvas people. And you needn't tell us at all about who wants to go. And if they do, then good riddance—the air here will be a little cleaner. Although it's because of them that suspicion tends to fall even on people like your husband. So when Ustinov calls us up and asks who to entrust with top secret work—Abramovich, Sigal, or Ivanov—what can I answer? Can I guarantee that Comrade Sigal won't end up completing his project somewhere in Tel Aviv? That's why I'm asking you to help, Anna. Not me or the KGB, but your friends and your husband. If we're sure that they can be relied on, what harm can come from that? If you say that someone is honest and a patriot, that's surely not denouncing him, is it? And especially if it's for the man's own benefit!"

Smart, Anna thought to herself. Very professional. How elegantly he put things, the son of a bitch!

Without thinking, she reached again for her glass. Barsky immediately topped it off for her with an unfussy but lordly gesture.

"I'll tell you something else, Anna," he continued in a more confidential tone. "We have the one hundred and tenth anniversary of Lenin's birth coming up soon. At one time the best films about Lenin were all made by Jews—Kapler, Yutkevich, and Donskoy. But the question is, who nowadays can be entrusted to make a new modern epic about Lenin? If we give the contract to some Auerbach or Heifetz, they might make the film and then hop off abroad, just like that sculptor. And that really would be a scandal. So you see the fix we're in?"

"And if I refuse?"

"Oh come, Anna Evgenyevna. Why turn this down outright? After all, I'm not putting any pressure on you. Although, as you realize, I could do that. Both because of the Rappoport case and through your father. You realize that? But all we're doing now is having a friendly chat, and I'm not asking for your answer today. You, dealing with your clients, don't make decisions without thinking through the consequences, do you? So just go on your way and weigh all the pros and cons. And in a week or so I'll call and we can have another chat. Not here of course, but in some neutral setting.

The main thing to understand, Anna, is that I'm not asking you and your husband to be informers. And, if you've noticed, I'm not trying to persuade you with any promises of career advancement either. Although, as you well know, we have ways of helping careers take off as well as bringing them to a sticky end. But don't take that too seriously. I know you're not the sort of woman who can be bought. I'm only suggesting that you and your husband might like to help your friends—and yourselves as well, of course—in holding on to your reputations as people that the state can rely on. As I see it, this is a rather noble assignment. Don't you agree?"

I have to get up, Anna thought. I have to get up and tell him to go to hell. What a bastard! No, I should say something worse, something really foul and put an end to this once for all! Come on, Anna! Get up and do it.

But some force—or rather, the hypnotic effect of the organization Barsky represented—kept her pinned down. Meanwhile, Barsky again put his own interpretation on her silence, smiled complacently, and clinked his glass against her own.

"Here's to our friendship, Anna Evgenyevna. I'm sure you'll make the right decision. Here's my business card. You can call me at any time. And as for that, er . . . that Israeli invitation, just put it out of harm's way. Okay?" He looked Anna straight in the eye, either as a warning or a command—she wasn't sure which.

Three

It was only when outside in the street that Anna realized how exhausted she was. She felt numb and feeble, as though a leaden ocean wave had crashed down on her and she had barely managed to struggle to the surface. But now she had her footing on land again, amid the bustle of a Moscow spring, and who knew of that oppressive underwater kingdom she had just visited? Cars rushed along Petrovsky Boulevard, honking; teenage girls in short dresses ate chocolate ice cream; by the Café Lakomka passersby bought bunches of early spring mimosas; in front of the Rossiya movie theater was a snaking line for the new film starring Vyacheslav Tikhonov; beneath the windows of the *Izvestiya* office a small crowd of idlers viewed recent photographs of world events and yet another caricature of Jimmy Carter with the caption "In the Service of Zionism." On Pushkin Square someone strummed a guitar, and young people crowded around the Pushkin statue waiting for their dates. Meanwhile tourists strolled along Gorky Street, all in a holiday mood.

Only a few hours ago, Anna had been just like any of them—a person with her own friends, her own absorbing job, and her own springtime hopes of someone new and romantic for the summer. And all of this—even her meetings in the solitary confinement cells with the criminals she was defending—belonged to her own private world, which no one dared encroach upon. And within this world of hers Anna lived easily, like a fish in water. She drove her own car, spent her own money, walked her own dog, went to her own gynecologist, and had her own circle of friends. But now she realized this was a delusion. All this time people had been following her: the weasel had been keeping a file of her successes and failures, and the KGB had been keeping track of her love affairs, her acquaintances, and probably even her abortions. And all so as to lower the net when the time was ripe and to fish her out and plant a tiny microphone under her gills, then toss her back into the water and say: "Go on, swim. Off you go. But don't forget that now you belong to us, and we are going to tell you how to run your life, what to think, who to meet, and who to make love with."

Anna was not even aware of crossing the street to Pushkin Square, sitting down on a bench, and lighting up a cigarette. Was she being followed just now or not? No, she didn't want to know. And anyway they could go to hell.

On the next bench a hippy strummed his guitar and serenaded three girls with a popular ditty about a Moscow streetcar that would take him "in any direction of your soul." The spring crowds drifted past, but to Anna they all now seemed to belong to a different world, one that was still free. They flirted, ate their ice cream, sniffed their mimosa, laughed, and lived a simple, natural life, just as they wished. And yet . . .

And yet perhaps she was wrong: in this crowd, too, there were probably men and women who had been marked out. Perhaps several of them. She felt in her purse for another cigarette, and her fingers closed on a stiff little cardboard rectangle and froze. Then she pulled out Barsky's business card.

OLEG DMITRYEVICH BARSKY
Telephone 243-1227

That was all. No affiliation, no rank or position, no address. The KGB was everywhere . . . and yet nowhere. "Are you still in touch with Maxim Rappoport?" But evidently they were not so concerned with Maxim, who had become a legend among the Jews of Moscow. They were more interested in her husband. "Can I guarantee that comrade Sigal won't end up completing this project in Tel Aviv?" That was the root of it! They desperately needed Arkady's brains to direct some major new project, so they had to tie both him and her down by making them KGB collaborators. Otherwise they would blackmail her over her affair with Rappoport and over her father's dealings. But what could they do now to an elderly alcoholic with a prison record? Probably nothing, and here maybe Barsky was bluffing. That left Rappoport. That was serious. Here they had the trump card that—heaven forbid!—could send her down under Article 88 for aiding and abetting illegal currency operations. So you had better stay calm, Anna Evgenyevna. You'll now have to become your own lawyer. So better smoke another cigarette.

Of course her affair with Rappoport violated that vital unwritten rule of the attorney forbidding any familiarity with clients, not to mention more intimate relations. When she was at university, Professor Shnittke had harangued them in his awful Jewish accent: "A lawyer has no emotions! A lawyer has no soul! A lawyer has no sex! Have you got that, you young people? And this is not Moses' Ten Commandments. When people break the commandments, they can just go off to church and make amends with a bit of hard praying. But when an attorney breaks Shnittke's rules, he ceases to be an attorney! And then heaven help that person! Have you understood that, you young people?"

Anna did understand. And she never broke Shnittke's commandments—not once, and not with anyone. Except with one client, Rappoport. For him she had made an exception. Because he had that same erotic power as the first man she had ever been with. And like him, Rappoport too had come sweeping into her life, passed through, and soon exited from it.

"Good day. My name is Rappoport—with three p's," he announced as he strode smartly into her office. His eyes shone with that glimmer of playful irony, which for her distinguished a grain of talent from the chaff of mediocrity. "I work in the shadow economy," he said, "and there are two indictments against me. You will be defending me. I don't care what the cost is, and I'll cover all your expenses. If you need assistants, consultants, or specialists, all that can be provided. Your job is just to win the case."

"All clients' payments have to go through our accounts department," Anna said coldly.

"Of course. I've already paid for everything."

"What exactly have you paid for?" Anna did not quite follow. Their accountant would never take even a kopek from a client without an attorney's countersignature.

"One thousand six hundred rubles. For briefing you on the case against me."

"Ho-ow much?!" Anna gasped. The top fee for briefing was thirty rubles.

Rappoport placed his black attaché case on the table. It was chained to a bracelet on his left wrist. Hmm, quite a dandy, Anna thought. Rappoport unlocked the bracelet, then bent down and picked up a large suitcase of light-colored leather. This too he placed on the table, unfastened its gleaming snap locks, and began hauling out a series of neatly bound fat volumes.

"What's all this?" Anna asked.

"Copies of the documents that the Prosecutor's Office has on me. Sixteen volumes for the first charge, and I'll bring the other twenty-two after you've gone through these. You wouldn't take on all this work for just thirty rubles, would you?"

"But how could they accept your money before I even agreed to take the case?"

"Anna Evgenyevna, my name is Rappoport—with three p's. And that explains everything."

And that's how it always was. The man was a genius in a realm of business unthinkable in a totally planned economy and under Communist dictatorship. Thirty-nine, of medium height, broad-shouldered, with short-cropped dark hair and a large hooked nose, Rappoport was a bundle of jubilant energy, willpower, and ingenuity, all directed toward one goal: making money. Or, as the criminal code termed it, "economic crime on an especially broad scale." Gold mines in Kolyma, black caviar from the Caspian Sea, antique ikons from the north, underground production of consumer goods in the Caucasus, denim fabric for counterfeit Levis made in Odessa, and even a special type of urea used in leather work. But nowhere in the thirty-eight volumes assembled by the Prosecutor's Office was there a single page that specifically implicated Maxim Rappoport in any crime. Other tricksters, speculators, manufacturers, chief accountants of national organizations, policy makers, factory directors, and even government ministers indulged in theft, or hid production, or diverted goods from south to north or vice versa, and sooner or later, through drunkenness, stupidity, or excessive greed, they came to the attention of the Prosecutor's Office. And at every interrogation the name Maxim Rappoport turned up—as the "chief consultant" who had thought up the scheme. But nowhere, not on a single document, could his signature be found nor any record that he had received even a kopek for his services. And that was his guiding principle.

"You see, Anna Evgenyevna," he explained after she had read the first sixteen volumes, "when you're dealing with this sort of folk, you have to realize from the outset that they are a bunch of plebeians. And eventually they're bound to screw up because of their weakness for vodka, women, or simply stupidity. But the name Rappoport—every letter of it, even the extra p—is dearer to me than the entire gold reserves of the Soviet Union. That's why I'm but a consultant. I've never handled a single business document. So you're bound to win this case, make no mistake about it!"

Rappoport's ingenious combination of underground businesses within the state economic system resembled a gigantic chess tournament. And as she read through the documentation, Anna realized that with his energy, organizational skills, and ability to grasp any industrial process, this man could have made a name for himself as a physicist, rocket scientist, movie director, or even a choreographer. He could have been a second Kapitsa, Koroloyov, Bondarchuk, or Grigorovich. A man like him could have built airplanes or bridges, split the atom, or made prize-winning films. But instead, he did one thing and one thing only—he made money.

"Of course I'm brighter than anyone in the Kremlin," Maxim agreed, as he explained to Anna later on, during their brief affair. "After all, these leaders of the proletariat can't remember their multiplication tables. But I can work out square roots in my head. They've been "building socialism" for sixty years. But I can turn around their grandiose plans in less than a minute, and using their own building blocks I can set up a normal business and make it work. But that's not the main paradox; it's that you Russians yourselves have made us Jews so clever. In a thousand years of beating you can probably even whip sour cream out of water. And that's what you did— you beat us so much that we were forced to become champions at whatever we did. But, now that I'm a grandmaster, how can I work for this bunch of dumbbells? To build their cretinous socialism they killed off thirty million people! And yet they still shout to the world that they're the leading lights of humanity! And they believe it too, I swear! Khrushchev believed that with his collective farm system he could overtake America; now Brezhnev believes in State Planning. So how can any self-respecting person work for them?"

Anna won her case. And she won it easily. First, because everyone who was already doing time—that is, all Rappoport's partners who were already in jail—denied the initial damning evidence they had provided against him. "That wasn't difficult," Maxim told her casually, once the trial was over. "All their wives get a decent pension now." And second, during the trial the state prosecutor was not at all aggressive.

"Did you really buy off the Chief Prosecutor?" Anna asked him the day after the trial, when they both took the night flight down to Sochi on the Black Sea. On his lap Maxim still held his perpetual black attaché case, still chained to his left wrist.

"Anna, dear," he replied, "that's not something you need to know. My name is—"

"Rappoport with three p's, I know!" she interrupted. "But do you have to drag that attaché case with you on holiday? It's all just for show! What's in there? Your secret codes in case of nuclear war, like President Nixon?"

"Do you want to see?"

"Yes."

"Right now?"

"Yes!"

"Okay." Without unchaining the case, and using just his right hand he set a number combination on the lock and opened the lid. "There you are," he said.

Anna gasped and then glanced at the passengers around them. But it was a night flight and they were all asleep. The attaché case was crammed with American dollars. Horrified, she clapped a hand to her mouth to stifle a cry of astonishment. There she was, a member of the Moscow Bar, flying off on holiday with her lover, who turned out to be a currency speculator! Who needed documentary evidence—that briefcase alone was enough to get them executed. And no lawyers could help. This was Article 88, part two: "currency operations on an especially large scale," which carried a sentence of from five years to execution.

"You're out of your mind! What do you need all this hard currency for?"

"It's not for me. It's going to a guy in Sochi. After that, we'll have the vacation that we deserve, and with unreal service."

That vacation was indeed one that Anna could never have imagined— not even from the movies she'd seen about American millionaires. They stayed on private estates not marked on any map of the Crimean peninsula. They swam from beaches unknown even to the Kremlin's favorite cosmonauts. They drove around in government limousines, stayed in luxurious government villas, and romped in powerboats that belonged to the commander of the Black Sea fleet. Moreover, the service was so unobtrusive that they never had to meet the masters of these villas, or the owners of the limousines, holiday estates, and powerboats. Anna was flabbergasted.

"Maxim, are we really in the Soviet Union?"

"Unfortunately, we are. But the worst of it is that we met too late for me to change anything. You know . . ."

She did know. She knew that in his attaché case he already had his exit papers, which he received within two hours of leaving the courtroom. Other Jews had to wait up to a year. But his name was Rappoport—with three p's! And he also had in his case a ticket for Moscow–Vienna flight number 228, on July 19, 1977.

Later, as she lounged with him on deserted beaches, or sprawled on the Turkoman rugs of government villas, or in the hunting lodges of Politburo members, she reflected on their adventures. "If I'd gone and lost that case for you," she said, "you'd have been traveling east instead of west, in spite of all your p's!"

But she had won, and in twenty days he was due to leave. And their awareness of that inevitable separation made their lovemaking ten times more intense than usual—just like it had been for her that first time, long ago . . .

"Can't you postpone your departure?" she asked. "After all your name is Rappoport!"

"Unfortunately, I can't. Twenty days is my limit, not a minute more. It's all been worked out."

At the time she didn't understand what exactly had been worked out. To her it seemed that a man like him could put off his departure for a year if he wanted. But later, after Rappoport's name had become a legend, she realized there was a time limit because he was being tailed, and he knew it. Even when he first came to her office at the Bar headquarters he was being tailed, and all during the trial, and also on the plane heading south. Only in Sochi did he manage to give them the slip, when a Chaika limousine without license plates whisked them from the plane's gangway and took them to a resort unmarked on any map. At that point all that the people tailing him could probably do was scratch their heads and throw up their hands.

But when Maxim and Anna returned to Moscow, they again began to tail him. He apparently realized this would happen, and that was why he told her at the airport: "That's it, Anna. As far as you're concerned now, I've left already."

"Why?" she asked in amazement.

"That's the way it has to be."

"You bastard!"

He looked her straight in the eye, and for the first time in their relationship there was no mischievous glint of genius in his eyes. There was only pain.

"Anna, dear, my name is Rappoport, as you know. But if I could only give up that name, in its entirety, three p's and all, and take you with me, believe me I would. I swear by the memory of my mother. But it isn't possible. Believe your old friend Rappoport."

Anna was furious. She drove home from the airport alone in a separate cab, as he insisted. Yet she was certain that in a day's time—or certainly no more than three—he would call her up and arrive with a bouquet of Crimean roses, or else burst into her office and announce: "Anna, it's all fixed—you're coming with me!" And right to the last day, the nineteenth of July, she waited anxiously each day for him to call or suddenly appear.

f o u r

Rappoport did not call. Nor did he reappear. And two hours before his plane was due to leave, she jumped into her little Zhiguli and hurtled off to Sheremetyevo Airport. But there was no sign of Maxim there. The Vienna plane was there; some Austrian tourists were; so was a crowd of emigrating Jews—sixteen families with all their children, luggage, and packages. But no Maxim Rappoport. She was about to enquire for him at the departure desk but stopped herself: she remembered the attaché case stuffed with dollars. She was an attorney and she knew the rules. The Kremlin might turn a blind eye to Rappoport's business crimes, but they were ruthless on the issue of hard currency. Even a "liberal" like Khrushchev got livid when he'd heard about the currency manipulations of Rokotov and Faibyshenko, and he'd ordered them shot without even a trial. And all Rokotov had was a mere two hundred thousand dollars.

Three weeks later Anna discovered exactly how much Rappoport had on him. Later, when the story became a legend, the figure grew and grew. But the initial sum bandied about at the time of his leaving was probably closer to the truth.

Rappoport was said to have had a million dollars.

That was just like him—he loved impressive figures. To leave the USSR with less than a round million would have been a blow to his pride. But more than that—a million plus small change—would not have been in character either. He was not one to nickel and dime. Anna believed the figure—Rappoport did have a million, all in hundred-dollar bills. He had bought them from black marketeers—both small- and big-time operators—in Moscow, Leningrad, Odessa, and Riga, paying almost any price in rubles, and up to 150 dollars in other hard currencies, for a one-hundred-dollar bill.

Of course, they began trailing him. That was inevitable. But—according to the legend—he carried on openly and brazenly, moving around Moscow and other cities with his constant attaché case chained to his left wrist, carrying wads money. He met up with currency touts and bought up their hundred-dollar bills, which he then took back to his apartment on Frunzenskaya Embankment. There he neatly stowed the bills in a hidden safe set into the wall behind the fireplace.

What exactly could the man have in mind? After all, the KGB's Political Security Department had a Tenth Section, one formed specially to deal with "economic criminals," i.e. speculators in foreign currency. They knew Rappoport's every move, and also of course about his application to emigrate. How was it they didn't pick him up and arrest him when he met up with the black-market boys? How is it they were permitting him to emigrate? They had to be aware he was not buying up currency to leave it in a Moscow savings bank.

All the same, they did not stop him from acquiring his million. And, according to the legend, when Rappoport and his mistress took off for Sochi, the investigation team personally counted the currency in the safe at his apartment. But at the time there was less than a million—about seventy thousand short. So they left it untouched. The reason was: their own ambitions. They wanted to pull in a round million. Why run around chasing petty speculators, arresting and questioning them, tearing up floors and disemboweling mattresses for a miserable ten or fifteen thousand dollars? That was the thinking of these KGB currency hounds. They would let Rappoport do the work for them, cobble together a round million, and then they would simply repossess the money as it crossed the border.

In other words, just like grandmaster Karpov, they were playing their own calm and confident chess game. It was because of that million that they asked the Chief Prosecutor not to be too aggressive at Rappoport's trial. After all, what was more important?—to send Rappoport to Siberia for his petty dealings in urea and caviar, or have him put together a million dollars for the benefit of the treasury?

Admittedly, the closer Rappoport's departure date came, the more anxious the KGB team became. They still had not worked out how he intended getting his million out. But then he did something that reassured them. On July 12, a week before his scheduled flight, he brought six enormous brand-new suitcases to the Kozhgalantereya leather workshop on Komsomol Square and asked the director, Aron Gurevich, to fit each case with a false bottom and sides. The next day, a certain Grisha Mendelson appeared at Sheremetyevo Airport and handed ten thousand rubles to the chief Customs officer with a simple request to bear in mind the name of Rappoport.

The KGB then concluded that the precious million had been assembled. Now they were left with the choice of either raiding Rappoport's apartment or waiting for the million to make its own way to Sheremetyevo, hidden in the lining of the suitcases. Obviously, they chose the latter. It was one thing to report to the Politburo that a million dollars had been found in the apartment of some crook named Rappoport, but quite another to announce that this sum had been seized by Customs from an emigrating Jew. "A Million Seized at the Border!" That would make headlines, an international event.

It would be a mark of the security forces' heroism and vigilance, which would translate into medals and awards, and it would provide a good reason to whip up another anti-Zionist campaign.

Meanwhile, Rappoport's behavior became more brazen by the hour. Four days before his scheduled departure, he threw a farewell party at his apartment for a hundred guests. The cream of society from Moscow, Leningrad, Riga, and Odessa all came. There was the famous poet-bard with his French actress wife; Gypsies from the Romany Theater, and half the corps-de-ballet from the Bolshoi; and an array of trendy artists, poets, movie stars, leading lights from the top TV shows, not to mention a sprinkling of diplomats from the embassies of Argentina, Australia, Nigeria, and the United States.

Of course, the whole of Rappoport's apartment house was staked out, but the event passed without incident. The guests drank champagne and whiskey and ate black caviar from the Gifts of the Sea food store and shish kebabs from the Aragvi Restaurant; they listened to the bard perform, and danced by firelight almost until morning with the Gypsies and girls from the Bolshoi; as a memento they also had themselves photographed with their host. From down below the KGB team watched the sixth-floor windows and listened in on the famous bard's performance via concealed microphones. And as they did this, the KGB officers couldn't stop marveling how in a country like theirs, where everything was so strictly controlled and people waited years to obtain housing, this speculator Rappoport had contrived to obtain a five-room apartment in a special A-category house that was built exclusively for elite Party members. And as they languished below in the dark and the dank that came drifting up from the river, they cheered themselves with a faint hope that after the triumph of this operation, they too might qualify for some upgraded accommodation. Maybe not in so splendid a house as this, but still . . .

Toward dawn, as Rappoport's guests began wending their way home, groups of specially detailed "street thugs" gave the diplomats a going-over as they left. But no wads of money were found on anyone. True, the bard had his guitar. But judging by the ease with which his wife carried it as she followed her inebriated husband to their Mercedes, it had to contain nothing. And the American and Australian diplomats, who were almost the last to leave, had cameras, but a million dollars could scarcely be concealed inside a few miniature Japanese cameras.

All the next day, Rappoport slept, recovering from his hangover. But on the seventeenth at two in the afternoon, he ordered a cab from the nearby taxi stand, loaded his six seemingly empty cases into it and took his seat next to the driver. "Let's go!" he said.

The stake-out team were right on his tail, of course. But there was no reason for panic—Rappoport could be taking his cases anywhere. Maybe the currency would not fit into the secret compartments, and he had decided to have more work done on them. However, after wheeling around the center of Moscow without stopping anywhere, Rappoport's cab headed up Gorky Street, past the Belorussky Station, and continued on along Leningradsky Prospect, further and further out of the city, past the River Port and construction sites on the edge of town. Where was he going?

To Sheremetyevo!

As the cab took the turn toward Sheremetyevo International, panic erupted on the airwaves: "What, has Rappoport gone crazy? Is he so hungover that he's mixed up the date? His flight isn't today, but the day after tomorrow. . . . What KGB guys are on duty at the airport? . . . What, there's an M. Rappoport on the list for today's flight 228, leaving at 3:20 P.M.? How can that be? . . . What? One Jew in six is named Rappoport? Damn it, could he really have two tickets—one for today and one for the nineteenth? . . . Is the head of Customs on duty? . . . Not there? . . . His day off? Lord, perhaps someone ought to tell this Yid he's leaving on the wrong day? . . ."

They did no such thing, of course. The KGB quickly managed to get themselves organized.

While Rappoport stood in line for the baggage inspection with other emigrating Jews, the entire KGB team that had been trailing him for the last seven months rushed out to Sheremetyevo and took positions beyond the Customs barrier. Major Zolotaryov, the chief of Customs, was dragged back from his dacha. And with good reason. After all, they were about to haul in the biggest currency operator of all time! And a Jewish emigrant to boot! One million dollars! Here would be proof of how these emigrants were cleaning the country out before they left!

Meanwhile six detectives kept their eyes riveted on Rappoport's precious suitcases. They practically surrounded them—each operative with his own suitcase to follow, and each man gloated at the mental picture of great wads of American dollars concealed behind the brown-tooled leather. And the senior KGB agents at a slight distance also felt that peculiar nervous frisson of the hunter closing in on a wild boar. Where did he have the money? All in one case? Or had he divided it up among the six?

Meanwhile the atmosphere in the Customs Hall was transformed beyond recognition. Those Jews who happened to be flying out of Moscow on July 17, 1977, could not understand why the inspectors suddenly stopped going over their baggage with a fine-tooth comb and no longer bothered confiscating items such as caviar, nickel-silver, medications, or even silver forks. Instead, officials hastily checked just one or two suitcases, quickly stamped their green travel visas, and hustled them on. "Next! Hurry up there! Go on through! Next!"

At last it was Rappoport's turn. He seemed to have noticed nothing untoward—neither his watchers, nor the haste of the Customs inspectors. And the bloodhounds of the KGB were enjoying that. They were filming him with concealed still and video cameras, and like a cat playing with a mouse before devouring it, they prolonged the process and allowed him to haul all six of his suspiciously light cases plus the ever-present attaché case to the inspection table.

"Your ticket?" the inspector asked.

Rappoport produced it.

"Your visa?"

With obviously feigned nonchalance Rappoport produced the document with its Soviet exit and Austrian entry visas.

"Unlock your cases."

"They're already open."

"What?"

"They're not locked."

"Hmm . . . Open this suitcase."

That was the signal. Six KGB officers together with Major Zolotaryov sprang behind the Customs inspector who was all primed for his heroic role as captor of a Zionist currency speculator.

Rappoport looked at them all in surprise, then flung open the lid of the first case. Inside lay seven male undershirts, and that was all. But the KGB team knew Rappoport's secret. The Customs inspector produced a lancet and with a practiced hand neatly slit open the bottom and sides of the case. Meanwhile a cameraman emerged from behind the glass barrier and with no effort at concealment aimed his lens at the eviscerated suitcase.

It was empty. Between the double bases and the double side walls there was absolutely nothing, not even a speck of dust. The inspector maintained his impassive expression and proceeded to cut apart the whole case, slicing through the middle of the base, the lid, and the sides.

Empty.

"Open the next case!"

Rappoport shrugged and opened a second case.

It too contained soiled undershirts, six in all, and three pairs of under-pants. The inspector carelessly tossed all this onto the floor and raised his finely honed weapon over the empty suitcase.

"Maybe that's unnecessary?" Rappoport asked with an expression of feigned innocence. "It's a good case. Why spoil it? I can give it to you."

But, in Soviet press parlance, "The enemy of our Soviet state failed in his fiendish attempt to provoke the steadfast officer of the Customs service. The frontiers of our nation are protected by staff unsurpassed in their training, experience, and vigilance." So once again, with practiced hand, the inspector slit open the base and sides of Rappoport's luxurious leather case.

It too, however, was completely empty.

"Next case!"

The third case also contained a secret compartment, this one covered by two pairs of worn-out jeans.

"Next one!"

It need hardly be said that the Customs and KGB staff began succumbing to a bout of blind fury. They slashed all six cases to shreds and literally hacked to bits his famous black attaché case. And needless to say, Rappoport himself underwent an exhaustive body search. He was X-rayed and also put through a humiliating inspection of his anal aperture. But apart from the ninety dollars that emigrants were legally entitled to, they found nothing of value in his pockets, his teeth, or even up his anus.

"You can take your things!"

Rappoport picked up his unwashed shirts, underpants, and jeans from the floor. One shirt and a pair of jeans he rolled up, and the remaining items he tossed into a garbage bin. Then, using his Austrian visa to fan himself in the heat, he made his way up to the second floor, to passport control.

There, at the departure gate, he was stopped by officers of the KGB.

"One moment, Rappoport!"

"Excuse me?"

"Where are the dollars?"

"Here . . . but you've seen them . . ." He pulled out his pathetic little bundle of ninety dollars.

"Don't mess with us! You know what dollars we're talking about! Look at this!" They handed Rappoport several large photos that showed him taking dollars from speculators in Moscow, Leningrad, Riga, and Odessa. "Either you tell us where the dollars are, or we take you off the flight."

"Oh, *those* dollars! So that's what you were looking for!" Rappoport exclaimed. "But my dear fellows, you should have said so at the beginning. Instead you've gone and cut up all those beautiful cases. I now have to leave empty-handed. I'll be ashamed to get off the plane in Vienna."

"Don't play the fool! Out with it!"

An expression of deep sorrow clouded Rappoport's nasal overhang.

"Do you mean to say you don't know what happened, comrades? Those swindlers tricked me. It's just terrible how they all deceived me. They planted masses of forged hundred-dollar bills on me. And I went everywhere to find them. I tried so hard—you can see for yourselves." He nodded at the compromising photos. "And d'you know what? Last night I almost had a heart attack! I showed all that goddamned money to some American and

Australian diplomats, and they told me right away that the whole lot was forged. Counterfeit! Even the Nigerian could see it. So I burned it all. What else was I to do? In my fireplace. Call up your people. They're probably already there in my apartment. Tell them to poke around in the fireplace. Those forged notes don't burn all that well, so you should still find a few fragments."

But they didn't need to call. They had already spoken with their colleagues, who had dashed over there as soon as Rappoport's third suitcase was reported empty. They had already heard that in the pile of ashes in the fireplace, 649 scorched fragments of U.S. hundred-dollar bills had been found. "He went and burned a million bucks!" they yelled over the phone.

"What could I do, my dear fellows?" Rappoport said sadly to the officers surrounding him. "As my old father used to say, one should learn to part with money with a light heart. Even with a million. Even a million, my father used to say, isn't worth a single "p" in our family name. . . . So can I go now?"

The KGB agents were speechless.

Rappoport shrugged, then turned and walked through the gate, still fanning himself with his visa and with his jeans and shirt rolled up under his arm.

And they kept on staring after him until the final moment, when the plane actually lifted off the tarmac.

The following day, KGB specialists reported the results of a spectrographic and chemical analysis of the charred scraps found in Rappoport's fireplace. They proved unambiguously that all the dollars had in fact been *genuine*! But even then the investigating officers failed to grasp what had happened. Could Rappoport with his own hands really have burned a million dollars?

According to the rumor, it was a week later that the head of the team woke up one night in a cold sweat. In some awful nightmare he realized how Rappoport had hoodwinked them. He really had incinerated a million— ten thousand hundred-dollar bills. And he'd done it in the presence of three American and two Australian diplomats. But prior to this, each of these diplomats had received from Rappoport a microfilm with photographs of each bill, and a list of their numbers. And they themselves had checked the list against the bank notes. Then they'd signed an affidavit confirming the burning of the bills, and they'd also captured the event on film with their cameras. Later, in the United States, on the basis of these documents, which were authenticated by representatives of two embassies, the Federal Reserve Bank would pay out to Rappoport one million dollars in exchange for the million he'd destroyed.

Naturally, the KGB rushed out to find the diplomats who had attended

Rappoport's farewell party. But it turned out that all five had left Moscow on the same day as Rappoport—July 17, 1977.

Of course, rumor might have exaggerated some of the details. But everyone who recounted the story rounded it off with one and the same phrase: the KGB, they said, had played off against Rappoport with all the confidence of Karpov. But he had outplayed and trounced them with the skill of Gary Kasparov—or to be more exact, with the skill of Rappoport spelled with three p's.

Sitting on her bench beneath the Pushkin monument, Anna tried to fathom why Maxim never had told her they were trailing him. Was his fleeting affair with her somehow vital for him to divert the KGB? No, surely not. Otherwise he would have kept her at his side right to the last day. Instead he'd deliberately pushed her to one side, out of harm's way. But then he'd gone and forgotten her. Two months later one of her "well wishers" told her that Maxim was in Boston and feeling on top of the world. But since the day he left, he had not once called or written.

Anyway, to hell with Rappoport, Anna told herself as she smoked what was probably her third cigarette. From now on, she had to think of herself. She had concealed her affair with Maxim from her husband. That was dishonest, despicable, and unfair to Arkady. Five years ago, at the most awful and desperate moment in her life, when she had been abandoned by her husband and rejected by her father, she was on the verge of God knows what—suicide or insanity. And at that point it was Arkady who took her in. He had brought her to his neglected bachelor pad and told her: "You can live here. You're going to finish university. And if you'd like, I'll give you a little dog too."

The dog, an Airedale terrier from some military kennel, was in fact presented to her within weeks—along with her wedding ring. And when she graduated from university, Arkady handed her the keys to a splendid new Zhiguli. It seemed to her then that a woman could want for nothing more: her husband was institute director, a doctor of science, and a State Prize winner, she herself working at the most prestigious attorneys' bar in Moscow; an apartment in the center of town; she had the latest model car; and even her dog was a golden-haired thoroughbred. But it turned out that over and above all these earthly blessings a woman of thirty needed something else. And that thing was love—banal though that might sound. Not that Arkady didn't love her. Indeed he did—but, as it were, from a distance. First of all, he would disappear for weeks and sometimes months to his top-secret institute at Chernogolovka, two hours away from Moscow. And secondly, even when he came home or she visited him at Chernogolovka, he was still "absent": he would sit at his desk for days doing calculations and neither saw nor heard her, nor paid her the slightest attention. Even in bed, at their most intimate moments, she sensed that in his heart and mind he still was not completely there. Mentally he dwelt in some other dimension—amid brain-racking formulae, experiments, physical and mathematical theories. Even at those moments that a woman holds most sacred, his super brain, which so fascinated the Ministry of Defense, remained preoccupied with heaven knows what other subjects. All this eventually turned Anna off. It simply phased out all her erotic power points, and finally her body ceased to respond. She no longer soared above their nuptial bed.

However, Anna remained at her husband's side, she could see that he loved having a young and beautiful *Russian* wife. He enjoyed visiting Science House in her company and inviting colleagues and friends back to their home. In moments when he was not madly working, he would take her to buy dresses and bring her flowers. But even during those infrequent shared diversions, it was she who accompanied her husband, and not vice versa. So sooner or later, Rappoport or someone was bound to come into her life and do what Vronsky did with her namesake, Anna Karenina. And all the untapped sensuality that had built up behind the dam wall of Arkady's indifference burst out and flooded over Rappoport. That was what brought them together in a frenzy on those Black Sea beaches and drove them wild with an insatiable sexual appetite. However, unlike Vronsky, Rappoport jumped in a plane and flew away alone, without his Anna. He left her struggling with a woman's most painful problem: what was she to do with her life and with her thirst for love? Her biological clock reminded her ever more loudly that she was already thirty-two. But even after Rappoport left she deferred any resolution of her problems and simply buried herself in work and in the social round. After all she already had a son—even if he lived in America; and a husband—even if he did spend most of his time in Chernogolovka.

However, Comrade Barsky only an hour ago had wrenched her out of this ostrichlike equivocation. He had revealed to her how utterly illusory her seemingly stable lifestyle was. What stability could there be, damn it, when under the very nose of the Chairman of the Bar, she could be blackmailed and recruited as a KGB informer? And there was no escape! If she didn't give in, Barsky would ruin both her own career and that of her husband. And if she did submit . . . No! The very thought made her gorge rise! From her work as a lawyer she knew all about the Barskys, Kuzyaevs, and other weasels in the service of this "world power." They could bind you hand and foot, and never let go, Anna thought bitterly. She didn't bother weighing all the pros and cons. What was the good if they knew virtually everything about her and could nail her with Article 88 for aiding and abetting a currency speculator? But where was the way out? Should she emigrate, flee? Maybe, like dozens of Jews she knew, she should try and get out. But she had already tried that once, and it was her own father who had all but killed her, refusing to sign the exit paper. "This is your country!" he'd shouted. "Your country is right here!"

She retrieved the last cigarette from her pack and lit up, narrowing her eyes as she pondered. No, this was not her country, and it was pointless trying to fool herself on that score. This was *their* country—it belonged to Barsky, Kuzyaev, Andropov, and others of their ilk. But over there, in America, she had a son. Even if he had forgotten her and now called some other woman his mother. Anna still had the right to be allowed to join him! Or, as she grimly reminded herself, she used to have that right. Why hadn't she gone earlier, before Barsky? Now it needed but a squeak about her right to leave the country for the Rappoport story to rear its ugly head and slam the door in her face. God, what could she do?

"You smoke too much," said the long-haired hippy with the guitar.

"This is my last. I'm quitting," she answered.

She got up, inhaled one last time, and ground the butt under her shoe. Then she looked up and suddenly, with a new sense of sharpened vision, she seemed to have a panoramic and hallucinatory view of the whole of Gorky Street, Tverskoy Boulevard, and Pushkin Square. Every detail minutely recorded—the hippy with his guitar, a sorrowful Pushkin surrounded by chains, the fountain, the line-up at the Rossiya movie theater, and the old-fashioned street clock. It was a farewell sensation and she was suddenly aware that soon she might have to leave all these things that were so dear. Her stomach clenched, her chest tightened, and she felt a surge of pity for herself. Who had given these bastards the right to ruin her life?

She set off for the underground walkway under Gorky Street. A sudden sharp trill of police whistles, stamping feet, shouting, smacking fists, and the dull thud of falling bodies made her look around. She froze halfway down the steps. Something dreadful was going on around the Pushkin memorial where she had just been. A group of men and women were standing in a tight circle behind the chains at the statue. Above their heads they'd raised placards with six-pointed stars and the handwritten words LET MY PEOPLE GO! The long-haired hippy who two minutes ago was peacefully strumming had joined them, holding his instrument aloft and displaying a blue star of David on its underside. Next to him stood a little gray-haired woman with a yellow star of David sewn to her breast, and there was also an elderly man who looked like the well-known comic actor Gertsianov.

"*Refuseniks*," said someone standing next to Anna.

She stood stock-still and watched as militiamen, volunteer guards with red bands on their sleeves, and athletic-looking young men in gray suits emerged from every side. They came running out of the underground walkway and jostled her as they rushed past. They also came from Tverskoy

Boulevard, Gorky Street, the nearby subway station, and the *Izvestiya* newspaper building. The first group lunged at the refuseniks, who offered no resistance. The men attacked without a word, swinging punches to the jaw and kicks to the stomach in totally random fashion. Then a second wave of attackers moved in, twisting arms, grabbing the placards, and trampling them underfoot. Somewhere a girl fell to the ground, and the hippy with his guitar yelled, "You're animals! Swine! Long live freedom!"

Out of the corner of her eye Anna saw a tall foreigner on the other side of Gorky Street raise a camera above his head. But he too was immediately knocked off his feet, and his camera was grabbed and crunched under someone's heavy heel.

A black militia van appeared from behind the movie theater and raced straight up to the Pushkin memorial. It bounced up the curb, onto the sidewalk, and screeched to a halt, a mere arm's length from the melee. Its metal rear doors swung open, and the beat-up and bloodied demonstrators with tattered clothes, shredded placards, and a smashed guitar were pushed, kicked, and hurled into the vehicle's dark hold. But still they struggled and resisted.

"This is a peaceful demonstration!" they shouted. "You signed the Helsinki Agreement!"

Anna stood two steps down the walkway staircase, benumbed and unable to speak or move. It all occurred as if in some nightmare. Pushkin Square was suddenly empty, as though a wind had swept the crowd away; the violence was over almost before it had begun. Clothes were ripped and teeth knocked out; the militia van swallowed up the whole group, slammed its rear doors, and sped off for Petrovka Street and the militia headquarters.

Abruptly it was over. The beefy young men quickly picked up the shreds of placard and a woman's shoe, used their boot soles to rub away the blood stains on the asphalt, and then dispersed, calmly lighting up cigarettes as they went; new waves of pedestrians flowed onto the square. People who had not seen the lightning pogrom continued laughing, chatting up the girls, eating their chocolate ices, and buying yellow mimosa from the flowergirls. And Aleksandr Pushkin, the Russian people's greatest poet, gazed down at them sadly and silently as before. A hundred and fifty years ago he too had asked the tsar for permission to go abroad, and the tsar had refused even him. So Russia's first literary "refusenik" was doomed to remain here, where he was later killed. Surrounded by a chain fence, his image now stood on a street that bore the name of yet another prisoner, Maksim Gorky. The great "proletarian writer" had asked another tsar, Joseph Stalin, to let him go abroad, but with the same result. Now the refusenik Gorky, also surrounded by cast-iron chains, stood at one end of his own street, on a stone plinth in front of the Belorussky Station.

Down in the walkway, Anna leaned back against the wall trying to get over the cottony feeling in her legs. God knows, it wasn't all that easy to leave this country—neither under the tsars nor the Communists. What if she too was turned down? After all she wasn't even Jewish. Would she too have to go through all this—bloody fistfights, broken teeth, and the dark maw of a militia prison van?

She was terrified.

With the same fear that had kept the nobleman Aleksandr Pushkin from antitsarist manifestations, and the tramp Gorky from making statements against Stalin. So where did these Jews find the courage to march out onto the square like that, with nothing more than a guitar and homemade placards?

How would she have the courage to confront the might of the Kremlin and risk her own row of pearly-white teeth? But all she could feel inside her was fear—a fear that filled her whole body and robbed her of all strength.

"Maxim!" her heart cried out.

"Are you feeling okay?" someone asked her.

She opened her eyes.

In front of her stood two little folk from Lilliput—a midget not much more than three feet tall, wearing a top hat and severe jacket, and with a cigarette jutting from his mouth, and an elegant little doll-like woman.

"Feeling queasy?" the little man asked again.

"Yes . . . very . . ." she said. "Do you have a cigarette?"

five

Every Thursday, as the ten-foot clock hands on Spasskaya Tower showed 9:58 A.M., a long black ZIL-110 limousine drew up onto Red Square. The car would stop by the old stone execution plinth, just a hundred paces from the Kremlin entrance, and out would get Mikhail Andreyevich Suslov. Behind his back people referred to the lanky, austere seventy-year-old Politburo member as the Kremlin's "gray cardinal," or as the "Red *Parteigenosse*." Dressed in a long gabardine dating from the fifties, a gray hat, and rubber galoshes that between September and June he never took off, Suslov looked at no one and steadily walked to the Kremlin on foot. In this he differed from all the country's other rulers who drove into the Kremlin, shielded from the populace by thick velvet blinds on the bulletproof windows of their armored limousines.

Knowing Suslov's "democratic" habit, the plainclothes agents of the Kremlin's external guard cleared all tourists and other idlers away from the area around the execution plinth in advance. Suslov then made his stiff-gaited transit of the square, passed through the checkpoint under Spasskaya Tower, and entered the Kremlin's inner courtyard. There in a niche in the wall stood two soldiers, tall as grenadiers and dressed in parade uniform. Together with the guard commander, on the stroke of ten, they would march out onto the Square to relieve the honor guard at the Lenin Mausoleum. This long-established procedure, which had down the years never changed, provided a certain reassuring feeling. Clutching their guns to their chests, the guard marched out in measured pace to watch over the embalmed body of the leader of the world proletariat. Meanwhile, the chief guardian of the purity of Lenin's theory paced across the Kremlin yard to the regular weekly meeting of the Politburo to supervise the realization of those immortal ideas. The holy silence of the Kremlin, Suslov in his perennial gray coat and galoshes, the marching soldiers in green with Kalashnikovs at the ready, the solemn bell chimes of the Spasskaya Tower built by Pietro Solario in 1491, and the gigantic red flag fluttering over the onetime tsarist Senate Building—all this reinforced a sense of the immutable permanence of that Communist empire that stretched from the river Elbe to the Kuril Islands.

It was the year A.D. 1978, and the eve of the sixty-first anniversary of the October Revolution and of Leonid Brezhnev's seventy-second birthday. The empire was at the zenith of its power. It held sway over more than a hundred nations in Europe, Asia, Africa, and South America; its intercontinental missiles with nuclear warheads were trained on every industrial center in the United States; its SS-20 rockets could reach every populated area in Western Europe, China, and Japan; in the guise of Arabs, Africans, Vietnamese, and Cubans, its pilots, commandoes, and tank troops supervised wars in the Middle East and were surreptitiously or openly establishing Marxist regimes in Angola, Algeria, Bangladesh, Laos, Cambodia, Mozambique, Ethiopia, Yemen, and Indonesia; and its diplomats toured the world dictating the Kremlin's conditions for survival. And the chief ideologue of this grandiose process was that ascetic elderly gent in his old topcoat and cheap rubber galoshes. And he was still two years from making his final fatal mistake in Afghanistan.

Suslov crossed the empty Cathedral Square, skirting the tall bell tower of Ivan the Great, the ancient Tsar-Bell, and the Palace of Facets, and made his way to the eastern porch of the ancient Kremlin Palace. An attentive guard opened the tall door with its polished brass handle, and Suslov entered the long, airy marble vestibule with its wardrobe on the left-hand side. There he removed his coat, hat, and galoshes and handed them to the courteous female attendant.

"Is everyone here?" he asked his assistant, who stood there waiting for him.

"Everyone's here as usual, Mikhail Andreyevich."

Suslov nodded and made his way up the broad, red-carpeted stair to the second floor, passing through the ornate walnut door into the anteroom with its green jade fireplace, and finally entering the celebrated Georgievsky Hall, a gigantic white marble room, sixty yards long and twenty wide. It had lofty forty-foot windows, and its ceiling and walls were decorated with marble slabs bearing the names of Suvorov, Kutuzov, Nakhimov, Ushakov, and other tsarist army leaders. The hall also boasted a bas-relief of St. George dispatching the dragon. Its gleaming parquet floor was composed of twenty rare varieties of wood—from Indian palisander to African paduka. Light was provided by six multitiered chandeliers in fretted gold, each weighing about one and a half tons. Before the revolution it was here that the tsars gave ceremonial balls, received ambassadors, and distributed the Empire's highest awards. After the revolution Communist Party congresses were held here, Stalin Prizes awarded, and specially solemn banquets, after the defeat of Germany for instance, or when Gagarin made his flight into space. And now, each Thursday, this Georgievsky Hall housed meetings of the Party's governing caucus—the Politburo. Suslov walked round the conference table and shook hands with each man present: Brezhnev, Kosygin, Ustinov, Gromyko, Chernenko, Kulakov, Andropov, and others. Then he took his seat to the left of Brezhnev, on one of the antique tsarist chairs with fluted golden legs and upholstered with silk the shade of the St. George ribbon. Putting on his glasses, Suslov drew toward him the sheet with the day's agenda.

At this point everyone—the Politburo members, Central Committee secretaries, and ministers, together with their assistants and advisors sitting at nearby lesser tables—came to attention and began rustling and readying their papers. Barsky, who was at one of the side tables, realized that as of this moment the meeting had begun, even though Brezhnev still continued his conversation with KGB chief Yuri Andropov.

"This morn'g the BBC were still talking about yes'day's Jewish dem . . . dem . . . demonstration on Pushkin Square," Brezhnev said. His speech clearly betrayed the impediment that plagued him in his later years.

"I know," Andropov answered calmly. He was a large man, balding and with a high forehead, and his heavy features were offset by a pair of fine spectacles.

"It turns out, hardly have we put Shcharansky inside, before the others start kicking up a fuss," said Chernenko. He was still only a candidate member of the Politburo, but as Brezhnev's friend and assistant, he sat on the right hand of the premier.

Before Andropov could reply, Fyodor Kulakov spoke up from the other end: "That's because Shcharansky should have been given the chop long ago, instead of us being so soft!" he grated. "Then everything would be nice and quiet!"

Andropov said nothing, and Barsky perfectly understood why. Two months ago the Politburo had discussed the Jewish activist Shcharansky, who had handed over to the West a secret map showing all the Soviet Union's forced labor camps and prisons. But unlike his treatment of another Jew, Edward Kuznetsov, whose gang had been arrested by Barsky in 1970 at Leningrad airport while attempting to hijack an aircraft, Brezhnev this time had not imposed a capital sentence, because he was afraid of forfeiting the favorable conditions offered by the United States for the purchase of oil-drilling equipment, computers, and grain. As a result, Shcharansky's trial had been continually deferred, and sensing Brezhnev's weakness, Jimmy Carter was threatening the USSR with diplomatic isolation. And as a result, the Jews had grown more brazen than ever in their demands to be let out.

"How is it they hold these gatherings by the Pushkin Memorial?" Kulakov stared hard at Andropov. "Who allows them to do that?" Kulakov was the most recent outspoken claimant to the Brezhnev throne. Sixty, he looked about forty-seven, was well-proportioned, broad-shouldered, with a strong peasant face. The touch of gray at his temples emphasized his relative youth alongside such obviously decrepit figures as Brezhnev, Chernenko, Gromyko, Suslov, and Ustinov.

Andropov shrugged, but his cold, serene eyes withstood Kulakov's stare. Barsky was familiar with that look—a gaze of tranquil vacuity that gave away nothing. Only heaven forbid that you're on the receiving end of that serene bespectacled stare.

"Okay, let's begin," Suslov said, coughing into his hand and formally opening the meeting. A Politburo member since 1955, on seniority it was always he who chaired. "The first item: Carter's diplomatic blockade and Jewish emigration. We have some introductory information on emigration from State Security in a report by Colonel Barsky, head of the Jewish Section. If you please, Colonel . . ."

Barsky stood up and opened his file. His hour had come: here he was, giving a report in the Kremlin! And in the hall where, in 1849, Emperor Nicholas I had conferred noble status on his forebear, the merchant Aristarkh Barsky. It was here too that in 1936 Joseph Stalin had presented a Stalin Prize to his father, the composer Dmitry Barsky. Now it was his turn, and he was being included in decisions of the leadership.

His entire report fitted on but one sheet of paper—that was the procedure. A few years earlier, when Brezhnev was in good health and enjoyed long discussions, the Politburo sometimes sat for six, eight, and even ten hours. But these days the old man and other leftover patriarchs were obviously wearing down; while they themselves liked to make long speeches, they weren't willing to listen to other people's reports for more than a minute. In fact, after the first hour of a meeting Brezhnev usually would slip away for a nap at Zavidovo, the closest of his out-of-town villas. So his assistants always tried to fit the most important questions into the first hour of any Politburo meeting. Barsky therefore confined himself to basics.

"Despite new pressure from the Carter administration, of eighty thousand Jews applying to emigrate this year, only eighty-one hundred and twelve have received permission to leave—all this conforming to our January decision to restrain the emigration process. No demonstrations by those who have been denied visas, or hysteria in the Western press, will influence the KGB on this. No one in our organization suffers from weak nerves. However, various aspects of the question deserve comment. The very fact that there exists an opportunity for part of the population to leave has an effect on non-Jewish groups. Evidence is provided by the incident when a group of Seventh-day Adventists burst into the American Embassy and staged a sit-in, demanding to be allowed to leave for the USA. At the same time, one observes a sharp rise in such activity by Volga Germans, Armenians, Carpathian Ukrainians, and Baptists. If earlier their requests were sporadic, now there are movements demanding emigration en masse. The CIA provides these groups with aid and overtly plans to use them as levers to overthrow Soviet rule. This is evidenced in an analysis of broadcasts by Voice of America, the BBC, and Radio Liberty; a campaign for so-called human rights now occupies a leading place in their programs. In addition, there is a sharp increase in attempts by Russian youth to leave the USSR by any means possible, including fictitious marriages. Especially active in this have been the population of the Caucasus, where the value of a 'Jewish bride' has risen to ten thousand rubles. . . ."

At this point Barsky looked up from his text and shot a rapid glance at the Politburo members, expecting laughter or at least a smile.

But the fathers of the Party did not smile. Their sagging faces remained expressionless. Barsky concluded that what he had said was already known to them, including the price of a Jewish bride in Georgia. The Politburo "youth"—i.e. the sixty-year-olds such as Demichev, Dolgikh, Kulakov, Mazurov, and Ryabov—sat there frowning, not grasping Andropov's drift or this report by his underling. To them, none of this required discussion. Emigration should simply be stopped and the country closed off.

Barsky decided he had best finish off quickly. So he hastily read out his last paragraph.

"It is essential to bear in mind also the international implications. Constant appeals by Soviet Jews, Germans, Crimean Tatars, and other groups to the United Nations, the American Congress, and to Western Communist party leaders with requests for assistance are compromising our state in the eyes of the peoples of South America, Africa, and the Middle East who are struggling to follow our own Soviet path of development. One can be sure that continuation of the Jewish exodus, and also the increasing activity of Zionists, as demonstrated yesterday on Pushkin Square, can only assist in reinforcing these deleterious processes and could have the most unfavorable consequences. Thank you for your attention."

Barsky closed his file and looked about anxiously. This "morning communion" by the apostles of Communism differed from Christ's Last Supper in its pompous setting and in the advanced ages of the disciples. But it did have one point in common: here too there was one person present plotting the downfall of his leader. Just now, with Barsky's help, this secret operator had made his first move. Barsky was amazed that he himself had realized this only now, at the very end of delivering his report, which Andropov had dictated to him yesterday. On paper the report had seemed far less provocative than when read aloud to the leadership. For a moment Barsky felt stifled, scared, aware that his chief had used him as a pawn to be sacrificed if need be, deliberately exposing him to the possible wrath of Brezhnev and his cohorts.

"Ahmm . . . ahmm . . ." Brezhnev cleared his throat and looked up at Barsky from under his heavy eyebrows. His face hung loosely as if made of dough. "So it turns out like in that funny story, eh? Everyone's going to leave, and only you and I will be left, eh? Is that it? Or are you going to leave as well?"

Barsky thought his end had come. He felt unable to utter a sound. The sudden shift from jubilation at taking part in top-level Kremlin decisions to this quaking fear paralyzed him.

"Well? Eh?" Brezhnev repeated insistently.

Barsky knew that Andropov was still reserving his main surprise for the Politburo, but he could see his boss was in no hurry to come to his aid. He swallowed hard. It was Suslov who stepped in.

"Leonid Ilyich, in the story everybody leaves, apart from you and *me*."

"Oh, *no*!" Brezhnev suddenly came alive. "I'm not staying here with you. You'll fuck me stupid with your Marxism-Leninism!"

The apostles roared with laughter. Even the perpetually surly Gromyko forced a smile. As chief Party ideologue, Suslov, however, didn't like the joke. His narrow lips compressed and his choleric features soured even further. But the Politburo members were outlaughed by their obsequious assistants and advisors, and Barsky caught his breath in relief—the crisis was past.

Barsky surveyed the Party leaders in turn, but his gaze halted when he got to Kulakov. Of all the Politburo, Kulakov was the only one who did not smile. His intense bull-like expression remained and he still stared at Andropov, clearly not fathoming his game. Had Andropov really swung round and joined his group, which was solidly opposed to any emigration?

Andropov, however, ignored Kulakov and his expression remained impenetrable while he waited for Brezhnev's coterie to finish laughing.

"Okay," Brezhnev turned to Andropov. "Yury Vladimirovich, you've fucked me up from hell to breakfast with these bloody Jews. Fucked me up completely. That decision was taken by all of us together. But as soon as there's someone to blame, then it's Brezhnev's fault. Is that it?"

Andropov shrugged.

"I'm not laying any blame on you or anyone, Leonid Ilyich," he said. "The decision on Jewish emigration certainly was made by all of us together. Our oil needed to become a source of hard currency, and we had nothing to drill for it with. And that's why the idea of 'Jews in exchange for oil rigs' seemed right at the time. So I share responsibility with everyone else."

"So then, why does the Party blame it all on me?" Brezhnev interrupted querulously. "And what are you suggesting now? That we stop the Jewish emigration just before the Olympic Games? So that not just Carter, but the whole world starts boycotting us?"

"I'm proposing nothing of the kind." Andropov answered, and picked up a document he had in front of him. "We've worked out a whole new program," he continued. "The idea is simple. You're right, we cannot halt the Jewish emigration, or even reduce it—not just yet. But what we can do is rig things so that the West loses all desire to take in any more of our Jews. How? Very simple. We adulterate the flow of emigrants with large numbers of sick people, invalids, alcoholics, and criminals."

"Excellent!" exclaimed Dmitri Ustinov, the Defense Minister, and half turned to face his friend Gromyko. "The Arabs are always complaining that we do nothing but reinforce the Israeli Army. But if we let out only alcoholics and invalids, what then?"

"And criminals!" Kirilenko put in briskly, another of Brezhnev's friends, rotund and smooth as a ripe tomato. "That's the way! Clean up the whole country! Send all our thieves to the West along with the Jews! Before the Olympics!"

"Well, we'll hardly manage that before the Moscow Olympics," Shchelokov smirked. "After all, we do have around two million crooks and bandits on our books."

"But who said that we have to stick to the American quota system?" Chernenko asked. "They let in thirty thousand Jews annually, but what if right now we let out a hundred thousand bandits, I mean? What about it?"

"Good man, Kostya! Absolutely right!" Brezhnev was suddenly trembling into life.

"But the bandits are not Jews," Shchelokov observed.

Brezhnev wheeled round to face him: "Are you sure about that? Couldn't they have some Jewish relatives in Israel? Eh? I mean if you look hard enough? Dig a bit deeper? You get it?"

"It's a great idea, Leonid Ilyich," Ustinov said weightily. "In that way we'll empty our jails of these parasites, and give the West a bitter pill to bite on. Especially the Israeli Army! Fill it up with drunks and screwballs."

"Yes," Suslov said pensively, as if reflecting aloud. "That would suit our Arab friends."

"Perhaps you'll let me read you just one paragraph," Andropov said, grinning at them like a group of noisy children. "Filling up the flow of emigrants with pensioners, criminal elements, and sick people will force the American Congress to reduce their immigration quotas, and cancel the Jackson-Benick amendment, immediately after the Moscow Olympics."

Andropov broke off and looked up from his text in surprise: the whole of the Politburo with the exception of Kulakov had begun applauding.

"Yeah, we'll send them such a truckload of shit that they'll be paying us to halt the Jewish exodus!" Kirilenko summarized the general view.

Barsky looked at them—their eyes shone with animation. Suddenly they all seemed a lot younger.

"They think that the Yids are a set of Einsteins, Moshe Dayans, and Svyatoslav Richters!" Chernenko grinned. "But instead of all these Richters we'll send them nothing but drunks and old women, eh?"

"Richter the pianist is not a Jew," said Sergey Igunov, the chief expert on Zionism, who was sitting over by the wall.

"Makes no difference!" Shchelokov dismissed the correction.

"Well, shall we vote?" Suslov asked.

"Why bother?" said Brezhnev, and turned to the stenographer: "Just write: Unanimously accepted."

"Wait a moment. I haven't finished," Andropov interrupted, and continued reading. "In addition, bearing in mind the dangerous influence of the Jewish emigration on other sections of our society, the Politburo proposed that the State Security Committee work out a program for restraining potential emigrants, including a system of refusal to those persons whose work is of interest to our adversaries."

"Bah, that's obvious to any idiot!" Brezhnev interjected wearily, his burst of vitality now over.

"That's something you can deal with, can't you?" Chernenko observed patronizingly, and looked benignly in Barsky's direction.

"Yes sir!" Barsky answered, delighted that the discussion had taken this favorable turn. Good God, he thought, trying not to smile openly, Andropov is so damn smart, a genius! He had them eating out of his hand, without their even reading what he wrote! And they'd forgotten all about yesterday's demonstration. Plus, the KGB now would have almost unlimited rights to take any action they saw fit against any Soviet Jew. Or even any Russians with pro-Jewish leanings. What possibilities! What operations his department could launch! And the first thing he'd do would be to deal with the Rubinchik affair!

"Just one moment," Kulakov said cooly but powerfully. Amid the general good feeling, everyone seemed to have forgotten him. "I keep sitting here and wondering . . . how long do we have to go on with this bullshit? I mean, paddling around in this Jewish shit, sorting out which of them is sick and who is an Einstein or a Landau? And if the KGB themselves admit it was a mistake to permit the Jews to emigrate, and that it's set a bad example to a load of Tatars, Chuchmeks, and others, then what's the good of any emigration policy at all? What about that?"

A tingling silence descended on the room. Kulakov loosened his necktie with a sudden jerk, as though shaking off some fetters that bound him. Barsky couldn't help noting his bull's neck and chest. It was plain Kulakov had only just realized how cunningly Andropov had outmaneuvered him: now *all* problems of the Jewish exodus would be dealt with not by politicians but by the State Security Committee—the KGB. And Dolgikh, Igunov, Kulakov, Mazurov, and the Kremlin's other campaigners against Zionism would have to take a backseat at least until after the 1980 Olympics. Now Kulakov erupted. He turned to those at the left-hand end of the table, including the candidate members—Demichev, Dolgikh, Gorbachev, and Shauro, and others of the younger generation.

"I don't believe this has anything to do with any Carter blockade!" he said. "Forget that nonsense! The Chinese have cut themselves off from the rest of the world and they're doing okay! And they'll continue like that for a hundred years! But if our country's falling apart just because of a bunch of kikes emigrating, then it's unthinkable to pursue any such policy! We could lose the whole country within ten years, and then no Olympic Games will do us any fucking good! And anyone who doesn't realize that is leading us toward disaster! We have to get the whole country back under control and close the frontiers! And not spend our time telling funny stories!"

Barsky was taken aback at Kulakov's open attack on Brezhnev. But most interesting was not Kulakov himself, but the people he had turned to for support. Their faces had turned into lifeless masks, as though they hadn't heard a word he'd said. Then Barsky understood what had taken place: Kulakov had jumped up without any prior agreement with anyone and without securing any support in advance, and now . . .

Barsky looked at his boss.

Andropov's face betrayed no hint of his triumph, not even a bit of a smile. He simply sat there beneath the bas-relief of St. George, who had just impaled the dragon, and his gaze conveyed the same vacuity as at the start of the meeting when he first looked at Kulakov.

So that was it. It was not he himself, Barsky realized to his relief, but Kulakov who had been set up. And Brezhnev confirmed Barsky's surmise. He champed his heavy jaw and addressed himself to Suslov in a tone suggesting Kulakov might as well not even have been there.

"Er, Mikhail," he said. "Continue with the meeting. What's the next item?"

"Afghanistan," said Suslov. "President Daoud has been killed, and it's time for us to decide who we want to put there in his place: Karmal or Taraki." Then Suslov turned to Barsky: "Thank you, Colonel. You can go."

s i x

The little Yak-28 banked steeply, and the ground could now be seen below the wing. The bare, icy wilderness resembled fried egg white, and in the midst of it, hoary-white in a fifty-degree frost, a small settlement could be glimpsed—the town of Mirnyy, diamond capital of Yakutia. It consisted of little more than a dozen short streets with houses built on concrete piles, snow drifts, ice hummocks, and—off to one side—three gigantic pits, like the craters left by a nuclear explosion. From the floor and walls of these great holes, excavators scraped out kimberlite, a mineral rich in diamonds and sometimes also containing the fossils of prehistoric mammoths. Operating in columns, like ants at work, forty-ton dump trucks could be seen hauling the kimberlite up to ground level and delivering it to the crushing and extracting plants—three huge, blank-looking aluminum box shapes, also covered in hoar frost and surrounded by a dotted line of barbed-wire fencing.

Further off, beyond the shaggy hummocks of the Siberian tundra, stood the snow-flecked trees of the taiga. Extending to the horizon, their expanse was broken only by the narrow ribbon of a winter trail that cut across from north to south. If ever space travelers reach Pluto or some other frozen planet, the unearthly landscape they find might well resemble this one. But these three great quarries at Mirnyy and five more slightly to the north, at Nadezhnoye, Aikhal, and Udachnaya, provided Russia with eight percent of its annual budget—in the form of diamonds. This was why journalists were more often seen here, at this coldest point on earth, than at the Bolshoi Theater.

As Rubinchik left the aircraft he was followed by two KGB captains—Faskin, a tall, blond thirty-year-old, and Zartsev, the same age and a specialist in karate. They both gasped as the frozen air stabbed into their lungs and froze the moisture in their nostrils. Their next feeling was panic at their seemingly total nakedness before the penetrating icy wind, despite their overcoats, sweaters, and long underwear. How in God's name was that son of a bitch Rubinchik going to succeed in screwing yet another of his women in a place like this? Why, even in May you could scarcely bend your legs in this frost and wind. As they ran toward the squat little terminal even their genitals turned to ice.

Faskin and Zartsev were already well briefed on Rubinchik's capabilities. They had spent more than a month working on him—or, more exactly, on the girls he had had in places like Pavlodar, Ust-Iliam, Paduy, Kostamuksha, Tarko-sal, and Kokchetav. From townships and settlements such as these, information had been received from local hotel administrators about the corrupt behavior of Moscow journalist Iosif Rubin, who had had girls in his room overnight. It was of course no secret that collaboration with the KGB was an essential part of every hotel manageress's work. However, their patrons all knew how to avoid being denounced—usually with the help of a three-ruble bill, a block of chocolate, or a gift of Polish cosmetics. Rubinchik used this method too, but he was mistaken in thinking it was foolproof. Because some of these hoteliers accepted their bribe and then still shopped you to the KGB. In fact, thousands of reports of drunkenness or immorality by men traveling the length and breadth of the USSR were received in Moscow every day. There they were deposited in the special archive of the KGB's Fifth (Ideological) Directorate, where they were sorted and filed by profession, employer, personal details, etc., and stored in an information bank. And whenever the authorities required compromising data, this priceless information was extracted. For, as everyone knew, there were no saints on this earth; and even the most saintly of saints could always be nailed for some minor offense.

Three months ago, Faskin had received from the Special Archive a routine crate of material on people with Jewish, or Jewish-sounding, surnames. Out of this he had pulled out two similar reports from Pavlodar and Paduy about the the "amoral conduct of Moscow journalist Iosif Rubin, of the *Labor Gazette*, who broke hotel regulations by allowing a girl to remain in his room after 2200 hours." An initial investigation revealed that "Iosif Rubin" was the nom de plume of a certain Iosif Rubinchik, and as soon as Faskin's superior, Colonel Barsky, heard this Jewish name, he sat up and took notice. He had a hunch that this information had great potential and, as with the Kuznetsov and Rappoport operations, he took personal charge of the case. He cabled the KGB in Pavlodar and Paduy to unearth complete details on Rubinchik's stay in these places and identify the girls he had slept with. At the same time the personnel department of the *Labor Gazette* confirmed that Rubinchik had joined the paper in 1968. Barsky then sent Faskin and Zartsev to the KGB operational library where they pulled out folios of *Labor Gazette*s for the last ten years. Thus, through reading Rubinchik's reports, it was possible to work out all his movements. On the basis of this research, an executive decree then went out to the KGB in every territory where Rubinchik had been, to question staff in hotels where he had stayed regarding any infringement of regulations. In addition, three staff members of the *Labor Gazette*, who were KGB informers, were invited in for questioning.

From all this, a remarkable picture emerged. In the Moscow offices of the *Labor Gazette*, Iosif Rubin had the reputation of being a devoted family man. Unlike colleagues who never took on domestic chores, he always went home loaded with groceries that he bought at the nearby food store or in their own office canteen. Furthermore, everyone knew how devoted he was to his family. His three-year-old son or seven-year-old daughter need only catch a slight cold for him to go running to the drug store or to the doctor, or else rush to buy fruit juice, honey, or lemons. There was no hint whatsoever of any affairs on the side.

But when away on assignments this same Rubinchik behaved quite differently. Once the local KGB bosses put the screws to them, both male and female staff of all the hotels where he had stayed began to remember vividly that, yes, there had been a Jewish-looking journalist from Moscow, and on the last night before he left a girl had spent the night with him. And they recalled this because in his room they always found a hastily laundered bedsheet with traces of blood on it. And there was little doubt where those stains came from.

Their next move was obvious to Barsky, Faskin, and Zartsev. They would find the girls whose honor Rubinchik had ruined in these various towns and villages. Then the affair could be blown up into a sensational public trial of a debauched Jew who went everywhere deflowering Russian girls. Offer the press a plum story like that and the whole thing would snowball. The papers would paint such a picture of this lecherous kike Dracula that the whole world would shudder! And it would be far more effective than any official anti-Zionist campaign.

To the amazement of Barsky and his assistants, though, almost all Rubinchik's victims who could be identified turned out to be already married. Furthermore, their marriages had been registered literally within a week or two of their visit to his bed. And immediately after marrying, they had changed their places of residence and gone off with their husbands as recruits to various northern or Central Asian construction sites. A human being, though, is easier to find than the proverbial needle in the haystack: because of the nationwide system of registering citizens' domiciles, the Central Address Bureau could quickly provide the KGB with the location of any Soviet citizen. At this point, however, Barsky reined in his tracker dogs. It was premature to establish direct contact with Rubinchik's victims, since any of them might still be in touch with him through amorous correspondence or some other means. And even without this, any of these young women could still call him up by phone to alert him, and that could blow the whole operation. At this preparatory stage, Barsky needed simply to establish the exact addresses of this fornicator's victims and to obtain not so much verbal evidence (there would always be time for that) as *material* proof of his depraved activities.

"We have to catch him in the act," Barsky told his two assistants. "Go with him on his next assignment, follow his every move, and catch him at the moment when he goes down on his next fair maid. But keep the whole job nice and clean—with witnesses, photographs, and have the militia there. All clear?"

Faskin and Zartsev loved the idea. This was far better than digging around in hotel guest books and registry office files. This was real action! And how convenient that Rubinchik's next assignment was to a place like this, in the tundra of Yakutia. Here every man and his dog were on display—just like these frost-covered placards on each side of the road honoring Brezhnev's recent visit to Siberia:

GLORY TO LEONID ILYICH BREZHNEV,

LEADER OF THE PEOPLES!

THE COMMUNIST PARTY—MIND, HONOR,

AND CONSCIENCE OF OUR AGE!

YAKUTIA GREETS LEONID ILYICH BREZHNEV.

WE SHALL BECOME A REPUBLIC OF COMMUNIST LABOR!

The director of the diamond plant had sent his little station wagon to meet visiting correspondent Iosif Rubin, and it heaved around over the hummocks and hollows of the tundra roadway as it brought him from the airport to the town's one and only hotel, the Polyarnik. Meanwhile the car belonging to Major Khulzanov, head of the Mirnyy KGB office, delivered Faskin and Zartsev directly to the town's supply depot. There they were issued warm fleece-lined suits, sheepskin jackets, felt boots, and fur-lined mittens. Then, after a short chat with Khulzanov, a crafty native Yakutian, the operation was worked out in detail, and the two agents were delivered to the same two-story hotel where Rubinchik was staying. Although the place supposedly had no vacancies (the vestibule was packed with newly arrived "recruits" from all over the country), Captain Faskin was assigned a room next door to Rubinchik's, and Zartsev the room opposite. Thus the trap was set, and they now simply had to wait for Rubinchik to bring in his next victim.

It turned out there was no need to dog his every footstep as Barsky had instructed: the town had but one hotel, one café-restaurant, one movie theater, and only one taxicab—and its driver was a KGB informer. In fact, the real problem was to avoid running into Rubinchik, since he too was taken to the supply depot to get outfitted with warm gear and then sent to the same self-service canteen. Here, instead of the one or two dishes served at most such provincial establishments, the menu offered borscht, bean soup, fish soup made with turbot, macaroni á la marine, venison ragout, fried fish, and even *pelmeni* dumplings. And there were also red bilberries with sugar and stewed apples. Not for nothing did Mirnyy supply eight percent of the gross national product!

Faskin and Zartsev ate their fill of fish soup, Siberian dumplings, and bilberries, all washed down with brandy supplied by Major Khulzanov. After that, with their senses dulled by the Siberian habit of heating every building as if it were a bathhouse, the two of them looked around: if they were in Rubinchik's shoes, who of this company would they try and screw?

In the evenings the cafe became a restaurant with table service and the alluring name Northern Lights. But at lunch time it was packed with drivers, engineers, crane operators, miners, and guards from the diamond processing plant. All these men and women were tall Siberians. And they appeared even more enlarged in their thick sweaters, quilted and fur-lined suits, sheepskin jackets and high boots. They also had mighty appetites. As they entered from the street amid clouds of frosted steam, all of them—men and women alike—took from the service hatch double helpings of the first and of the main course, plus buns, blancmange, stewed fruit, and bilberries. And while they conversed raucously amid thick tobacco smoke, both men and women would lick their platters clean.

How would that little Jewish squirt, Faskin and Zartsev wondered, ever manage to seduce one of these female buffalos? Aha, there he was—talk of the devil—already fitted out in fleece-lined overalls and sheepskin jacket, but still wearing his Moscow fur cap with earflaps. As Khulzanov immediately explained, Rubinchik's companions were the chief female architect of the town, two young female geophysicists, and a young militiawoman guard from the processing plant who, though no older than twenty, was in charge of all local amateur entertainment. And although the women were all taller than he, Rubinchik held himself with a sense of poised sophistication, radiating self-assurance and had an appetite second to none. He ate slowly, watching and listening to his companions. Occasionally he would make a note. Or he would offer some pithy comment on what they were telling him, which sent the whole company into gales of laughter. And he himself grinned with his crafty little Jew eyes that seemed full of dark fire and energy.

Faskin and Zartsev glanced at one another. Which of these ladies would Rubinchik bring to his room tonight? The architect could be eliminated outright—already thirty and not his sort of game. The geophysicists too—though younger, were clearly no virgins. The fair-haired girl from the militia looked more his type, although she was at least six feet tall. So if they were to catch him tonight in the act, they'd have to be extra careful, since the girl could well be armed.

But Rubinchik confounded all their expectations. Neither that day nor the next did he bring in either the six-foot militiawoman, or the geophysicists, or any other of the local skirted buffalos. According to Khulzanov, he spent the first day at the kimberlite quarry, at the crushing plant, and on a reconnaissance tour of the town. The second, third, and fourth days he spent at the urban architectural center and construction plant, where he inquired about who was responsible, and why, for the more than four years' delay in building the "domed city"—an interesting scheme for putting a single roof over a whole complex of living quarters including a nursery school, hospital, stores, and greenhouses. Evenings Rubinchik spent either at Northern Lights or visiting local engineers and geophysicists. He would return to the hotel toward midnight, and much to the chagrin of his watchdogs, he was always alone.

Faskin and Zartsev started getting bored. They were fed up with waiting for their "love-kike," as they called him, to choose himself a girl and let them fulfill their mission. They were sick of the cold, which prevented anyone from taking a decent breath, because the frozen air would almost literally stab their lungs. They were turned off by Major Khulzanov, by the drunken nightly snorting of other travelers on both floors of the hotel, and even by the Siberian dumplings and sugared bilberries. The only thing that helped sustain their morale was Khulzanov's brandy and vague promises by the perky hotel manageress to drop in "for a cup of tea." On the fifth evening this luxuriant beauty with her ample bosom and two gold teeth did actually call in to see them, which led to a show of tipsy enthusiasm and a loud toast by Khulzanov "to the lovely ladies!" She, however, damped their fervor straightaway by curtly announcing:

"Your correspondent's leaving the hotel!"

"How do you mean he's leaving? Where to?" The news immediately sobered them. Barely twenty minutes before, they themselves had seen him roll up to the hotel in an official truck and go up to his room.

"How should I know where?" she said. "But he used my phone to call a cab."

The manageress was warm, mellow, and clearly in the mood for a drink, but the three of them grabbed their jackets and caps and left her sitting there. They raced downstairs, sprang over the travelers asleep on the floor of the vestibule, and ran outside just in time to see Rubinchik's taxi set out into the inky blackness of the taiga night. Fortunately, though, Khulzanov's Land Rover was standing by with its motor running and with the young soldier-driver snoozing in the cab. Khulzanov and his two companions dived inside and yelled: "Get after that taxi! Quick! Step on it!"

So Rubinchik had set up his lay, and now he was heading to her home— an apartment or somewhere in a dormitory. Now they had only to find out where, and who. Then, once there, they could take their time, call the local militia, gather witnesses, and collect their cameras from the hotel. There would be ample time for all that—they had the whole night ahead of them.

But they saw the taxi reach the end of the dark, snowbound street without turning off at any of the houses. Nor did it head toward the airport. Instead it rushed on straight out toward the taiga.

"Where the devil's he going?"

"He's making for the winter highway." Their driver was the first to realize.

Indeed, the taxi was hurtling toward the intersection with the winter trail. Along that seasonal road heavy trucks plied day and night, bringing up from the Lena River to the south everything needed for survival in the tundra: fuel, foodstuffs, construction material, vodka, machinery, and medicines. In summer, once the tundra melted and turned into a mushy bog, the roadway disappeared. That was why tons and tons of freight had to be delivered during the winter.

"Why in God's name is he heading that way?"

"Because," said Khulzanov, "once you're on it, you can go anywhere you want—south down to Lensk, or up north to Aikhal."

"But in a taxi? Why?"

"He's obviously trying to lose you. He's figured out that you're on his tail."

Once the taxi reached the winter road, however, it turned neither north nor south, but came to a halt at the roadside.

"Stop! Put your lights out!" Khulzanov ordered.

Immediately the frozen darkness closed in. A red moon could be seen hanging low over the horizon. Ahead, at the intersection, the taxi stood with cones of light ramming the darkness ahead, and a feeble glow came from its yellow tail lamps. Nobody got out. The KGB team couldn't figure it out. What was Rubinchik doing? Where was he heading?

On the winter trail, the headlights of a gasoline tanker heading north appeared. Rubinchik jumped out and stood at the intersection with his hand raised. The tanker immediately slowed down and came to a halt. Rubinchik stepped up onto the high footboard and sprang in next to the driver. The KGB team waited, and so did the taxicab. Then, ten seconds later, with a roar of its engine, the tanker headed north again into the Arctic night; the taxi then turned round and drove off back to Mirnyy.

"God damn it!" the Moscow captains swore. Major Khulzanov got out of the car and flagged the taxi down. Faskin and Zartsev jumped out after him.

"What's his game? Where's he gone?" Khulzarov asked the cab driver.

"He wants to spend a night on the road and write an article about the long distance drivers," the cabman explained.

Faskin and Zartsev looked at one another.

"But he has a ticket for Moscow leaving tomorrow!" Zartsev remembered.

"Let's get after him!" Faskin stoutly ordered Khulzanov, and they bounded back into the car.

"Why? Whoever is he going to find out there on the road?" Khulzanov asked, surprised.

"He'll find someone!" Zartsev said confidently and, by way of explanation: "This is his last night here! And he always screws his girls on the last night. Then he flies away!"

"Okay then, let's get going!" Khulzanov told his chauffeur. Descended from generations of hunters, he too was excited by the prospect of this new sport, the hunt for the love-kike.

Anna Evgenyevna?"

Anna caught her breath. Barsky! All last week she had lived in the secret hope that somehow he would disappear like a bad dream—that he would change his mind, vanish, fall under a bus, contract syphilis, or fly away overseas. But no, there he was on the other end of the line. Why? After all, thousands of people do die everyday from heart attacks, cancer, automobile accidents. . . . So why not KGB agents?

"Hello?" the baritone voice said impatiently.

"Yes?"

"Anna Evgenyevna?"

"Yes?" She had now achieved some control of herself. Holding the phone in her left hand, she pushed away the nose of the Airedale that kept nuzzling against her and rummaged on the kitchen table for her cigarettes and lighter.

"This is Oleg Dmitryevich Barsky."

"I'm listening."

"How are you?"

There was a pause. The rat was waiting for her to return his greeting and enquire after *his* health! There was no escape.

"How are you," she said abruptly, without any more personal address. She lit a cigarette. He of course heard the click of the lighter, and there was now a smile in his voice:

"You smoke too much, Anna Evgenyevna."

There was another pause. He clearly was trying to adopt a friendly informal manner, as though he had already recruited her. But she was not going to cave in.

"Hello!"

"Yes?" said Anna.

"I was saying, you smoke too much."

"I heard that."

"Hmm . . . Well, excuse me for calling on a Sunday. If you remember, we agreed to get in touch in about a week? I waited all week for your call, and then decided it wasn't going to come. So the mountain has to come to Mohammed!"

There was yet another pause. She sensed he was hoping she would laugh. Screw him!

"Hello!" he said again.

"Yes?"

"You clearly have your armor on," the baritone spoke respectfully. "But all the same, we really should meet, Anna Evgenyevna. How does tomorrow look for you? We could have lunch—"

"No," Anna interrupted. "I'm completely booked up until the end of the week. I'm in the middle of a trial, as you probably already know."

"Very well," he seemed ready to agree, although they both knew she was simply putting off the meeting. "What about a week from Tuesday? Let's say, around three o'clock. We could have some lunch then?"

Anna sighed. There was no getting out of it. She would have to meet him.

"Where?" she asked, wondering where the KGB took out its agents for their first meeting.

"Well, what about the Armenia? Do you know it? They have wonderful trout. How do you view the prospect of some trout?"

"With interest." She grinned.

"What's that? What's that?" Barsky guffawed. "Anna Evgenyevna, you're a marvel! So that's next week, Tuesday, at three. At the Armenia. By the way, I know you're never late. So . . . till Tuesday. Best wishes meanwhile!"

"Bye." She slowly put down the phone. There was something in his voice—something hard to name, but which an experienced woman could detect, like a violinist when a string is out of tune. He was playing up to her. That meant he needed her. Well, not so much herself as Arkady. And not even Arkady so much as the new missile system her brilliant husband had devised. He'd been in Moscow less than a day, and prior to that had been away for almost two weeks. When she pressed him on why he was straining to get back to Chernogolovka, his answer was, "You see, Anna, during the last month's war games our missiles launched from submarines in the White Sea flew as far as Kamchatka and landed within a kilometer of their target. Over so vast a distance, that's not bad, especially if the missile has a nuclear warhead. One kilometer wouldn't make much difference, and just three years ago we got a State Prize for this system." He paced the room, his hands thrust in the pockets of his favorite, well-worn velveteen pants. Then he tossed back his curly head and smiled the smile that had conquered her five years earlier. "But," he went on, "I've come up with a new idea. If we can make it work, it will mean our missiles can hit their target bang in the center, no matter the distance—even if they've had to circle the globe. Can you imagine? A rocket straight in through the window of Carter's oval office in the White House—or else the star on the Spassky Tower of the Kremlin. Admittedly, at this stage the idea's still raw, and I'm not sure myself how to accomplish it technically. But last night I had a few ideas, and I urgently need to test them out in the lab."

After that Arkady had left again. She could, of course, have told him about the conversation with Barsky in the weasel's office. Why, she could even have told him about Rappoport (though not the full story, of course!). But even if Arkady had forgiven her three times over—what difference would it make to her life? "Last night I had a few ideas . . ."—and there lay the root of her problems. So what was she to do?

Her cigarette had burnt right down to the filter and was now scorching her fingers. With a shudder, she took one last draw, then stubbed it out.

The roar of motorboats on the Klyazma Reservoir could be heard through the trees along the shore and on the highway beyond. The unexpected heat of late May had driven Muscovites out of town, and the wooded bank of the reservoir was lined with tents, branch shelters, and huts thrown together from cardboard and planking. Tens of thousands came here on weekends, and in defiance of posted prohibitions they built fires, held picnics, got drunk, swam, bathed their dogs, and tore around the lake in motorboats and homemade launches. Other pastimes included shooting at bottles and cans with hunting rifles and a fishing technique that involved an underwater explosive to knock the living daylights out of the fish, which could then be simply scooped up from the surface.

Anna turned off the highway and after slowly driving down a rough and twisting forest road, she stopped at a fork and wondered whether she was going the right way. But just then she saw a foreign car heading toward her—a Ford or Lincoln—lurching over the potholes and ruts of the dirt road. Anna relaxed: she was going right. First, though, she had to back up and give way to this foreign cruiser and ignore the bald Caucasian at the wheel who brazenly looked her up and down before sailing away with the look of an Oriental potentate. He was just another black marketeer who'd bought his car by paying a huge bribe to the UPKD, a directorate that serviced the diplomatic corps. Western diplomats and correspondents were not allowed to sell their vehicles on the open market—not even when they returned home, or when their cars were smashed up or simply died of old age. Instead, they were required to turn them over to the UPDK for a mere pittance. The waiting list to acquire these elderly secondhand Fords, Volvos, and Volkswagens was huge, and it included famous actors, producers, scholars, and prize-winning scientists. As a reward for their loyal services the authorities allowed only these dignitaries, the crème de la crème, to purchase some beat-up Ford or Mercedes, fix it up, and parade around Moscow with it.

Admittedly, over the last few years the head of this body assigned more and more such cars not to Lenin Prize winners but to individuals from the Caucasus who had contributed nothing more than provide Moscow's black market with cut flowers, apples, or tomatoes. Every few days, a tow truck would winch some rusting wreck from the Director's lot—the sort of car any Westerner would have dumped at the junkyard. In Moscow, however, these were delivered to the so-called "Pit," an underground repair shop run by Ivan Lopakhin. It was here that Anna's father worked.

Lopakhin was a loudmouthed, overweight former actor from the celebrated Taganka Theater. Right now he was standing at the edge of the Pit, a gentle slope leading down into a manmade basin, and shouting at two of his workers. They were busy unloading a mass of twisted wreckage from a truck. With an effort of imagination, the wreckage was barely recognizable as the remains of a BMW or maybe a Toyota. But when Lopakhin saw the yellow Zhiguli with Anna at the wheel, he dropped what he was doing and strode over to her. He wiped the sweat from his round freckled face and spoke loudly like some Brechtian actor.

"Good Lord, Anna darling! How many summers have passed! So you haven't forgotten us poor sinners? My God, what a woman! Veritable queen that you are! The dream of Andalusia!"

"Cut the bullshit, Lopakhin!" Anna could not restrain a smile. "Is father here?"

"Of course, my princess. Your father is here, in this fresh forest air! What could be better for a Soviet worker and pensioner? Shall I call him?" He gestured toward the bottom of the Pit, where several cars rested in pieces. There, under a slate-roofed awning stood a little elderly man in faded pants and worn checked shirt. He was using a felt hammer to beat out the accordianlike crushed fender of some vehicle. The man was Anna's father—a former tank major on the Second Ukrainian front, former head of technical services in the Moscow KGB, and—since the death of his wife—an alcoholic who had drunk away even his medals.

Anna was continually horrified by the story of her father's life. In 1934, when Stalin wanted to set up the first Soviet automobile factory, he sent a group of brilliant young engineers for a period of work study to one of the Ford plants. One of the group had been twenty-four-year-old Evgeny Krylov, Anna's father. In 1935, after returning, he told a neighbor that the best car engines in the world were made by Ford. The next day he was arrested for spreading "anti-Soviet propaganda," and after being sentenced by a secret tribunal, was sent to Siberia.

Admittedly, they were not yet transporting prisoners in cattle cars, and her father and a dozen other "enemies of the people" rode to Siberia in a sleeping car supervised by just one escort. When they had passed Chita, at some hamlet out in the taiga, the escort produced a sealed envelope marked "E. K. Krylov, 1837 km." He handed it to her father and pointed to a watchtower standing out in the wilds.

"Go to that tower," he said. "That's the camp area. Hand them this packet and they'll fix you up."

Krylov did as he was told. The orderly on duty opened the packet and read father his sentence: ten years in a labor camp.

In fact, at the time no camps yet existed; Stalin's infamous Gulag was still being constructed—by these same "enemies of the people." A week after his arrival, two thousand more prisoners were brought there together with a vehicle loaded with axes, saws, and other tools. The commandant summoned Krylov and spread out a map of the surrounding taiga.

"Take six hundred convicts, a hundred axes, and a guard squad," the commandant said. "And you go just here . . ." He poked a finger at an area of pine forest. "You have a week to set up quarters and saw benches. And in a week you start producing planking, door, and window frames. If you don't get it done, I'll have you shot. Any questions?"

"Yes," Anna's father said. "What size do you want the window frames?"

The commandant stared at him long and hard.

"Barracks size, goddamit!" he said. "We're building prison camps!"

For four years her father nourished the mosquitoes with his blood and produced planks and door frames. Then, in December 1939, he and another hundred thousand convicts were herded on foot from all over the countryside to Chita. There they were lined up on the station square to hear a speaker from Moscow shout from a podium:

"Dear comrades! A tragic mistake has been made! You were sentenced quite mistakenly! Your country owes you an unpayable debt! But our motherland is now in mortal danger! Finland has invaded us! Finnish forces are marching on Leningrad, the cradle of the Revolution! Everyone must help defend the motherland! Everyone on board these trains!"

The same cattle cars that brought the "enemies of the people" to Siberia now transported them westward again. At Kolpino near Leningrad, they were issued rifles made in 1913 and each man was given ten cartridges and immediately hurled into the fray. Getting more ammunition was their own responsibility. Get more arms or perish—that was their choice.

Eventually the "triumphant" Red Army picked its way over the bodies of its own dead former prisoners and burst through the Mannerheim Line, and Molotov signed a peace accord with the Finns. After that, any surviving former "enemies of the people" were disarmed, again loaded into cattle cars and . . . sent back to Siberia! Men who had helped save their country didn't even get their sentences commuted by the period of their army service. Construction of the Gulag continued—Stalin's empire needed slaves to mine gold in Kamchatka, coal in Vorkuta, copper in Kazakhstan, and nickel in Norilsk.

However, in October of 1941, two years later, there they were again back at the Chita rail station, again thousands lined up on the station square, again a platform festooned in red, and the same words:

"Dear comrades! There has been a tragic mistake! The country owes you an unpayable debt! But the country is in mortal danger! Hitler's forces are approaching the Volga, Moscow, and Stalingrad! Everyone must defend our motherland! Everyone on board these trains!"

For Anna's father the war began near Stalingrad, where he was an army driver, and it ended up on the river Elbe, where he was commander of a repair battalion in Marshal Timoshenko's tank division. At the outset, he was wounded for the first time near Stalingrad, and thereby with his blood he "washed away his guilt to the motherland," as the phrase had it. That sacrifice opened the way for his eventual promotion. Then, while he was in the hospital, his plight melted the heart of Olya, a seventeen-year-old nurse, who became his wife and later Anna's mother.

In 1946, he returned from Germany driving his own Opel, with a row of medals on his chest and a major's stars on his golden shoulder tabs, and in the Prague Restaurant he hosted a noisy celebration of his marriage. Twenty-four hours later, during the night, state security agents turned up and took him away to the Lubyanka. It turned out that his earlier conviction had been quashed only "nominally" for the duration of the war. Nine months later, Anna was born. But she first saw her father only in 1954, after the "leader of the peoples" had died, and when she was eight years old.

However, after all this, the most surprising thing was that Anna's father still remained a fervent Stalinist. On returning from Siberia, he managed to secure a complete exoneration and the return of all his decorations; his military rank was restored, along with his Party membership. He found work in the KGB garage where he rocketed up in rank, and from an ordinary mechanic he quickly advanced to manager of technical services. He and his family became the recipient of special Kremlin-supplied rations and a house in the country, and Anna spent the rest of her childhood well fed, living in the lap of luxury, and beneath a portrait of Generalissimo Stalin, which hung in their apartment in a prominent position.

In 1967, Anna brought home her first husband, artist Ilya Kantorovich, to meet her parents. And it was then that she learned that apart from an unquenchable love for Stalin, her father had also brought back from Siberia a burning hatred of all Jews. Although she was pregnant, when he clapped eyes on Kantorovich, he not only threw her out of the house but did his level best to ruin her marriage. With his KGB connections, one phone call would have sufficed to obtain an apartment for them. Instead, Anna and Ilya and their newborn son had to camp out in storerooms and basements. Although her father could easily have had an avant-garde artist like Kantorovich removed from the KGB file of politically "unreliable" artists, her husband couldn't find work even as an illustrator of children's books. In addition to his pay, her father also had access to a special food center on Khmelnitsky Street, but not a crumb found its way to Anna and her family, who for months at a time subsisted on a starvation diet. And although her father had a dacha outside Moscow and could secure admission to any sanitorium or resort from Karelia to Samarkand, they and their asthmatic infant son could never get away for a vacation, not even in the oppressive Moscow summer heat. Whenever her father found out that Olya had secretly brought clothes and fruit to her grandson, he threw tantrums cursed with all the foul language of the camps and sometimes even beat her. Then, in 1971 American billionaire Armand Hammer suddenly bought up half the works of the Moscow artistic underground, including nineteen Kantorovich paintings. It was then that they decided to apply to emigrate. Anna's father, however, refused to sign the permit that would allow her to leave the country.

"Father, little Anton suffers from asthma! He needs to live somewhere like Arizona! This is his only chance of survival!"

"Okay, let him go. I'm not stopping him."

"But what about me?"

"You're staying here in your own country."

"Father, you must be mad! He's my son! And Ilya is my husband! D'you want them to leave without me?"

"Because of that kike that you call a husband, they refused to make me a general! Let him get the hell out of here, but you're staying!"

"I shall curse you forever after, I swear it! I'll never set foot in this house again!"

But he risked losing his job and feeding at the KGB trough if she were to leave, and he remained immovable.

Strangely, though, Fate came and punished him. Not long afterward, he began drinking. Perhaps he could not cope with knowing that despite all his efforts, his only daughter, whom he had so loved as a child, had for the second time married a Jew. Or maybe it was his awful loneliness. But in 1972, right after Anna's mother died, her father began drinking, and with a blind and grim fury that typified former inmates of the labor camps. Within three months he drank away everything—his job, his car, his Party membership, his furniture, and even the Stalin portrait together with his military medals. Everything, except for his talent. A drunken genius like him could assemble a T-34 tank out of two sewing machines, which is why he'd been taken on by Ivan Lopakhin, resurrecting beat-up foreign cars far more skillfully than any normal mechanic.

Early each morning Lopakhin came personally in his little gray Fiat and picked up her father on Peschanaya Street. Lopakhin also brought with him a bottle of vodka, and the day began by pouring out a glass.

"That's your ration for now. You get the rest at lunch," he said.

Obediently Anna's father would get into Lopakhin's car and travel out to the Pit with him. There he straightened, welded, and soldered the bodywork and mudwings of cars so buckled and smashed that not even Henry Ford himself would have bothered resurrecting them. Over lunch her father would finish off the promised bottle. Then for the rest of the day he would continue transplanting Renault gearboxes into Fords, or hammering out twisted bodywork with an array of wooden hammers. So what did Barsky's threat, "through your father," mean? Would he take away the old man's pension because of his "unearned income"—income amounting to a mere three glasses of vodka per day?

Anna edged her Zhiguli down the slope into the Pit and pulled up a few feet away from her father. Since her mother's funeral, they had seen each other only once a year, at the cemetery on the anniversary of her death. But even then, at her mother's graveside, when Anna tried to talk to him, he was curt, unfriendly. He had vodka on his breath and would tell her to leave him in peace. After which he would leave. For the last two years he had missed even these annual dates.

Anna switched off the engine, got out, and walked over to him.

He had seen her of course. But he said nothing and continued working intently, beating out what resembled the rear fender of a Mercedes. Anna too said nothing and simply watched him. He was unshaven, and his gray hair was awry. His neck was shaggy, his checked shirt faded, his pants dirty and baggy at the knees, and his shoes almost worn through at heel. He also reeked of vodka, and his eyes continued avoiding hers.

At last he stopped hammering, picked up the piece of metal, and took it over to the frame of a dismantled car and placed it over the rear wheel. Then he hauled a welding unit out from under the awning, fastened a protective shield over his head and prepared to weld the part in place. She stepped right up to him.

"Father, we have to talk."

He said nothing. No doubt he realized that she had come here specifically to see him. So he could hardly just tell her to leave him in peace. But he still said nothing and fiddled with the welding torch.

"Can you hear me?"

"Yeah, I can hear. Go on then. What d'you want?"

"I want to leave."

He shrugged indifferently.

"Forever," she said. "I want to emigrate."

He flicked the flint lighter and a thin blue hissing flame burst from the torch.

"Father!"

"Go wherever you want! Only leave me alone!" he said and began welding the fender to the chassis.

She patted him on the shoulder.

"Dad, I need your permission," she said. "You know that. They don't let people out without their parents' permission."

Abruptly he turned to face her and pushed back the welding mask. In his blue eyes she saw an intense flame, like that of the welding torch. "Don't call me Dad. I'm not your father. Get it?"

"No, I don't get it," she said shaking her head. "You can call me a Jewish trollop, or kike's hooker, or whatever you like. But it doesn't alter the fact that, apart from me, you have nobody else in this world."

He turned away and resumed working. But now the weld was going out of line. His hand was shaking.

"Dad," Anna said quietly, "tell me honestly. That neighbor of yours who denounced you back in 1935, was he a Jew?"

Her father still said nothing, now trying to correct the uneven weld.

Anna seized him by the shoulder and jerked him round to face her.

"Come on, tell me! Admit it! You hate the Jews because forty years ago some Yid wrote in denouncing you to the KGB! Is that it? Am I right?"

"Get your hands off me!" He tore himself free and turned away, obstinately trying to continue working.

The roar of a motor launch on the lake filled her ears, and her eyes ached from looking at the blaze of her father's torch. Suddenly he seemed pathetic, sad, helpless. She was feeling a great sorrow for him.

"Come on, Father, let's go and have a drink," Anna said.

He turned round to her in surprise.

"What's that?"

"Let's go and have a drink, Dad. Come on."

He switched off his torch and sighed hoarsely.

"It's too late, Anna. I'm all shot to hell!"

"Daddy!" Anna impulsively put her arms round him and pressed him to her. And she was suddenly aware how small and frail he was—like a child. She realized, too, that he was weeping as he pressed his unshaven cheek against her shoulder.

"Dad! . . ."

"It's too late, my dear. . . . Too late. . . . They've ruined my life. . . ." He pulled away from her and wiped his wet face with a fist.

"Who? The Jews; or the KGB?"

"Same shit! . . . If you . . . If you want to go, then you can go. Get out of this shitty country. You see what they've done with my life? Go on, I'll sign anything you want. Only will they let you out? Your husband's a scientist."

"I want to go alone, father."

He stepped back and looked her in the eye.

"But who's going to let you out without your Jewish husband?"

But she let the question pass without answering.

"Dad, I need your help. There's this guy in the KGB, a Colonel Barsky. I need to know everything about him—absolutely everything there is to know, okay? You still have a few friends back in that company—I mean, your drivers from the garage there. Chauffeurs always know all their bosses' business."

He shook his head.

"No, my dear. You don't play those sort of games with that crowd."

Anna seized her father firmly by his shirt collar.

"Father, just look at yourself. They loused up the whole of your life then dumped you in this shithole. *They* did that . . . not your Jewish neighbor! And now they're worming their way into my life to do the same with me! Do you want me to end up another KGB whore? Are you going to let them do that?"

"Hey!" Lopakhin suddenly shouted from above. "Hands off your father, princess! Why, not even Cordelia raised a hand against her father, King Lear!"

"Up yours!" she snapped back.

"Hush, Anna!" There was fear in her father's voice. "Be careful when he's around! He's in the KGB too!"

Anna sniggered. "No kidding! Otherwise they'd have shut this place down long ago!" Then she shouted up to Lopakhin, "Vanya! I'm taking Father off for a few days. We're holding a family celebration!"

eight

Rubinchik was not quiet sure what it was that drew him out to the winter trail. His three pads were already crammed with notes—more than enough for a series of articles on life in frozen Siberia. Although each month Mirnyy supplied the state treasury with two hundred kilograms of diamonds, half the local laborers and engineers still lived in wretched barracklike huts, where walls and ceilings were covered in frost despite powerful central heating systems and several electric stoves. Meanwhile the other half of the workforce squatted in what was called "Shanghai"—a residential area consisting of dugouts, oil-drum shacks, and crude homemade huts. All this, despite the fact that five years ago at the Montreal International Exposition, young local architects had won the Grand Prize with their project for a "domed city," providing normal human living conditions for two thousand workers. To realize this project, the local management had obtained colossal funding, materials, and technical backup from Moscow. Before long, though, all this disappeared—it sank in the bogs, rusted away in the taiga, or was embezzled and whisked away by the bosses to build dachas for themselves in Yakutsk, Vilyui, Lensk, and in Mirnyy itself.

As he gathered this information, Rubinchik was not in the least surprised. He had seen the same thing happen at the site of the Bratsk Hydroelectric Station, the Siberian gas pipeline, and dozens of other so-called "Communist construction projects." The striking feature of Mirnyy, though, was that here you could see socialism on display as it really was, pure and without the frills: here it squeezed diamonds out of a workforce paid in paper rubles, just enough to buy vodka, basic food, and—the dream of a lifetime—an annual one-month holiday on the Black Sea.

Despite its title, however, even the so-called *Labor Gazette* could never publish such a series. Rubinchik would be lucky if he managed get even ten percent of the outrageous information filling his notebooks past the censor. This meant that instead of chasing all around, he could just as well have spent a quiet night in the warmth of the hotel and flown home to Moscow the following morning. In fact he'd already started packing when he was stopped in his tracks by a keen sense of what newspaper men call "journalist's instinct." Something made him look at his watch, scratch his head, and then haul on his fleece-lined pants, boots, cap, and sheepskin jacket; then he called the local taxicab. Five days before, as he flew into Mirnyy, he had noticed the thin ribbon of the winter trail threading across the taiga from north to south. Seen from the plane, the few trucks crawling along the trail appeared so tiny and abandoned in that snowy wasteland that he imagined himself at the wheel of one of them—alone in that boundless icy wilderness like some hero out of a Jack London story. What did those drivers think about at the wheel? How did they live? Where did they stop? And what attracted them to the far north? Just the money? Or was it that vague call emanating from somewhere in the depths of the tundra that even an outsider like himself could sense with every fiber of his being?

But like a gourmet leaving the tastiest morsel till the end, Rubinchik saved his trip to the winter trail for the very last day. Every day in Mirnyy, though, he felt the call of that road, especially at night when he was unable to sleep, what with the drunken snores that echoed through the hotel. The cell-like rooms had no showers or toilets, and there was only one communal facility down on the ground floor. The rooms were crammed with geologists, mining experts, and traders of various sorts, living three or four to a room and sleeping on bunks. And people slept in the corridors too, but on individual camp beds. And each of these taiga shit-kickers seemed to see it as their sacred duty to consume a bottle of vodka before turning in, after which they would hit the pillow and snore in an appalling chorus.

Rubinchik also enjoyed his drink, and in good company he could put down plenty, but he could never understand the urge of these people to actually get drunk. Yet he saw it on all his travels. And that inexplicable feature of the national psyche placed a limit on his sense of kinship with his countrymen. But in all other respects, he felt, he understood this open, cheerful, and trusting people, and he was fond of them and regarded himself as one of them. What sort of Jew was he after all? Right now, for instance, after sitting in at least six different truck drivers' cabs, he was delighted at how easy it was to make contact with these travelers of the taiga. And he was amazed at the plainspoken and confiding accounts of their life stories, after no more than two minutes of general preamble.

"I came from the Urals originally, like. . . . After the army I went to the Sverdlovsk Technical College. I dreamed one day of becoming an astronomer and making telescopes. That was my great passion—telescopes—ever since I was a kid, like. Anyway, I fell for this young virgin during my senior year—head over heels I was. I just wanted her, and that's all there was to it, damn it! Anyway, we got married. And I was happy—no man happier in the whole of Russia, no kidding. But how could two folk live on just one student grant? When I was on my own, I boiled up a packet of dumplings, and it just cost thirty-eight kopeks. As a first course, for soup, I'd drink the broth they were cooked in—you could have that with bread. Then, for a main course there were the dumplings proper. In short, I could survive on one ruble a day, even eighty kopeks! But a man can't feed his wife on the broth from dumplings, right? Right, so I started attending evening courses and drove a taxi in the daytime. We rented one room, and from three pay packets I bought her a fur coat, and altogether I just waited on her hand and foot—no kidding! And she loved me for it too—no doubt about it! Same in bed too. In winter I'd come home from work frozen solid—no buses after midnight where we were—you know, fucking Commies, with all their 'concern for the people,' right? Anyway, she'd always be there to meet me with a bowl of hot water, and she'd sure warm my feet up for me in no time at all, no kidding. But d'you know what? Once the driveshaft on my engine went, and instead of midnight, I arrived back home next day at three in the afternoon. I open the door and let myself in, thought I'd give her a surprise. I walk in and find she's in bed with our neighbor, fuck it! And the two of them were so caught up with each other, they didn't even hear me come in. Anyway, naturally, I got a bit worked up, like. In fact, I took a kitchen stool to them and did them both in, good and proper, like. It was a fairly heavy stool, made of oak. So I got eight years for murder on grounds of jealousy. I did time not far away from here, in Lensk. But once I got out, I never went back. No point really. Pity about those telescopes though. I left six of them back there in Sverdlovsk. . . ."

If only we didn't have this damned censorship, which always serves the truth up in driblets! Rubinchik thought as he sat with these drivers. What an array of subjects, what human tragedies and dramas you encountered at almost every step!

"In our village there's not even a cat left alive now. Some of the old folk died, some of them moved south. And all the young 'uns went their ways long ago. That was when Khrushchev told everyone to plant corn in the water meadows. So that our corn crops would overtake America. Can you imagine it—planting corn in a water meadow? That takes some thinking up, that does! Anyway, that way they ruined the whole of Vyatka province. And time was when it provided butter and cheese for half Europe. But now there ain't no butter, no corn, no cows, no folks, no nothing! The whole place is empty! Last year I went on vacation to the Black Sea, and on the way I dropped in back home, 'cuz I wanted to find my old folks' grave. Are you kidding? Huh, no way! They've even ploughed up the graves to make room for the corn, darn them!"

Over to the left of the cabin as they drove, a bright moon scudded low over the tops of the dark taiga pine trees, like a polished brass plate. Battering the fog with its headlights and hammering the icebound trail with its chain-clad wheels, the heavily loaded truck carefully made its way northward.

At the hundredth kilometer from Mirnyy, the driver swung off onto a parking lot. It was lit by a garland of lamps. About thirty trucks and tankers stood with their engines roaring and churning out exhaust vapor. Just beyond, where the actual Urman taiga began, stood two buildings of fresh-cut logs.

"This is Beryozovy Service Station," the driver announced. "We can get tanked up here."

The trucker left his engine running—"so she doesn't seize up"—and jumped down into the scalding frost. He ran over to the station office, his felt boots squeaking on the snow. Rubinchik hurried after him, surprised at his unaccountable sense of excitement and exhilaration. This feeling of bittersweet anticipation was something he recognized, and it had never let him down. So this was what summoned him here! Yet these male wolves driving the winter trail had probably screwed everything in sight that was even half recognizable as female. So where on earth could any "ikon diva" appear here in the tundra?

At the entrance, Rubinchik scraped the snow off his boots with a fir branch and followed the driver in through the double felt-padded doors. He found himself in a large and well-heated dining room. At two long wooden tables sat the drivers of the trucks that stood roaring away outside. Their quilted coats lay on the floor or hung over the chairbacks, and on the table each man had in front of him plates of borscht, goulash, pancakes, and the inevitable red bilberries. This evidently was their late supper or an early breakfast. Over in one corner was a washstand with a wet gray towel (for use by all comers), and at the far end was a service counter and beyond it the kitchen. A few recent arrivals lined up at the counter. Meanwhile from the kitchen came the aromas of boiled venison, fried onion, pancakes, soup, buckwheat gruel, and goodness knows what else. In the dining room these smells mingled with the fumes of diesel fuel, tobacco, and male sweat.

But through the tobacco smoke and the thick moist blend of these vapors Rubinchik caught sight of her immediately—behind the counter, standing next to the fat cook. Slender with an elongated neck and gray eyes, she wore a white laundered pinafore, and her fair hair was tucked up in a headscarf. She was by no means beautiful, but she showed a hint of some beauty yet to be—like the outline on a film negative. One of the drivers was serving up the usual chat:

"All right, Tanya! So, to celebrate our friendship, I'll have two borscht, three plates of goulash, pancakes, two glasses of sour cream, and four teas. And if I can down that lot, then the two of us will get married tomorrow. Is that a deal?"

"But if there's no wedding, will you be any less hungry?" she asked with a laugh.

She got her answer in the form of a gale of laughter from the other drivers, who egged one another on:

"Take no notice, Tanya. He's got three wives already at various points along the road!"

"What's this goulash made of? Venison? Tell me, how much did this deer have on the clock before it landed in the goulash? Okay, Tanya, forget the goulash! Give me some borscht, there's a good girl. Some goo from the bottom and some fat off the top! And don't forget about our journalist! This guy here is a journalist from Moscow—so give him some off the bottom too. D'you ever read the *Labor Gazette?*"

She didn't answer that one. But she did look up, saw Rubinchik, caught his glance, and with some inner vision of her own she seemed to recognize him, too. The smile left her face and her gaze became serious, scared, and yet curious.

"I'd like just pancakes and tea, please," he said.

"How many glasses?" she asked quietly.

"Just one."

Only minutes ago, out on the road, he had no idea what impulse had brought him here to the edge of the universe, to this frozen tundra landscape. Now, though, as he took the aluminum dish of pancakes from her hand, he sensed an electric charge in every cell of his body. Here she was! It was Her! It was Her! There, standing behind the counter!

At that moment the door banged open again. Amid billows of frosty air came a short thick-set Yakut in a fur jacket with a KGB major's shoulder tabs. With him were three others. One a young soldier dressed in a greasy driver's tunic, The other two, judging by their new-looking jackets, were visitors to these parts. Rubinchik thought he had already seen them somewhere, but he couldn't think where.

Everyone seemed to know the KGB major. At the sight of him, the whole company fell silent. Then the conversation gradually revived, but the truckers now talked in low voices and quickly finished their meals. Meanwhile the four newcomers joined the line at the service counter. As Rubinchik collected his tea and pancakes and turned to find a seat, his eyes met theirs. They immediately looked away, but there was something stabbing in their hostile stare. Taken aback, Rubinchik walked past them to the other end of the almost empty dining room and sat down with the driver who had brought him here. To his right sat a young driver with a round face, talking to another elderly man with pockmarks and a pointed nose.

"My buddy and his tanker have come off the road at the bridge. Some shit-ass overtook and knocked him in the middle. The poor bugger's ended up in the ditch. He turned right over and landed back on his wheels. It's okay. He's all right, but he's mighty cold. Can you drag him out?"

"That's what we're here for," the pockmarked one said vaguely. "Is he far away?"

"About fourteen miles. You know the bridge over the Ulakha? There's a steep turn and a fork. You turn right for Aikhal, and left to Nadyozhny."

"Sure, I know it. Only how did he manage to actually come off the bridge?"

Rubinchik realized that the pockmarked guy was the driver of the powerful tow truck he had seen in the parking lot. It was equipped with a winch, chains, and hawsers, specially designed to rescue vehicles that landed in the bog or a ditch, or had some other accident. From a professional viewpoint, it sounded interesting to Rubinchik. He introduced himself and invited himself to go and assist the capsized tanker. He finished off his pancakes and tea, and they were soon on the road. As they bowled northward, he listened to his driver complain about "those young jerks" who hadn't really learned how to drive but were already tearing up and down the winter trail.

"Just the other day one was going at such a lick that his back flap flew open. But he never noticed, and as he turned his whole cargo flew into the ditch. And it wasn't just any old crap. He was carrying champagne—three hundred twelve cases. Three thousand bottles dumped in the taiga! Half of them broken of course."

In the darkness of the cab Rubinchik noted down the story, but he found he was listening without concentrating and writing semiautomatically. He was already nursing a vision of that princess of the taiga he had seen at the canteen, with her gray eyes, excited, questioning, and appealing.

"Look at that! Just look how they drive!" His companion pointed at the road ahead. "He should get a kick in the ass for driving like that!"

In front of them the rear lights of a vehicle could be seen veering from side to side.

"Is he drunk or something?"

"He's not drunk, just hauling a trailer. Only he's no brain in his head! Oh well, he'll just end up one of my customers." With that, Rubinchik's pockmarked driver swung into a steep turn and off to the right, while the truck with its swinging tail lights disappeared up the trail to the left. Minutes later the tow truck inched its way over an improvised bridge that spanned a frozen brook. Down below Rubinchik could see a small fire that someone had lit in a bucket. Not far away lay the gasoline tanker, its wheels buried in a snowdrift.

"We're here," said Pockmark and turned round to look back. "I wonder why the KGB are tearing off up to Nadyozhny on a night like this? They'll never make it in a little car like that!"

"What KGB? Where from?" Rubinchik asked, puzzled.

"That was our local boss, Major Khulzanov," Pockmark said. "I thought at first they were looking after you, but they've turned off toward Nad-yozhny."

"After me?" Rubinchik laughed, and then remembered the sharp, un-friendly glances he'd gotten from the foursome in the cafe. "Why should they be watching me?"

"Who can tell with you guys?" the driver said. "You birds from the capital—you're big game out here. And they were sure giving you some nasty looks back in the cafe." Then, as the tanker driver rushed forward to greet them, Pockmark steered his heavy truck down the slope, flattening a pathway through the deep snow.

Rubinchik felt an unpleasant chill run down his spine. He now recalled where he had seen the KGB major's companions—at the room next to his own in the hotel, in the Northern Lights restaurant, and at the Diamond Club. But so what? Perhaps that was why they stared at him in the cafe, because they recognized him as their neighbor from the hotel? After all, there was only one hotel, one restaurant, and one club in the whole of Mirnyy.

Pockmark had meanwhile attached a towing cable to the tanker, hauled it back onto the road, and was ready to head back. At that moment, though, another truck from the north braked and halted right where they were. The driver announced that about seven miles north another tanker had skidded off the road and needed help.

An hour later, though, they made it back to the Beryozovy transport station. From the doorway Rubinchik spotted his new diva, her cheeks aglow and her eyes sparkling. But as Pockmark stepped inside, one of the other truckers called out:

"Hi there, Uncle Vanya! Don't take your coat off! Just after the Nad-yozhny turn-off, there's a KGB car waiting for you!"

"So, what's up?"

"They were overtaking some truck with a trailer. And our guy bashed them side-on with his trailer and spun them off the road. They've already been sitting in the ditch sunbathing for an hour!"

Rubinchik felt a weight fall from his mind. So that's who the KGB were chasing.

"Okay," said Pockmark. "Let 'em sunbathe some more. I'm having some tea first. You see," he complained to Rubinchik, "that's what it's like on this job. Are you going to come with me, or have you had enough for today?"

"No, I guess I'll head back to Mirnyy," he said.

Although it turned out the KGB were interested in somebody else, Ru-binchik was still eager to avoid another encounter with the Yakut KGB major and his team's cold, hostile stares. And also he felt uneasy in this dirty café out in the frozen tundra, God knows where, somewhere up in Yakutia, beyond the Arctic Circle! Especially since the girl had now disappeared into the back room.

He sat in the far corner, drinking his tea, warming his hands on the hot cut glass, and watching the door where she had disappeared. But she didn't come back. So he picked up a recent *Pravda* that someone had left lying on the next table. On the front page he saw the punchy headline that someone had circled with a pen:

PUNISH THEM AS THEY DESERVE!

Anatoly Shcharansky, Yury Orlov, and their accomplices concocted vile and libelous statements, in which they openly and brazenly slandered our Soviet country and social system. Anti-Communists and opponents of détente, of whom there are many in the West, joyfully seized on their malicious inventions, and they are now trying to present these liars and slanderers as "campaigners for the rights of the oppressed Soviet people." This was Shcharansky's aim. In fact he long ago decided to abandon his motherland and desert to the West. Fortunately, however, the logic of treachery handed over this "human-rights campaigner" to our special agents and revealed him to be a common spy. Both personally and through his accomplices, Shcharansky collected secret data on the location of enterprises vital to our military defense. The whole Soviet people demand that such traitors and spies be harshly punished. . . .

At this point the stout lady cook appeared behind the serving counter.

"Who ordered pancakes? There are just a dozen left. Then that's it— we're closing till seven A.M.!"

Rubinchik looked at his watch. It was five to five. Three truckers were finishing up, and Pockmark had already gone out to his vehicle. But now, even if the gorgeous Tanya reappeared in the dining room again, he no longer had a longing for romance. The *Pravda* article reeked of vile malice and clumsy fabrication. Spies—if they *were* spies—would never dare write lampoons against the country they were spying on! Those overstuffed oafs at *Pravda* didn't even know how to lie convincingly! The only "enterprises vital to our military defense" that Shcharansky had ever talked about were prisons where convicts were kept busy sewing military overcoats and mittens! Who, he wondered, could have left that paper here, and marked that report with a circle? Some driver or other? Or was it . . . ? No, he had to clear out, clear out before Pockmark brought those KGB skunks back with their gimlet stares.

Rubinchik got up to go.

"Are you heading north or south?" he asked the truckers who were also on their feet.

"We're going north. Which way do you want?"

"South. I'm going to Mirnyy."

"Just walk out to the roadside. Anyone will pick you up."

"You're right." Rubinchik donned his heavy jacket and tied the laces on his earflaps, now again hoping that Tanya might put in an appearance. But then the cook emerged from behind the counter with a mop and began cleaning up. He had no choice but to leave with the drivers. Heaving on the outer door, he again found himself in the open air with its lung-scorching frost, and he felt disappointed and exhausted. To hell with the taiga, the diamonds, and all this Arctic exotica! He'd had enough. Now he'd pick up the next truck going his way, return to Mirnyy, collect his bags, and then head for the airport, Moscow, and civilization! How great it would be to take a shower, put on normal clothing, eat normal food, and see his wife and children.

"Are you leaving already?" a gentle, low voice spoke from the darkness.

He looked round. On the flattened snow, standing in the moon-cast shadow of a tree, stood a short, thick-set figure in a fur hat, dark jacket, quilted pants, and felt boots. Was this the dainty young waitress? Even her voice sounded lower in the frosty air. But Rubinchik realized, it was her.

"Yes, I'm leaving," he said. "Are you going to Mirnyy too?"

"No, I'm just taking a walk. After work I always come out to breathe a bit of taiga air. Do you like it here?"

"It's hard to say. . . ." he was lost for an answer, and he could already feel his cheeks stiffening in the cold.

"I love the taiga!" she said. "In the fall, the grouse run around here, just like people out for a walk. And the chipmunks love music. Yes, it's true! I take my recorder out with me, and they follow me quite openly, and they listen. Honestly! And sometimes I sing to them."

"You write songs?"

"Yes. Would you like me to sing you something?"

"Right here?" He watched an empty truck roar past, heading south.

"No, nobody could sing in weather like this!" she laughed. "But for so long I've wanted to try my songs on someone who understands poetry. Do you have some time? What's your name?"

"Iosif."

"That's nice. Like Stalin." She turned off the trail and went in among the trees. In pitch dark, under spreading pines that shut out the moon, she made her way through the thickets along a path that only she knew.

"It's true," Rubinchik said surprised. It had never occurred to him.

"That was Stalin's name. Though, really, it's a biblical name. Where are we going?"

"It's quite close. Don't worry." Her voice ahead of him seemed to smile. "There's an old hunter's shelter. Nobody's lived there for ages. I discovered it. I keep my guitar there, and my poems. I had a feeling that today you'd come—I've had the heat on since last evening." Suddenly she turned to face him and looked keenly into his eyes. "Have you been in Mirnyy for long?"

"Five days. Why?"

"How odd," she said. "For five days I've kept the stove burning there. But your cheeks are going to freeze. Rub them with snow. We're nearly there though."

A few paces away, beneath a gigantic pine, he saw the dark shape of a tiny low-roofed dwelling—a little log-shelter, sunk in snow up to its eaves. A path had been dug through the snow right up to the door, which was secured with a wooden bar.

Tanya bent down to inspect the tracks by the doorway and laughed.

"The sable have been here," she said, "and Bruin too. This is where I put carrot out for the sable, and the old bear must have been upset." She slid back the bar and pushed the door open. "Come in. I'll light a lamp."

He gave a laugh and recited: "And in their country the cold is so great that each of them digs for himself a pit, and on it they place a wooden roof and scatter earth upon the roof. And in such dwellings they live. They kindle fire, and on their fires they heat stones until they glow red. . . ."

"What was that you said?" she said, surprised.

"Those aren't my words. They were written by an Arabian traveler describing the people of old Rus in the tenth century. You see, I was trained as a historian."

A few minutes later, a kerosene lamp and sticks blazing in the brick stove lit up the tiny room. The wooden beam walls were decorated with bunches of onion and a portrait of Pushkin, and there was also some shelving. A worn deerskin carpeted the floor, firewood was piled in one corner, a cast-iron pot stood on the stove, and Tanya had settled herself on the low oak sleeping bench. Strumming her guitar, she sang softly to Rubinchik, who sat there still in his fur jacket on the deerskin rug.

Thank you, Lord, that I abide
With deer in taiga stillness, in the forest wide!
A rarer gift I could not find!
Thank you, Lord, that I'm alive.
I hold myself in meekness and anticipation;
Ready for the fateful day and inspiration,
I hold myself.

In the wild woods,
In the silence
I hold myself.
I am intent,
I won't relent,
I'm ready for the fateful midnight inspiration.

Rubinchik listened to this half song, half recitative. Hardly real poetry, it tried to imitate the style of popular modern Russian bards. But the inspired air with which she sang filled his heart with tenderness. It was as if someone had spun a thread connecting her soul and body with his own. As the final chord of her song died away, Rubinchik rose and stepped over to where Tanya sat. He bent over, looked into her gray eyes, and kissed her on the lips.

She did not shy away, and her own soft lips answered him with a gentle response.

He closed his eyes, sensing a triumphant surge of desire in his limbs, like the call of a bugle. O Lord, I thank Thee! I thank Thee for the miracle of the taiga, for this gentle body pulsating with passion, spread out on a deerskin pelt in the glow of the fireplace, for the mounds of her breasts and her arching spine, for the quickness of her tongue, the hoarse breath of ecstasy, and the narrow throat of her magical cleft.

"Don't hurry, my love. Do not hurry."

The Rus then pour water over these stones heated in the fire, and from this comes a steam that heats up the dwelling until they remove even their clothing. And in such dwellings they remain until the spring.

Why did he suddenly remember this?

At that moment Major Khulzanov's KGB Niva rolled into the empty parking lot at Beryozovy in the wake of the tow truck. Three sullen gentlemen—Captains Faskin and Zartsev, and Khulzanov himself—got out and walked over to the cafe entrance.

"Where's the journalist?" they asked the cook, who was sweeping the floor.

"What journalist?" she asked.

"There was a Moscow journalist here an hour ago. With a big nose . . ."

"Oh, that one. The Jewish-looking one, you mean? He left a long time ago."

"Where to?"

"I heard him say he was going to Mirnyy."

The officers looked at one another. But Faskin was suspicious.

"And where's the girl, the one that helps you?"

"Tanya? She's asleep, I suppose. She went to bed a long time ago—in the hostel next door. Shall I call her?"

Without answering, the officers went out, and with their boots squeaking on the snow walked over to the wooden building next door. Naturally, they found no Tanya in any of the four rooms where the other staff were sleeping. Her bed was neatly made, and on the bedside table were a few books and a photo of her in a summer dress. On the next bunk the girl who worked as her relief was asleep.

"Tanya?" she said, when they woke her. "She's not back from her night shift yet. . . . What's the time?"

The officers took Tanya's photograph, checked both buildings again, then walked back to the parking lot. Nearby, in the uncertain light of a tundra dawn, trucks, vans, and tank trucks kept roaring by.

"That bloody Jew! He's gone and abducted the girl!" Faskin swore. "Put out that cigarette, and get going!" he ordered the driver when they got back in their car. "Back to Mirnyy. Fast as you can!"

Rubinchik reappeared in Mirnyy only toward the end of the day, just before the last flight for Krasnoyarsk. He looked exhausted. As they took off, he looked back at the receding lights of Mirnyy and happened to catch the eyes of Faskin and Zartsev, who were three rows behind him. Oh yes, they knew only too well that supposedly casual look of the quarry when pursued. And actually, Rubinchik was keeping up his end nicely. Or had he screwed himself so blind last night that he simply didn't have the energy to get scared?

Rubinchik looked away and gazed out of the window. Down below, the lights of the diamond town gleamed in the Arctic night, and to the west, amid a black ocean of taiga, was a dotted line of yellow specks—the headlamps of trucks rolling along the winter trail. A few minutes later the dim lights of the Beryozovy transport station could be seen flickering. Once these had drifted away, Rubinchik settled down against the hard back of his aluminum seat and dozed, drifting into the satisfied sleep of a man who had fulfilled his duties both as a male and a professional.

Three rows away, unlike Rubinchik, Faskin and Zartsev were in no mood for sleep. In fact they felt like slinging the damn Jew out of the plane then and there. But for now there was nothing they could do. Sooner or later, they knew they'd get him for good. After all, apart from mere surveillance, the KGB had lots of more aggressive tricks.

nine

Of course Rubinchik got very little sleep. How could he sleep with the KGB looking daggers at him and seeming to threaten to beat him up? Like that time eight years ago when he was mauled by a weightlifter in Kaluga after taking the man's fiancée to his hotel room on the eve of her wedding. Since then he had stopped pursuing girls. Instead of going after them, he now did no more than let them come to him of their own accord. And that, of course, had the piquancy of a far greater challenge. These KGB agents could not have seen him with Tanya—he'd gone off with her before they'd arrived at Beryozovy. Yet all the same, he had a sense of their eyes filled with hatred and focused on the back of his neck. As though they'd already lined him up in their gun sights.

Rubinchik pretended to sleep, but meanwhile he thought feverishly: What was wrong? What did they want? Okay, so they didn't catch that idiot with his trailer—but where did he come into the picture? Surely they didn't take him to be an accomplice of that bandit? No, he was just panicking. A wretched Jewish coward, that's what he was! Of course, he'd made yet another lovely Russian girl into a woman (and what a woman!). But so what? People's sleeping habits, thank God, were hardly KGB business—they were after dissidents, saboteurs, American spies. Also, this morning, when he bade farewell to Tanya, there wasn't a soul around her little taiga shelter, only a tiny trail of squirrel paws on the snow. He had walked out onto an empty roadway, flagged down the first truck heading south, and five hours later, he was back in Mirnyy. Admittedly, the first people he'd met back at the Polyarnik Hotel were those two agents with their glaring eyes. But so what? Probably they'd failed to catch some bandit, or some courier of stolen diamonds, and now they felt like venting their anger on the first Jew that crossed their path. That was typical in Russia—even Gorky had written about that feature of the Russian character.

However, no amount of reasoning seemed to calm him. Also the whole plane reaked of garlic sausage, homebrewed vodka, unwashed feet, sweat, sheepskins, and carbolic acid from the toilet. Someone had taken his boots off and was drying his foot bindings by winding them round the legs of his damp felt boots; someone else was smoking vile-smelling cigarettes; and up front another loudmouth was declaiming about "this Jew Abraham who comes home and finds Sara in bed with the neighbor . . ."

Because of the filth, stench, and the threat posed by the two agents seated behind him, Rubinchik lost all his former sense of being a pioneer explorer of exotic lands. Instead, he felt like an orphan abandoned on a barbarian planet. Also, he now changed his view of the country he had traveled all these years. For instance, the crepe towel by the washstand at Beryozovy was simply black with dirt, with only one towel for all the drivers who came—because the other hundred-odd needed in such a place had been stolen by the manager. And those torn gray bedsheets at the Polyarnik Hotel, which were changed every ten days for another set just as torn and gray, were so awful because the new sheets had been sold off by the manager for booze. And in the "Shanghai" of Mirnyy, hundreds of families with children lived in ice-covered shelters made out of metal drums and plywood, because the construction materials for their "domed city" had been carted off by the Party committee to put up villas for themselves. And that was how things were everywhere, from the Arctic to the Pamirs, from Khabarovsk to Moscow. Here was this sweaty, unwashed, brutish state with its imperial ambitions and anti-Semitic stories, building space rockets while looting everything that wasn't nailed down; a country mired in bribe-taking, corruption, and cruelty; a country whose leaders "at the request of the workers" were ready to execute those who spoke a word of truth about their regime, and whose slavish population was drowned in alcohol. This was the vision Rubinchik now saw. And he was terrified. And if those KGB agents were to arrest him here and now, on the airplane, on some whim instead of the bandit who'd given them the slip, there was nothing to save him. If he were to disappear, nobody—not even the editor of his paper—would risk inquiring where he was. He would simply vanish into some Siberian labor camp.

Rubinchik opened his eyes and glanced out the window. Siberia, as usual, was covered in a blanket of cloud from horizon to horizon. Only occasionally was there a glimpse of the snowy taiga, the rocky clefts of some ravine, the blue twisting ribbon of a frozen river and a yellow-gray crust of ice covering the bogs.

"Will you be having breakfast, Comrade?"

Rubinchik looked away from the window and saw bending over him a young stewardess, no more than seventeen, with eyes of cornflower blue in her little round pimply virginal face. She wore a short uniform skirt and blouse, with gray woolen stockings and felt bootees and was holding a cellophane packet. Rubinchik squinted and saw the two KGB agents turned in his direction like zealous parents. He looked at the stewardess and shook his head.

"No thank you," he said.

"I'd take it if I were you!" she spoke with sudden jauntiness, and looked him in the eye. "There's Finnish servalat and Bulgarian apples! Very tasty. Incidentally, this is your third flight with me. I read your articles in the paper. If I were you, I'd have some breakfast. You'll not regret it! My name's Katya, by the way."

She fitted the table into some slots in the armrest and put down the breakfast package. As she did so, she bent over so close that her flaxen hair touched his face. "Would you like tea or coffee?"

Rubinchik noticed his KGB neighbors turn livid with either fury or jealousy.

"Tea, please."

"Quite right," Katya said approvingly. "The coffee will keep you awake. But you'd do well to eat something and then sleep. It's another six hours to Moscow." Then she turned to the KGB team. "Will you be having breakfast?"

"Yes," they grunted.

"In a moment," she said, speaking in a curt, formal voice, and then went off down the aisle.

Rubinchik could not help smiling and turned back to look out of the window. All his fears seemed to fade. Of course, this was a barbaric country. But they knew him here, they read him, and even recognized him! And in such obscure locations—and even aboard this plane—one could still find the glinting genetic outcrops of that former Russian-Nordic beauty that had only once revealed its secret to him—long ago, seventeen years before, on a benighted shore of the Volga. Yet ever since, this vision excited him. So much so that every month he roved Siberia, the Urals, and the Altay in search of it. Maybe it was this which, without realizing it, the Germans, the French, the Poles, and the Swedes—and long before them, the Jews in the sixth century—had been seeking when they came here?

And our ancestors fled from Persia . . . And they were taken in by the Khazarian people. Because the Khazarians who dwelt on the Ityl lived in those days without any law. And our ancestors became the kinsmen of those who dwelt in that land and learned their ways. And they became one people with them.

As ruler they placed over themselves their military commander, the man who achieved victory at war. And this continued until that day when the Jews went to war along with them. One Jew displayed on that day unusual strength with his sword and put to flight those foes that had attacked the Khazars. And the people placed him at their head. And they renamed him Sabriil and made him king over them. And then the fear of God was upon those peoples that dwelt around us, such that they did not go to war against the Khazarians . . .

But in the days of the evil Roman, ruler of Macedonia, there was persecution of the Jews in Constantinople. And when the Khazarian king heard of this, he cast down many of those in his kingdom who were uncircumcised. And Roman the Evil sent great gifts to Igor the Old, Tsar of the Rus, and urged on him to make war on the Khazars. And Igor went at night to Samkerts and took it by stealth, because its governor rab-Hashmonai was not there. And this became known to the venerable Pesakh, chief captain of the Khazarian king, and he moved against Roman and took Samkerts and three more towns. And from there he advanced on Cherson and made war against it, and saved it from the hand of the Rus, and smote all those remaining there. And from there he advanced upon Igor's capital. . . .

That was it! Amid the background roar of the engines, it occurred to Rubinchik that this must have been a tragic turning point in Russo-Jewish history! Why the devil had Pesakh made war on Kiev? Wasn't it enough that he'd won back Samkerts and Cherson and three other towns? Why did he have to go and make war on the capital of Old Rus?

"Why aren't you eating?" Katya sounded upset. "I've brought you some tea."

He looked into her eyes. And again—as on the winter trail—the inner depth of her cornflower-blue Polovtsian eyes opened up for him. He'd need only some gesture or small sign for this Katya to step up to him in front of these staring KGB agents, press her cheek against his shoulder and become his new mistress. Right there on the plane.

"Thank you, Katya," he said, and he took the glass of tea in its aluminum holder from her tray.

ten

Blood stains are most easily washed off from an oil-based paint. So in Soviet jails, the floors and lower walls of interrogation rooms were always finished in a thick ochre oil-paint, to match the color of blood. The upper sections of the walls would vary. Some were painted an impersonal gray, others a cheery blue, while others an anguished yellow. But the ceilings always had a lightbulb with no shade, in every room hung a portrait of Brezhnev in blue marshal's uniform, and on every window an iron grill. The prison courtyards were adorned with placards saying things like EARN RELEASE WITH A CLEAN CONSCIENCE! and it was there that the convicts exercised and lined up for their roll calls.

"What are you talking about, Comrade Warden?! I'm no Jew. I'm Russian," was the protest of every convict summoned to the warden's office at Moscow's Butyrki Jail when issued with his new passport.

"You've been sentenced for theiving four times now. And in here you're always shirking and dodging. What sort of Russian d'you call yourself?" the warden sneered. "I'll make it brief: I just had confirmation that your sentence is being extended by another six years for your part in a group assault on another prisoner."

"But I didn't do that. I was nowhere near the guy at the time!"

"Don't interrupt. You assaulted him! So you now have a choice: either you go to Siberia to feed the mosquitoes for six years. Or else, you take your new passport and Israeli visa. And you clear out of this country tomorrow! Got it?"

"Israel? Warden! Who's going to let me in there? I've never even had my dick snipped!"

"You can have that done when you get there! And they'll let you into America even without it. But the main thing for you to remember is this: one squeal that you've done time, and that'll be the end of you. No America, no Israel, or anywhere else. Keep quiet and the world is yours—you can even go on a thieving spree to Australia! Or if you want to be circumcised now, we can fix that too: I'll tell the medic—"

"No! No, Warden! Thank you, I'll go as I am."

Barsky, however, was not amused by these interviews. He was even disconcerted at how readily these men agreed to leave Russia. Of course, they were incorrigibles, the scum of society. But all the same, weren't they Russians?

Although he enjoyed brandishing an occasional Yiddish expression, Barsky himself was pureblooded Russian, in fact of noble origin. His mother, who'd died only two years ago, was of peasant stock from Vyatka, and she was a singer of Russian folk music. His late father's ancestry went back to Novgorod merchants who had made their fortune under Peter the Great. In the 1930s, of course, when his father received a Stalin Prize, his noble origins had to be concealed. But later there had been a revival of imperial traditions. Among the new Soviet elite, to be of noble descent was a sign that someone was ultrareliable and had a history of loyalty to Russia. And the Barskys had always served their country. But Oleg Barsky was no idealist. He could see for himself how corrupt and incompetent the Brezhnev regime was. Yet despite all that, he believed, things could be put right: once Andropov took control, he would haul Russia out of this crisis. For all the rumors that Lenin was syphilitic, Stalin a maniac, and Khrushchev a drunkard, the fact remained that these men had built an empire that Russians for centuries had always dreamed of. Russia was now a superpower. And if to maintain its stability a few thousand Jewish rebels had to be imprisoned, why then Barsky was ready to do the job.

It was of course one thing to make such decisions in the luxury of the Kremlin, but quite another to carry them out in wretched Butyrki, and other Moscow jails.

"Comrade Colonel, there's a phone call for you."

"Who is it?"

"From the Committee, the duty officer."

Barsky took the receiver.

"Hallo, Barsky speaking."

"Colonel, do you listen to Voice of America?" the KGB duty officer asked.

"What's up?" Barsky asked, surprised. "Why should I—"

"One moment. I'll switch on our tape."

Barsky could hear the familiar tones of a Voice of America announcer loud and clear above a background of Soviet jamming:

"Moscow. The trial began in Moscow yesterday of Professor Yury Orlov, charged with making false statements about infringements of human rights in the USSR. A protest of Jewish women refuseniks is reported to be taking place outside OVIR, Moscow's central Visa office. The well-known activist Inessa Brodnik is said to be leading the demonstration of a hundred and fifty or so other women. They are demanding a meeting with the head of OVIR, General Bulychev, and . . ."

"Damn it!" Barsky swore, slammed the receiver down, and rushed out and dove into the black Volga that waited by the sidewalk.

"To OVIR, the central Visa Office! And make it fast!" he said, and the driver gunned the engine.

Again the Yids were making a fool of him! And this time a bunch of fucking Jewesses. That Brodnik broad seemed dead set on becoming a Yid Joan of Arc. Barsky wrenched free the cell telephone and began talking.

"This is Twenty-four-seventeen. Get me the head of OVIR . . . No, I don't know his number. Get it from the directory. General Bulychev."

From informers and from bugging foreign correspondents' phone calls, Barsky had learned yesterday that some of the more fanatic women refuseniks were planning something, possibly trying to force an audience with Bulychev and then hold a sit-down protest in his office, and they'd invited Western correspondents to witness the spectacle. But Barsky had planned to thwart them and had told Bulychev to treat them politely. The female officer at reception was to accept their request for an audience and tell them that a date with Bulychev would be communicated to them by mail within the next ten days. All perfectly normal, as in any civilized country. Brodnik would thus look like a fool, along with the Western journalists. Later, in about three weeks, once the trial of Orlov was over, Bulychev might then agree to see these women—singly, of course, and not in a group.

"I'm about to connect you," the operator finally said. By this time Barsky's car was racing along the streetcar track past Novoslobodskaya subway. Then another female voice came on the line:

"Visa Office Reception. Hello . . ."

"This is Colonel Barsky of State Security. Give me Bulychev. It's urgent."

"One moment." She sounded unruffled, and Barsky heard the receiver thump down on her desk.

Bulychev evidently had no switchboard, and his secretary had run and told him who was calling. The cell phone was a brilliant invention, but high technology was useless with a bunch of dimwits. He'd probably arrive there before he was finished with the phone call—by now they were passing the Soviet Army Theater, halfway already!

Irritated, Barsky loosened his necktie and only now recalled why he'd even put on his starched white shirt: today at three he was due to meet Anna Sigal. Anna! He thrust a hand in his pocket and pulled out two packets, Dunhill and Stolichnye. But with a squint at the chauffeur he put back the Dunhill, and lit up one of the Russian brand. He inhaled. Not to worry, he reflected—he still had a few trumps against these Shcharanskys, Brodniks, and Rappoports. Compared with this, the "Frontier Million" operation and the arrest of Kuznetsov's hijackers would seem like a sedate picnic.

"Bulychev here," a voice finally announced.

"This is Barsky. What's going on?"

But, by now, Barsky's car had already emerged onto Olympic Prospect, and he could see for himself what was happening in front of the three-story Visa building. The roadway was blocked by a crowd of women holding placards reading LET MY PEOPLE GO!, YOU SIGNED THE HELSINKI AGREE-MENT—NOW OBSERVE IT!, STOP THE ANTI-SEMITIC PRESS CAMPAIGN! PUT THE ANTI-SEMITES ON TRIAL! and so forth. Several women had children with them, and foreign reporters with TV cameras swarmed like crows around a piece of carrion. Nearby, on the sidewalks, were their husbands. Closer, though, a line of militiamen stood uncertainly pawing the ground along the edge of the sidewalk.

"I've accepted their petition, but they won't leave," Barsky heard General Bulychev say helplessly. But Barsky had no chance to reply, because at that moment there was a howl of sirens behind them. Barsky turned and saw police cars and canvas-covered militia trucks tearing toward the Visa Office, and on Tsvetnoy Boulevard a squadron of similar trucks and cars also appeared on the other side of the demonstrators. Seeing this, the women grew alarmed, their husbands raised a shout, and the foreign journalists aimed their cameras at the advancing vehicles anticipating an appetizing spectacle of fistfights and arrests.

"Stop! Quick! Turn around!" Barsky told the driver. With a scream of brakes, Barsky helped the driver to swing the wheel all the way over, so he managed to position his car between the demonstrators and the militia trucks. Then he jumped out and ran toward the leading truck and with a commanding gesture raised his hand holding his ID.

"Back off!" he shouted.

"What's up? Who are you?" A militia colonel with a terra cotta complexion stuck his head from the truck's cab.

"KGB, Fifth Directorate!" Barsky jumped onto the footboard and shoved his papers in the colonel's face. "Get out of here right now! All of you! Give me your radio!" he said with quiet authority, literally wrenching the mike from the colonel's grip. "Who've you got on the line?"

"Petrovka Department, duty officer," the colonel said.

"Duty officer," Barsky spoke into the microphone. "This is Barsky of KGB Fifth Directorate. Tell your Black Marias to get the hell out of here, right now! And order your men to cordon the area off, but no arrests. There's to be no use of force! Have you got that? Confirm. Over."

"But I have orders from Deputy Minister Shumilin! Over!"

"I'll talk to Shumilin later! Meantime just carry out my order!" Barsky chucked the microphone back at the colonel. "And don't forget, Colonel: if your fucking vehicles aren't out of here in one minute, I'll come and rip your shoulder tabs off personally. Have you got me?"

Without waiting for an answer, Barsky jumped down and returned to his car. The moronic militia, always trying to show off. It was mere luck that he'd managed to stop those cretins. Only idiots would have sent in such a swarm to arrest a hundred Jewish women. Imagine the glee *that* would have given those Western newsmen!

He got back in his car.

"Let's go," he said.

"Where to?"

"Straight on. To the Visa Office. Where else?"

"But these women are . . ." the driver hesitated and nodded toward the crowd barring their path.

"Not to worry. They'll let us through. Give 'em a honk."

Barsky was right. Seeing the militia vehicles reverse away again following his command, the women let the KGB Volga pass through their midst, and it delivered Barsky directly to the main entrance.

The doors were shut, and two militiamen stood on sentry duty. Barsky turned away from the Western cameras as he quickly got out. Two paces took him past the guards, and once inside he ran up the stairs to Bulychev's office on the third floor.

"Perhaps I should see them?" Bulychev asked as Barsky walked in. Bulychev was standing by the window and watching the noisy crowd below from behind his muslin curtain.

"And what will you say to them?" Barsky objected, joining him at the window. "They'll sit right down, and you'll have a sit-in on your hands for weeks. Or will you drag them out by the hair?"

"What if we let in just five or six?"

"No way!" Barsky was definite. "If you give so much as an inch, you'll have a thousand people here every day! From all over the country!"

"So what do we do?"

Barsky said nothing and stood watching the Jewish women. Most of them he'd never met, although from the photos in their dossiers he knew almost every one of them. Strange, in the seven years his Section had existed, he'd never managed to recruit a single Jewish woman as an informer. The men were no problem—he had more than a dozen in Moscow alone. But no women. Aha, there was Inessa Brodnik—the little gray-haired one. Despite the heat she was wearing pigskin boots and a gray quilted jacket with a provocative yellow Star of David. All prepared to be arrested, and she was reading from today's *Pravda* to some Western television man:

" 'During the last hundred years there is no political crime to which the Zionists have not stooped. During the war they worked side by side with the Gestapo. Many Zionists worked as guards in the death camps . . .' You see? They print filth like this every day."

Barsky frowned. *Pravda* had overdone it. But when you tried to find out where stuff like that originated, you discovered it came directly from Suslov's Central Committee Propaganda Section. Or from the other young Kremlin hawks, who wanted to prevent the KGB from having a say in molding public opinion.

Barsky then turned his attention to the women standing next to Brodnik. There was Zina Gertsianova, wife of the famous comic actor—she, incidentally, was of pure Russian blood and almost thirty years younger than her husband, yet here she was, in a Jewish demonstration! He could also see Natalya Katz, whose three-month-old daughter was allegedly dying and urgently needed treatment available only in the United States. And Raya Goldina, whose application to emigrate had been turned down three times. Shameless bitch, breast-feeding her infant in full public view!

"Not bad-looking, that one!" Bulychev suddenly commented. He closed the double-glazed window to cut out the noise.

Barsky looked him straight in the eye, and the general was embarrassed.

"I didn't mean the one with the tits. I meant the wife of Gertsianov. She's Russian. . . ."

Barsky could tell, though, from the gleam in Bulychev's gaze, that it was the Jewish woman Goldina he had in mind. That was also something that grated on him: how was it almost all Russian men got so worked up over Jewish women? Just scratch the surface, and you discovered half the elite were either married to Jewish women or had a Jewish mistress. Barsky thought himself above such things and prided himself on never having been turned on by a Jewess.

"That's one thing I don't understand," Bulychev said, trying to divert suspicion of his prurient interest in Jewish women. "You'd think that Ivan Ivanovich gets enough hints in the papers to get all aroused and beat the hell out of the Yids. They're virtually told that nobody'll say anything. But there's not been a single pogrom! Just look there." Bulychev pointed toward Samotyochnaya Square, where the militia had erected barriers to prevent the demonstration spilling onto the crossing. "Guys go walking past. They might curse at these Jews, but they still don't. And look at those construction workers." Bulychev nodded toward a nearby site across the street. "They've stopped work, and they keep staring and spitting down from their scaffolding, but nothing more!"

This was a paradox that perplexed the entire KGB directorate. Newspaper articles and broadcasts on the so-called "international conspiracy of

Zionist fascists" did generate some heat, and there was a sputtering of anti-Semitic outbursts here and there. But no sign of a storm of popular wrath in the form of pogroms that would have channeled and hopefully discharged the growing general public discontent with the regime.

A telephone trilled, and Bulychev hastily picked up the receiver. It was the white "hotline" phone emblazoned with a Soviet coat of arms. He listened, then handed the receiver to Barsky.

"It's for you . . . Shumilin."

"Boris Tikhonovich," Barsky immediately squared up to his caller, determined to avert any tongue-lashing despite his peremptory cancellation of the Deputy Minister's order. "Boris Tikhonovich, it was quite out of the question to arrest more than a hundred women in full view of those Western newsmen. That was exactly what they wanted us to do. Each of those bitches sees herself as a Joan of Arc. There would have been a free-for-all, and tomorrow the press would have been plastered with it. And then the first heads to roll would have been yours and mine."

"So what do we do?" the Deputy Minister asked, now seeing the disaster that Barsky had saved him from.

"I think I have an idea," said Barsky, glancing at the construction workers who were still lounging on the half-completed roof of the nearby building. "What we need is about three hundred militiamen dressed in overalls and construction helmets. They should look like angry workers. It has to seem like public anger, as if ordinary people have come to settle things in their own way. It stands to reason, after all. If the KGB and the militia couldn't handle the situation . . ."

"I get it!" said Shumilin, heartened. "I'm very indebted to you. Hold on, your workers are on the way!"

"Only warn them: no beating up!" Barsky said hastily. "Although if they accidentally trample a few Western cameras, that can't do any harm."

"Brilliant!" Bulychev commented.

Barsky replaced the receiver and felt satisfied. To have the Deputy Minister of Internal Affairs in your debt was not a bad thing. But what was he thinking about before Shumilin's call? Oh yes, pogroms. Now, if this Rubinchik could be publicly tried with a procession of Russian girls who had been dishonored by this Jewish monster, that would deeply impress every Russian who had a daughter or a sister. It might even have an impact overseas. But inside the Soviet Union, it could detonate something more explosive even than the "blood of Christian infants" that the Jews were supposed to drink, and which had unleashed those pogroms at the turn of the century.

"Do you have anything to drink?" Barsky asked.

"You insult me even by asking!" Bulychev laughed cheerily. He opened his safe and took out a bottle of Napoleon brandy, then pressed a button under his desk. "Valya," he said as his secretary appeared—she was young and tall, like a volleyball player, and wore a miniskirt and scarlet lipstick. "Fix us some glasses and . . . well, whatever you can come up with. Only make it snappy!"

Barsky followed Valya with his gaze. Then he eyed the leather settee adorning Bulychev's office.

"Specially made to size, was it?"

Bulychev pretended not to understand.

"How do you mean?" he asked, then picked up the hotline phone, which was ringing. "Yes . . . Good day, Yuri Vladimirovich . . ."

Barsky tensed. That was Andropov.

"Yes, he's here. I'll just hand you over," Bulychev said respectfully.

Andropov wasted no time on greetings.

"What are you up to?" he asked.

Barsky explained his idea. No longer a KGB reprisal, it would seem like an ordinary workmen's response to the excesses carried out by these Zionists right in the heart of Moscow.

"Well, okay . . . Only don't get too carried away," Andropov said. "With the trial of Orlov, the situation is tense as it is. We don't need people going off the deep end just now."

"I know, Yuri Vladimirovich. That's why this Brodnik woman has grown so brazen."

"You can settle her hash later on," said Andropov.

Barsky rejoiced inwardly: Andropov himself had approved his plan! But in that case . . .

"One moment, Yuri Vladimirovich," he said. "I have another new scheme that I'd like to put to you. . . ."

The pause at the other end of the line could mean one of two things: either Andropov was assessing the enormity of Barsky's insolence, since he couldn't bear KGB staff who went over the heads of their superiors to get his attention. Or else he was simply leafing through his desk diary for some available time. In all his years with the KGB, Barsky had only once requested a meeting with Andropov. That was in May 1970, after he had pulled out a note about a Zionist called Edward Kuznetsov from a pile of provincial reports. Kuznetsov had just been released from jail and was apparently getting together a group to hijack a plane and fly it to the West. At that time, it was something utterly new, an act of unheard of boldness. Any other KGB operator would have arrested Kuznetsov and his band there and then. But Barsky discerned some special possibilities for his organization in this scheme for a *Jewish group hijacking*. It was then that he'd managed to secure an audience with Andropov.

"My assistant will call you back. Will half an hour be enough for you?" Andropov's voice asked abruptly. Barsky's spirits rose.

"Absolutely! Thank you, Yuri Vladimirovich!"

The line immediately went dead. But Barsky was not in the least put out. His chief didn't like wasting time on idle chatter. He smiled, and without thinking took one of Bulychev's cigarettes from the packet on the desk and lit it.

At that point the door opened again, and the secretary brought in a tray with two bottles of mineral water, two cognac glasses, and a plate of sandwiches. As she placed the tray on the table, she stooped so that the neck of her blouse parted, briefly revealing her bare breasts. She then stood up and looked at her boss.

"Anything else, Kirill Fyodorovich?" she asked.

"Yes. Put on your bra," Bulychev said sullenly.

"And if possible, cut us some lemon," Barsky added.

"Right away . . ." She cast Barsky a provocative glance and walked out again with a swing of her lanky thighs. "Well, one tries to teach them . . ." Bulychev muttered as he poured the brandy.

"Perhaps you don't teach them the right things?" Barsky smirked, still nursing the memory of Andropov's friendly tone and his question, "Will half an hour be enough for you?"

At that point there was a hullabaloo out on the street. Barsky peered out the window. Another black Volga had been let through the militia barrier and was making its way through the crowd toward the Visa building.

"Who's that?" Barsky asked, but Bulychev merely shrugged. A moment later Barsky recognized Sergey Igunov, the Central Committee's chief specialist on Zionist affairs, who swung his way majestically toward the entrance. Igunov had a doctorate in history, he was the author of books such as *Fascism Beneath the Blue Star*, *Zionism Revealed*, and *Unarmed Invasion*, and also edited a dozen other similar works.

"Shall I clear this away?" Bulychev asked, nodding toward the brandy bottle.

"What for? He's a Russian, isn't he?" Barsky laughed.

"Valya!" Bulychev shouted. "Bring another glass!"

A minute later, Igunov appeared. He was young, no more than thirty-five, tall, and solidly built, with a round face, turned-up nose, and his smooth ash-gray hair was brushed straight back. His eyes were light gray and their protruding lids betrayed either a liver condition or a propensity for alcohol. He was wearing a light summer suit and Apache-style shirt.

"So," he said without a word of greeting. "It's come to this, damn it! Can't even drive down the street because it's blocked by kikes!" He took a glass of brandy from the tray and downed it in one, as though drinking water. "So, and what are we going to do?" he asked Barsky.

From his use of the word "we," Barsky immediately guessed Igunov's game. Fyodor Kulakov, on whom Igunov had staked all his bets, had blundered at the last Politburo meeting, and Igunov was now looking for some way of contact with Andropov.

Barsky had no chance to answer. At that moment Bulychev's secretary appeared again, bringing a third glass and a plate of clumsily cut lemon. She was the same height as Igunov, and the two of them eyed one another like a pair of pythons meeting on a forest path.

"Hmm . . . well, we have the following situation. . . ." Bulychev began. "Comrade Barsky has proposed getting rid of the demonstration using so-called workers. . . ."

Valya and Igunov visually disentangled themselves, and she walked out. Igunov then turned to Bulychev.

"Is that the bench where you do your hammering? Or might I be free to have a go?"

Although he was Bulychev's junior by fifteen years, Igunov's position allowed him to be familiar even with generals.

"Well . . ." Bulychev was stuck for a reply.

"Why so coy?" Igunov said. "Peter the Great wasn't shy about fucking his secretaries in full view of the court—and also at dinner, between the soup and the meat pie." He turned to Barsky: "Well, so how are we going to liquidate this little gathering?"

Barsky disliked the "we." He curtly told Igunov of his idea with the "workers" and mentioned that at any moment they were due to arrive.

"Good. We'll wait then."

Igunov poured himself a full glass of brandy, pulled up a chair and placed it by the window. Then he sat down with outstretched legs and stared down at the noisy throng of women. Through the double glazing, they heard only occasional shouts about the Helsinki Agreement, freedom of emigration, the illegality of the visa refusals, and other nonsense. Igunov sipped his brandy, then suddenly spoke.

"Well, you guys, which one of them would you screw if you had the chance? What about you, General? Come on, be honest!"

"W-well . . . I don't know . . ." Bulychev said, confused.

"Oh yes, you do know!" Igunov insisted. "You know all right! Don't try and fool us! What Russian doesn't dream of screwing a Jewess, if only once in his life! In fact, that's where all our troubles began!" Suddenly Igunov closed his eyes and began quoting: " 'And it was the habit of the Khazarian king to have twenty-five wives, of which each was the daughter of the ruler of some neighboring tribe. And King Joseph took them willy-nilly!' And that," said Igunov, "is a piece of history. Even in the tenth century, the

Yids used to shaft all our Polovtsian princesses, do you get it? And that's why we all dream of having a Jewess! Isn't that right, Colonel? As head of the KGB's Jewish Section, you've certainly come across a few Jewesses. So what's your impression?" Igunov held his empty glass out to Bulychev. "Let's have a refill, General . . . That, incidentally, was why I came today—to take a squint at all these Yids. So here they are, like a curse of leprosy on our country! Where else can you see so many Jewesses all together?"

Barsky did not buy Igunov's explanation of why he was here.

"By the way, Sergey Sergeyevich," he said, "just before you came we were discussing a curious question . . ."

"Oh yes?" Igunov asked, without turning from the window.

"How best to put it?" Barsky wondered aloud. "Let's call it the inadequate public reaction to the anti-Zionist efforts of the press, and . . ."

"Aha, so that's your drift!" Igunov interrupted with a laugh. "Why not come to the point? You mean that however much we keep yelling 'Beat the Yids!' there's still no sign of a pogrom. Do you know what Father Sergey Bulgakov had to say on that subject? 'Between Russia and Jewry there exists a mutual attraction and a spontaneous link. . . .' "

He was interrupted by a loud chorus from outside. The women had all joined in singing "Hava Nagila."

"Look at them, the bitches!" Igunov said leaning forward. "Well, Colonel, where are these so-called workers-cum-militiamen, damn it?"

"They should be here any minute . . ."

"Excellent! How very splendid!" Igunov said sarcastically, still watching the singing women. "Just look at them! In the middle of Moscow, our Russian capital! Incidentally, Colonel, you know what song this is, don't you? You should know, after all they know all of our songs! It's a hymn to the sun. Anyway, on the question of pogroms. You're right, of course, mere newspaper articles won't get us anywhere. You should tell your boss that I have one or two other practical ideas. So we could pool our resources and work together." He gave Barsky a sober stare. "Would you like that?"

Barsky felt the pit of his stomach freeze. Could Igunov really know of his secret plan involving Rubinchik? Or did he have some schemes of his own? But no chance to answer that, however, because at that moment the singing outside suddenly broke off and there was shouting and the tramping of feet. Now, a dense dark crowd of "workers" decked out in smart new canvas overalls and sporting plastic helmets could be seen moving down from Troitskaya Street to the north. They moved in on the demonstrating women in a solid cohort. Meanwhile, behind the crowd, militiamen hastily began clearing away their barriers and reopened Samotyochnaya Square to traffic.

"Aha!" Igunov brightened and moved closer to the window. He undid the catches and flung open first the inner panes, then the outer storm windows. Cool spring air, the noise of the crowd, women's cries, and the oaths and swearing of the "construction workers" came flooding into the office. At that moment the "workers" reached the demonstrators and began pressing and forcing them back toward the road traffic that was now rushing along Samotyochnaya.

"Come on, move it, fucking Jews!" they yelled. "Clear off to Israel! Hold your demonstrations there! We don't want you fucking bitches here! We're running this place—us workers!"

"Be careful, there are kids here! How dare you!"

"Come on, clear out! Take your kids home! Get your fucking kike brats away from here!"

"This is an outrage! What sort of workers are you! You stink of vodka! Call yourselves men! Charging at women like this!"

"Shut up, you bitch! I'll show you what sort of a man I am! D'you want me to?"

"Get your asses out of here, you Jewish bitches! People need to get past! These sidewalks are for working people! This isn't the fucking place for fucking demonstrations in front of fucking Westerners! Come on, guys, let 'em have it!"

"Once more the sons of Israel are persecuted, they who only yesterday appeared triumphant. . . ." Igunov pronounced with ironic pathos.

Barsky didn't know whether this was another of Igunov's quotations, or something of his own.

Meanwhile, out on the street the husbands rushed to assist their wives. But from goodness knows where Inessa Brodnik produced a megaphone and shouted out to them:

"Get back! Get back! Don't you understand? They want to provoke a fight! Get back! Don't come near! Girls, we're going to move off! Start moving away gradually!"

The women began backing off. The ones in the rear moved out onto the roadway crossing the square and began waving their arms, trying to stop the cars that came flying toward them with horns honking.

"Fuck you, you Jewish bitch!" one of the "workers" yelled. He jumped up and began forcing his way through the demonstrators, reached Inessa, and grabbed her megaphone. His attack parted the crowd, and the "workers" rushed into the gap and piled on the pressure. They managed to split the crowd in two, and then again. Jeering and whistling, they then chased the scattering women across the square and up Tsvetnoy Boulevard. On the way they knocked over TV cameras, trampled some underfoot, and here and there landed an elbow in some journalist's stomach or a knee in the groin. The only hitch occurred with the old comedian Gertsianov, who managed to get up onto one of the tall circular pillars that displayed theatrical posters.

There he stood poised above the battlefield and loudly declaimed out of some book:

"The Jews of socialist countries are completely free from any national or social oppression! The vast majority live in harmony with the rest of society and actively participate in the building of socialism!"

"The bastard!" Igunov swore merrily as he stood at Bulychev's window. "He's reading from *my book*!" He reached for another refill of brandy. "And you tell me you can't work the Russians up to carry out a pogrom. Nothing could be easier. The only thing they need is a good hard shove."

In fact, what had just taken place was hardly a pogrom. No women had been killed or violated, and their children's heads had not been smashed. They had merely been gently kicked in the stomach and pushed into the traffic on Samotyochnaya Square.

Gertsianov continued his recital:

"Soviet working Jews respond with anger to the slanderous fabrications of Tel Aviv about the supposed 'difficult situation of Jews in the USSR,'" Gertsianov kept shouting as the action played out below him, and he waved a copy of Igunov's book *Zionism Revealed*. But at this point the "workers" managed to dislodge him. The celebrated comedian was punched in the kidneys and then sent flying head first onto the sidewalk.

Barsky looked at his watch and suddenly felt awful. It was 14:59. In one minute he was due to meet Anna Sigal at the Armenia Restaurant! He knew that if he was not on time, she would not wait.

e l e v e n

Anna sat at one end of the almost empty dining room and looked at her watch in surprise. If Barsky so desperately needed Arkady's missile systems, why in God's name was he late? Of course, she could perfectly well get up and go. It was now 3:06. P.M. And had Barsky not been a colonel in the KGB, she would have. But as her father said, people don't play games with the KGB. Once on your tail, they never let go. So she thought it best to wait and fight out this first round. Also, in addition to his KGB brazenness, there was something odd about Barsky that caught Anna's interest. Maybe not so strange as enigmatic. That first time, in the weasel's office, he had that imperious manner typical of the Soviet elite. But in their last phone conversation his voice had a slight tremble and a pleading tone. As though he was less setting up a business meeting and more trying to make a date. That chink in his armor led Anna to believe that she might well discover some compromising information on him. After all, who among today's leaders didn't take bribes or have some dark secret—a mistress, illegitimate children, an illegal dacha, or undeclared income from the so-called "shadow economy"?

To Anna's amazement, however, Barsky had turned out to be pure as the driven snow. At least, according to the information picked up by her father from his former KGB driver pals. Apart from a divorce ten years ago, Barsky seemed to have a history beyond reproach. A star pupil at the Nakhimov Naval College, and then at the KGB Senior College, a member of the Party, a workaholic officer, according to the chauffeurs, he was neither a womanizer nor a drinker nor a closet homosexual, and had taken no bribes from Jews seeking permission to emigrate. He had no country villa, no car, he owned no expensive furniture, and didn't even live in a decent apartment. Probably that was why his wife had left him for some diplomat. She'd gone off with him to Cuba, leaving Barsky in their one room with their eight-year-old daughter and his elderly mother. Only when he got his colonel's stripes, two years ago, did Barsky get a three-room apartment vacated by some emigrating Jews. His mother and daughter had immediately exchanged this for two one-room apartments, imagining that Barsky could now live an independent life again and eventually remarry. KGB drivers had in fact begun noticing indications of that. For instance, a year ago he'd begun dressing in expensive, fashionable foreign-style suits that cost a fortune even in the KGB's special store. His mother, however, had passed on to the next world without seeing her son set up with another woman. Once his daughter entered university, Barsky, now totally freed of domestic chores, spent all his leisure time not with women but at the Lubyanka, often staying at work till almost midnight.

So, although Anna's father had taken a great risk to wheedle out this information, what he'd come up with was totally disappointing. On the other hand, Anna had not studied with old Professor Shnittke for nothing. Shnittke's second law, expounded with characteristic bluntness, maintained that "There is no such thing as a saint! Only angels can be saints, and we don't put angels on trial or defend them in our courts! And if you ever need to compromise a witness, even if he's the Apostle Paul incarnate, keep on at him! Keep digging! Work him over, then his children, and his parents, and his ancestors, back to the seventh generation. Keep foraging, and somewhere you are bound to find liars, lechers, bribe-takers, enemies of the people, members of the Vlasov Army, or—for lack of anything better—alcoholics. Remember that not even the Immaculate Conception has ever been proved!"

On more than one occasion Anna had discovered for herself the truth of Professor Shnittke's law. The trouble was, however, that deep biographical "excavations" required time, and now the most she had was a week. That was why yesterday she'd abandoned her business, sat Charlie, her Airedale, in her car, and set out for Chernogolovka and the top secret Institute of Modern Technology where Arkady worked. She'd never actually been inside—admission even to the grounds required top-level clearance. But whenever she'd come even as far as the entrance gate, she'd been struck by the huge scale of the work that Arkady was responsible for. The little Jew in his worn velveteen pants directed a vast enterprise of multistory hangarlike workshops, other gigantic buildings, mysterious towering constructions, and even an internal railroad! Therein had to be the top-secret rockets of which he was so proud. And because of them, the whole place was surrounded by a continuous concrete wall topped with barbed wire, and guarded not by ordinary militia but by special forces. It was no surprise that the KGB wanted to make doubly sure of the loyalty of the director of this institution.

"Good afternoon, Anna Evgenyevna, please forgive my late arrival."

Anna looked up.

Wearing a well made French-cut suit, but with his shirt rumpled and necktie askew, Barsky looked tired as he slumped onto the chair opposite her. He immediately reached for the menu, as if to conceal his tired eyes behind it.

"Well, I see you haven't ordered anything yet. Waiter! We'd like two bottles of Narzan mineral water, please, and . . ." For the first time he now looked Anna in the face. "What are we going to drink? Brandy?"

"Not before dinner," Anna said.

"Oh, yes, of course!" Then he put on his glasses and again retreated behind the menu. "What are we going to have to eat? I see they have Armenian Ararat shish kebab, Georgian chicken tabaka, skewered sturgeon . . ."

Anna studied him with increasing interest. She'd spent all last week researching his past, feeling constant fear and hatred. At the same time she couldn't help notice her involuntary, and female, interest in him as a man who personified authority and strength. But now this "relentless agent" was appearing before her as a tired and perfectly ordinary human being. Or was this just another of his games?

"Had a heavy day, Oleg Dmitryevich?" she grinned.

He pulled himself together and took off his glasses.

"What? What makes you think that?"

"You forgot, we already discussed the menu. On the phone. We decided on trout."

"Oh yes! Damn it, so we did!" He laid the menu aside, returned his glasses to his pocket, leaned back, and exhaled loudly. "You're right, I have had a helluva day. But never mind!"

Anna could see the effort it cost him to get a grip on himself. She also noticed how quickly he put away his eyeglasses. Aha, she thought, so we have a little inferiority, do we? Embarrassed at wearing glasses? So our Comrade Colonel has one weak spot after all.

Meanwhile Barsky was addressing the waiter in an expansive manner. "Be a good guy, just bring us whatever you recommend for hors d'oeuvres and salad. And then we'll have trout for the main course. And a bottle of Tvishi—nice and cold, of course." Then he turned to Anna and put on the leonine look she recalled from their first meeting. "You know, Anna," he said with a smile, "Life really is splendid, and full of surprises! Don't you agree?" He offered her a Dunhill.

Anna did agree—to herself. She turned down his offer. And I too have a surprise for you, she thought. Her spoken answer, though, was cautious. "That rather depends on what you're referring to," she said.

"All sorts of surprises," he fired back, as if her answer was exactly what he'd expected. "Here the two of us are, sitting in this restaurant. Who would have imagined that a year ago?"

She now realized why he'd chosen the Armenia. This of course was where she'd most often been with Rappoport! God, what a bastard! First those phone calls to her home—to show that she couldn't hide from them even in her own apartment! And now the Armenia with its ornate ceiling, to pile on the psychological pressure.

Her earlier attraction to Barsky evaporated in a trice and was replaced by loathing.

"Oleg Dmitryevich," she said, "I'm not going to have dinner. You and I are here on business, not for some tryst. You wanted to know whether my husband is thinking of emigrating to Israel. So here you are."

She took from her handbag a small black Grundig tape recorder, and laid it on the table. This little electronic novelty had cost her a month's salary.

"What's that?" Barsky asked.

"It's a conversation I had with my husband. I taped this without his knowledge. You could maintain, of course, that we simply playacted. But once you listen, you'll know that no one could fake *that* sort of conversation."

She switched on the device. At first there was the usual blank tape hiss, then the indistinct voices of various staff from her husband's institute making their way out through the gate, then the roar of a truck driving past, and finally a series of joyful dog barks, and at the same time the approaching voice of Arkady Sigal:

"Anya, what's happened? Hi there! Is anything wrong?"

"No, nothing special. Charlie, be quiet!"

"But for you to come out here! That means that something has to have happened?"

"No, nothing has happened . . . I just got sick of sitting there on my own! And I want to talk to you. Charlie, will you be quiet!"

"Let him out of the car. He just wants to say hello! Okay, Charlie boy. Calm down! It's great to see you! Unfortunately I can't invite you into my office. Let's go someplace to eat—you're bound to be hungry. Just fifteen minutes from here there's quite a decent restaurant, the Atomic Age."

"No, thanks," Anna's voice answered. "We're not hungry . . ."

"Well, you never know with Charlie!" Arkady interrupted teasingly.

"Let's just take a walk here, in the woods," Anna's voice continued. "I hope you don't keep any of your secrets in there . . ."

"Oh yes, we have fine woods! Full of mushrooms and rabbits! It's a bit too early for mushrooms though. But Charlie will love it. Off you go, Charlie! Enjoy the woods! This way, milady. Along the path here."

"Arkady," Anna's voice continued, "a week ago I had a meeting with a gentleman. From the KGB, a Colonel Barsky. . . ."

Barksy made a gesture of displeasure and was about to speak, but Anna raised her hand and said quietly: "Listen." Her voice continued:

"They're interested in why we didn't hand in that Israeli invitation to the Party committee."

"There you are, you see!" Arkady's voice exclaimed.

At that moment Anna had to switch off, as the waiter appeared bringing wine and hors d'oeuvres.

"I'm not going to eat," Anna said.

"Never mind. Serve it up anyways," Barsky told the waiter. While the latter was dishing out the food, she lit a cigarette and wound back the cassette deck a short ways. Then, as soon as the waiter left, she turned it on again.

"... They're interested in why we didn't hand in that Israeli invitation to the Party committee."

"There you are, you see!"

"Yes, you were right. They really do test a person's loyalty that way. But that isn't the point. They have some information. . . . Not on you, but on me. To put it briefly, I have something to confess to you. Last year, in spring . . . Well, I got interested in a certain person . . ."

"Don't tell me, Anya . . ." Arkady interrupted in a voice suddenly quite different, gentle and pleading.

"I have to tell you. If they know, then you have to know too. His name was Rappoport."

"I know, Anna."

"What do you know?!" Her voice sounded amazed.

"I know it's my fault. I keep disappearing here, into the Institute. I don't pay you enough attention. And you're young and beautiful, so sooner or later this was bound to happen. But I heard he left already, last summer. . . ."

"And you knew everything then, at the time?"

"No, not then. I was away at those rocket tests, remember? But a month after he left . . ."

"How did you find out? Oh my God!" The tone of her voice conveyed her pain . . . as though she was going back in time and sensing what an effort it had cost him to say nothing for a whole year and to pretend that nothing had happened.

"Well, that Rappoport became a sort of Jewish legend," Arkady said. "And part of it was a beautiful female attorney. It wasn't hard to put two and two together. Did he really have a million bucks?"

"Arkady! Oh lord! I feel like such a shit!"

"Stop that! He's left, let's forget the whole business. I got over it. Well, partly anyway. But never mind about me. This KGB guy, what does he want? What exactly is he after?"

"He wants me to inform them as to who of our Jewish friends is *not* about to emigrate to Israel."

"*Not* about to emigrate? Interesting. So that means that the rest of them, those you don't report on, are . . . So in essence, they're trying to recruit my wife as a stool pigeon, and they're blackmailing you. Well, well . . ."

There was a long pause, the crunch of dry leaves and twigs beneath their feet, then a whistle, and Arkady's voice:

"Charlie! Come here, boy! Come here! Leave it. It's only a

squirrel!" Then, after a pause, Arkady's voice sounded grave, as though he'd thought this over and made a decision. "Okay, listen, Anna. In two weeks I'm flying off again to Severodvinsk for rocket tests. Ustinov is going to be there. I'm going to tell him that some KGB agent—what did you say his name was?—is interfering and getting in the way of my work."

"Arkady, this is the KGB. You can't mess around with them!"

"Anna, just get this straight. Even without that Rappoport business, which they screwed up themselves . . . Even if it was you that made off with a million dollars, all that's peanuts compared to what I'm doing for them. And nobody, no one on this world except me, can build them a rocket guidance system like mine. Not even the Americans have anything like it. So just think: if I tell Ustinov that some KGB guy is pestering my wife and hindering my work, you know what'll happen? That guy will forget all about you! So don't you worry. If he calls again, just tell him to go to hell. Okay?"

"Arkady, maybe we could go away ourselves?"

"Where to?"

"Well, I mean . . . emigrate. To Israel or America. You are Jewish."

"Anna, are you joking?"

"But I do have a son there. Of course, they wouldn't let you out—not right away, I mean. They'd turn you down, deny you a visa for a year or two. But we'd get by somehow. And before the Olympics they'll probably start letting scientists out."

"Anna, forget the whole idea!"

"But what kind of country is this? With the KGB peeping through everybody's keyholes!"

"D'you think it's any different over there? You think the FBI doesn't keep tabs on their scientists? And they've got plenty of political prisoners too, Anna! It was Pushkin who said it was the devil's luck to be born with talent in Russia! But I don't regret it! It's even turned out to be good luck. There's no knowing who I might have become over there, but here I am God and king! I can ask them for anything—a cyclotron (an atom-cracker, that is), a rocket launch station, plutonium, even an apparatus that we don't have here. And then the KGB will steal it for me from Japan, or America, or wherever!"

"But they're just using you!"

"Or maybe I'm using them? Think about it: in this world there are two teams trying to put a man into space. One is sitting in Huntsville, Alabama, and the other is here in Chernogolovka. And both these teams pretend that they're really making rockets for the military. And both superpowers are showering billions on us. 'Yes, go for it! Anything else you need? Just say the word!' And we're doing what Korolev once did: he promised Khrushchev a super-rocket, and in fact he sent a sputnik and Gagarin into space."

"But you've already put together so many of these goddamned rockets, you could blow up the whole world."

"Bullshit, Anna! We're not going to let any war get started! We're not idiots who'd destroy ourselves! My new navigation system will not just allow us to pop a rocket through the window of the Oval Office. That's peanuts. It can also dock spaceships out in space! Nobody's ever done that, but we're going to. It's fantastic, don't you see? And as long as they let me sit here with a pencil and paper in my hand, I'm not going to leave this place. Besides which, I have everything I want here—a pair of pants and a beautiful wife. What else could a man need?"

"Wait . . ."

Anna switched off the recorder.

"What comes next?" Barsky asked.

"That's not important. I erased it. So are you satisfied? All your questions answered?"

"Well, not quite all. . . ." Barsky drew the recorder toward him and removed the cassette.

"What are you doing?" Anna was suddenly frightened.

He placed the cassette in his pocket and then looked her in the eye.

"What I usually do. Well, so now you've started working for us. Thank you."

Anna was struck with horror. Unwittingly she'd walked right into a trap. She had denounced her own husband to the KGB. And not just him, but all the other scientists working with him.

"Give me back the cassette," she said blankly.

He said nothing, but looked her straight in the eye, plainly enjoying her fright. She sensed he had her in his power, with *material* evidence of her treachery, her weakness, and her collaboration with the KGB. Even more, he had proof that she'd been broken morally, that he'd made her dance to his tune.

For him, such a moment, when the victim cracked, was supremely delicious, almost orgasmic.

"Please give it back. . . ." Anna said, not even suspecting what sensual pleasure he was getting from her pleading.

Any other KGB officer in his place would have calmly pocketed the cassette, knowing that from now on he could blackmail Anna and force her to bring in goodies from the entire world of Jewish activists and dissidents. But Barsky's plans were different. He needed more than just another routine informant acting under pressure. He pulled out the cassette from his pocket and with one finger slid it across the table toward Anna. As he did this, he smiled condescendingly, like a chess master who delights in sacrificing a rook to achieve a branch of his opponent's defenses that totally escaped the latter's notice.

"There you are, Anna," he said, trying to sound generous. "Since you ask for it. And there's nothing dreadful on it, really. All your husband says about our scientists has been known to us for a long time."

Anna hastily put the cassette and recorder back into her bag. She sensed that her agitation, her pleading tone, and even Barsky's show of magnanimity were somehow all wrong, and that all this could have awful consequences for her later on. But she couldn't help herself. At that moment she longed more than anything to run away and destroy this dangerous cassette, as if it had never existed.

She got up.

"Can I go?" she asked, without looking up at him.

"Oh, of course, Anna Evgenyevna." Barsky courteously rose. "If you're really in a hurry. I'll give you a call sometime."

twelve

Daddy, what is a little kike?" six-year-old xenia asked over supper.

Rubinchik and his wife, Nelya, were dumbfounded. Xenia, though, was oblivious and went on stirring her mashed potato with a spoon. Only three-year-old Borya noticed his parents' confusion. Sitting on his high chair, he gazed at them intently with eyes suddenly full of adult interest.

"Where did you hear that?" Rubinchik asked at last. He'd always explained any new words his children picked up on television or out in the street. But a word like that!

"Oh," Xenia explained, "We were singing 'May There Always Be Sunshine' at school today. And I sang louder than everyone else, and the teacher said to me 'Not so loud, little kike!' " Xenia stared at her father with her dark cherry eyes. "So what is a little kike?"

Rubinchik was racking his brain for some harmless, explanation, but Nelya spoke first.

"It's a bad word, Xenia. You know, there are always bad people who are jealous of good people and who think up nasty names to call them. And some have thought up 'kike' as a nasty name to call us Jews. Come on, eat your potato."

"I don't want to be a Jew," Xenia answered, chewing and paying no attention as a train roared past somewhere outside.

"Oh, why not?" Rubinchik asked.

"Because they all tease me and keep saying, 'You're a Jew! You're a Jew, and you killed Jesus!' So is it okay for me not to be a Jew?"

"And me too!" Borya said categorically, shaking his head from side to side. "I'm not going to be a Jew either! No, I'm not!"

That night, after the children were asleep, Nelya and Iosif settled down on the convertible in their living room. Lying and gazing up at the ceiling, she said, "You know, it's become impossible at work. Parents are taking their kids out of my class. The director of the Conservatory just pulled my best pianist, Vitya Tarasov, out of a competition because he might have taken first prize and because he has me, Rubinchik, as his teacher! Jewish pupils are being deliberately flunked in their exams and expelled. And the director himself said to me, 'Why spend money on them? Sooner or later they'll all leave for Israel.' That's what he said—to *me*, can you believe it? And it's like that everywhere you turn. Half of my friends have already left. But with your profession . . ."

"I'm not going anywhere!" Rubinchik retorted—more sharply than he'd intended. He got up and took a pack of cigarettes from the night table. Then, slinging a jacket around his bare shoulders, he stepped onto their narrow balcony with its clutter of empty jars, car tires, and Borya and Xenia's old toys. He never smoked inside, and even when he went out on the balcony, before lighting up he always checked that the vent to the children's room was tightly closed. Now, too, by force of habit, he tested it with his hand and pulled it taut, so that no smoke could reach the children. After that, he struck a match and inhaled hungrily.

Between him and the gray obscurity of the suburb of Odintsovo stood an array of identical six- and eight-story apartment blocks. Cheaply built during the Khrushchev period, their joints were sealed with some sort of black mastic and they resembled a series of dominoes standing on end. Beyond these apartment blocks, on some vacant lots, were two dark rows of cooperatively owned garages where Rubinchik kept his own old Moskvich. Beyond that a tract of forest was cut through by the railway where trains passed by so often that the Rubinchiks, like all the other residents, never even heard or noticed them.

Now, however, in the middle of the night, Rubinchik both saw and heard a train go by. For the first time in the four years they'd lived here, he realized that all the trains rolling past were heading toward the West. For four years—every day and every hour—trains, wheels clattering, had passed beneath his window. Like this one now, its whistles seemed to sound a summons. Beyond the yellow smudges of their windows, they were transporting Jews and their children out of Russia—away from questions such as "Daddy, what is a little kike?"

But he, Iosif Rubin, was a *Russian* journalist. He had no thoughts whatsoever about emigrating and avoided all conversations on the subject. Like Moslems who avoid entering a Christian church, and religious Jews who not only abjure pork, but won't even mention the word. Whether "to go, or not to go" occupied the minds of many a Russian Jew, but he had a further reason for avoiding the topic. Anyone who associated with these "renegades" and "national traitors" was immediately categorized as "dubious," "unreliable," and "politically unstable." And that meant the end of one's career. It didn't mean arrest or internment, just that you would quickly be removed from all work connected with the press. Put more crudely, it meant you'd be cut off from the food trough. Only the most faithful of the faithful were allowed to sup from the "trough of plenty."

On the other hand, his daughter's questions were not easily brushed aside. "Daddy, I don't want to be a Jew." Yet did he himself want to be? All his adult life—and especially after obtaining his journalist's license—Rubinchik had tried in vain to clarify his own origins. But he'd got no further than a record for 1941 in the register of an orphanage in Saratov. It read simply: "Rubinchik, Iosif. Age—five to seven months; weight—3240 grams; condition—emaciated; distinguishing features—circumcised extremity; birthmark, 2 mm. below left shoulder blade; brought from children's reception center on Kazan Railway, without documents, 20 October 1941. Surname and first name given at reception center." And that was all. Where were his parents? Who were they? No trace. The only thing he'd managed to establish was the origin of his surname. It turned out that the woman in charge of the orphan center on the Kazan Railway in 1941 was a certain Esther Rubinchik. This woman had had a son, Iosif Mikhailovich Rubinchik, who died in the war, and she gave his name to every circumcised baby found among the trainloads of refugees bombed by German warplanes. In the records for the period Rubinchik discovered eighteen more of his namesake "brothers," who'd been dispatched to orphanages all over the USSR. But Esther Rubinchik was no longer alive. In 1949, during a routine campaign against "cosmopolitanism," she had been sent to a labor camp for some alleged Jewish "national diversionary" activity.

Thus, apart from the record of his "circumcised extremity" and birthmark, Rubinchik had no information whatsoever about his origins. Yet all his childhood and youth had been poisoned. Why was he forced to suffer, just because someone had snipped away a scrap of skin when he was a baby? When he was a little kid, why did the others rub his lips with lard? Why did they beat him till he bled, call him a "Yid" and a "kike" and refuse to let him join the orphanage football team? And why, later, was he turned down by the Aviation Institute and Leningrad University?

Had he personally crucified Jesus Christ?

He had never known his parents, but until he became a student he hated them. Why had they punished him this way?

And now, "Daddy, what is a little kike?" So it had come to this! Tomorrow he'd go to the nursery school and blow up at the woman in charge! And he'd see to it that the scum of a teacher who'd called Xenia little kike was fired!

But then he suddenly recalled the two KGB agents on the plane when he flew back from Mirnyy, and the predatory looks they had given him. No, complaining at the nursery school would be pointless. After all, those articles in *Pravda* about the Jews supposedly working for the Gestapo were a clear invitation by the Kremlin to incite the pogroms.

A cold shiver ran down Rubinchik's spine. Angrily he threw his cigarette butt off the balcony and stepped back inside. Then as was his habit, he went to check that the children were all right. He pushed open the door and the wretched thing gave a squeak, causing Xenia to toss in her sleep. He was always forgetting to oil the cursed hinge. He and his wife had given up their bedroom to the children. First he felt Borya's eiderdown slip and checked his son's diaper. Hurrah, still dry! But Xenia was a problem, constantly throwing off her cover, then catching chills. There she was again, with her bare legs tucked up under her chin.

Rubinchik covered his little girl, tucked both sides of the cover under the mattress, then stood looking down at his children. Did they have to undergo the same humiliations, beatings, and ostracism that he had to suffer? Or should he take them and leave the country? Yet how would he feed them over there, in the West? Who needed a journalist whose only language was Russian?

He picked up Borya's plush teddy bear from the floor and laid it on his son's pillow, then went back to the other room. Nelya was already asleep, and her long, slender body lay spread out across the open divan. In the semidarkness he could see her white shoulder, her cheek on the pillow, and her lips half-parted like his daughter's. It always surprised him that he'd chosen a Jewish wife, when sexually, as he himself put it, he was a russophile and anti-Semite. Could all his affairs with Russian women be some kind of revenge for his childhood that had been poisoned by kids and adults who hated Jews? Maybe, when the time came to marry, he had chosen a Jewish wife subconsciously? Or was it Nelya who had chosen *him*?

Rubinchik gently lifted one corner of the blanket and lay down, now cocooned by Nelya's warmth and the scent of her breasts, hair, and shoulders. Without opening her eyes, she sleepily nestled up against him. Immediately he sensed desire rouse within him, causing even his shin muscles to tense. Ever sensitive, Nelya opened one eye and looked quizzically at him. Over the last three years, since Borya was born, their sex life had cooled somewhat, but the occasional erection would sometimes wake Rubinchik in the middle of the night, and they then enjoyed each other with almost the same pleasure and abandon as before they were married. It was as if they managed to forget their children, his too frequent travels, their domestic quarrels, and all the vile scum that floated to the surface of their everyday life.

At that moment, too, Rubinchik threaded his arm beneath Nelya's head and powerfully drew her to him. And with his other hand he helped her remove her nightdress. But just then the distant clatter of a train came rolling from Moscow toward Odintsovo. Another express on its westward flight was forging a path through the predawn mist, and as it passed beneath their windows it drowned the whole vicinity in the powerful shriek of its siren.

Rubinchik lay back and relaxed again.

Nelya froze and opened her other eye in surprise.

"I'm sorry . . ." Rubinchik said.

She closed her eyes, gave a sigh, and turned over with her back to him. He lay there and listened to the receding clatter as it disappeared toward the West.

Thirteen

The motor cruiser Mikhail Sholokhov nosed its way along the Moskva River in the bright summer twilight. On the open upper deck, KGB Chairman Andropov lounged in his deck chair and inspected the photographs Barsky had delivered to him. They were pictures of young beauties from the provinces that Rubinchik had seduced on his assignments around the country. Barsky closely watched his boss's expressions and also his hands as he leafed through the photos. Andropov seemed to linger over the task. He was reflecting on the scheme that Barsky had proposed. But this time, unlike with the Kuznetsov operation, he was not rushing into a decision. This worried Barsky. Last time, when Andropov had read his brief report on the hijacking planned by a group of Jews, he had needed less than a minute to perceive exactly what Barsky had seen: a pretext to stamp out the entire Jewish campaign for their right to emigrate. Andropov had assigned Barsky a team of the KGB's best agents, given him carte blanche, and Barsky had not let his chief down.

They had stalked Kuznetsov and his accomplices with meticulous care. On no account must Kuznetsov be given cause to abort his scheme. And heaven forbid that Israel use its own channels to halt the plan. And no overzealous militia was to be allowed to spoil things by prematurely arresting the Kuznetsov group for holding Zionist gatherings.

Was Kuznetsov ever aware of these goings on?

To judge by his brazen behavior, he must have been. Barsky thought that Kuznetsov saw his hijacking as a way to incite the United States to demand that Brezhnev permit the Jews to leave. But at the same time, Andropov needed the sensation of this affair to pursue his campaign against anti-Soviet elements and thus to get the Politburo to grant him extraordinary powers.

Working in tandem, Barsky and Kuznetsov had conducted operations like two secret partners in a poker game. They had managed things with elegant precision right to the very last move, when Kuznetsov's team boarded the plane at Leningrad Airport on June 15, 1970. Barsky had even let Kuznetsov get on board, remove the official pilots, replace them with his own pilot, taxi the plane out to the runway, and even begin its take-off run.

But the one thing the Jews couldn't do was get the plane to lift off. For twelve minutes they taxied up and down the runway. Barsky earlier had briefed his engineers to choke the fuel supply into the engines. Kuznetsov and his pals couldn't exceed forty miles an hour. Once the attempted hijacking was plain for all to see, a voice rang out over the runway loudspeakers: "So, gentlemen, have our gang of terrorists enjoyed their ride? Now, all of you get out of the plane one by one with your hands behind your heads!"

Yes, that was indeed a beautiful operation. It was followed by a sensational press report on the "Unmasking of Zionist Agents"—described by the foreign media as a "Grand Act of Desperation by Soviet Jews." Here the public read accounts of a "Political Diversion Preempted"—while abroad people learned of a "Daring Bid for International Attention." Here there was "Vigilant Protection of State Frontiers" while Westerners read about the "Trial of the Century." Each side got what it wanted. Kuznetsov obtained international recognition of the Jewish wish to emigrate, world celebrity, and a capital sentence. Andropov brought about the most acrimonious meeting ever of the Politburo. But the ever-cautious Brezhnev, even with his back to the wall, managed to maneuver and appease both sides. Kuznetsov's death sentence was at the last moment commuted to fifteen years' internment, and the KGB obtained additional funding to set up new sections dealing with Zionism and airborne terrorism. A thin trickle of Soviet Jews was allowed to leave, and the Soviet Union obtained American grain and technology at favorable prices.

But it was Oleg Barsky who emerged with the richest personal prize. For his brilliant apprehending of these Jewish air pirates, he received a major's star, and he was made head of the new Jewish Section in the KGB's Fifth Directorate. Admittedly, later on he suffered certain setbacks. The greatest was the failure of his whole Rappoport operation, which damaged his reputation in the KGB. For that reason, he was moving cautiously against the Love-Kike. On the other hand, it boded well that Andropov had chosen to see him here, during an evening cruise, rather than in his office at the Lubyanka.

"And doesn't he want to leave and go abroad?" Andropov asked suddenly, still gazing at the photographs.

"Who?" Barsky asked, wrapped in his own thoughts.

"This what's-his-name? Rubin?"

Barsky grew both hot and cold. Damn it, how could he have missed that? Of course! Getting Rubinchik to apply for a visa was precisely the trick that would enable the KGB to keep a firm hand on the safety valve. As if to say: we are not putting *all* Jews on trial or trying to provoke a pogrom; the man being charged is a renegade element. This would show Soviet Jews that as long as they worked and went along with the system, then the system would disregard their minor peccadillos. But let them once turn their eyes westward, and they would get quite different treatment.

"Well?" Andropov asked and looked intently at Barsky over the top of his spectacles.

"I get it, Yuri Vladimirovich. We'll go to work on it."

Andropov nodded.

"That's the first thing," he said after a pause and in a tone that suggested the question of Rubinchik's emigration was firmly settled. "Now for the second point. It's obvious this trial shouldn't be our affair. It's not KGB business, we'll need an open public trial. So who'll act as public prosecutor? Any good candidates?"

Barsky did not show it, but inwardly he shrank and gave a shudder. Andropov was touching on the most sacred and secret part of the operation he had contrived. Barsky's answer, though, was noncommittal:

"I've several people in mind. But I held off starting work on that until I heard your decision about the whole operation."

Even under torture, Barsky would never have admitted that he'd conceived the whole trial of Rubinchik not so much as a means of combatting Zionism, but as a way of involving the one person he had lined up for the role of prosecutor—Anna Sigal. He had mooned over Anna ever since he'd first seen her with Rappoport.

"It should be a woman," Andropov said abruptly, as though reading Barsky's thoughts. "An ordinary Russian woman. From the provinces."

Barsky said nothing. He felt himself to be the teacher's pet of this master of intrigue, someone whom Andropov was counting on in his secret bid for the Kremlin throne. But Barsky also had his own goal. Anna Sigal was not from the provinces, and she could hardly be called an *ordinary* Russian woman. But she had other qualities that were vital for such a public trial— she was young, had a striking appearance, had professional skill and wit, and the ability to counter arguments with a single brilliant retort. To find all these abilities in an ordinary provincial attorney would be impossible.

Andropov laid aside the photographs, leaned back in his deckchair and watched as the cityscape floated past him. Moscow was bathed in peace and summer lassitude. An occasional convoy of cars drove across the Stone Bridge, along Kropotkin Embankment, and past the Kremlin walls. But Andropov saw further than those walls—his sights were aimed at the very heart of that stout rampart.

"You know, this country of ours is sick, very sick, Oleg Dmitryevich," he said quietly. "Everything is bogged down in lies and corruption. Everything—from top to bottom. Girls come to the hotels to become whores. Nobody wants to work, and all they do is make demands on the state—give us this, give us that, give us the other! Every important position is up for sale, even the post of minister. Will we ever manage to clean Russia of all this filth?"

Andropov's question might have been rhetorical, had the cruiser not been sailing past the Kremlin at that moment. And had Barsky not worked in the KGB, knowing that even Brezhnev himself accepted bribes—diamonds from his ministers and local Party secretaries, and Rolls-Royces from the secretaries of Western Communist parties.

"Of course, the Jewish emigration was a concession to the West. And it was a mistake," Andropov continued after a pause. "All the rulers in history who allowed the Jews to depart then perished. It happened in Persia, in Spain, and not so long ago in Germany. But we're not going to allow this to turn into a mass exodus. Your idea of putting this 'love-kike' on trial is a good one because there are no politics mixed up in it. And I doubt there's a single Jew in the whole country who hasn't had an affair with a Russian woman. So it'll give all our Jews a bit of a scare. But it has to be based on unimpeachable evidence, and with all these girls and their parents and the hotel managers taking part. All of them! And this Rubin has got to be nabbed and nailed down, just like you did with Kuznetsov."

"I understand, Yuri Vladimirovich."

"You were saying Igunov is feeling out some way of making contact with us? Well, you can let him in on the plans for this. So that the Central Committee doesn't try and spike our guns later on." Andropov handed the photographs back to Barsky. "Okay, get to work. By the way, how is my 'goddaughter'?"

In fact Barsky's daughter was not Andropov's "goddaughter," and he had seen her only once—fourteen years ago, when Barsky took her to the May Day demonstration on Red Square. But then, with childish directness, the perky four-year-old had gotten to know Andropov's son Igor and was introduced to his dad, who picked her up and was then immediately referred to as "Uncle Yuri." Ever since, whenever he met Barsky, Andropov had always inquired after his "goddaughter."

Barsky was flattered and smiled.

"Thank you. She's at university now!"

"Really? So soon?" Andropov was surprised. "Have you got her photo?"

"Not on me, unfortunately." Barsky gestured his dismay.

"Why's that?" Andropov said, disappointed. "You carry around photos of these sluts, and don't have one of your own daughter."

"I'll have one next time we meet, Yuri Vladimirovich, definitely," Barsky said, feverishly trying to recall whether Andropov's son was married or still single. Could Andropov have had him in mind when asking to see her photo?

"Hmm, yes . . ." Andropov finished off their meeting decisively. "This

Rubin has got to apply to emigrate. And then we've got him, he's in the bag! But all the evidence has to be collected before that, understood?"

Barsky rose and stood to attention.

"Yes sir, absolutely, Yuri Vladimirovich!"

Barsky maintained a serious expression, but his heart was leaping: Andropov had again given him complete carte blanche! Just as with Kuznetsov!

"There's just one thing, though," Andropov said. "The title 'Love-Kike' is something we can't use in the documents. We'll have to find some cleaner-sounding name. Let's say 'Operation Virgin.' "

part two

the trap

fourteen

TOP SECRET

Per your instructions, I hereby present for your approval details of Operation code-named "Virgin."

1. For its execution an investigative team shall be set up in Sector E, Fifth Central Directorate with powers appropriate to a high level assignment (SIA). Team director—Colonel Barsky; assistant—Captain Faskin.
2. The team shall be granted the services and technologies of other KGB Directorates by agreement with them. In particular: Sector B, Second Operational Directorate shall place at the disposal of the Fifth Directorate a civilian female operative capable of supplying the investigative team with indisputable proof of the corrupt activities of journalist I. Rubin (Rubinchik). The said person shall also take part in the public trial as a victim of these activities.
3. To facilitate the Rubin (Rubinchik) family's decision to emigrate, the operational team shall be permitted to:
   a) provide the Rubinchiks with an invitation to emigrate to Israel;
   b) use moderate physical force on the Rubinchiks (i.e. without causing bodily harm).
4. The investigative team shall be empowered to bring to Moscow all women seduced by Rubin (Rubinchik), and also staff from hotels where Rubin met his victims, so as to permit the court appearance of these persons. Further, the said persons shall be provided with a guard, a per diem allowance, and accommodation in a Moscow hotel.
5. The investigative team shall approach the Kostroma, Yaroslavl, Gorky, and Moscow Bar of Attorneys to select a candidate for public prosecutor at the said trial.
6. When the case is ready for trial, the KGB Directorate of Investigation and the USSR Chief Prosecutor's Office shall become in-

volved, and by agreement with the Public Information Section of the CPSU Central Committee (Comrade S. Igunov), arrangements shall be made for the case to be heard in the Union Hall of Columns with wide publicity in the press and on television.

> KGB Colonel O. Barsky,
> Head of Sector E, Fifth Central Directorate
> Moscow, June 7, 1978

DECISIONS:
Agreed and approved—Gen. Sviridov
Confirmed, approved for action—Yu. Andropov
June 8, 1978

CODED TELEGRAM

To: CHAIRMAN, COMMITTEE FOR STATE SECURITY (KGB),
UKRAINIAN SSR,
GENERAL V. FYODORCHUK.

Tomorrow, June 10, an investigative team with SIA authority, led by Colonel Barsky, is flying out to Kiev. The team consists of eight men. Give them your Committee's full cooperation, including accommodation in a hotel to be chosen by Col. Barsky, and any transport and technical backup they require.

This team operates under personal control of Yu. V. Andropov.

> General V. Sviridov,
> Chief, Fifth Central Directorate
> Moscow, June 9, 1978

DECISION:
To General Sushko, Asst. Chairman:
Approved for action, under your personal control.
Kiev, June 9, 1978   Fyodorchuk

f i f t e e n

It was the first time Rubinchik had flown on assignment to Kiev. As one of the *Labor Gazette*'s leading writers, he had long ago been allowed to choose the subjects and the destinations for his assignments. So it was easy for him to avoid trips to places where he believed the chances of his meeting a genuine Russian diva were zilch. But he hadn't been able to turn down this trip to the Ukraine. Having read his story about the Mirnyy diamond workers, a group of 140 female weavers in Kiev had sent his paper a collective letter addressed to correspondent I. Rubin, inviting him to visit the Dawn of Communism weaving mill where they worked, and also their hostel, club, and canteen. Their letter described the splendors of the weavers' life—workshops so dusty with cotton waste that asthma and tuberculosis were guaranteed after five years' employment; a filthy hostel in which six women had to live in a room designed for two; and a canteen where the cooks stole everything, even the salt. Rubinchik had no doubt that everything described in their letter was the truth, and he suggested to his editor that the letter be forwarded either to the Trade Union Committee or the Ukrainian Party Central Committee, or else to the cosmonaut Valentina Tereshkova, who chaired the Committee of Soviet Women. But the editor shook his head.

"No, I'm sorry. There's a price to pay for fame, old boy. We're the *Labor Gazette*, and if the laboring people ask for Rubin, they're going to get Rubin, even if you were planning to go climb the Eiffel Tower!"

"But why? The censor will cut out everything that these women are complaining about!"

"Look, you may decide not to even write a story. But you have to go. And look at the bright side, a hundred and forty women all *wanting* you! What more could you ask?"

Rubinchik sighed and put himself down for a two-day trip. A place like Kiev wouldn't be worth more than two days. And since he had forty-eight hours to fill in there, he'd take some time off to look at the St. Sophia Cathedral and the Babiy Yar ravine.

"Excuse me, will you be having lunch?"

Rubinchik broke off from reading the *Labor Gazette*'s front page story—

about the awards to Brezhnev, Kosygin, and Gromyko of the Peruvian Sun Golden Cross, the top award of the Peruvian Communist Party. He looked up and went numb, astonished: here was another miracle of nature, a little flower of not yet ripened womanhood. There at his side stood Alyonushka, straight out of the old Russian fairy tales, dressed in a blue Aeroflot uniform and holding out a tray. She had a slender neck, green eyes wide open with innocence, a corn-colored braid on her splendid little head, and breasts like two small fists that ever so gently thrust forward her Aeroflot tunic.

"Yes, please," he replied, although he'd eaten only two hours before. He looked her in the eye. "What's your name?"

"Natasha." She was slightly flushed as she handed him a tray with the standard Aeroflot lunch of bread and butter, servalat sausage, an apple, and cookies. In her embarrassed shyness she reminded him so much of that Siberian stewardess who'd served him breakfast on the plane from Mirnyy that he automatically looked round to see whether the same two KGB agents were sitting behind him. Of course they weren't, but elsewhere in the cabin other passengers were impatient to hand her their empty trays. But Natasha was in no rush to serve them. "Would you like tea or coffee?" she asked Rubinchik.

"Tea, please," he said with a smile. "Have you been flying long?"

"No," she said. "This is my first flight. Excuse me, I have to run." And she dashed off down the aisle, as impatient calls came at her from all sides.

"Natasha, can you come here for a moment?"

"Natasha dear, can I have a tea?"

"Stewardess!"

"Natasha, you've forgotten me!"

A few minutes later, as she poured the tea into Rubinchik's glass and holder, Natasha sweetly complained, "It's simply awful how hungry everyone is!"

Before Rubinchik could respond, his neighbor, an elderly invalid with a row of war medals on his jacket lapel, spoke up, "Uh-huh! Especially hungry for stewardesses!"

The whole cabin echoed with laughter. Most of the passengers were men traveling on business, supply agents, Party workers, engineers, and army officers. Strangely, from among all this male company Natasha had singled out Rubinchik and was constantly stopping to offer him tea, cookies, or an apple, and so on.

"Congratulations!" his neighbor said. "You got one on the hook there!"

Rubinchik could see for himself that this fish was biting. A surge of adrenalin set his blood racing. He straightened his shoulders and took on a look of bold self-assurance. Damn it, that Russian religious philosopher must have been right when he wrote that "the Jews experience a mysterious and quite surprising attraction toward the Russian soul, and the latter in turn feels a reciprocal gravitation toward the Jews." Not for nothing did the Kievan princes of the tenth century impose a fine of ten golden rubles on Russian men unable to restrain their wives from secretly visiting the Jewish quarter. And so it was just now. What was it that caused this green-eyed daisy to single him out among forty others and casually ask him: "Is Kiev where you live, or are you going there on business?"

"Business trip," Rubinchik said. "And are you based in Kiev or in Moscow?"

"In Moscow. But we've a one-day stopover in Kiev."

"Oh, what hotel are you staying at?"

"I don't know yet. They'll tell us when we get to Kiev."

"Would you fancy going to the theater this evening?"

"I don't know Ukrainian, unfortunately."

"Then let's walk down Kreshchatik—that's Kiev's Broadway?"

She shrugged, looking embarrassed, but he was already writing down the phone number of the *Labor Gazette*'s local correspondent. Then he tore off the sheet of paper and handed it to her.

"Take this," he said. "I'll expect your call at five o'clock." He looked her straight in the eye, and again, as always at those sacred moments of encounter with some Russian diva, her soul seemed to open up to meet his gaze.

"Thank you," her small childlike lips pronounced almost inaudibly. But the green eyes had lit up with an inner fire.

It was all over quickly. Then, as though scared by her impulse, Natasha turned and dashed away down the aisle. Rubinchik meanwhile felt his legs weaken, his breath taken away, and his heart pounded like a galloping cavalry squadron.

He leaned his head back and closed his eyes. And his lips spontaneously parted in a smile as he blissfully anticipated regaining that paradise for which he had searched the length and breadth of the country for seventeen long years. Could she be it? Would he now rediscover again that miracle of years ago at the Sputnik pioneer camp, on the banks of the ancient river Ityl? And fool that he was, to think that he hadn't wanted to go to Kiev! Tonight on the sacred hills of old Kiev, first capital of ancient Rus, he would embrace that youthful Polovtsian body, those pliant little breasts, and play on the lyre of her belly and the magical little thicket that concealed the imponderable, divine, and breathtaking wonder. And she, frightened, timid, but obedient, would arch and twist her slender spine. With the little tongue fluttering in her tiny nightingale throat, she would thrash in ecstasy and bite his shoulders and fingers like a frenzied small animal.

The vision of this approaching nocturnal feast was so palpable that Rubinchik's manhood grew tense and erect, like a Mongolian horseman ready to lunge into attack.

O Lord, he cried out silently, do You see what is happening? How can I ever go away and leave this blissful country?

sixteen

As always on a wednesday, Nelya left the conservatory at three, right after her class with her favorite young pupil, Vitya Tarasov. But today even working with such a prodigy gave her little pleasure. All day she'd been nervous and on edge. She found her thoughts constantly wandering away from her pupils and their lessons. The reason for all this was quite clear. That morning, after Iosif left on his trip, she had gone down in the elevator to take the children to nursery school. On her way out she noticed something strange through the slot of their mail box—an unusually long, nonstandard envelope. But the kids were late, so she left it and opened the mailbox only on her way back. As she took out the envelope, she already sensed something wrong, and felt a premonition of danger.

First of all, it was not a Soviet envelope. It was a thick beige packet of obviously foreign origin. It had two foreign stamps on it and the address was printed in fine type:

USSR—Moscow
24 First Cosmonauts' Street, Apt. 67
Mr. I. M. Rubinchik

Nelya examined the envelope, and turning it over found English lettering on the reverse side:

Ministry of Foreign Affairs
Israel

Nelya's heart sank, and she looked about anxiously. She could guess what it contained. Before any of their neighbors appeared in the hallway, she ran to the elevator and pressed the fourth floor button. Only when the elevator door closed behind her did she unseal the envelope. In it was a thick sheet of paper folded in three. It read:

The Ministry of Foreign Affairs of the State of Israel hereby confirms an invitation issued to Iosif Mikhailovich RUBINCHIK (born 1941), his wife Nelya Markovna RUBINCHIK (born 1950) and their two chidren Xenia and Boris to emigrate and take up permanent residence in Israel, and to join their relative Esther COHEN, residing at 12 Gilo Street, Apt. 7, Jerusalem. This invitation is valid for a period of one year.

Signed—Arye Levy,
Head of Repatriation Department,
Jerusalem, Israel.
May 16, 1978.

On the letter was a red ribbon and wax seal.

The elevator door opened. Quickly, as though it were contraband, Nelya slipped the invitation under her jacket and dashed inside the apartment. There she reread it several times, then hid it in the closet, on the top shelf beneath a pile of underwear. After that she hurried off to work. But all day she'd been haunted by a sense of guilt, as though she'd stolen something, or as if her very appearance showed that she had betrayed her country and was emigrating. At the same time the eight-line text of that invitation kept dancing before her eyes, like the magic words in a children's fairy tale. And the words "Ministry of Foreign Affairs of the State of Israel" seemed to resound with a solemn and sublime music, like Vivaldi's "Gloria." And with the curt phrases of the invitation she had a vision of the biblical gardens of ancient Jerusalem, with the sunlit sonorities of string music.

But who could have sent it? Nelya had heard that Jews who went to Israel informed the government there of the names and addresses of other Jews they knew. Yet, how was it the invitation had arrived precisely when only a few days ago she and Iosif had first talked of emigrating? It was almost as though someone had eavesdropped on them.

Yet what if this was not pure chance? What if it was a sign from fate? Perhaps there was some good reason. Only a few days ago Rebecca Gilel, one of the elderly violin professors, had taken Nelya by the arm during a break and led her to the Announcements, Instructions, and Information board, where the director posted his daily instructions, headlines from *Pravda,* and any material about performances by former graduates. Three pages had been pinned up from a recent article in *Ogonyok*, the popular national journal with a five-million-copy circulation.

"Have you read this?" Rebecca asked Nelya, sotto voce. "Just read it. It's terrible!"

The three pages contained whole paragraphs that had been underlined in red by the director:

> Arming themselves with Jewish dogma, the Zionist obscurantists strive to inspire Jews with a hatred of all non-Jews. "Do unto others as you would that they should *not* do unto you!"—that is the working rule of modern Zionism. All Zionist terrorist gangs are led and directed by the intelligence department of the World Zionist Organization's executive committee . . .

Nelya turned away disgusted.

"Terrible!" Rebecca Gilel whispered. "Just like it was under Hitler in 1936!"

It was then that Rebecca had fled Germany and come via Poland to Russia, where she was soon picked up as a German spy and exiled to Siberia. She was twenty-eight and had taught violin at the Berlin Conservatory, like Nelya today.

Nelya left the Conservatory carrying her heavy briefcase and walked out to her trolley bus stop. When it came, she got in with several others and sat in the back, on the one free seat by a window. As she did so a broad-shouldered young oaf reeking of garlic and vodka settled down next to her and promptly fell asleep. Nelya traveled everyday on Moscow's buses, and like the other passengers poring over their magazines and newspapers, she was used to ignoring these annoyances. She now noticed however that four fellow-passengers were reading *Ogonyok*, all open at the page emblazoned with the anti-Zionist headline.

She felt uncomfortable, as though something foul was pressing in on her. She decided to shield herself by reading something herself. From her briefcase she took a slim English edition of *Jonathan Livingston Seagull*, opened it where she had left off, and engrossed herself in it. Despite her limited English, this was a book that she was enjoying.

"Garden Ring. Next stop—Moscow Zoo," the driver announced. "Incidentally," he continued, "yesterday they brought a new macaque to the zoo. From Ethiopia. They say it's a gift to Brezhnev from the Ethiopian communists. It's supposed to be wildly funny!"

Some of the passengers stood up and moved forward to the exit. At that moment the reeking hulk who was dozing next to Nelya begin shifting and jabbed her painfully in the side.

"Would you please be more careful!" she said.

"What?" The hulk awoke, infuriated, and began shouting. "You filthy Jewish scum! You sit here reading one of your kike books, and on top of that you dare to tell me off! I'll show you, you Jewish bitch! Get your ass out of her! Get off to Israel and read your bloody kike books there!"

Nelya turned cold with shock and terror.

"This book . . . this isn't a Jewish book. . . ." she protested feebly.

"Don't bullshit me, you bitch! Think I'm blind? All you scum have grown fat, eating the bread off our plates. Israeli vipers, that's what you are! Get the hell out of here, you Jewish whore!" He suddenly got up and jerked Nelya by the shoulder with such force that she fell off the seat. "Get out and read your books in Israel, Jewish cunt!"

"What's this?! You're crazy. . . . I'm going to call the militia. . . ." Nelya mumbled, trying to rise. But the hulk was now in a frenzy. He grabbed her briefcase, hurled it toward the door and began shoving Nelya in the same direction.

"Come on, get the hell out of here. We're not having any of you stinking Jews on our buses! Sitting reading your books! Fucking Zionists!"

The entire busload of passengers meanwhile continued reading. They said nothing and sat with their noses in their newspapers, pretending not to hear or see. The driver, who'd been so garrulous a moment ago, also said nothing. As they drew up to the next stop, he opened the doors and waited impassively. Meanwhile the oaf hurled Nelya's briefcase off the bus along with her book, which he had ripped apart, then he kicked Nelya herself out the door.

"Fucking Jewish bitch! Dares to tell me off! Get off to Israel and try telling your own kind off! Fucking whore!"

The doors closed again and the trolley bus moved off. The last thing Nelya saw framed in window was the young drunk still flailing his fists, and the heads of the other passengers sitting there like dummies.

Nelya watched, flabbergasted, as the bus drove away. It had all happened so quickly that she'd had no chance to gather her thoughts or say anything back. But that was the least of it. Far worse was the other passengers' cruel passivity, or even approval of that drunk. Not one had turned his head or said a word.

Nelya swallowed back her tears and began gathering the scattered pages of her book and the sheets of music that had fallen from her briefcase. Meanwhile gusts of laughter drifted over from the barred enclosure of the Moscow Zoo. The Ethiopian macaque was making faces and keeping the Moscow public amused.

seventeen

Attention all passengers, please return to your seats, fasten your safety belts, and kindly refrain from smoking. We are now making our final approach into Kiev Airport. Kiev was the first capital city of our Russian state, founded in the seventh century by the Scythian-Varangian Prince Kiy, and by the ninth century it became a major trading center. In the tenth century Prince Igor and his successor, Princess Olga, succeeded in uniting all the neighboring Slavonic tribes under the rule of Kiev."

As he listened to the ritual Aeroflot incantation and thought of the heat in Natasha's appealing yet frightened eyes, Rubinchik tried to calm his mounting flesh and glanced over his neighbor's shoulder toward the window. As their plane banked, beneath its wing appeared a panorama of the great city spreading over a series of gentle hills, drowned in greenery and etched by the meandering ribbons of the Dnieper and Pochayna rivers. The broad avenues of the city center had a rectilinear Stalinist severity; probably laid out immediately after the war, replacing the ruins left by Nazi bombing. But the little suburban lanes, descending from the hills of apple and cherry orchards, had retained their ancient Ukrainian charm. Damn it, Rubinchik thought suddenly, it was on these very hills that the venerable Pesakh, first military commander and khakan-bek of the Khazarian king, had stood in A.D. 941. It was here that he had overtaken Prince Igor after earlier seizing Samkerts and three other cities from him, not counting a "great multitude of small townships." But where exactly had he been? Over there, on the steep riverbank, where the Dnieper Bridge now loomed? Or was it just below, opposite the gilded cupolas of St. Sophia, that began just after the Kievan Rus had been converted to Christianity? No ancient chronicle recorded these details, and Soviet historians kept silent about any defeats suffered by Russian princes and tsars; they also said nothing about the Khazarian empire. But at the Saratov Teachers' Training College, Rubinchik's alma mater, there was a library that had survived from pre-revolutionary times. And he remembered historians Klyuchevsky and Solovyov's accounts of the baptism of the Kievans in the Dnieper by the dissolute Prince Vladimir, grandson of Igor, and the dethronement of the pagan god Perun, whose gigantic image had been "dragged through the dung" by the new Christian converts and thrown into the Dnieper, and an even more ancient chronicle about the battle between Pesakh and Igor somewhere in this area, near Kiev.

But what was the rumbling suddenly filling Rubinchik's head? Why had his vision clouded? Why was his heart pounding so? He felt as if his cranium was about to burst.

"Not feeling well?" His neighbor's voice reached him as though through the glass of a fish tank.

"It's okay, I'm all right," Rubinchik said lamely and leaned his head against the backrest. He feebly stroked his brow, and large drops of cold sweat from his forehead wet his hand.

"It sometimes happens," his neighbor said condescendingly. "If you're not used to it. When the plane comes down quickly."

Not to me, Rubinchik thought. But he lacked the strength to pronounce even those few words. His head was bursting, like a balloon engorged and overflowing with blood.

"She'll be bringing the candies round in a moment. Probably she's forgotten," his neighbor said. "Aha! Here she comes. Natasha, over here please!"

Natasha appeared in the aisle with a tray of candy that was usually served on takeoff and landing to help passengers ease the pressure on their eardrums.

"Over here, Natasha!" his neighbor called again.

Natasha came over and got a fright when she saw Rubinchik's pallid face.

"Oh, what's the matter?" She looked around in confusion. "He's sick. We should get a doctor. . . ."

There was no doctor on board however, and the war veteran reassured her in the commanding tone of an experienced air traveler.

"Keep calm! It's nothing serious. Bring him some water. And some smelling salts from your first-aid kit, if you've got any."

Natasha ran off and quickly returned bringing water, smelling salts, and a pillow, and began fussing over Rubinchik as though he were the love of her life. Her cool slender fingers unbuttoned his shirt. She supported his head with a hand as he drank from the glass, and her frightened eyes were right next to his own as gradually he came round.

"Feeling better? What else can I bring you?" She showed such concern, as though he mattered more to her than anyone. Then, the aircraft suddenly banked, and Natasha rolled into Rubinchik's lap.

"Now he'll really feel okay!" his neighbor said, and Rubinchik gave a wan smile. Indeed, as the plane moved away from the city and began its approach to Kiev Airport, he did gradually begin to feel better.

. . .

Ignat Dzyuba, correspondent of the *Labor Gazette* in the Ukraine, was there to meet Rubinchik. He was a typical Ukrainian, broad shoulders, large frame, an ash-gray forelock, and dense whiskers, and he wore an embroidered Ukrainian shirt. He drove Rubinchik into town in the sidecar of his motorbike.

"You probably had too much to drink yesterday!" he hollered above the engine's roar. "So we'll put off today's visit to our lady weavers. We'll go tomorrow instead!"

"No, I didn't have anything to drink," Rubinchik answered limply, as he jolted up and down in the bucking sidecar.

"What's that?" Dzyuba leaned down to hear his answer.

"I'm okay now!" Rubinchik called, though none too loudly.

"You sit still! Okay indeed! Just look at yourself!"

But there was no way Rubinchik could do that. The wind was slamming into his face like a sailcloth and filling his nostrils with a mixture of cool riverside smells and the odors of summer gardens and burnt gasoline from the trucks that roared past them. Involuntarily his eyes fixed on the portraits of Brezhnev and the gigantic banners with Russian and Ukrainian texts that lined the roadside:

GLORY TO LEONID ILYICH BREZHNEV,

VETERAN LEADER OF THE PEOPLE!

IN TWO YEARS THE UKRAINE WILL BECOME

A REPUBLIC OF COMMUNIST LABOR!

OUR UNBOUNDED LOVE AND GRATITUDE TO

LEONID ILYICH BREZHNEV

FOR HIS FEAT IN ACHIEVING THE PEOPLE'S HAPPINESS!

Goddamn it, Rubinchik cursed to himself, gripping the sidecar rail as though it were the pommel of a saddle. There was never such ass-kissing even in the days of Nebuchadnezzar! The Roman Empire never had roadside portraits of its emperors. Instead of all these stupid slogans and portraits of Brezhnev that plastered the country from Yakutia to the Baltic, why couldn't they build a few decent hostels for their weavers? But try and write anything of that sort.

At that point, after bypassing the suburbs, the highway suddenly mounted a bridge across the Dnieper.

"The first completely welded bridge in the world!" Dzyuba proudly called out. "Not a single rivet!"

Rubinchik couldn't think why welding was better than riveting, or why one should be so proud of that fact. Green-and-blue streetcars and rows of cars and buses trundled across this bridge just as over all the others he had seen. To one side, behind a railing, bicycles and pedestrians moved along a metal sidewalk. The shores were empty, but three speedboats roared across the smooth blue expanse, and there was a heavy barge loaded with sand slowly moving downriver.

"That's St. Vladimir's Mount!" Dzyuba pointed out ahead. His ashen whiskers fluttered in the wind beneath his black goggles. "Look to the left! Look down at the Podol! That's where they baptized us a thousand years ago! Now look to the right, at the bend in the river. Do you see the church? Olga founded it! With her own hand!"

Rubinchik glanced at the white church with its green dome and golden cross. Suddenly, however, his pulse began roaring and his heart started pounding even more violently than before. He closed his eyes and let go of the sidecar's rail.

"Hey! What is it? Iosif!" Dzyuba shouted as he saw Rubinchik keel over and almost fall out of the sidecar.

"Wait! Hold on!" he yelled, and veered to the right so sharply that the cars behind him honked furiously. But Dzyuba took no notice and pulled up by the pedestrian walkway. "Iosif!"

Rubinchik tumbled from the sidecar like a sack. Jumping from the saddle, Dzyuba grabbed him under the arms and dragged him clear of the roadway. Then, laying him out on one of the welded plates of the walkway, he tried to flag down one of the oncoming cars.

"Stop! Help! Stop! I've got a sick man here! Help!"

A gray minibus labeled *Repairs* tore past at full speed and then halted about a hundred yards ahead. But nobody got out, so Dzyuba swore and tried waving to others.

Rubinchik, meanwhile, lay spread-eagled facedown on the metal sidewalk. As if in his death throes, he clung to that first welded bridge in the world, which roared and trembled beneath him like a drumskin. It felt as if hordes of horses were pounding by. He also had a feeling as if someone was forcing him out of this world and into some other dimension. Or else he himself was falling, falling, falling from the bridge into the water, and at any moment his pulsing veins would burst and the blood would spray from the back of his head as it cracked open. It seemed as if only gripping and holding on to that ridge on the walkway could save him from collapsing into total oblivion.

Dzyuba meanwhile had failed to stop any of the vehicles racing past. So he now stepped out into the roadway, almost under the wheels of an oncoming truck and yelled: "Be a friend, will you? Call us an ambulance, please!"

"Bloody drunks all over the place, fuck it! Even on bridges!" Swearing, the truck driver steered around Dzyuba and drove on.

"What god-awful people!" Dzyuba lamented and rushed to try and stop the next car.

Meanwhile, the people in the repairs van that had stopped a hundred yards ahead were perhaps not all that insensitive. Indeed, as they peered through their rear window, they showed a high degree of concern for Rubinchik.

"You went and poisoned him! What did you give him, you little bitch?" Captain Faskin shouted at Natasha.

"I didn't poison him with anything! Have you gone crazy?" Natasha retorted bravely. "The Comrade Colonel had the same things to eat—bread and butter and servalat and apple. Colonel Barsky, tell him to stop shouting at me."

"Quiet! Cool it!" Barsky ordered. He had already summoned an ambulance by radio telephone and now turned to the war invalid who had sat next to Rubinchik in the plane. "What's up with him? What d'you think?"

The elderly man shrugged.

"The whole flight went perfectly okay, nothing out of the ordinary. And then suddenly . . ."

"Huh! They go and palm this pathetic weakling off on me, and then have the nerve to yell at me!" Natasha grumbled, as she applied scarlet Hungarian lipstick to her pouting Lolita lips.

"He'll show you tonight whether he's a weakling or not!" Faskin growled, his eyes still glued to the rear window.

"We'll see which of us shows what and to whom. Just you wait!" Natasha smirked.

"Only you . . . Don't get too carried away!" Faskin warned her sternly. "Don't forget to give us the signal, when . . . Well, you know when."

"No, I don't know when. You tell *me*," Natasha said, needling Faskin. "Do you mean when we're in bed? Is that what you mean, Comrade Captain?"

"Yes, yes, of course!" Faskin answered nervously. He had never had any dealings with these female specialists from the Second Directorate. Most of their work was with top-level foreign diplomats.

"But you'll turn up with a doctor, won't you?" the young nymphet continued tormenting Faskin. "So as to catch us good and proper. That's right isn't it?"

"Yeah, that's right," Faskin confirmed sulkily, anticipating another of her jibes.

"I mean, he has to make a woman out of me, doesn't he? Or am I wrong?"

"Otherwise you wouldn't be a woman!" the old veteran smirked.

"For all you know, maybe I'm a woman six times over. But for your little Jew I have to be a virgin, right? So he'll have to put in a bit of work on me. Is he up to it, though? What do you think, Comrade Colonel?"

Barsky didn't reply. He was in no mood for joking. Just an hour ago, sitting in the back of the plane, he'd been delighted with the way this young she-devil worked. She had snared Rubinchik in no time at all. Yesterday he learned that Dzyuba, Rubinchik's local colleague, had reserved a room for him in the Moskva, Kiev's best hotel, and Barsky, with the help of the Ukrainian KGB, had booked rooms there for his whole team, with a separate room for Natasha on the same floor as Rubinchik. So it would be easy for Rubinchik to get her to his room. Or else she could have flirted and enticed him into hers. The other arrangements—the doctor, the militia, the witnesses, and the cameras—were simple matters. Joyfully anticipating his success, Barsky had not attached any significance to the small incident in the plane when Rubinchik felt lightheaded. Now, though, as he looked from the window of the van at the figure spread out on the sidewalk, he began thinking Natasha was probably right—Rubinchik seemed hardly in shape to demonstrate his masculine prowess tonight.

Barsky's thoughts were then distracted as an ambulance appeared at the far end of the bridge. With siren howling, it rolled up to where Dzyuba stood waving his arms. As the medics jumped out with a stretcher, Natasha sighed.

"Well, we can say good-bye to that one. So I'll be staying a virgin, I guess! Rotten luck!" The medics were now bent over Rubinchik, checking his heart and pulse. "What's the good of their feeling him up? He's had a heart attack! I once had another client like that—a Frenchman from Switzerland. And they took him straight from my bed to Sklifasovsky Hospital. But he at least held up for an hour, but this one?! The Jews are a feeble race. That's right, isn't it, Captain? I looked him in the eye just once, and that got him going—he had his hooves in the air!"

"Shut up!" Faskin exploded.

"I'll be submitting a report on you, Captain. Your rudeness is offensive! There I was, all set to play the innocent with him, and you come at me like that! And the Comrade Colonel isn't helping any . . ."

Barsky, however, was totally preoccupied. He watched as the paramedics shoved Rubinchik, strapped on the stretcher, into the ambulance, which then roared off with its siren wailing. Barsky turned to their driver.

"Get after that ambulance! And keep up, don't lose him!"

The cavalcade of vehicles, led by the ambulance, with Dzyuba following on his motorcycle and with the repairs van trailing them a hundred yards behind, moved off across the bridge.

"Don't be upset, Comrade Colonel," Natasha consoled Barsky. "If this Jew doesn't get to screw me, another will! You know, there are plenty more where he came from!"

As soon as Rubinchik felt himself being lifted from the walkway's metal plates onto the stretcher, he let himself lose consciousness and drift off into the history he so loved.

eighteen

Wearing a white cloak with crimson lining, the venerable Pesakh, military chieftain of the Khazars, sat mounted on his black Arabian filly. Shielding his eyes against the July sun, he calmly observed from a stand of oaks as an armada of multicolored Rus skiffs and barks came speeding upstream toward the sanctuary of the Kiev fortress. Sweat pouring down their necks and backs, the Rus heaved on the oars with all their strength, rowing against the Dnieper current, and every now and then they glanced at the sloping, sandy left bank where Khazar cavalry moved abreast of them under fifteen-year-old Joseph, son of Khazar King Aaron. But the hooves of even the strongest chargers kept sticking in the sand. Lashed on by eager bearded warriors, the horses were covered in sweat and foam and kept falling, exhausted. But the hot-blooded and still unbearded Khazar heir spared neither horse nor rider. In his inexperience he couldn't accept that the perfidious Rus were escaping him, and he urged his men on with whiplash and shout.

The Rus could see that they were ahead and gaining. And the sight of the Kiev fortress ahead on the hilly right bank, with its welcoming open gates, and the cheers of its women and children on the wooden towers and ramparts, gave them new strength. They pulled on their oars even more furiously, and the terror that pursued them after their disastrous rout at Samkerts and Cherson folded as they breathed in the vitalizing hope of an imminent sanctuary.

"Come on! Pull those oars!" Igor the Old urged them on. The Kievan Prince was a tall, blue-eyed, and weather-beaten Norseman, still strong for his sixty years, and he displayed one distinctive lock of hair on his otherwise shaven scalp. His bark was decorated with a wooden figurehead of Valkyrie, the Norse goddess of war. As they approached the shore, he was first to spring from his boat and stood up to his waist in water. As guards made the vessels fast, he urged them on with shouts and heaved with his own sinewy arms.

Pesakh bided his time. Smoothing his small curly beard with his right hand, and steadying his impatient filly with his left, he counted Igor's force. Of the five thousand skiffs and barks in which the prince of the Rus had like a brigand arrived in Samkerts one month before, there remained no more than a hundred. So, no more than two thousand warriors could have survived. And these men were exhausted, starving, and they'd torn their hands till they bled heaving on their heavy oars. Those warriors could hardly wield a sword. But it was not the Rus who now alarmed the venerable Pesakh.

As he gazed at the distant opposite bank of the Dnieper, he grew angry. Young Joseph had forgotten he was the son of the great King Aaron. Like some savage, like a Pecheneg, or the ataman of some band of brigands, he had raced ahead of his forces, urged his foaming steed into the river, and holding its withers with one hand, was swimming across to the right bank to give chase to the escaping Rus.

Pesakh, of course, understood the royal heir's impetuosity. After so exhausting a chase, to give up the prince of the Rus and let him fall into the hands of the Alans or Kipchak tribesmen was frustrating. But this had been part of their original ploy: to send the elite royal cavalry, led by young Prince Joseph, in open pursuit of the Rus along the sloping left bank and thus lead Igor to believe that this was the entire Khazar army. Meanwhile Pesakh, leading a troop of Alans, Burtas, Kipchaks, and Kasogians, would overtake the Rus along the high right bank and skirt Kiev in a broad loop from the the west and north. Then, once his horses had rested, he would wait for Igor to disembark below the Kiev fortress, so that in full view of the Kievan Slavs he, Pesakh, could destroy the barbarian prince and his Varangian troops.

But now, impetuous Joseph was ruining that splendid plan. The Rus on the last six skiffs had noticed him, and instead of continuing their flight back to Kiev, they had turned their boats and raced to meet Joseph. Surrounding him as with a net, they were making ready simply to pluck their quarry from the water.

"Kadyma ts'ad!" The venerable Pesakh waved an arm, and immediately his command was repeated with a thunderous cry by two whiskered giants—the kondur khakans, Pesakh's aides, who raced forward on their chargers clad in fine chain mail. At this signal, there came a mighty crashing noise from the great northern forest, and from its thickets emerged a numberless lava of cavalry, composed of undersized and crafty Kipchaks wielding short swords, an army of simplehearted Burtas bearing heavy lances, Kasogians with curved sabres, and squadrons of ruthless Alans with their Persian yataghan daggers glinting in the sunlight. The Dnieper and Pochayna rivers echoed to the thunder of hooves, terrified squawks of gamebirds in the heather, and cries of horror from the walls of the Kievan fortress. The Khazar forces surged down in four streams toward the Dnieper, cutting off the footbound Rus both from the fortress and from the river. As they closed in, the Khazars crushed the Rus's feeble resistance, scything off their heads as they rode, slashing them from shoulder to hip, flooding grass, earth, and water with their blood, and also smashing the sodden wood of the bulbous Rus rivercraft with their axes, and holing and sinking them with their lances.

All around were the groans and mortal gasps of the Rus, the ring of lance and sword blade, the triumphant shouts of the victors, the neighing of horses rearing in fear while smashing human skulls under their death-dealing hooves, rivulets of blood. . . .

The venerable Pesakh loosed his reins and allowed his filly to advance toward the already quieting battlefield. He moved at a slow prance befitting his rank as first chieftain. He had seen the six boatcrews suddenly forget all about the Khazar prince and race to get away down the Dnieper. Meanwhile a Kipchak cohort lead by a giant kondur khakan leapt from their horses onto the shoulders of Prince Igor, seized his sword, and bound his arms with strong rope. And the ruthless Alans finished off the guards at the fortress gate with their bloody daggers.

The battle was over more quickly than a skilled cook could slice a head of cabbage. Pesakh's hirelings—the Burtas, Kipchaks, Alans, and Kasogians—raced up the spur of hillside to the gates of the Kiev fortress, which stood open and helpless. Then, as was the custom, for three days and nights they pillaged the homes of the vanquished and satisfied their lust with their wives and daughters.

"But no fires! And no children killed, as those Rus savages did in Samkerts!" Such was Pesakh's warning.

"If you had perished, what would I have said to King Aaron? Could I have stayed alive and faced his gaze?" Pesakh reproached the young heir that same evening as they sat in his tent with its light, transportable rugs. "Remember, Joseph. You are our next king, and a king should not fight at the head of his troops. Not even the most valiant. Valor may prevail in single combat, but it is wisdom that wins battles. A king has the right to go into battle only once—as the very last, and then only in order to die in a manner befitting a king!"

With eyes downcast and aware of his guilt, obstinate Joseph said nothing. He was a youth of average stature but strong in the shoulder and broadly built, with prominent brow, large head and nose, and wiry black hair. The fine woven chain mail emphasized rather than concealed his broad chest. He wore a short Roman sword on a leather belt, and his strong hairy legs, like those of a young bull, were enclosed in short, reversed leather boots. Indeed the whole of him resembled a young Sumerian bull that had just begun to mature and swell with the raw energy of manhood. The gold fastenings on his Greek satin cloak seemed somehow to constrict the continuing growth of his body.

"Shev, bevakasha. Please be seated," Pesakh said.

Not daring to contradict the great chieftain to whose authority his father had committed him, Joseph sat at Pesakh's camp table with its inlaid mother-of-pearl and ivory, one of the old spoils of his campaign against Chorasan.

Sitting by the light of dripping candles, Pesakh broke off a piece of bread and dipped it in a goblet containing red wine.

"Borukh Ata, Adonai Hamotsy," he began, closing his eyes and rocking back and forth in prayer.

"Blessed art Thou, our Lord God, Ruler of the World . . ." Joseph took up the prayer with some constraint.

". . . Who hath sent us victory over the enemy of Israel, over his city and his tribe," Pesakh continued. Closing his eyes, Joseph repeated: "Over his city and his tribe . . ."

"It was not we who came to him with sword and fire, but he who forced us to make war. Bless, Almighty God, our fallen warriors and accept them into Thy kingdom, Adonai Ekhad!"

"Adonai Ekhad," Joseph echoed.

"And bless, Almighty God, our king on this earth, the venerable Aaron," Pesakh continued without pause, "and Joseph, his bold son, who for eight days and nights chased the Rus brigands that laid waste to our cities and killed our wives and children. Bless him, Adonai, as our future ruler and heir to his father, and allow me, his slave, to live to see the day of his wise rule, so that I may serve him with my body, heart, and counsel, even as I serve his father, Aaron, Amen!"

"Amen!" said Joseph, blushing at this flattery by the great Pesakh.

"And now, Joseph," Pesakh said, "go back to your tent. You are tired and you deserve to rest. Go to your tent. You will find a gift from me awaiting you there."

Joseph rose, but paused before bidding Pesakh good night. Pesakh looked at him in surprise with his large and slightly protruding eyes. No one dared contradict the great chieftain, but Joseph, the son of the king, had other rights.

"What will you do with the prince we have taken captive?" Joseph asked, blushing at his own daring. "Will you kill him?"

"We do not kill prisoners, you know that," Pesakh said. "I shall make him bow down to the will of your father."

"And if he refuses?"

Pesakh did not answer, but his faint smile conveyed that this was a silly question.

"I want to see him," Joseph said, blushing again and throwing back his large head. "When will you be talking with him?"

"I shall speak with him this very night. But you cannot be present."

"Why?" Joseph's eyes suddenly blazed angrily.

"You are our next king. A king should not demean himself to speak with a barbarian prisoner. Leave that to your servants. Apart from which, I hope you will be too occupied with my gift to be distracted by such trifles. Shalom!"

"Shalom!" Joseph was forced to respond. Leaving Pesakh's tent, he sprang into the saddle, whipped his horse, and furiously galloped through the camp and down to the Dnieper. No, once he became king, the first thing he would do would be to fire this kagan bek. Nobody was going to talk to him as though he were a little boy. Not even the great Pesakh!

. . .

As the night drew on, chilled from swimming, Joseph returned to his tent. The camp spread out below the hill on the Dnieper shore was brightly lit by the glare of fires blazing inside the Kiev fortress and by hundreds of campfires by the waterside. From these came waves of spicy aromas—the Moslem Alans were roasting mutton, the pagan Burtas were preparing horsemeat cut from animals slaughtered in the battle, and the Kipchak and Kasogians were cooking pork. Standing, sitting, and lying by their fires, they talked and laughed, tearing off lumps of meat with their teeth, drinking the intoxicating honey *nabiz* produced by Kievan peasants and Greek wine from the cellars of the prince's guard. Meanwhile they also were dividing their plunder—gold, silver, amber, various weapons, and, most valuable of all, the soft furs of marten and sable, in which the forests of the Slavs, Severyanians, and Derevlians were so rich. And in the darkness beyond the fires, they were satisfying their lust raping the young wives and daughters of their vanquished enemies. Indeed, well aware of the custom, many of these women willingly submitted themselves.

Joseph slowly led his horse along the riverbank, hardly noticed by the feasting warriors. The groans of women and aromas of roast meat aroused him, but he kept his distance from the campfires. It was not fitting that he should take part in the festivities of commoners, or that he inhibit them by his presence. Furthermore, his heart was troubled by a strange compassion for their victims. He knew, too, the origin of this feeling—it came from that interest that the Rus had aroused in him ever since he was a child. Whenever they came to Khazaria with merchandise, they struck everyone with their stately physique and their white skin, which was decorated with strange figures from their toenails to their necks—drawings showing birds of prey, wild animals, and pagan gods. Hardly had they moored their brightly ornamented craft before each of them disembarked, carrying with him bread, meat, onions, milk, and *nabiz*. And all this was offered to Volos, their god of cattle and trade, whose effigy was carved from a wooden beam and placed upright in the earth. As they bowed down to this idol, they would say, "O my lord, I have come from a distant land, and with me so many girls, and so many slaves for sale, and so many sable, and so many pelts," and they would enumerate all the goods they had brought. Placing their offerings before the idol, which had a human face, they would continue: "And here I have come to you with this gift, and I wish that you should grant that a merchant come to me who is rich and has many dinars, and that he should buy everything from me at the price that I shall name." After this they would set up wooden dwellings on the bank of the river, lay out their goods—pelts of marten, fox, and squirrel, and mead and wax—and they would sit next to one another, together with the lovely girls they had brought to offer to their customers. But soon, as Joseph had been told by his father's servants, one of the Rus would grow impatient for a buyer for his girl or his other wares, and he would begin to copulate with her himself. As his friend watched and saw the strength of the girl's passion, he too would become aroused. Sometimes then a whole group of Rus would gather and couple with their girls this way. Eventually, when some merchant turned up to buy goods, slaves, or girls, the

Rus would be incapable of doing business. They couldn't tear themselves away from their girls because of the magical power of their *fardja*, which had the strength of a python's jaw.

Joseph had heard from Arabian envoys who passed through Khazaria after visiting the Rus that in their own country the Rus had little trust of one another, always carried their swords with them, and that treachery and deceit were part of their everyday dealing. If any one of them succeeded in obtaining even a modest property, his own brother or friend would soon become jealous and try to kill or rob him. They didn't even go alone to relieve themselves, but went with two or three companions and took their swords, which they laid beside them. According to other stories, if anyone in their country saw a person who showed alertness and some special knowledge, they would say: "This man is most of all worthy to serve our God." And they would take him, put a rope about his neck, and hang him from a tree. The Rus were also said to be abusers of *nabiz*, drinking it day and night, so that often some of them would die with the goblet still in their hands.

But were these tales true? Now, when he saw their corpses and heard their dying gasps and cries, all that he had heard about their strength, daring, and uniqueness seemed most unlikely—like so many other tales thought up by the Khazar merchants who roamed the entire world from torrid Hispania to mysterious Cathay. But more than ever, Joseph longed to see with his own eyes the fortress walls of Kiev and the life of these people, tall and handsome as palm trees, who for so many years had aroused fear and trembling with their raids on Bulgaria, Germany, and even on the great Byzantine Empire. However, this too he had to deny himself. It was not fitting that he, the son of a king of Judah, should force his way into Kiev along with a pillaging horde of Alans and Kasogians.

Finally, Joseph reached his tent, which stood a hundred paces from that of Pesakh and his kundur khakans. The Kipchak stableboy ran out to meet him, seized his horse's bridle and immediately led the animal away to rub it down, wash, and feed it. As he walked along, Joseph threw his wet garments to his servants and made his way to his tent. There he stopped short, amazed. Seated on cushions and traveling carpets before his tent sat twelve Rus maidens, with fair hair and skin, lovely of countenance, with slender waists and round embossed cases on their breasts. At Joseph's appearance, the beardless Persian castrato, chief eunuch of the great Pesakh, shouted to them and they all jumped to their feet.

"What is all this?" Joseph asked him in Persian.

"It is a gift sent to you by my master." The eunuch raised his lantern for Joseph to inspect the row of captives who stood there with averted gaze. "Look at them, my lord! Fair goddesses of the north! Each more beautiful than the last. Their skin is like ivory, their hair like honey, and their breasts . . ."

Joseph was overcome by a rush of anger.

"Get them away from here!" he shouted, realizing what Pesakh was hinting at when he said Joseph would have no time for negotiations with the prince of the Rus that night. No matter if Pesakh is three times as great a commander as he is, how dare he mock me this way!

"Take them away from here immediately!" Joseph repeated his order in Hebrew.

The eunuch, however, shook his head.

"I don't want to lose my head by contradicting you, O Prince," he said in Persian. "But hear what I have to say. You cannot refuse this gift. The great Pesakh plucked them out of his own heart, for I selected them for him and not for you." The crafty Persian once more walked along the line of girls with his lantern, illuminating their slender figures and downcast faces. "Of course, he could have sent you gold or furs. But what is gold to Pesakh, or to you, the son of a king? Pesakh has given you the sweetest spoils of all. See! If you chase them away, you will offend the first kagan bek of your father! You do not need to take them all; you can keep just one for yourself, but to refuse such a gift . . ."

Thinking, Joseph began to accept that he could not treat Pesakh rudely, after he had that morning saved his life. Furthermore he had pursued the Rus prince for eight days and nights and chased him into a trap. So part of the spoils should be his—it was his right as a warrior, and not just as the king's son.

Joseph looked up and gazed at the girls who stood there with downcast eyes and listened in alarm to the guttural sounds of the Persian tongue. Now that his anger had abated he could examine them properly. Naturally, he was already a man. From his father's harem he had known three Persian women and one Greek virgin, but his heart was now filled with boyish shyness. For he had never seen such beauty. Everything about these girls was unusual, exciting, and new to him—their honey-colored silken hair, their fine white complexions, their shoulders the color of ivory, their small breasts covered with round embossed cases made of pure gold (the sign of their belonging to a wealthy society), their bodies tall and slender as some marine plant, and their shapely legs. And for the first time in his short life, the spoilt heir to the Khazar throne felt shy. He stood stock-still, utterly perplexed. All of them were lovely as Nordic goddesses, and they appeared just as inaccessible, although they stood before him with their eyes averted.

Suddenly one at the end of the row, with three strings of large green beads around her neck, each worth one sable skin, and with gold cases on her breasts and gold pendants on her arms and legs, raised her dense eyelashes and looked Joseph straight in the eye. Her eyes were blue, or blue cast with grayish-green, like the hoarfrost on a winter morning, and so fathomless that Joseph immediately felt weak at the knees, his tongue went dry and his thoughts grew confused. It was like plunging into some icy depths, through a hole in the ice of the River Ityl in winter. There in that chill he felt bathed in a flood of hot blood.

At that same moment the eunuch raised his plaited lash to strike this prisoner who dared look the king's son in the eye. But with a gesture Joseph restrained him.

"This one!" he said, and with that rushed into his tent, all confused.

He did not hear or see the irritation of the Persian eunuch, who with the words "A royal choice!" struck the girl with the back of his podgy, heavily ringed hand.

Later that night, when Joseph summoned him, Pesakh's eunuch brought the girl to him. She now looked even paler and more lovely than before. She had been washed clean by the eunuch's female assistants, adorned in golden and transparent Turkish silks; she smelled of Arabian herbs and her honey-colored hair was combed and held back with an ivory comb set with green stones. But in her blue eyes with their straight, firm gaze there was neither the terror of a slave nor the fear of a prisoner. She now looked older than fifteen, and to Joseph's surprise turned out to be taller than he, but only by a little—perhaps a mere third of a hand—but even from that height the look she gave him was proud and imperious.

The girl's stature and her gaze perplexed Joseph so that he forgot the ritual of dealing with women that he had learned in his father's harem. There, both the experienced Persian women and the Greek virgin had not dared raise their eyes to the son of the great Khazar king. They had removed his boots and clothing and with their knowing caresses had inflamed his flesh and then satisfied him. But this Rus was not bending to unbind his footwear. She held him at a distance with her cold Nordic eyes, like two steel blades.

The unexpectedness of this arrogance in her eyes and bearing caused Joseph to freeze. He stood stock-still, like a calf as it confronts some strange wild animal. And there the two of them stood, facing each other without a word—two antipodes of the human race who had been heading toward this meeting for a thousand years—one an Israelite scorched by the sun of the Levant, and the other a cold, Nordic Russian diva. Fate had brought them across burning sands and icy fjords via bloody battles and nomadic wanderings, face to face just here, on a steep bank by the River Dnieper on a late July night in 941. But neither of them saw their meeting as a sign that their gods were making peace, or that this justified the thousands of corpses that led to their coming together.

As they eyed one another, they were like two animals encountering one another on a woodland path, and in total silence, disturbed only by the flicker of candles and the sizzle of molten wax in the candleholders, they watched each other's every gesture, even the flutter of an eyelash.

Of course, had this really been a chance encounter, this Rus diva would have been the first to turn haughtily away and retreat into the thickets of her inscrutable northern existence. Any princess who knew her own worth would have turned her back on a timid, callow youth. But this girl was a prisoner, a trophy, part of the spoils of war. Her only choice was between the ruthless elderly Pesakh and the young and inexperienced Joseph. And for choosing the youth she had been struck by the eunuch. But she had outsmarted him, and now she was summoning up her last weapon of defense, her pride.

Joseph, however, soon recovered his regal bearing. He stood erect and threw back his large curly head.

"Take off my shoes!" he ordered her in Persian.

She did not move a muscle. He then realized she did not know Persian.

"Take off my shoes!" he repeated in Greek, and gestured toward his plaited sandals.

But she gave no response and stood silent like a statue, like a goddess, an idol of northern loveliness.

Perplexed, Joseph walked around her. Everything about her was beautiful—from the front, from the side, and from the rear. Almost completing a circle around her, Joseph put out a hand and undid the golden fastening on her shoulder and then quickly drew back. That single clasp evidently secured her entire dress, which then fell about her onto the carpet, revealing to him her incredible white body, slender as a reed stem, with satin skin, little marble breasts with carmine nipples, smoothly curving stately thighs, fine golden bracelets on her hands and feet, and green pendants on her neck.

Her gesture was instinctive rather than conscious as she covered her breast and the golden down of her *fardja* with her hands. Then, almost provocatively, she dropped her hands and stood there amid her fallen garments like the proud figure of the Valkyrie on the prow of a Varangian boat.

Joseph by now had regained his confidence as lord and master.

"Lie down," he said to her, again in Greek, since he knew no languages except Greek, Persian, and Hebrew.

In response to his gesture she obeyed.

After hesitating, he then undressed himself and lay down next to her.

"Caress me," he ordered.

She seemed not to understand.

Then, after a pause for thought, he himself began to stroke her body and her breasts, her nipples, belly, and the margin of her *fardja*. And the fortress of her pride could not resist that incursion. Her eyes closed in ecstasy, and her body rose in an arch on the silken mattress with its ornate colored pattern of fawns.

Finally Joseph reared above her, triumphant and excited as the young bull depicted on a Greek amphora. But as he spread her loins with his knees and moved his wand of life toward her, a hoarse rasping cry suddenly broke from her lips and she began thrashing in his embrace, crying and imploring him in Greek:

"No! Don't do that! I implore you by your God! Don't do that!"

Surprised, Joseph delayed the final decisive thrust.

"What? So you know Greek?"

She did not answer, but continued to pray and beseech him as she lay there under him.

"No! Don't do it. Don't enter me!"

"Are you a virgin?"

"Yes! I implore you! Don't do this!"

"Have no fear. It isn't painful. I have done this before." And with the condescending air of an experienced man he lowered his key of life toward her *fardja*, searching for the hallowed opening.

At that instant, she jerked her thighs with a wild, pantherlike, almost masculine strength, slipped away from him, sprang to her feet, and darted away. As she reached the tent flap, however, she stopped short. There was no escape. Outside stood a guard quite capable of finishing off what she had forbidden to Joseph. Joseph himself felt a rush of blood to his head and limbs, and to the masculine root of his oxlike strength. Going after his prisoner, he was on the verge of springing at her when she cried out.

"Wait! Wait! I will give you three whole cities! Only spare me! Korsun, Novgorod, and Chernigov!"

Joseph leapt at her with the powerful spring of a furious lion covering some obdurate young lioness. Knocking her off her feet, he turned her on her back and laid his whole body on top of her, parted her legs and thrust his powerful bull's phallus blindly at the cherished aperture.

"Five cities!" she cried out in despair. "Six! Even Pskov you can have! Only don't enter me! You may take the whole left bank of the Dnieper!"

In amazement, Joseph held off a second thrust.

"Who are you?" he asked.

"You don't need to know that! But you'll get everything, just as I said!" She spoke hurriedly, still lying under him.

He pressed his loins hard forward and thrust into the hidden opening of her *fardja*.

"Who are you! Speak!" he said again insistently.

She said nothing, though, and closed her eyes.

"Well?" he shouted, failing in his inexperience to understand the reason for her silence. "What is your name?"

"Volga," she said softly.

"You lie! Volga is the wife of Igor, Prince of the Rus."

She was silent again.

"Come on! Speak!" He threateningly prodded her *fardja* again with his pulsating organ.

"I am Volga, the wife of Igor."

"But you are a virgin! You said so yourself! Speak the truth! Or I shall . . ."

"I am a virgin."

He smacked her face with the back of his hand with such force that her whole head twitched as she lay there on the carpet.

"And the wife of Igor?" he said in a frenzy.

"And I am the wife of Igor."

He hit her again with even greater strength.

"And you're a virgin?"

"And I am a virgin."

"And what about the wife of Igor?" He beat her again.

"I am the wife of Igor," she repeated. Suddenly she opened her eyes again and looked him straight in the eye. "I am the wife of Igor and I am a virgin. I swear it by the gods."

He sat down at her side and blinked in surprise.

"How can that be?" he asked at last. "Does he have other wives? Or does he not love you?"

"No. He loves me," she laughed bitterly, still lying on the carpet. "He loves me very much! And I am his only wife. For three years now. It's simply that he cannot do what men do."

"Why?" Joseph was even more astonished.

She shrugged her white shoulders, and from the bitter little wrinkle at the corner of her mouth he suddenly realized that she was older than he was.

"How old are you?" he asked. He now relaxed and lay down next to her. Not only did he now feel pity for this Rus princess, but the hardness of his vital root had also begun to abate.

"I shall soon be seventeen."

"And you have not known any man?"

"No. I am my husband's wife. But nobody knows about what I have just told you. I am sorry for you, Joseph."

"Why?" he asked.

She did not answer.

The candles in the silver holder melted and went out, and still they both lay there in the half-darkness, and he had no idea what to do next. The Kievan princess and wife of the Varangian Prince Igor lay next to him naked, and somewhere nearby, a hundred paces away, the mighty Pesakh was interrogating her husband—a man who knew how to wage war, seize cities, kill, crucify, pillage, enslave, and exact tribute from those he conquered, but who could not do what other men did. What a sad life this Princess Volga must have lived.

Suddenly he felt through the hair on his chest the gentle, barely perceptible touch of a hand.

He lay quite still.

His stillness was that of a wary and sensitive animal, halting on a woodland path as it hears a sudden sigh of wind in the treetops.

The sensation continued—the slow and careful touch of a light female hand moving across the hair of his chest, then his belly, lower and lower. And it sent the blood thrusting through his limbs so powerfully, as though the drums of war had sounded. His pulse surged with new blood, and his heart was swept into the galloping onslaught.

nineteen

Rubinchik regained consciousness in a hospital ward from the touch of a hand that held his own and seemed to soothe and draw away all tension. The gallop of his heart also abated and his racing pulse calmed.

He opened his eyes.

Nelya was sitting there, bending over him and holding him by the hand. She was dressed in a freshly laundered hospital smock and a grayish-white cap with an amusing ink stencil in Ukraininan that read *Kiev Hospital No. 39.*

"Where am I?" he asked.

"You're in Kiev. Everything's all right. Lie there and keep calm," she said gently.

He squinted to the side: in the same ward six other patients lay in their beds.

"What? Did they make you come all the way to Kiev?" he asked, amazed. "What happened to me? Was it a heart attack?"

"No. But your blood pressure is two-forty over one-eighty. And it was even higher."

"What does that mean?" All his life Rubinchik had believed he was perfectly healthy, and he had never had his blood pressure taken.

"How are you feeling?" Nelya asked cautiously.

"Okay. My head feels a bit heavy, but otherwise . . . I could even get up." He stirred and tried to raise himself, but she anxiously restrained him.

"No, no! You must lie there!" She motioned to someone with her hand. "You can come in now. He's come round!"

Ignat Dzyuba, who was waiting out in the corridor, stubbed out his cigarette and walked in.

"So there he is! At last!" he said with the jaunty air people adopt when visiting someone gravely ill. "You gave us quite a fright, old boy! The doctors were saying people pop off with blood pressure that high! But I told them: 'Come on! He's got a hundred and forty weaving women waiting for him! He's bound to live! He'll soon be enjoying a drink with us.' Won't you, Iosif?"

"Have you got a bottle with you?" Rubinchik asked.

"There! You see?" Dzyuba said to Nelya. "I told you he was only kidding around! And if we let those weaving women in here with their flowers and goodness knows . . ."

A nurse, as severe and stuck-up as the plaster on the wall, appeared at Rubinchik's bedside. Without a word she took his arm, wound a rubber band just above the elbow, and began taking his blood pressure.

Rubinchik, Nelya, and Dzyuba all stared at her worriedly.

"How much?" Dzyuba asked as she unwound the rubber arm-wrapper.

"Two-twenty over one-sixty," she said.

"Well, so now we know he'll survive at least!" Dzyuba said cheerfully. He looked at his watch. "Are you flying back today?" he asked. "Or tomorrow?"

"I'm not flying," Nelya said. "I'm scared of airplanes."

But Nelya's fears were not a deciding factor. The doctors refused to let Rubinchik travel home by plane. Two days later, when his pressure was almost back to normal, he was discharged, but only after Nelya solemnly promised to take him home by train.

Once in the train and settled in a comfortable compartment, Nelya said, "Could you have guessed that this was your last business trip?"

"Why?" Rubinchik was astonished.

"Because soon we'll be leaving this country. We've had enough."

She told him about the invitation from Israel, about the Bulletin Board at the Conservatory, about old Rebecca Gilel, and the article in *Ogonyok*. She also recounted how she'd been attacked and thrown off the Moscow trolley bus.

"Once the Nazis began beating up Jews in the streets, Rebecca didn't sit around and that's why she stayed alive," Nelya said. "And we've got our kids to think about too. But for some reason we're still sitting around waiting!"

"But what am I going to do in Israel?"

"I don't know. But if you won't come, the kids and I are leaving. So you'd better decide."

Lying there on his bunk, Rubinchik listened to the clatter of train wheels and saw the steel supports of a bridge flash past—they were crossing the same bridge where five days before he had lost consciousness.

twenty

At the Moscow offices of the *Labor Gazette*, a long corridor led from the café-restaurant in the northern wing to the chief editor's office on the southern side. Just a week ago, before his trip to Kiev, Rubinchik had walked the length of it in half a minute. Today it took him almost half an hour, although hardly an hour ago he'd given Nelya his word that he wouldn't stay here more than ten minutes. He'd come first thing in the morning, simply to place his letter of resignation on the chief's desk and request a work reference. That document was vital. Without it, and without the permission of any parents remaining here, without a note from one's place of residence, from the military enlistment office, from the trade union confirming no debts were unpaid, from the library, from the telephone exchange, and so forth—without all these documents the Passport and Visa Office would not accept any applications to leave the country. But though it was clear more or less why all these goddamned clearances were required, Rubinchik was baffled and angry at the requirement to show a report from his place of work. Why in hell's name did they need it? And what was it supposed to say? "So-and-so is morally stable, politically literate, dedicated to the task of building Communism, and therefore is hereby recommended as a fit person to leave the country and take up permanent residence in Israel?" What else could such reference say? And if he was an anti-Soviet slacker and a drunkard, would they refuse to let him out?

The real reason for that requirement wasn't hard to guess. When any Jew asked for such a reference, he had to admit to his employers why he needed it. And whatever reason he gave, it branded him as an odd man out, an outsider, a leper, and a traitor to his country.

Rubinchik could not imagine himself doing that. For Nelya it was easy. The Conservatory director was openly anti-Jewish. She would even enjoy throwing her resignation in his face. And as she demanded her reference, she could even afford a smile of contempt. But here Iosif had felt close to his colleagues for ten years; simply announcing his departure would hurt their feelings. Especially today, when he first came in, journalists, photographers, clerks, and typists had poured out of every room with delight, to give him a hug, pat him on the shoulder, and welcome him back.

"Well, old man, are you okay again? Thank God! Welcome back!"

"Iosif, come on, quit all this hospital nonsense! We need you here!"

"Oh, Iosif, I'm so glad to see you! We were all about to fly off to Kiev to visit you in the hospital."

"What, so you've got high blood pressure? Listen, the brother of my mother-in-law is a specialist in extrasensory healing! Absolutely fantastic! Incredible! He'll cure you, free of charge, honest!"

Rubinchik never suspected that his being sick for a week would cause such a stir. Going down the corridor, he stopped at every office, thanked them, listened to their joking congratulations, and caught up on the latest gossip. With every step he took toward the chief's office, he realized more and more how fond he was of these people, these office walls, the rattle of typewriters behind each door, the chorus of ringing phones, and the pungently acidic smell of those long proofs—the galleys of tomorrow's issue that the secretaries scurried to deliver to various offices. Here, along this corridor, ran the pulse of the nation. Here they knew everything (or almost) there was to know about events from Kamchatka to the Baltic. Here, as best they could, they slid around the Party censorship and each day managed to force through a few grains of truth onto the printed page. And they rejoiced at this minuscule success as though it were a great victory. And it was here that Rubinchik found his true calling, and even moments of glory. So why should he have to bid them farewell? Why should he, with his own hand, cut the umbilical cord that connected him with the whole of life and with his wonderful work? If he did that, where would he end up? He would be alone in space, like an astronaut who had lost touch with the earth!

"Iosif! Why've you come back to work?" An angry voice sounded behind him.

Rubinchik wheeled round. It was the chief, dressed in a light foreign-cut suit and holding out his hand. He was younger than Rubinchik, but he'd already suffered two heart attacks.

"Hi there! Come with me a moment!" he said, leading Rubinchik off toward his office and talking all the time. "Listen, Iosif. I've fixed it up with Chazov—that's the Kremlin directorate in the Ministry of Health. You're going to let Chazov have a look at you. At the Kremlin Hospital. And no arguing! If you need any medication from abroad, you know we've got our correspondents around the globe, and we'll get it for you at our expense. Another thing. If Chazov will let you fly, you're going off immediately—to Sochi, to a film festival. You'll go instead of me, as a member of the jury. What else? If you need cash, don't be afraid to ask. Sit down."

When they reached his office, the chief hung up his coat, then opened a double door and produced a bottle of French Napoleon brandy.

"Just remember," the chief said, "every day you need to take fifty grams of this stuff. It expands your arteries. So come on!" He poured the brandy into two vodka glasses and clinked glasses with Rubinchik. "I'm really glad you're on the mend," he continued. "What's that Jewish toast you have? L'chaim? So let's drink to life! Now you realize what these things are like? It's like having your first car crash—until it happens, you think you're driving a tank and that nothing can touch you. Then, once it does happen, you realize that any car can be crunched like an eggshell! And only after you've had your first heart attack do you realize what life is all about! So once you've turned forty, the main thing to do is look after your health! Here, have a refill."

"Andrey," Rubinchik interrupted quietly, and looked sadly at the wall behind the chief's chair, which was plastered with the still-damp proofs of tomorrow's edition. "D'you know what? If you really want to make me a present, then send me off on a trip."

"I've already said so!" The chief sounded surprised. "If the doctors will let you, you can fly straight off to Sochi! Perhaps even tomorrow!"

"No, not to Sochi."

"Where to, then?"

"Siberia, or the Arctic—it's all the same to me. Only today, right now."

"Something gone wrong at home?"

"Well, almost." Rubinchik answered evasively.

With a broad gesture the chief pointed to the huge wall map of the Soviet Union and grinned.

"Iosif, you know what they say on such occasions in America?"

Rubinchik shook his head.

"Be my guest!" he said.

Ninety minutes later Rubinchik was out at Bykovo Airport, which served the whole east of the USSR. It was summer, and the terminal was crammed with travelers. He forced his way through the crowd to the mail and telegraph office and handed in his wire. Mouthing the words with her dry, unmade-up lips, the fat woman cashier read out the text as she totted up the words with her ballpoint pen:

" 'MOSCOW—24 FIRST COSMONAUTS ST. APT. 67—NELYA RUBINCHIK—LEFT URGENT ASSIGNMENT IN ARCTIC FIVE DAYS—DON'T WORRY—THIS IS MY LAST TRIP—LOVE AND KISSES YOU AND CHILDREN—IOSIF'. That's thirty words. One ruble fifty kopeks. I don't have any change."

Rubinchik handed her a green three-ruble bill.

"I just told you: I've got no change!" The woman exploded. "Or don't you understand Russian?"

"But I don't have any change either. And I'm boarding one minute from now. I've got to get the Tyumen' flight."

"That's none of my business! Take your telegram and clear off!"

"Just take the three rubles! And keep the change!" he pleaded.

"Did you ever see anything like that?" The cashier addressed the people lining up at her window. "Trying to buy me off! Huh! Rubinchik!" Then, turning malevolently to Rubinchik himself: "Take your stinking money and get out! You dirty Jew! Filthy Zionist!"

Rubinchik had no time to retort, or even become enraged, as the waiting crowd pushed him away from the window and out of the line. At that moment a rusty metallic voice sounded over the intercom:

"Attention please. Departure of the Moscow–Tyumen' flight has been delayed and put on hold due to weather conditions at Tyumen'. I repeat . . ."

"Goddamn it!" Rubinchik swore. There was the motherland up to her old tricks. He stuffed the telegram into his jacket pocket and went back to his friend in the booking office to exchange his ticket for another flight— to Salekhard.

Twenty-one

Over all of salekhard, capital of the Nenetsk region—land of the Soviet eskimoes—a thunderous cannonade could be heard as the ice on the river broke up. Slightly to the north, the huge eight-mile-wide bay of the Ob River flowed into the Arctic Ocean. In winter the river froze to a depth of thirty feet. But now this mighty, rutted expanse of ice gave out a menacing crackle and crunch as it swelled up in the warmth of June. Under pressure from water flowing from the south, the ice cracked, exploding and rearing up with thunderous noises. Ice floes, each the size of football fields, overlaid one another like giant walruses at mating time. Crushing one another with their incredible weight, rising up on end, and then pushed by powerful currents, they rammed into the still-unbroken ice on the bay to the north of Salekhard, causing a deafening roar as they finally broke up.

When this happened, everyone came out onto the banks of the Ob and stayed there from morning till late at night. The entire population—Nenets men and women in gaily colored dearskin jackets, Russian geologists and

oilmen with their quilted jackets unbuttoned, helicopter crews wearing fur-lined flying suits, hoards of drivers on snowmobiles with caterpillar tracks or with chains around their wheels, children driving sleighs and dog teams. The only beings that took no interest in this springtime festival were domestic cats and wild animals. The cats hid inside in fright, and the wild animals—squirrels, arctic foxes, martens, wolves, and bears—all moved off into the taiga and tundra. But it was a time when both animals and humans relaxed. Nobody worked, the schools were closed, and even the authorities were powerless with the onset of sunlight and warmth that softened everyone up. Managers forgot about pressuring their workers, and they too relaxed, climbed into their four-wheel drive cars, and brought beer and *stroganina**
with them and joined everyone else on the steep banks of the Ob.

During those few days, the arctic spring reduced everyone to one level. You could see a drunken old-timer with PARTY SLAVE tattooed on his fore-head (obviously a relic of life in a labor camp) walk straight up to the head of the Salekhard militia, who was busy enjoying his beer, and say: "Come on, buster, give us a swig." And the militia chief actually handed him a bottle!

Rubinchik wandered around among this colorful crowd. He stopped at a bonfire lit by a team of young geologists, some strumming on guitars. He paused to watch a group of Nenets who had just slaughtered a deer and were relishing a bowl of still hot deer's blood with strips of the animal's liver floating in it. He stopped to watch some Nenets boys trying to feed their dog team with frozen fish, who snorted and refused to eat the stuff. And a group of Nenets girls in festively trimmed jackets, who were smoking pipes and drinking an eau de cologne called Red Moscow straight from the bottle. . . .

Rubinchik found all this fascinating. Instinctively he felt for his note-book in the fur jacket presented to him by the local natural-gas consortium—a gift for the visiting Moscow correspondent. He couldn't find it, though, and then realized he didn't need it. This was his last mission ever, and he wouldn't be writing any story. When he got back he would be handing in his resignation. This thought depressed him, and he headed off towards the Ocean Wave Restaurant that jutted up on the crest of the riverbank. There he ordered "a glass and a chaser"—a hundred grams of brandy and a mug of beer together with a plate of *stroganina*. And he sat, sullenly hunched over his drink, spirits flagging, intuition switched off, blind to any divas that might be around.

The night, more like the milky twilight of an arctic day, drew on. Ru-

*Finely sliced fresh, frozen salmon.

binchik trailed off to the wooden two-story Sever Hotel. There, drunk, discombobulated, and feeling sorry for himself—as though soon to die rather than just to emigrate—he rolled into his bunk. Like all the other hotel guests, he slept fully dressed, and even the rumble of the ice floes was inaudible above the sound of his snoring.

Three such days passed. By the fourth, the cannonade of breaking ice had quieted, and only isolated ice floes together with tree branches, shattered barrels, and other debris now drifted down the Ob towards the Arctic. The drunken festival was over, the oilmen had flown back to the tundra in their helicopters, the Nenets had driven their deer herds off to seek out the moss on the thawing hillocks, and the children had gone back to school. And on that same day, not far from the hotel, Rubinchik suddenly came across Natasha—the same stewardess who'd been on his flight to Kiev and who had missed out on promenading with him along the Kreshchatik.

"Oh, it's you! Hi there!" She was the first to recognize him, and even blushed with pleasure at their unexpected meeting. "I've been transferred onto these northern flights," she explained. "By the way, I called you up that time, in Kiev. But there was no answer."

"I'm sorry, Natasha. I had a sudden high-blood-pressure attack, and I ended up in the hospital."

"Really?" she said, full of concern. "How are you feeling now?"

"I'm fine," he said. "Are you here for long?"

"No, only till tomorrow."

"Perhaps we could take a walk along the Ob? Have you seen the ice already?"

"No. We only got here last night, and this is my first trip here."

"Oh, then let me be your guide! It's not quite like the Kreshchatik, but still . . . Come on, I'll show you where the Arctic Circle passes through here. There's actually a little pillar with an inscription."

"Just one moment! I'll just tell our commander that I'm with you, so he won't get alarmed."

"What commander?"

"Our flight commander—from the plane. I'll be right back! Ooh, look there! Look at those boys with their dog team!" She ran off into the hotel, flopping comically on the wooden sidewalk in her heavy fur boots.

He stood and waited for her. Suddenly all the dross fell away from him—the misery at being forced to emigrate, and the hangover from yesterday's booze. His head was filled with a spring freshness, joy and uplift. A feeling bubbled within him like champagne. Once again he had that foretaste of the miracle that would reprogram all the atoms of his body and fill him with a spurt of new energy. A warm glow returned to his cheeks, his hunched Jewish shoulders opened, his spine straightened, and he almost felt himself grow taller. And once again his eyes glowed with the fire that had led his ancestors across the Sinai and the sands of Persia, and brought them to Russia.

When Natasha came out, she had exchanged her Aeroflot coat for a coquettish Bulgarian sheepskin. Paying no attention to a twitch of curtains in the hotel windows, Rubinchik took her by the arm and with an air of authority led her off past the collapsing snowdrifts towards where the Ob emptied into the blue expanse of the bay.

Everything on that warm polar day was like a fairy tale. They walked by the river; rode out with some fishermen in their deep-hulled vessel and ate their freshly made fish soup with them; wandered among the hillocks of the tundra, gathering snowdrops; admired the blue-and-silver fox at a fur farm; rode in sleighs pulled by dogs and reindeer and drank tea in a Nenets hut; and they went up in a helicopter for a bird's-eye view of Salekhard, and afterwards they wandered again by the bay. Rubinchik was in good form. His *Labor Gazette* ID was sufficient to get them the best table at the Ocean Wave, with a view overlooking the river; at the fur farm they were shown storerooms crammed with first-quality pelts for export; and the helicopter pilots took them into the depths of the tundra to see the oil rigs. As he pointed out to Natasha the beauty of the tundra, the mighty Ob, the Eskimo mores, and the earth's mineral treasures, Rubinchik felt like a king revealing to some young princess the secret treasures of his kingdom. He himself liked everything he saw here—and especially that he had easy access to all these splendors. And at each new revelation, the gleam in Natasha's cornflower-blue eyes brought him to wave after wave of new inspiration. Strolling by the Ob, he recited poetry to her, amused her with funny stories from his life as a journalist, and quoted her passages from Arabian and European chroniclers who visited ancient Rus a thousand years ago:

" 'I have seen the Rus when they arrived to do trade and set themselves up by the River Ityl. I never saw folk with more perfect bodies than theirs. They are tall like palm trees, fair-haired, with fine faces and white bodies. . . . As for their women, they are all beautiful. Their bodies are all white like ivory, and each of their breasts is enclosed in a small case in the form of a circle made of iron, or of silver, brass, gold, or wood, depending on the wealth of their husband. They wear these breast cases from childhood, so as to prevent their breasts from becoming too enlarged. Round their necks they have necklaces of gold and silver, and a knife that hangs down between their breasts. . . . If the head of a family dies, his kinfolk say to his girls, "Which of you will die together with him?" And the one who loved him most announces she is willing. . . .' "

Rubinchik never lavished so much attention on any of his previous liaisons. But this Natasha was the final, farewell diva that Russia would present to him. From her shining eyes and the way she clung to him as they walked, he could sense that she was already his, that he could lay her down in the snow or the tundra and take her there and then. But he was in no hurry. He led her on and on, among the hillocks, into the tundra, and into the depths of Russian history, using all his charm. And he, too, relished her increasingly languid mien, and his infatuation with this, the last Russian-tundra snowdrop of his life. His performance was like that of some superb jazz musician captivating an audience with one improvisation after another, prolonging the pleasure, coming up with new variations, each more dazzling than the last, as he himself was transported into some beatific realm.

In the lucent twilight of the pale arctic evening, on their way back to their hotel, either from weariness or because of her reluctance to part with this magical day, Natasha began walking more and more slowly. She let him move on ahead of her, and then suddenly called to him:

"Iosif . . ."

He turned round.

She stood there on the path, looking indecisive and with a strange torment in her eyes.

He walked back to her and bent to look into her eyes.

"What's wrong? Are you tired?"

Suddenly her gaze flashed with the same passion that he had seen in her eyes two weeks before. It was the sort of look that caused men to lose their heads, their honor, their liberty, their wives and children, and even life itself. Only this time, it was not the brief flash of some mirage, but a call from the very soul.

"I . . ." she began. Then she looked around, as though in that tundra desolation, lit only by the unsetting sun, someone might overhear them. But then she took the plunge and declared, "I want to run away with you somewhere! Right now!"

"Run away?" He smiled indulgently as though talking to a child. "Where to?"

"Wherever you like, Iosif!" she rushed on. "To the ends of the world! Only right now! This moment! Please!"

There was such urgency in her voice that he couldn't help but laugh.

"But we're at the very ends of the earth right now, my sweet! This is the Arctic Circle. Have you forgotten?"

"Iosif! . . ."

"Yes, my dear?"

But she said nothing and just gazed into his eyes. Either she was actually pleading with him to run away with her, or else by her look she was trying to convey something else. But what? For perhaps the first time in his experience, a sort of veil over a woman's eyes prevented him from looking into them and feeling the pulse of her thoughts. Earlier all was so clear. But now in her voice he heard something strange—a note of torment, heart-rending and almost desperate.

"What's wrong, Natasha?" he asked again.

"Nothing really. . . ." She then relaxed, as though acknowledging defeat in the interaction of their glances. Then: "Kiss me," she said.

He bent down to her, as though she were a little fawn, helpless and in distress. Immediately he felt her hands stretch out and entwine themselves about his neck, her tender childlike lips clumsily thrust toward his chin, and the full length of her slender youthful body pressed against his own, from the lips down to her knees.

"Come, let's go home. You're frozen," he said.

"I don't want to go back there," she said. "Not there! Let's go away from here, Iosif!"

"And where on earth can we go to, silly?"

They kissed until their limbs went weak. Then, almost forcing her, he took her by the hand and led her back to the hotel. It was midnight. The hotel resonated with waves of mighty Siberian snoring and with the aromas of alcohol and strong tobacco. Tiptoeing past the sleeping hotel manageress, they made their way up to the second floor, and Rubinchik led Natasha to his room. But she pulled her hand away.

"There we are. Good night!"

"Wait! Where are you going?" He caught her by the elbow. "No! No! That's it!" she protested, almost in a panic. "Bye!"

In tears, she ran off down the corridor toward her room.

He remained true to his rule and made no attempt to pursue her. In any case, she was sharing a room with two other women. But he had no doubt that she would return. In all his experience, the girls he had discovered in Siberia, the Arctic, the Urals, or central Russia had never betrayed his expectations. Sometimes they came later, occasionally after a whole hour. But they always came, and of their own accord.

He opened his room, went in, lowered the blind and switched on the light. It was a standard room in a standard hotel in the Russian outback. Long and narrow like a box, it had neither a shower nor toilet, but only a chipped enamel sink. The only furniture was a narrow bunk with broken springs and a tiny table with cigarette burns, and the flimsy wallpaper was peeling away because of the steam-powered central heating.

Rubinchik left the door slightly ajar, so that in the darkened corridor a thin strip of light revealed the whereabouts of his room. He peeled off his outer garments, and settled down on top of the bed just as he was, in his vest and underpants. He lay with his hands clasped behind his head and gazed up at the ceiling, trying to calm his arousal. On the ceiling he saw stains left by champagne and stubbed-out cigarettes. Good lord, he thought, where in God's name have I landed this time? What am I doing here in no-man's-land, the Arctic Circle, in this wretched hotel with its snoring and stench of raw vodka? Back in Moscow my daughter gets called "little kike"; my wife gets beaten up in a bus; and in today's *Pravda* yet another of Igunov's pieces with its vile anti-Semitic howl reaching every corner of the country. Then Rubinchik recalled that woman in the telegraph office at Bykovo Airport. It was clear that these articles had worked people up to a state where the tiniest flare-up, the slightest incident—an isolated Jewish terrorist act, or even just a car crash caused by a Jewish driver—might well be enough to spark off a nationwide pogrom. Hadn't Hitler and Goebbels fed the Germans on exactly this kind of fodder?

Just then the door opened. It was Natasha, in bare feet and dressed only in a light cotton dressing gown. She dodged inside, immediately locked the door behind her and switched off the light. Then in the half-darkness, she dove onto the bed, discarding her gown. Immediately he felt her hot and naked body press against him, her little pliant breasts, her nipples warm and aroused, the hollow of her belly, the curve of her thighs, and her tense leg muscles.

"Natasha!" he gasped as he felt her embrace him and inhaled the milky perfume of her young body. Forgetting all else, he tenderly began planting fairy-light kisses on her lips, eyes, and neck.

But she tore herself free. "No! Quickly! I want you right now! Be quick!" she whispered furiously.

Without any invitation she dived down to his groin and with a quick movement extricated the rigid sword of life from his underpants. She covered it with rapid, moist caresses of the tongue, then drew him deep into her mouth, right down to the full depth of her little throat and beyond.

Rubinchik gasped. Never had he experienced such an immediate, rapid cascade of bliss. It was as if his soul were soaring high above this world, and his body also strained upwards. But Natasha gave his body no chance to fly up to his soul. As Rubinchik lay on the bunk, she rose above him. And he had not time to say anything or even throw off his undershirt before the wonderful lightness of her pulsating body descended onto him, and despite the darkness and the needle-eye of her open gallery, she located precisely the blazing tip of his erection.

"No! Wait!" he managed to force out, trying to restrain her, and realizing that this was not at all the way to do things; she was not yet open or ready for him. "Wait a moment. . . ."

"Hush! Don't say anything! Not a thing!" she asserted. And suddenly he felt her minute aperture open out its moist and tremulous lips, pressing down on him with the full weight of her body, and admitting the rod of life into the vital, hot, and vibrant passageway to some otherworldly bliss. Farther and farther, ever deeper. Heavens, half of him already! And still farther, till she had him whole. And Lord, yet further still? Yes, one more millimeter, another micron. . . .

He gasped, then ceased to breathe, or see, or hear. He forgot his mission and destiny to be the Teacher, First Man, High Priest, and Poet of Lovemaking. Because this child Natasha, this youthful snowdrop, turned out to be a High Priestess herself, and a Teacher, or whatever else one wished. More exactly, the whole of her body turned out to be a single boiling crater of passion, a fantastic instrument of ecstasy, filled like an organ with little hammers and strings which, without releasing him, began pulsating along the whole length of his rod, touching, squeezing, playing some unearthly rhythmic melody of her own.

Suddenly, though, this music was drowned out by a powerful drumming, the roar of some new ice slip or a thunderstorm.

Down from the heavenly heights Rubinchik plummeted and landed on his bunk, now realizing that someone was hammering at the door.

"Wait! Someone's knocking!" he said.

"No! Don't move!" she replied in a furious whisper, pressing against him with all her body and accelerating her gallop.

"Open up! Militia!" a voice shouted as the hammering continued.

Rubinchik started up and was about to shout that they had made a mistake, but Natasha suddenly gagged him with a strong pair of hands. Her legs locked around his thighs in a convulsive grip, her body seemed to turn into a single craving and pulsing muscle, and her mad gallop increased in fury.

"Quiet! Quiet! Quiet! Quiet!" she whispered hotly in his face in time to her thrusting.

At that moment a powerful blow shook the wall and wrenched the door from its hinges. Figures in militia uniform came bursting in, lighting the room with flashlights and a blinding flashbulb. Rubinchik was deafened by their raucous yells.

"Aha! At last!"

"The game's up, Comrade Rubinchik!"

"Come on, get up, you filthy cunt-chaser!"

"Fucking shit-ass! . . ."

Rubinchik looked from one man to the next in shock, still unable to escape from Natasha's pincerlike grip. Meanwhile someone switched on the light. Another man sat at the table and began filling in some official form. A third tried dragging Natasha off him and continued cursing:

"Get up off that bed, you bastard! That's enough fucking for tonight!

That'll do!" And he grabbed Natasha by the hair and continued shouting. "Let him go, Natasha, come on! You've had your bit of fun!"

Then it began to dawn on Rubinchik.

No, not quite everything.

One thing he could not understand—neither when they were hauling her off him, nor later on when he mentally reviewed the day's events. Why had Natasha, who evidently was nothing but a KGB slut, clung to him with her whole of her beautiful, eagerly pulsating body, and why had she wept and shouted "No! No! You promised to come in only an hour! Get out, you bastards! I love him!"

And at the top of her voice? After all, none of that was necessary for their police report.

The three militiamen eventually hauled Natasha out of the room. While she kept sobbing and swearing at them because they "promised to come only in an hour, instead of now!"

"Get dressed, citizen Rubinchik!" The speaker was a forty-year-old man dressed in a stylish foreign suit.

"Who are you?" Rubinchik asked. The man had brown eyes and a walnut visage, with a profile often seen on imperial coinage. Rubinchik immediately sensed an aura of power and authority radiating from him, and also an icy hostility.

"Oh, I do beg your pardon!" the man said with a mocking smile. "I came in without introducing myself! But never mind. Everything in its time. Right now, though, you can put your pants back on!"

twenty-two

The most unpleasant part of working in the KGB's Jewish section was that Zionist activities usually tended to peak on Saturdays. Just when normal people were resting, going out of town on fishing trips, or simply playing with their kids, the Jewish refuseniks would put on their skullcaps and gather at Moscow's only synagogue on Arkhipov Street. And not so much in the actual synagogue as on the street around it. There on the sidewalk they whispered, arranged secret gatherings, exchanged Zionist literature, swapped cassettes of Kol Israel broadcasts, and gossiped about arrests and searches carried out by the KGB. This was also where addresses were passed on to which further invitations to emigrate were to be sent.

Since Arkhipov Street was in the center of Moscow, these Saturday gatherings became an eyesore to the Party rulers, and on more than one occasion the KGB received angry phone calls demanding that the synagogue either be shut down or moved out to the suburbs. But Barsky did all he could to resist these pressures. To exile the synagogue to the city outskirts would raise yet another international row, and nothing would be gained: the Jews would simply continue gathering as before. At least on Arkhipov Street, they were easily watched, and in an apartment on the second floor of the house opposite the synagogue Barsky had long ago set up an observation post with motion picture and still cameras equipped with telephoto lenses. But what he lacked was the apparatus that made it possible to listen in on conversations on the other side of the brick wall. But only the KGB's First Directorate, which "ran" the American Embassy, had been issued with these liquid ampoule microphones. Barsky had to make do with conventional equipment and agents posing as Jews.

These agents were then on duty, standing around among the various groups gathered in front of the synagogue. Their task was simply to listen and remember. They had to hear every word and find out from the slightest chance remark when and where the Zionists were planning to pull their next dirty trick. Yet no microphone nor even a team of superagents could guarantee that Barsky and the Kremlin leaders would enjoy a quiet life. Since there were several thousand Jews—and as refuseniks, these were not stupid people—and since day and night they were scheming to pull off some new stunt against the KGB, even with his forty-eight staff agents and another hundred informers, Barsky still couldn't preempt all the escapades thought up by these Slepaks, Brodniks, Katzes, and Lyubarskys. For instance, there was no advance warning of yesterday's stunt in broad daylight on Gorky Street, when Vladimir Slepak suddenly unfurled a large handwritten placard from the balcony of his apartment saying LET MY PEOPLE GO! Of course, it hung there for only seventeen minutes, until the militia broke down his door, which Slepak had barricaded from within. But seventeen minutes had been enough for foreign journalists to come rushing there, photograph the placard, and then sound off on Voice of America and various other "voices." The correspondents had been waiting for the signal, of course, which meant that somehow or other they had been forewarned. So how had it escaped Barsky's agents? That would be the question General Sviridov would ask next Monday at one of his routine give-him-hell sessions. And what was to be expected today? Henry Kissinger was coming to Moscow allegedly on an unofficial visit. But clearly this was no innocent fishing trip. Anything at all could happen. There was some reason why all the ringleaders were here—

Brodnik, Gertsianov, Katz, and Karbovsky, waiting for Kissinger. But clearly not to join him in offering prayers to their Jewish God. They probably had some of their brazen placards up their sleeves ready to unfurl. Or else they wanted to use Kissinger to pass on another list of "oppressed" Jews to the American Congress or to President Carter. Yet even if Barsky brought in the entire Dzerzhinsky Division, he could still not prevent some Jew or other from slipping a petition into the pocket of one of Kissinger's suits, or from handing it directly to Kissinger himself during prayers in the synagogue.

Barsky suppressed his annoyance and walked away from the window. But the secret cause of his fury, he knew, was not Kissinger, but the unforeseen collapse of Operation Virgin. It was to have radically changed world sympathy for the "oppressed" Soviet Jews. And back in June, when Barsky finally apprehended Rubinchik in Salekhard, everything seemed set for a brilliant conclusion to the affair. The debauchery of journalist Rubin, corrupter of Russian virgins, had been documented in photographs and in militia records in the presence of witnesses; and two days prior his wife, Nelya, had resigned from the Conservatory and secured a work reference for her application to leave for Israel. Nothing seemed to stand in the way of the Rubinchiks' applying to leave the country. And Barsky's next strategy had been thought through and prepared: all Rubinchik's victims would be summoned to Moscow; the Prosecutor's Office and Igunov would swing into action. And in Rubinchik's public trial, which was planned to arouse a worldwide sensation, the crowning touch would be Anna Sigal.

It was Anna who'd become the object of Barsky's dreams and deepening infatuation ever since he finally broke her down in the Armenia restaurant. Ah, the sweetness of that conquest! Quite different from merely following her and Rappoport from some KGB monitoring van and sitting in torment under Rappoport's window, imagining the two of them in bed together. In more sober moments, Barsky realized he was behaving like a dog in heat, aroused by other animals' mating. But he was powerless to suppress his obsession with Anna. Of course, he never interrupted her affair with Rappoport, although he could have. One phone call would have sufficed to have her removed as his attorney. However, so as to pull off the Frontier Million operation, Barsky had held himself in check, suppressing his jealous lust with casual encounters or—more frequently—by taking a five-mile jog and a cold shower before turning in.

But after Rappoport fled, leaving nothing but the ashes of his dollars, Barsky swore he would get even. The Ministry of Communications was instructed to block Anna Sigal's domestic and work phones from all overseas calls. And the same Ministry's postal section was detailed to intercept and hand to Barsky any letters addressed to her from abroad. Next, after allowing Anna to cool down after her affair with Rappoport, Barsky began seeking ways of approaching her. He could, of course, have staged some chance meeting and then pressed his attentions on her. But what chance did he really have? He was no black-market millionaire, like Rappoport, nor a brilliant scientist like her husband, nor was he a Jew of the sort for which Anna showed such a strange preference. He was a rank-and-file KGB colonel—even though after the arrest of the Kuznetsov group and before the fiasco at Sheremetyevo he was regarded as a man of talent. But that was all. No, a mere chance meeting didn't suit Barsky, even if it led to some banal affair. He was, after all, descended from a noble family, the son of a Stalin Prize winner, and he was going to get more than the leftovers from someone else's table.

Within his injured soul he nurtured truly grandiose designs, all meant as a fitting comeback to that Rappoport with his three p's who had run rings around the KGB as easily as Kasparov trounced Karpov. But Barsky knew how to survive being punched and to come back fighting, and he was going to prove it to the KGB and to the whole of Moscow. Anna Sigal, the one-time mistress of Jewish titan Rappoport, was going to become Barsky's own mistress and a KGB informant; and on top of that, she was going to be public prosecutor at the trial of that Jewish Tartuffe Rubinchik—and it was going to be aired on TV all around the world!

And at that point—no earlier, no later—Barsky was going to place a direct call to Boston. It was there that Rappoport now lived and from where he kept showering Anna with love letters so stimulating that even a corpse would have been fired with passion. And Barsky would say to him in a benevolent voice, "Mr. Rappoport? Rappoport with three letter p's, right? This is KGB Colonel Oleg Barsky. Do you remember me? We met at the Sheremetyevo Customs on June seventeen last year. You recall? Well, now open up a copy of your *New York* fucking *Times*. Do you see the photo of that woman, the prosecutor in the Rubinchik case? As far as I recall, you refer to her in your letters as 'my one and only love.' Is that right? Well now, just switch on your little kike imagination and prick up your ears. Because tonight I'll be fucking her!"

After which he would hang up. And even if the KGB fired him for mouthing off like that, too bad! It would, at least, be the best possible Russian-style conclusion to the Jewish legend of Rappoport with his three p's! For that, it was well worth the months of searching for this fail-safe strategem—all starting with a seemingly banal denunciation of a minor journalist. It was well worth scouring all of Siberia to find the victims of this love-kike, and even worth stooping to plant that little tart Natasha on Rubinchik. To Barsky it was also worthwhile risking everything with Andropov in serving up Anna Sigal instead of some simple Russian female attorney from the provinces!

But now, just when everything was laid out for the final onslaught, the animal refused to emerge from his lair! Rubinchik neither handed in his resignation at work, nor did he apply for permission to emigrate! And without these, Andropov had decided, Rubinchik could not be touched. Thus, the whole operation that had moved along with such elegance and speed, now came to a halt. The whole affair had been blown to hell, and Barsky was up shit's creek!

Barsky realized where he had gone wrong. Rubinchik had been terrified by the incident at Salekhard. But unlike those other slippery Jews who had an investigation hanging over them, he had not gone rushing off to the Visa Office. Nor did he do what any normal journalist of his level would have done—try and use his contacts to have the whole business swept under the rug. Instead, Rubinchik had simply gone on the bottle! And he drank the way people do in Russia—instead of turning up for work, each morning he went off to the beer bar in Sokolniki Park and got tanked in the company of a mix of alcoholics and other flotsam and jetsam. Then, toward evening he would go on the subway to the Journalists' Club on Suvorovsky Boulevard. There he would beg a ruble apiece from various friends (after all, he was known to the whole profession in Moscow), and then proceed to reduce himself to an inebriated stupor.

When the first reports reached Barsky that Rubinchik had taken to the bottle, he was inclined to dismiss them—after all, there weren't any Jewish drunks! It was only after a team of observers confirmed Rubinchik's daily drinking bouts that Barsky got alarmed: damn it, would the man they were about to charge turn out to be nothing more than a dipsomaniac?

Beside himself, Barsky ordered three raids on the Sokolniki beer bar, and each time Rubinchik was picked up and hauled off to the cooler along with various other froth-blowers. There, doctors pumped his stomach, put him through various unpleasant blood tests for alcoholism, and sobered him up with a freezing shower followed by the ordeal of a literal "night on the tiles" in a prison cell. After that, they called Rubinchik's wife, made her pay a fine and come take him home. On the fourth such occasion, Barsky watched from a parked car as Rubinchik came out of the jail. It was then, from Rubinchik's triumphant gesture as he unfurled the warrant confirming his detention at a sobering station, that Barsky realized the game this scoundrel was playing with him. By drinking himself silly Rubinchik was managing to evade his wife's demands that they apply to leave the country. And by ordering his arrests and detention, Barsky, it seemed, had been aiding and abetting Rubinchik's tricks!

Caught red-handed and with the sword of Damocles hanging over him, this vile, lecherous little love-kike still was unwilling to get out of Russia! It was unthinkable. It defied all logic. The man's wife had now been mauled three times in the street by anti-Semitic hooligans (though without any actual violence); his children had been branded "little kikes" at their nursery school; yet there he was, still clinging to his Soviet citizenship!

It took Barsky three sleepless nights before he came up with an explanation. First, ever since they settled in Kiev under Prince Igor, the Jews for nearly a thousand years had held onto Russia for all they were worth. And none of Khmelnitsky's witch-hunts in the seventeenth century, nor the notorious pogroms in Ukraine and Belorussia at the turn of the century had succeeded in removing them from Russia. It was almost as if they had a honey-sweet existence here!

Secondly, there was the problem of what Rubinchik would do in the West. Of what use was a journalist who could speak and write only Russian? And—most important—over there he would never find such a profusion of teenage beauties stupid enough to jump into bed with him for God-knows-what reason and protest that they loved him, like that little tart Natasha!

So now how could he force Rubinchik into deciding to emigrate? The scoundrel had been plastered for three weeks, and Barsky didn't have the nerve to report to Andropov that Operation Virgin had failed. That would be a disaster, the ruin of his career!

"Comrade Colonel! Oleg Dmitryevich!" Captain Zartsev called excitedly. He had been watching the Jews outside the synagogue through his telescope.

"What is it? Has Kissinger arrived?"

"No, even better! Come over here! Please, hurry, Comrade Colonel! Look!" Zartsev moved aside to let Barsky look through the telescope. It was trained not on the doors of the synagogue just opposite; instead Zartsev had aimed it toward the southern side of the humpbacked roadway.

"What else is there to see?" Barsky asked limply and put his eye to the lens.

Used as he was to Jewish tricks, even Barsky was amazed. Coming down the street toward the synagogue was a thickset individual wearing a dark suit with a white shirt and necktie. The man moved along with a sober, deliberate, and purposeful stride. It was Iosif Rubinchik.

twenty-three

Where do people go for help when there is no help?

Who do they turn to for advice, when there is no one to advise them? They turn to God.

No matter whether we are atheists, agnostics, or criminals, it's all the same. And when there is utterly nowhere for us to go, we go to church, or to the mosque or the synagogue. We turn to our priest, our mullah, or our rabbi.

Iosif Rubinchik, who so astounded Barsky by his appearance on Arkhipov Street that Saturday morning, had been a confirmed atheist since his orphanage days. But now he no longer had the strength nor the money to buy booze; the mere sight of vodka made him retch; and worst of all, he could no longer bear the looks of surprise and fear in his children's eyes whenever he dragged himself home, dirty, unshaven, stinking drunk.

"Daddy," they asked anxiously, "what's the matter with you? Are you sick?"

But he never answered. He simply rolled onto the folding bed that Nelya had put up for him and collapsed into a sleep that was like some deep, foul, stagnant pool. And just before he sank into the depths he would hear Nelya tell the children, "Don't touch him! Go to sleep!"

Nelya had not talked to him since the day he returned from Salekhard and confessed to his secret vice. This, he alleged, consisted of "drinking orgies" whenever he was away on assignments. He also maintained that while he was potted in Salekhard, some whore had got into his hotel room, and a moment later the militia had burst in and charged him with immoral behavior. Of course, there would be repercussions at his job, and if they now applied to emigrate, there would be complications with the Visa Office.

Nelya was skeptical. She figured that he had gone off on the trip and made up the whole filthy story in a last-ditch effort to delay their leaving Russia. And she despised him for his cowardice at the prospect of starting life all over again in the West. But Nelya was also afraid, and she felt incapable of divorcing him as she had once threatened, and of leaving without him. Besides which, even if a father was an alcoholic or a criminal doing time, no one could take his children abroad without his permission.

Rubinchik knew all this. And in his secret battle with the KGB he kept putting off the decisive moment when he had to step into the ring. For the time being he simply practiced with a series of arrests and visits to the cooler, almost like a sportsman psyching himself up for a big match.

In this particular competition, Rubinchik's prowess would rest precisely on his most vulnerable point—his dependence on alcohol. He was unaware of Barsky's plans on his behalf. But he did know better than anyone—better even than Barsky—the whereabouts and the number of little "love beacons" he had lit up across the Soviet map. And, in his uncertainty, he saw danger everywhere. In Salekhard, after he had signed the police report, Rubinchik was left on his own and he had done some hard thinking. Something inside him—some basic animal instinct—told him that the flat almond face of the man in the expensive foreign suit posed a terrible threat to him. Yet who was he? The head of the local militia? The head of the Salekhard KGB? He had not arrested Rubinchik, nor had he made him sign any undertaking to remain in the country. All the same, that break-in to his room was no routine raid by a workers' "moral vigilante" patrol. After all, whoever it was had already tried palming off that Natasha girl on him in Kiev! But why? What were they up to? What did they want from him? And who were "they"? The KGB? Were those the KGB agents who were trailing him all that time back in Yakutia?

Terror-stricken, Rubinchik couldn't sleep or even remain alone in his room. He looked cautiously out the window. There was no sign of any militia cars, the nightbound street was empty, and a milky glow came from the unsetting Arctic sun. He went to the door and opened it slightly. The corridor too was empty, and the whole hotel rumbled with Siberian snoring. He got dressed and a moment later walked out of the hotel. A watery sun flowed along the horizon like a broken egg yolk. It spread a deathly flat light over the wooden sidewalks, over the roadway roughened into ridges by the caterpillar tracks of cross-country vehicles, and the long, low houses sunk waist-deep in dirty snowdrifts that had fossilized over the winter. In the yards behind, reindeer slept, and there were poles jutting up with turned-out dog-skins, hung out to air before being made into boots.

Without knowing where he was going, Rubinchik set off toward the Ob and the restaurant. A herd of gaunt, blue-eyed stray dogs resembling wolves came toward him. They sniffed at his pockets, like a gang of street raiders, but not scenting anything edible they trotted away. The Ocean Wave was closed. Another herd of homeless Siberian huskies lay sleeping by the entrance, guarding their territory from other canine intruders and waiting for morning and the arrival of the chefs. Rubinchik was about to turn back. At the squeak of his steps, however, a gray mound of snow suddenly shifted, and Rubinchik saw it was no snowdrift but a line of reindeer asleep on the ground. From the center of the mound a human figure looked up, wearing a reindeer jacket and thick hood.

"You wanta drinka?" the hood asked in a soft Nenets accent.

"Yes, me wanta drinka," Rubinchik admitted.

"But you has Russian passport?"

"Yes . . ."

"And you has moneys?"

"Yes. What have you got? Vodka?" Rubinchik was suspicious.

"I not has own vodka," the Nenets said as he scrambled out of the heap of reindeer. "We go shop. We go waken up Svetka. You show Russian passport. You buys vodka, but you give bitta vodka to Nenets Sanko too."

Rubinchik now realized what business this man was in. One of Stalin's strokes of genius had been to devise an internal passport system. But no Soviet eskimo people—the Nenets, the Khanty, Chukchi, and Mari—and in fact none of the country's rural populace were allowed passports or any other ID. They were kept on their collective farms or other places of residence. Without an ID nobody could travel, get a hotel room, rent living space, or even buy an air ticket. And even before the Revolution, the Nenets had been turned into hopeless drunks by the Russian merchants who bought up bundles of mink and sable skins from them for next to nothing—for a bottle of vodka. And so the Soviets invented a way of preserving this tribe that was dying out from alcoholism, tuberculosis, and syphilis: shops were not permitted to sell them any strong drink, including eau de cologne and methylated spirits.

But by sleeping close to the restaurant and bringing the salesgirl Svetka thirsty nocturnal customers, Sanko had devised a way around the law. Ten minutes later, after paying double the price, Rubinchik held in his hands a half-liter bottle of spirits and a snack, two pickled cucumbers and a hunk of liverwurst.

Oh, the searing and benumbing power of alcohol! Healing every pain, fear, suffering, and sorrow and a sense of I-don't-give-a-damn. Inspiring men to tears of repentance, insane sacrifice, thoughtless murder, and easy acceptance of death. Only a soul oppressed by suffering can understand the healing blessing that alcohol can bestow!

That night Rubinchik the Jew and Sanko the Nenets communed in fathoming the essence of existence and the freedom that comes from telling the whole of creation to go fuck itself. They woke up Svetka three more times that night, and shared generous portions of liverwurst with the stray dogs. And after they'd spent all of Rubinchik's travel allowance, the two of them fell asleep against the warm flanks of Sanko's reindeer.

The following morning, at the airport, the two of them drank up the dregs of their fourth bottle, and Sanko presented Rubinchik with a farewell gift, which he claimed was made from the bone of a walrus's penis, after which Rubinchik boarded his plane. By good fortune he didn't know any of the stewardesses and made a safe return to Moscow.

With Sanko's help, Rubinchik had discovered a means of liberation from Soviet rule, the militia, the KGB, and the much-vaunted wise policies of the Communist Party. Now his defense against any accusations of immorality would rest on that simple excuse so hallowed in Russia—drunkenness. Indeed, all of Salekhard had seen how on his first three days there he had done no work, conducted no interviews, and wrote not a line in his notebooks. He had done nothing but drink. And on the fourth day, by which time he was pie-eyed, shot to hell, and in an alcoholic stupor, if he really had screwed some stewardess, what claim could be made against him if he was nothing but a down-and-out drunkard? And his previous escapades—if they were known to the KGB—could be ascribed to his alcoholic vice. And the fact that he was a pathological drunk was now confirmed by reports from an official Moscow rehab station.

So it was that alcoholism, which until recently had aroused in Rubinchik nothing but contempt, now struck him as a brilliant invention of the Russian nation. It could be used to write off and explain absolutely anything—Prince Oleg's stupid campaign against Constantinople, the collective orgies at the Ityl bazaar, centuries of isolation from world civilization, the drunken escapades of Peter the Great, the murder of the Emperor Paul, the explosion on board a nuclear submarine, the death of Yury Gagarin, anti-Semitic hooliganism in the streets—indeed absolutely anything! And neither tsars nor the Communist Party had managed to deprive the Russian people of this privileged indulgence.

But Rubinchik was not a native Russian, and he couldn't drink forever without stopping. Sooner or later, he had to end his debauch, and he did so on that Saturday morning of July 8, 1978.

And as he emerged from his alcoholic haze, he turned to the ultimate source of refuge, his Jewish God. More precisely, he went off to see the rabbi.

When he awoke that morning, he found neither his wife nor children at home. There was no money in the house and no note from Nelya, either. But he was not alarmed—this was not the first time in the last month that Nelya had left and gone to stay with her parents, pointedly leaving behind her a mountain of unwashed dishes, unmade beds, and general disorder.

Rubinchik gazed for a long time in the bathroom mirror at his crumpled, unshaven features, the bags under his eyes, the white layer on his tongue, and the collapsed muscles of his shoulders. Then he spent a long time cleaning his teeth, gargled, shaved, took a cold shower, and rubbed himself down with a thick towel. Then he took another critical look at himself in the mirror.

After that he brewed some tea, lit a cigarette, but then stubbed it out and took the remainder of the pack to the bathroom, crumbled the tobacco into the toilet, and flushed it.

Satisfied with this decisive start, he then knocked back the remains of a bottle of yogurt he found in the otherwise almost empty fridge and washed it down with tea. Returning to the bed-cum-living room he took out his one and only anthracite-gray dacron suit, a white nylon shirt, clean socks, and a necktie. After dressing, he then went back to the bathroom for one more self-examination in the mirror.

Of course, he now looked better than an hour ago, and this raised his spirits. He foraged in the bottom drawer of the desk and found his spare keys to the garage (his main set had long ago been hidden away by Nelya). Then he put his driver's license and Journalists' Union ID in his pocket and left. The patch of wasteland was turning green in the warmth of June as he crossed it and made his way toward the cooperative garage that stood among rows of wooden, brick, and sheet-metal sheds, all with gigantic locks on their doors.

As he reached his garage, the noise of a train on the line from Moscow caught up with him. The clatter of its wheels on the nearby track and the long-drawn wail of its siren struck him as a good omen. As usual on a Saturday, various of his garage neighbors lay underneath their Moskviches, Zaporozhets, and Zhiguli sedans, changing oil, or applying antirust sealant. At Rubinchik's approach they all respectfully emerged from under their chariots and waved greasy paws to salute and welcome him back from his alcoholic excursion, as if he were an astronaut back from outer space.

"Well, old man, that was some binge!"

"Welcome to the club! But you know, I can't keep that up for more than a week these days. Goddamned liver won't take it!"

"Just look at him! The guy was soaked for a whole month, and he still looks fresh as a daisy! And they say Jews can't drink! You're a tought nut! Anyway, Iosif, don't get mad, that was meant as a compliment!"

Rubinchik wasn't offended. He felt a sense of triumph at the success of his scheme. He acknowledged their congratulations with a modest nod. Then he opened up his garage, sat in his old gray Moskvich and at the third attempt managed to get it started. He picked up his cap from the passenger's seat and put it on to shield his eyes from the sun, and the neighbors all waved him off.

Moscow's vistas opened out to greet him. The summer streets were half-empty because it was Saturday. They had been rinsed by an overnight shower and were also sluiced clean by city sanitation trucks. Everything seemed familiar and dear. Rubinchik knew every pothole in the road, every traffic light, and also every speed trap. He switched on the radio, and either in honor of Kissinger's visit or else as a piece of Saturday mischief by the youth radio station, the air was suddenly filled with some rhythmic Beatles song.

As Rubinchik drove, he was aware that with his four detentions he had scored a victory over the KGB. What could they charge him with now? Interfering with a stewardess? But it was she who had come to his hotel room! And his previous conquests? But who had seen them? Where were they? It had been a mistake to panic and admit to Nelya what had happened in Salekhard. His so-called crime had still not been reported to his boss. Otherwise his friends at the *Labor Gazette* would have told him, on one of his visits to the Journalists' Club.

No, old boy, everything is okay. Everything's fine, he kept reassuring himself as he drove. Life had its black-and-white patches—like a zebra—and its ups and downs—like a ride on a roller coaster. And right now he was coming up out of a dark valley and heading for the sunny heights. That was all. The main thing was to put himself in a positive frame of mind, and set his mind on winning. Of course, he desperately wanted a smoke, and he could have done with a morning snifter too—his stomach was gripped with longing for a drink. But he was not going to give in. He'd manage without. And tomorrow he would start jogging again, he'd take the kids to the zoo. Tonight he'd give Nelya such a night that she'd forgive and forget. Okay, he'd wandered off the straight and narrow. And, yes, in a drunken moment he'd fallen for the advances of some whorish little flight attendant. But who doesn't go off the rails sometimes? And what's more, he hadn't got anywhere with the girl because of the militia. And as for his drinking, well, he'd already signed on to get himself dried out, and he was ready to take his medicine. Nelya would forgive him all right. She'd do that for the kids' sake. And anyway, she couldn't leave the country on her own with just the children!

Rubinchik veered off Manezh Square onto Karl Marx Prospect, drove across Sverdlov Square—dedicated to the first chairman of the Council of Peoples' Commissars—past the granite memorial to Karl Marx, past the Bolshoi Theater and Metropole Hotel, eventually reaching the top of the rise and emerging on Dzerzhinsky Square. Here, though, at the sight of the giant gray statue of Iron Felix, the founding father of the KGB, and the massive headquarters of that organization looming behind it, his courage and jaunty confidence evaporated like a child's punctured balloon. Of course, for someone like Sanko, settling down to sleep with his reindeer in the frost, it was easy not to give a flying fuck about anything, including the KGB. But as a trained historian, Rubinchik knew well the power of the secret police. Not only at his paper, but at *Pravda* too, and even in the Central Committee building, staff members were afraid to open their mouths anywhere near a telephone. Everyone knew they were bugged and served as the ears of the all-powerful Andropov. George Orwell, in his famous novel, created a system of total scrutiny in a tiny country like England and only in 1984. But the KGB had made this awful fantasy come true over the whole Soviet Union, and a good ten years earlier! Here a person could get three to five years in the Gulag merely for listening to a reading of Orwell's novel on Voice of America or the BBC.

Like every other driver who had to cross Dzerzhinsky Square, Rubinchik shuddered and reduced his speed to ten kilometers less than the limit. Then, under the eyes of the brawny sentries guarding the Committee building on Old Square, he made his way carefully along Kitaisky Passage to Nogin Square, and five minutes after that turned off into the short, humpbacked lane that bore the name of General Arkhipov.

Rubinchik parked his car a hundred yards from the synagogue and looked in surprise at the crowd gathered there. Not only had he not expected to see such a crowd, but here, for the first time in his life, he found himself looking at a gathering of self-avowed Jews. He had grown up in a Russian orphanage, had a Russian schooling, served in the Russian Army, studied at a Russian institute, worked for a Russian paper, had traveled the length and breadth of the country, and lived all thirty-seven years of his life in an all-Russian milieu. Like others of his kind, he had learned not exactly to conceal, but certainly not to advertise his Jewish origins. And now, in the Russian capital, a mere stone's throw from Dzerzhinsky Square, here was this crowd of a hundred or more men, provocatively bearded and side-locked and wearing long-hemmed jackets and skull caps. And even the nonreligious ones— the men and youths without beards—deliberately wore their shirts open to display glinting gold chains with the six-pointed star. And women too. And children. And the language they spoke . . . what was it? Heavens, was that Hebrew they were talking? People talking Hebrew openly on the street, here in Moscow!

Rubinchik could not grasp how he could ever be at one with *these* Jews. But at the same time he no longer felt like a lone swimmer in the ocean, engaged in solitary combat against the whole might and force of the Soviet Union. He now sensed he was among his own people, in the company of friends and allies. He made his way through the crowd toward the door of the synagogue. At that point he was stopped by a small red-bearded Jew wearing a long lapserdak coat with a white fringe hanging from inside his jacket, and thin leather thongs wrapped around his hands.

"*A yid?*" the man asked.

To his joy, Rubinchik suddenly realized that he knew the word. But he didn't know the Hebrew for yes, and therefore simply nodded expansively, as he did to the doorman at his office, and walked into the synagogue.

To his surprise there were far fewer people inside than on the street. In the center of the large hall stood about forty men. Their heads rocked fervently back and forth like a set of woodpeckers, and they gently muttered a guttural prayer.

Rubinchik respectfully took off his cap and gazed into the depths of the hall. Facing the group stood a tall, dark-haired, bespectacled rabbi with a white tasseled prayer shawl over his dark suit. To Rubinchik's surprise, the rabbi was young, not more than forty. He recited the prayer aloud with his eyes closed, and also rocked. But periodically he would open his eyes and without interrupting his recitative would cast a sharp glance at the doors.

Praying next to the rabbi and also facing the worshippers stood two bewhiskered Jews of giant stature. They too wore white prayer shawls and had a Georgian or Armenian appearance. Set into the wall behind their backs was a tall glass cabinet with doors decorated with stained glass behind which white scrolls could be seen, and a thick book lying on a cushion.

The elderly Jew standing close to Rubinchik bore a surprising resemblance to the famous actor Gertsianov. Rubinchik wondered why the man kept glancing at him with an accusing stare. He inspected himself. No, everything was as it should be—he had respectfully removed his cap, just as one should in church. Okay, he would simply take no notice.

The murmured prayer continued, and Rubinchik thought with horror that he would never manage to learn this language. But then he reassured himself—he had no need of it: he was not going to be praying, neither here, nor over there.

Rubinchik began studying the young rabbi. Was he a KGB agent or not? From his journalist's vantage point Rubinchik understood well the secret workings of the ideological apparatus, that the priest of every Russian church was granted his parish by agreement with the Religious Affairs Directorate. And that was only a label. In reality that whole department was staffed by the KGB, and not a single priest, including the Patriarch of All Russia himself, could occupy his post without some form of collaboration. Not even Orwell had imagined such control over the soul. So maybe a rabbi was also planted as a KGB informer?

Suddenly the rabbi raised his voice and continued in Russian, "Since our honored guest has been delayed, we are granting the honor of carrying out the Torah to our Georgian brothers Irakly and David Katashvili. They have each contributed two thousand rubles to our synagogue. So I call upon you, Irakly and David!"

The rabbi opened the ark and with the words "Vayehi binsoa haaron, vayomer moshe . . ." He picked up a torah scroll in a white silk cover with gold embroidery and handed it to one of the two Georgians. He gripped it with his mighty gold-ringed fingers and carefully raised it and began carrying it round the crowd of worshippers, his brother and the rabbi following behind, chanting.

Now, as the rabbi came close, Rubinchik saw he had an elongated, Christlike face, a small beard, and large, slightly protruding eyes with a benign and faintly jovial expression.

Meanwhile, everyone the Georgians passed kissed the Torah's silken cover or touched it with the white tassels on their prayer shawls. But when the scroll reached Rubinchik and he tried to kiss it, the Georgian abruptly bypassed him, not letting him touch it. Rubinchik, however, did not take offense. God knows, he thought, maybe they had a rule that only those who had contributed money to the synagogue were allowed to kiss the Torah.

After the Torah reading and another hour of prayers, the worshipers began moving around and talking among themselves. Rubinchik realized their service was now over, and he was about to make his way through the throng to the rabbi, when the clergyman raised a hand and began speaking in Russian:

"Brothers! Before we all go on our way, I want to remind you that when the Lord gave the Torah to Moses, he commanded us to *celebrate* the sabbath. So, no matter what's happened the six days before, we should enjoy life's pleasures, sing, make merry, eat good food, and drink good wine. God has given his people fifty-two shots of optimism, which strengthen us to cope with the bad stuff of the coming week! And in addition, we have another dozen reasons to be joyful: Purim, Hanukkah, Pesach, Simkhat Torah, and so on. What other people has so many celebrations of life? Scores of tyrants have taken away our money, our homes, our cattle, our land, our right to wear Jewish clothes, publish our books, speak in our own language, and teach it to our children. And they could not understand why, when we'd lost everything, we still remained Jews. But the answer is simple: a man who rejoices in life even once a week cannot be destroyed! And a whole race even more so. Just think: could we have survived through the ages if we were always gloomy, malicious, and lived in filth, immorality, and envy? And what sort of people other than monsters could be conceived in an atmosphere of anger and aggression? For Jews, even the intimate moment when a new life is conceived is a feast consecrated by God. That is why we give birth not to murderers and Hitlers, but we produce Einsteins, Chagalls, and Gershwins."

Heavens, Rubinchik thought in amazement, wasn't that exactly what he always told his Russian divas: copulation is a feast, a gift of God! And that was why he always stemmed their impatience, switched on the light, and offered them wine or champagne—in order to sanctify that moment, turn it into a feast. . . .

"And as long as we continue to celebrate the gift of life," the rabbi continued, "and to thank our Creator, if only on the sabbath, then we shall remain Jews—no matter what!" And with that he suddenly began beating out a rhythmic motif with his hands on the podium rail, like at a pop concert, and started singing.

The entire company took up the chant and began swaying and clapping their hands in time to it. Rubinchik understood not a word, but he too felt his body pulse and move to its rhythm.

The young rabbi completed his song in Russian, then said, "That's all, my brothers! I wish you a happy holiday! *Gut shabes!*" With that he turned and headed toward an inner door behind the Torah cabinet.

Rubinchik hastened after him.

"Excuse me, please!"

The rabbi turned and looked at Rubinchik over the top of his glasses. In his slightly protruding dark eyes there was a spark of jollity, and something else that Rubinchik recognized and felt was almost familiar. Rubinchik came straight to the point:

"I'm getting ready to emigrate, and I'd like to read something about Israel. The thing is that I . . ."

Suddenly the rabbi who had been so warm, stepped back and threw up his hands.

"How dare you! You want to incriminate me?" he shouted. "We don't deal with such matters here!"

"No, you don't understand!" Rubinchik was taken aback. "I honestly mean that. I simply don't have any information on Israel though, but I—"

"Get out of here! Out!" the rabbi shouted again and with exaggerated theatrical wrath pointed toward the door.

"Hang on! Wait a minute!" Rubinchik pleaded, "The thing is that I have another sort of problem. With the KGB. And I wanted—"

At this point the two Georgian Jewish giants seized him by the elbows and began moving him toward the door. Their voices were quiet but menacing.

"Get out of here! Get out! You're an agent provocateur!"

"No! I'm a Jew. I swear it!" Rubinchik insisted, struggling to turn and address the rabbi. "My name's Rubinchik! I'm a Jew!"

Never before had Rubinchik shouted out his name in the hope that this might help him. On the contrary, he'd always felt awkward about it and even signed his articles Rubin, the Russified shortened form.

"Quiet!" the two giants spat, lifting him by the elbows and carrying him toward the exit. "Or we'll circumcise you and really make you into a Jew!"

"But I am circumcised! Do you want to see it?" Rubinchik said furiously.

But by now the mighty brothers had flung him out onto the street—followed by his cap, which he'd dropped.

The entire crowd gathered in front of the entrance turned and stared at him with silent contempt. One—a shaggy-maned young man who looked like a hippy and carried a guitar—struck a mocking arpeggio as Rubinchik was flung out and landed on all fours.

But Rubinchik was in no mood to give up. He jumped quickly to his feet, like he'd always done in fistfights at the orphanage. He looked around at all the Yids. Fuck the lot of you! You're all Jews, and so am I! You want to get out of here, and so do I! And so what if the rabbi doesn't believe me! Maybe he shouldn't! Who knows how many of you are KGB agents! Well, Rubinchik would show them he was no spy. His ID, under Nationality it said Jew. Shouldn't that help him at a place like this?

"*A yid?*" asked a voice right next to him.

"Yes, *a yid!*" he answered truculently.

"What did they call your father?"

"I don't know. I'm an orphan."

"What about your mother?"

"I told you. I don't know. They were all killed in the war."

"Keep your voice down! Are you circumcised?"

"Do I have to show you?"

"No, keep it to yourself. Do you want to put on tefillin?"

"What's that?"

The red-bearded man didn't explain. From the pockets in his overcoat, he pulled out some fine black leather straps to which a tiny black box was attached. He laid the little box on Rubinchik's forehead, and with his left hand wound the straps about his head. As he did so he shook his head in sorrow.

"What sort of Jew is it who drives his car on the sabbath? And to the synagogue! And takes his cap off inside the synagogue! Oy-oy-oy! You've forgotten everything!"

Only then did it dawn on Rubinchik why he had been taken for an agent provocateur.

"Repeat after me!" the red-beard ordered him. "Baruch ataw . . ."

"But I need information about Israel," Rubinchik interrupted. "And I need someone to give me a whole lot of advice."

"Quiet. Don't shout. We'll give you everything you need. Books, and advice. But now just repeat after me. Baruch ataw adonai."

"Baruch ataw adonai." Rubinchik repeated, struggling with the unfamiliar sounds.

"Leanikh tefillin."

"Leanikh tefillin," he echoed.

The others stood around and watched the two of them.

"Shema Yisrael!"

Rubinchik met their glances, filled his lungs, and exhaled assertively.

"Shema Yisrael!" he proclaimed.

"No need to shout!" the man said in Russian. "He can hear you anyway. Speak calmly: 'Adonai Elohainu, Adonai Ekhad!'"

"Adonai Elohainu, Adonai Ekhad," Rubinchik repeated, amazed at himself. It seemed to him as if sometime, long, long ago, he had spoken these words. But where? When?

The hippy guitarist and a little woman with gray hair nodded their heads approvingly.

Meanwhile, on the opposite side of the Street, Barsky stood with his eye glued to the telescope and smiled. The ice had broken, things were going as planned, and his soul was singing. Rubinchik had evidently emerged from his binge and was now joining the most desperate set of Jewish activists—Karbovsky, Brodnik, Gertsianov, and others. With his Zenith camera and a telescopic lens, Captain Zartsev had zealously recorded all this on film.

Even had he tried, Rubinchik could hardly have presented the KGB with a better gift.

twenty-four

Where are we going?" her father asked nervously.

"Don't get excited. You'll find out right away," Anna said as she raced her car along the Danilov Embankment toward Avtozavodskaya Street. It was evening, and a breeze from the river cooled the road that had basked all day in the sun. Above the old houses built in the 1930s, neon signs glowed, FORWARD TO THE VICTORY OF COMMUNISM! At the Ulan Batur movie theater people were lining up to see the newly released *Slave of Love*.

"Where are you taking me?" her father asked again.

"Don't you recognize where we are?" Anna had pulled up by an elm tree whose trunk had split with age. They were standing in front of a large four-story apartment house. Lights shone in the open windows, and people were sitting out on their balconies drinking tea and beer and watching television. Below, next to the children's sandbox, some old-timers were sitting on a bench and playing dominoes.

"Why have we come here?" her father asked.

"Come on!" Anna ordered.

He made no movement.

Anna got out, walked around and opened the door on his side.

"Get out!"

"Why?"

She grabbed him by his sleeve and pulled him out.

"Have you gone crazy or something?" He jerked his arm free and looked at the old men on the bench. "Why should I go in there?"

"Because!" Anna said. "This man denounced you. Now you're going to confront him! Which floor did you live on?"

"Anna, this is stupid! That was forty years ago! More than that!"

"You mean you've never been back here?" She had to all but drag him toward the entrance. "Why? You were released twenty-five years ago!"

"But they're probably gone."

"No, they're not. I called up the House Commission. Come on, straighten up, Colonel!" She led him inside.

There was no elevator. The stair was lit by a dim lamp on the ground floor; the second-story landing was dark, and the sound of smooching could be heard. A young man was holding a buxom girl pressed against the wall in a long, drawn-out kiss. As Anna and her father appeared, the girl wrenched herself free and ran past them down the stairs with clacking heels.

Anna's father looked after her, amazed.

"Riva?!" He spoke the name without thinking.

The girl, who was about fifteen, stopped just below. She too was surprised.

"Is it me you want?"

"No," he became embarrassed. "I made a mistake . . ."

"You bet!" said the young man as he walked past them. "That's what they call her grandma!"

The door banged, and the young man and his girl dashed out laughing.

"And you thought they'd moved. Come on!"

But Anna's father shook his head.

"Why?" she asked.

"Let's get out of here." He turned to go down, but she intercepted him.

"Wait. Hang on. It was that girl's grandfather who condemned you, right?"

"I don't know. Come on, let's go."

"Grandma!" They heard the girl's voice calling from below. "Granny, you've got guests! Put on the light for them!"

"Too late, Comrade Colonel!" Anna laughed to her father. And then the light came on on the second-floor landing, and an apartment door opened. Framed in the brightly lit entrance stood a tall sixty-year-old woman who resembled the girl they had just seen.

"Good evening," Anna said. "Are you Riva Kogan?"

The woman didn't answer but fixed her myopic gaze on Anna's father.

"Is it you, Evgeny?" she asked in a weak and cracked voice. Anna's father said nothing, so she repeated, "Is that you, Evgeny?"

"Er . . . yes." Anna's father opened his toothless mouth and caught his breath.

"Are you still alive?"

"As you can see . . ."

"And did they . . . did they let you out a long time ago?"

"Same as everyone else. In fifty-three."

"Mamma, who's there?" a woman's voice inquired from inside.

"Nobody. No one. Only a neighbor," the elderly woman said and began to close the door.

"Wait!" Anna pushed back on the door. "I don't understand. We wanted to talk to Semyon Markovich Kogan. He wrote a letter denouncing my father!"

"Semyon was killed in 1943," the woman said. Then she gave Anna's father a bitter laugh. "Well, thank you for visiting, even after twenty-five years."

With that she closed the door.

Anna, puzzled, looked at her father.

"Dad, I don't . . ." she began. And then it dawned on her. "You had an affair with her! You slept with her! And that's why he denounced you! That's it, isn't it?"

But at that moment the light went out again. She couldn't see her father's tears. But she could hear the soft whimper of an old man.

She found him in the dark and put her arms around him.

"Right, Dad, now we really do need to go and have a drink. Come on."

twenty-five

After Rubinchik's visit to the Moscow synagogue several curious events took place.

First, after he'd repeated the Shema Yisrael, he was approached by the hippy with the guitar, a small hazel-eyed woman in her fifties, and several others. The hippy introduced himself as Ilya Karbovsky, and the woman turned out to be Inessa Brodnik, who according to *Pravda* was a "virulent Zionist," while the Voice of America referred to her as the "Mother Teresa of Soviet Jewry." They asked Rubinchik if he needed an invitation to emigrate, who was in his family, and where he hoped to go to—Israel or the United States. On hearing that he had not yet decided, and that he was "the same Rubin"—the well-known *Labor Gazette* journalist—they decided that he must come back with them to Inessa's home, where he could pick up all the information he needed.

In breach of the sabbath commandment, Brodnik, Karbovsky, and a few others squeezed into Rubinchik's car, and they headed off toward the Danilov Market, where Inessa Brodnik lived. As he drove, Rubinchik kept looking in the rearview mirror.

"Iosif, stop it!" Inessa Brodnik yelled at him. "I've been tailed by the KGB for eight years, and I've found it even has advantages. At least, I never get molested by stray hooligans!"

That little woman turned out to have the energy of an Ariel Sharon tank brigade combined with a childlike optimism. Her three-room apartment resembled the site office of a construction project in Siberia. There was a constant chatter from two typewriters and a telephone kept trilling. While in the kitchen two kettles were boiling and potatoes constantly frying in two huge skillets "for one and all." And most noticeably, every few minutes, the apartment door kept opening to let in a series of hurrying messengers from every corner of the country. And unlike the construction offices that Rubinchik knew so well, these typewriters were not rattling out reports on construction completed in record time. They were printing petitions to the United Nations, the European Parliament, President Carter, and personal pleas to Leonid Brezhnev, about the denial of rights to Soviet Jews, the arrest of Jewish activists, and also of Baptists, Seventh-day Adventists, and Catholics, and about every other Soviet breach of the Helsinki Agreement whose text had still not been published here. And three radio receivers—one in each room—were tuned to the BBC, Kol Israel, and Radio Liberty. Also, unlike the the engineers at a communist construction site, the visitors here did not burst in cursing about the shortage of spare parts or fuel oil; their first word was always *shalom*. After that, though, they did switch to Russian. And they brought news about who had been refused an exit visa, and where and why; who had managed to obtain a review of his case, and where and why; and who had been interned, together with all the whys and wherefores.

After spending a few hours in Inessa's apartment, Rubinchik understood that this information was processed here, and in each case someone made operative decisions and took practical steps. Within a few minutes of its arrival, news about visa refusals and arrests went out—carried at a sprint by some courier. Nothing was passed on by telephone, and it was all committed to memory. And a few hours later, seemingly invisibly, the news got passed to Moscow's foreign journalists, left Russia, and came bounding back over the BBC, Kol Israel, Radio Liberty, and other stations.

"You are listening to Vladimir Martin in Washington for the Voice of America. Secretary of State Cyrus Vance has canceled his visit to Moscow as a response to the trial of Anatoly Shcharansky and Alexander Ginzburg, due to begin in Moscow next Monday. Ginzburg is head of the Solzhenitsyn Fund, set up to assist the families of Soviet political prisoners. Speaking at a session of the Supreme Soviet, Prime Minister Aleksey Kosygin accused the West of unwillingness to establish normal trade relations with the Soviet Union, but he made no mention of the trials of dissidents. In Kiev, agents of the Ukrainian KGB arrested Mikhail Portnoy, a teacher of Hebrew . . ."

When such broadcasts came in, everyone in Inessa's apartment ran to the radio and listened intently to the announcer's voice, which could only be heard above the sound of Soviet jamming stations.

"According to information from Moscow," the distant Washington announcer continued, "thirty-two Jewish activists have been arrested in the USSR since the first of July. In view of this and with the imminent trial of Shcharansky and Ginzburg, the American Jewish Congress, the Jewish Defense League, and other Jewish organizations have decided to hold a mass protest tomorrow, Sunday, in front of the Soviet Embassy in Washington. . . ."

"Hurrah!" A wave of rejoicing spread around the apartment, and champagne was suddenly produced from he had no idea where. Everyone congratulated everyone else, as though tomorrow's American demonstration was totally on their behalf. Which it was.

To his surprise, Rubinchik quickly felt at home here and soon was editing petitions to the U.N., to Brezhnev, and news releases for Western radio. He was in his element again, writing and editing. Only the material was different, and here there was no censorship and no need to present the life of the country in some wrapping of upbeat phraseology. At the same time, the need for high-toned journalism was gone, along with trendy subjects, vivid dialogue, and other nuances that Rubinchik saw as his distinctive style. The petitions required plain expression and a precise selection of facts so as not to obscure the main thrust of the document. They had to be as accessible as possible for public reading or publication in any Western media.

Rubinchik realized this when Inessa asked him to help "the girls"—Raya Goldina and Zina, the wife of actor Gertsianov. The two were at the typewriters, typing a long message to the World Association of Women on conditions in a women's camp in Mordovia, where Russian, Jewish, and Tatar dissidents were being held. Contact had been established after Inessa went there and brought a parcel of provisions for the prisoners. Squatting at the kitchen table, Rubinchik took half an hour with all that Zina and Raya had written and condensed it to a third of its original length. His new text had Inessa in tears, even though all the facts were drawn from her own account and from secret letters now arriving through a channel she had set up.

"That will read beautifully over the radio," Inessa said as she continued peeling potatoes. She asked the two girls to type out a final copy with four carbons for UNESCO, Amnesty International, the Red Cross, and correspondents of the *New York Times* and *The Guardian*. Inessa had been refused permission to emigrate in 1970, and she had organized or taken part in all the major Zionist initiatives—starting with a hunger strike in the reception hall of the Supreme Soviet in 1971, and most recently with the demonstration in front of the Moscow Visa Office. And the reason the KGB had not apprehended her, Karbovsky explained to Rubinchik, was that this apartment had been visited by foreign heads of state and scores of foreign journalists. Which means, Karbovsky said, "if they send her off to a camp, there'll be a colossal uproar! Although now, after the Orlov trial, who knows what they'll do. . . ."

Toward evening, after Karbovsky had produced from a hiding place slim brochures on Israel and on the Jewish religion, printed on tissue paper, and Rubinchik was getting ready to leave, Inessa led him off into an empty room.

"So what has brought you to us?" she asked.

But Rubinchik could not have told his own mother of *all* the fears they'd raised in him, so he said simply:

"Well, about a month ago I was away from home on a trip and . . . well, the KGB found me with this woman. But I was drunk!"

"And now you're having problems with your wife?"

"How did you guess?"

"That's the first thing the KGB try to do to us—break up our families.

Because the whole secret of Jewish survival in the diaspora lies in the family. Perhaps you're laughing and thinking that sounds too banal? Right? But everything long-lasting has to be banal, or it wouldn't go on forever. Incidentally, the KGB broke up my family too. I'll tell you about that some day. But just now, take this." Inessa opened a chest and produced from it a brightly colored box with a foreign label "Matzo," a bottle of red wine marked "Manischewitz," and a red candleholder, and all this she handed to Rubinchik. "There, hold that," she said.

"Why? What's this for?" he asked.

"It's matzo and sabbath wine, so you can celebrate shabbat. And you can read how in the book that Ilya gave you. And my advice is: read it *before* you go home, okay? And here's fifty rubles from our fund. Take it, take it. This isn't my money. It's from over there. And when you and I are over there, then we'll keep helping those that are left behind, right?" Inessa peered curiously into his eyes.

The second major event of that Saturday occurred three hours later, when Nelya and the children came home. They found the place clean, which in recent weeks was unusual, and the apartment was brightly lit; a festive sabbath table had been set with a white tablecloth, candles in a holder, a bowl of fruit, matzo on an elegant plate, an open bottle of Manischewitz, and wine glasses set out at each place. At the head of the table sat Iosif wearing his best dacron suit, a white shirt, and a white skull cap on his head. Syllable by syllable he slowly mouthed the Hebrew words of a sabbath prayer, comparing the text with its Russian transliteration.

"Daddy, what is all this? What are you doing?" the children cried. "Is it your birthday?"

Rubinchik raised his head and looked at his wife who stood there in the doorway, rooted.

"Yes," he said, looking Nelya in the eye, "today is a birthday—the birthday of our sabbath tradition. Wash your hands and come and sit at the table. Mamma will light our sabbath candles."

That night, as they lay in bed, Rubinchik told Nelya about his visit to the synagogue and his meeting with Inessa Brodnik, Karbovsky, and the other Jewish activists. Suddenly, she said, "You've got to remember all this, right down to the last detail."

"Why?" Rubinchik wondered.

"Once we get over there, you're going to write a book about them."

He was flabbergasted at her brilliant idea. Lord, why hadn't he thought of that? Of course! In America, millions were putting on demonstrations to defend Soviet Jews who were strangers, with no name or face. But if he were to write a book about Inessa Brodnik, Slepak, Begun, and Karbovsky as real people, about their daily war with the KGB, their demonstrations, hunger strikes, Inessa's trips to Mordovia and other prisons, the KGB arrests in the dead of night, the secret delivery of news to Western journalists—as in some spy novel—the trials of Orlov, Shcharansky, Ginzburg, and the foreigners who smuggled through Soviet Customs these flimsy brochures on the sabbath rites, Hebrew textbooks, and cassettes, secreting them on their person as if they were explosives . . . Why, all this was more powerful than any novel! This was a Jewish "Gulag Archipelago!" good enough for the Pulitzer Prize. What better subject for a journalist?

The train whistle outside roused him to his feet. His wife lay there asleep, but Rubinchik hauled himself out of bed and went out onto the balcony, all excited. He was desperate for a smoke. He thought of going down and begging a cigarette from some neighbor or passerby. But no, damn it, he had started a new life! Yet could it all be ruined, along with Nelya's brilliant idea, just because he got involved with that goddamned stewardess in Salekhard? And that could so easily happen, so very easily! The Soviet regime was invincible and utterly ruthless. Even Yury Orlov—who was a *Russian* physicist—had gotten seven years in prison and five years of exile, despite the international uproar! And Shcharansky was being threatened with the death penalty.

Standing on the balcony next to the window where his children were sleeping, Rubinchik looked at the grubby vacant lot and the forest and the distant glow in the night sky above Moscow, and he felt scared.

twenty-six

Within two days Barsky heard of what Rubinchik had been doing at Inessa's. Three informants (including the little red-bearded *a yid* from the synagogue) had reported to him. Admittedly, Barsky could never totally rely on these agents. They too were Jews and possibly fed only part of their information to the KGB and sometimes held back the most important items. Otherwise how could that demonstration have occurred on Pushkin Square without any warning? And how had Brodnik managed to elude her surveillance and turn up in Mordovia on International Workers' Day, when even the drunken camp guards could not refuse a May Day food parcel for the prisoners? And, most crucially, who, after the trial of Scharansky, Ginzburg, Begun—and yesterday of Slepak—was managing to supply the Western press with news edited by Rubinchik, which was being broadcast from overseas?

Not one of the refuseniks recruited by Barsky was able, or willing, to provide this information—not even in return for permission to emigrate.

But Barsky was good at waiting. He did not loaf around, nor was he on tenterhooks like a boy waiting for some prey to fall into his snare. Barsky was like a gardener who didn't wait for the fruit to fall, but cultivated his orchard until the harvest time, watering and fertilizing the soil and removing weeds and pests. In all his previous missions against major Jews, Barsky invisibly but cunningly trailed his quarry right up to their arrests. In professional parlance this was referred to as "active waiting."

However, in the security agent's trade there was also a different kind of waiting. This was the war of nerves, invisible to the outside observer, in which each side lay low, waiting for the other to make the next move that could decide the whole contest. Operation Virgin had now attained that decisive phase. Now there could be no question of scaring Rubinchik off, or preempting things by another hooligan attack on his wife. Like a river's strong current pulling along a swimmer, the Jewish activists around Rubinchik would have to lead him to apply to emigrate. That was inevitable. Or in two or three weeks Brodnik, Gertsianov, Karbovsky, and all the others would suspect him of being either a coward or a KGB agent.

In previous similar situations, he had always enjoyed this pause in the game. For instance, even after the failure of the Frontier Million, he was consoled by having managed to get the United Jewish Appeal, the American Jewish Congress, and Amnesty International to outfit the entire management of the Fifth Directorate with fashionable French and Italian suits, shearling and tufted overcoats with raglan sleeves. It had not been difficult. All the refuseniks received parcels from Western organizations via the Red Cross containing clothing and footwear that were hard to come by here. Some of these things they sold on the black market, and with the money from just one shearling coat one could live comfortably for two or three months. Moreover, the longer the KGB denied them their exit visas, the more they acquired an aura of martyrdom in the United States, and the more frequent and opulent were the parcels arriving from abroad.

The sixteen refuseniks who secretly collaborated with the KGB wrote letters of thanks to the Red Cross, and in them informed their benefactors of the sizes that they supposedly took in boots and clothing. These sizes, of course, were given to them by Barsky. How ironic that the head of the KGB anti-Zionist section and all its top staff, up to and including General Sviridov, now wore watches, suits, shoes, jeans, and shearlings supplied from abroad by die-hard Zionists. But if this irony ever struck anyone as humiliating, Barsky derived only pleasure from it. He loved setting small traps in the process of a large-scale operation; to him they were a sign that any setback he might suffer meant only one point lost in the overall contest. And even when the traps snapped shut without catching anything, he never grieved for long. He was like an experienced chess player during a nerve-racking competition—tomorrow there would always be a new game, a new hunt for Jewish knights, rooks, and queens.

However, like any grand master, Barsky also never forgot his defeats. And his one defeat—the fiasco of his life—he regarded as the Frontier Million operation. His secret stake had never been Rappoport's million, but Anna Sigal herself—the woman that he lusted after with every cell in his forty-year-old body.

For Barsky, Operation Virgin was now just as crucial. On no account could he blow this operation—and risk losing Anna along with it—through some hasty or clumsy move. Yet to just sit and wait till that scum Rubinchik handed in his goddamned documents at the Visa Office—that somehow required more strength and patience than Barsky could summon!

On Friday, at the end of the working day, Barsky pulled the Rubinchik file from his safe and began preparing what in the trade was called a "weeded file." This was what the KGB used when they needed to consult outside specialists not permitted access to company secrets. Such people might be physicists (if, for instance, they were dealing with a formula stolen from Silicon Valley), or sewage specialists (if they needed to calculate the number of staff at the American Yokohama naval base using Japanese press information on the water supply), or they might call on Kim Philby in person (if the failure of Soviet agents in Britain made it necessary to pinpoint the exact whereabouts of some espionage leak).

In Rubinchik's file there were no such secrets. Barsky's work amounted to erasing Rubinchik's name, surname, press pseudonym, and place of work from each and every report coming from hotel administrators, from interrogations of the girls involved, stewardess Natasha Svechkina's statement, that of the Salekhard militia, and other such reports. Any of these would have revealed to Anna Sigal ahead of time who it was that Barsky was preying on. This was routine work that any member of his staff could have done, but Barsky did it all himself, sitting until midnight. This was personal, his own precious brainchild.

"The Committee for State Security hereby calls on Anna Sigal, leading member of the Moscow Bar, to provide a juridical assessment of various documents pertaining to the case of citizen X, accused of corrupting more than one hundred young girls all around the USSR."

That was all. Nothing more. A simple official request to an attorney to familiarize herself with materials from an operational file. Anna could not refuse to render an expert opinion—especially after Barsky had so generously returned her cassette of that provocative conversation with her husband.

Once he'd finished, Barsky stretched, feeling satisfied, and he loosened and cracked the numb joints of his shoulders. The nerve center of the KGB never slept and was forever vigilant, but Barsky's day was over. He returned the Rubinchik file to his safe. A few minutes later he handed back his keys to the duty office, and walked out of the building. At this late hour the Kuznetsky Bridge Street was almost deserted. He could have waited for the official bus that left each hour and took home any officers who'd worked late. But Barsky only used the bus or an official car during winter or when the weather was bad. Now, it felt pleasant to step out and stretch his legs and walk down through the center of town to the Sverdlov Square subway. A few passersby might have noticed the open, dreamy smile on his face. But the young lovers that strolled through Moscow on a summer night were too absorbed with each other to see such things.

Like the tired gardener inspecting and admiring his work after a long day's weeding, Barsky walked through his favorite city with a proprietary sense of having done a good job, and with wild sexual fantasies of Anna Sigal. Here in the street he felt no need to wear a stonewall expression to conceal these imaginings. In fact, to him these visions were a sign that far from him lusting after Anna, he now had fallen in love with her, like a youth. It was rightly observed that from love to hate is but a single step. Though the reverse, from hate to love seemed even shorter. And the more Barsky worked himself up with cunning plans to draw Anna into Operation Virgin, the more completely he felt drawn into the whirlpool of his infatuation.

When he got to the Petrovka, by the Bolshoi Theater, he dropped a kopek into a vending machine and enjoyed a glass of clean, cold soda water. Like all Muscovites, he believed that nowhere in the world was there such a tasty drink—not even in the vaunted country of America where all those Jews were striving so hard to get to . . .

Twenty-seven

FROM THE CENTRAL COMMITTEE OF THE CPSU, THE PRESIDIUM OF THE SUPREME SOVIET AND THE USSR COUNCIL OF MINISTERS

The Central Committee of the CPSU, the Presidium of the Supreme Soviet, and the USSR Council of Ministers sorrowfully announce the sudden death on July 17, 1978, at the age of sixty, of Politburo member, Secretary of the Central Committee, Deputy of the USSR Supreme Soviet, Hero of Socialist Labor, Fyodor Davydovich KULAKOV. His death has removed from our ranks a prominent campaigner for the worldwide construction of Communism. On the night of 16–17 July the deceased developed a severe cardiac insufficiency followed by sudden heart seizure. . . .

Moscow was shaken by the news of Kulakov's death. And a day later the fact that his funeral was not attended by either Brezhnev, Kosygin, or Suslov reduced all of Moscow to a state of shock. People crowded around the newspaper display stands and said not a word as they read and reread the few lines published there. But the Kremlin service staff of cooks, typists, guards, chauffeurs, gardeners, and cleaners were no longer isolated as they'd been in Stalin's time. Through hints, rumors, and slips of the tongue, Moscow always knew what was going on—who was allied with whom, and what changes were in the offing; new taxes, price rises, currency reforms, etc.

The public therefore immediately connected Kulakov's obituary with a rumor that circulated only two months before about his open criticism of Brezhnev at a Politburo meeting. The KGB's special laboratory for manufacturing poisons to dispose of political opponents was a "Kremlin secret" that the Moscow public had always known. In fact, they sensed it with their skin. The unexpected death of Kulakov, who was known to be healthy as an ox, and the ostentatious absence of Brezhnev at his funeral spoke for itself.

But in the death of Kulakov there was, after all, nothing sensational. The real sensation—and a terrible one at that—was the fact that once again, as in the 1930s, the KGB had been granted the right to use poison and the dagger to eliminate opponents of the Kremlin leadership. The public also knew that the death of such men was usually followed by a wave of terror. And it was this dire omen that frightened people.

Sitting in her office at the College of Attorneys, Anna Sigal read her *Izvestiya* then placed it on the desk feeling numbed. She sighed. Matters were coming to a head; the noose was being drawn ever tighter around her own neck, and she had to do something.

In his *Pravda*, Barsky read Gorbachev's farewell speech over Kulakov's coffin twice. Then he took out his treasured packet of Dunhills, which he reserved for special occasions. He inhaled, narrowed his eyes, and blew smoke rings up toward the open window. He always knew that his organization was a serious one, but even while following the duel between Andropov and Kulakov from a few feet away, it never occurred to him that it would be this serious. The Technical Section was a mere two floors below, and although it was possible it had nothing at all to do with Kulakov's death, nevertheless ... Cardiac insufficiency could be caused by a poison called ritsine, which had been perfected in the KGB technical laboratories six years ago.

In Inessa Brodnik's apartment everyone crowded around one of the radio sets. Above the howl of the jammings, they listened to Vladimir Martin speaking from across the ocean:

"Moscow. According to reports from the Soviet capital, people there have reacted with extreme suspicion to the announcement of the sudden death of Fyodor Kulakov, who until recently was regarded as one of the prime contenders for the Kremlin leadership. Two months ago, rumors of his conflict with Brezhnev caused agitation in Moscow. . . ."

"Congratulations," Inessa said quietly to Rubinchik. "He's reading your text, word for word."

At that moment the phone rang in Anna Sigal's office. Anna gave a shudder, as though she'd been caught reading anti-Soviet literature and not just Kulakov's obituary. Then she picked up the phone.

"Hallo?"

"Anna Evgenyevna?" asked a familiar voice. "This is Oleg Barsky speaking. How are you?"

"Okay, thank you."

"I'm calling because we need some advice on a small judicial matter. If I come round to see you right now, could you give me a couple of minutes?"

twenty-eight

As he got off the trolley bus at samotyochnaya square and set off toward the Visa Office—only three hundred yards up Olympic Prospect—Rubinchik felt he was losing his grip. All his determination and energy seemed to ebb away. It seemed as if across the street, by the entrance to the Visa Office, where a forlorn group stood holding folders and portfolios, there was a radioactive zone. To cross the square and join that line-up with all of Moscow watching made him imagine walking into the Warsaw ghetto and pinning a yellow Star of David on his breast.

Here on this side of the square, you were still your own person, a Soviet citizen, perhaps slightly disadvantaged by your Semitic appearance, but basically you still belonged. You could argue with a militiaman or run to him for protection. You could talk loudly, laugh, and joke with a girl selling ice cream, flirt with other girls passing by, or swear at the driver of a car who refused to let you pass.

But once you were over there, among that group . . .

A powerful and almost visible aura of contempt for these "traitors," "outsiders," and "Yids" seemed to hover over the assemblage lining up each morning at the Visa Office. They stood there supervised by three militiamen, with a further unknown quantity inside. The militia watchdogs maintained no order in the queue. They also never heard or took notice of the insulting shouts of "scum" and "Judas" hurled at the applicants by passersby. They were simply watching for "Zionist anti-Soviet demonstrations." Even at a distance, therefore, anyone seen approaching the Visa Office was subjected to scrutiny and checked for any banner or placard that might be jutting from under his jacket.

As he stepped down from the sidewalk, Rubinchik's feet became leaden, and the thin folder containing his documents hung like a deadweight under his arm. He made his way across the square and took his place at the end of the line without a word. It felt as if at any moment they would be raked by machine-gun fire. He drew his head into his shoulders—and everyone else in the queue also stood that way. But no shots were heard, and a few minutes later he breathed more evenly. The row of people beneath the windows of the Visa Office was the strangest line he had stood in in all his thirty-seven years, although like any other Soviet citizen, he'd had more than his fill of standing in line. Starting with his orphanage, where the older boys used to make the little ones drink ten glasses of water and then occupied and barricaded all the toilets. Then there were the bread lines at night during the 1950s, where you had your own four-figure number written in ink on the palm of your hand. Then there were the several-day line-ups for subscription editions of Jack London, Chekhov, Balzac, and even Sholokhov. And the several months you had to wait to get a carpet, sewing machine, furniture, or a fridge. And the years spent waiting on lists for an apartment or a car. And every day of the year the lines for meat, fruit, beer, and pharmaceuticals. In sixty years of Soviet rule these lines had become a ritual for the Russian people—like the American's morning shower or the Frenchman's coffee and fresh baguette. There were even customs for standing in these lines: people made one another's acquaintance, flirted, exchanged news and anecdotes, began love affairs, and even offered their hearts and hands in marriage. As a young man dreaming of becoming a writer, Rubinchik had once thought of writing a play about a ticket queue at the fashionable Taganka Theater: a set of complete strangers began queuing up for *Hamlet* one evening, and by the time the box office opened in the morning, it became not a line of strangers but a family of sorts, with its conflicts, love intrigues, betrayals, political disputes, and its own KGB plant who was tormented by whether or not turn in the girl with dissident views with whom he had fallen in love.

But the line-up here was different. Not one conversation! And it was all the more strange, since this line was all Jews—people famed for their volubility. Here, among their own blood brothers, one might have expected their affability and sharp repartee to come into their own. But no way! As he stood there with militiamen's eyes focused on him like searchlight beams trained on an enemy aircraft, Rubinchik too felt in no mood for jokes. Holding his document folio pinned under his elbow, he rehearsed his story for the umpteenth time and wondered whether it would sound sufficiently convincing—this was number 23 in the biographical questionnaires, where one had to explain the geneological blood ties of the relatives in Israel whom one was preparing to join. In all previous questionnaires—when signing on with the Army, entering an educational institute, or registering for work— he had written: "No relatives residing abroad." Ah, you see, comrade inspector, Esther Kogan, who sent us the invitation, is the Israeli aunt of my wife; she is the daughter of her grandfather's brother who left Russia before the Revolution. Of course, had he known that there would be a Soviet revolution in Russia, and such a happy life for everyone, he would never have left! But he left in 1910, got caught up in the savagery of capitalism and died there of homesickness. But he had a daughter who still lives in Israel.

She's old, sick, and lonely. It was she who found us through the International Red Cross and has been deluging us with letters, pleading for us to come and help her during her last few years. It would be heartless if we refused her. Here are her letters. See for yourself!

The closer Rubinchik came to the entrance of the Visa Office, the greater were his doubts about this story. The letters from "Aunt Esther" had been written by him and Nelya; they'd been smuggled out by people leaving for Israel, and then mailed back to them with Israeli postmarks. But now they struck even him as too obvious a forgery. Still, everyone knew that the Visa Office inspectors couldn't care less about the applicants' stories. If the KGB decided to turn you down, you wouldn't be allowed to join even your own mother, and the reason would be the same as in all other cases: insufficiently close relation. Yet all the same, your story ought to sound convincing so as not to give them some additional reason to object.

With spirits fading as he approached the door, Rubinchik anxiously went over his other documents, comparing them with his real life story. Then he began thinking of the afterworld, standing in line to see the Apostle Paul at the celestial visa office—or so rumor had it. And there, in that line, people would recall the whole of their lives and timidly wonder which of their sins were known to the heavenly clerk and which forgiven or forgotten because they were committed so long ago. But if God could forgive or overlook one's faults, the KGB was quite another matter.

A cold cramp gripped Rubinchik's stomach as he recalled the militia reportage at Salekhard. Where was that record now? In Salekhard? In Moscow? And where was that character in the dark blue foreign-made suit with the sharp and impenetrable expression? And who was he for that matter?

"Hey! Are you asleep? It's your turn!" said the militiaman standing by the door.

With his heart pounding, Rubinchik stepped inside the tall wooden door. Ahead of him was a stairway roped off and marked STAFF ONLY. To the right was a small office with windows marked DIPLOMATIC VISAS, CASH OFFICE, FOREIGN PASSPORTS. Rubinchik headed that way but was pulled up by a shout:

"Where are you going? To the left! Jews to the left!"

Rubinchik almost stumbled. That shrill sound of "Jews to the left!" jarred on him as if he were watching a movie of himself at Auschwitz.

Turning left, he found himself in a small corridor where all the office doors were open. In each sat the inspectors, all dressed in the Customs service's gray tunics. Each would-be emigrant was seen by them individually and his documents checked. And the doors were all kept open—as Rubinchik immediately surmised—so that none of the Jews would think of trying to offer a bribe.

He was met by a tubby young Jew wearing a T-shirt and sloppy-looking jeans who came out of one of the offices marked INSPECTOR A.P. PIROGOVA. The young man's eyes gleamed and he made a victorious gesture conveying that he'd got his documents and his story accepted. Inspector Pirogova was young, thin-faced, and flat-chested. Her tunic was adorned with sergeant's shoulder tabs. Silently she put a hand out to take Rubinchik's folder.

"How do you do," he offered.

She took his folder and opened it.

"Sit down," she said dryly. "So . . . Rubinchik, Iosif Mikhailovich. Profession: boiler man." She gave a sudden laugh. "Good grief, another one!" And she half-shouted to a colleague across the hall: "Hey, Sergey. I've got another boiler man!"

"Me too!" came back the merry answer.

Pirogova turned her head and hemmed: "It looks as if all you Jews have become boiler men! If you all leave, who's going to stoke the boilers and keep us warm?"

At any other time Rubinchik might well have made a joke of this and perhaps written a short piece for his paper. But not here, not now. Three weeks ago, with Ilya Karbovsky's help, he had actually managed to sign on as a stoker on the night shift of some boiler room. Many Jewish scientists and academics did that before filing their applications to emigrate. First, so as not to need work references from their high-level institutions. And second, because janitors and boiler tenders were at the bottom of the Soviet social scale. Nobody was fired from such jobs, even if he was a dissident.

"What about your previous position? Where's our copy of your work record?" Pirogova mused to herself as she leafed through Rubinchik's dossier. "Aha, here it is. Right at the bottom. Well, what do you know! A correspondent with *Labor Gazette*, released last June at his own request." She flashed him a look of mock surprise. "What made you do that all of a sudden? From a job like that, straight down to the boiler room? Eh?"

He could see in her eyes that she was mocking him, but he had his explanation ready.

"You see," he pulled out of his pocket a report from the detox clinic. "I've got a drinking problem."

Pirogova looked mistrustful, but her interest seemed genuine as she began looking through the militia reports of one I. M. Rubinchik apprehended in an intoxicated condition, and the various medical reports. This appeared to be the first time anyone had produced this type of document for her.

"Hmm . . . you keep hitting the bottle? How long did you work for your paper?" She looked again at his employment document, which recorded all his jobs with the dates when he began and finished. "Ten years! Oho! I read the *Labor Gazette* quite regularly, but I don't remember that name. Or did you write under another name?"

"Well, yes. . . . Occasionally. . . ." Rubinchik felt his palms and the lower part of his legs sweating.

"What name did you write under?"

"Rubin."

"Ah, so you are Rubin!" Pirogova exclaimed. Her tone suggested that now something had clicked in her mind, and she had put two and two together. Then she lowered her voice and looked down at the documents. "Of course, I remember, I read things by you." She abruptly placed Rubinchik's documents back in the folder and closed it. "Very well," she said, "You can go. You'll be notified through the mail, as usual."

Rubinchik got up, not knowing whether to rejoice like the tubby young man or to sink into despair. Nevertheless, as he left the Visa Office, he felt an enormous sense of relief. The endless ordeal of deciding whether to go or not to go, apply or not apply was now over. And also, having filed his application, he now felt a certain pride in having done so. As if he had sewn a yellow star to his lapel and heroically stepped out onto Unter den Linden in 1940. He imagined that in all of Russia, such a feeling had been felt only by the seven dissidents who carried placards into Red Square to protest the crushing of the Prague Spring in 1968 by Soviet tanks. Of course, they were heroes of a higher level. Yet every Jew who applied to emigrate was also spitting in the face of this whole cruel empire with its tanks and sputniks, free medicine and the best ballet in the world.

As he left the Visa Office, Rubinchik felt a glow of pride. And to those militiamen before whom he had stood hunched an hour ago, he now imagined himself saying: "Now you can do with me whatever you like! Knock my teeth out, put cuffs on me, and send me to Siberia, as you've done with Shcharansky, Ginzburg, Slepak, and so many others! But I no longer belong to you. I'm no Soviet, and I'm not a slave to your Communist Party! I've made my choice!"

He looked the militia thugs in the eye with a brazen air. And for the first time that day he also exchanged a friendly smile with his kinfolk waiting in line. What he could not know was that Inspector Pirogova had already gone up to the third floor office of the director and silently laid his folder on Bulychev's desk. It now carried a stamp that said: "Application number 078/R741." And in copperplate female hand:

I. M. RUBINCHIK (RUBIN)

General Bulychev looked up at her.

"Is that our man?"

Pirogova nodded.

Bulychev lifted the receiver of the yellow telephone and dialed a four-digit number on the KGB internal network.

"Is that you, Colonel?" he asked with a smile. "This is Bulychev. I've got a present for you. Citizen Rubinchik has just filed his application."

part three

the attack

twenty-nine

Splintering the ice along the water's edge with its hooves, the white stallion galloped along the river Dnieper, heading toward Kiev, which languished on its hilltop in the April sun. The rider, fourteen-year-old Prince Sviatoslav, leaned against the horse's mane and whipped his mount along, directing its headlong progress through the exercise area with its fences, ditches, wooden archery targets, and straw dummies in Khazarian dress on which his personal troop practiced their swordsmanship. The short wedge-shaped lock of fair hair on his shaven scalp fluttered in the wind. Sviatoslav's troop of Nordic and Slavonic bodyguards and warriors, all teenagers like himself but without his princely lock, sprang out of his path and looked at the boat sailing down the Dnieper that had sparked the prince's sudden anger.

Standing by the gunwale of the boat could be seen the shapely dark-haired seventeen-year-old Malusha, attendant to Princess Olga. Her round Slavonic face was marked by a fresh brown scar, as though struck with a lash; her lips were puckered miserably, and her eyes full of tears. Powered by sail and twelve powerful oarsmen, the boat headed away from Kiev on the first spring high water, still streaked with ice.

Turning toward Podol, at the Kiev outskirts, the stallion and rider sped up the ascending roadway, galloping past merchants' carts that rushed right and left to get out of Sviatoslav's path. The horse splashed springtime mud into the shacks of the merchants, potters, and tanners who lived along the road beneath the walls of the Kiev fortress. In the Khazarian quarter he knocked over the trading counters of the merchants with their forelocks and headed toward the bridge by the Golden Gate, where the Kievan guard collected a tithe on all goods brought into the city. Here, confronted by throngs of people, carts, and drays filled with geese, ducks, cranes, and pigs, even a prince's steed would have had to moderate its pace, if not come to a halt. But instead Sviatoslav let out a wild yell and jabbed his steed in the spleen with his hobnailed boots. The rider's fury communicated itself to the young stallion, which had grown up under its young master's saddle and whip. With a desperate spring he cleared one of the carts, smashing another loaded with geese as he bulled his way past, and with steel hooves thundering he charged across the wooden bridge right past the frightened guards.

Inside the Kievan fortress beyond the Golden Gate, the dirt and clay roadway was mushy with mud from the April rains. Here too there were rows of traders' stalls and counters laden with meat, fish, and poultry, smoked sides of bear, layers of lard, sacks of grain and salt, pitchers of milk, honey, wax, and *nabiz*, bundles of leather and fabrics, and splendid weapons from far and near. The whole area was crowded with people. But like lightning, the shouts of "Look out! The prince is coming!" set off a panic, and people raced to clear the road.

Hugging his sweating steed, now gray with foam, the prince flew past the stalls. Yellow clay and slop from the gutters splashed and spattered the richly dressed boyars in their colored satins and the coarse garb of the peasants, all of whom hugged the side of the road. Come, come on! Faster, faster! Past the wooden palaces of Kievan boyars and Varangian noblemen, past the sacrificial altar with its silver-haired and golden-whiskered statue of Perun the thunder god. Now Sviatoslav headed toward the two-tiered brick and stone palace of his mother, where the guards, forewarned, had already opened the heavy brass-bound gates. Across the court he charged, with its scared janitors and other menials, and made for the broad galleria with its columns of marble from Cherson. Here, before the galleria and its oaken doors, the horse came to a halt, as was its habit. But a furious lash of the whip and its master's shout of "No! Come on! Gee-hup!" caused the stallion to rear on its hind legs and then drive onward, across the portico's fine Greek marble.

The powerful thrust of the horse flung open the front doors and shook the whole palace—the lower, stone structure built by Prince Kiy, founder of Kiev, and the upper story in red brick added in recent years. Horse and rider burst into the antechamber, from which hallways led to the Princess's banquet room, the servants' quarters, and the broad arched oak staircase, which led up to the Golden Hall of the palace. Again lashing his horse, Sviatoslav drove it up the stairway and swung down under the animal's belly to dodge hitting the jasper-set archway. Stretching its neck forward like a swan and rasping the oaken steps with its hooves, the stallion too cleared this obstacle and bore its young master out onto the marble paving of the Golden Hall. There, at the far end, on the steps of the rostrum to her throne, thirty-three-year-old Olga stood waiting.

Incensed by Sviatoslav's brutal incursion, she had come here from her chambers all alone. Her flaxen hair was caught up hastily in a golden hoop. Her fine features were pale with anger, which emphasized the cold blue of her steely gaze. Her simple dark dress of Greek velvet sewn with pearl did not hide the honeyed ripeness of her shoulders, the proudly held long neck, and the diamond cross upon her breast. The April sun beating through the stained glass of the large round windows played on the facets of her cross and threw daggerlike reflections on the gilded cupola, the silver lanterns on each side of the golden throne, and the high walls decorated with the swords, spears, battle axes, and shields of Oleg Ryurik and Igor the Old.

Olga did not mount the dais. She watched as her son clambered from beneath the belly and onto the croup of his stallion. The horse meanwhile snorted, turned its head to one side, its frenzied eye asquint, foam dripping from its badly rubbed sides. It came to a halt only inches from her.

"You!" Sviatoslav shouted at his mother. "You've dared to banish Malusha! Now bring her back!"

Olga, who'd been gazing at the hoof-scarred floor, now looked up at her son. The fury in his dark eyes made them glow like coals. He was fair like Olga and all those who had come to this land from Norway. But his face was not the elongated Nordic type, and his general appearance was unlike any northern *Konung*. Of medium stature, with broad shoulders, a short and powerful neck, heavy brows, a fine and slightly arched nose, he had on his thin, obdurate upper lip the first signs of youthful down. He reminded her of fiery Joseph, Prince of the Khazars, but Olga quickly banished the memory. She simply continued looking at her son in silence.

In his right earlobe, like all young Kievans of noble blood, he wore a gold ring with two pearls and a ruby set between. But he had no tattoos on his head and body—this, thank the gods, Olga had managed to prohibit.

Breathing heavily, as though he had carried his horse into the Golden Hall and not vice versa, Sviatoslav stared down at his mother, his look was full of hatred.

"Yes," Olga answered calmly, "I banished her. She was my attendant, not yours."

"You beat her!"

"Yes, I did. She is my slave."

Shifting on his excited steed, Sviatoslav didn't take his eyes off his mother for an instant. Their looks conveyed more than words. Both knew what was at stake. Malusha, his mother's slave, had made Sviatoslav a man that winter, and at the time Olga had turned a blind eye. Didn't all princelings become men in the harems of their fathers? But Olga had no harem, and hearing of her sons's nocturnal visits to Malusha's quarters, she herself removed the night guards from the northern wing, where the young woman lived. Olga was prepared to give her gifts of furs and fine garments in recognition of Malusha's care for her son. But that worthless creature—"cur's blood," to use the Polish phrase—had sought to rise above her status and, good for nothing that she was . . . she had conceived a child by Sviatoslav! That Olga could not tolerate. Summoned that morning before the princess, Malusha was whipped on the face and immediately expelled to distant Buguchan. There she was to be married off to an elderly former bodyguard, who for a generous reward had agreed to shelter and bring up the royal bastard as his own. Sviatoslav was on no account to be told of Malusha's whereabouts. Olga had her own plans for her son.

"Bring her back!" Sviatoslav yelled, and whipped his horse so it moved even closer to his mother.

Olga turned even paler but stood her ground.

"Come on! Gee-ho!" Sviatoslav kicked the horse and lashed it with such force that the stallion sprang forward. But as it met Olga's dagger-like gaze, it reared up in front of her and gave a snort that echoed all through the Golden Hall.

The horse's hooves came down again, passing a hair's breadth from her left shoulder, and Sviatoslav too was now close at hand.

"Get out of here, you young whelp!" she said in an even voice.

"No, you bitch! You're going to bring her back!" Sviatoslav jerked the horse's muzzle into his mother's face and lashed it once again. Now, though, either from fear of the princess, or sheer fatigue, the stallion retreated a pace, lifted its tail, farted loudly, and deposited a load of shit on the marble floor.

"Get him out of here!" Olga laughed contemptuously. "Before he starts pissing!"

Her mockery inflamed the youth even more. He hauled a sword from the wall display and lifted it above his mother's head.

"Bring her back, or I shall kill you. I swear it by the sword of my father!"

Now at the peak of his fury and with his hand raised to strike her, she couldn't help again seeing a vision of the man who one night sixteen years ago had ferociously, gently, deliciously made love to her in a Khazarian battle tent lit by flickering silver lanterns. But again she swept away the memory.

"That's not his sword, you know," Olga grinned dismissively. "His sword is in the hands of the Khazars. That's only there as a substitute—to keep the Slavs down." She teased her son, as though playing with a young bull.

"So this is not his sword, and I am not his son? Is that right?"

"No, you are his son."

"You're lying, you bitch!" Sviatoslav swung the sword and clouted his grandfather's shield that hung above his mother's head. "I am the son of Sveneld! You were involved with him even during my father's lifetime!"

"You see! You said 'during my father's lifetime.' Igor was your father."

"You lie! Nobody believes that! He was more than three score when I was born! Whose son am I? Speak! Sveneld's or Pesakh's?"

"You are the son of Igor!" she responded coldly.

"But you were a prisoner of Pesakh! For a whole night!"

"That's ancient slander. And I've hanged all those who dared utter it," Olga retorted with contempt. "You are the son of Igor. And now get out of here." She wearily turned away to her courtiers and guards who had at last ventured into the Golden Hall. "Lead the horse and child away!" she ordered.

One of the guards was about to seize the horse, when Sviatoslav raised his sword.

"Hands off! I came in here on my own and I'll leave the same way!" Then, turning to his mother: "Watch out! Your days are almost finished! A year from now and I'll be in control! And I'll bring Malusha back!"

Olga merely shook her head. She had different plans for her son.

The primary Russian chronicle states as follows: "In the summer of the year 955 Olga came to Constantinople. The emperor then was Constantine Porphyrogenitus, the son of Leo. And Olga came to him ..." But according to *De ceremoniis Aulae* by Constantine VII, the princess was received by him not in A.D. 955, but on Wednesday, September 9, A.D. 957. She was shown to a seat close to the emperor, where "she spoke with him of those matters she found necessary."

"For the whole season from April to October, Olga and her followers remained at large in the waters of the Bosphorus. But despite her persistence she did not obtain what she wanted of the proud family of Porphyrogenitus," reports Kartashev in his two-volume history of the Russian church. "She evidently dreamed of [. . .] some marital ties for her barbarian dynasty with the Porphyrogeniti, so to rise up from the status of mere 'barbarians' and become dynastic aristocrats. In the world of that century, the only undisputed aristocrats with status equivalent to Caesar Augustus were the Byzantine descendants of Basil I. . . . In Constantinople, Olga proposed that they offer her a Byzantine princess as wife for Sviatoslav, and that she herself should thus become a relative by marriage of the Byzantine court. She waited for several humiliating months. Olga could avenge her failure [. . .] only by the feeble gesture of dismissing their envoys from Kiev."

These events are commented on even more curiously by Lev Gumilev, modern Russian historian. He writes: "The Khazarian King Joseph can hardly have been pleased when authority in Kiev passed out of the hands of a Varangian *Konung* (Sveneld) into those of a Russian prince (Sviatoslav). But he did not repeat Pesakh's campaign . . . Joseph saw fit to refrain from campaigning against Rus, but the delay availed him little."

However, even the most resourceful scholars have not been able to disguise the fact that Sviatoslav, son of Olga, was not the son of her husband Prince Igor. In the same way, the next Russian prince, Vladimir, was born not by the lawful wife of Sviatoslav, but by the slave Malusha, and Vladimir was able to claim the throne of Kiev only when he had killed his brothers, the other sons of Sviatoslav.

As for Malusha, historians do not concern themselves with her. Regrettably so. It was the son of Malusha and Sviatoslav, Vladimir (the Shining Sun), who became the greatest and most dissipated of Russian princes: having seized the throne of Kiev, he raped Julia, the pregnant Greek wife of his brother, also the Nordic princess Rogneda, daughter of a Polovtsian prince he had killed, and dozens of virgins. Then, in exchange for the hand of the Byzantine Princess Anna, he forcibly baptized the whole of Rus. And by this marriage he finally realized the bold plan of his grandmother Olga, who had always dreamed of a link with the imperial line of Porphyrogenitus and had for that reason banished Malusha.

The only thing that remains unclear to modern historians is why Joseph of Khazaria did not repeat Pesakh's example and attack the Rus while Olga and her enormous delegation were away in Constantinople for almost half a year, and when fifteen-year-old Sviatoslav suddenly ceased paying tribute to the Khazars. What was it that stayed the spear of Joseph, at a time when he ruled half the world, from the Dnieper to the Aral Sea?

Thirty

Bulychev's telephone call was the signal that Barsky had been waiting for. Like the commander's single gesture that launches hoards of cavalry into the fray, one order from Barsky sent the whole of his team swarming forth.

INSTRUCTION

SECTION OF THE FIFTH DIRECTORATE, USSR KGB
To implement Operation Virgin all operatives now dispatched to collect evidence from I. Rubinchik's (Rubin) victims. Evidence to be collected at victims' place of residence; if necessary use confrontation with staff of hotels where victims met with I. Rubinchik. After collection of evidence, secure signed agreements from witnesses of willingness to appear and give evidence at Moscow trial.

APPENDIX: List of operatives with areas where they will be sent to execute the above.

IN CHARGE: Captains Faskin and Zartsev.
     Signed—Head of Section, KGB Colonel O. D. Barsky
     Moscow, August 7, 1978.

At the same time a coded cable went out to all area and regional KGB directorates in Siberia, reading as follows:

URGENT. SECRET.

TO AREA AND REGIONAL MANAGERS
As part of Operation Virgin, carried out on instruction from the chief of KGB, an agent from E Section of the Fifth Directorate is being sent to your locality to conduct operations. You are to give him complete cooperation. The operation is under control of Yu.

    V. Andropov.
    Director of Fifth General Directorate, A. Sviridov.
    Moscow, August 7, 1978.

Thirty-one

As she sat in her office reading the weeded dossier that Barsky had brought her, Anna was haunted by a strange sense of alarm, like the insistent rhythm of Ravel's *Bolero* beating inside her. And it seemed to have no connection with the disparaging accounts of some debauched journalist that had been addressed to Barsky from almost every corner of the country. After more than four years as an attorney, Anna was no longer surprised by a denunciation, anonymous letter, or even evidence of a national epidemic of sexual promiscuity. In a country where the people were under pressure at all times, they had long ago discovered the one secluded corner not under Party control were their own or other people's beds. Fleeing from the all-seeing eye of the KGB, people searched for any space where they could lock the door and cover themselves with a blanket. This was how young people found an outlet for their frustrated emotions. And they devoted to sex all those energies that in other countries people spent on public life, political debate, or dancing at all-night discotheques and rock festivals. And for those lacking a sexual safety valve, self-expression often took the form of some perversion. This was why domestic violence, marital infidelity, and drunken orgies had become the order of the day in civil courts. Yet the censorship blocked all attempts by the press to deal with these subjects. After all, all Soviet people were earnestly engaged in building communism and were not meant to be distracted by such trifling negative issues.

But in the dossier that Barsky brought her to inspect, Anna saw signs of something else besides a commonplace instance of some man's screwing around. It was something that Anna could not quite grasp—possibly because every mention of the name, characteristics, and position of the lecherous journalist had been carefully blacked out. It was only when she got to the evidence from a certain Natasha X. that Anna's heart missed a beat and she had a sudden sinking feeling, as though she had suddenly tripped over some unseen obstacle.

> ... during our walks around Salekhard and along the Ob [erased] told me about his newspaper and about some Khazarians and ancient Russians who made war on one another a thousand

years ago. From his stories I gathered that in olden days the Russians all used to wear tattoos, and that they produced nothing at all and just murdered and robbed their neighbors; they drank themselves stupid and burned their wives . . .

Heavens! Anna thought. It's him! It couldn't be anyone else!

She nervously lit a cigarette and scrutinized the even handwritten lines, the penmanship of a teenage girl:

And the first Russian princes were all rapists and debauchees. For instance there was some prince—either Vladimir or Sviatoslav, or someone else, I can't remember exactly—who screwed and raped everything that moved, even the pregnant wife of his brother. And at the same time, he gave banquets for the whole of Kiev. They were such banquets that people came from everywhere around, and they stuffed themselves for a whole week, and got drunk and had sex. And if some Russian died, they burned him together with his favorite wife, who agreed of her own accord to be put on the fire . . .

Anna closed her eyes and leaned her head back against the wall of her little office. Holy Christ, this was Rubinchik. It was Iosif Rubinchik, who all the girls had nicknamed "the Saint" or "the Historian." And it was there, at that Sputnik pioneer camp, that she'd chosen him for the honor of being her very first. Although, at the time it had not been quite so obvious or conscious a choice. At first she'd simply fallen in love—with that hungrily desperate teenage need. But "fallen in love" was not quite the right term: she had *longed* for him. Yes, that was it. She had longed for, desired him as she sat by the campfire at night and listened to his inspired stories of the ancient Rus, Slavs, Khazars, and Byzantians. She hungered to soak up and absorb that dry and lambent flame that blazed in Iosif's eyes, and which ever afterward she had searched for, and which she'd found—in Jewish men.

Yet how had it happened then, seventeen years ago? Why was it she, of all people, who on that last night had gone to Iosif's tent to seduce him? Back then he was just a bashful student troop leader, and on the beach he was even too shy to look at his bare-legged female charges, and they deliberately tantalized him with their revealing bathing suits, languid looks, and seductive poses.

"Do you know what it means to be a Russian woman?"

After her first week there on the Volga, it emerged that in her troop of forty girls aged fourteen to fifteen, she was the only virgin. What a blow to her pride. But she'd rejected outright the hints and even propositions she'd gotten from the muscular lifeguards who were visited at night by the other girls—sometimes in groups of three or four. She had made her choice. On the day before they broke camp, when the girls were playfully drawing lots for Joseph "the Saint," for who was going to go to his tent and make a man of him, Anna loudly claimed that she too wanted to take part. The others began making fun of her, "Mom's little virgin," and they didn't want to let her in on it. ("How's he ever going to screw you? Have you ever in your life held a dick?") Then she got furious (or maybe jealous lest anyone else get her beloved Iosif), and she insisted on participating. And then . . .

Anna still could not understand how she'd managed to win. Probably, the other girls had rigged it and planted the winning ticket on her to enjoy a laugh at her when she screwed up. That must have been why the whole crowd of them escorted her to his tent. But Iosif was not there, and after waiting about twenty minutes, they all wandered off to their lifeguards.

Anna waited, however, and eventually Iosif turned up. She looked him straight in the eye and told him that she had won him in a lottery for the whole night. He laughed and said, "Well, yes, it's hard to fall asleep on your last night at camp. Come on, let's go down to the river for a walk and a talk. Would you like that?"

The two of them went off down to the river, to its sandy banks, with the distant lights of timber rafts floating by. They walked for an hour, for two, and three . . . Iosif told her about his life in an orphanage, his army service, and his dream of becoming a historian or archeologist and of discovering the vanished ruins of Khazaria, and then maybe Atlantis.

And as she listened to him, she thought and wondered—when, oh when was he going to kiss her?!

"I'm tired, Iosif," she said. "We've walked a long way."

"Oh, you're right. We'd better turn back."

"No, let's sit down. It's so peaceful here. And it's chilly . . ."

"Are you cold?" he asked.

How did they manage to end up kissing? There on a moist sandy bank of the Volga, on the very edge of that water from which, according to Iosif, all life came, how did the two of them—both he and she—for the first time in their lives come to experience the miracle and bliss of sexual union? Their mating was one in which the crazy age-old polarity of their races somehow brought on the seemingly electric flashes of hungering ecstasy and the insatiable animal energy of an all-night orgasm.

The following morning she left for Moscow, and he went back to the Saratov Teachers' Training College. Two months later, she secretly paid twenty rubles and had her first abortion. Afterward she burnt the paper with Rubinchik's address and tried to forget it, but she remembered it and thought of him often. She imagined he'd gone somewhere in the provinces, working as a history teacher in some school, or at best, as an archaeologist at some distant excavation. But now it turned out he had become a newspaper correspondent. But where? In which paper? She had never seen his name in print. Or maybe this wasn't him? How could a shy young man like Iosif "the Saint" turn into a Casanova, a debauched monster and sexual maniac?

As Anna closed the file, she noticed its official heading: "USSR KGB. Investigation Case No. 578/E67." With that she placed it in her safe and walked out into the suffocating August heat. Twenty minutes later her little yellow Zhiguli had crossed Moscow and pulled up on Suvorovsky Boulevard in front of the iron railing surrounding the old three-story building of the Union of Journalists. Showing the doorguard her Bar of Attorneys ID, Anna was directed to the accounting office on the second floor. The room was stacked with shelves and card files. In the center, at a table heaped with files, a corpulent elderly woman in thick horn-rimmed spectacles sat at a typewriter.

"Good afternoon," Anna said. "I am from the Moscow Bar of Attorneys. We are looking for a journalist called Iosif Rubinchik. I believe he is a member of your union."

"Not now, he isn't," said the woman.

"How is that?" said Anna, surprised.

"He's applied to emigrate," the woman said brusquely. "As soon as they tell us about any such traitors, we expel them straight away, automatically."

"But do you still have his address?"

"Of course," and the woman produced a card and handed it to Anna. "Here you are."

The card had already been crossed out in thick red ink. In the lower left-hand corner was a passport photo of Rubinchik, probably taken ten years ago, and the details that Anna needed:

Rubinchik, Iosif Mikhailovich. Pen name: Iosif Rubin.

Place of work: *Labor Gazette.*

Home address: Odintsovo, 24 First Cosmonauts' Street, apt. 67.

Telephone: 921-17-02.

Admitted to the Union of Journalists: October 1970

Expelled: 7 August 1978.

Anna gave a snort of laughter. The second commandment of Professor Shnittke had proved correct: he who seeks shall find! But how was she going to find the slightest mote of compromising material against this Colonel Barsky? But it was now a matter of life and death.

Thirty-two

I'm sorry, I don't know anybody called Rubin."

"His real name is Rubinchik. Iosif Rubinchik. Here's his photo. Two years ago, on the night of January 17, 1976, you spent the night in his hotel room at the Hotel Bolshoi Ural in Sverdlovsk. Here's the evidence given by the hotel manager and the chambermaid. They saw you on that occasion, and they've identified you from photographs."

"This is a mistake. I have never been in the Bolshoi Ural Hotel. Apart from which, on twenty-nine January of seventy-six I got married."

"Precisely! On seventeen January you were in the hotel; on the twenty-ninth you were married, and immediately afterward you and your husband enlisted to go and work in Bratsk, and on eighteen September you gave birth to a child. That is, eight and a half months after you were married, but precisely nine months after that night you spent in the hotel with Rubinchik."

"That's your reckoning, not mine. I wasn't aware that the KGB even kept an eye on the course of someone's pregnancy. According to the papers, that happens only in China."

"Just a moment! No need for you to go off the deep end, my dear. We have nothing personally against you. On the contrary, we want to help people like yourself. Figure it out for yourself: here we have this stud traveling around the country corrupting and dishonoring Russian girls. These girls are your sisters, you understand? And there are dozens of them. Here, look at their photographs!"

"It's pointless, my looking at them. None of this is any business of mine."

"Wait a moment. Neither your husband nor anybody else will ever know anything about this conversation of yours. I give you my word as an officer. But you have to help us stop this swine and his tricks! All the other girls have already admitted it. Look, we even have pictures of him in bed with one of them! Do you see?"

"What I can see is that you're trying to drag me into some filth and pornography. But you've got the wrong address. This business has got nothing to do with me. Now, if you'll excuse me, I have to go."

Captain Faskin watched dejectedly as yet another of Rubinchik's victims left. This was his sixth fiasco in the five days he had spent in the Irkutsk region, which had many new construction sites at Bratsk, Angarsk, Ust-Ilim, and Paduy. Faskin and his colleagues had flown the length and breadth of the country collecting evidence against the love-kike and everywhere they reported the same failure. Yet this was not because they did not know how to pile on the pressure with their interviewees. They were very skilled at that. After all, they were professionals, well used to extracting evidence from dissidents and Zionists as well as ordinary criminals. But they had never interrogated women such as these before. As soon as each new victim of Rubinchik's crossed the threshold of their office at the local KGB head-quarters, Barsky's agents realized they had screwed up and been thwarted yet again!

Because each time they found they were not dealing with some dim-witted girl from the provinces who had either been whoring around or else been downright careless and managed to cover matters up by a shotgun marriage. In the obscurity of the taiga or the filth of some Siberian con-struction site, they came across something quite unexpected and exceptional: they found themselves dealing with yet another Russian madonna, a genuine fairy-tale beauty, an ancient princess with slim waist, high breast, proud bearing, and the eyes of a northern goddess. And it was pointless to raise one's voice at them, or try using foul language or blackmail. Quite the con-trary, as soon as these girls appeared, your first instinct was to call them "Highness," click your heels like a hussar cavalier, and simply rejoice that such female beauty still survived in Russia. At the same time these goddesses radiated such sexual allurement that one glance into those unfathomable eyes was enough to take your breath away and send you weak at the knees. Yet it was amazing that such gorgeous creatures could work as crane operators, tally clerks, cooks, draftswomen, and surveyors, when their real place was in Hollywood—or, at the very least, the Russian equivalent in Mosfilm. What sort of fiendish instinct was it that enabled that parasite Rubinchik to find these pearls of great price in the murky depths of Russian provincial life? What sorcery or hypnosis did he use that turned them into such faithful admirers that at the sound of his name their eyes lit up and flashed dreamy rainbow fire? And after that, they glazed over with an icy impenetrable shield and totally denied everything: "I do not know . . . I was not there . . . I never saw . . ."

Like all Barsky's other colleagues, neither Faskin nor Zartsev doubted at all who was the father of those children growing up with Russian names and living in Russian families in dozens of Siberian towns and villages. But how could they prove that when even Tanya, the waitress from Beryozovy transport station in Yakutia, turned up to be interrogated hand in hand with her young husband, a strapping six-foot Siberian driver!

Zartsev failed to recognize her at first. Where was that unimpressive, flat-breasted gray mouse of a girl in her laundered apron, who only four months ago had served them venison ragout and weak coffee in that grubby dining room on the winter trail? The person who appeared at his office at the KGB headquarters in Murmansk was a lovely, queenly figure—a veritable Claudia Cardinale of the tundra, with head held proudly and the mysterious smile of an expectant Mona Lisa.

"Can we come in?" her husband asked in a deep voice.

"Yes, certainly. What is your name?"

"Nikolay and Tanya Rykov. You wanted to see us. Here's the summons."

"Well, actually I called only Tanya. Maybe you could wait in the corridor while I talk with her?"

"I never leave my wife alone. Nowhere. She's expecting."

"I see. Congratulations. Have a seat. What month are you in?"

"This is the fourth month. Why?"

"Well, to be honest, I just have one formal question for her. If we'd known that Tanya finds it difficult getting about..."

"She doesn't find it difficult. I carry her myself. So what do you want us for?"

"A very small matter..." With some constraint, Zartsev opened the drawer of his desk and from the packet of photographs used for his interrogations he pulled out just one—a picture of Rubinchik. "You see," he said, "We're looking for a particular person. Maybe you have met him. Take a look." Zartsev glanced at her intently. But not an eyelash trembled on that regal countenance. She shook her head.

"No. I've never seen him."

"Wait a moment!" her giant husband said suddenly. "I've seen this guy." He turned to Tanya. "Isn't this that correspondent guy that was knocking around in Mirnyy in the spring? Just before the two of us met... D'you remember? Then he wrote an article about how the authorities had robbed half the town. Everyone read it, d'you remember?"

"No, I don't remember," she said and looked Zartsev straight in the eye. "I don't read the papers."

"How d'you mean you don't?" her husband exclaimed. "Tanya, why so modest all of a sudden? You even write poetry! And damn good poetry too!"

"Yes, I write poetry, but I don't read the papers," Tanya answered calmly, her faintly mocking gaze fixed on Zartsev.

"Anyway, what's this guy done? This journalist?" her husband asked.

"Nothing in particular, never mind," Zartsev said and returned Rubinchik's photograph to the drawer. "It doesn't concern you."

He realized of course that Tanya, like all Rubinchik's other conquests, was simply lying. But when they had been seduced and abandoned by this rake from the capital, how was it these queenly young women defended and covered up for him? In their envy of Rubinchik, both Faskin and Zartsev spent sleepless nights. They would have dearly loved to screw even just one of these girls for themselves. Sometimes they actually tried turning the interrogations into a form of flirtation and invited some girl for supper at a local restaurant and even tried luring them to Moscow. But their reward was always the same contemptuous, proud smile. In the evenings, therefore, they simply got tanked up to the gills in some local dive and swore that one way or another, whatever the price, they were going to *get* that love-kike. How they would grill that bastard in Lefortovo jail once they turned him in! They'd have that bloody kike's balls on toast, and when he screamed in fear and agony, they'd get a genuine thrill!

After the first two dozen reports of his men's failure with Rubinchik's victims at various points around the country, Barsky himself flew out to Siberia. But to begin with even he couldn't crack any of those madonnas. They simply refused to answer his questions. "Pardon me, Comrade Colonel, but I'm eighteen years old, and even my mom doesn't ask me questions like that any more. Good-bye!"

"Just one moment, Nina Petrovna!" Barsky managed to stop her from leaving. "Exactly how old is your child?"

"Three. So what?"

"Girl or boy?"

"He's a boy. What of it?"

"Do you happen to have his photo with you?"

The young mother looked embarrassed and said nothing.

"Never mind," Barsky said. "*We* have a photo of him, and also one of your husband. Have a look."

Opening a file, he produced from it and laid on the desk photographs of the young woman's round-faced fair husband, of their large-eyed dark-haired son, and of Rubinchik. The child's similiarity to Rubinchik was so obvious as to be beyond dispute.

"Now sit down!" Barsky told the woman harshly.

She obeyed and sat down on the chair by his desk.

"This is the choice you have: either you write down here and now, in my presence, an honest confession as to where, when, and in what circumstances this bastard seduced you and deprived you of your innocence. In which case, you have my word as an officer, we'll take the matter no further—your husband will never know who the child's real father is, and

I'll tear up these photographs and destroy the negatives in your presence. Or else ... well, you can guess the alternative. So decide!"

"And what are you going to do with my evidence?" the woman asked in a feeble deadpan voice.

"Oh, nothing at all! That's only for our own internal use. We need it to halt this Rubinchik in his tracks and withdraw his rights as a journalist. That's all. What more can we do to him? After all, he didn't rape you, did he? Eh?"

"No."

Barsky laid a clean sheet of paper in front of her and began dictating.

"So write this down: I hereby declare that I, Nina Petrovna Uvarova, born 1956, met with journalist Iosif Rubin on 27 April 1973 at Ust-Ilim in the Tyumen' Region ..."

Once he had broken the young woman, it took Barsky only another hour to extract from her all that he required. Afterward, he briefed the men under him:

"That's the way to work with them. And if some of the kids aren't like Rubinchik, and if their mothers deny everything, that doesn't matter either! After all, their denials simply confirm the deep *psychological* effect Rubinchik has on them. They simply worship him. And we'll base the whole trial on this factor. This won't be just the trial of some Jewish Casanova, but of a kike who is corrupting, debauching, and enslaving the souls of our Russian girls, affecting their morality and their state of mind, turning them into members of his secret sect! And it won't matter if they deny it a hundred times over. Once we present them before the court, the public and press are going to hate him just as you do—simply because these dolls are so luscious!"

When Barsky returned to Moscow, however, another matter distracted him from Operation Virgin.

URGENT. SECRET.

TO: GENERAL A. K. SVIRIDOV, HEAD OF FIFTH DIRECTORATE

OPERATIONAL ORDER

In connection with the arrival in Moscow on 21 August of PLO leader Yasir Arafat, and in order to preempt undesirable excesses, measures should be taken to isolate from 20 through 25 August all Zionist activists, and also any others who could jeopardize Arafat's visit.

Please inform of measures taken.

Major General S. Tsvigun,
First Deputy Chairman of the USSR KGB
Moscow, August 17 1978.

218 / Edward Topol

RESPONSE: to Colonel O. Barsky, Head of E Section
IMMEDIATE ACTION! INFORM ME DAILY OF SITUATION.

> (Signed) Gen. Sviridov,
> Head of Fifth Directorate.

Reading this, Barsky sighed. Arafat was coming to Moscow because of the treachery of Anwar Sadat. Without warning, the Egyptian leader had outlawed the Communist Party, ejected all Soviet advisers, and begun direct negotiations with Israel. These Yids didn't know how lucky they were! That bastard Rubinchik didn't even suspect that he would enjoy an extra few days of freedom thanks to Yasir Arafat.

Thirty-three

At the Taganka food store, there was a line for peaches. It was like any other in Moscow—one of the hundreds that sprang up as soon as Bulgarian tomatoes appeared on sale, or Finnish footwear, Turkish halvah, or Cuban bananas. There were more of these in summer—for such things as apples, cucumbers, watermelons, potatoes, cherries, strawberries, and so forth. And on the off chance of suddenly coming across such a sale, people never left home without taking along a bag, carrier, or folder, just in case. And everywhere in Moscow—on the subway, in buses and streetcars—you could find people lugging their acquisitions back home.

This queue was for peaches—beautiful large ones from the Crimea, with their skins tanned by the southern sun and covered in fine down. Rubinchik saw that he was in luck: there were only about forty people waiting. That meant he would not have to stay long—maybe half an hour. But on Sunday, they would enjoy a rare feast when he went to see the children out at Lyubertsy.

"Are you the last one?" he asked a woman at the end of the line.

"Yes," the back of her head answered. She had fair hair done in a bun and glasses looped over her ears.

"What's the quota?"

"Three kilos," the hair and bun muttered, obviously buried in some reading matter.

"What? Three kilos each, or for the whole line?" Rubinchik jested. He was in a good mood.

Put out, the head and bun turned. In a flash, as soon as Rubinchik saw her face, a hot surge of blood shot through his veins and took his breath away. It was as though he had gripped a high-tension wire.

I've got to get out of here! was his first thought. He had to escape—this was another trap!

But some strange force kept him in his place. Calm down, Iosif. Don't be such a coward. Don't panic. The KGB can't plant goddesses in every queue in Moscow. How could they have known that just then, at 9:27 in the morning, as he left his boiler room and headed for Inessa Brodnik's, he would look out of his Moskvich, see people coming out of a food store with peaches, and decide to buy a few kilos for his kids? Furthermore, there were no traditional Russian beauties in Moscow—this girl was no doubt from the provinces. Damn it, before, working for his paper, he never had a spare moment in Moscow, never noticed a change in the weather, let alone some girl.

Now, though, he had tons of spare time. Nelya and the children had fled from the heat and gone to stay with her parents at Lyubertsy. And now for the first time ever he was living the life of a genuine writer. In the mornings, at Inessa Brodnik's, he would edit reports on the Jewish struggle to emigrate from the USSR. Then he would sleep till evening. Then in his boiler room at night he would write his book about the Jewish exodus from Russia—a work that, he told himself, was going to stand alongside Solzhenitsyn's *Gulag Archipelago* or Pasternak's *Doctor Zhivago*.

What was the girl reading? No no, he was not going to tempt fate yet again. Once bitten, twice shy. . . . Actually, she was reading a book by Waliszewski—he could tell from the binding. *Peter the Great* by the Franco-Polish author Kasimierz Waliszewski, first published in 1912. Since then it had never been reprinted. Strange that she had managed to find this rare book. Damn it, why wasn't the line moving? Another ten people had lined up behind him, but he hadn't advanced one step.

The girl turned a page, and looking over her shoulder, he managed to see a chapter heading called "Women." Could he recall anything at all of Waliszewski's book, or had he forgotten it completely? He closed his eyes as he used to at school exams as a boy. In a moment a page from the chapter about women in Peter the Great's life appeared before his mind's eye—just as if it lay before him on a table in the Saratov Library, where he had read it fifteen years ago:

"He was too preoccupied and too crude to make any mistress worthy of his name or even a suitable wife," he quoted out loud. "He fixed a price on the caresses lavished on his soldiers by the Petersburg lovelies, and the charge was one kopek for three kisses. And after each meeting with Catherine, his future empress, he paid her one ducat . . ."

The girl turned round in bewilderment, and now he saw her eyes—impassive, cold blue-green, slightly enlarged by the round lenses of her spectacles.

"Beg pardon. What did you say?" she asked in a gentle low voice.

"Nothing, nothing really . . ." he exhaled feebly, and in the nape of his neck he again felt the same clattering rhythm he had experienced in Kiev.

She turned away and looked down at her book again. Then she turned to him.

"Do you really know the whole of Waliszewski by heart?" she asked, and then smiled. "Or maybe you were cheating and you looked over my shoulder? Right?"

She was no younger than seventeen, but she had an open and confiding smile—like a child at the circus for the first time, ready to see some marvel. Her openness and spontaneity after her earlier aloofness reassured Rubinchik, and he felt a refreshing sense of calm and well being. After tumbling into some chasm, it felt now as if he had landed in the warm waters of some familiar lake. He rose to the surface, breathed in a lungful of air and continued swimming with easy confidence.

"Of course I cheated," he admitted. Then still looking her straight in the eye, he continued: " 'In love he found satisfaction neither in his own virtues nor in those of any woman, and he was too lacking in self-possession to be satisfied with mere decorum.' Want to hear some more?"

"Yes!" she begged.

"Very well: 'Take, for example, the following story recounted by Baron Poelnitz about the tsar's behavior at Magdeburg in 1717. Since the king of Prussia had ordered that Peter be shown every imaginable honor, various state institutions turned up with their entire staff to pay their respects. The Count de Koczerdzy, brother of the grand chancellor, at the head of a deputation from the Regency to greet Peter, found him in the embrace of two Russian ladies, and the Russian monarch continued thusly while the speech of greeting was addressed to him. Also in Berlin, when meeting with the Countess of Mecklenburg, his niece, the tsar ran straight up to her, embraced her tenderly, and led her into a separate room where without locking the doors and paying no heed to the other people in view, including the Duke of Mecklenburg himself, he conducted himself in a manner designed to show that his passions were utterly insatiable . . .' "

The girl listened, her childlike lips parted in amazement. The dark crystal of her eyes suddenly opened wide, like the aperture of a camera when the flashgun fires, and a powerful stream of radiant energy engulfed him. He felt himself plummet into those orbs, and his knees grew weak.

"Say, how do you manage that?" she asked. "Is it telepathy?"

"No," he admitted. "I once studied at the history faculty. But that was a long time ago, and I've forgotten a lot."

"Oh, I'm studying history too!" she lit up. "But I'm awfully dumb," she announced sadly. "I can't even remember the dates of Party Congresses."

"Oh, well, that is terrible!" Rubinchik playfully mocked her dismayed tone, and she had to laugh.

"No, it's true though! I have to develop my memory somehow, but I don't know how." She looked at her watch and sighed. "It's no good, I can't wait any longer for those peaches. I'll be late for work."

"I'm going to go and find out what the trouble is," Rubinchik said firmly. "I've no time either. Only don't you go away, okay?"

She nodded, and he dashed inside the store, inspired, forgetting his fears, and even the fact that he'd applied to emigrate. Inside he immediately saw what was the matter. Behind the counter and surrounded by crates of peaches stood a corpulent young woman in dirty overalls. But instead of weighing the peaches and selling them, she had turned her back on the line and was chattering on the phone.

"And what did he say? . . . You don't say! No, you're kidding! He really said that? Well, I never! And what did she do? . . . No, I know her though. She'll run after him hand and foot. . . ."

A queue of forty-odd people stood along the wall and the length of the counter and stoically listened to this twaddle. Some had their faces buried in newspapers and magazines. But Rubinchik couldn't take anymore.

"Look here, miss!" he banged on the counter. "There are people standing here waiting. Are you going to start doing some work?"

But the clerk never so much as turned in his direction. She flapped a hand dismissively as if shooing off a fly, and continued:

"Sochi? No, I've been to Sochi. Me and Sasha were thinking of the seaside at Riga . . . So what about the Lithuanians? Or Latvians, or whatever they call themselves! I'm not going to talk to them even in Russian!"

"Okay then, where's the manager?" Rubinchik exploded, still thinking of himself as a journalist with some clout.

But, instead of calling the manager, the saleswoman suddenly planted a notice on the counter with the words CLOSED FOR LUNCH and carried on her chatter.

"Amazing!" Rubinchik said. "Here are people standing in line, it's nine o'clock in the morning, and she has her lunch break! Never mind! We'll deal with this."

He was just setting off to find the manager when a loud male voice called out from the crowd.

"Hey, if you don't like it, clear off to Israel!"

Rubinchik turned round, amazed. At least half the men and women in the line were looking at him with undisguised hatred.

"Huh, he doesn't seem to like waiting with the rest of us!" one woman commented.

"A real smart-ass too! Quoting books by heart!" someone said from further down the line.

"Pity Hitler didn't finish off the whole bunch of them."

"Never mind, the Arabs will finish the job!"

Horrified, Rubinchik looked around and felt like a cornered animal. Malevolent faces glowered at him from every side, while the rest of the crowd continued impassively reading their magazines and pretended not to hear.

"And if anyone in their country saw a person who showed alertness and a knowledge of things, they would say: 'This man is most of all worthy to serve our God.' And they would take him, put a rope about his neck, and hang him from a tree . . ."

Rubinchik turned round, blindly made his way out of the store and headed toward his car. Fuck them! To hell with all of them, and their peaches, and their Russian divas too! Contemptible slaves! He was going to get out and take his children with him. And let these vile lackeys stand in their queues and put up with their impudent sales clerks and their mobster regime. That was all they deserved!

He flopped into his seat and nervously started the engine. But at that moment a figure flitted in front of the car, and he put on the brake.

"Wait!" In the side window he saw the youthful face of his recent companion. "Stop!" she said. "I heard what they said to you. It was disgusting. Please, forgive us!"

"It's nothing to do with you!" he answered gruffly.

"Yes it is. I am Russian too. But that's not the point. Don't get upset. Please don't take any notice! I wish you all the best!"

She stepped back onto the sidewalk and walked smartly away toward the subway, with Waliszewski tucked under her arm. Maybe she was embarrassed at her impulsiveness.

Rubinchik watched as she walked away. There she was, disappearing in the distance, walking out of his life. The morning breeze blew her loose gray dress against her body, picking out her breast and the smooth curve of her tall thighs.

He let in the clutch, accelerated, and caught up with her at the corner. There he jumped out of the car, and despite the angry honking behind him, he stepped over to the sidewalk and shouted to her.

"Hi there! Hallo!"

She looked in his direction.

"Come with me!" he called her. "I'll take you wherever you're going."

She shook her head. Further conversation was interrupted by the long blast of a police whistle. The traffic controller at the intersection was heading their way. With a meaningful gesture he pulled a wad of traffic tickets from his pocket.

"Quick!" Rubinchik called, opening the door. "Get in, or they'll fine me!"

She quickly sat in. But by that time the burly cop was standing in front of the hood.

"Well," he said sharply, "shall we pay our fine then?"

Rubinchik pulled his red journalist's pass.

"I'm from the *Labor Gazette*, officer!" he explained.

"But that doesn't mean you can drive along the sidewalk!" the militiaman scolded. Then he changed his tone. "And, by the way, it's time someone wrote that they should give us a summer uniform. We're baking alive in this outfit!"

"Yessir! We'll see to it ! Call in at the office and we'll write it up!" Rubinchik answered.

"Okay! On your way then!"

Rubinchik started up.

"Where are you going?" he asked the girl.

She smiled.

"It's all right," she said. "I've a long way to go. I'll get out here. I only came in to save you from getting fined."

Her face radiated such simplicity and charm, Rubinchik's diaphragm tautened.

"What does a long way mean?" he asked. "New York? Paris? Tokyo?"

"Almost. Kuskovo." She smiled and pointed to a bus stop. "If you'll stop here, I can get the bus."

But Rubinchik kept going, turned a corner, and then sped away down Enthusiasts' Highway.

"Where are we going?" the girl sounded scared.

"Kuskovo. Where is it you work?"

She gave him a long, studious look, but he pretended not to notice.

"Why are you doing this?" she asked softly.

"Doing what?"

"Taking me all this way?"

"Aha, you probably think I'm some Jewish Casanova," he said. "And you think I'm going to pester you and ask for your phone number. Don't worry, I shan't do that. I just have this hobby—ferrying girls from the History Faculty around Moscow. Seriously though, you rescued me today. Otherwise I don't know what I'd have done. Probably gone and got drunk!"

"Are you a journalist?"

"No, I stoke boilers."

"Seriously though . . ."

"I am serious. You think Jews don't ever stoke boilers?"

"But you showed the cop a pass for the *Labor Gazette*. I saw you."

"It's an old one. I did work there once. But then they fired me for drunkenness. But there again, you don't believe me! A Jewish boiler man—and a drunk too—highly improbable. Although, incidentally, we're just passing where I work. Here in this building, the boiler room of the Institute of Glaciology. Night shifts, nine at night to nine A.M. It's work for a man that has nothing better to do. What about yourself? Hey, wait, though. Let's think. What have the Polish Waliszewski, the Russian Emperor Peter the Great, and the region of Kuskovo in common?"

She smiled.

"Count Sheremetyev."

"Absolutely right," he said. "And you're doing your summer job in the Palace-Museum of Count Sheremetyev in Kuskovo. And on the q.t. you're using the museum library, although it's strictly forbidden to take books out of the museum. According to the Criminal Code, the penalty for abusing one's official position is six months of forced labor. What have you to say in your defense?"

"You are a dangerous man."

"That's the first thing. What else?"

"And you too abuse your official position—what's more, a position that you no longer have."

"That's the second point. What else?"

"I can't think of anything else."

"A very poor defense! However, considering your youth and especially because of your love of Russian history, the court will pardon you.

"Do you see, that's the fourth bread van we've passed. Did you know that under Stalin they used those vans to transport arrested 'enemies of the people?' And it never occurred to folk like you and me just walking along the street that inside those trucks there might be our own relatives and friends. Incidentally, if you're interested in Peter the Great, then you should read not Waliszewski, but the letters and papers of Peter himself in the archive of Prince Kurakin. The commentaries and notes are even more interesting than the actual text. Although, unfortunately, our libraries don't have these books."

"Why?"

"Because Stalin wanted to be called 'the Great.' And so to avoid comparisons with Peter's despotic regime, he set a halo around Peter and removed from his biography all evidence of mass suppressions and other savagery. But he couldn't rewrite the letters from Peter and his contemporaries. So they were simply not published, and the old editions were taken out of the libraries. Even while Peter was on the throne, the poet Khomyakov wrote that Peter had destroyed the old Holy Russia, and that by following Peter we had 'renounced the heart, and all the sacred things of our native land.' Anyway, here we are at Kuskovo. And you said it was a long way! Well, it was a long way for the emperor when he came to visit Boris Sheremetyev—but he rode on a Prussian trotter. Whereas you and I are using a steed produced by the Moscow Likhachev Car Plant. And here we are!"

Rubinchik stopped in front of the quaint old cast-iron gates of the famous museum and estate of Count Sheremetyev, one-time field marshal and friend of Peter the Great. Just inside was a wooden hut billed as the ticket office, and next to it sat an elderly watchman. A long sandy path planted with ancient oaks, firs, and maples led into the enormous park with its marble sculptures of naked Venuses.

"Thank you," the girl said and remained seated another few moments, expecting probably that he would ask for her name and phone number. But he didn't. "Good-bye," she said, and got out.

"All the best!" he said and watched sadly as she showed the watchman her pass, stepped inside the gates, and walked away down the path lit by the morning sun, receding ever further into the distance and bathed in a tremulous sunny haze.

Rubinchik sat there and continued gazing down the path, even after the girl had disappeared. Of course he would never see her again. The ball is over, Comrade Rubinchik!

Thirty-four

"Tell me, Oleg, is this debauched journalist of yours a Jew?"

Barsky looked Anna firmly in the eye. How could she have worked that out? He had blacked out absolutely every clue to Rubinchik's identity. The only thing he had left in was his profession, and there was no point in erasing that. Who after all, apart from a journalist (and a KGB officer) could travel all over the country every month? But there were hordes of journalists, several thousand in Moscow alone.

"I don't think that's relevant at the moment," Barsky replied. He tried to soft-pedal his answer. He didn't want to spoil the relaxed and intoxicating sense of intimacy that he'd felt from the very start of their meeting. They were at the Race Course restaurant. Along the brightly floodlit cinder tracks outside the windows, tall, slender-legged horses could be seen elegantly cantering, harnessed in multi-colored two-wheel traps with Lilliputian jockeys. On the stage in the restaurant a quartet was playing something quiet and relaxingly bourgeois. Anna had slightly made-up her eyes, her thick eyelashes were turned up, and her fair hair was smoothly combed back like those hairdos of the forties. All this gave Barsky a sense of the unreality, as though he were watching himself in the movies. Or else this was some dream vision of his own mother in her youth. Anna herself had selected this restaurant, and Barsky at first was surprised by her choice. Yet those horse races outside the window could hardly have formed a better frame for her regal beauty. Nor was there any affectation on her part—she did not demean herself with any coquettishness. But in response to his hearty "Anna," she immediately began calling him Oleg. The first bottle of champagne was disposed of quickly and pleasantly. Could she really be mine? The thought drummed in his brain and throbbed in the pit of his stomach. Could she already be mine? Today?

"Well, I think it's highly important," Anna said. She was wearing a dark evening dress with open shoulders that drove Barsky mad. Only an effort of will prevented his reaching out to touch and caress them.

"After all, both my first and second husbands were Jews," she continued. "If I appear as the prosecutor, it would be easy to accuse me of some bias."

"On the contrary, Anna. On the con-tra-ry!" Barsky responded with a conviction fired partly by champagne and partly by her closeness. "That's one of the main reasons why the public prosecutor has to be you. Apart from your talent, of course! Nobody on earth could suspect you of being anti-Semitic. I think that would be great in your opening speech. You can disarm everyone by saying 'I can hardly be suspected of prejudice, if only because both my husbands have been Jews!' An opening gambit like that would slay them!"

"So he *is* a Jew then?"

"Yes, he's a Jew all right! What d'you expect? Seduced a hundred girls! And only Russian girls! And those are only the ones we know about, going by where his trips have taken him. But how many more are there we don't know about? The man's a sexual Russophile! What are we going to drink now? Champagne or brandy?"

"Another bottle of Abbrau-Durseau. That is, if your firm can afford it."

Barsky grinned, but he liked her boldness.

"You're a dangerous woman!" he said.

"Right," she agreed. "But if you want, you can still cut and run."

As if he would even consider it.

"Oh no," he said. He felt like he did as a little boy, unable to tear himself away from the woman selling chocolate ices. "I think I'll stay. Waiter! We'd like another Abbrau-Durseau. Incidentally, Anna, did you know that the Abbrau-Durseau vineyards used to belong to the imperial family, and their champagne tasted even better than the French stuff?"

"Really? So we're drinking imperial champagne?"

"With such a regal woman, one drinks only royal wines. Your health!"

"Thank you. Do they teach you compliments like that at the KGB Academy?"

That put Barsky on his guard. How did she know about the KGB Academy? He had told her he was a Moscow University graduate.

But first he invited her to dance. During the tango he gripped her firmly by the arm, like a child that has finally managed to grab its favorite candy. Only then did he ask her:

"Anna, who told you that I studied at the KGB Academy?"

"Oh, that's not difficult to work out," she grinned. "You're embarrassed about wearing glasses. And yet you have the figure, gait, and bearing of a naval officer. So, at very least, you probably studied at the naval college and dreamed of becoming a captain and cruising around the world. Right? You're ambitious, and so you got top grades. But at some point in your third or fourth year, your sight went and you had to leave. But you didn't graduate from the Law Faculty. You lied to me about that. I checked it. So where was there for an ambitious young guy with an incomplete officer training to go, if today he's a colonel in the KGB?"

"Hmm . . . Quite!" Barsky was no less amazed at this accurate pinpointing than at the closeness of her body, her breasts, and her legs. "I see you've really been to town on me."

"Of course," she confirmed. "You have with me, so I made a study of you. I'm a serious attorney, Oleg. If I take on a case, it's to win it. Remember that. And that's why, before taking on one, I have to see the victims' evidence. Incidentally, has your defendant been arrested, or is he still at large?"

"For the time being he's still walking free. But his arrest is a matter of weeks, no more than that."

"And these girls—did they consort with him willingly, or were they coerced? Were they aged eighteen at the time, or younger? That's important, and I don't have their statements. You gave me only the first file with denunciations and official reports."

"I know, Anna. Only at the moment I'm busy with Arafat. But you'll get all that. And don't worry: he coerced them all right. He hypnotized them."

"Is that all? But every man does that. You've been trying with me since last May."

"Precisely. But without success, because I'm a mere dilettante. But he is . . ."

The tango came to an end and they returned to their table.

"Believe me, Anna," Barsky continued, "when I bring these girls to Moscow, you'll see that Don Juan and Casanova couldn't hold a candle to this man. These girls are real princesses—the best women in Russia! Now, I'm not anti-Semitic—no, it's true! And I know your attitude toward the Jews. But you are Russian and—between ourselves, Anna—let's make no bones about it: the Jews just make use of us Russians. Everywhere and always, they take the best that every country has to offer for themselves: the women, the jobs, the houses and apartments, and the valuables. Just look around: do you know of one Jew who works on a collective farm? Who drives a tractor? Of course, you don't. But who are all the doctors? The scientists? The musicians? And the theatrical producers? Somebody once put it very well: the Jews fasten onto the most vital, succculent roots of whatever people they live with, they become part of them and feed on their sap until finally they suck it dry. And then they move on—from Spain to Germany, from Germany to Poland, and to Russia."

"That's probably a quote from Hitler."

"No, not necessarily. In fact it was said by some Russian philosopher, either Bulgakov or Rozanov, who, incidentally, was fascinated by Jewish sexuality and maintained that with them it had been sanctified by religion. Which brings us back to what this case is all about. Come on, have a drink. I didn't think we'd end up having such a serious discussion."

"But Oleg, this is just the littlest beginning. If you really want to involve me in this, we'll need hours discussing it. So I can counter any arguments raised by the defense."

"It'll be a pleasure. I'll provide you with the sort of literature that—"

"Oh no, not that!" Anna interrupted him with disdain. "What they print in *Pravda* and *Ogonyok* is . . ."

"Anna, what do you take me for? What they print in *Pravda* is written by amateurs. And we'll soon be taking that sort of work out of their hands. No, I'll give you serious stuff. For example, what the Japanese keep publishing nowadays: *How the Jews Achieve World Power*, *The Jews and Capital*, *The Secret of Jewish Power*, and so on. I hope you don't suspect the Japs of being anti-Semitic? There isn't a single Jew in the whole of Japan. The Japs simply study the Jews so as to apply their methods for themselves."

"So you read Japanese?"

"*I* don't. But we have a section that translates. As soon as you sign our agreement to collaborate on this case, you'll have access to everything."

"Even Solzhenitsyn?"

"Everything!" he said with conviction. "So? When can we start?"

"You know, Oleg, I'm one of those women who don't like to be pressured. Give me a few more days to study this case."

As they left, there was an awkward moment when Anna turned out to have a car, and Barsky was without transport.

"Perhaps we can go on somewhere else?" he suggested.

She laughed.

"Comrade Colonel, this is Moscow and it's midnight. The nearest bar that's open is in Helsinki. Get in and I'll drop you off at the subway. Where do you live?"

He realized that if ever she was to be his, it would not be tonight. But he was not put out. In fact his soul sang at the mere thought of her presence. And this was only the start! No, he told himself, he mustn't rush.

In the car she had more questions.

"But if the Jews are so harmful and dangerous, how is it you hold on to them? Why not send them all off to Israel, like the Poles did?"

"The answer's simple, Anna dear," he said, leaning back and relishing the fact that she, Anna Sigal, was his chauffeur. "Because the Poles are anti-Semitic. But we aren't. Of course, it's true that the Jews have harmed us. And because of that we're getting rid of all the Jewish slag and garbage. But by all means let the useful Jews stay here. Russia is a big place. And nobody will oppress them, believe me. That is, of course, if they behave reasonably. I mean, does anyone persecute your husband because the Jews set up the Gulag?"

"The Jews did that?" Anna was surprised. "I thought it was Stalin."

"There you are!" Barsky said. "Everyone goes on about Stalin, Beria, and the KGB! But have you read Solzhenitsyn's *Gulag Archipelago*? No? Well, you shall. I'll let you have a copy. You do at least believe Solzhenitsyn? He tells who the real organizers of the Gulag were. And who do you think stood behind Dzerzhinsky when the Red Terror first began? Eighty percent of the first Soviet government were Jews! And you want us to let them all go? No, let them first do a bit of work for Russia's benefit and help us put right the faults in the system they created for us!"

"I can see you're something of a dissident as well."

"No, Anna, I'm a Russian nobleman. A patriot. The dissidents want to destroy the system, but I believe that another revolution is more than Russia can take. It would tear us apart. What our country needs is a slow process of renewal. With everyone helping, even the Jews. After all, while our love-kike was a modest journalist, nobody touched him."

"What? What was that you called him?"

"Well, love-kike is the name we call him among ourselves. Another name we have for him is 'goat-kike.' But that's not the point. While he was just an ordinary journalist, everything was fine. Even if he did a little fucking on the side—who knows, maybe he doesn't love his Jewish wife? But there's a limit!"

"What limit? I'm serious, Oleg. What limit would you yourself set on a husband's playing around on the side?"

"Well, if I had a wife as lovely as you, I'd have every unfaithful husband shot," Barsky said with smooth assurance.

Anna grinned.

"Pushkin too had a beautiful wife. They say she was the most beautiful woman in Petersburg. But if I'm not mistaken, he notched up a list of one hundred twenty-six conquests on the side!"

"Well, first of all, Pushkin was an Arab," said Barsky. "And secondly, you remember where it got him? Killed in a duel!"

At the subway station, he chivalrously kissed her hand and made one last feeble attempt: "Such a warm night! Maybe we could just stroll for a bit?"

"Oleg," she said gently. "You've forgotten: I have a husband waiting for me at home!"

He knew she was fibbing. Her husband was at the rocket range at Severodvinsk. Together with Ustinov, the minister of defense. But she did have her father at home—she had moved him into the apartment—and her golden Airedale terrier. But Barsky didn't argue. Still holding her hand, he said:

"Anna, you know, before the war my father was a well-known composer. And he was friendly with a poet called Iosif Utkin—who was also a Jew, incidentally. And Utkin had some lines which went as follows:

No, there is something nobler, higher
Than parting and your icy hand.
I saw you and I heard you, lying
Injured in a foreign land.
And when the light of life burned dimmer,
I brought you back within my heart,
Just like the sick doll of an infant,
A soldier with an injured arm.
And at the turning in the road
You're neither friend, nor kin, nor brother.
But I know you will not leave me! No,
I know that you are mine forever! . . .

Barsky suddenly interrupted himself. "Anyway, Anna, good night! I'll call you next week." And with the cultivated deportment of a naval officer, he headed off into the subway.

When Anna got home, Charlie the Airedale rushed to greet her, but she pushed him aside. Without a word to her father she went to her bedroom, took off her dress and threw it in the hamper. Then, kneeling in front of the toilet, she stuck two fingers down her throat and vomited up all she had eaten and drunk. Then she took a long time to gargle and rinse her mouth and took a shower—almost as if she had slept with Barsky rather than merely danced with him.

Yet even after all this, the line still echoed in her head: "I know that you are mine forever!"

She flung on her dressing gown and went out to her father who was sitting in the living room with a book.

"Papa, do we have anything to drink?"

"Any amount!" he grinned, and got up and opened the fridge.

It was stacked from top to bottom with bottles of Narzan mineral water. Anna smiled: she had learned this unique method of curing alcoholism from one of her former clients, an alcoholic cab driver who never left for work without downing half a liter of vodka. For eight years he took his daily half liter before work, and for twelve hours a day he drove his passengers around Moscow without incident. Then something happened, or, as he explained to Anna, his store of "antialcoholic isotopes" was used up. One day he ran into a telegraph pole when his own three-year-old son was with him. Fortunately both son and father survived. "But I realized that was an order from on high: it was time to quit!" he told Anna. "So I stocked the fridge with Narzan mineral water and told my wife to lock me in the apartment and never let me out. And every hour, as soon as I had this craving for a drink, I'd open the freezer and see all those goddamned bottles of Narzan, so I drank that instead of vodka. One or two bottles at a time! And what d'you think? Inside two weeks I'd washed myself clean of all that alcoholic infection! And now I never touch a drop of it, and don't even feel the urge. But they still want to put me away for five years because I smashed up that taxi. But it wasn't me that did that! It was that alcoholic soak that they gave the car to for eight years without even checking his condition! But I'm a different man now, I'm a teetotaller!"

Anna was using the same method. She threw out everything containing alcohol, including her own perfume and eau-de-cologne. And she filled the fridge with mineral water and told her Airedale not to let Father out of the apartment. The first four days were the worst—Father went crazy, cursed and swore and threatened to jump from the balcony or smash all the dishes. But the dog lay there in the middle of the floor and watched his every step. And Father needed only to move toward the balcony or the door for Charlie to give a gentle warning growl. Once Dad actually got to the door, but Charlie jumped up and barred his way and growled fiercely. In a temper, Father swore and put a hand out to the knob, and instantly the dog gripped his wrist in its huge jaws and squeezed—not painfully, but firmly, like a pair of pincers. And he snarled and fixed Father with his intelligent matte-brown eyes.

After that, Father never so much as approached the cabinet where the porcelain was kept. He became a passionate reader. Anna and Arkady had a splendid library, a whole wall lined with books, and her father, a mechanic, became a keen reader of science fiction and read Tsiolkovsky, Asimov, Efremov, and Ray Bradbury. And when the craving for a drink got too much, he opened the refrigerator and drank mineral water, and at least satisfied his swallowing reflex. Two weeks later Anna hardly recognized him. He looked younger, stood with his shoulders back, held his head high, and even began taking an interest in the women who walked past their window.

Now her father stood by the open fridge.

"Well, what would you like, dear? Brandy? Vodka? Champagne?" he asked ironically.

"Gin and tonic!" she said.

"Certainly. Maybe a double?" Father produced a bottle of Narzan, opened it with the opener that lay ready, and poured Anna a full glass.

"You must join me!" Anna said.

"Of course!" and he poured himself a glass.

They clinked glasses and drank. Her father sniffed the water with a show of relish, as though it were vodka, and Anna laughed. Then she went to the bookshelves and from the second shelf pulled out a volume of the *Great Soviet Encyclopedia*, leafed through it, and on page eighty-two found the following short entry:

"BARSKY, *Dmitry Igorevich (1903–37), Soviet composer, author of 'March of the Victors,' et al. Stalin Prize winner.*"

Of course, that Stalin prize had earned Barsky his two lines in the *Soviet Encyclopedia*. But there was something—maybe the year of his death—which struck Anna and caught her attention.

"Father, do you know the 'March of the Victors'?" she asked.

"Of course I do. Why?"

"Sing it to me."

"Why?"

"Just sing it. I'd like you to."

"We stand on guard for Stalin, the Kremlin cavalry . . ." her father began and then interrupted himself. "What do you want to hear all this for?"

"What other songs by Barsky do you know?"

"Oh, so that's why! Well, you know, at that time even we weren't too clear about which songs were by Barsky, or someone else like Dunayevsky, or Solovyov-Sedoy. They all wrote that sort of stuff. And we sang it." And he began singing again: "Oh, it's great to live in our Soviet land! It's great when your country loves you too!"

"Wait!" Anna interrupted. "And who exactly used to sing these songs?"

"Everybody sang them! I'm telling you, the whole country sang them."

"No, I don't mean that. Who performed them? Which singers? Are they still alive?"

"God knows! Later on, sooner or later, Stalin put everyone in prison! Ruslanova, Kazin, even the singer Mikhailova, who was married to Budyonny!"

"But are any of them still alive?"

"I don't know. I think Leonid Kashchenko's still alive. I heard him not long ago on radio. But why in God's name do you want to know all this?"

"And did Kashchenko perform these songs?"

"Of course. Kashchenko was a leading singer at that time. Like Joseph Kobzon today. What the hell d'you want to know for?"

"I'm not quite sure," Anna said pensively. "I'm not sure yet . . ."

Thirty-five

Why had he come here? At one time in these stately halls of the Sheremetyev Palace, royal guests had dined till they hiccupped and choked. Peter the Great had shorn the beards of his boyars and forcibly poured vinegar down their throats. It was also here that Peter publicly made free with his secretary between the soup and the kulebyaka pie course, and also slapped the daughter of his vice-chancellor Shafirov and clouted the writer Tatishchev with a club. But what was Rubinchik looking for in these empty halls?

Now there was no trace of those groaning boards, stacked with roast quails, larks' tongues, crane with apple, pheasant au vin, sides of wild boar, and flagons of Siberian vodka. There was no sign, either, of those long-legged, narrow-muzzled borzoi hunting dogs that used to sleep on these same waxed parquet floors. No trace either of the serf musicians who played here. No vestige of the grandees with their decorations of satin ribbons and diamond pendants, and the boyars and marshals in their jabots and Dutch camisoles, who once banqueted here. And no reminder of those women in luxuriant crinolines, tight bodices, and lice-ridden wigs, with whom they fornicated here.

All that remained were the portraits, "improved" by obsequious restorers and hanging in heavy gilt frames and gazing down from the walls—luxuriant still-lifes and a profile of Peter squinting with his crazed and bloodshot eye. Also the polished and gleaming gold and silver tableware from which they had once eaten and into which they spat, now placed neatly in heavy mahogany cabinets. And the velvet camisoles and gilded swords were also on exhibit.

Rubinchik slowly wandered from one hall to another, gazing at the female portraits. He tried to find some similarity with the women he had sought and found in Russia. Now he felt as if he were inspecting a farewell parade of these girls and of their youthful great-grandmothers, and a gentle tingling at the nape of his neck confirmed this feeling. There was Tanya from Yakutia . . . here was the stewardess Natasha . . . this was Katya from Khabarovsk . . . and here was Marina of Norilsk . . . Heavens, and here was the KGB agent who was on the plane as he left Mirnyy! No, truly, exactly the same face! And who was this? But, no, damn it, to hell with these boyars, and these marshals and Peter's barons! He had come here to see that girl from the peach line at the Taganka food store—simply to gaze at her. He wanted nothing of her, just to see her. Heavens, all these women in wigs and crinolines couldn't hold a candle to that girl still almost a child! What was it that she said to him? "Forgive us!"

And he forgave. God knows, Barukh Ataw Adonai, he had long ago forgiven this country everything, there on the banks of the Volga. For the sake of that mad, blissful copulation—beyond the power of words—with young Anna Krylova, and for all the subsequent delights this country had bestowed on him. He had forgiven it for its Jewish quotas that came from the government, and for the anti-Semitism of its common people. Weren't those Russian peasants right when they beat us till we bled, and chased us out of their country, and passed their impotent hatred on to their sons? After all, for ten centuries since Pesakh's campaign against Kiev, the Jews had taken from the Russians their sweetest, youngest, and most beautiful women.

But she wasn't there. A few guides were conducting the first tourist groups through, trotting out the standard phrases about Peter's desire to "serve the glory of Russia" and "open a window into Europe." Rubinchik couldn't listen to this garbage and went out into the park. How splendid, how magical it would be if he could meet her out here, on the lonely path by Peter's grotto. But she wasn't out here either.

It was such a golden day, with oak leaves etching shadows on the warm sand of the paths, little intimate summer houses as in Corot paintings, pure air, white butterflies soaring over the marble statues, a nearby woodpecker, and a distant cuckoo. And such a magical day being wasted! How many days like this were left before his departure? He had imagined his life here unmeasured and eternal. And suddenly . . . how fleeting those final days were! There was no knowing how many remained. If they let you leave, you normally got ten days to pack and make ready. And that was it! Beyond, nothing but obscurity, a harsh life in the capitalist jungle. No more Russia, and there never would be! No more singing birches, no more of this air, this lazy sunlit dust hanging over the stream, these half-dark gazebos, and the drumming of the red-headed woodpecker and the sweet sound of that invisible cuckoo somewhere in the distance.

Where could she be? She had saved him that day, literally, from being arrested! If he had not brought her out here to Kuskovo, and if he had gone to Inessa Brodnik's as he'd intended, he would have been scooped up with all the others. Every refusenik and Zionist activist had been rounded up that morning and, according to Radio Liberty, been ferried out of Moscow. When he saw those bread vans, probably they were the vehicles transporting Inessa Brodnik, Efim Gertsianov, and Ilya Karbovsky out of town.

She wasn't here! Neither in the palace, nor in Peter's grotto, nor in the orangery. She wasn't here, and he couldn't even ask for her by name.

With a sigh he made his way to the exit.

"Leaving already?" the old man at the gate asked. "Done enough walking?"

"Yeah."

"Got a cigarette?"

"I gave up smoking. This is my third week," Rubinchik sighed. "Otherwise I'd have one with you."

"They all say that," said the old man. "Look after their tobacco like a Jew with his gold."

Rubinchik let that go by.

"By the way," he said, "Two days ago I gave a girl a ride out here. A student. She's here on a summer job. Perhaps you remember her?"

"Everyone comes here with their girls, damn it! I can't remember them all."

"You're right. Well, I have to go."

"On your way then. Bye, nonsmoker!"

Rubinchik walked out of the iron gates, sat in his Moskvich, and then . . . suddenly he saw her. She had just got off the bus that had arrived, and she stood there delighted and watching him from across the road.

Twenty minutes later they were gliding across Count Sheremetyev's lake. Olya—for that was her name—had not only managed to borrow the museum's row boat, but even an ancient silk parasol. Sitting under it, she looked like one of the Empress's ladies-in-waiting and her happy gaze glinted blue-green like the lake.

"Iosif, tell me something," she said.

"What, for instance?"

"Something about Peter the Great."

"Well, I never made a special study of him. But I did once hear a sermon by Bishop Nathaniel. He had an interesting view of Peter. Would you like to hear about it?"

"Of course."

"He maintained that Peter's importance in Russian history was equal to that of Prince Vladimir. It was he who in A.D. 989 forcibly baptized all the Rus and made them Christians. Until them, the Russian Slavs had no national consciousness, no culture of their own, not even their own gods. It was in return for the hand of Princess Anna that the dissolute Vladimir brought the untouched souls of the Slavs as a Christian offering. And as you know, the newly converted always pray with threefold fervor. And so the Slavs followed Christ like the ancient Jews followed Moses, without a backward glance. And one generation later, there were more churches, monasteries, and holy books in Rus than in Byzantium itself. Women made Christ their romantic idol, and men their hero. So, thanks to his marriage to a Christian princess, Vladimir's debauchery was expiated by the whole Russian people's striving after sanctity.

"So you can just imagine, Olya, that Peter the Great appeared to be the Antichrist incarnate, when he began breaking up, destroying, and violating this patriarchal land of 'Holy Russia!' When he began mocking Christian places of worship and erecting marble statues of naked Roman women and so on. But Nathaniel saw Peter's greatness elsewhere that in his short life he created a powerful empire from what was hitherto an obscure Muscovite province at the edge of civilization. He built a navy, opened an Academy of Arts and Sciences, started a ballet, theaters, ministries, schools, and he even introduced potatoes and tomatoes! And when Count Golovkin—if you've heard of him—gave Peter the titles of Emperor and 'Father of the Fatherland,' he said, 'By your untiring efforts and leadership, we have emerged from the darkness of ignorance into the theater of worldwide glory.' In other words, Peter made Russia into a superpower of the eighteenth century. Only nobody, not even Soviet historians, like to admit that Peter allowed the

Russians no freedom, not even the nobility. He dressed them all in western wigs and camisoles, and closed off the country's frontiers. And," Rubinchik continued in an ironic vein, "that forces us to draw comparisons with modern times, and especially with the so-called 'great' Stalin. But that's the subject for another conversation, next time, because now it's time for me to go and get some sleep. I have to be at work soon."

With that, he brought the boat to shore by Countess Sheremetyev's orangery.

"Can't you manage just ten more minutes!" Olya pleaded like a child.

"I can't," he said. "Someone in this country has to work—you in your museum, and me in my boiler room. So, Princess Olga, forward march to work! I'll count up to three. One . . ."

"But you will come again?"

"Definitely. Two . . ."

"Thank you!" She planted a childish smacking kiss on his cheek, jumped out of the boat, and ran off in the direction of the palace.

"Three," Rubinchik said to himself sadly as she left. "And if you ever do come back, you bastard, you'll ruin this one last fairy tale."

Thirty-six

The thick dark beer gushed into the glass mugs. unexpectedly a consignment of Senator Czech beer had come on sale, and a noisy throng had gathered under the faded awning of the beer pavillion in Sokolniki Park. A crowd of men, and a few women, pressed around the bar as a couple of sprightly barmaids held tankards under the spurting streams of beer, barely half-filling them before the foam frothed up over the brim. The women handed these half-mugs to the customers and flung the sodden coins into their till. When Karbovsky asked for a top-off, the saleswoman glared at him and passed his two tankards to someone else.

"Svetlana, he's with me! He's with me!" Rubinchik cried on his friend's behalf. Not so long ago he had been here everyday, so he knew the barmaids.

"So what's all this crap about getting a fill-up?" The woman took another beaker and held it directly under the spigot so the beer foamed even more than before.

"He's still a youngster! Only just been let out!" Rubinchik explained.

"Oh, well, that's different. You should have said so! Otherwise I'd give him some fill-up!" Svetlana's anger instantly evaporated, and she filled Karbovsky's glasses to the brim.

"What did they do you for?" she asked genially.

"For Arafat," Karbovsky answered reluctantly.

"Oho!" she said respectfully. "What'd you do to him?"

"Nothing so far. But I've the whole of life ahead of me yet..."

"There you Jews go!" She jerked her head round. "Swilling vodka and fighting Arabs!" Then, as Rubinchik brought back another fistful of glasses: "Anyway, where have you been? Ain't seen you for a month!"

"I gave it up," Rubinchik explained. "Only today my friends got let out, and we had to celebrate." He paid for the beer, grabbed his glasses—three in each hand—and followed Karbovsky to the end table that Efim Gertsianov was holding for them. The seventy-year-old actor had just had his head shaved at the Nogatinskaya Penitentiary. With a copy of *Pravda* spread out on the table in front of him, he was busy breaking up a dried carp with his tobacco-stained fingers. His helper in this was the even more famous film director Andrey Koltsov, who at thirty-six had won the prize at Cannes; and Gertsianov had starred in all his productions until he filed his papers to leave for Israel. The fish was tough as old wood and was giving them problems. But they kept at it, while continuing the never-ending dialogue between the Jewish and Russian intelligentsia.

"You see, old man," Gertsianov said to Koltsov, who was half his age, "Whatever I do here, I'm still an outsider. If I go and tell the Russians that they're sitting in shit because of their Soviet rulers, they hate me for telling them that, since I'm a Yid." He began clouting the dried fish on the beer-sodden tabletop, and finally managed to snap it. "And when I play some kindly, long-suffering Russian in one of your movies, they don't like that either: they say I'm trying to curry favor and kiss Big Brother's ass. And none of them realize that this whole regime is propped up only by the goddamned good-heartedness and patience of the Russian people! You Russians would be better off if you turned nasty!" Gertsianov finally managed to split the carp. He handed a sliver to each of his drinking partners and lifted his glass. "Okay, then, here goes! It's great to be free! Even after only five days in there!"

They all drank. Koltsov wiped the foam from his lips with the back of his hand and began reflecting in a dreamy voice: "Perhaps I should try and clear out too? Send the whole lot to hell, eh? I could bang the door so loudly, there'd even be a rumble over there in Cannes."

From his tone of voice, it sounded as if this was an idea he'd already considered. Rubinchik could well imagine the sort of rumble Koltsov had in mind. "Andrey Koltsov, famous Soviet film producer and jury member at

Cannes, refuses to return to the Soviet Union and is requesting political asylum . . ." It would make headlines around the world.

"No, you mustn't leave!" Karbovsky said with conviction, dipping his fish in the beer. "You are telling people about the human soul, conscience, and mercy, and *they* go on about friendship with Arafat and raising productivity. And every time that they shove one of you out of the country—Solzhenitsyn today, Tarkovsky tomorrow, and you the day after tomorrow—each time that happens, you lose some of the people to them. No, if I was a Russian, I wouldn't leave!"

Koltsov grinned.

"It's easy for you guys to talk, when in fact you are about to leave."

Gertsianov looked at Koltsov with his little hazel eyes.

"You're a dick," he said sadly. "You're a streak of stupid Russian crap, that's what you are!" He stroked the stubble on his shaven scalp and lit up a Yava, a coarse cigarette without a filter. "First of all, we ain't goin' nowhere. We've been turned down. That's the first thing. Secondly, you think I have no feelings for Russia? You think I understand Tchaikovsky less well than you? Or don't I know that there aren't and never will be any women better than Russian women?" Gertsianov leaned down and pulled out an already-started bottle of Moskovskaya vodka. He then poured it into his fiends' empty beer glasses. "And just so you know," he continued, "I'm still quite capable of getting it up, and my wife, who is Russian, is thirty-seven years younger than I am! But you'll never know what it means to be a stranger in your own country. And that's a theme from Shakespeare, old man! Even better than Hamlet!" He lifted his glass. "So here's to it! Here's to freedom! *Our* freedom and *yours!*"

He downed his vodka in one gulp, banged his glass on the table and said sadly:

"Bastards! It's two years now since they pulled the ground from under me—I can't get onto the stage or the movies! People no longer even recognize me, they just think I'm a drunk."

"Don't worry," said Karbovsky, "once you're over there, you'll start again."

"Yes, I'll start acting again out there!" he exclaimed.

"In what language?" Koltsov asked. "Parlez-vous anglais? You speak English?"

"Never mind!" Gertsianov waved the question drunkenly aside. "Art is like beer—it's international. And there's never enough of it." He pointed to their empty glasses.

"Okay, I'll see to it." Karbovsky caught the hint.

But Koltsov stopped him.

"No, it's my round."

"I'll come with you, or they'll short-measure you," Rubinchik said. The two of them gathered up the empty glasses and went off to the bar.

Gertsianov gnawed at the dried fish and looked around. Over the thirty-odd tables there was a hum of conversation mixed with the fumes of beer, vodka, and green-pea soup. There were local drinkers with their mouths full of metal teeth, unshaven business travelers with briefcases, naval commandos, students wearing Odessa's answer to American Levis, heavily made-up stout-legged women. But these people were "his" public, who only two years ago knew him by sight and recognized him as a celebrity.

"Yessir! And lots of people think it's hard to be a Jew in the Soviet Union," Gertsianov said suddenly. His voice was not loud, but he projected it in a "public" manner—with the aplomb of a master performer who knows the audience will listen even if he whispers. "But in fact, there's nothing easier. Now, it *was* hard being a Jew in tsarist Russia. . . ."

"Efim, don't!" Karbovsky begged.

But Gertsianov continued:

"My grandfather, for instance. In order to be a Jew, he had to live in the Pale of Settlement! Secondly, he had to go to the synagogue! Thirdly, he had to keep the sabbath! Otherwise who would have considered him a Jew?"

"Efim, don't get wound up," Karbovsky implored again, glancing all around them.

Gertsianov seemed to be talking softly, just to Karbovsky, but everyone at the neighboring tables had fallen silent and turned to look at them. Gertsianov seemed not to notice though, and carried on:

"But in our country today it's far easier to be a Jew! If my mother and father are Jews, then that makes me a Jew, and I need do no more about it. I don't even need to get circumcised. It's true, isn't it—nobody's going to check whether or not I've been snipped."

Some people laughed uncertainly, not sure how to react. The group of rowdy students tuned in immediately, though, and realized some fun was in store.

"Come on, then, tell us, Grandpa! Tell us more!"

"Of course I'll tell you." Gertsianov now turned to face his public.

"Efim, they've only just let us out!" Karbovsky moaned behind him. But Gertsianov wasn't listening, and kept on addressing the public, like a practiced master of ceremonies:

"Whether I am circumcised or not is not important," he said. "Nor whether I know Hebrew or not. Or whether or not I eat pork. I am a Jew, and that's that. I don't even need to go to a Jewish school—there aren't any in the country anyway. We only need to be born of Jewish parents, and that makes us Jews for all eternity!"

"Hey, that what's-his-name? That actor . . . you know . . . Gertsianov!" The young naval commandoes now recognized him.

But Gertsianov lifted a hand and quelled the excitement as people recognized him. Then he began moving among the tables as though he had left the stage and was walking among his audience.

"It's true, of course. A few of us try to get away from our Jewish origins and hide them. Some people change their names. And for a substantial bribe, the militia will even write in your passport, in the "nationality" section, that these people are Russians, Ukrainians, or Uzbeks. But that's of no help whatsoever. As the saying goes, it's our faces that get beaten, not our passports! I'm right, aren't I?"

"This is a provocation!" a little Tatar woman commented loudly. "We should call the militia!"

"Let the guy talk if he wants!" her fancy man objected. He was a tall, handsome type in a leather coat.

"Yeah, go for it, boss!" the drunken students egged him on. "This is a free country! Let the man talk!"

"Thank you!" Gertsianov nodded to them and then turned to the Tatar woman. "And so far as your beating our faces and not our passports is concerned, well, that old saying came from experience, like every other proverb. But imagine how often you get your face flattened before a saying like that comes into being!"

People laughed, and there was a shout from a group of workers at the far end who had just come from their shift.

"Here you, comedian, come over here! We'll stand you a drink! But tell us the whole truth! And give it to us straight, like a good Communist!"

Gertsianov's face now wore a faint smile of satisfaction. By now they'd all recognized him. Then Koltsov emerged from the crowd around the bar with three glasses of beer in each hand. When he saw what was happening he stopped dead.

"Efim, come on, stop it!"

"Keep away!" Gertsianov said quietly from the corner of his mouth, then loudly to his audience: "A funny thing happened to me recently. It was in Kiev. I was riding along in a streetcar, and suddenly a woman got on with a little dog. And the dog, begging your pardon, went and pissed. Right there in the streetcar. Yes! Well, the passengers of course began to get annoyed. It's a disgrace, they said. Filthy smell! And since when are dogs allowed in streetcars? Then up gets this passenger and says in broad Ukrainian: 'What's all the noise about? We tolerate kikes in our streetcars, so we can certainly put up with a few dogs!' "

Gertsianov waited for the laughter to subside and then continued:

"So, as you can see, it's easy to be a Jew here. You don't even need to do anything. Because people can tell the difference between dogs and Jews just the same."

"No, this is an outrage!" the Tatar woman started up again, but most people just laughed.

Gertsianov now picked issue with the Tatar woman:

"Why is it an outrage, my dear?" he said. "Surely you realize that you are a Tatar? When my grandson was only seven, his friends in the street explained to him that he was a Jew. They ambushed him on the way home from school and rolled him in the snow and shoved lard in his mouth and said, 'There you are, you little kike! Have some of our lard! Enjoy it!' But of course, they are only children, so there's no way of getting back at them. But I remember when I was performing on the Southern Front during the war, an army colonel came round to see us backstage—"

"Efim! We can do without all this. . . ." Andrey Koltsov pleaded behind his back.

"Leave me alone. *I* can't do with out it!" Gertsianov shot him an aside and turned again to his audience, which had now begun to expand as people began walking up from the surrounding paths. "Anyway, yes . . . So this colonel came backstage and he had these colossal *eyebrows* . . ."

This one word Gertsianov pronounced with exactly the same intonation and speech defect as Brezhnev, so that everyone realized who he meant. A worried hush descended as they recognized the old actor's incredible daring:

"Well, he talked with our women performers, and then invited me to his office. And he personally poured out a drink for me and he said to me"— At this point, without any makeup Gertsianov became a living replica of Brezhnev and continued impersonating his voice—" 'Well, you Yids really are so talented, . . . u-u-uck me. If I could be so funny, I'd be getting it on with all the telephone operators!' "

Everyone burst out laughing, even the naval commandoes.

"So," Gertsianov resumed, "the Jews in Russia have no problem about retaining their nationality. Furthermore, the government shows special concern for us. For instance, just a few days ago Comrade Arafat paid us a visit, and as you know, he's not the Jews' greatest friend. So the day before he arrived, they collected all of us and transported us out of town and, as you can see, shaved our heads. This was to insure we didn't get infected with lice. From our cellmates, I mean . . ."

The pavillion shook with another round of laughter. The show was now attracting the Sokolniki Park prostitutes looking for trade, and courting couples who emerged from fumbling with one another in the shrubbery.

"And the training we get!" Gertsianov went on, reveling in his success.

"Under the tsar, you know, there was a five percent quota in universities for Jews. Now it's just half a percent!"

"Come on, that's enough! This isn't a theater!" the barmaid yelled. They were miffed that the crowd had turned their backs on them to watch Gertsianov. However, nobody—neither the public, nor Gertsianov—took any notice. Svetlana then produced a phone from under the counter and with furious jerky gestures began dialing.

"No need for that, Sveta," Rubinchik said. "He's just had a few, so what?"

"If he's tanked up, let him go home and put his show on there! I'm responsible for what goes on here!" Svetlana swept her hair back resolutely and pressed the receiver to her ear. "Hello! Comrade Captain! This is Solovyova from the beer bar. We've got an actor guy here making speeches..."

Abandoning his glasses of beer on the counter, Rubinchik dodged behind the performer's back to where Koltsov and Karbovsky were standing.

"We've got to get him out of here. The militia will be here any moment!"

Koltsov grinned.

"Ever try dragging an actor off stage? Especially with a success like this!" he said. Indeed Gertsianov was enjoying a veritable triumph.

"And the government's concern for the Jews has reached such a pitch," he announced, "that none of them are allowed to go and live abroad. Well, you know yourselves, that if you, or some Uzbek or Ukrainian wrote an application and said you wanted to leave for the West, they'd put you straight in an asylum! But here the Jews again get privileged treatment. Especially if you happen not to be a very useful Jew—say, a thief, a loafer, or if you're subnormal. And if you want to go to America, wonderful. Off you go! Or Australia? Good riddance! Or Israel—by all means, off you go, you bastard! But intelligent Jews, scientists and scholars and the like—no, no. They can jolly well stay in Russia. This, surely, shows real concern for the purity of the Jewish race!" Gertsianov watched as a young commando officer left his group and made his way to the exit. Then he continued: "Incidentally, a friend of mine—who was also a sailor, by the name of Ivanov—went to the Visa Office to see General Bulychev and demanded to be let out to Israel. The head of the Visa Office was astounded. 'What?' he said, 'What sort of Jew are you? Your name is Ivanov. You're Russian!' But Ivanov said, 'But I *feel* that I'm a Jew!' Bulychev said, 'But both your father and mother are Russians!' All the same, Ivanov maintained, 'I *feel* that I'm Jewish, and that's all there is to it.' So do you see how far things have gone? Russians are even signing on as Jews! Ukrainians too. And even Georgians!

And why? Because they've grown lazy. They don't want to 'build Communism' any more. They'd rather travel West and have a rest."

"Look out! The militia!" There was a sudden shout from outside, where a militia van had rolled up with a red flasher on its roof.

Thirty-seven

The van hardly had time to brake before six men in uniform jumped out and rushed into the pavillion. But at that instant all the lights went out in the bar and everywhere else in Sokolniki Park. In the darkness, as frightened women shrieked, two of the commandoes dragged Gertsianov over to Karbovsky, Rubinchik, and Koltsov and said in low voices, "Be quick, take your comedian and beat it—fast! Through the bushes! We'll cover you!"

Karbovsky, Koltsov, and Rubinchik grabbed their friend under his arms and dashed out. Behind them, they could hear the militiamen's whistles, shouts, the thump of falling bodies, and the crash of broken glasses.

But the naval commandoes evidently were better trained than the militia. Nobody came chasing after them, and a few minutes later they managed to get out of the park. Five minutes after that, they were all sitting in Rubinchik's car heading away from Sokolniki and driving though the Moscow evening. Cooling down, Koltsov turned to Gertsianov.

"And you go on about Russians not liking the Jews. Those young guys that saved you were Russian commandoes!"

"Thank the Lord. That was just a rare exception," Gertsianov said. "If everyone loved us like *they* do, we'd have been assimilated long ago."

"There's no way of getting it right for you, is there?" Koltsov laughed.

Rubinchik set his friends down at the subway station and headed off toward his boiler room. He was in great form, and last night he had made real progress with his book. His work at the furnaces required no effort. His predecessors had also been Jews—engineers and technicians, all of them, waiting to emigrate, like himself. Thanks to their efforts, the gas supply and the temperature in the water boilers had been regulated and made fully automatic. The whole job was reduced to watching four pressure gauges, which a three-month-old chimpanzee could have done. And to enable this chimpanzee, or his human substitute, to sleep, read Proust, or do academic work, the alert on each pressure gauge was connected to an alarm clock. At the time there were several hundred such boiler rooms in Moscow, which enabled the Moscow Gas Company to save millions of cubic meters of gas. The directors of Mosgas took credit for this as stemming from their skill in regulating the city's heating systems, and every few months they won commendations. The emigrating boiler men, however, didn't ask for any bonus. They were content to set up their boiler rooms as studies, Hebrew language classrooms, or as meeting places for clandestine seminars.

Rubinchik shared his particular furnace room with a day-shift partner called Shulman, a microbiologist. Their premises were equipped with a large industrial fan the size of a jet-engine turbine, an old folding bed, a dozen microscopes of various sizes, a closet laboratory with Shulman's test tubes, a writing desk, and—inherited from earlier generations—a super-powerful homemade radio. It could pick up any Western station regardless of Soviet jamming, because the aerial had been run to the top of the furnace-room chimney. In addition, there were cunning hiding places built almost into the furnace and boilers concealing Jewish prayerbooks, Cecil Roth's pocket *History of the Jews*, a volume of Jabotinsky, Menachem Begin's memoirs, two volumes of the *Jewish Encyclopedia*, and a book of Jewish fairy tales—the Haggadah—all of which had been smuggled into the USSR by intrepid Western tourists.

Rubinchik had brought his typewriter here. Now, as he listened to Dave Brubeck and Louis Armstrong and fortified himself with strong coffee, he sat writing accounts of episodes from the Soviet Jewish saga: the secret Hebrew schools, Inessa Brodnik's visit to the prisoners of Mordovia, which read like a detective story, the women's demonstration outside the Visa Office, the stool pigeons in the Jewish synagogue, and the baking of Passover matzo in a "mobile bakery" that the KGB had been hunting down for eight years, in much the same way as the tsarist Okhranka had searched for the underground Bolshevik press that produced *Pravda*. That night Rubinchik wrote a dramatic account of the refuseniks' arrest on the eve of Arafat's arrival in Moscow, and of Gertsianov's crazy performance in Sokolniki Park. His book was written "from life," and the dissident and refuseniks' ongoing battle with the KGB provided a subject and plot worthy of John le Carré. As a professional reporter, all he had to do was disentangle the main thread from a mass of minor incidents.

As Rubinchik put together this by-no-means-exhaustive account, he was left in no doubt: the authorities were furiously seeking ways of subduing and intimidating their citizens. It reminded him of the orphanage where he grew up, where teachers treated any disobedience by locking up the children and thrashing and starving them. While he sat there in his cellar, he realized that this country was not a great sovereign power with just a few minor defects, but a monstrous combination of an orphanage and a concentration camp. Here children were offered alcohol instead of mother's milk, poisoning their genetic memory and obliterating any recall of the goodness and mercy implanted almost a thousand years ago by Christianity. Everything in Russia that had been nurtured by her Christian priests, since the time of Prince Vladimir, had been broken, ruined, and erased. Once again, as a thousand years ago, this was a country where men could kill and be killed for a fur hat or a glass of vodka.

Admittedly, in this jail with its two hundred million inmates, it was still possible to meet a few hundred people of conscience. Yet even one of the best of them, Andrey Sakharov, had been forced with his own hands to create and explode an atomic bomb, before the human feeling revived in him and he realized with horror what he had done.

It was only Russia's women, those divas scattered around the provinces, who still preserved in their souls and in their DNA a few secret flickerings of a former Christian humanity and Russian beauty. But what difference could they make? Even if a thousand teachers and poets such as himself roamed the empire, seeking out these fading flames, fueling them with Jewish vitality, all such efforts were trifles, bagatelles, mere drops in the ocean. All the Jewish spermatazoa in the world could never revive this nation. What was needed was a new intervention, for maybe three hundred years, by some Anglo-Swedish horde that would fertilize all the women here with a healthy new set of chromosomes.

But in that case why in God's name had he delayed emigrating? Why had he not left seven years ago, as soon as Kuznetsov, Dymshitz, and other Zionist pioneers managed to breach the Iron Curtain? Why had he decided to move only when he was in a jam?

He knew perfectly well why, of course. The bend of Olya's thigh, her radiant, shining eyes, childish lips, the fair lock over her little ear—all this promised a repeat of that miracle on the River Ityl seventeen years ago. All these years he'd been chasing these mirages the length and breadth of Russia. But now he was putting it all behind him. He would not go to Kuskovo again, he would not put his book or his emigration at risk for just one final seduction. Liberty was more important than pleasure!

Proud of his decision and of his book, which would show Russia to the world and make him famous, Rubinchik sat at his typewriter and rattled off a final paragraph about Gertsianov's unexpected deliverance by the naval commandoes who turned off all the lights in Sokolniki Park. Then he returned his manuscript to its hiding place above the boiler. Looking up at the window, he saw the first signs of dawn and began putting on his yellow doeskin track shoes. Nocturnal jogging around Moscow had become part of his preparation for a new life in the cruel world of Western competition.

And off he went. Yesterday's blazing heat had now abated, and the streets were filled with cool air from the evergreen forests around the city. At times like this he felt an overpowering impulse to breathe in and fill his lungs and go out and run. With his vest and runnings shoes on, he again felt "with it," young, and vibrant.

He realized of course, once he got to the West, there would be no more Olyas, and he would never find a Russian diva to equal Anna Krylova. His wife might think that he was abandoning only his profession. But in fact he was leaving behind his secret "temple of love" whose female apostles carried him in their hearts almost like the name of God. But he never permitted himself any reunions. If the Angel Gabriel had appeared to the Virgin Mary *twice*, even he would have appeared no better than a commonplace cupid; then there would have been no Bible, no Christianity, no divinity.

But anyway, to hell with them, these Olyas and all the other Russian beauties! Rubinchik rallied his spirits as he left the boiler room. He locked the door and left a small cardboard notice: BACK SHORTLY. God had to be served, art demanded sacrifices, and Rubinchik's own book required abstinence from earthly blandishments. After all, what awaited him here if he were to stay? In a year or two, at the insistence of Arafat and the Kremlin's other Arab friends, Andropov and Brezhnev would slam the door on emigration altogether, just as Stalin did in 1928. And in ten years' time Xenia would come and ask him, "Dad, you had the chance to leave and take us away. Why did you decide to stay? What on earth for?" And he would answer, "Because I was afraid they wouldn't let us out." "Why, Dad?" "Because in the town of Salekhard I had an unpleasant set-to with the militia." "But you could at least have tried!" Xenia would say. And she would be right.

"No, we're going to leave, we're going to leave!" Rubinchik told himself as he rounded the corner and turned off onto the Garden Ring. They will let us out! And I *will* write my book! And for the sake of this book, God will allow me to emigrate. Of course, I still have that gnawing fear that I could get turned down. And end up a janitor, a social outcast. But why would they want to keep back someone who is only a journalist? Or a pianist like Nelya? Why?

Rubinchik's thoughts were disturbed by a heavy pounding of feet behind him. He turned round. A tall male figure was moving up and would soon overtake him. For a moment he took fright—was this some hoodlum? Three years ago in Chelyabinsk, he'd almost been beaten to death by teenage marauders who couldn't undo the metal clasp on his watch. Or was this guy from the KGB? That was it—they'd found his manuscript in the boiler room and were now going to arrest him and dump him in one of their bread vans.

Panicked, he stopped. There was nowhere to run to, and he was alone on the Garden Ring. Three hundred yards ahead was a militiaman's post. No, pointless to run. They were everywhere. It was their country.

The tall stranger was pounding toward him like a sprinter, his feet slapping the cinders. Rubinchik came to a dead stop, caught like a rabbit in the headlamps of an oncoming train. And then the sprinter became visible in the cone of light from a streetlamp, and Rubinchik felt a weight lift from his shoulders: the other man also wore a running vest and shorts. But Rubinchik was no match for him. He had long powerful legs, took broad strides, and his shoulders and head were thrown back like a running deer. On his head he wore a sports cap with the words "Soviet Wings." An Olympic runner! Rubinchik felt relieved and envious, and he stepped to one side to clear the way.

"Shalom!" the man said as he ran past. As if this was a routine greeting! Rubinchik gazed after him, flabbergasted.

And as the Olympian disappeared in the haze of dawn, he waved a hand in the air. Without turning he shouted out in English:

"Next year in Jerusalem!"

It was a summer night like any other.

The capital of the world's proletariat slept its sleep, drank its vodka, made love in cramped apartments and in dark hallways. In secret laboratories it also worked to strengthen its might. It stalked and hunted dissidents and Zionists, and jammed Western radio stations, and with September just around the corner it also printed new textbooks with portraits of Brezhnev on the opening page. And at this quiet hour before dawn, here and there on the streets of Moscow men appeared wearing running vests and shorts, sweating and panting as they ran, with a look of grim concentration. Traitors to their country, they were training and preparing themselves for another life, in a different world, in the cruel world of capitalism.

At about the same time, another man left the so-called "Prize Winners' Nest," an eight-story brick edifice with a spacious lobby and airy apartments, and emerged onto the sleeping, deserted expanse of Vasilyevsky Street. He was neither a runner nor a Jew, but an ordinary, slightly elderly gent with a cap on his head and wearing worn pants and a freshly laundered checkered cowboy shirt. It was Evgeny Krylov, Anna Sigal's father. He carried a bag with a dozen or so empty bottles, and his route took him to the nearest wine and liquor store at Belorussky Station, where empty bottles could be exchanged for a quarter liter of vodka or a half of Algerian wine.

There were at least four hours to go before the store opened. Yet despite the early hour, a dozen or more suffering alcoholics had gathered by the heavily bolted doors, holding a variety of domestic articles—a silver glass holder, a meat-mincer, school textbooks, and a porcelain teapot. They were trying to hawk these goods for "just a ruble, sir" to the early risers hurrying to work.

Old Krylov stood with them for a quarter of an hour or so, gazing around him. Then, tormented by alcoholic thirst, he wandered off to another store on Krasnopresnenskaya, hoping it might open earlier. But there was a notice there, SALE OF ALCOHOL BEGINS AT 11:00 A.M. After standing around for a while with a second group of drunks, he headed off to a place where bottles could be traded in by the subway station on 1905 Street. From there, some ten minutes later, he trecked off to the beer kiosk at Barrikadnaya subway. There, too, however, everything was closed. And if anybody had been following Krylov, they would have seen that the old boy was in utter despair.

Seemingly, though, no one had bothered following him. So after a sigh and a groan and another chin-wag with the local boozers, he disappeared into the subway. Down there his behavior became curious. First he made a call from a phone booth, but hung up without waiting for a reply; then he joined the throng of Muscovites on their way to work and made his way on the circle line to Kursk Station. There, he seemed to change his mind. He jumped out of the car just as the doors were closing, and as in some spy movie, he rode back in the opposite direction. At Novoslobodskaya he repeated the maneuver. Every now and then he would dial a number from a public phone, hang up before any reply came, and continue traveling around on the crowded morning subways until he was convinced he had shaken off anyone that might have been trailing him, or—more likely—watching his daughter's apartment.

Thirty-eight

At 9:00 A.M. Rubinchik handed over his duties in the boiler room to Shulman the microbiologist and left for home. He intended to sleep for about three or four hours, then go down to the market for some fruit, and after that drive out to Lyubertsy to see Nelya and the children.

The road home took him via Kutuzovsky Prospect onto the Mozhaisk Highway. At that time—between nine and ten—there were convoys of ZIL limousines going in the opposite direction. Surrounded by a motorcycle escort, they were bringing VIPs back from their dachas at Rublyovo to the

Kremlin. While they raced down the axial Kutuzovsky route, the militia halted all traffic in both directions and moved all cars up against the curb. Swishing over the asphalt with their black polished armor glinting in the sun, these "V.I.P. mobiles" swept past the locals, who could only guess as to who might be sitting behind those heavy plush curtains. Could it be Kosygin? Or Gromyko? Or Andropov? Or even Brezhnev himself?

After three such corteges, Rubinchik finally got to the fork of the Mozhaisk and Rublyov Highways. Now he was in a working-class area, with six-and nine-story high-rises containing a honeycomb of tiny flatlets and standing like up-ended dominoes among the feeble saplings of the green open spaces. Here, he turned off to the northwest and a few minutes later, he rolled up the dusty track across the vacant lot to the garage compound. He stopped and got out. He undid the padlock, then heaved to push open the heavy gate. Just then, he saw a frail-looking old man in a cap, worn pants, and faded checkered shirt carrying a bag. The man appeared as if from nowhere—either from the empty watchman's hut or from behind some boxes of trash. Without a word he began helping Rubinchik open the gate.

"Thank you," said Rubinchik in surprise and tried to recall whether he had ever seen the man before.

The old man said nothing, but held the gate open as Rubinchik drove into the compound. He also waved Rubinchik on as he stopped to close the gate behind him.

"Go on, go on! I'll close it!"

Rubinchik drove up to his garage. Through the rearview mirror he saw the old man carefully close the gate, then follow him down the track, glancing all the while to left and right as if looking for someone. But who could he be looking for here, on an ordinary weekday, and at ten in the morning? Rubinchik opened up his space and drove the Moskvich in. As he locked the car and walked out, he again bumped into the strange old man as though the latter were waiting for him.

"Are you looking for someone?" Rubinchik asked.

"Uh-huh," the old man said. "I'm looking for a man called Rubinchik—Iosif Mikhailovich Rubinchik."

"Who? What's that?"

"Are you he? Are you Rubinchik?"

"Yes . . ."

The old man looked around him again, then stepped swiftly into the half-dark of the garage.

"Quick! Close the door!" he ordered.

"Why? What's up?" Rubinchik grinned—the old man only came up to his shoulder and was too old and shortsighted to be a mugger. But to be on the safe side, Rubinchik took a spanner off the shelf.

"Leave that alone! Don't fool around," the old man said. His voice was calm but had the authoritative tone of an army officer. The man began rummaging in his bag and there was a clink of empty bottles. Then from under them he pulled out a bundle wrapped in newspaper. Opening it, he produced a thick gray document folder and handed it to Rubinchik.

"This," he said, "is your case file from the KGB. You've got to read it, right now, and then give it back. So are you going to do this where everyone can see you? Or are you going to close the door?"

The man's voice was not loud, but he spoke in such a way that those at nearby tables could hear. Dramatist Iosif Prut was tall and impressive-looking with a head of completely gray hair.

"The other day I was at the doctor's," he said. "And I told him, 'There's something not quite right with me,' I said. Well, he examined me as he usually does. Then he told me, 'You're impotent, my friend!' And do you know . . ." At this point Prut took a long theatrical pause, to insure he had the attention of everyone in the room. "And do you know," he resumed, "it was like a weight off my shoulders!"

A chorus of friendly laughter filled the dining room, and Anna too smiled. She sat there by the window, enjoying the view of the large deserted park with the Yauza River just visible in the distance. The morning sun played on the river with a flash of glistening fish scales and also drove oblique shafts of light through the tall windows of the semicircular dining room.

The club here at Bolshevo belonged to the Filmmakers' Union. Anna had heard about similar such estates belonging to the unions of architects, writers, and composers. Since most people couldn't afford their own country dacha, the Soviet artistic elite had created these inexpensive resorts where union members could come for a month's holiday once a year. Here they had inexpensive lodging and enjoyed three meals a day among the company of their colleagues. Some even contrived to come for two months. Also, as Anna learned from the local Don Juans who fastened onto her as soon as she arrived, this particular estate, situated just forty kilometers from Moscow, had been a gift to the union from Stalin during the 1930s as a reward for the first Soviet blockbuster movie, *Chapayev*. Stalin evidently thought that filmmakers should be able to retreat here from the hassles of Moscow to dream up more celluloid masterpieces. Which they did. It was in Bolshevo that such acclaimed movies as *The Cranes Are Flying*, *Ballad of a Soldier*, and *Moscow Doesn't Believe in Tears* were conceived. A selection of stills from them decorated the corridors and halls of the main two-story house and the four cottages in the adjacent park.

Unlike the other guests, Anna Sigal had obtained a reservation here not to write a film script, nor to prepare a new role like Tatyana Samoilova at the next table. Samoilova was memorizing her lines as a Soviet weaving woman. Earlier she had made a big name with her role in *The Cranes Are Flying*, but then she'd become unrecognizably plump, largely from misery after the Kremlin refused to allow her to play the title role in a Hollywood version of *Anna Karenina*.

Anna Sigal's secret aim here was to gain the trust of singer Leonid Kashchenko. Since the 1930s he'd been as famous in Russia as Frank Sinatra in the States. And it was on this legendary old man that she was pinning her hopes in her secret duel with Barsky. She had followed old Professor Shnittke's commandments, and his belief that "there are no saints—dig deep enough, and you shall find!" In particular she had fastened onto the two lines on composer Dmitry Barsky in the *Great Soviet Encyclopedia*, and she was now carefully tugging on this slim thread. In a library copy of the three-volume *Soviet Musical Encyclopedia* she had found not only several lines on Barsky, but also a small, passport-size photo of him.

"BARSKY, Dmitry Igorevich, 1903–1937—popular music composer; Stalin Prize 1936; author of 'March of the Victors,' 'Morning of the Motherland,' 'Stalin's Falcons We . . . ,' etc.; film music for *Eastern Sunglow, Field of Gladness, Mountain Spring*, and others."

Anna had never heard of him, and it was not his works that interested her as much as his photo. She'd looked hard at the snub-nosed face, with its broad cheeks and the almost Tatar slant of its deepset eyes, and then recalled the visage of Colonel Oleg Barsky. Try as she might, she saw nothing in common between the Barsky she knew and the miniportrait of his father.

Anna had replaced the *Musical Encyclopedia* on its shelf and left the library. Outside she lit up a cigarette, inhaled deeply, and closed her eyes, as though trying to detect where her intuition was leading her. Some sixth sense—what Professor Shnittke called the "secret orgasm of the genuine investigator"—told her she was on the right track. Where it would lead, she had no idea, but within an hour she was at the office of the Union of Composers, and after that she visited two music booking agencies—Moscow Stage and the Russian Concert Agency, Roskontsert. Here she discovered that the only surviving performer of songs by Barsky was Leonid Kashchenko. But after the recent death of his wife he no longer lived in Moscow, nor at an out-of-town dacha (which he no longer possessed), nor at the Composers' Union hostel, which was a hotbed of infighting between Kremlin "court musicians." Instead he lived at the Filmmakers' club at Bolshevo. The rest was simply a matter of knowing how to work the Soviet system:

To Comrade Maryamov, Secretary
Filmmakers' Union

Dear Grigory Borisovich,
The Moscow Bar of Attorneys earnestly requests your cooperation
in helping attorney Anna Sigal obtain a booking at your Bolshevo
resort for a period of one week. The Bar of Attorneys will be glad
to return this favor to the Union of Filmmakers in the form of
priority attention to any requests for legal consultation, et cetera.

By now, her fifth day at Bolshevo and sitting just four tables away from
the great Kashchenko, Anna realized why he and other legends of the Soviet
arts scene chose this place as their last refuge. It was a cheery community
and provided an atmosphere in which people could unwind.

In the mornings the denizens were awakened by the cry of philosopher
and film critic Valentin Tolstykh:

"Rise and shine, celebrities! Gabrilovich has already written two pages!"

Tolstykh was a lark among men. He rose at five in the morning and
spent the next three hours scribbling philosophical tracts. After that, with a
sense of having dispatched his duty, he would hang around the producers'
and scriptwriters' rooms, distracting them with his lofty observations or
tempting them with walks in the nearby wood, or, if worst came to worst,
a hike to the nearby village of Pervomaika to buy a bottle of brandy.

By seven in the morning all the guests older than fifty were out in the
park. There, before breakfast, they'd stroll round the two circular paths that
were referred to as the lesser and the greater hypertonic circles. The first
and "leading" group on these walks were four Jewish founders of the Soviet
cinema, Evgeny Gabrilovich, Yuly Raizman, Sergey Yutkevich, and Mark
Donskoi, the pioneer of neorealism. Between them, these four men created
all the early classics of Leniniana—from *Lenin in October* and *A Man with a
Gun* to *The Communist* and *Lenin in Paris*. Still, this had not saved them from
being branded "rootless cosmopolitans" in 1949, and they'd been hounded
out of every movie studio until after Stalin's death.

Behind these elders, odd groups of other celebrated warhorses walked
and discussed their latest ideas. There was the Jewish Aleksey Kapler, who
in his youth had done ten years in a Siberian camp for having an affair with
Svetlana Stalin; dramatist Nikolay Erdman, who had received a sentence in
1935 for his play *The Suicide*; Evgeny Dombrovskii, who had served three
sentences for nothing at all; and also such great film authors as Yuly Dunsky
and Valery Fried, two Jews who had been thrown into a camp in 1944 at
the age of seventeen for allegedly organizing a "plot to assassinate Stalin."
Each had survived thanks to their ability to "pull out novels." That is, they

used to retell the tales of Alexandre Dumas and other authors to the bandits and murderers; they also kept them amused with a host of fascinating invented stories. Doing this, they so perfected their skills that later they could effortlessly "pull out" film scripts that now amused the entire socialist world.

By chance, some talents of the cinema had missed out on the Stalinist camps and were not used to rising so early. While others exercised, these fellows were still only waking up, cursing Valentin Tolstykh, and supping their yogurt to recover from the previous night's boozing.

By nine, however, everyone came trooping into the dining room for breakfast. This entire beau monde, including Kashchenko and the composer Nikita Bogoslovsky, would sit down and enjoy their cottage cheese, boiled eggs, and toast and marmalade. At this point into the dining room, walking with the gait of a tired Roman emperor, came the aging Soviet Bob Hope and Charlie Chaplin, the one and only Arkady Raikin. He too, of course, was a Jew.

In fact, ninety-nine percent of the old elite of the Soviet movie world were Jews. These pensioners sat for days on end on the veranda, chattering and recounting amusing stories and episodes from their eventful lives. Another favorite pastime was playing cards together with the house director Aleksey Bely. The latter was a former colonel who had helped liberate Prague. Now, however, he had so succumbed to the corrupting influence of his guests that he never reported them either to the KGB or even the Film Union Party committee. Not once had he informed on them, although at night through the doors of the guest rooms you could clearly hear the "enemy voices"—the BBC, Radio Liberty, and of course Kol Israel. And the following morning at breakfast everyone openly exchanged whatever news they'd heard the night before "from over the hill." The old waitresses, cooks, and cleaning women also never reported anyone—possibly because they remembered each of these giants from their younger days, or else simply because Bely had managed to gather a team that was watertight.

The Bolshevo moviemakers' club was clearly a veritable wasps' nest of Jewish activity. And if ever any anti-Semite from the movie world chanced to visit here, he saw living confirmation that Jewish domination of the cinema was no empty theory, and he usually left in a fury, never to return. But these men here were the patriarchs and teachers of several generations of great Russian filmmakers. Thus, despite vicious campaigns against the Jews, nobody touched this preserve of Jewish film relics. Probably their enemies were just waiting for them to die off of their own accord.

But these old-timers were not very good at dying. They basked in the Bolshevo sun, gossiped, played billiards, watched Soviet and Western films in the little screening room in the basement. And they patronizingly mocked their own eminent pupils whose youth still permitted an assault on anything in skirts that happened to land in "strawberry acre." Such as Anna Sigal.

The wives of these veterans would enjoy an afternoon jaunt around the local country stores in search of imported clothing. It was unclear why, when they'd already traveled the world, these ladies still needed Czech outfits, Hungarian shoes, and Polish cosmetics. But for whatever reason, they simply loved buying things. And at that time, as an incentive to collective farmers, they were allowed by Kosygin to make direct deals with other socialist countries; in exchange for tractors and furs, they brought to these rural areas goods that otherwise were in short supply. The best items of course were never displayed, but were disposed of via the back door. Anna knew about that from one of her clients—the director of a store in the next village of Tarasovka. Indeed, it was thanks to her defense that he avoided landing in jail for six years for embezzling so-called "high-priority goods."

But Anna had no need for Bulgarian tights or Vietnamese sandals. By her second day she had doped out the local timetable and knew what went on and where, on this, that, or the other veranda. She politely turned down invitations from Tolstykh, Govorukhin, and other forty-year hotshots of the cinema to accompany them on delightful walks in the woods, or to join them "for tea." She was waiting for a chance to get into the company of the legendary elders, where Leonid Kashchenko was to be found. But the wives of these old masters somehow protected their husbands' peace and quiet. But also the elders never allowed anyone in on their company, which usually gathered on the lower veranda. They would fall silent when anyone walked past who was not a member of their group. Of course, they were always exaggeratedly polite and showed pointed courtesy in giving way in the corridor, surrendering a chair in the TV lounge, or a seat in the screening room. But it would go no further than that.

Even on her fifth day, as Anna sauntered along the paths in the park, sunbathed in a deck chair reading pulp fiction, or joked her way out of various come-ons, she was beginning to despair. She still felt like a fish out of water and could find no way of penetrating the impassive armor of Raikin, Raizman, Yutkevich, Kashchenko, and company.

Despite that joke about her patronymic being "Evreyevna," these Jews would not let her into their circle and they distrusted her. She was no closer to her goal than when she arrived a week ago. But time was passing, and the grace period Barsky had allowed her was coming to an end. In another day or so he would be phoning looking for her and expecting an answer. Damn it, how could she latch onto Kashchenko while he was sitting there yet again with Raizman, Prut, Yutkevich, and Raikin, while all their wives were busy getting into Stolper's car for another cruise around the stores? But her attorney's intuition—what Professor Shnittke called "canine instinct"—was staying with her—as in the party game "hotter, hotter, colder, colder." She was convinced that these movie mastodons must have known the composer Barsky, and that they held the key to her salvation. But how to find an approach to these men?

Thirty-nine

Anna watched from the upper veranda as Stolper's white Volga drove away. Then she decided to go into the park. As she crossed the lower veranda, like a well-bred schoolgirl she bade a decorous "Good day" to the elders seated there. As her glance happened to rest on Kashchenko, the old boy was obliged to respond with the rest of them.

"Good day, my dear, good day!" he pronounced in his familiar thick baritone, with its trace of Jewish Odessa intonation.

"Oh, so they've not taken you with them shopping?" she asked, testing the water.

"No, my dear, they don't take us such places anymore. No more demand for the product," he said, and his companions laughed.

"Would you like me to take you? I do have a car."

"Thank you, my dear, that's hardly necessary," Kashchenko said. Then, as if to soften his refusal, "They haven't stocked our sizes for a long time now."

There was another gust of laughter.

"As you wish," said Anna, sensing there was no point in pressing. "I was just about to go to Tarasovka. I once defended the store director there. I think he might be able to find something for you."

Kashchenko glanced at his companions.

"Maybe I should go?" he half asked them, still with that inimitable Odessa intonation.

"Definitely go!" Prut said. "If such a young lady invited me, I'd go with her wherever she wanted!"

"Despite the doctor's advice?" Raikin said, and looked at Anna enviously. "Are you taking only singers?"

"No, I'll take you too with pleasure," Anna blushed at her success, and at this chance to talk to the famous Raikin in person.

· · ·

Ten minutes later Anna had quickly changed and grabbed her bag. Driving out the gate, she turned right and headed northwest down the lane toward Tarasovka. In her little yellow Zhiguli she had three of the greats: Kashchenko, as a portly seventy-year-old, sat in front, and in back were the one and only Arkady Raikin and Yuly Raizman. In American terms, it would be like having Frank Sinatra, Bob Hope, and Sidney Lumet all together. Anna was awed at the responsibility for conveying so precious a cargo, and she drove so slowly that Kashchenko began to rebel.

"My dear, people only drive this slow to the cemetery!"

"Oh, there was a speed limit sign," Anna volunteered as justification.

"Anna dear," said Kashchenko, "For us there aren't any limits any more. We've gone beyond them all."

"Apart from Prut's illness, of course," Raizman said from the rear.

Anna quickly discovered that all their old men's humor turned on this single theme. She could, of course, have taken the bull by the horns and asked Kashchenko there and then about his relations with Dmitry Barsky. But she decided not to hurry. She was enjoying the unexpected delight of conversing with these great artists and listening to the mock-jealous verbal dueling of Raikin and Kashchenko, whose sole aim, barely concealed, was to make an impression on Anna. Raizman took no part in this and just kept smiling with the thin lips and browless eyes of a wise turtle.

They came to a fork, one branch of which led to Tarasovka but had a barrier across it and a sentry and was marked MILITARY ZONE. With a sigh Anna began turning onto the other lane to follow the sign which said: TARASOVKA—DETOUR 15 KM.

"Stop, my dear!" Kashchenko said. "Where are you going?"

"To take the detour."

"No need to. Drive straight ahead."

"It really is the shorter route," said Raikin from the rear.

"But it's a prohibited area!"

"Of course it is. This whole country is a prohibited area," Kashchenko said. "Just drive straight on, dear. Listen to your elders."

Anna obediently drove on, imagining the old men had some sort of permit. She stopped by the barrier, and a lanky young soldier with a machine gun sauntered out of the sentry hut to meet them.

"Where are you going? Let's see your permit!" The young soldier's manner was brazen, once he saw there were no officers in the car.

Anna looked round at Kashchenko and Raikin, and the guard followed her gaze and also looked at them. Suddenly his face changed, his eyelashes fluttered and his jaw fell in mute astonishment. He couldn't believe his eyes—Raikin and Kashchenko, large as life!

"Open your barrier, there's a good boy," Raikin said gently.

In confusion, the guardsman suddenly jerked to attention, saluted and bawled: "At your service, Comrade Raikin! May I proceed?"

"Do just that, buster. Do just that," Kashchenko said.

"Yessir, Comrade Kashchenko!" The guard rushed to open the barrier, and as soon as he had, he again stood at attention, his hand glued to the peak of his cap.

"Thank you." Kashchenko gave an imperious nod as they rode past.

"Serving the Soviet Union!" the soldier bawled back at the top of his voice.

Barely controlling her laughter, Anna drove away while Kashchenko jealously turned round to Raikin.

"Well, d'you think it was because of you that he let us through, or because of me?" Then, to Raizman: "Rabbi, what would you say?"

Raizman the Wise gave his verdict: "You're a couple of kids!" he said accusingly.

In the Tarasovka store the same situation was repeated a little differently. The manager and all the sales staff were thrown when they saw the live apparitions of Kashchenko and Raikin. So much so that they immediately closed the store and served only their celebrated customers. From secret stockpiles they hauled out Brazilian moccasins and Finnish suits with fancy double-stitched lapels. And while Raikin, Raizman, and Kashchenko grunted and wheezed in the bookkeeping office, which was turned into a fitting room, the manager himself tore off to a nearby restaurant and brought back some ten-year-old Armenian brandy, champagne, roast sturgeon on a skewer, and various other snacks, which he served on his office desk.

"Anna Evgenyevna," he told her, "I shall always be in your debt for introducing me to such people! Please, persuade them to have just one drink with me! I'll be able to tell my grandsons who I've had a drink with!"

After a glass of brandy and delighted with their purchases, the elders and Anna drove home. On the way back they completely softened up. Kashchenko began humming in his familiar rusty Satchmo voice.

"What's that song you're singing, Leonid Iosifovich?" Anna enquired cautiously.

"That's Dunayevsky's 'March of the Nakhimov Men,' " Raizman answered for him.

"Rabbi," Kashchenko turned round in his seat, "You're always right, of course. But when you're not quite sober, you're not quite always right. That was as much Dunayevsky as I am a Bolshoi ballerina. That tune, Anna dear, is a Jewish dance called 'Ha sher,' which Dunaevsky *cribbed* to compose the 'March of the Nakhimov Men.' "

"In that case," Raikin said, "all the Soviet marches of the 1920s were derived from Hebrew melodies."

"Do you know how it began?" Kashchenko asked, and went on without waiting for an answer: "It started with Monya Grass! In 1918 a fifteen-year-old Jewish boy called Moishe Grass turned up at the headquarters of the First Cavalry Army. He said he needed to see Commander Semyon Budyonny. Are you listening to this, Anna?"

"Of course, Leonid Iosifovich!" Anna replied, and slowed down slightly.

"Well, of course they wouldn't let him anywhere near, and told him to clear off. But he insisted. 'I want to see Budyonny on an important matter!' So again they told him: 'Get out of here! We can't be bothered with you at a time like this! The whole army's being gobbled up by lice!' But still he went on about wanting to see Budyonny on important business. So finally they let him in. And Budyonny asked 'Whaddaya want?' And Monya tells him, 'I'm a composer, and I can write you such a song that it'll lead your men into battle as well as any general!' Budyonny twisted his mustache and said, 'Well, I'll probably lead my men into battle myself. But what I do need is a march that'll lead those scumbags off to the bathhouse! The buggers simply won't get washed, can you believe it?! Can you write a march like that?' 'Sure thing!' says Monya. And he gets up and rolls his little Jewish eyes and suddenly starts marching on the spot, and to the tune of a Jewish freilechs-dance he sings:

> Forward march!
> Ich geihn in bod!
> Kratz mir on die pleitze!
> Nein, nein,
> Ich well nit geihn
> A daink dir far on eitze!

" 'Well,' Budyonny said, 'I like the tune, it's a good jaunty melody. But what does it mean?' Then Monya rolls his eyes again and switches from Yiddish into Russian:

> Forward march!
> I'm off to the baths!
> Just you scratch my back!
> Oh, no, no!
> I will not go!
> I'd rather be pole-axed!

"Well, Budyonny liked it so much that ever since then the whole Red Cavalry went to the bathhouse singing it. And so Moishe Grass became the first composer to the Red Army! And he and his brother Abram wrote all their songs to the tunes of Hebrew freilechs!"

"And not just the Grass brothers," said Raikin.

"And did you know the composer Dmitry Barsky?" Anna at last managed to ask. Holding the wheel with her left hand, she began fumbling in her handbag.

"I hope you're not going to smoke?" asked Raizman, who had a sharp eye and never missed a detail.

"Oh no, Yuly Yakovlevich," she answered, taking her hand out of the bag and putting it back on the steering wheel.

"Hear that, Arkady?" Kashchenko laughed. "Here we are talking about the Grass brothers, and she asks me did I know Mitya Barsky! And do you know why it was that Barsky got the Stalin Prize?" he asked.

"It was for the 'March of the Victors,' wasn't it?" Anna asked cautiously.

"You're dead right! And who was it who sang that song to Stalin? Who was the first performer? D'you know?"

"Was it you?"

"Right again. And do you know how that song came about?" Kashchenko said and turned to Raizman and Raikin. "I don't think you ever heard this *meintze*? It's part of the same story really. In 1935, Anna—before you were even on the drawing board, so you won't remember any of this—Stalin began getting rid of certain cultural figures. Babel, Goldberg, Mandelstam, and others. Because you realize who these people were? Eighty percent were Jews. And how do you think he managed to nab them? He demanded that every artistic Union—the composers, the writers, and the others—should name all 'enemies of the people' among their membership. And if the Union leaders didn't find the required quota and expose them, then they themselves were sent to the camps as accomplices of these 'enemies.' So there was Mitya Barsky, then a young secretary of the Composers' Union, almost the only Russian among all that musical *mishpoche*. Are you still listening, Anna?"

"Yes, I certainly am."

"Well, anyway, there was Mitya Barsky—an honest young guy from an old noble family and stuck in an awful situation: he had to turn somebody in, or else he'd land behind bars himself! So what did he do? He just sat and drank! Every evening we met at his dacha in Pakhra, and he was tearing his hair, and he sat drinking vodka and weeping: 'I'm a nobleman! I'll have to shoot myself! I can't write denunciations!' Well, it was clear, the NKVD were not going to wait. Almost every night they came round and scooped up someone or other. And any day they would come for him, because he wasn't reporting anyone and he wasn't writing any songs either. Meanwhile Isaak Dunayevsky wrote a new song every day, and so did the Grass brothers, and so did Blanter, and Solovyov-Sedoy—all of them! Trying to stay in the public eye so nobody would arrest them. But all Barsky did was drink. Well, his wife Varya was quite a beauty—not the world's best singer, but she did have a voice. Do you remember her, Yuly?"

"Of course," said Raizman. "She did a small part for me once."

"Well, anyway, one day she set the table with caviar, mushrooms, and vodka, and she invited us over. She said: 'You guys have got to do something! You've got to save him! Tomorrow there's a concert for this workers' congress, and everyone's going to be there with their new songs—Dunayevsky and Solovyov-Sedoy, but Mitya can hardly stand up! Help him!' So what do you think the Grass brothers did? You see, Anna, they were from a klezmer family, that means a Jewish band from the shtetl. There were five brothers, all talented as the devil. Two of them became Soviet musicians; two ran off to America in 1920 and to this day they're writing musicals for Broadway; and the fifth was some sort of technical genius killed in the war. Anyway, the two of them, Abram and Moishe, sat down there and then with me watching began hammering out some old freilechs-dance tune and putting words to it, just like Moishe once did for Budyonny. Only this time it sounded like this: 'We're the Stalinist guard, we're the Kremlin army! The whole world we conquer, both land and sea!' and so on and so forth. And by about midnight the thing was finished, and we went over to the dacha next door where the poet Iosif Utkin was staying, and we asked him to write some lyrics. Well, he wasn't having any. 'I'm not kissing Stalin's ass, and that's final!' he said. (Anna, please excuse the word kissing, okay?) And I said to him, 'Iosif, what's Stalin got to do with it? We have to save this guy. So just do it for my sake! Nobody'll know you wrote it!' Anyway, I persuaded him. He left the first two lines in about Stalin, just as it was in their first draft and he wrote some appropriate stuff to go with it, without any Stalin. And the next day I appeared at this concert for the workers' conference in the Hall of Columns, and who do I see sitting in the first box? Comrade Stalin and Comrade Ezhov, the head of the NKVD! And so I announce: 'A new song by Dmitry Barsky—"Song of the Victors." ' And I sang it. And what happened? Do you remember, Arkady?"

"I sure do," said Raikin.

"Toward the end of that song, Anna, the entire hall got to its feet and began singing along with me! And then afterward, when we'd finished, the Great Leader himself got to his feet and applauded. And we realized that Mitya Barsky's life was safe, and that his Stalin Prize was also in the bag."

"But he died in 'thirty-seven. So that means he was arrested after all?" Anna said casually, trying not to sound too intent.

"No, he wasn't arrested," Kashchenko said. "But that's another story. . . ." He turned away to the window.

"Leonid, that's no way to act with a young lady," Raizman commented.

"Or else *I* shall have to tell her," Raikin threatened.

"Okay, I'll tell her then. But it's not a happy story, Anna." Kashchenko uttered a heavy, laborious sigh. "Well . . . there it was. Mitya Barsky got his Stalin Prize. But, again, it wasn't all sweetness and light. On the one hand his conscience troubled him, and on the other hand he had to keep up his reputation as the creator of that triumphant march. So what did he do? Once a week he'd get tanked up, and then summon Moishe and Abram Grass. And he'd say something like this: 'Ezhov and the NKVD are pressuring me. They want to know any enemies of the people among our composers. Quickly, write me a couple of marches—one to save your own skins, and a second to save mine. Otherwise I'll have to report you.' So what choice did they have? They sat down at the piano and began work, and Varya, Barsky's wife, helped them since she specialized in performing Russian songs. That way they wrote both the music and the lyrics, and she would sing it back to them so they could hear their music 'from offstage' as it were. Meanwhile Barsky sat at the table and downed one vodka after another. And what do you think came of all this, Anna?"

"I don't know. 'The Harvesters' March,' I guess?"

"Well, yes, that was a matter of course," Kashchenko said dismissively. "But when a beautiful young woman works at night at the piano with two brilliant young composers, while her drunken husband is slumped with his face in the salad, to coin a phrase, what came of all this, my dear, was not just a 'Harvesters' March.' A splendid little boy also appeared. But he had just one defect: a small birthmark under his left armpit—in just the same spot where all the Grass brothers had a birthmark. And when Mitya Barsky was bathing his baby son and saw that, all hell broke loose. I've never seen a man beat a woman so hard. How he thrashed her, it was dreadful! If the neighbors hadn't come, he'd have killed both her and the child! But they managed to restrain him and shove him under a cold shower, but he still was blazing with anger. Then he called up Ezhov and said, 'Nikolay Ivanovich, this is Barsky calling, Stalin Prize winner. Two of our enemies have wormed their way into Soviet music and are undermining it with the corrupting influence of tunes from the Jewish shtetl . . .' Ezhov told him 'Thank you very much. Just give me that in writing.' Well, to make a long story short, the two of them—Moishe and Abram—were picked up the next morning. That day, Mitya Barsky came to his senses and clasped his head in horror. But it was too late. Well, after that he took to drinking in earnest. And he drank without let-up. Out of sheer horror at what he'd done! Inside three months he practically burnt himself up, and he died in a bout of delirium tremens. Abram and Moishe Grass got twenty years each. They were carted off to Siberia and disappeared there and perished. And that, Anna, is the whole sad story. What d'you think, Yuly, could you make a movie out of that?"

"Maybe in two hundred years," said Raizman sagely. Meanwhile Anna slipped her right hand into her handbag and switched off the little dictaphone.

Professor Shnittke had proved right as always.

f o r t y

Mustering all his willpower, Rubinchik dashed off the sidewalk, straight under the wheels of an oncoming truck. Too late! With a squeal of brakes, the truck halted, and the petrified driver jumped from his cab and dragged Rubinchik up from beneath the bumper. But once the driver saw he was alive and not even injured, he became livid and began beating him. In fact, he clouted him with such fury that Rubinchik barely managed to get away.

Ending your life turned out to be harder than it seemed. Especially if, in order to spare your children, you tried to make your suicide look like an accident. After reading his KGB file, Rubinchik was in a worse state of shock than with his blood pressure attack in Kiev. But still he could not bring himself to jump under the wheels of a car. On two occasions in the subway, too, alert platform guards had dragged him back from the edge just as the train came screeching into the station.

These failures occurred possibly because Rubinchik felt he still had time to spare. The old man who brought him that dreaded file had refused to identify himself, but he did tell Rubinchik he had a week before he was to be arrested. Evidently, whoever had sent that elderly messenger reckoned on Rubinchik using the respite to secure protection in high places, organize his defense, or simply flee. But ever since he'd applied to emigrate, there was no question of any high-level protection. And where could anyone hide from the KGB?

Rubinchik walked around Moscow in a blind stupor, realizing he was seeing these streets for the last time. He drew deeply on a cigarette (before he died, he could permit himself that luxury again). So all his maneuvers—

going on the bottle, getting fined for being drunk and disorderly—turned out to be nonsense, a childish game, a boy's tomfoolery. That Colonel Barsky to whom those reports and denunciations were addressed had collected a file on him that left no escape. Maybe half the apostles of his secret Love League had been broken and testified against him. The journalist Rubin had allegedly enticed them into his hotel room and deprived them of their virginity in a manner forbidden by Article 120 of the Criminal Code—"for the satisfaction of his sexual passion." This lecherous monster, who had also derided Russian history and the great Russian people, was represented as a foul degenerate that Rubinchik himself would readily have executed.

Aware that his earthly existence was coming to an ineluctable end, Rubinchik was filled with a poignant sense of the world's beauty: its lofty blue heavens, wind rustling in the dusty poplars, the acrid taste of tobacco smoke, and the amazingly cute physiognomy of a streetcar that suddenly came hurtling round the corner with a jangle of its bell. Everything around him that he earlier despised and hated—the stupid slogans praising the Communist Party, the awful, scandalous lines at the stores, the brutish bribe-taking militiamen—everything suddenly acquired added color. Like in one of those 3-D movies, where you put on special goggles and see the images on screen in sharp relief. But there you cannot reach out and touch the brilliant phenomena, and Rubinchik too felt that he no longer belonged to this world; he felt like an outsider, a disembodied spirit visiting from some world beyond.

He felt as if he had already died. True, a certain physical envelope remained. It had legs and carried him through the streets and boulevards. But he himself—the journalist, would-be emigrant, father of two, mentor of a constellation of beauties—*that* Rubinchik had died, dissolved into space. And in another few days the remaining physical husk would be destroyed. Because there was no other way out, none at all . . . Lord, how stupidly he'd spent his time on this beautiful planet. He had written nothing, created nothing. All he'd done was chase after Russian girls, believing this was something ordained by Providence. But having reviewed his life through the eyes of the KGB, Rubinchik saw what devastating material they had against him. The Dreyfus case, the Beylis case, and other anti-Semitic calumnies had been contested in the courts and later refuted in the press. But what Emile Zola, Maksim Gorky, Heinrich Böll, or Simon Wiesenthal was going to stand up and deny what was irrefutable? Who would defend a man who did nothing but corrupt innocent Russian girls? And even if the philosopher Sergey Bulgakov had proclaimed there was a mystical, divinely ordained attraction between Judaism and the Russian soul, what did the KGB care?

The trial would make him into a sexual maniac, and this stigma would attach to his children and to all other Jews like a shameful tattoo. Well, to hell! He would not let it happen. Ilya Gabay had the strength to hang himself after a KGB interrogation; Solzhenitsyn's typist was desperate enough to jump out of a window when the KGB broke into her apartment to search for the *Gulag Archipelago*; and Musa Mamut, the Tatar activist, had the strength to burn himself alive after the authorities' refusal to return the Crimean Tatars to their homeland. So if they all could do it, Rubinchik too would find the courage. All he need do was sit in his car with the garage doors closed and fall into a drunken sleep.

One evening in his boiler room, Rubinchik decided that was the best way. The simplest and least painful. He retrieved the folder with his manuscript from its hiding place, all set to burn it. He stepped over to the furnace, opened the cast-iron door, and looked at the leaping jet of flame that roared and sputtered. He had once read that Jack London used to write only a thousand words per day, that is, two pages of typescript. But Rubinchik's manuscript already consisted of three hundred pages, and in his folio he had about another hundred sheets of notes and sketches. But for him these were more than four hundred sheets of densely corrected typescript. This was his first genuine book—sixteen chapters that brought to life the characters of Inessa Brodnik, Ilya Karbovsky, Vladimir Slepak, Efim Gertsianov, Anatoly Shcharansky, Raya Goldina, and a dozen other personalities, real and invented. To burn them all felt tantamount to throwing himself into the furnace.

Rubinchik looked around. He had to have a drink. Somewhere in Shulman's work cabinet there had to be some alcohol that he used to clean his slides or to preserve his amoebas and worms. He laid his manuscript to one side, opened Shulman's cabinet, and there among the test tubes and retorts he saw a flask containing a transparent liquid. It had a handwritten label with a skull and crossbones drawn on it and the words POISON! DO NOT TOUCH! Nonsense of course—it was the everyday practice of chemists and biologists to protect their alcohol against random pillaging by drunks. Rubinchik took the flask, opened the cork, and sniffed. It smelled of spirits all right. Though—goodness knows—maybe it was high-tech and not the sort one could drink? Now, though, it hardly mattered. He lifted the flask to his lips, swallowed a gulp, and suddenly heard a female cry.

"What are you doing?"

He turned round.

There was Olya in the doorway, with a look of horror on her lovely face.

"What are you doing?" she said again, and she ran toward him and grabbed the flask. "Are you mad? That's poison!"

"It's pure alcohol, Olya dear," Rubinchik grinned. "Want to try it?"

"Alcohol?" she was slightly embarrassed. But then she took the offensive again: "And even if it is, surely you don't have the right to drink while you're on duty?"

"Olya dear, I told you before that I was an alcoholic. How did you get here?"

She did not answer. She gazed around the boiler room and her eyes lighted on his typewriter and the folder with his manuscript.

"Aha," she said, bending over to look and covering her embarrassment. "I can see what sort of alcoholic you are. Iosif Rubin. *The Jewish Road*. Goodness, how messily it's typed. I knew you were a writer. Would you like me to type it out decently for you?"

He stepped up to her and took the manuscript from her.

"How did you find me here?" he asked.

"You yourself told me where you worked. That first day, do you remember? At the Institute of Glaciology. And I live just around the corner, above the Taganka food store. I used to live with my grandmother before, but now I'm on my own. Maybe I could sit down?"

He looked at her and did not answer. The glowing flame from the open furnace door lit up her face—or was she blushing at the boldness of her nocturnal visit to his cellar?

"I've been writing my practical paper on 'The Ethical Reforms of Peter,'" she said, and broke off. "Listen, if you're going to look at me like that, I'm going. I'm afraid . . ."

"Olya," he said, "do you realize who sent you here this evening?"

"Nobody sent me! Honest! I'm telling you: I was writing this paper of mine, and it suddenly occurred to me that probably you weren't very happy here. Don't you believe me?" Her wide eyes suddenly filled with tears— tears so childlike and innocent that he felt a sudden shock as a rush of hot blood coursed through his limbs.

"Yes, I believe you," he said, realizing full well that her arrival was a gift from heaven. Only God could have sent him such a precious consolation when he was on the brink of suicide. So he could pour forth all his vital essences into this magical vessel, so that his body would remain an empty envelope, and he could then wing his way from this beautiful earth as lightly as an angel. "Yes, I believe you," he repeated. "So, do you want to show me what you've been writing?"

forty-one

Barsky was interrupted at his work by the phone. He picked up. Who could be calling him at midnight? Surely not another emergency? After all the Jews did their mischief during the day, when they had an audience.

"Barsky speaking."

"Comrade Colonel, this is Zubovsky Boulevard, Captain Zhuravlyova," a female voice said. "We have a caller by the name Anna Sigal who's just booked an urgent call to Boston, USA. Do we connect, or do we block it?"

On Zubovsky Boulevard stood the huge faceless concrete building that housed the Ministry of Communications' central telephone exchange; two stories were occupied by the communications department of the KGB. Last year, this department had received an order from Barsky to block all calls from abroad for Anna Sigal and to monitor all her foreign calls.

"Boston?" Barsky said in surprise, and frowned. "What number?"

"No number was given. Sigal requested a directory inquiry, for a Mr. Maxim Rappoport. What do you want us to do?"

What? A call to Rappoport! At a time like this! On the eve of their decisive meeting! Why?

"Can I monitor their conversation from here?"

"No. We don't have the equipment for that. You can either come over here, or else I can send you a tape."

Barsky thought hard. Should he sit here not knowing what Anna was talking to Rappoport about and simply wait to get a tape? No, that passive stuff wasn't for him. Besides, his presence at Zubovsky Boulevard could be crucial: if Anna dropped even a syllable about Rubinchik, he'd have to cut her off. He got up.

"Wait for me," he said. "I'm coming over."

Carefully, neatly, almost with reverence, he tied the laces on the second and third folders of the Rubinchik file, which contained all the statements and photos of the love-kike's victims. He was proud of this collection and reveled in its value. Of the 114 women interrogated, fifty-two below the age of eighteen had confirmed they had sexual relations with Rubinchik, and twenty-nine had confirmed that Rubinchik was the father of one of their children. To amass this had taken four months of wearisome labor. Barsky felt the weight of the three folders with a glow of satisfaction and returned them to his safe. He felt like an author priding himself on the heft of his manuscript and recalled the story of Pushkin, who on completing *Boris Godunov*, supposedly exclaimed "Good man, Pushkin! What a great son of a bitch!" Of course, there'd been plenty of missteps, but now it was all tied up, the prepatory stage complete. Those nice fat files could have been handed over to the Prosecutor's Office and a criminal action launched yesterday; Rubinchik could have been arrested, and witnesses and victims already summoned to Moscow. But Barsky had decided to delay for a few days, until he got Anna Sigal's final agreement to act as public prosecutor. But what suddenly had prompted her to call Rappoport?

Barsky locked his safe and walked out of his own office into the adjoining room. The space there was cramped and tobacco smoke filled the air. Nine officers on night shift manned the two phones at six bulky desks and worked on the files of Jewish emigrants that had been brought in from the Visa Office. Because of the sharp rise in applications, Barsky's section could no longer cope with checking through the flood of documents during normal working hours. But he was putting off asking for more staff until Operation Virgin was over-the-top. Now he'd get nothing. But once this was a success, they'd give him everything he asked for—extra staff, two more rooms, and new phones and some Finnish furniture.

"Hallo! Hallo! Vladivostok!" one of the staff yelled into his phone. "Can you hear? You've got to turn Guberman down! No, not Kuperman—Guberman! The trawler captain! Hallo!" Angrily he chucked the receiver back into its cradle, and looked up at Barsky. His eyes were red from exhaustion and the smoky atmosphere. "You know, Oleg Dmitryevich, it's impossible to work like this! I can hear them, but they can't hear me! This is supposed to be the world's best intelligence service, but our equipment's no better than what they have in Papua, New Guinea!"

"Just be patient for another month," Barsky said as he walked past, continuing down the long, dark, echoing corridor into the other wing, and then down the stairs to the Duty Office. There he offered the general on duty a Dunhill, made out a one-time pass for the Communications Control section, and minutes later a black staff Volga whisked him through the sleeping city to Zubovsky Boulevard.

On the third floor of the telephone exchange, the staff were also in the middle of a busy day. The large, broad-gauge tape recorders were of almost prewar vintage, and on them were recorded all incoming and outgoing foreign calls from Moscow and the Moscow region. (Other areas of the USSR were covered by their local exchanges.) Because of the time differences between Moscow and Paris, London and Washington, and because of better audibility at night, Western correspondents dictated their copy then, and foreign businessmen called their home offices, and their wives and mistresses. But in the course of some routine report or seemingly amorous chatter, any one of these people could be passing secret information. Therefore these huge, slowly rotating reels recorded every message that left the USSR on the open lines; and later the analysts and code-crackers of the KGB would sift out any suspicious information.

"The American dealer Jay Crawford, representing the International Grain Fund, has been declared guilty by a Soviet court of illegally exchanging eight-and-a-half thousand dollars for twenty-five thousand rubles on the black market in Moscow. The prosecutor has asked for a five-year sentence. It is expected that the Soviet authorities will exchange Crawford for two Russian staff members at the U.N. who have been accused of spying. . . ."

"The Moscow militia have arrested seven American members of the International Antiwar League for attempting to hold a disarmament demonstration on Red Square. . . ."

"Jewish activists report a sharp rise in the number of Soviet Jews applying to leave the country; this is linked with an increasing wave of anti-Semitism. They note that during the eight months of this year one hundred thousand Jews have applied to leave, whereas during the whole of 1977 only seventy-eight thousand applied, of which only seventeen thousand were allowed to leave. . . ."

Bastards! thought Barsky irritably. Where did they get their figures from? True, those that actually did leave were registered and counted in Vienna. And the Jews leaving had only one route—Moscow–Vienna—whether by plane or train. But how did they find out the number of applications? Could someone in the Visa Office be working for them, like that army colonel, Filatov, who'd worked for the CIA? Or might there be some mole in his own section?

Barsky shuddered at the thought.

"Colonel, Boston has Rappoport on the line. I'm connecting this woman Sigal for you. Hello, Moscow! Boston on the line, go ahead!"

Then the sound of Anna's voice—that chesty voice with its ironic banter. At the sound of it, Barsky caught his breath and felt weak at the knees.

"Hello? Is that Rappoport? The one with three p's?" she asked mockingly.

"Anya!" Rappoport gasped on the other end. "Where are you?"

"In Moscow, at home. Where else?"

"Did you get my letters?"

"I've never heard a word from you. But hold on. I'm calling on a business matter. I have a request for you. Terribly important, as they say. Are you listening?"

"Yes. I'll do anything you ask. Shoot!"

"Get hold of the *Musical Encyclopedia* published in Moscow three years ago. That shouldn't be too hard for you: loads of Jewish musicians have left here and they all take books with them."

"Okay, I'll find it," Rappoport said. "What then?"

"Open volume one to page fourteen and then to page forty-two. And it will all become clear. And if the two of us don't see each other in a month's time, feel free to use this information however you like. You might even show it to the *New York Times*. You understand?"

"No, not a word. But I can get that encyclopedia in two hours. No problem there. So how are you? Are you thinking of coming over here?"

"When you read the encyclopedia, you'll understand. And if for some reason you don't, then call me up. It won't bankrupt you."

"Anna dear, you're crazy! I've been calling you every week! Your telephone is . . ."

Barsky pulled the jack from its socket on the switchboard.

"Hello! Hello! Maxim! Hello!" Anna's voice came over on the speaker.

"Don't shout, caller!" the operator said brusquely into her microphone.

"I've been cut off! I was speaking with Boston!" Anna said.

"Not at this end. It's the Americans. We've lost contact. Please hang up."

The operator pulled the other plug from its socket and turned to Barsky.

"Do you want your copy on broad or narrow track?" she asked.

Barsky shrugged. It was all the same to him, and in any case his mind was elsewhere: where could he find that encyclopedia at one o'clock in the morning? Crawford had gotten five years for exchanging a mere eight-and-a-half thousand dollars; and here was Anna Sigal calling Rappoport and openly communicating secret information! And to spite him, all Moscow's libraries were closed at night, and the KGB library too. The simplest thing would be to call up Butyrki and get the chief guard to open up the prison library. But would they have the *Musical Encyclopedia*?

Half an hour later, the assistant duty officer at KGB headquarters reluctantly opened the library for Barsky and watched sceptically to see whether he'd find what he was looking for. But it turned out to be quite simple. The volumes of the *Musical Encyclopedia* were standing together with the medical, Great Soviet, and all the other encyclopedias.

Opening volume one at page fourteen, he immediately saw alongside composers Bach and Balakirev a photograph of his own father, Dmitry Barsky, together with a short entry on him. But what could this mean to Rappoport, and what had it to do with Glinka and Gounod, whose portraits appeared on page forty-two?

That was a riddle Barsky could not solve, even though he ignored the duty officer's protests and took the volume up to his office and sat poring over pages fourteen and forty-two into the wee hours. In the morning the tape of Anna's conversation with Rappoport would go off to the code-crackers of the KGB's First Directorate, and if they were . . . No, the very thought was horrifying. He had to contact Anna. He had to find out.

forty-two

finally Rubinchik rediscovered the marvel he'd been seeking for seventeen years! This was what he had hunted for all over Siberia, the far north, the Urals, and the Far East. For this he'd kept abandoning his wife and children, had frozen in the taiga, had been beaten up in Kaluga, and had fallen into a fatal KGB trap at Salekhard. But, as the Bible says, the Jews are a stiff-necked people. And now, in the last hours of his life, God was revealing to him His secret and had sent him this miracle. Like a brilliant turquoise found in the mesozoic layers of Yakutian kimberlite, such a wonder occurred but once a century. In fact, one could read about this marvel only in the writings of Ahmed ibn-Fadlan, who had visited the Rus in the year 921.

There she lay before him—a young, white, warm body lying in the moonlight that streamed through the window. Her straight fair hair fell down over her bare back. Her lips, slightly swollen from kissing, were open. Her tired arms embraced the pillow. The line of her back joined her waist in a gentle curve, rose steeply to her thighs, and then descended smoothly again to her slightly raised bare feet. Her childlike face was calm, and the ikon-green of her eyes no longer blazed at him with reproach or tearful entreaty.

Rubinchik sat by the bed and looked at Olya in a state of panic. Damn it, to all appearances she was hardly different from all the other girls that had come his way during his travels. Indeed, to be honest, Olya was no match for some of them—she was small, she wore plain shift dresses that hid her figure, and old-fashioned glasses that covered her brows, and her way of walking was less than graceful. Rubinchik alone could recognize the swanlike diva concealed in this ungainly duckling. Similarly, at Mirnyy, amid the stream of dirt and kimberlite fragments on the conveyor belt, only an experienced sorter could detect the gray rice-grains of unworked diamonds. Yet it took only rubbing, washing, and grinding for these gems to flash with a thousand facets and adorn royal crowns. And Rubinchik was also such a sorter, polisher, and gemologist, searching among the rural shearlings, coveralls, cheap quilted jackets, and lab coats, finding those rare diamonds of femininity that had not yet been ground down by Soviet drudgery. And in a night he transformed them from drab girls into women of great beauty. He was the first to drink from these artesian wells, of course. But the next morning they walked away with a different gait, a different posture, and a different look in their eyes. It was as if they had been magically rescued from degradation and restored to their own true dignity and splendor.

But while he rejoiced in his discoveries, much like a poet over each felicitous line, Rubinchik realized that these transformations did not fully satisfy the aim of his quest. What he sought was a miracle, rare as a turquoise brilliant, whose phantom haunted him ever since he first chanced across it one night seventeen years ago on the banks of the Volga that once bore the ancient Khazarian name of Ityl. It was this miracle, fleetingly mentioned by Ahmed ibn-Fadlan, that had bewitched him. And in his pursuit of it, he had disdained moral standards, the rules of society, even his own family.

Yet although aware of the aim of his search, he was nonetheless shaken when this rough diamond yesterday evening slipped into his boiler room so shyly and wearing the same old shift dress, and later brought him to her one-room apartment with her grandmother's ikon hanging in the corner. All the treasures of Russia seized by the Communists—even the 120-carat "Mountain Moon" diamond of the tsars now kept in the Kremlin diamond trove, or the eighty-five-carat "Shah's Brilliant," or the "Pole Star," a pale red ruby of forty carats—all these were nothing, mere cold stone, compared with the living, magical being that Rubinchik had seized that evening almost under the very nose of Colonel Barsky! And the dossier that that strange old man had handed him yesterday was trivia, too, compared with the wonders of last night. For those, and for Olya, Barsky could torture him, kill him, break him on the wheel, and leave him to rot in his KGB dungeons.

But she really loved him. Lord, he could not even imagine being loved so intensely. Of course many girls had been infatuated with him. They'd blushed or paled when they met him and had come to him in his hotel as if under a spell. And sometimes they'd even wept when they parted. But had any loved him like this, so unconsolably and heart-rendingly? What had possessed him to open up so totally, and, to the sounds of such gross music on her cheap record player, and to the tasteless "Soviet Champagne" she'd found in the refrigerator? As in previous such ceremonies, he poured champagne into a couple of glasses, and he raised his glass by its slender stem and gazed into Olya's trusting eyes, slightly enlarged by her spectacles. Then he suddenly grinned and came out with something he'd never said before.

"My dear," he said with a sigh, "Wish me luck!"

His voice, though, conveyed something else, something bitter that didn't go with his assumed role of Sage and Teacher. And Olya was scared.

"Is something the matter?"

"No. Nothing really," he said in a forced way. "It's just that . . . well, I didn't tell you this before. But the fact is I am leaving here. Forever."

"You . . ." her voiced cracked like a dried branch. "Are you emigrating?"

"Yes," he lied, unable to admit that he was planning to kill himself from the exhaust in his own garage.

And then it happened.

She looked at him for about a minute, her eyes getting wider and wider, her gaze blank. Then suddenly she fell, collapsing to the floor in a dead faint. Rubinchik was frightened to death. He'd never before seen anything like this.

"Olya! Olya!" he called. "What's the matter? Oh my God!" He knelt down, cradling her head and looked around. He knew that probably she needed smelling salts and water. But there were no such things at hand. So he stretched a hand out to the table, picked up a glass, and splashed her face with cold champagne.

She opened her eyes, but there were no pupils in them. It was horrible, worse than a horror movie—her eyes had no pupils. They were blank and gray-white like hard-boiled eggs. Several long seconds passed, maybe half a minute, before her pupils began to float back from somewhere beneath her brow.

"Olya! Olya!" He shook her head and shoulders. The idiotic music— was it Saint-Saëns?—kept on playing. But then Olya fixed her eyes on him, and with a sudden jerk hugged him around the neck with hysterical strength and burst out sobbing.

"No! Please! No! Don't go away! I love you! Oh my God! It'll be the death of you! Don't leave, I beg of you!"

Her tears wet his face, and he almost choked in the vice of her embrace.

"Wait!" he said. "Let me go! Olya!"

She let him go as suddenly as she'd embraced him. Indeed, she didn't simply release him, but thrust him away. Then, like a small animal, she crawled into a corner on her hands and knees and sobbed loudly, rocking from side to side, howling and uttering incoherent words, as though lamenting over someone's grave.

"No! I can't go on living! I won't! I love you! I realize you're married. I never asked you for anything, and never called you. But I knew that you were here, somewhere near, in Moscow. But if you leave, I can't go on living!"

Rubinchik couldn't imagine what to do. He switched off the record player, brought her a glass of water, and tried to lift her up from the floor.

"Stop it, Olya. Wait . . . I'm not dead yet, after all. Have a drink of water!"

"It would be better if you'd died! No, if I died!" she cried.

He felt irritated that everything was turning out so hysterically, as in some overinflated women's novel. But he couldn't just leave. How could he abandon her there, sobbing on the floor, looking as if she really was weeping over his grave?

"Olya." He knelt down before her and tried to embrace her, but she began struggling in his arms.

"No, no! I don't want your pity! I'm going to die! I want to die!"

"Olya!" He managed to press her arms back with his elbows. And he took her face, wet with tears, and held it between his palms, and kissed her on the lips.

She moaned and tried to tear free. But he did not let go of her lips, nor did he release her arms, although she continued pushing him away with manic strength. Only after a long struggle—minutes—did he feel her resistance weaken, and she began to go limp and melt in his arms. He continued kissing her wet eyes, her lips, then her eyes again. She did not respond, but she no longer was pushing him away. The hysteria was subsiding, her body relaxing, seemingly indifferent to him. Only a gentle childlike whimpering led to spasms in her breathing, and then turned into hiccups.

"Water . . ." she said, blindly waving her arm in the air with its slender bracelets. He brought her some, and she drank with her teeth chattering on the rim of the glass. But the hiccups did not subside. Leaning with her back against the wall, she threw back her head and continued hiccuping, whimpering, and shedding tears, talking quietly and bitterly.

"For . . . forgive me . . . I'm . . . I'm sorry!"

He was touched beyond words.

"Oh my God, Olya!" He knelt down in front of her and started kissing her again. But she remained passive, her arms dangling lifelessly like lengths of rope. Only her shoulders kept twitching with her hiccups. He unbuttoned her dress and bra and began kissing her slender bare shoulders, neck, and breasts. The hiccups subsided and ceased, and he wiped her face and swollen nose with a napkin. Then he laid her—submissive and unresponding—on the carpeted floor. He unbuttoned the rest of her shift and removed all her clothes—her silk slip, tights, and panties.

She didn't react and simply lay there on the carpet—a slender alabaster

Venus—with her eyes closed, dark nipples, light-colored curly down on her mound, and two silver bracelets on her left arm.

How could he just have her here on the floor? This, the last Russian woman in his life, who turned out to be so deeply in love with him?

Rubinchik picked her up and carried her to the little bathroom. He stood her under the shower and began washing her like a child, with a soft pink sponge. He stood beside her under the spray, naked and with water running down his hairy torso. In the confined space he almost had to touch her with his body, and his battle-ready sword of life rubbed against her buttocks and her thighs. But he still felt no sexual pressure. Rather, he felt like an oriental eunuch, proud that in a huge dirty slave bazaar he had found this white pearl, this shy young pagan princess with slender legs, golden mound, tender belly, soft hips, childlike breasts, long slender neck, blue eyes, and flaxen hair like fresh honey. There were no such women in Persia, in Iran, or Israel. Such divas lived only far away, beyond two seas and three khanates, north of the cunning Armenians, the wild Alans and other such tribes, and even further north than the Bulgars and the Lachs. The Greeks called their tribe the "Russos," and said that their tongue was like that of the Teutons. Even the name of their chief river had a German sound— Dnieper. These Rus also did not know the One God—they worshipped fire, wind, stones, trees, and idols.

But in the final reckoning it didn't matter what language they spoke and what gods they worshipped. The important thing was that this slave girl shivered like a fawn, was pure as moonlight, and fearful like all pagan girls.

As he bathed his new find, Rubinchik imagined himself a eunuch preparing a new concubine for his Jewish king. The one difference being that he himself was this ruler, and thus . . .

He began kissing her warm wet lips. Streams of water sprayed down their faces, his hairy body pressed against her soft wet breasts, and his erect rod prodded against the lyre of her belly and pressed its length against her from her mound up to her navel and beyond, almost to her breasts. His tongue entered her wet mouth and began tenderly licking the roof of her mouth, teeth, and gums. His hands slowly reached down her back, fingertips sliding along her spine, like the fingerboard of a cello. His hands reached down to her buttocks, seized them, parted her legs, slightly raised her light wet body, and set her astride his heated phallus. He did not enter her, no, not yet. He simply wanted to warm her on his flaming cudgel and get her used to it. But she immediately pressed her legs around it, as if it were a great thermometer. And through his own heat, Rubinchik felt the intense warmth of her fissure, which, snail-like, suddenly extended its soft warm lips and suckers and began drawing him in with an unmistakable and irresistible strength.

Rubinchik was rooted to the spot.

He had experienced such a thing only once before—on the banks of the Volga, seventeen years ago. He stood beneath the stream of water, not believing what he was feeling. He was both cold with terror and hot with delight.

The hot snail between her legs continued wrapping itself around his shaft and slowly drawing on it. Suddenly her lips also pressed against his mouth, and her tongue followed and began repeating what he himself had just done—licking his gums, teeth, and the roof of his mouth with avid tenderness. Then her tongue withdrew, pulling his own tongue with it, and began sucking it in—further and further, down to the root, until it hurt. At the same time, down below, the irresistible force of those little hot tentacles continued dragging his flesh into her own.

The nape of his neck grew frigid with fear. His breathing stopped, and his legs turned weak. He moaned, shook his head, and with an effort pulled himself free. Stunned, he stood there looking at this youthful princess.

She was beautiful and innocent.

She closed her eyes and leaned back against the tiles. Covering her breasts with her slender white hands, she stood in the the middle of the tub like Rodin's Venus in the Pushkin Museum. Only her rapid breathing caused her wet, girlish lips to open and reveal her teeth, gleaming with a soft whiteness. Streams of water ricocheted off her finely wrought body, spurting up from her collarbones and glimmering in pearly drops in the golden down of her mound.

Rubinchik gazed at her and could not believe what he had just experienced. This shy and slender, modest little virgin with her still-undeveloped breasts and . . . had a kind of inhuman, snail-like hunger and force in her mouth and between her legs. So Ahmed ibn-Fadlan was right when he wrote that "so lovely are the Russian girls, and so strong is their *fardja* that nothing can tear a man away from coupling with them." Another anonymous Arabian traveler had written even more candidly: "The *fardja* of a Russian girl is like a voluptuous python that draws a man into it with the strength of a bull."

Rubinchik turned off the water and rubbed Olya down with a fluffy Cuban towel bearing a large portrait of Fidel Castro. There was a special piquancy in drying her rear with that image, but this was no time for jokes. He took Olya by the hand.

"Let's go," he ordered.

She opened her eyes. With her slender legs she stepped over the side of the tub and followed him into the bedroom. Rubinchik snatched the spread, blanket, and top sheet from the bed in one sweep.

"Lie down," he ordered.

"Can I switch the light off?"

"No. You mustn't do that."

"Kiss me . . ." she begged.

"Later. Lie down."

"I'm scared."

"Me too," he grinned. "Lie down."

"Will it be painful?"

"It will be beautiful. But not just now. Later. Lie down. Don't be afraid."

She stretched out on the bed and turned her face to the wall—like a child in the hospital, turning away so as not to see the needle.

"Come on, silly!" Rubinchik smiled. He had now slipped back into his role of First Man, Teacher, and Instructor. Now after seventeen years, he was no longer that repressed youth driven crazy by the ravenous *fardja* of a fifteen-year-old girl at the Sputnik pioneer camp.

"Where's our champagne?" he wondered with a smile. "And the music?"

Among her records he found Ravel's *Bolero*, switched it on, and poured out more champagne. On the eve of his suicide, fate had presented him with such a pristine Russian beauty. This was something to celebrate with ceremony. He sat down beside Olya with his legs tucked under him, oriental-style, and made her drink a few swigs of champagne. He too drank a full glass. He still had not recovered from his fear of that snail of hers. But he was also gripped by curiosity, and he decided to do without all the ceremonial speeches and other details, and get right to the essentials.

Laying Olya across the bed, he knelt down before her, parted her legs and placed them on his shoulders, and with scientific curiosity inspected the thick silky growth that concealed the ravening snail of her pagan temperament.

But everything there was quiet and calm, except the pale cream bud lacked that crumpled look of all his earlier princesses. Higher up, beyond the downy mound, everything too was familiar—Russian, beloved, and dear to him—an expanse of warm and tender white skin running to the gentle hollow of her belly, the two hillocks of her breasts, the long swan's neck, and her upturned chin.

Taking courage, Rubinchik began gently parting the soft growth before him, and laid it out on either side of her rosebud. Then, as careful as if he were approaching a flame, he brought his lips down onto it. But at the first touch of his lips Olya seized his head with her hands and tried to push him away.

"No! You mustn't! Don't do that!"

He seized her hands and pressed them back until it hurt.

"Hush! Forget everything! Listen only to yourself! And say nothing!" he commanded in his usual manner.

And he carefully licked her rosebud. The silent miracle that can be seen only on film came to pass before his astonished gaze. The bud awakened. The movement was minuscule, yet it was so obvious that Rubinchik caught his breath, expecting to see—as on film—how the petals of the bud expanded and rose on their own accord, as on a tulip. However, there was no more movement. It was like a child who after being kissed in its sleep, stirs and sighs, then returns to its gentle slumber.

With a chill running through him and hardly daring to breathe, Rubinchik ran his tongue once more over the closed petals of the bud. And then again. And once more.

Then the miracle continued—like an Indian fakir causing a snake to rise to the sound of his magical pipe; like petals of an enchanted flower opening in an animated film; like the first leaf unfolding on a young apple tree in spring. After every touch of his tongue, those sensitive sleeping petals slowly opened in time to Ravel's *Bolero*. And they filled with life, flesh, color, and the juices of desire.

Rubinchik forgot all about that old man yesterday with his awful KGB file. In fact, he forgot about everything—emigration, suicide, and even his wife and children. His soul filled with joy and merriment. He felt like a magus, fakir, Walt Disney, Michurin, Casanova, all together. He began playing with Olya's rosebud, and his tongue tickled the folds as they opened. He licked them, teased them with a fleeting touch of the lips, and lightly dipped his tongue into that little fatal crater. As he did, he failed to notice that the rest of her body too was stirring. The power of the Dnieper flowed through her, she breathed hoarsely, ground her teeth, twisted and tossed, undulating with the paroxysms and pangs of her own desire. But Rubinchik saw none of this. Absorbed, he became the orphan boy of long ago, who after years of neglect and poverty had been given the most magical toy in the world.

Suddenly, at a moment when his tongue once again approached her tender, moist crater, Olya's white legs closed like a vice around his neck and her knees pressed against the back of his head with a frantic, inhuman strength and forced his face into her loins.

Not only couldn't he tear himself free, but he could barely breathe. Then, as he fought for breath, he felt those soft, warm petal-folds of her rosebud acquire a new fierce and hungry strength, clasp his tongue and begin drawing it inside her, pulling it in like a piston, further and deeper into the bittersweet depths of her crater. In much the same way a python wraps its coils around its prey to consume it.

Rubinchik could no longer hear Ravel's *Bolero*. He didn't groan but braced himself against the bed frame with all his might, trying to escape. But he managed only to drag Olya's body an arm's length down the bed, and that was all. She pressed against him and her hungry snail swallowed him deeper and deeper, pulling his tongue out of his larynx. Rubinchik, like a drowning man, began jerking his whole body chaotically and flailing his arms against her, scratching her with his nails. But these desperate movements lacked strength. He was choking and dying. His lungs felt as if they were bursting, his head had grown huge and was ringing, blood ran from his nose, and his eyes were popping out of their sockets.

In her throbbing crater, the muscular coils had already dragged his tongue to the precious membrane and were trying to draw it all the way through. But his tongue lacked the firmness for this. Realizing this, the coils relaxed, the crater enlarged, and the gentle folds released Rubinchik's tongue from their ferocious embrace. Olya's legs stretched full length in a final convulsion and collapsed.

Rubinchik fell to the floor like a dead man. He lay facedown, his arms spread out as though embracing the earth that he had already departed. He hardly had the strength to breathe, he could barely catch some air with the edge of his disabled lungs, and he palpated his wretched tongue that had almost been wrenched from him. Minutes later, though, through the deepening roar of his own pulse, he again heard the triumphant beat of Ravel's *Bolero*, growing louder and inescapable as fate. He rolled onto his back and opened his eyes.

An ancient ikon in a dusky frame stared at him from the corner of the room. Rubinchik's eyes met those of the crucified Christ, and as he lay on the floor only now did he realize what torment it is to be a teacher to the heathen.

In time he got his breath back and finally felt sure that he had survived. He looked at Olya. She lay on her side with her eyes closed, curled up like a child, like his daughter Xenia. Her lips were open as if she were asleep. Her hair had dried and it now spilled over her tender little knees, and nothing about that peaceful adolescent body seemed to belong to the wild forces concealed between her white legs. Nothing, that is, apart from the sharp curve of her thigh.

Rubinchik got up and went to the kitchen. He opened the refrigerator and on a shelf in the door found a bottle of Stolichnaya, a third full. Taking a glass, he poured the contents into it. Then he breathed out and drank the almost full glass of vodka in one shot. He closed his eyes, sniffed his fist, and felt the vodka run down to his stomach, reviving him. He shook his shoulders. Then he opened his eyes and stood leaning with his back against the fridge. God damn it, what a gift Russia had presented to him, and just as he was on the verge of death!

He returned to the bedroom and disconnected the plug of the record player. The needle rasped out a last pathetic dying bar and then fell silent. He glanced at the window. Below lay Moscow, plunged in gloom. In the darkness an occasional window gleamed, a patch of light. A solitary truck trundled across empty Taganskaya Square, the wind swept a few scraps of paper along the sidewalk, and under a lamp post a drunk sat and dozed peacefully. This, Rubinchik thought, was his Russia, his beloved homeland, and he recalled the lines of a Romantic poet's love for those "decrepit peasant huts . . ." and other simple delights.

But suddenly, with the glow of the alcohol, a furious energy rose in him. No, he was not going to part from life! No, it was not going to be like that!

His face became lit with a wild and angry smile—the kind men show picking up a glove when challenged to a duel; when diving from a cliff into the boiling ocean surf; the smile of a toreador holding his short sword when stepping out to fight a bloodied and maddened bull. He drew the curtain, reconnected the record player and headed toward her bed to the rhythmic pulse of the reanimated *Bolero*.

Olya lay as he had left her. But her gray eyes now were open and watched him from the pillow with innocent expectation, and her pupils sparkled with a childish radiance.

He stopped in front of her, naked. A challenge radiated from his dark Semitic eyes and from his whole short being. But he was not yet ready. He stood there before her, breathing loudly and feeling how the strength he needed was gradually mounting in him.

The *Bolero* still rang out.

Bam! Para-rara-ram-para-ram! Bam!

And as the music reached a crescendo, so too his rod, the shaft of life, began to rise and come alive. Para-ram-tarara-aam-ram! Bam! He saw Olya's eyes move from his face down to the rising symbol of his manhood, and he saw terror, undisguised terror, in her childike face and her gray rainbow pupils. That prompted a burst of triumphant adrenalin into his blood, and his sword swung up, as a signal to begin.

Parira-rira-rira-tam! Ta-ta-tam!

But he did not leap. He approached with the soft tread of a leopard, panther, or tiger. Without letting her lose sight of his erect weapon, covered in gnarled, rootlike veins and crowned with its blazing violet onion-dome, he slowly and gently ran it over her shoulder, breasts, and hip—like a skilled horseman stroking the withers of a wild young filly he has lassoed, before leaping onto her back.

At his touch Olya fell onto her back, and their eyes met.

There was now only fear in her childlike gaze, nothing but fear. She raised a hand instinctively to shield her breast and belly. But her so-called innocence no longer deceived him. Now he knew her better than she knew herself. There would be no foreplay, no fellatio, no chatter about eternity and stars. "Kadyma ts'ad!" Seizing her hands, he spread them apart and leapt onto her, his bare buttocks resting on her chest, his scrotum resting in the hollow between the two budding hillocks, and his sword quivering inches from her frightened eyes.

"Are you afraid?" His voice was slightly hoarse and mocking.

She did not reply, but she looked both entranced and terrified. Pagans must have looked at their gods this way as they rose up before them out of fire and stone. Pressing her hands to either side of the pillow, he slowly began sliding down her body, toward her belly and her mound. And when she lost sight of his hot weapon, she looked up into his eyes.

"Don't! Please don't!"

"I must!" he answered hoarsely, and forced apart her clasped legs with his knee.

"No! Please! Don't do it!"

Her soft voice was so full of pathos that he paused. He had never before done this by force. But then he remembered that ravenous snail between her tightly clasped legs. And the boys at the orphanage, when he was a child: "Eat dirt, little kike, eat dirt!"

He then thrust his other knee between her legs and fully parted them.

The *Bolero* was still pounding and echoing. It had now reached its climax and rang out like a call of destiny.

Para-ram-tara-ram! Bam!

Rubinchik pushed himself up and raised his thighs above hers, rising as it were from the saddle as he always did at this decisive moment and rearing triumphantly. But before plunging into the maelstrom of her ravenous crater, a sudden cowardice or curiosity prompted him to glance down betwen her pale legs. From this angle he could see neither her rosebud, nor its cleft, but only the golden thicket of her mound. And once again, from the far distance of the pillow a faint entreaty reached him:

"No, you mustn't. . . . Please . . ."

But he already knew the password, the "open sesame!" With a twisted, vengeful smile, he gently applied his rod just once to the warm, hidden folds of her slit and rubbed it along them, as if with a violin bow.

Her body froze and her breathing ceased.

This gave him added, intoxicating strength.

Gradually, as if in a slow-motion sequence, he moved the lower edge of his swordpoint along the folds of her bud–once, twice, three times . . . And at last those warm, sleeping folds stirred as though from a deep sleep. But now Rubinchik was on the alert. He raised his weapon above those danger-ous petals, to prevent their seizing him in their hungry grasp. Then again he faintly touched them, and again, and again . . .

Olya's body lay silent.

Only the crater of her groin kept opening wider and wider, like a living tulip. Rubinchik even felt like starting a countdown, as if at a rocket launch: ten . . . nine . . . eight . . . seven . . .

But he had not reached five, when she opened fully, and her pink folds stretched out to greet his sword with a carnivorous eagerness.

Still the *Bolero* roared and thundered.

Rubinchik smiled, arching lower, and prepared for a thrust into the center of the crater, bracing his back and thighs, when suddenly . . .

"No-o-o-o!"

A wild cry broke from Olya's throat.

"Yes," said Rubinchik quietly, more to himself than to her.

"No-o-o!" With animal strength her body began writhing beneath him, her arms tensing, her thighs pulling away to one side. "No! You shall not! No-o-o!"

"Yes!" Rubinchik said again hoarsely. With steely grip he pressed her arms behind her back, and with his legs he parted and raised her thighs.

Now she could neither stir nor escape. And—at last!—he again began to approach her burning crater with his incandescent tip.

But he could not let this moment pass without fixing it in his memory. Still holding Olya firmly, he watched as his sword made its approach.

Suddenly Olya raised her head from the pillow.

"No!" she shouted with hatred in her voice and in her gaze. And then—she spat in his face with the same malice as they once spat on him after beating him up in Kaluga, or recently when the anti-Semitic telegraph clerk shouted at him at Bykovo Airport.

"You little bitch! There!" Rubinchik exploded, and with a single furious motion he embedded himself in her, putting all his strength and weight behind the thrust. He even thought he heard her hymen split, amid the thunder of the final bars as the Bolero exulted and finally expired.

"Oh . . . o-o-oh!" A deep sigh emptied Olya's lungs, as her whole body stretched out and went limp. And her eyes closed.

And there too, in the depths of her belly, in her burning crater, every-thing went quiet.

Then Rubinchik fell on her and wiped the spittle from his face onto her face and lips. And so, they lay motionless as the music died away. But then, as the last chord faded into the exhausted silence, Rubinchik felt a quiet new life starting up in the living scabbard that surrounded his still erect sword.

The tight, warm, moist crevice gently tautened and drew him deeper inside with slow undulations that gradually grew quicker and quicker. . . .

The sensation was incredible, unthinkable, unreal.

Yet this had happened to him seventeen years ago on the benighted shore of the Volga. And now again here, on this bed, high above Taganskaya Square. Here again these muscular waves of female flesh rippling and sucking the whole length of his phallus!

What talentless masturbators do with their hands, and what the world's most skilled women do with their tongue and lips, this teenager was achieving with the muscles of her crater. And the pleasure was incomparable even with what had happened on the Volga long ago. Who said that after completing the creation of the world, the Creator rested on his laurels? Surveying the six-day labor of his hands, the Almighty doubtless awarded Himself a highly satisfactory grade. But that alone would not satisfy a true Creator. Most probably, the Almighty One merely prepared His canvas during that first week, and then there were further days of creativity. And then He began to experiment, and He created Leonardo da Vinci and Michelangelo, He breathed genius into Paganini and Wolfgang Amadeus Mozart, and He invented Edison and Einstein. And after these, He created the golden tonsils of Edith Piaf, the eyes of Giulietta Mazzini, and the legs of Plisetskaya. But the Creator could hardly have rested content without also implanting something of genius in other areas of the body.

"Again . . . More . . . More . . ." Rubinchik's lips whispered deliriously. He embraced Olya, squeezed her in his arms, rolled with her onto his back, and relaxed, now allowing her crater to do whatever it wanted with him— pull or suck him in, squeeze its coils of flesh about him and send its undulating waves ever further up his organ.

"Lord!" he whispered to himself, stretching out beneath Olya like a string, throwing his head back and opening his mouth in a muted cry of ecstasy, fearing to breathe. "Lord! You have excelled even yourself in creating this!"

But down below the hungry waves of her muscular spasms stimulated him constantly, accelerating their heated flow, striving to squeeze and suck out all his seed, his very blood and soul. Resisting, his fingers found her breasts. They squeezed her nipples, twisting them to cause great pain. But to no avail. In that crater there boiled an avid, incandescent magma.

"No!" Rubinchik's fading consciousness shouted to him. "No! Hold on! Prolong it! Keep on holding! Keep on!"

Hands now braced against her shoulders, he began forcing them away from him, prying away her body that had fastened onto him and clove to him with all its skin like a leech. She gave way, reluctantly, yielding to his strength. But even then, as her breast drew away, she drew up her knees and settled down on him, throwing back her upper body and hanging on. Now the whole of her had turned into an extension of her crater, which kept working away like the blazing forge of a smithy.

Life seemed to go out of him. He could neither breathe nor feel his heart beating. On the fringe of his awareness, the thought floated by that maybe he was close to those sensations felt by women during similar convulsions of male flesh inside their own motionless craters.

Rubinchik stopped thinking, controlling himself, or being aware of what was happening. He turned into a tree with its crown somewhere high above the clouds, growing upward from the juices down in its roots. He had turned into an underwater plant stem, pushing up through dense tropical waters toward some other form of life—a lofty form of life in a clear atmosphere of birds and clouds. It was there, in that cloudless height, that the Jewish God Yahweh lived, resplendent and untouchable. Rubinchik suddenly had a clear vision of Him, close by and lit by bright sunlight, and beside Him, on the next cloud, was his own young mother, round-faced, happy, and with little dimples of laughter on her cheeks.

He rose in an arc on the gun-carriage of the bed, and soared up like a rocket with his whole body ringing. And his ears popped at that ascent, his veins burst, and his soul broke free. But as he approached the Godhead and had almost reached Him, he felt all strength abandon him, the impetus of the flight fell away, and—

—an explosion shook his body . . .

—a white cloud burst from him into the crater of Olya's *fardja*, which hummed with flame . . .

—the mushroom cloud grew and grew, giving off more and more explosions and clouds . . .

But even when Rubinchik collapsed onto his back, breathless and emptied, still the hungry and jubilant furnace of Olya's flesh continued pulsing, squeezing, and crushing his phallus and sucking in and absorbing everything he had left.

Turning his head helplessly on the pillow, Rubinchik knew that he was empty, that even his soul had slipped out of him and had burned up in that blazing crater. And that all that was left of him lying on the bed was an empty, weightless husk for which even he had little use.

Meanwhile the pagan goddess remained motionless, like some Indian Buddha in a museum. She did not abandon him, did not release him, or leave him to expire on the rumpled bloodstained sheets, as barbarians leave their conquered foe on the steppes. No, the temperature of her glowing furnace merely diminished a bit, as did the pressure of her muscular spasms. Now the coils of her flesh became softer and more tender, their motion slowed and made him think of the gentle surf that follows a ferocious storm, stroking him like one who's been injured, like a loved one, or like an infant at the breast.

He felt Olya lie on top of him, and her moist lips damped his own parched mouth with a gentle dovelike kiss.

And suddenly, to his terror and delight, he felt that in the tender, moist, and quivering heated depths of her undulating mine shaft, his own lifeless empty sword was beginning to revive, filling with a new strength from goodness knew where.

Much later, after they had passed through every stage of ecstasy, and when they had died tenfold deaths within one another and then been resurrected— calmly, without savagery, and as though waltzing together in inexhaustible delight; and when he afterward had bathed her again in the bathroom, and when she, like a true pagan, had kissed him all over, as though he were a god, kissed the whole of his body down to the tips of his toes, only then did he wonder to himself: So is this the end? Do I now go and finish myself off? Go away and die? Leave this world forever? He felt filled with horror and his whole body broke out in frozen goose flesh. As the day began to dawn, he sat by candlelight with Olya as she slept. He was tormented by desire for a smoke. Lord! he thought, how can I die, now that I've found this treasure, this miracle I've sought for seventeen years? "And the name of these people is Rus. They are a numerous people, and nowhere in the adjacent lands and countries are there pagans more handsome than they." Such was ibn-Fadlan's record in the ninth century.

The dawn light lit up the window pane. Rubinchik lay down next to Olya. Warming himself with her body heat and realizing that he could not sleep, he took a book from the little pile that lay on her bedside table. Its title had been stamped in dusky gold letters on the tawny cloth cover:

The Letters and Papers of Peter the Great
(FROM THE ARCHIVE OF PRINCE FYODOR KURAKIN)
Saint Petersburg, 1890

Curiously he glanced at Olya sleeping there at his side. Where did she get this book, he wondered? He opened the heavy tome, and his eye was immediately caught by a large ink stamp on the title page:

LIBRARY OF THE

USSR STATE SECURITY COMMITTEE (KGB)

THIS BOOK NOT TO BE REMOVED.

INVENTORY NO. PK. 674/75

Rubinchik looked down at his beloved, stricken with terror. He made an unconscious, instinctive move away from her. So abrupt, in fact, that she stirred and stretched in her sleep and then snuggled up to him. But he again backed off.

"Where did you get this book from?" he asked.

"From my dad. It's from his library," she said without opening her eyes.

"Does he work for the KGB?"

"Yes. Why?" She opened her eyes. They were full of sleepy, childlike innocence.

"What does he do there?"

"I dunno. Probably catches spies. He lives on his own. I told you: my mom divorced him ten years ago, then remarried a diplomat, and now she's in Cuba."

He looked at her, afraid to let in the awful thought that flashed though his brain.

"What's your last name?" Rubinchik asked.

"Barsky," she said. "Why, do you know my dad?"

Rubinchik got up to light a cigarette and nervously began breaking matchsticks and throwing them out of the open window. Moscow lay before him, coming awake and brightened by the rising sun. Here in this city, he finally had discovered the ideal of Russian beauty and femininity. Furthermore, he had fallen head over heels for this girl. And now she turned out to be the daughter of the same Colonel Barsky to whom all those denunciations and reports about him were addressed. If this guy was to discover that Rubinchik was sleeping with his own daughter, he would rip his balls off, have him hanged, drawn, and quartered in the Lubyanka cellars without ever bringing him to trial!

"Do you have a photo of your dad?" Rubinchik asked.

"Of course." Olya came up to him from behind and clung to him with all of her beautiful warm, naked body. With her left hand she opened the bookcase, took a photo album off the shelf, threw back the cover and held it up for him to look. On the first page was a photo of that same hard-faced man who'd led the militia raid on Rubinchik's hotel room in Salekhard.

"You don't need to worry about him," Olya said. "My dad's a splendid guy. He won't do us any harm, I swear!"

Rubinchik gave a sarcastic grin.

"Of course! And Andropov is a splendid guy too."

"Oh, Yuri Vladimirovich? Do you know him?" Olya exclaimed happily. "He really is marvelous! He's my godfather!"

Rubinchik spun around in amazement.

forty-three

This time they met not at the empire-style Armenia Restaurant, nor the elegant Race Course, but at the functional business café on the ground floor of the National Hotel. The room had huge plate glass windows looking out onto Manezh Square and the Kremlin. Its stucco ceiling, snow-white tablecloths and embossed silver cutlery wrapped in starched linen were relics of the time when this was a rendezvous for such men as Bulgakov, Dunayevsky, Eisenstein, Mayakovsky, Meyerhold, Mikhoels, Stanislavsky, and other stars of the prewar period. The story had it that once when the poet Mikhail Svetlov was tanked up and leaving the hotel, he encountered an admiral in dress uniform and mistook him for the concierge or bellboy and told him, "Porter, get me a taxi!" The man was affronted. "I'm not a porter," he said, "I am an admiral!" "Okay, then," Svetlov said, "get me a dinghy!" Another denizen of that café allegedly once turned up in a sweater with a horizontal line drawn across it. When asked by one of the waitresses what the line represented, his answer was: "That, my dear, is my liquid level."

In those days long past, the waitresses too were three times younger and quicker off the mark. Now they had put on weight and become arrogant. The public, too, was less impressive and consisted mainly of businessmen from the provinces, wheeler-dealers, and middle grade Party officials. But it was the starched tablecloths, haughty waitresses, and high prices that still prevented the National from plummeting from its once elevated status and becoming just another public eating place.

Barsky chose this rendezvous as a sign to Anna that this was to be a serious meeting. He turned up with a fat tome of the *Musical Encyclopedia* in his attaché case and wasted no time before getting straight down to business.

"Three months ago, Anna," he began, "you said that you had no more dealings with Rappoport. Yet last night you called him up in Boston and talked to him in all sorts of riddles. You realize of course that all conversations with the USA are monitored. So what are we to make of this? Was it meant as an open challenge to me and the whole KGB? Or what?"

"Well, almost," Anna grinned.

"How d'you mean 'almost'?" Barsky frowned deeply. He did not like her self-assured manner. "What's that supposed to mean?"

"Well, it's hardly in my power to throw down a challenge to the *whole* of the KGB," Anna said, and allowed an eloquent pause to ensue. Unlike their last meeting, she was dressed in a no-nonsense manner and wore a dark attorney's jacket, a plain gray sweater, and a skirt of the same dark shade. Instead of a handbag she carried a briefcase. Yet even this severe and unadorned turn-out enhanced her looks—like a lovely face against the dark background of a Rembrandt canvas. It took Barsky a considerable effort not to throw caution to the wind and tell her straight out that he was crazy about her.

"So it's meant as a challenge to me? Personally?" he said, dismissing the buxom waitress who had just served their lunch.

"Yes," Anna said.

"Really? Very interesting!" Her outspokenness made Barsky lean back in his chair and stare at her. Lord, any moment now he would simply drown in those eyes of hers! But he took himself in hand and with another effort forced away the alluring sexual mirage and put on an expression of mocking superciliousness. "Well, let's have it. What exactly is Rappoport meant to understand from a photo of my father along with the biographies and photos of Gounod and Glinka?"

"Do you mind my asking a personal question?" Anna said, surprising him.

"Ask me a hundred if you want!"

"No, just one. Do you have a birthmark under your left armpit?"

"Yes," he said, surprised. "So what?"

She pointed to his attaché case.

"Can I borrow your *Musical Encyclopedia* for a moment?" she said.

Barsky grinned at her astuteness. Damn it, this woman had her game worked out three moves ahead. What trump did she have up her sleeve?

He opened his attaché case and handed Anna the heavy volume he'd brought.

She leafed through it and found page fourteen, and then suddenly ripped out the whole page.

"Hey, what are you doing?" he said, taken off guard.

"We can stick it back in later," she said nonchalantly, and began leafing through the book again. She turned up pages 42–43, and with the same calm demeanor ripped out that double-page spread.

"Anna, this is a library copy!"

"What? From your departmental library?" she laughed. "Never mind, you won't lose your job. Look here." She laid the double page in front of

Barsky and pointed a polished nail not at page forty-two but the next one, where between two portraits of Gluck and Grieg there was a photo of the Grass brothers.

"Well? So what?" Barsky was puzzled.

"Have you never heard of these composers?"

"Well, I've heard of them of course. They were songwriters, before the last war."

"But you've never seen their photograph before?"

"No. Where's this leading, Anna? None of this makes sense."

"Uh-huh . . ."

He could feel her looking at him with the sort of compassion people have for a cancer patient, and he grew more nervous.

"I still don't understand this . . ."

"Oleg," she said, "show me your ID."

"Why?"

"Just for a moment. I won't run off with it."

Reluctantly he produced from his pocket a little dark-red leather binder with KGB USSR in gold embossed lettering. Anna took it and opened it. Inside was a black-and-white photo of Barsky with personal details filled in with India ink: "*Barsky, Oleg Dmitryevich. Rank: Colonel, State Security.* Office: *Head of Section.*" It also had a round stamp from the KGB Personnel Directorate.

Anna placed Barsky's open ID between the photo of his father on page fourteen and the similar-sized photos of Abram and Moisey Grass on page forty-three.

No specialist in facial types was needed to see the obvious.

The photo of thirty-four-year-old Dmitry Barsky showed an open, round, snub-nosed Russian face with broad Tatar cheeks and deeply set light eyes. The faces on the other three showed remarkably similar facial types—an elongated, oval-shaped head with a high-domed forehead, slightly balding, with dark protruding eyes, and a straight nose with broad nostrils. True, none of these showed characteristic "Yiddish" features—curly hair and hooked noses. But at the same time none of them looked very Russian either, particularly now, when two had Jewish surnames printed underneath.

Barsky said nothing. He gazed hard at the photographs, breathed noisily in rapid pants, and his face, ears, and neck grew red with horror.

"How did you find this out?" he asked in a hollow voice, avoiding Anna's eyes.

Anna said nothing.

"Who . . . who else knows about this?" he asked.

"I think that nobody does, apart from Rappoport and myself."

"No ! This is some kind of madness ! It's a chance coincidence!" Barsky tapped one of his Dunhills from its packet and began rolling it nervously in his nicotine-stained fingers.

Anna opened her briefcase and silently got out her little portable Grundig dictaphone, and pressed Play. The throaty Louis Armstrong voice of an elderly Russian singer said:

"... Did I know Mitya Barsky! And do you know why it was that Barsky got the Stalin Prize?"

"It was for the 'March of the Victors,' wasn't it?" came Anna's cautious question.

"You're dead right! ... And do you know how that song came about? ... It's part of the same story really. In 1935, Anna,—before you were even on the drawing board, so you won't remember any of this—Stalin began getting rid of certain cultural figures. Babel, Goldberg, Mandelstam, and others ..."

Anna watched Barsky. Any moment now he was going to hear the secret of his birth—a secret that had been kept from him for four decades. What was going on in his mind? His arid features now had hardened even more, his eyes were pinned to the dictaphone, his right hand still gripped the red packet of Dunhills, and with the fingers of his left he continued rolling his cigarette, but the tobacco was falling onto the tablecloth and his pants.

Kashchenko's voice picked up the story at a later point:

"When a beautiful young woman works at night at the piano with two brilliant young composers, while her drunken husband is slumped with his face in the salad, to coin a phrase, what came of all this, my dear, was not just a 'Harvesters' March.' A splendid little boy also appeared. But he had just one defect: a small birthmark just under his left armpit—in just the same spot where all the Grass brothers had a birthmark."

The Dunhill packet crunched in Barsky's right fist. He chucked it aside and nervously lit up his cigarette, which had lost half its tobacco. His face was obscured by smoke.

"... All hell broke loose," Kashchenko's voice continued "I've never seen a man beat a woman so hard. How he thrashed her, it was dreadful! If the neighbors hadn't come, he'd have killed both her and the child! But they managed to restrain him and shove him under a cold shower, but he still was blazing with anger. Then he called up Ezhov and said, 'Nikolay Ivanovich, this is Barsky calling, Stalin Prize winner. Two of our enemies have wormed their way into Soviet music and are undermining it with the corrupting influence of tunes from the Jewish shtetl. . . .' Ezhov told him, 'Thank you very much. Just give me that in writing.' Well, to make a long story short, the two of them—Moishe and Abram—were picked up the next morning. That day, Mitya Barsky came to his senses and clasped his head in horror. But it was too late. Well, after that he took to drinking in earnest. And he drank without let-up. Out of sheer horror at what he'd done! Inside three months he practically burnt himself up, and he died in a bout of delirium tremens. Abram and Moishe Grass got twenty years each. They were carted off to Siberia and disappeared there and perished. . . ."

Anna switched off the dictaphone and summoned the waitress.

"Bring us some vodka, please. Two hundred grams."

Barsky was shaken and gazed blankly out the window. Outside on the broad expanse of Manezh Square there was the usual morning flow of traffic. Workers were stringing up some banners, a summons from the Central Committee to "intensify the struggle for peace" and "raise labor productivity," in honor of the forthcoming sixty-first anniversary of the October Revolution. Meanwhile on Red Square the slow, dull peal of the Kremlin chimes could be heard—one, two, three, four . . . They seemed to go on for ever. Five, six . . .

The waitress came with a small carafe of vodka. Anna poured it all into a glass and slid it across the table toward Barsky.

"Thanks," he muttered, still without looking at her, and downed it in one gulp.

The chimes struck ten and fell silent.

Anna got up and laid on the table a folder from her briefcase.

"What is it? What's all this?" Barsky asked hoarsely.

"My documents to emigrate. Here's the Israeli invitation, this is the work reference and note about my leaving work, here's the divorce certificate, this is a note of permission from my father. And so on, and so forth. You heard what I told Maxim Rappoport, that if he and I don't meet in a month's time . . ."

"Yes, I heard. You want to leave so you can blackmail me from over there. Isn't that right?"

"Oleg Abramovich . . . Or is it Moiseyevich . . ." Anna began harshly. "I gave you an honest warning not to tangle with me. But like all Jews you're persistent. And now you've no choice. Either you take me at my word—that I will not blackmail you—and you let me out to join my son, or else . . ."

"But you're not even Jewish," he said, looking up at her at last. He took back his ID from her hand. "You can't have any relatives in Israel."

"I have a son."

"He's in America."

"So far as you are concerned, he's in Israel. And we're not going to haggle over it, Oleg." Anna removed the cassette from the dictaphone and flicked it across the table toward Barsky. "If you don't want your superiors to get a copy of this tape, you'll find a way of phrasing the permit for me to leave."

"And how do I explain to State Security your call to Rappoport?"

"Tell them the truth," Anna grinned. "Tell them I used that to get you to meet me this morning." She placed her dictaphone back into her briefcase, snapped the lock, and stood there waiting for his answer. "Well?"

"Very well," he said reluctantly. "You'll get your exit permit. In a month's time."

"One last question, Oleg. About Iosif Rubin. Is he really such a . . . such a monster as you make out? Or is this just another of your rigged cases? Like with Shcharansky?"

"That no longer concerns you," Barsky said brusquely. "You can go."

"Good-bye," Anna said.

"Farewell," he answered, and turned toward the window.

forty-four

All his life Barsky had taken pride in his pure and ancient Russian lineage and his descent from the Petersburg nobility as though this were some medal of honor. His ancestry could be traced back to the Novgorod family of Barsky-Vyazmitinov, merchants of the First Guild who lost all their money under Ivan IV, but regained it under Peter the Great, thanks to their enterprise and several advantageous marriages. Of course there were some Western historians, such as Kasimierz Waliszewski, who claimed that if you give a good shake to the genealogical tree of most Russian aristocratic families, among the luxuriant foliage you would find evidence of not just Norman, Tatar, Polish, and German stock, but also Jewish connections! For instance, it was well known that all five daughters of Peter the Great's vice chancellor, Baron Shafirov, married into Russian noble families. Indeed there was quite a contest among the suitors, since the highly aristocratic clans of the Vyazemskys, Tolstoys, Yusupovs, and others considered it an honor to become in-laws of the influential vice chancellor, to whom the emperor himself owed his life. Yet everyone knew that Shafirov was a baptized Jew whose real name was Shapiro. Thus, through his daughters, the vice chancellor managed to "adulterate" at least five ancient genealogical trees in the Russian aristocratic garden with the blood of a Shapiro. Not to mention his own dallyings in the shrubbery of that garden, which are beyond the reckoning of any modern historian.

But all these admixtures of Norman, Tatar, Swedish, Franconian, German, Jewish, and Polish blood were long ago dissolved in the powerful Russian homebrew from the steppes. Nowadays narrow Tatar eyes, large Jewish ears, or Norman fair hair were rare among Russian children and quickly disappeared with age.

Barsky had brown hair, his ears average, his nose straight and narrow with no trace of a Jewish hook, and his eyes were hazel. From childhood on he had never had the slightest doubt about his Aryan ancestry, and since the 1970s he had not concealed his noble origins. On the contrary, the USSR was now reestablishing its imperial traditions. Among nomenclature, to be a nobleman was not only fashionable—it had become a token of reliability and loyal service, like a good reference when you joined the Party. And the new elite, descended from the proletariat and working peasantry, suddenly began searching family albums and museum archives for possible traces of their own aristocratic roots.

But Barsky had no need to dig around in archives. The nineteenth-century book *Decrees and Deeds of the Emperor Nicholas I* recorded that his great-great-grandfather, the manufacturer Aristarkh Barsky, had been made a hereditary nobleman, and during the First World War Aristarkh Barsky's sons had made millions from supplying the Russian Army with greatcoats, underwear, and hospital sheets. Family legend had it that Oleg Barsky's great-grandfather had also been friends with Rasputin and even taken part in some of his orgies. But when Rasputin and the Empress began secret negotiations with Germany for a separate peace—which would of course have affected textile supplies to the army—the Barskys threw in with the revolutionaries and began funding those striving to overthrow the autocracy. In 1916 the intrepid escape of seven Bolsheviks from the Kiev jail was financed by the young factory-owner Igor Barsky—and that was no family legend but was documented by a letter from the Bolshevik Romanenko to Lenin, now on display in the Museum of the Revolution. Igor Barsky had also provided funds to help purchase equipment for "Iskra," the underground Bolshevik press on Moscow's Lesnaya Street.

The Barskys' contributions to other political parties—the Socialist Revolutionaries and the liberal Kadets—will never be known. But their friendship with the Bolsheviks, plus the fact that Oleg Barsky's grandfather, together with fellow millionaires Eliseyev, Babayev, and Sliozberg, voluntarily gave the Soviets all his factories, served to protect the family during the first years of the Revolution. Igor Barsky had also been a member of the first People's Commissariat of Education.

Now, suddenly, this powerful family tree on which Barsky had leaned all his life, and which had helped build his career with the KGB, had been uprooted and come crashing down. There was, of course, his mother, the Russian singer Varvara Dymkova, who had died just two years ago. There was no doubt about the purity of her Russian origins—she was from a Vyatka peasant family. And Barsky had spent his childhood after the war on the Vyatka River, in the village where all the Dymkovs hailed from—his grandfather, uncles, aunts, and cousins. But they were all simple folk, and certainly no match for that noble line to which Barsky had for forty years believed he belonged. And now, suddenly . . .

After his meeting with Anna, Barsky put all his other business aside and toward evening of that same day managed to locate the file on the Grass brothers in the KGB archives. It contained just five papers: a letter from Dmitry Barsky to NKVD director Ezhov concerning the "secret machinations of the composers Abram and Moisey Grass, who are deliberately poisoning Soviet musical culture with Jewish religious melodies"; the confessions of the Grass brothers that they had been carrying out assignments for British intelligence; a "Conclusion of the Prosecution" signed by the prewar head of the NKVD Fifth Directorate; and an "Extract from the record of the Special Commission of the NKVD" with the sentence, "Confine to corrective labor camp for period of twenty-five years for anti-Soviet activities." The fifth and final document was a copy of a statement sent in 1957 to a certain Sonya Moiseyevna Grass to the effect that her father Moisey Grass and his elder brother Abram Grass "were in 1936 held criminally responsible for a crime against the state *without foundation* and died in the year 1939 in Siberian camp No. 601 on a Tyumen–Norilsk railroad construction site." There was no information about the cause or circumstances of their deaths.

That was how Barsky discovered that somewhere he had either a half-sister or a cousin called Sonya Moiseyevna Grass.

She turned out to be a petite forty-eight-year old brunette, a professor of physics at the Moscow Institute of Steel and Alloys, and she lived in the Arbat, where in the sixteenth and seventeenth centuries there had been an artisan quarter. This history was preserved in the names of several lanes, Skatertny, Khlebny, etc., which denoted the former presence of traders in tablecloths, bread, and other goods, and of carpenters, grooms, and furriers. Since the eighteenth century the area had been inhabited by the nobility and had been nicknamed the Faubourg St. Germain of Moscow. But from 1917–20 the Arbat nobility fled abroad, along with the White Army, or was liquidated in the first wave of Red Terror. Their houses had been converted into apartment "beehives," in which the appointees of the new order—engineers, doctors, writers, and People's Commissars—were accommodated. Then, beginning in 1935, many of these had been taken away each night to the dungeons of the NKVD.

From his first minutes of observing Sonya Grass from his official car, Barsky sensed in her gait, her spectacles, the angle of her head, and even her manner of dressing, something that was familiar. It felt as if he had known this woman for a long time, as a girl even. But that was impossible. In 1941, when he was only three, his mother had taken him to Vyatka, to her parents in Dymkovo, a village famous for its brightly painted children's toys. Out there, there had been no Grass family, and not a single Jew; everyone had the same name, Dymkov. Barsky had lived there until he was nine, after which he returned with his mother to Moscow, studied at a boy's school, and had nothing to do with any girls until he was sixteen, when he went to the Murmansk naval college. So no Sonya Grass could ever have figured in his childhood and youth. Yet nevertheless . . .

From inside his car, Barsky followed his sister or cousin. He had not the slightest desire to get to know her. But an integral part of his professional skill was what Anna Sigal called his "Jewish persistence," or what in the KGB was called "tenacity." He had to find out which of the Grass brothers was his father, and this woman was the only connecting thread. So he followed her as though on a leash, first along the Arbat lanes; then he almost lost her at the crossing on Garden Ring, but then picked her up again on the western side of Zubovsky Boulevard. Did she really go all the way to work on foot? From the Arbat to Leninsky Prospect? Four miles! But no, she then turned off Zubovsky onto Komsomolsky Prospect and . . .

Barsky could barely believe his eyes. Sonya Grass, the daughter of Moisey—or Moses—Grass, made the sign of the cross, and walked into the Church of Saint Nicholas the Miracle Worker!

Amazed, Barsky got out of his car and followed her into the church. There he saw her praying before the ikon of the Holy Virgin Mary. He walked almost right up to his sister or cousin as she stood immersed in prayer. Then suddenly he realized why he had the impression of having known her since childhood—because her way of holding her head, the wisp of hair at the nape of her neck, and the round spectacles drooping from her sharp nose all reminded him of his own daughter, Olya. Although he had always believed Olya took after his mother, she turned out in fact to resemble more this unknown aunt of hers—at least in her gait and posture, if not facially and physically.

When Sonya left, Barsky approached the priest. One glance at his KGB ID was enough to persuade the clergyman to tell all he knew about her. It emerged that Sonya Grass had become a Christian in 1957, on the day she heard that her father and his brother had perished in the Gulag. On that day she had renounced her belief in the Jewish God to whom she had secretly prayed for the last twenty years—ever since she was seven—asking him to watch over and preserve her father.

So Barsky had at least one consolation: although his father came from a family of Jewish musicians, Sonya, Barsky's half sister or cousin, had renounced Judaism and become a Christian. But did this change anything for him? For believers it was simple: you could change your religion and become an instant Christian, Muslim, or Buddhist. But Communists were supposedly above religion. And if your father was a Jew, then you too were a Jew from the moment of your birth forever and ever, Amen!

But Barsky could not—and would not—be a Jew! In the empty church of St. Nicholas, he mentally raised his voice and shouted at those ikons and images: Oh Lord God, I do not want to be a Jew! Just because of a tiny birthmark under my left armpit, do I really have to go through life bearing in my soul the curse of being a Yid?

In the evening Barsky called up his daughter but did not find her at home. How long since he last saw her? Three months? Four? Even those books that she asked him to get a long time ago—various things by Khomyakov, Bilbasov, and from the archive of Prince Kurakin—had been passed on to her via the duty officer at the Lubyanka. He himself had no time. Because of those Jews and Yasir Arafat, he had not had time to see his own daughter! She had been abandoned ten years ago by her mother, and now her father too. Where was she? Who was she with? What was she doing? And Barsky wondered whether he himself still had any friends, home, and family. Like some maniac, he had surrendered himself totally to his work, to the State Security Committee. But what had he gotten for it?

Keeping up his spirits with brandy, Barsky dialed Olya's number over and over. But she was not at home. Not surprising. The semester had begun, and she probably was disappearing into the library again. He walked over to his mother's portrait, his favorite picture of her—a still from the film *Snow Hills*. Since 1934, that picture was the one she had used for all her concert flyers and for the jackets on the records she'd made. He always used to hold his picture of Olya next to it and rejoice that she was growing up to look like not her own mother, who had run off with a diplomat, but like his, Barsky's, mother—the beautiful, talented Varvara Dymkova. But after about fifteen, Olya began losing her good looks; stopped growing, began wearing glasses, and had burst out with teenage pimples. He had wondered then why both he and Olya had problems with their eyes. Now it was clear. Their Jewish heritage, it came from the Grass family—after a thousand years of reading prayerbooks, generation after generation, the vision of all Jews was genetically impaired.

Barsky grinned to himself gloomily. Just when his mother had her affair with one of the Grass brothers—or was it both of them?—Stalin had branded genetics a false science! What else had he and Olya inherited from their Jewish genes? And how was it neither of them had an ear for music? Because one way or another, his father had been a composer, and his mother a singer. And he had so loved his mother! Throughout his childhood and youth, and to the end of her days, she had been like a saint to him. For his sake, he believed, she had not remarried, although she was widowed so early—at twenty-two. And the most eligible men had sought her hand—attorneys, military men, academics, and scientists. But she had turned down each and every one of them, and she even laughed as she told him about it when he was a boy. Did it now turn out that this was not so much self-sacrifice on her part, but an attempt to atone for some secret sin? Yet if that was the case, what an awful life this woman must have had, knowing that three men had perished because of her.

As he sat with his brandy in front of his mother's portrait and gradually got drunk, Barsky kept addressing both himself and her, repeating the words: "Mama . . . Mama . . . Why was it necessary? Bloody Yids! Nothing but kikes wherever you turn! Even I am a kike!"

He got one of his mother's old records from the cabinet and placed it on the turntable, and he drank and listened to his mother's youthful voice as she sang:

Do not scold me, don't upbraid me.
For I could not help but love him . . .

Well, he would have his revenge. He would have his vengeance on all of them! For seducing his mother, for depriving him of his father, for making him a half-breed and taking away the woman he loved most! For all this, he would avenge himself a hundredfold! As his prosecutor he would find a fire-eating woman attorney, and of pure Russian blood, someone whose eloquence would cause Cicero, Robespierre, and Vyshinsky all to turn over in their graves with envy. He would sell his soul to Igunov if need be, but for his show-trial of Rubinchik he would secure the best venue in Moscow—the Hall of Columns in Union House, which used to be the hall of the Noble Assembly, right next to the Bolshoi Theater! And he would put on such a trial—an event with all foreign correspondents admitted—that Jews worldwide would regard the Dreyfus affair or the trial of Ariel Sharon for the carnage in Lebanon as a mere school picnic!

His finger trembled as he dialed his office.

"Zartsev speaking," his duty officer answered.

"This is Barsky."

"How can I help, Comrade Colonel?"

"Where's our what's-his-name? Our love-kike?"

"I don't know, Comrade Colonel. We stopped trailing him once he sobered up, you remember. I think he's probably at work, in his boiler room."

"Get a team after him!"

"What? Right now?" Zartsev had noticed the slurred speech of his boss and seemed to doubt his word.

"You heard what I said! Get him under surveillance right now, and we'll bring him in in the morning!"

"Very good, Comrade Colonel," Zartsev said. Five minutes later, though, he called back. "Comrade Colonel, the dispatch officer won't give us the men without your personal written order. Perhaps we can leave him till the morning? He's not going to run anywhere!"

Barsky chucked the receiver back into its cradle. Zartsev had tactfully tried to convey to him that in his state he should not try to requisition a surveillance team by telephone. Barsky got the message. He poured himself the remains of the brandy and drank it down.

"You see what luck these kikes have!" he said, addressing his mother's portrait. "But never mind! I'll find a woman attorney. I'll find such an attorney, that . . . !"

Then he remembered his daughter and dialed Olya's number again. But there were the same long beeps as before and no answer.

He peeled off his shirt and staggered along to the bathroom to inspect himself in the mirror. On his left side, under his arm, and so far back that it was only visible using a mirror, he could see that small brown birthmark, no larger than a bean. He tried scratching it with his finger, but it would not scratch off. He pressed his nail hard into it and winced with pain. His "Yiddish" birthmark could not be removed.

"Fuck it!" He punched the mirror with his fist—so hard that he almost dislocated his hand.

f o r t y - f i v e

To the USSR General Prosecutor,
State Counselor of Justice.

Comrade A. M. Rekunkov:

The USSR State Security Committee (KGB) hereby refers to your attention file No. 578/E67 in order that a criminal case be brought against citizen Iosif Mikhailovich RUBINCHIK, residing at 24 First Cosmonauts' Street, apt. 67, Moscow, in accordance with Article 120 of the Criminal Code concerning mass corruption of minors and other infractions of public morality. Initial investigation has been carried out by E Section of the Fifth Main Directorate of the KGB under Colonel O. D. Barsky.

In view of the extreme crimes committed and because of evidence collected by the KGB on I. M. Rubinchik's connections with Zionists and his anti-Soviet activities, we request that a warrant be issued for the arrest of citizen I. M. Rubinchik, providing for his detention under guard in preliminary confinement at isolator No. 2 (Butyrka Jail), and also a search warrant for I. M. Rubinchik's apartment at 24 First Cosmonauts' Street, apt. 67, and his place of work: boiler room of the Institute of Glaciology, 27 Enthusiasts' Prospect.

We also request that the KGB be permitted to conduct the case, prepare it for trial in open court, and also select a suitable public prosecutor.

> Head of Investigation Board of the USSR KGB
> Lieutenant-General of State Security R. Medvedev
> Encl. Case file No. 578/E67
> Moscow, September 7, 1978

OFFICE OF THE USSR GENERAL PROSECUTOR
RESOLUTION CONCERNING INITIATION
OF CRIMINAL CASE

Moscow
September 7, 1978

Having reviewed the investigative materials of case No. 578/E67, submitted by the USSR State Security Committee (KGB), I instruct as follows:

1) Criminal case to be opened against citizen I. M. RUBINCHIK, resident at 24 First Cosmonauts' Street, apt. 67, Moscow, under Article 120 of the USSR Criminal Code.

2) In view of the extreme character of the case, its investigation is to be placed in the hands of the KGB.

3) Investigative Board of the KGB to be issued with arrest warrant for I. M. Rubinchik permitting his preliminary confinement in penitentiary No. 2; warrant also to be issued for search of Rubinchik's apartment and place of work, as per the RSFSR Code of Procedure.

4) Upon completion of investigation of the above by the State Security Committee, all materials relating to the case to be passed to the USSR Prosecutor's Office for prosecution to be prepared, and confirmation of public prosecutor.

5) Preparations for public trial of the above mentioned to be handled jointly by the State Security Committee (KGB) and Office of the General Prosecutor, and also by agreement with the Propaganda Section of the Central Committee.

USSR General Prosecutor
Judicial Counselor, A. Rekunkov

REPORT
by State Security Captains Faskin and Zartsev

To: HEAD OF E SECTION, FIFTH DIRECTORATE OF
USSR STATE SECURITY COMMITTEE, COLONEL O. D. BARSKY

According to your instruction and acting on the basis of a warrant from the Prosecutor General, at 2110 hours today, September 7, 1978, citizen I. M. Rubinchik was arrested in the boiler room of the Institute of Glaciology (17 Enthusiasts' Prospect). At the same time the said boiler room and apt. 67 at 24 First Cosmonauts' Street were also inspected, together with Rubinchik's cooperatively owned automobile garage and his vehicle, a Moskvich-407.

Careful examination of all these sites failed to disclose the presence of any illegal publications, foreign editions, manuscripts, notebooks, telephone books, or even the personal typewriter of I. M. Rubinchik.

The only materials that might relate to the current investigation are two undeveloped rolls of film, found in the boiler room among Rubinchik's personal possessions. These were placed in a packet and sealed in front of witnesses and are appended to this report. Although the arrested man refused to identify what was recorded on these films, the fact that they are his property is specified in the search report. When signing the search report, the arrested man stated emphatically that the films in question should be developed and printed personally by Colonel Oleg Dmitryevich Barsky. The arrested man refused to disclose the source of his knowledge of your name. However this fact, and also the total absence of incriminating materials, led to the conclusion that I. M. Rubinchik was expecting his arrest and had prepared for it.

The arrested man has been delivered to the Butyrka Penitentiary, where he is in solitary confinement, pending interrogation.

> Captain Faskin
> Captain Zartsev
> Moscow
> September 8, 1978

forty-six

The pages had been neatly typed, with even margins, on alternate lines, and were obviously the work of a careful typist:

Iosif Rubin

THE JEWISH ROAD

Chapter Seventeen:
The Rise and Fall of KGB Major Seda Ashidova, Head of Freight Customs

Epigraph: "Hell and heaven and earth all look with special sympathy upon a man when Eros enters him." (Vladimir Solovyov)

Up until a few years ago, the post of Head of Moscow Freight Customs was regarded as a dead-end job. It involved little but listening to endless profanities from packers and loaders, and unpleasant arguments with the railroad traffic control.

But in the early 1970s, when the Jewish emigration began, that cramped office, without even a secretary, on the third floor of the four-story building at number 1-A Komsomol Square became a coveted workplace. But it was also fraught with danger. Even the most fervent and uncorruptible up-and-coming young people in the Party and KGB, who had a burning desire to build a career based on their integrity, lost their innocence within a week of moving into that office. In official parlance, they became "trapped in the web of Zionism and fell victim to their own acquisitiveness." Put more simply, they began taking bribes.

How indeed could one avoid taking bribes, when money and jewelry came bursting in at your office door at seven in the morning and continued throughout the day? These were riches beyond the comprehension of any ordinary employee. Of course not every Jew intending to emigrate was an underground millionaire. Not everyone had made a fortune through the shadow economy in the southern republics, or through manufacturing "homespun" jeans and polyester raincoats somewhere in Riga. But the average emigrant never found his way up to the office of the head of Customs. The main things the average emigrant wanted to take with him were his books—an enormous collection of Russian books without which no Jew could imagine living in Israel, America, Canada, or Australia. These bookworms usually resigned themselves to the removal from their baggage containers of such heirlooms as grandmother's silver spoons or mother's china, whose export was forbidden. But they dug their heels in and created a scene whenever they were told not to take with them works by Sholokhov, Mayakovsky, or Nikolay Ostrovsky, published in the USSR before 1946 and thus banned for export as "antique editions." These bibliophiles were a strange crowd, there was no getting away from it. Some of them slipped hundreds of rubles into the Customs inspectors' pockets—simply to avoid being left with nothing to read when they landed abroad.

Barsky laid the page aside and covered his eyes, aghast. The recent death of Major Seda Ashidova, one of the KGB's best officers, had caused a sensation not just within the KGB but throughout Moscow. But that was not what upset Barsky. Nor was it that this bastard Rubinchik had evidently obtained information about the circumstances of her death. It was the place where he had discovered this manuscript. An hour ago, standing in the red glow of the KGB dark room and bending over the plastic cuvettes, large as bathtubs, in which the prints of Rubinchik's films were being developed, he had suffered his first-ever cardiac spasm. It happened at the moment when the prints floated to the surface of the developer and the light and dark tones began to differentiate, and he saw Rubinchik posing against a Moscow summer townscape, seemingly embracing Barsky's own twenty-year-old mother. That was how it looked! At first, when the contours of her face emerged on the photos, Barsky thought he was going mad—it was his mother, his mother in her youth, as she looked in photographs of the early thirties. And it was only a minute later, when the picture emerged in detail, that he recognized her as his daughter.

He leaned over the developing tray, unable to believe his eyes. But it was her, his own Olya! Olya and Rubinchik with their arms around one another! And that was all there was—everywhere on all seventy-two frames of the two rolls that Faskin and Zartsev had confiscated in the boiler room of the Glaciology Institute. The pictures showed Olya smiling, thoughtful, and laughing. On Red Square, Lenin Hill, the Crimea Bridge, and even kissing Rubinchik on Dzerzhinsky Square with the KGB headquarters in the background—an obvious mockery and challenge to Barsky.

Barsky was overcome with fury and horror, and for a moment he was blinded. But he was alert enough to realize that no one, not even the photo lab assistant, must see these pictures. So that was why that son of a bitch had "stated emphatically" that the film should be developed by Barsky in person! He stepped quickly across to the switch and put on the light. All the prints in the developing trays immediately darkened and turned black. The girl who was busy at work with the enlarger, swung round with a look of astonishment. But he made no attempt to explain things and simply took the two rolls from her and walked out, suppressing an urge to run. He then went down, got into an official car, and sank into the seat.

In the car he struggled to fight down the pain that gripped his chest. Twenty minutes later he bowled up to the food store on Taganskaya Square and dashed up the stairs to Olya's apartment on the third floor. Nobody answered his knock. Undeterred, he aimed a kick at the lock and the door flew open. Olya was not home, but one glance told him that that bastard had been here, regularly. There was a photo of him on Olya's bedside table; there were cigarettes lying on the window ledge, and on Olya's desk there was a typewriter and a pile of typed pages next to it, including this chapter seventeen.

Barsky chucked the papers aside and began ransacking the place, flinging open drawers, the medicine cabinet in the bathroom, and a box with cosmetics. From innumerable searches in the apartments of dissidents and Zionists, he well knew where women concealed their contraceptive pills. But there were none in Olya's apartment, and not knowing whether this was a good or a bad sign, he walked over to the window. Where could she be at twelve midnight, when Rubinchik was now in solitary at Butyrka?

He switched on the radio atop her chest of drawers beneath a small ikon of Christ—shortly before her death his mother had become religious and attended the local church in Kotelnichesky Lane. Of course the radio was tuned to the BBC, and through the rasp of Soviet jamming he heard an announcement that talks had started in Camp David between Israeli Prime Minister Menachem Begin, U.S. President Jimmy Carter, and the Egyptian President Anwar Sadat. Iran had declared martial law in twelve cities, and in the United States wire tapping had been prohibited, except in special cases, by a new law. And American Senator Edward Kennedy was preparing to come to Moscow for a meeting with Brezhnev to discuss the fate of Soviet dissidents and Jews who had been denied exit visas.

Irritably Barsky switched off the radio. Kennedy in Moscow—that was the last straw! These kikes would become totally brazen if American senators started coming to Brezhnev! And where the hell was Olya, damn her? Lord, how had he deserved such punishment? His mother, Anna Sigal, and now his own daughter cohabiting with kikes! What attraction did these Jews have for all the very best Russian women?

He lit a cigarette and returned to the desk. Rubinchik's anti-Soviet manuscript lying in the apartment of his own daughter—in his worst nightmare he couldn't have imagined anything more vile. He drew deeply on his cigarette and began reading through the clouds of smoke.

. . . The scandals involving run-of-the-mill emigrants and their petty bribes normally never left the Customs Hall. The third-floor office was visited only by people who wanted to arrange in advance for their baggage to be cleared "without obstacles," that is without any inspection. Usually these visitors announced themselves by tapping on the office door with a large gold signet ring on their right hand. Then they inched the door open and poked their heads inside.

"May I come in?" The question usually came in a thick Caucasian or Central Asian accent. Then the man would enter, pointedly and firmly close the door behind him, and sit down on the chair facing the head of Customs. Conversation would then begin:

"My dear man, do you have any children?"

"Why do you ask?" the officer would reply.

"No, tell me as a friend. Do you have children, and a wife?"

"Well, yes, of course . . ."

"That's great! I have here a small memento for your children. This little ring here, with a two-carat diamond. I would really like your daughter to wear it when she grows up. Wait a minute! No need to blush, my friend, this isn't a bribe. I am not offering it to you. It's for your daughter. It's no use to me anyway. I can't take it out of the country. It's forbidden to take diamonds out. So what am I to do? Throw it away? If you want, I'll throw it out the window right now, okay? Right now, in front of you, I swear on my mother's tomb. So why not take it for your daughter? Don't deprive her of such a treat!"

After such a foray, the remaining moves to clear one's baggage without inspection were mere technicalities. As soon as the Customs chief dropped the ring or pendant in his pocket, the visitor would continue:

"Listen, my friend, when is your wife's birthday?"

"Oh, not for a long time."

"What a shame! Well, maybe I could send her some flowers in advance? That surely won't make you jealous? I'm leaving, after all. What's your address?"

It should be noted that none of these visitors ever gave presents—not even a cigarette holder—to the head of Customs himself. Only to his wife and children. They were the ones who that same evening received cases of Armenian brandy and White Horse whiskey, cartons of Marlboros, gigantic cream cakes, and baskets of grade-A fruit. And at the doorway the visitor, as if by accident, would slip a fat envelope full of 100-ruble notes into the pocket of the boss's coat hanging on its peg.

After a few months of such intense Zionist pressure, the head of customs would despair at the loss of his honor and start drowning the remnants of his Party conscience at the Aragvi and Uzbekistan restaurants, enjoying juicy shish kebabs, liters of vodka, and the attentions of young beauties from the Komsomol register in the KGB's Second Operations Directorate. Sooner or later he would rent a one-room apartment for one of these Komsomol girls somewhere on the outskirts of Moscow, and there in an orgy of self-reproach, lamentation, and breast-beating, he would confess to having "sold out to the Yids."

The rest was routine. The offender would be fired, or else transferred to other work and receive a Party reprimand, but never brought to trial. Why draw attention to someone who had accidentally fallen into a Zionist trap?

After that, behind the frosted glass door of the Chief Customs Officer a new man would appear, self-assured and with an unstained reputation, long years in the Party, and with a dozen endorsements of his patriotism and efficiency. Unfortunately, though, and unaccountably, within a month he too would start appearing with a redness about the eyes, and his hands would tremble. And a month later the Second Directorate would receive an anonymous note from one of the Customs inspectors reporting the misdoings of his senior officer, or a report from one of the Komsomol girls.

Finally, these musical chairs in the Freight Customs department attracted the attention of none other than General Tsvigun, Andropov's deputy. As a hardboiled character, Tsvigun had lambasted the head of the Freight Customs Section in his own inimitable way and ordered Barsky as head of the Jewish Section to halt these diversionary activities of emigrating Jews. It was a simple matter to give orders, but an entirely different one to see them through. Barsky gave the problem some thought, then called up General Katorgin, who was head of the Directorate of Corrective Labor Institutions—an organization better known by its former name, the "Gulag."

"Can you find us a reliable person?" Barsky asked, after briefly outlining the situation.

One week later Katorgin sent him the files of three commandants of Siberian labor camps. These candidates—two men and a woman—were known to the criminal world as the "Mad Dogs." Moreover, each of their files contained reports from the Camp Inspectorate describing them as incorruptible. Reluctant to take the final decision himself, Barsky brought these to Tsvigun. Having examined them together, both men chose the female candidate. As men in the prime of life, they both recognized that there was no male on God's earth who was absolutely incorruptible. But as for women, damn it, the jury was still out!

Major Seda Ashidova, the commandant of Siberian Women's Camp No. AS/527, was a Tatar. Age forty-two, unmarried, and a Party member, she'd been awarded two medals for "Outstanding Work," seven certificates for "Irreproachable Service," and three cups for first place in the competition of Siberian Corrective Labor Institutions. She had also been presented with a Makarov-type pistol engraved personally with the signature of Interior Minister General Shchelokov. The convicts had also rewarded her—with a range of appellations including "Rabies," "The Bitch," and "The Fascist." Both Barsky and Tsvigun decided that there could be no better candidate to withstand Zionist temptations and blandishments.

Seda Ashidova thoroughly justified the hopes placed in her. During her first week, the underground millionaire, Gutman from Baku, died of a heart attack in her office. During the second week, the same thing happened to Rozentsveig, the last in a long line of Saratov dentists. The pockets of each man held jewelry worth three to five thousand rubles, and envelopes each containing ten thousand rubles. The containers with their baggage revealed, among other restricted items, ancient handmade Persian rugs, gold and silver vessels fit for a museum, and gold coins and diamonds, all concealed in household items.

Ashidova's third week in office brought a harvest of four heart attacks, three fainting fits, and an attempted suicide, a man trying to jump from her office window.

When rumors of her incorruptibility spread and the flood of visitors knocking at her frosted glass office door subsided, Seda moved down to the general inspection hall and there too rapidly established the same model penitentiary system. A windowless concrete wall was erected to separate the inspectors and loaders from the actual owners of the luggage, and she herself prevented any contact between the two groups.

Major Ashidova was a squat, slant-eyed woman, with bow legs and a slightly pockmarked visage and high cheekbones. She would stroll up and down in her calfskin boots between the huge crates of baggage, and tap her boots with a riding crop as she watched, hawk-eyed, for the slightest suspicious move by any of her subordinates or clients.

"Take that back! What was that you were passing over? Come here! Show it to me! Open that crate! I don't care if it's already been inspected! Open it. I'm going to inspect it myself!"

Within another week, doctors at the nearby Sklifasovsky Hospital knew that every ambulance call from 1-A Komsomol Square meant another emigrant heart attack, brought on by despair at Seda Ashidova's remorseless methods. And if her past fame had been narrowly institutional, she now became a national celebrity. Every Jewish businessman from Kiev to Vladivostok knew there was no way of getting around her. To her existing nicknames, three new ones were added: "Genghis Khan," "Stalin," and "The Morgue." Furthermore, the first two of these were invented by her own staff—the Customs inspectors who now found themselves done out of their regular harvest of small bribes.

Several Jews delayed their departure because of Major Ashidova. They needed to take countermeasures. In their reckoning: "If she can't be bought, there are just two ways out. She has to be either killed or screwed."

The substantial funds these people had would have made either of these options feasible. In practice, though, neither proved possible. As to murder—the motive would have been too obvious: Seda had been in someone's way and that someone had taken her out. Whether or not the CID found the actual killers, there would be widespread reprisals against the Jews. For that reason, the first scheme was ruled out from the start.

As for the "screwing operation," both amateurs and professionals tried their hands at it. Among the amateurs were those who, for a few gold trinkets hidden among furniture or in the electric iron, were prepared to close their eyes to Ashidova's pockmarks (a feature she had in common with Stalin) and give her the benefit of their hot Jewish blood. Among the professionals were four well-known Moscow playboys of various ages, hired by a group of Jewish big shots. One was a tenor from the gypsy cabaret at the Romany Theater; another a famous movie star who had taken to drink; the third a comedian of French-Armenian appearance; the fourth an outright gigolo who passed himself off as a celebrated Georgian artist.

But the frontal attacks by the amateurs in Ashidova's office, and the professional attempts to meet her, as if by chance, in the metro or on the street, met with no luck. She didn't go for an invitation to the Romany Theatre, nor for a show with the famous comedian Arkady Raikin, nor even for a private showing of Fellini's *La Dolce Vita* at Film House. She failed to respond to suggestive looks, jokes, French-Armenian glamour, or even the luxuriant whiskers of the giant Georgian. In fact she froze every attempted advance with a scornful look of her narrow lynx eyes and a few unprintable oaths from her prison camp lexicon. After such rough rejections both professionals and amateurs came to the same curt conclusion: "Fuck her."

But people still had to leave.

Dozens had already obtained their precious exit permits. But now, instead of engaging in commerce in Tel Aviv, walking the clean streets of Vienna, or sunbathing on the beaches of Ostia or Ladispoli, they were compelled to postpone their departures, while still retaining their visas, by getting themselves admitted to hospitals with fictitious pneumonia, simulated strokes, imaginary jaundice, and make-believe blood in their urine. And worst of all, there was no hope of immediate recovery!

Major Seda Ashidova, a little Tatar weighing just a hundred pounds, and known to certain parties as the "cunt in epaulettes," had achieved what the fiercest Politburo hawks had failed to do: check the Jewish emigration. The departures were not halted altogether, but once she had corked up the Moscow Freight Customs depot, the number leaving tailed off sharply.

At that point someone voiced the suspicion that since she was commandant of a women's camp, Ashidova was most likely a lesbian. So a series of women of various shapes and sizes were sent to test her. But because of her previous job, she had no trouble in identifying that kind of woman and she threw them out with even nastier curses than she used on the men.

And then they guessed: "She's a virgin!"

And a general groan went up in Jewish emigrant circles.

"What can be more dreadful than a virgin KGB major!" some lamented. Others uttered a more colorful curse: "May she not only dry up, but let weeds and tall grass sprout from that part of her body!"

But whatever anyone said made little difference. As director of the Moscow Customs, Seda Ashidova had stuck not only in the collective throat of would-be Jewish emigrants. She had become a challenge to a whole people—yet another ordeal visited by God on the Jews of Russia.

But, just as God is generous with His ordeals, so He can be generous—to give Him His due—in offering deliverance.

In this instance, deliverance came in the form of a noisy crowd of dwarfs that one day burst into Major Ashidova's office. These Lilliputians were from Dreamtime, the only midget theater in Europe, on the payroll of the Moscow Philharmonic Society. Since dwarfs are people with few manners and considerable nerve (in this respect outdoing both Jews and Gypsies), they burst into Seda's office without knocking and immediately created a tremendous ruckus.

"Don't let him go!"

"Keep him here!"

"Do something to stop him!"

One female midget, who bore a striking similarity to Walt Disney's Snow White, leapt up onto Seda's desk and crossed her miniskirted legs.

"I planted some diamonds in his baggage," she whispered in Seda's ear. "In the toothpowder. They're not real of course, but you can say that they are. And hold him for smuggling. Please! It won't cost you anything! Without him we're finished!"

At that moment one of the dwarfs played a heartrending melody on the violin. Another was walking along the window ledge on his hands, yelling, "If he leaves, I'm going to jump!" Three other weeping Lilliputians settled themselves on the floor, opened a bottle of Kakhetian wine and took turns drinking it from the bottle, wiping tears from their cheeks.

Seda lost her cool. For the first time in her life she found herself dealing with people not taller than she, but half her size. And these little folk were asking her not to clear someone's baggage but, on the contrary, to hold it back.

"Hold who back? Who are you all?" Seda asked.

"Our director! Hold our director back!" whimpered the little Snow White as she sat facing Seda on top of her desk. "We're actors from the Dreamtime, the only professional midget theater in Europe. He created it, brought us together from all over the country, and now he's leaving!" The little woman burst out sobbing again and comically wiped away her large tears with a tiny doll-like fist.

"So what about it?" said Seda. "Is he a Jew?"

It had never occurred to her that there might be Jewish midgets. But on the other hand, why not?

"Of course he's Jewish!" said a handsome little gnome who looked like a prince. Even in his top hat, he was no higher than the desk. "Who else could have thought up a name like Dreamtime? And then put on performances of *Anna Karenina!*"

"We even played to full houses in England!" Snow White said. "Please, don't let him go! It's easy for you. And the scoundrel never said a word about leaving until today!"

"If he leaves, they'll close us down!" a tubby individual wearing a red embroidered velvet jacket and felt hat with plume intoned tragically. All the dwarfs now started to wail in chorus.

Well, thought Seda, I can maybe do them a favor and hold up this dwarf for ten days or so. But no longer than that.

"Okay, so suppose I do hold him up for a couple of weeks," she said with a smile—perhaps for the first time in her life. "That still won't help you."

"It will! It will!" all twenty exclaimed at once, throwing their top hats and other headgear in the air, leaping up and down and turning somersaults. "Then we'll have time to persuade him! And we'll get our salaries. And then we'll be off on tour to Mongolia, and he won't be able to emigrate from there!"

Seda saw their naive joy. She smiled and did not even bother to remove the lipstick that a grateful Snow White planted on her cheek. Of course, she would hold back their director. For once she could permit herself to be a little softer— and not for a set of crooks or kikes, but for these little folk.

"All right," Seda said, and was getting up when the door flew open, and in stepped an utterly improbable figure—a seven-foot, forty-five-year-old Adonis wearing a long black leather coat, white scarf, white kid gloves, and with the glare of Mephistopheles.

"And what exactly is going on here?" he said to the dwarfs in a loud and stern voice. They all fell silent. "What's this performance you're putting on here? Apologize at once to the Comrade!" In an aside to Seda, he added, "I'm sorry, madam, I don't know your name. They're just like children." He then turned to Snow White: "Isolda! Come here at once! Come over here, you bad girl!"

Snow White stood up on Seda's desk and with her eyes downcast, walked across it toward the giant. Even standing on the desk, she barely reached up to the diamond pin that glistened on his necktie.

The giant took from his pocket a round cardboard box marked SVEZHEST— FRESHNESS, a Soviet brand of toothpowder. Disdainfully he opened it with the long fingers of his white kid gloves.

"What is this?" he asked Isolda.

In among the toothpowder the dull gleam of some make-believe diamonds could be seen.

"Isolda, I ask you!" the giant said in his fruity baritone. "What on earth is this? Have you ever seen me use Soviet toothpowder? And anyway, do you all want me to land in jail?"

"We don't want you to go away," Isolda said quietly as the others stood by in gloomy silence. "We love you!"

"Yes! Yes!" the other little folk broke in. "We love you! And there you are, leaving us! How will we manage without you?"

Seda gazed at them all. Or, rather, at the giant in the leather coat. This was the first time she had ever seen a man like that. It was also the very first time she had ever relaxed and dropped her guard. And it had to be at the very moment when into her office walked not another of your Emmanuel Katzmans from Tashkent, but this splendid figure—Venyamin Bruskin.

Isold-cum-Snow White turned to Seda.

"Remember, you promised!" she said in a theatrical whisper. But there was no need to remind Seda of her promise. Lord, what do we know of the female heart? When God created the first woman out of Adam's rib, probably not even He suspected what surprises were in store for Him.

Seda Ashidova was a major in the KGB, promoted from the Directorate of Labor Camps to take charge of Moscow Customs, given government awards, an engraved gun, and nicknames such as "Genghis Khan." But now she had fallen in love at first sight with Venyamin Bruskin, director of the midget theater—like girls in the eighth grade in the 1950s fell in love with Marlon Brando or his Soviet equivalent, Vyacheslav Tikhonov.

How could she possibly let him emigrate?

"Excuse me one moment," she said, and left her office. She felt an unfamiliar burning sensation all through her body as she flitted downstairs into the general hall.

"Where's that actor's baggage?" she said. "You know, what's-his-name. That director of the midget theater?"

"Oh, Bruskin?" said the inspector on duty. "It's over there. Two crates, nothing out of the ordinary. Books, Czech furniture, a Weltmuller accordion, and a Yava motorbike with a spare engine. There was a box of false diamonds in some toothpowder, but I gave that back to him."

"We have to find something!" Seda interrupted feverishly.

"In order to fine him or arrest him for smuggling?"

"Just to postpone his departure, that's all."

"You've got lipstick on your face, Comrade Major. Holding him up is no problem. You simply order his bike to be dismantled—on suspicion that it contains contraband. That'll hold him up for a good three weeks. Who's going to take a Yava apart here? We don't have any mechanics. And you could hide two pounds of real diamonds in a Yava!"

"Great! Write up a report and bring it to me!" Pleased with herself, she rushed off to the storeroom where confiscated items were kept. It contained everything—from sixteenth-century mirrors in gilded frames to modern French cosmetics.

Some twenty minutes later, when Seda left the storeroom, she was transformed. Though still dressed in Customs uniform—gray jacket, gray skirt, and calfskin boots—her eyes, eyelashes, lips, and hairstyle were all different. Even her pockmarks had mysteriously disappeared, and her cheeks had acquired a new rosy tint. The loudspeaker system, which most of the time rasped incomprehensibly, as in every railroad station, burst into song. Loud and clear came the "March of the Toreadors" from Bizet's *Carmen*. "Toreador, march boldly off to war! Love awaits you there!" And to this music, Seda, now seductively transformed, flitted back up to her third-floor office. The inspector was there waiting for her with his report requiring a further examination of Bruskin's motorcycle.

Bruskin sat there surrounded by his midgets, who had now subsided like children tired after a bout of exuberant play.

"Comrade Major," he protested, "This will be the death of me! I have a ticket for tomorrow's flight to Vienna!"

"I'll help you change your ticket. No problem," Seda cooed in her newly adopted turtledove tone. She picked up the phone and dialed: "Hello? Sheremetyevo Customs? Major Zolotaryov, please. Comrade Zolotaryov, this is Seda Ashidova here. Sorry to bother you. I have to detain a man here, and his ticket is for tomorrow. Could you change it for a flight in about ten days?"

"But my visa's running out!" Bruskin exclaimed.

"We'll extend that too. Don't worry," Seda cooed again, covering the mouthpiece with her hand.

The Lilliputian in the red velvet jacket stepped up and kissed her hand.

"Goddess!" he intoned in his deep voice. "We're all going to go straight from here to the Aragvi Restaurant! You will of course accompany us, I hope?"

"Oh, certainly," Seda replied in her new voice. "Only let's drop by my apartment, so I can change."

Rumors that The Morgue had been cracked spread like wildfire. But few Jews believed it. The hotshots were cautious by nature and sent their agents to Customs to check out the rumors. They found Number 1-A Komsomol Square in an incredible state. The inspectors were doing exactly as they liked, taking bribes openly, right under the nose of a totally transformed Seda Ashidova. She herself fluttered through the Customs building in a chiffon blouse and bright-colored skirt, caught up at the waist with a dark-colored broad belt. Her hair was curled, her cheeks glowed, her eyes gleamed, and her lips were constantly whistling or singing some airy melody.

In fact, it was no longer an easy matter to find Seda in the Customs hall. She appeared at various times in the middle of the day for an hour or so, signed everything put before her, and immediately disappeared. Either the dwarfs picked her up in a taxi, or she hailed a passing "gypsy" cab.

But the agents were paid to find out the fine details. Nor was it all that hard to do—Seda and Bruskin made no secret of their tempestuous affair. On the contrary, they partied openly in the most fashionable restaurants—the Aragvi, the Uzbekistan, the Sovetskaya, Theater House, Film House, and then back to the Aragvi. They spent their afternoons in the bars in Sokolniki Park, at the Journalists' Club House, and on the Arbat. And soon everyone who needed to know knew everything, that Bruskin had practically moved in with her at 9 Grokholsky Lane; that every morning she rushed off by taxi to buy fresh fruit for his breakfast; that after breakfast he had a nap, and she jumped back into bed with him and rode him so hard that the chandelier in the apartment below had fallen from the ceiling three times. "You see," said the experts, "if she was a virgin till she was forty, she has to go like crazy to catch up on all she's missed."

When the big shots received confirmation of all this, they discharged themselves from their hospitals, packed up their belongings, and came to agreements with the Customs inspectors. They then began spending their evenings at the Aragvi and other restaurants, hoping to see with their own eyes the transformation of Seda The Morgue, and in the company of their savior, Venyamin Bruskin. When Bruskin and Seda arrived, the most distinguished Jews were there to open the car doors for them. Once inside, they would call Bruskin aside, whisper their gratitude, and thrust wads of 100-ruble bills into his pockets. At first Bruskin couldn't work out why they called him "our Yiddish knight in armor," nor precisely what service he had performed for the Jewish people. But when it was finally explained, he laughed heartily, even took pride in it, and began accepting money and other small gifts with an easy conscience.

But all things, as the old books say, have a beginning and an end. Seda Ashidova's happiness lasted exactly a month and six days. Twice she exchanged Bruskin's ticket for Vienna; three times got him a visa extension. But Bruskin's stay with her could not be measured by the extent of her love or her connections. On July 10, at their general union meeting, the members of the Dreamtime Theater presented him with a cake on which was written, "Next year in Jerusalem!" On the twelfth they all quietly flew off to Ulan Bator without Bruskin. And after he had seen them off at Sheremetyevo, Bruskin told Seda there and then that he too now would have to go.

She knew it would happen sooner or later. Her beloved was proud that he had never done any manual work but had become the creator and director of a whole series of astonishing enterprises, from a traveling show called "Motorcycle Wall of Death" to *Anna Karenina* performed by midgets. Now his thoughts were occupied with another grandiose project: to bring from Odessa to America the whole Bruskin clan—thirty-nine brothers, sisters, nephews, and nieces—and to form in the States a corporation called Bruskin and Family. He, Venyamin Bruskin, was to leave first and prepare everything for the arrival of the rest of the family. It was to them that he owed his life. In 1942, as a boy of nine, he lost his whole family during a German air attack on Kharkov and had been taken to the hospital with a concussion. There Major Matvey Bruskin, an army surgeon, had saved his life. He had adopted him, given him the Bruskin name, and sent him off on the next train to join his own family in Samarkand. However, young Venyamin never made it to Samarkand. At some station in the Urals a squadron of cavalrymen heading for the front heard him singing "A Fire Burns in the Narrow Stove," the most popular song at the time. Captivated by his talent, they enticed him into joining them with the promise of his own horse and sabre. While mounted on that horse, some time later the boy was surrounded by enemy troops. By a miracle he and ten other men escaped and made their way to the famous partisan brigade led by Medvedev. Venyamin became a scout for them, and as a lad of ten he was sent behind German lines, pretending to be a goatherd looking for his goat, or a poor orphan playing the harmonica.

It was not until a year later, in the winter of 1944, that a commissar from the First Belorussian Front flew in, and while enjoying a steam bath with the partisans, observed that the young scout had been circumcised. The commissar bawled out the whole unit for keeping a Jewish lad among them. Had he been caught, the Germans would have recognized him as a Jew and tortured him till he revealed their location. The commissar took Venyamin back with him by plane. On landing, however, they were caught in another bombardment and Venyamin was hospitalized again with burns on his back. After discharge, he made his way at last to Samarkand and joined his new relatives. There Major Bruskin's wife, Revekka, fed him on southern fruits, dressed his wounds, and surrounded him with warmth and affection. Later, after the Crimea was liberated, she took him back to Odessa with her own six children to live in their quiet little house on Third Fontan Avenue.

But by now the boy had the partisan spirit in his blood, and he fled Odessa with a band of runaways. He roamed the country traveling on the roofs of freight cars, and with another bunch of runaways he was caught stealing a sack of sugar from a barge on the Volga. For that he got six years in a children's punitive labor colony. Then, after a brief interval of freedom, he landed in an adult camp for his part in a dance-hall fight.

At twenty-five, Bruskin got out of labor camp vowing to give up crime, and the only place he could find a roof over his head was that crowded little home in Odessa. Strangely, they took him in again without a word of reproach. Perhaps in memory of Major Bruskin, who never came back from the war. Or maybe it was simply the kind heart of Revekka Bruskin, who by that time had raised six children of her own. But without education, and with the same partisan virus in his blood, Venyamin was incapable of slaving in a nine-to-five job. So he got into the arts. He started as a circus administrator. Then he invented the first of his own routines, which involved being shot from a cannon onto the back of a horse as it galloped around the ring. Then it was the flying motorcycle. And so on, culminating in the motorbike "Wall of Death" and the midget theater.

However, through all his escapades, Bruskin never ceased to love and cherish his adoptive mother. And when Revekka Bruskin decided that "the whole of Odessa is leaving, and it's time for us to go," Venyamin dreamed up a fabulous plan—to take all the Bruskins to America, not just Revekka and her children and grandchildren, but the whole extended family.

His affair with Seda Ashidova delayed things for a month. But finally he could no longer put off his departure. Thirty-nine adult relatives and their children, and all the rest of the *mishpoche*, as he put it, were breathing down his neck.

"When do you want to leave?" Seda asked him demurely, as they stood at Sheremetyevo and watched the Tupolev-134 take off for Ulan Bator with the only midget theater troupe in the whole of Europe.

"I have a ticket for August 17, you know that," Bruskin answered.

"You don't want to take me with you?"

"You're joking, of course."

"Of course," she said. "Where shall we have dinner? At my place or in the Aragvi?"

Seda took time off for the remaining five days before his departure and spent every minute with her beloved.

On August 17, at 3:20 P.M., the Tupolev-137 on Aeroflot flight 228 took Venyamin Bruskin, "savior of the Jewish people," away to join the Jewish emigration.

That same day, at 4:50 P.M., the ambulance controller at the Sklifasovsky Hospital received an emergency call.

"That's Seda at work again!" he commented. "It's quite some time since she was up to her tricks!"

His words turned out truer than he'd thought.

When the medics arrived at Customs and made their way up to the third-floor office, the door had already been broken down. They found the militia already there, a sad crowd of Seda's colleagues, and the lifeless body of Major Seda Ashidova. Although the militia detained everyone who was at the Customs office at that time, one glance at the corpse was enough. This was suicide. Seda had shot herself in the chest—straight through the heart—using her own pistol engraved with the signature of Interior Minister General Shchelokov.

On hearing Colonel Barsky's report on the suicide of Major Ashidova, Tsvigun asked whether he had begun an investigation.

"The militia have started one," Barsky answered. "But to be honest, there isn't much to investigate, Comrade General. It's quite clear. She got in the way of the Jews, and the Jews got rid of her!"

As he got to these lines, Barsky sensed that someone was standing behind his back.

forty-seven

Barsky turned. Evidently Olya had been standing there for some time, watching him as he read. She smiled as their glances met.

"Do you like it?" she asked.

He did not answer, simply looked at her. Slowly, he took in the fact that this little girl—his Olya, who always wore her hair in a bun, never used makeup, and was a hermit, most at home in libraries poring over history books—this Olya was now no longer little, but a beautiful young woman in the full sense. This transformation had not been so obvious in the photos in the dull red light of the darkroom. But now it was apparent in every curve of her body, it oozed from every cell of her peachy skin, and gleamed in her gray-green eyes. Had Paradise been located in Russia, doubtless Eve would have looked just like her after tasting the fruit from the tree of knowledge. The young women in Botticelli's paintings also had that look. And so did Barsky's own mother in prewar photographs. He had also seen the same look in those radiant Russian divas he interrogated in Siberia while on the trail of the love-kike.

"Dad," Olya began, "I've been wanting for a long time to introduce you to the author. But why have you broken my door down?"

She had no time to finish. Barsky took a pace toward her and dealt her a hard slap across the face.

"Dad!" she choked in horror and surprise.

But he hit her again, harder. She fell to the floor. But he grabbed her like a puppy by the scruff of its neck, and clouted her once again. He never heard her cries nor saw her face, and whenever she fell, he picked her up again and beat and kicked her over and over. And he hated himself for beating his own daughter. And his fury was all the more intense because it was she, the little bitch, who had provoked him into beating her like this!

Finally, unable even to cry out, she silently crawled away on all fours, trying to escape his blows. At length she made it to the bathroom and by some miracle was able to close the door and bolt it.

"Open up, you little slut! Open up, or else! I'll murder you for going with that fucking kike! Open the door, Yid hooker! I'm going to slaughter the two of you! And he's going to rot in Siberia! Down the uranium mines! Open the door, you slut!"

Olya neither opened the door nor answered. Neighbors looked in at the doorway, frightened by the noise and shouts, but Barsky chased them out, swearing and brandishing his pistol. "Get the hell out of here! Clear out!" He slammed the door and went to the kitchen to try and find some drink to cool himself. But in the fridge there was only an already-open bottle of wine. He took a swig and suddenly thought of how forty years ago his father had beaten another young woman in exactly the same way—his own mother. The stabbing thought came like a cardiac spasm, and he reeled back against the wall and closed his eyes. Lord, he cried out silently, why are you doing this to me? And what am I doing?

The fury leaked out of him like water from a punctured vessel, and his soul filled with despair. No, I'm not a Jew, the thought flashed through his mind. Jews don't beat their children. At that point, his ear caught another different sound, water running in the bathroom. He heaved a sigh and went back to the locked bathroom door.

"Olya, open up!" he called.

No answer.

"Olya, open the door. We need to talk."

Silence again, only the sound of flowing water.

"Olya, what are you doing in there?" he asked. Then suddenly he saw and felt the floor awash beneath his feet. The water, tinged pink, running out from under the door. "Olya!"

He put his shoulder to the door and forced it open. Olya lay there fully dressed in a bath full of water. Her eyes open and staring. She had slashed the veins in her right wrist and was holding the razor with her left. Blood-stained water came frothing up over the side of the bath.

"Olya!" Barsky yelled in horror, and he pulled the belt from his waist and wound it tightly around her right arm.

The following morning, Olya woke up in the hospital. She opened her eyes and saw her father sitting by her bed. Her gray lips barely moved as she spoke.

"Dad, if you lay a finger on that man, I shall do it again just the same."

Barsky said nothing.

"Did you hear me?"

"Yes, Olya, I heard you," he said, struggling to say the words.

"Now go," she said. "I want to sleep. You're disturbing me."

She closed her eyes, and her face relaxed again. She really was like his own mother—just as he recalled her in his earliest memories. Just as she was in 1941, when she dropped everything, took her toddler son, and left Moscow, with the Germans just fifteen kilometers from the city. His memories of their flight were unclear as to what he remembered himself or what he'd reconstructed from his mother's stories, because all his memories existed as fragmentary visions, like a series of color slides, or as in a dream: crowds of crazed people looting stores and carting off armfuls of condensed milk in tins, cocoa, and blocks of butter; men in Stalinlike green service jackets being dragged out of police cars and beaten; militia vehicles being pushed into the Moskva River; torn-up books with the bearded profile of "Uncle Lenin" stamped on the front being thrown from balconies and windows onto the roadway, and passersby laughing and stamping on them.

It was only much later, while studying at the KGB Academy, that Barsky learned what had really happened: On October 15–16, 1941, Moscow was abandoned by the retreating Soviet troops, and all trains heading east were crammed with Party and government officialdom and their families; the legendary Marshal Budyonny, in charge of the defense of Moscow, had lost his headquarters; and the German General Keitel passed on to his troops the will of Berlin in the form of a special directive:

> The Führer has decided that the capitulation of Moscow should not be accepted, even if offered by the opposing side. One has to reckon that in Moscow and Leningrad there is an even greater risk to our troops than there was in Kiev, due to the likelihood of time bombs. Not a single German soldier therefore should enter these cities. Before these cities are seized, they should be destroyed by artillery and air attack. It is impermissible to use German troops to save Russian cities from fire, or to feed the population at the expense of our German Fatherland.

As he studied these directives at the KGB Academy, Barsky always remembered his mother and that day, when she ran around the panic-stricken city carrying her son in her arms together with a plush teddy bear, which he of course could not abandon.

Now a reincarnation of his young mother lay there before him, pale and with her right arm bandaged and linked up to a drip-feed apparatus behind the bedstead.

Barsky got up and left. On his way out he spoke with the doctor on duty at the end of the corridor.

"Don't worry. She'll recover okay," the doctor assured him.

"And no visitors!" Barsky ordered. "Is that clear? Absolutely no one apart from me!"

"Absolutely, Comrade Colonel."

Barsky left the hospital. Seated in his official Volga, he took the seven-round PM pistol from his under-arm holster and returned it to the glove compartment. Then he roared off through the rainy dawn, heading for the Butyrka Jail.

ꜰoɾʈy-eiϱhʈ

Rubinchik recognized him well before the door of his cell swung open. Awakened by the thunder of his step in the corridor, he sat up on his folding bunk. Had he really managed to doze off? There was no mattress, pillow, or blanket, and he lay there on a hard plank that the guard folded up and locked during daytime. But at night, his body had curled up, trying to retain a residue of warmth in that cold damp cell. Now, as he woke, his knees and shoulders and all his joints were aching.

The bolt clanged, the cell door swung back, and a male figure lit from behind by the light in the corridor burst into Rubinchik's cell. Rubinchik grinned to himself. This was Barsky. Now the bargaining would begin for which he had agreed to dictate the remainder of his book to Olya, and to photograph himself with her all over Moscow.

But before Rubinchik had a chance to rise, a fist dealt him a stunning blow on the ear and hurled him onto the floor. Taken by surprise, he had no chance to fling out an arm and defend himself as he fell to the concrete and landed painfully on his shoulder. Still dazed, he felt Barsky twist his arms behind his back and clip handcuffs on his wrists and ankles. Then he was grabbed by the hair and dragged out into the corridor. The pain as his hair was torn out was excruciating. Moaning in agony, he tried to help himself by scrambling to his feet and walking in the direction he was being dragged, but the shackles around his ankles prevented that.

In the corridor, a warder tried either to waylay Barsky or else help him drag Rubinchik along. But Barsky barked at him: "Hands off! Get out of the way!" And he humped Rubinchik single-handedly like a deadweight all the way out of the cell block. Cracking several of Rubinchik's ribs, Barsky dragged him without stopping down the back outside steps, wet with rain, to the open rear door of his car that stood waiting. Still holding him by the hair with one hand, Barsky used his other hand to grab him by his pants, which had had the belt removed. He then hurled Rubinchik onto the back seat of the car and took his place in the driver's seat.

"Could you please sign here, Comrade Colonel!" The young duty officer dashed up holding the prisoners' register.

"I'm his investigator," Barsky said.

"I know, Comrade Colonel. It's just so the books are straight. To say that you've taken him."

Barsky signed hastily, then accelerated away. The Volga roared out of the prison gate and turned off toward the Belorussky Station. Moscow at dawn was empty and streaked with damp autumn rain. The only people around were groups of hopeful sufferers gathered by the wine and liquor stores. Before reaching the Station, Barsky swung out onto the wet tarmac of Leningradsky Prospect and tore off toward the northwest, heading out of town. They passed the Dynamo subway station where he had recited his poetry to Anna Sigal. Past the Airport subway, an area where many of the Jewish dissident elite lived. Past the Northern River Station where he had joined the Mikhail Sholokhov for his river trip with Andropov. Farther and farther from the center . . . Now they were passing the last suburban residential areas. After that the roadway was flanked by a strip of dense woodland broken by occasional narrow dirt roads leading off to the Khimki Reservoir. Hardly braking, Barsky veered off down one of these tracks and headed through the forest. The car bounced on the rutted surface, and behind him he heard Rubinchik slither off the back seat and onto the floor, but he did not bother to turn and look. The wipers scudded across the rain-streaked windshield. Barsky narrowed his eyes in fury and gripped the wheel, and the engine screamed as he gunned the Volga into third gear along the narrow slippery track. Through a gap in the trees the gray expanse of the reservoir could now be seen. Barsky braked hard, and the car skidded off the track toward the water's edge and halted.

Barsky got out, wiped his sweating face with the back of a hand, and looked around. Not a soul in sight and everything absolutely still. The only sounds were the swish of autumn rain on the withered foliage and the rumble of the KGB Volga's hard-driven engine. Barsky broke several matches as he tried to light a cigarette. To make sure, he walked around the nearby bushes. But no sign of mushroom gatherers, fisherman, or campers. There were hardly likely to be any on a rainy day in midweek.

By now Barsky had cooled down and felt calmer as he walked back to the car. He took one last pull on his cigarette then ground it out with the toe of his boot. Then he opened the rear door. Rubinchik was lying on the floor between the seats. Barsky grabbed him by the collar and dragged him out, then stood him up with his back against the car.

"Stand up, you bastard! Can you stand?"

Rubinchik stood there, and the rain continued falling.

"Now look at me. Do you know who I am?"

Rubinchik said nothing.

"You know well enough, son of a bitch! So you thought I was going to make a deal with you, right?"

Rubinchik nodded.

"Okay, we'll see about that!" Barsky grinned. And suddenly he kicked Rubinchik with all his might right in the groin.

The blow was such that Rubinchik choked out a silent scream, folded up like a jackknife, and crashed facedown into a puddle.

With a jerk, Barsky grabbed him by the scruff off his neck and tried to stand him up again. But Rubinchik would not straighten up. He instinctively sensed Barsky's intention and tried to use his shoulders, upper body, and even his head to shield his loins.

"Stand up, you bastard!"

But Rubinchik couldn't and slithered to the ground again. It took an upward blow to the chin to straighten him and throw him on his back, thus laying him open to a further attack. Barsky kicked him again in the same accursed spot.

"So here's your deal!" Barsky said. He no longer tried to haul Rubinchik to his feet. Unhurriedly, and in businesslike fashion, he took careful aim with his heavy muddy boot. Straight in the groin . . . straight to the groin . . . into the groin, and only there.

"Is this deal okay then? This is for Olya! This for Anna! This for mother! This for Seda Ashidova! This is for Tanya on the winter trail! And this is for all the women you've had with this dick of yours, you bastard!"

Rubinchik did not cry out. He hadn't the strength. With each kick Barsky rolled him over the wet ground, until finally he fell into the water, and Barsky's foot could no longer reach him.

By the time he had finished, Barsky was soaked to the skin. He felt in his pocket and got out his cigarettes. With an occasional glance at Rubinchik, he lit up and squatted on the car bumper. Rubinchik lay still in the water, like a sack. Barsky continued smoking, shielding his cigarette from the rain, and every now and then he would glance at his victim. Rubinchik's body did not stir, and he lay there in the water. His mouth was open and his eyes were closed, and the rain streamed down over his face.

Barsky threw his cigarette away, got the keys to the handcuffs from his tunic pocket, stepped into the water, and bent over Rubinchik. He undid the cuffs on his wrists and ankles, then with a swing he flung them far out into the reservoir. Without a backward glance, he returned to the car. With its engine screaming again, the vehicle roared out of the mud and back up the embankment.

part four

the reckoning

forty-nine

By early october, night frosts were starting to bite in Moscow. By the end of the month, snowy blizzards begin preparing the way for the Russian winter.

At that time, though, hardly anyone paid attention to these natural phenomena. Instead, the city's population was bustling to prepare for the anniversary of the Great October Revolution. In honor of that hallowed date the authorities upgraded supplies, and people hastened to stock up their refrigerators with everything their government had obtained for foreign sales of oil, gas, furs, and MIG-24 fighters. Even the dissidents, Jewish refuseniks, and criminal elements knew of the Kremlin's intolerance for any disruption to the November seventh festivities; so they too reduced their activities and joined everyone else in laying in supplies for the winter. And the lucky few that obtained their exit visas during those few days had no time even for a farewell glance at the country they were leaving behind.

In that epoch and that season of the year, the early snowy twilight began at two in the afternoon and the city was lit up by the patterned glow of neon signs. The great imperial capital of Communism decked itself in glowing colors like a prima donna in her spangled concert stole. The neon-lit twilight masked the bureaucratic hustle common to any state capital; and in another hour or so the same gathering twilight would reduce the working pace of those hundreds of ministries, directories, consortiums, boards, and committees with whose help the Kremlin ruled the Soviet colossus. By this time the Central Committee had vetted the opening pages of tomorrow's issue of *Pravda* from which half of humanity would discover what the Kremlin had decreed as the truth, and what was to be regarded as imperialist scheming and insinuation. The day's activities had also seen elaboration of detailed schemes for improving the potato harvest in Siberia, the production of fermented mare's milk in Kirghizia, the catch of fish in the Sea of Okhotsk, the range of intercontinental nuclear missiles, and the underwater operational range of atomic submarines. Now, however, as evening set in, Moscow could afford to relax, acquire a first powdering of snow, and enjoy a sense of deep moral satisfaction and a well-earned rest.

At this point Moscow turned on the lights of its theaters, state circus, restaurants, and cafés, and people on their way home hastily dashed into the various food stores. There, after standing in line for a mere thirty or forty minutes, they could purchase Finnish and Kievan sausage, Hungarian chicken, Latvian fish, Bulgarian apples, Moldavian cheese, Bashkirian honey, Cuban sugar and rum, Syrian bananas, Armenian brandy, and Algerian wines. But, the main thing was that Muscovites drank their own vodka— Moskovskaya or Stolichnaya—and thus felt themselves true rulers of the world, from Pacific depths to cosmic heights.

Having gathered the offerings of the State Planning Department from the nearby food store, Muscovites were then quick to relax. The elderly settled in front of their TV to watch serials; working-class youths headed for the dance floor at their factory clubs; and students and bohemians made for Gorky Street and the cafés and bars on the New Arbat. Business travelers from all over the Union sat around with their pickup dates in cheap restaurants, at the circus, or some stage show. The elite—top officialdom, nomenclature, and the artistic beau monde—would make for the fashionable theaters, Sovremennik, Taganka, or the Moscow Arts to attend premieres. Or they would go to foreign movies at private clubs.

In fact, life in Moscow was constantly on the boil, though all this contrasted starkly with the puritanical "Moral Code of the Builder of Communism." Along the paths of parks, and even on the snow-covered benches of the square in front of the Bolshoi, young people flirted, drank liquor, got into jealous squabbles, and kissed one another till their heads reeled. In the State Universal Store of GUM and in Petrovsky Passage, artful Muscovite playboys would wait around for a likely pickup. Their particular targets were buxom young girls from the provinces, members of the Communist Youth League, who had come to attend university conferences and who spent their spare time lining up to buy Hungarian stretch tights, which in the boondocks were not to be found. In hairdressing salons women had their hair curled and nails manicured. Outside the concert halls, music-lovers in snow-covered hats loudly pleaded with concert-goers to sell them a spare ticket. And celebrated actors emerged onto the stage to applause from capacity audiences that hung on each word, searching every line for some veiled critique of the regime.

The only thing that thousands of Muscovites lacked, which would have given them a sense of superiority over the rest of the world, was "a house with a roof," their own apartment, or at least a private room where they could entertain their girlfriends, enjoy a drink with company, or write their Ph.D. dissertations.

Yet who actually groused if Hungarian chickens at one ruble twenty kopeks disappeared from the food store, when there was Bulgarian stew meat at eighty kopeks a kilo? And who was angry when the bar ran out of Czech beer if the local brew was still available?

The only malcontents were the dissidents and the Yids, that was all!

However, almost all dissidents, including that imperialist lackey academician Andrey Sakharov, had already been dispatched eastward by the KGB, and the Yids were heading West of their own accord. And that not only cleared the air, but was freeing up a whole lot of living space.

That particular day, among the line of people wanting to leave the country was Anna Sigal.

It was a merry little crowd who still could barely believe their good fortune. They had been *released*! For months they had lived in fear that they might be turned down, and that for the rest of their lives they would be left to scrape a living on the lowest rung of society—as street cleaners, watchmen, and garbage collectors. "Like that Shulman, you know? He's only a doctor of biological science. What secrets are there in biology? Yet he's gotten refusals for six years now!" "Biologist indeed! Do you know the actor Gertsianov? You might wonder what secrets an actor knows? But this is his third refusal! And I'm a specialist in power engineering. I couldn't sleep a wink for the last month, and I went through two packets of tranquillizers!"

Fear had become part of these people's lives. It had soaked into their skins and their souls along with the sedatives. But now their faces had lost their frowns, their backs were straight, they held their heads high, and despite the freezing wind, their coats were unbuttoned. One would never recognize that these were the same Jews who six or eight months ago had stood in line with their heads in their shoulders, silently tolerating the spittle and the insults of passersby. Their names, of course, were the same—Rabinoviches, Rozenbergs, Finkelsteins, and Dankeviches. And the faces usually matched the names. But their faces now had wholly different expressions—those of people who had lucked out in a game of Russian roulette.

"Lord, if I'd known I was going to get permission, I'd have gone to Leningrad to see the Hermitage!" one woman lamented next to Anna.

"Never mind the Hermitage! We ought to have learned a new language!" her neighbor pointed out.

Indeed, each of these Jews who came to the Austrian Embassy was superstitious in quite a Russian way. They had done nothing to tempt Fate. But now that Fate no longer had them in its gunsights and they had their exit visas, they now berated themselves in quite a *Jewish* way for not being ready to leave!

"Okay, we'll learn the language when we get there," said another slightly younger woman. "But there are so many good men getting left behind! If I knew I'd be let out, I'd have played the field a bit more!"

The crowd laughed. There were not many—about thirty. And there was space for them all in that Soviet-style queue behind the iron barrier of the embassy that was issuing their transit visas. But these people, who'd spent their lives demurely standing in long lines, could now barely stay put for more than a minute, no matter how the militiaman on guard shouted at them. Eventually he lost his cool and yelled, "Clear the sidewalk so pedestrians can get by! Or else I'm not letting any of you in!" Only then did they line up in a remotely orderly fashion, as if doing him a personal favor. But he needed only to walk back to the embassy entrance for them again to cluster in a crowd, filling the sidewalk and spilling out onto the roadway.

"Have you heard! The Customs at Brest are letting people through with coral necklaces. Word of honor! My brother went there specially to reconnoitre. They're letting through coral beads, amber, measuring instruments, and even canned goods. But at the Sheremetyevo Customs nothing gets through! Not even sandwiches for your children!"

"Do you know how a friend of mine fooled them? He's a dentist, and he works with gold of course. But, if you can imagine, he took nothing with him but an ordinary tool kit. Screwdrivers, pliers, hammer, an adjustable spanner, and screws. Yes, about ten pounds of screws and bolts. And at the Customs they asked him why he needed so many screws. And he says: 'What sort of future have I got in the West? Do you think they'll let me touch their teeth? I'm going to be a plumber, so I'm taking my tools with me.' And they let him through. And what do you think? Half of all those screws were gold! He cast them himself!"

"No kidding! My sister left last year, and they even took the wedding ring off her finger!"

Anna smiled to herself. Only yesterday, these people couldn't sleep at night and were swearing to God that they would leave everything and, if need be, walk naked out of this Communist paradise! But as soon as the Almighty granted them an exit permit, they forgot all their oaths. Not that their Jewish God blamed them. He could see these people had slaved all their lives, so why should they have to bequeath their apartments, furniture, silver forks, wedding rings, and savings accounts to this anti-Semitic empire? The state even charged a fee of five hundred rubles to relieve them of their Soviet citizenship—half a year's pay for a schoolteacher or engineer.

"Have you heard whether they let Airedale terriers out?" Anna asked the expert whose brother had gone to get the lay of the land at Brest–Litovsk.

"Only with a Canine Club permit," came the qualified answer. "And if the dog is younger than ten and won more than two medals, the Club won't give you a permit. But that's not the main problem. Give him a bribe and any vet will write you a certificate saying the dog is over forty! The main problem is getting the dog into Austria. They require a certificate to prove the animal is fully vaccinated."

"D'you mean they're not worried about our own health?" someone asked.

"Correct," said the ombudsman. "They realize you're not going to infect any Austrian girl with some nasty disease—you couldn't afford that! But they have other taxes covering dogs."

"Next five!" called the militiaman, and Anna walked to the embassy entrance.

People indulged in the same sort of chatter in the line at the Moscow Freight Station, whence the emigrants' baggage would leave. And at the Central State Bank, where they could pay 136 rubles and in exchange receive ninety American dollars. And it was the same at the Intourist office where they bought their airplane tickets for Vienna.

Colonel Barsky's thoughts, however, were not occupied by routine emigrants like these. His first concern was official and quite different—to avert totally and completely any disorders or demonstrations targeted at Arab guests arriving for the Revolution Anniversary. To this end, his section—along with the entire Fifth Directorate—had been put on twenty-four-hour alert. With the same purpose, Inessa Brodnik, Ilya Karbovsky, and other rebellious elements had been dispatched to Siberia; old Gertsianov had been put under house arrest; and all Barsky's informers received instructions to keep watch in the synagogue and report immediately any suspicious conversations or gatherings.

But the colonel had a second and secret concern, his own personal anguish. The whole city was in a festive state, alive with bustle and meetings, flirtations and flowers. Yet there was no one with whom Barsky could go to the theater, sit in a bar, play a round of cards, or go skiing. A month ago he had taken his daughter straight from the hospital to Dymkovo, to stay with her maternal aunts and uncles; and he had instructed them to give her fresh milk to drink and generally cosset and care for her, and never take their eyes off her till he himself returned to collect her. Now he was tormented by loneliness and the senseless hassle of his KGB activities. It was as though someone had pulled the plug on his life-support system. Of course, he did have a few possible diversions. He could call up and get that Natasha Svechkina to come and spend the night with him, or he could join some of his colleagues at the bar. But his KGB buddies were boring, and they irritated him with their perpetual anti-Jewish jokes, and little sluts like Natasha Svechkina filled him with disgust.

And the person to blame for all this was that bastard Rubinchik!

Barsky had not actually killed the scum that rainy September morning, mainly because he feared Olya's threat.

And either that little kike with his nine lives had scrambled out of the water, or else some fishermen had picked him up, but after lounging a few weeks in the hospital, Rubinchik was discharged and walking again—albeit with a cane. And he was also driving around in his dilapidated Moskvich, probably thinking that when he flew out on November 4, he would smuggle out his book about the Russian Jews. Barsky had been forced to give him an exit visa, as he had to Anna Sigal. That was the only condition on which Olya would agree to leave Moscow and not return before Rubinchik left. Besides, how could he put Rubinchik on trial now, if it came out that he had been cohabiting with Olya and that she was involved in helping with his libelous anti-Soviet scribblings? But he was damned if, on top of everything else, Rubinchik was going to take his manuscript with him as well! Barsky had given Olya no promise about that, and he now personally checked all the passenger lists on the Moscow–Vienna run, so there would be no screwup as there had been with Rappoport. He himself with his own hands was going to shake out Rubinchik's baggage. Our little author would see who had the last laugh!

With these thoughts in mind, Barsky turned up his collar and wandered along the Arbat amid a crowd bent on festive pursuits. But he never really saw them and their bags and parcels, or the shop windows with their pyramids of canned food, or the snowflakes that whirled beneath the streetlamps, or the Central Committee's festive exhortations to the public to fortify the socialist camp with their fervent labor. For the last twenty-four hours he had been haunted by a strange snatch of un-Russian music—a blues motif— which he had heard the other night on Voice of America, "music from the film *My One and Only Love*; and the composer was George Grass," the announcer said. God damn it! The thought cut Barsky to the quick: Could he, a colonel in the KGB, actually have an uncle in the USA?

"Hallo there, Colonel!"

Barsky looked up. In front of him stood Valya, General Bulychev's secretary. She was wearing a short sheepskin jacket, a sweater that clung to her firmly thrusting breasts and came down just below the thigh, and foreign-made boots that rose above the knee and emphasized the length of her graceful legs. She was carrying two heavy bags, and her little round face glowed like a sunflower. Barsky smiled as he recalled how they had learned at the Academy how to read personalities from the features people chose to emphasize in their dress. Valya's main virtue, of course, was her figure and its sex appeal.

"Happy holiday!" she said. "How is it you're looking so glum? Have the Jews been getting you down? Help me get a cab, would you? With these heavy bags I can't get a hand in the air! Can you imagine? I've managed to get six jars of Bulgarian peppers! And a bottle of Cinzano!"

Barsky relieved her of one bag, and they stepped off the sidewalk and began flagging down passing cars.

"Where've you got to get to?"

"Chertanovo," she said. "We're having a little party. Why don't you come with me, Comrade Colonel? I've got a friend—she'd be just right for you! You like blondes, don't you? She's a schoolmistress—you know how sexy they are! Incidentally, your buddy's going to be there. Igunov, remember him?" Then, as she got into a car: "Well, are you coming?"

"I can't, I'm afraid. Thanks all the same," said Barsky, handing her the bag with the Cinzano.

"That's a pity," Valya said, obviously sincere. "Well, I hope you have a good holiday. Give us a call some time." She rewarded him with a long and expressive look, then turned to the driver. "To Chertanovo."

Barsky slammed the taxi door and watched as it disappeared along the Arbat amid a whirl of snow. He was not quite sure why he had turned her invitation down. Was it because Igunov was going to be there? Or because, like a masochist, he preferred tormenting himself with thoughts of Anna Sigal to the sound of blues written by his American relative? Or else because this was his third day of wandering around the Arbat for hours on end, trying to think of a way to knock at Sonya Grass's door?

Something else he did not know was that at that moment the Kirov–Moscow train had pulled into platform four of the Yaroslavsky Station, and out got Olya, his daughter; she had run away from her relatives in Dymkovo, and returned to town.

fifty

If anyone had told Rubinchik a month ago what he would go through in his last days before leaving Russia, he would have simply laughed at such prophecies and dismissed them as a melodramatic fantasies. A month ago, as he lay in the Pirogov Trauma Clinic, he had sworn to God that he would never again go anywhere near Olya Barsky, or any other woman, including his wife. A vow like that was not hard to keep: the doctors believed it would be a miracle if his sword of life ever again saw active service. But he himself was not worried by that. He simply cleared his mind of carnal thoughts, never looked at women, and concentrated on just one thing—his book. It was a natural reaction: once he has kicked the habit, a former chain-smoker cannot stand even the smell of tobacco; similarly, after a heavy drinking bout, many an alcoholic is revolted even by the display in a liquor store window.

But Rubinchik's book was something special. He was obsessed by it and even saw a sign of divine providence in his injured masculinity. Nelya's parents had taken the children to stay with them for one last time. Rubinchik could thus sit day and night in their half-empty apartment and fill sheet after sheet of paper with his fine handwriting. When he began three months ago, he intended writing only about the Jewish activists. He never guessed how the book would expand of its own accord. But it proved impossible to confine his story to the Jews. Russian dissidents, Lithuanian nationalists, Crimean Tatars, Volga Germans, Ingush and Chechens, Ukrainian Catholics, and Seventh-day Adventists kept bursting into the narrative, in much the same way as those Baptists last spring had broken through the militia cordon and forced their way into the American Embassy. And once Rubinchik put all these groups in his manuscript, he realized that under the Soviet empire's monolithic crust there was a boiling mass of magma and lava. As yet, these elements did not form a single geological tectonic unit. The Jewish refuse-niks tried to remain apart from the Ukrainian Catholics, and the Chechens and Crimean Tatars had no links with the Lithuanian nationalists. But all these diverse groups were stoking the subterranean fires, and despite the threat of internment in labor camps and psychiatric wards, the KGB could not cool the magma. Rubinchik, too, could not withstand the pressure of all this material. The same miracle occurred that in ancient times transformed Jewish shepherds into prophets and apostles—he began to believe in his *mission*. He was well read in Jewish literature and, like all writers, had mystical inclinations, and he believed that Providence had kept him alive to finish his book. And to this end it had also freed him from carnal temptations.

Nelya, of course, felt differently. She believed it was because of his "goddamned book" that the KGB had beaten him up. And now he had gone totally round the bend. In a bout of pure Jewish obstinacy he was now trying to finish it here in Russia, just to spite them. "But no one needs another Solzhenitsyn!" she yelled. "I want to get out of here alive, not as an invalid! Isn't it enough that they damn near kicked your balls off?"

Rubinchik frowned at such vulgarity. Some women could forego sexual pleasure for years without losing their dignity, but Nelya evidently couldn't go a week. But he did not rise to her outbursts. How could he ever tell her the price he had paid to obtain their exit visas? On the other hand, he did exploit his weakness on coming out of hospital, and left all the departure preparations to Nelya: selling the furniture, packing the cases, gathering the paperwork, going to the Austrian Embassy, obtaining a permit for Xenia's violin, and so on. He tore himself away from his work only once—to buy their tickets for Vienna; as he explained to Nelya, he still had a bit of pull with a friend from his journalist days in the railroad offices. But the trip for the tickets took only a couple of hours, and after that he sat down on their already packed suitcases and continued working.

Nelya observed the latter-day Dostoyevsky in silence until their final day before leaving. That morning she found him engaged in an unusual activity. Overnight he had turned the kitchen into a darkroom. He had photographed all four hundred pages of his priceless manuscript, and a dozen thirty-six-frame films were now hanging out to dry on a clothes line. Nelya could no longer contain herself.

"If you insist on trying to smuggle your shitty book across the frontier," she shouted, "I am going to leave separately with the children *before you*! Is that understood? I'm not putting the children at risk because of that load of crap!"

"Calm down," Rubinchik said as he cut the film into short lengths of six frames each. "I have a channel I can use. And my book isn't shitty. And it was your own idea."

"Yes, that was my stupid fault!" Nelya said. And she walked out, slamming the door.

But Iosif had fibbed about the "channel." He had no special means of getting his manuscript out, and no prospect either. If he even went near any foreigners, he risked arrest: all Shcharansky had done was hand a package to some foreigner, and the KGB had given him thirteen years! And if Shcharansky's package had contained a book like this! Also if they arrested Rubinchik handing a manuscript to foreigners, then even Barsky would be unable to get him off. On the other hand, if he sat quietly until his departure, not only would Barsky be unable to touch him, he would be forced into acting virtually as his guardian angel. Only a month ago Rubinchik had dictated his book to Olya and had let her keep just one chapter at a time in her apartment. That had been his only way of saving it. Indeed, that had to be why God had sent Olya to his boiler room that night: to save the book and its author. And all Barsky's fury, and even that bloody beating at the reservoir were signs of Barsky's impotence before the will of God, which was to help Rubinchik accomplish his mission. But Barsky was like Pharaoh, who first released the children of Israel and then came chasing after them.

At the last moment, at the frontier, he would do everything in his power to prevent Rubinchik from taking abroad a book about the Jews and their campaign—a campaign directed against him, Colonel Oleg Barsky.

Immersed in these reflections, Rubinchik worked away without feeling the cold of that first November day. He stood at the homemade bench he had set up in his garage. Together with his car it had already officially been turned over to a new owner, and tomorrow, the day of their departure, the car and garage would actually change hands. But today Rubinchik still had the keys, and he stood at his bench using a small chisel to hollow out the handle of a shoe brush. The idea of photographing the manuscript was not his. He had borrowed it from the Rappoport legend. But *he* had the idea of carefully splitting open the brush handle along a seam and hiding his films in it, and he intended to tell no one, not even Nelya. The second part of his plan was also an improvement on the legendary battle between Rappoport and the KGB. Rubinchik had booked *air* tickets for Moscow–Vienna flight No. 230 on the last day permitted by the Visa Office—at 1520 on Saturday, November 4. But for Friday, November 3, he had carried out Nelya's wish. She was afraid of air travel, and he'd bought train tickets to Brest, ordinary domestic tickets on sale at the station without the need to show any documents or register any names. The idea was to be at Brest by eight A.M. on the fourth of November and join the emigrants leaving the country on one of three westbound trains that left Brest before one P.M. that same day. This meant that by the time Barsky turned up at Sheremetyevo for the three-twenty flight to Vienna, Rubinchik would already have left the country. And even the Comrade Colonel's long arm would be too short to reach him once he was outside Russia.

Naturally, rather than a mere few hours, it would have been better to have a few *days'* head start and leave Moscow on Thursday or even Wednesday. But that was impossible. The Rubinchiks' neighbors were already lining up to get hold of their apartment, and any one of them was bound to report to the house manager that they had moved out. This person would then dash off to the militia to register that he was moving in; the militia would tell the KGB, and within hours Barsky would know they had left. But on Friday evening no neighbor could find a house manager. By that time the superintendent would be gone and probably drunk, and on Saturday the militia did not register changes of address, and the neighbors would have nobody to report to. He had thought all this up while still in the hospital, and after Nelya came rushing in, beaming with happiness, to announce that the Visa Office had granted them exit visas. "Would you believe it? And it took just three months! Some people have to wait up to a year." Rubinchik said nothing. He realized someone was keen to get him out of the country.

Now he had to put his plan into action. After prying off the part of the brush with the bristles, he placed the other half in a vice. Then he proceeded to carve out the inside with what he imagined the care of a Stradivarius fashioning his violins. In an hour he had chiseled out a hollow sufficient to accommodate the precious strips of film. He wrapped them tightly in cellophane and laid them in the brush handle. With the two halves of the brush pressed together, however, he saw there was a visible gap between them. He took a piece of fine sand paper, smoothed out the hollow, then fitted the two halves together again. A perfect match! Now with a brush he applied a thin layer of joiner's glue to each side, blew on the surfaces, waited a minute, then pressed the two halves together and clamped them in a vice.

"Bless us, O Lord!" he prayed aloud with eyes closed. "Adonai, work a miracle and let this get through Customs. I pray Thee! Bless this work of my hands!"

Now for the manuscript.

Rubinchik walked out of his garage. The low clouds scattered crystals of snow. Car owners in the nearby garages were preparing their Zhigulis and Moskviches for the harsh winter ahead—changing carburetors, adding antifreeze, and covering chassis with antirust, fitting antiskid chains, and so on. Every now and then, they stopped for a smoke and warmed at little fires kindled from scraps of wood. So Rubinchik had no hesitation in starting his own small fire. He laid a metal sheet on the ground at the garage entrance, squatted down and began burning his manuscript, ten to fifteen pages at a time.

From the distance came the rumble of a train, and the noise grew as it approached. Suddenly it was thundering past. Rubinchik stood up and watched as it disappeared toward the west. Through a gap between the garages he could see the glow of lights in the receding cars, while the engine blasted the snow-covered landscape with the wail of its siren.

"Okay, I can hear! I can hear!" Rubinchik grinned.

He squatted down again and stuffed another wad of papers into the flames, watching as the fire consumed his chapter about Inessa Brodnik's trip to the Mordovian women's camp. How his life had changed in one summer! He was no longer a correspondent for a Moscow newspaper, nor a hunter of Russian divas. He was an outcast, an emigrant, a traitor. But, also the author of a book! Tomorrow he was going to leave this country, with its anti-Semitism, perpetual obscenities, and Byzantine pretensions to be the torch-bearer of progressive humanity. To hell with its percentages for "persons of Jewish origin." In the West his children would grow up without hearing "Yid" and "kike," and that alone would be worth the privileges he once enjoyed here. What did they amount to anyway? Being able to buy Hungarian chicken at the *Pravda* publishers' buffet, or drinking beer at the Journalists' Club without having to stand in line? Watching American films in the editors' screening room? What should have been aspects of normal life had been turned into privileges by the Communists! And in order to pick up these crumbs, he had spent almost twenty years unable to write what he wanted.

Now, though, he was finished. Here was his first real book! Let others take their cameras, coral necklaces, nickel-silver forks, and measuring instruments—he was going to take his book. And he would see what happened when he got to the West.

Large snowflakes drifted into his fire and melted in the white flames. None of his neighbors paid him the slightest attention as he calmly burnt his manuscript. He stirred the ashes and scattered them around and put some in a garbage bin. "And how are we feeling, Mr. Gogol?" he asked himself with an ironic grin, remembering how the great author had burnt the manuscript of his epic *Dead Souls*. Indeed there was something almost offensive in the way his manuscript had burnt—not at all like when Gogol destroyed his work in the blazing hearth of a genteel residence on Suvorovsky Boulevard. Rubinchik's work had simply been consumed on a sheet of scrap metal outside a dirty garage with a philistine bunch of Muscovites as indifferent onlookers. Anyway, to hell with them!

He extracted his shoe brush from the clamp and rubbed a few soft lumps of glue from the seam. Next, he brushed on some varnish. While it dried, he tidied up the garage, then dusted the brush down with a dirty rag and put it in his briefcase and placed the briefcase on the back seat of his car. After that, he locked up the garage and looked at his watch—Good Lord, already almost five! He had spent the whole day messing with his negatives and this shoe brush!

His work complete, Rubinchik drove out onto the street. Before evening there was still time to dash to the Eliseyev store, and thanks to a long-standing friendship with the manager he hoped to buy something festive for the children, since Nelya was bringing them back from Lyubertsy that evening.

He rolled along First Cosmonauts' Street and was turning off toward the Molodyozhnaya subway station, when suddenly . . .

Was that really Olya?

He could not believe his eyes.

It *was* Olya. She had just gotten off the bus and was walking down the street, stumbling through the still-uncleared snow on the sidewalk and peering shortsightedly at the house numbers that were plastered with snow. She was wearing a strange heavy, peasant-type coat, rough boots, thick knitted stockings, and a gray headscarf. But it was not her odd garb that disturbed Rubinchik, but her pale and tense expression, as though her features were made of wax, like the face of a saint on some ancient ikon.

"Olya!" he shouted and stopped the car.

She turned and a happy smile lit up her eyes and melted the frosty tautness of her cheeks.

"Hallo there!" she said, running up to his car. "So you've not left yet. I was so afraid I might not catch you in time...."

"How is it you're here?" he asked.

"I ran away from Dymkovo. You know, the place where father took me to get me out of Moscow?" She spoke animatedly. "But I simply had to see you! I want to ask you something: take me with you!"

"Olya, what on earth are you saying!"

"Iosif, I beg you!" she suddenly shouted out loud.

He looked at the other passersby. God, on his last day this was all he needed. Her hysterics had to be stopped, there and then, and no nonsense! He got out of the car. But instead of mouthing harsh words, he took her by the hand and talked to her gently as though to a sick child.

"Olya, dear, I can't do anything at this stage. I'm leaving tomorrow. Do you understand? So just be a sensible girl and go back home, I beg you. Will you do that?"

"Yes," she said after a pause.

"There's a good girl! And I wish you a bundle of happiness!" He planted a kiss on her cold cheek where some snowflakes had settled without melting. Then he sat back in the car and started the engine.

He was about to let in the clutch when suddenly, to the left of him, something collapsed into the snow and a pair of white hands slapped against the side window.

"Iosif!"

A chill ran through him. Olya was kneeling there in the dirty snow, her hands pawing at the car door, and everyone passing on the sidewalk halted to watch the spectacle.

He stood on the brake and with his left hand he wound down the side window.

"Cut out the hysterics!" he said sharply. "And stand up!"

"Iosif," Olya whispered, "I ... I'm pregnant."

fifty-one

"My name is Terentyev. I called you up yesterday," Barsky said. The door in front of him had four buttons with names written in dark ink: Grass, Romanov, Chaplygo, and someone else.

"Yes, yes, come in please." Sonya Grass quickly ushered him inside. "You're from security?"

"Yes, the State Security Committee." He removed his officer's coat, wet with snow, and looked around. The hall was crammed with small cabinets containing old shoes and children's sledges, and a floral basket hung from the ceiling. "Where can I hang this?" he asked.

"Better in my place. There are children here," Sonya said timidly and motioned toward the neighbors whose heads were peering from every door along the long corridor. "It's all right," she said, "he's my guest!" Then, to Barsky again: "This way." She led him past the communal kitchen and down the corridor lined with old cabinets with padlocks.

Barsky was wearing his tunic and shoulder tabs, and he knew when he dressed like this no one would ask to see his documents. And if Sonya Grass had plucked up the courage to ask for his ID, he had three of them, under different names and for all contingencies. He walked into her room and looked about. It was large and spacious with three windows, probably a former drawing room, or—judging by the wall that abutted the window—part of a former drawing room. But there was enough furniture in this one room to fill a three-room apartment. There were several old bookcases in dark wood, a grand piano, a pier-glass, a buffet, a broken-down leather chesterfield, a dark bed spread, a dining table, a few cabinets, and some lamps. The wide desk by the window was loaded with books, and above it in a glass frame hung a large portrait of Moisey Grass—young, with a broad forehead, and a forelock in thirties style. Next to it was a small ikon in a silver case.

"Do have a seat," Sonya Grass pointed to a chair by the dining table. "To what do I owe this visit?"

Once in her own room, she regained control. Or rather, adopted a manner of cold politeness.

"Thank you." Barsky sat down and forced himself to look away from the portrait. "As I told you on the phone, we're studying various cases with a view to compensating victims of the Stalinist repressions. I would like to get to know . . ."

"Comrade Colonel," Sonya interjected, "What sort of compensation are you talking about? You seem like an intelligent man. So tell me, who can compensate me for the loss of my father? What money will do that? I don't want anything from you."

"I understand, Sonya Moiseyevna. I understand your feelings. But today's KGB is not the same as the NKVD in 1937. And we may not be talking about money. But I look here at this room you live in. You're a professor, and yet you live in a communal apartment. I imagine this probably used to be your parents'—the whole of it, including the other rooms?"

"Of course," she said. "When you arrested my father, we were forced to give up some space, and they brought these people in." She nodded toward the partition and the corridor.

"Well, there you see," he said gently, pretending not to notice the provocative "*you* arrested." "I don't want to promise anything at this stage, but . . ."

"Excuse me, Colonel," Sonya interrupted, "but how should I address you formally?"

"My name is Oleg . . . Oleg Ivanovich."

"Listen, Oleg Ivanovich. I know that you people are trying to move the old residents out of the Arbat and settle them in places like Chertanovo, and then take over our apartments. But forget it. I'm not moving out of here, even if you offer me three rooms."

Barsky grinned.

"You're a tough nut, Sonya Moiseyevna."

"Yes. And if they'd arrested your father before your very eyes and taken him away forever, you wouldn't be so soft either. And anyway, with those shoulder tabs and your rank, you're hardly an angel."

"Well," Barsky said. "So, as you can see, we have something in common. In our characters, I mean. How about if we drop the subject of apartments and talk about a possible edition of your father's works. There were songs and film music by him. What else?"

She sat down on the chair opposite him.

"Are you . . . are you serious?" she asked quietly.

"I did say: at this stage. I can't promise anything. What's the matter?"

She was weeping. And as she wept, her shoulders began quivering. She removed her glasses and rubbed the tears from her eyes with her hands, like a child.

"Forgive me . . . Just one moment . . . Oh my God! Forgive me, but if only you knew. . . ."

He had seen Jewesses weep before, and the sight had never moved him.

But this woman . . . She looked so like little Olya when she wept that he felt like jumping up, putting his arms around her, and telling her there and then that he was her brother. By now he had no doubt. But he remained where he was.

"If only you knew how many times I've tried to get even one piece by him published!" she continued. "God alone knows where I haven't tried—the Composers' Union, the Ministry of Culture, State Music Publishers. After all, the whole country used to sing father's music. I have it all collected here. Look!" She got up, opened a bookcase and laid several laced-up folios out on the table. "This is all his film music. These are operettas. These are his songs, marches, and cantatas. But, you know, as soon as one breathes father's name and that of Uncle Abram! Why is that? After all, even Prokofiev wrote some Hebrew Melodies! Can you really help? No, I can't believe it!" She suddenly placed her hands over the folios, as though afraid he was about to take away her riches.

He looked her in the eye. Yes, she was his sister. A month ago he had received her file from the Institute of Steel and Alloys, including an autobiographical sketch. Born in 1930. In 1937 both her father and uncle had been interned. Then, in 1941 her mother, grandfather, and other relatives had perished in a bomb attack while being evacuated. From 1941 to 1946 she was kept in a home for children of enemies of the people in Kazan. There she heard, in 1942, that her uncle Lev Grass had been killed at the front, in the Kursk salient. In 1948 she returned to Moscow, where she worked on a construction site, attended evening courses, and graduated from technical college. Then she became an external student at the Mining Institute, and in 1965 defended her doctoral dissertation. She was unmarried and had no children.

Yet, despite all these years of losses and loneliness, this woman had preserved the music folios of Moisey and Abram Grass.

"Sit down, Sonya Moiseyevna," he said. "I'm not going to take anything from you. I don't understand music anyway. All I know now is that you have your archive, and I'll think what can be done with it. But before I leave, I'd just like to have a look at some illustrative material. That's something I do understand. Probably you have other photographs in addition to this portrait, which could be used for an edition?"

"Oh, of course! I certainly do! I have whole albums of photos." From the bottom shelf of the bookcase she took out several weighty albums. "They all loved taking photos of one another in those days! Maybe you'd like a cup of tea?"

"Maybe," he said with a smile.

During the next half hour he heard the whole story of the enormous Grass family. He saw photos of Sonya as a ten-year-old sitting on the lap of her (and his own) grandpa, Aron, and pictures of her (and his) American uncles in their youth—Hershel and Isaak. There was also twenty-six-year-old Lev Grass, who served in an engineering regiment and had perished in the war; he was wearing his major's uniform and had his arm around his young wife, who was expecting. There were pictures of Abram and Moisey Grass, who had died in the Gulag before they were thirty. There were also photos of them with Marshal Budyonny, with Mayakovsky, and Iosif Utkin, and with producers Meyerhold and Stanislavsky, the singer Leonid Kash-chenko, and with composer Dmitry Barsky.

f i f t y - t w o

But this is her first pregnancy! No, Iosif. You know the respect I have for you, but I can't . . ." Dr. Yablonskaya pushed away the two gift-wrapped packages of food and champagne from the Eliseyev store that Rubinchik had placed on her desk as he entered her office at Sokolniki Hospital.

Seventeen years ago, Rubinchik, still a student in Saratov, worked free-lance for the *Labor Gazette*. On the day of Yury Gagarin's flight into space, he came rushing to the Saratov hospital and with the connivance of Dr. Renata Yablonskaya he had suggested to all the new mothers that they name their newborn sons Yury. Then he wrote a piece about the patriotism of these families in bringing eleven new Yurys into the world. And there were also flattering words about Dr. Yablonskaya. All this had an immediate beneficial effect on her career. She was promoted to senior doctor, and a year later moved to Moscow and became director of obstetrics at Sokolniki. Later on, after Rubinchik got married, it was she who took charge of the births of his children, Xenia and Borya. And although she never took bribes, he had rewarded her with generous gifts. All this was preamble and excuse for Rubinchik to break all the rules and turn up at the maternity unit late that evening. However . . .

"We Jews do not destroy our own seed," Yablonskaya said, "and I'm not performing any abortions!"

"Renata Borisovna!" Rubinchik was desperate and began fumbling for his wallet.

"Iosif, are you crazy? Put your money away this minute. I'd never expect this of you. And anyway, what's all the rush? In a couple of weeks, if she decides that she still doesn't want the child, then come back and we'll discuss it."

Rubinchik raked a hand through his already ruffled hair.

"Renata Borisovna," he said, "I don't have two weeks! Look here." He laid his exit visa and train tickets on the table. "I'm leaving in sixteen hours. For good."

The sixty-year-old doctor looked him in the eye and sorrow and torment clouded her face.

"Goodness me!" she said quietly. "You too!"

"Now you understand," he said. "I can't leave this child behind."

"What are you going to do over there?" she asked, with a pained expression as though Rubinchik were heading for the African jungle and some imminent catastrophe.

"I dunno. Something or other." Bitterness crept into his voice. "God will help me over there. But here and now, please, I need your help."

She stared at him with pain and sorrow, as though gazing at an already dead body. Then she sighed and put the two packages into a drawer in her desk.

"Iosif," she said, "you are forcing me to commit a crime."

"Thank you!" he said.

Rubinchik walked out of her office and returned to Olya who was sitting in the empty corridor. Her eyes had the trusting gaze of a child. That for him was the worst thing that had happened to the two of them so far.

He sat down next to her and held both her hands. He felt like an executioner, a monster, an utter scoundrel.

"Everything will be okay, my love. They'll give you an anesthetic and an injection of phenamine. You won't feel a thing, word of honor!"

She smiled.

"Why won't you let me keep the child? I'll bring him up as your son, honestly. I'll bring him up myself."

"Olya, come on. Let's not talk about that!"

At that moment the office door opened and Yablonskaya emerged.

"Come with me, my dear," she said to Olya, and set off down the corridor ahead of her.

Rubinchik and Olya got up and followed, but she swung round.

"Iosif, you stay here," she said curtly.

He let go of Olya's hands, and she followed after Yablonskaya. Then Olya stopped, took off the two slim bracelets from her arm, handed them to Rubinchik and again followed Yablonskaya, moving with that slightly ungainly walk of hers. After a few steps she looked round again. Her large gray-green eyes showed no sign of fear, only doubt and questioning.

It was the look of a child, gazing back at her father as she walks into the doctor's office.

Rubinchik smiled back wanly. When she had gone, he sat down again. Gripping her two bracelets, he leaned his head back against the wall and closed his eyes.

"Heaven help us!" a voice inside him seemed to cry. "Why is all this happening? Why? What for?"

Somewhere in his head a strange roaring and tolling of temple bells began. It was as if this abortion were weighing down on him and forcing him into some other dimension—somewhere he had never been before, as bad as when he'd collapsed in Kiev. He clasped his hands behind his neck and tried to massage himself and somehow reduce the surge of blood pressure. But it was in vain. He suddenly passed, or burst his way, through an insubstantial wall of pealing and ringing darkness and light. He found himself in a strange airy space with a clear and lofty sky that was turquoise and transparent and seemed itself to ring.

Before him lay an endless expanse of steppe with a tall growth of dry feather grass. And across the steppe a mighty army was advancing. Out in front rode the vanguard of cavalry with heavy forged armor, sharp spears, and brightly colored pennants. Behind them came the foot soldiers carrying blazing torches and a gigantic gold shield that glowed in the sun. Then, in the wide space between these warriors and the rest of the column, came a rider mounted on a white horse ornamented with gold brocade. Of medium stature and no older than forty, he wore a sky-blue cloak with golden lining. He had a high forehead and well-groomed beard and wore a gleaming helmet. Rubinchik recognized him immediately, like someone he'd known all his life. This was the king of Khazaria, Joseph Togarma, son of Aaron. Behind him rode his cavalry headed by the khakan-bek: thousands of warriors, divided into companies of a hundred men advanced in formation. And behind them, as far as the eye could see, was a host of infantry, camel trains, teams of fresh horses, and droves of sheep and rams as provender for this army.

Suddenly something disturbed the advance of this immense procession. A flurry ran like a wave through the columns, as though a mile long serpent had been gripped by a convulsion that finally reached Joseph Togarma himself. The king turned round. What he saw was a gray-haired half-dressed barefoot rider tearing toward them on his foaming steed and rending the air with his cries.

Joseph reined in his horse and turned to face the rider. He recognized him. It was the kundur-khakan, deputy of the khakan-bek, who had been left behind in Ityl to govern the city and defend it. And when Joseph recognized the khakan-bek's own deputy and saw his disarray, his heart was gripped by the cold hand of fear, and terror pierced his ribs like a spear.

The kundur-khakan had flouted ancient tradition, had abandoned the city, and instead of reporting to the khakan-bek came directly up to the king, approaching brazenly close and falling before the hooves of the king's own charger. All this forebode news that was terrible.

The venerable khakan-bek raised a hand and halted the entire army in its tracks.

"Speak!" the King ordered quietly as the kundur-khakan lay in the dust before him.

"The Rus!" he said. "The Rus have burnt the city of Ityl!" the kundur-khakan cried without looking up from the dusty ground with its scattering of horse dung. "The Vyatka and Burtas tribesmen let the Rus through along the Great River and they have burnt the city! Everything ruined, your entire kingdom perished, oh Great King! The God of Israel has forsaken us!"

King Joseph grew dark in the face.

"Tell me more!" he ordered.

"They came in their boats, at night, when your troops were asleep, oh King! Thousands upon thousands! Their host was without number, like the sand of the seashore; they were fierce as wolves of the steppe; and they showed no mercy to our men, or to their wives and children!" The kundur-khakan spoke rapidly, swallowing dust. "They sacked and pillaged everything by the river and around it. They burnt the synagogues, churches, mosques, bazaars, and bathhouses! They killed everyone they found asleep and drove nails into the heads of those who woke! They put out the eyes of the rabbis, mullahs, and priests. Your whole kingdom has perished, oh king of kings."

"And who was leading them?"

"Sviatoslav, the new prince of Kiev. He is young, like a youth, yet strong as an ox."

"Be silent now. You know what you have to do," the king interrupted him and slowly turned his horse back to join his army, whose countless ranks stood ranged before him with their battle pennants fluttering.

Meanwhile, behind him, as he lay in the dust, the kundur-khakan drew the dagger he carried at his waist, embedded its handle in the ground, and then fell upon it with his chest.

King Joseph did not even turn as his kundur-khakan uttered his last mortal gasp. He rode up to his troops. At a brief sign from him, the khakan-bek raised his hand again. And the Khazarian army fell silent, and even their horses ceased pacing and churning the ground with their hooves.

"Hear, O Israel!" Joseph Togarma said to his troops in a loud, clear voice. "Once again, as he did twenty-two years ago, the Russian prince has entered our kingdom like a thief in the night. And by sword, fire, and torture, he has slain our children, our wives, and our fathers. And now I shall lead you against this vile man and against his host. May your hearts be strong! Fear not, nor tremble before them, for the Lord our God is with us and will fight for us. Baruch Ataw, Adonai Elohainu! Melech Hawolam! Scatter our enemies like straw in the wind. Consume them like a forest before the flame! Chase them with Thy storm and strike them with Thy tempest! May they be seized by fear and dread! By the might of Thine arm and when Thy people strike them, Oh Lord, let them fall like silent stone! My warriors, we are not in retreat, we go forward! Advance in the name of the Lord! And He shall crush our foes! Kadyma!"

"Kadyma ts'ad!" the khakan-bek cried, drawing his sword from its gilded scabbard.

"Kadyma ts'ad!" a thousand throats cried in answer.

Then King Joseph lashed his white charger with his whip and rode forward. But they did not turn back to Ityl. And a moment later Rubinchik understood the maneuver of his great forbear. Without breaking ranks, the whole column moved off at a canter behind their king, and he led his army in a great arc, turning first toward the west, and then to the south, toward the city of Ityl. The foot soldiers and supply trains remained almost stationary and were easy to turn toward the south. But the cavalry did not wait for the infantry and were flying forward behind their king and God.

Rubinchik's eye was blinded by the sun glinting on their armor and helmets. And the thunder of hooves set the steppe a quivering, like a gigantic membrane, deafening his ears. And out of this light and noise arose the sound and motif of fate, familiar like Ravel's *Bolero* or the freilechs. And strange words were heard of some unknown though painfully familiar text. It had no beginning, and there were words and whole sentences missing, but Rubinchik could see it, and he could read and hear, as though he himself had written these same words a thousand years ago in the ancient Hebrew tongue:

> And the Khazarian people took them unto themselves. . . . And they became kith and kin with the inhabitants of that land. . . . And they always went to war along with them and formed one people with them. . . . But the prince of the Rus, and the king of the Turks went to war against them, and only the king of the Alans offered assistance to the Khazarians. . . .

The circle of the Khazarian host grew narrower, and Joseph Togarma led his cavalry in an ever sharper curve toward the south, and the thunder of their hooves rolled ever nearer to Rubinchik. He was deafened by the roar, then picked up like a splinter in a flowing river, hauled up into the saddle, and carried away. And in the thrill of the attack, terrified by impending death, he too was forced to shout in ecstasy: "Kadyma ts'ad!"

The noises echoed louder and louder over the steppe, over the battling cavalry and armored tanks, over the bayonettes of the Grande Armée and the firing of Messerschmidts. And all the time Rubinchik was fighting against unknown foes—Frenchmen, Germans, Swedes, Lithuanians, and Japanese. "And they became kith and kin with the inhabitants of that land, and they always went to war with them and formed one people with them. . . ."

"Iosif! Iosif Mikhailovich!" A woman's voice hauled Rubinchik back from the depths of history.

He opened his eyes, not aware of where he was, what part of the globe, what century.

Dr. Yablonskaya was standing in front of him in the Sokolniki Maternity Hospital corridor, the passage lit by a cold fluorescent glow. He realized he was back in the twentieth century and still in Russia.

"You can go," Yablonskaya said.

"Where to?" he asked, surprised at the sound of this language, which he seemed to speak so easily. Only a moment ago he had been thinking in ancient Hebrew.

"You can go home. You're leaving soon."

Only then did his memory come back: Olya, Colonel Barsky, his children, his wife, and their emigration tomorrow. Or was it already today?

He let out such a heavy sigh that Yablonskaya looked anxious.

"You're not sick are you?" She laid a hand on his forehead, and he felt the cool of her palm. "No," she said. "You can go."

"But . . . but what about Olya?"

"She's asleep. Everything's okay. You don't need to worry. She'll sleep for six hours, maybe even eight. And I'll keep her here for a day or two. But you have to go."

He got to his feet.

"Can I see her?"

"No," Yablonskaya said, harsh all of a sudden. "No point to it. You should be on your way. It's already ten o'clock."

"Thank you," he said and set off toward the stairs. There was a burning pain in his left shoulder. But in his head and his right hand—the hand of a scribe, or a journalist in modern parlance—there still floated splintered fragments, the alien phrases of a long forgotten language. Who had written them? Who dictated them to him?

> We are far from Zion, but a rumor has reached us that through the multitude of our sins, all reckoning is awry. . . . I myself live at the mouth of the Great River, and I will not permit the Rus who

come here on their ships to enter our land with the sword. . . . I wage a constant war against them. . . . If I left them in peace for one hour, they would come and destroy our land. . . . In the month of Nissan we leave our city and each one goes to his own vineyard and field, and goes to work in the fields. . . .

Rubinchik walked out of the hospital unable to recall where he had learned that text. Sokolniki, on the northeast fringe of Moscow, was covered in snow. All around was the darkness of a winter night. Wind had blown the snow from the branches of the blackened trees, but the rooks' nests still clung on to them like tumors. Rubinchik shivered as he drove along the darkened Luchevoi Passage. God knows, he said to himself, this just isn't my country! What have I been doing here for the last thousand years?

Suddenly the wheels hit a patch of ice, slippery as glass, and the car skidded left toward oncoming traffic. "Steer into the skid!" Rubinchik remembered the driver's golden rule too late. He spun the wheel and squeezed the brake, but the car refused to respond and careened toward the curb. Rubinchik realized there was nothing to stop him from smashing into the concrete base of a telegraph pole.

"No!" he cried out to God, but the cry was strangled, and he had a glimpse of Olya's eyes as they'd looked when she was going for her abortion.

Then his cry was drowned out by the crunch of metal against concrete.

fifty-three

Three blocks away, a quite different mood reigned at the large apartment in the Prize-Winners' Nest where Anna and Arkady Sigal had their home. In the drawing room, Dixieland jazz was playing, champagne corks hit the ceiling, and several dozen friends had gathered to say good-bye to Anna. Farewell toasts were drunk, there were snacks with caviar and salmon, and awkward remarks were made, Anna was given the phone numbers of several friends abroad "just in case," and details of the latest sensation were recounted—how the Bulgarian dissident Georgy Markov had been murdered in London with an umbrella tipped with poison.

Meanwhile, Charlie the Airedale terrier ran nervously around and got under the feet of all Anna's guests. His little dog's heart could sense there was trouble in the air. He could see it in the sad looks of his master and of the old man who was again drinking bottles of fizzy mineral water with its smell of iron and sulfur. He could hear it in the unnatural loudness of his mistress's voice, and see it in her exaggerated gestures, and when all the women embraced Anna and plastered her face in red lipstick. Almost all of them gave off a strange feeling that Charlie did not find at all friendly—like a disguised desire to gobble up his mistress, her husband, or goodness knows what else. Confused by the fact that Anna kept hugging these poisonous ladies, Charlie scuttled around the apartment, trying to ensure that these strange visitors at least did not march off with any of the property.

The telephone was constantly ringing.

Anna would lift the receiver and kept saying "Thank you!" and "Definitely!" and "Absolutely!" to whoever it was, and hardly had time to hang up before the phone rang again.

"Anna Evgenyevna?"

"Yes," Anna was so taken aback to hear *that* voice that her voice cracked, and Charlie froze.

"I think you recognize my voice," he said.

"Yes, of course. What is it?" she asked curtly.

"Oh, don't worry. This is not an official call," Barsky sounded amused at her cautiousness. "It's simply that your time here is running out, and your name still isn't on any of the Aeroflot passenger lists. I just wondered whether you need any help?"

"No, thanks. I'm leaving by train."

"When?"

"Tomorrow." Anna's voice had by now recovered its usual vitality, and Charlie had relaxed and was nuzzling her thigh. She absentmindedly scratched him behind the ear.

"Oh, tomorrow?" Barsky sounded surprised. "Why by train? It's far simpler by air!"

"I have a dog with me. Aeroflot insists that they go as freight, and they have to be drugged and put in a cage. So we're going by train instead."

"But bear in mind that our Customs are very strict in Brest. And I can't be of any help to you there."

"Thank you. I wasn't expecting you to help. I'm not taking anything out which . . ."

"Oh, I didn't mean in that sense. I meant in general. Is anybody seeing you off? I mean, traveling to Brest with you?"

"No. Why?"

"No special reason. There are long lines there."

"I know. That doesn't matter. Thanks for your concern though."

"Okay. Well then . . . bon voyage."

"Thank you."

Barsky hung up. Although his black Volga stood just a few steps away with its engine turning over, he kept standing there in the darkened phone booth on Gorky Street, just a few blocks from the Sigal residence. He clung to the receiver as though it were the last thread connecting him to Anna. For a long time, more than a month, he had struggled with the temptation to call her and ask to meet her. But he'd conquered his feelings and held out until this last day, when it would have been stupid even to mention seeing her. She was leaving. And that was good, it was splendid, because it was only her departure that was going to save him. Otherwise . . .

It had gone on for the whole month, thinking of her all the time—a week ago, three days ago, yesterday, and even today at the operations meeting with the head of Fifth Directorate. And now, she was in his thoughts—night and day, at lunch in the officers' canteen, at the wheel of his car, on the street, and of course in his lonely bed. Damn it, he had never worked out why it was that these beautiful Russian women went for the Yids! It was ridiculous to suppose that the large number of Russian-Jewish marriages occurred merely because Jews tended not to drink. First of all, the Jews did drink. That bastard Rubinchik, for instance, drank like a fish. Secondly, among the fifty million Russian men one could find at least a million who didn't drink. And that was exactly how many Jewish men there were in the country. Yet how was it that these sober Russians married Jewesses?

Barsky would have liked to discuss this with Anna—or even just chat with her about it, if only in jest. But it was too late. "Between Russia and Jewry there exists a mutual attraction and a spontaneous link"—Igunov in his cups had once quoted that. And now it turned out that Barsky himself was one of those, another secret nexus of that Russo-Jewish magnetism. Was that inexplicable and unquenchable hankering after Anna the Jewish soul in him? Was it the call of the blood, which flowed in him as part of his Grass inheritance? And just as he was drawn toward Anna, so probably Moisey and Abram Grass had been drawn toward his mother, and Rubinchik toward his own daughter.

But this was dreadful! Monstrous! He did not want to be a Jew! He had never been a Jew and was not going to be! He was the son of a *Russian* composer and a *Russian* singer, and he'd be damned if he'd hear about "spontaneous links." To hell with Anna Sigal, and Rubinchik too! Two days from now he was going to make sure that bastard did not leave Sheremetyevo with any goddamned manuscript about Jewish freedom fighters! Or even his own family photos! Instead of those, when his wife opened her handbag in

Vienna she'd find quite a different set, pictures of her husband with Natasha Svechkina in the Salekhard hotel. And even if that was a dirty trick, petty, spiteful—what the hell! It would be Barsky's little farewell gift.

That was the only way. He needed this to burn away those feelings that almost overcame him yesterday in Sonya Grass's apartment. Only such a nail could drive out the one that Anna Sigal had hammered into his heart!

Barsky finally let go of the receiver, left the phone booth, and crossed the slippery sidewalk to his car. It was warm inside the car and there was music on the radio. On the front seat sat General Bulychev's secretary, Valya, with her long legs tucked up cozily beneath her chin. Her high boots lay on the floor. She swayed her knees in time to the music and in anticipation of further, more earthly pleasures. Barsky had his hand on the gear shift when another wave of despair came over him. Lord, he wondered, why am I being tormented like this? After all, it would be quite a simple thing for him to drop everything, fly to Brest, and meet Anna there with flowers, a gigantic bouquet of roses. And he would at last say to her those simplest of words, and admit that he was in love with her, and then he would travel on with her to Vienna, Rome, New York, or even Israel! Why in God's name should he be forbidden to travel further than the Berlin Wall? Why should a few youths in frontier guards' uniform have the right to stop him? And by what right did all these Brezhnevs, Chernenkos, Andropovs, and Gromykos—and before them every Russian tsar since Ivan the Terrible—set up these goddamned frontiers with their barbed wire, ploughed strips of no-man's land, and guards with machine guns? Had the Lord not given the whole earth to each and everyone?

"Let's go, Oleg Dmitryevich!" Valya said impatiently.

Barsky looked at her. Her little brown eyes were not darkened by a single thought, apart from the play of juices in the slender stem of her young body. Her scarlet lips were slightly parted, her pliant young breasts thrust their nipples against her tight-fitting blouse; under her unbuttoned sheepskin coat her loins in their dark tights were visible right up to the narrow line of her panties; and she beat out a jazz rhythm with her thin typist's fingers.

Barsky felt a bitter lump in his throat and swallowed hard. So now he would take this beauty home, fill her up with champagne, and screw her till morning, stirring himself up with megadoses of brandy and angst. Meanwhile Anna would be packing, saying farewell to friends, and tomorrow she'd be setting off for Brest, and from there to the West. Forever. To join Rappoport. And there wasn't a thing he could do about it, not a damn thing.

"Come on. Let's go, Oleg!" his young diva ordered playfully.

"R-r-right," Barsky drawled bitterly, more to himself than to her. "Let's go."

He switched on the headlights and wipers, cleared the snow from the windshield, and moved off. The Volga joined the stream of traffic up Gorky Street beneath an arch of lights with the slogan THE PARTY IS OUR HELMSMAN!

fifty-four

The following morning, Nelya busied herself stuffing their cases with essentials that had appeared from nowhere—bed linen, oatmeal, footwear, medicines, washing powder, kitchen items, soap, and goodness knows what else might be needed in the West. Meanwhile seven-year-old Xenia was able to play her violin one last time before they left. Her little music stand looked desolate in the completely empty room. Both her bow and violin had been marked by the Ministry of Culture export commission with lead seals, and Xenia made a face as she drew her bow across the strings.

"Mom!" she called moodily through the kitchen door, "I can't play on this violin! It doesn't sound right!"

They'd had to buy a new violin, to replace her Italian instrument that the Ministry had decided could not be taken out of the country. At any other time Nelya would have found some comforting words to reconcile her daughter to this Soviet-produced matchbox. Now, though, her nerve cracked and she ran into the nursery and shouted.

"Whoever said that it had to sound right?" Then she saw Xenia's eyes wide with fright, and caught herself at the point of slapping her—as though Xenia was to blame for her own frenzy. Or for the fact that that son of a bitch had got so carried away playing a Jewish Solzhenitsyn that he'd probably been caught handing his films to some foreigner and been arrested. And on their very last night!

Then something in Nelya broke—cracked like glass—at the realization that she had turned into a common swine about to hit her daughter. She leaned against the wall, closed her eyes, burst out sobbing, and collapsed to the floor.

"Mom! Mamma! It's all right! I'll manage to play! I will . . ." Xenia ran to her mother and was now even more frightened. Still sobbing, Nelya spread her arms to embrace her child and clung to her.

"Forgive me. Forgive me, my dear. Forgive me."

At that moment, they heard the scrape of a key in the lock. Xenia joyfully rushed out to the hall.

"It's Daddy! Daddy's here!"

But it was Nelya's parents bringing back Borya, who had spent the night with them. They also brought two heavy bags of groceries, which Nelya's mother had obtained somewhere. Or she had hauled her own winter supplies out of the fridge. Xenia loudly greeted her grandparents.

"Well?" her grandmother said provocatively. "Where's your father?"

"I don't know. Mamma is crying . . ."

"She should have done that ten years ago!" muttered her grandmother, who had always opposed her daughter's marriage to Rubinchik.

"Fira! How can you talk like that?" her husband called her to order. "He's obviously been *detained*."

"One moment," the elderly woman said taking off her boots. "If the KGB had got him, they'd have been here with a search warrant. Otherwise, if it wasn't for the children, I could tell you who's picked him up!"

"What are you going on about! He's only just back from hospital!"

Nelya's mother brushed the objection aside. "It only needs some dirty little *shiksa* . . ."

At that moment the front door opened again, and there stood Rubinchik. His forehead was plastered with a dirty bandage, his unshaven cheeks and hands had cuts and gashes, and there were patches of dried blood on his jacket.

"Daddy!" Xenia cried in fright.

"It's okay. It's nothing, darling," he said and gave a faint smile. "I'm still in one piece. Only my shoulder is a bit . . ." He read the silent question in the eyes of Nelya and his parents-in-law and explained: "I smashed the car up. Complete write-off."

Xenia and Borya ran to look out the window.

Down below, they could actually see the driver of the tow truck loosening the chains from the smashed-up Moskvich. The whole front of the car was crushed.

"Where did it happen? What happened?" Rubinchik's father-in-law asked.

"Yesterday evening. It was slippery, I smashed into a telephone poll," he explained, trying to remove his jacket and wincing with the pain in his left shoulder.

"Couldn't you at least have called?" Nelya asked brusquely.

"I was unconscious," he said and looked her directly in the eye. "But I've handed the films over. You needn't worry."

"And there you were going on!" Nelya's father reproached his wife, then hurried to assist Iosif. "Wait a moment! Looks like you've sprained your shoulder! Don't take anything off! I'll take you off to see a guy I know. He does extrasensory healing. He can work miracles. Otherwise how can you leave? Your train goes in six hours!"

"And who's going to pay for the car repair?" his mother-in-law asked.

"Gosstrakh, the State Insurance company," Rubinchik said and placed his briefcase containing the shoe brush alongside the already packed suitcases.

fifty-five

It was a dark November night. The Moscow–Triest express was approaching the western frontier of the Soviet Union. A few hours earlier it had left Moscow, and it was due to arrive at Brest the following morning. The usual complement of a hundred and forty men, women, and children occupying the last two cars were emigrating to the West. There they would no longer be citizens of the mighty state. Behind them on the platform of Belorussky Station they had left their closest relatives and the precious few friends who had dared to come and wave good-bye to these traitors to the motherland.

The Rubinchiks were seen off only by Nelya's parents. But among the passengers on the platform she recognized people she had met in various lines during the last few days. There was the redheaded blue-eyed Levite artist with his two strapping sons, the book illustrator Grigory Bouis with his numerous relatives, the portly string player, and several others she recalled from the Austrian Embassy and the State Bank. The period the KGB allowed all these people to pack was limited to the few days before the October Revolution anniversary, so it was no surprise that they were all leaving at the same time.

Of course, there were other passengers on the platform too—foreigners, Soviet diplomats and their families, and army officers returning from leave to rejoin their divisions in Poland, Hungary, Germany, Czechoslovakia, and other countries. Their ruddy faces, full dress uniform, and astrakhan hats, their imperious air and the shearlings of their wives were better evidence than any ballistic missiles that the Communists had in sixty years realized the thousand-year-old dream of Russia's princes and emperors. The power of Moscow outshone that of Rome, Constantinople, Berlin, and all the other imperial capitals in history.

The foreigners and holders of Soviet foreign-travel passports were all in the front ten cars. They had no need to change at Brest, and they did not mix with the hoi polloi. The emigrants and other passengers had tickets only as far as Brest, and occupied only the last two cars. In Brest the emigrants had to go through Customs and then board the train for Vienna. Rubinchik stood on the step of their car and watched the Jews' nervous haste as they climbed aboard. "Mamma, where's the brown case?! Dad, you forgot the thermos! Just check, have you got your visas? Call us from Vienna as soon as you get there! D'you hear? Monya, where's the bag with our pies?!" He watched them shouting, all steamed up and sweating from lugging their overweight crates and valises; then he looked at the Soviet diplomats and military who disdainfully skirted the crowd of Jews and headed for the cars at the front; then he looked at the Jews again. There was something absurd about their fuss and commotion, but only their children and dogs sensed this. The children acted out, the dogs tore at their leashes, and the irritable adults gave both animals and kids a good scolding. Then, for the umpteenth time, they would recount their suitcases, turn down parcels thrust on them by parents, and even shout back: "That's enough, Mamma! We can't take any more! That's it!" And only when the train moved off did they quiet down, glue their eyes to the windows, and realize that they had just said good-bye to their near and dear ones—probably forever.

"Next year in Jerusalem!" someone shouted from the platform. Rubinchik recognized the man—it was the Olympic athlete he had met on one of his nighttime training runs.

"Nelya, lift Borya up! I want a last look at him!" Nelya's mother suddenly shouted hysterically. Her cry still rang in Rubinchik's ears hours later, as their train passed through dark forests. The whole car finally was pacified—sleeping children and tired women lay on the benches with blank and lifeless looks in their still open eyes. The men crowded onto the platforms at the ends of the coaches, smoking relentlessly and exchanging information about the voracious Brest Customs, the reception immigrants got in Israel, the United States, and Canada, and the latest news on the BBC.

Rubinchik did not join in any of the conversations. Another concern kept him lying on the top bunk. That morning when his father-in-law took him to see the extrasensory healer, he had never believed in any auras, biofeedback, telepathy, or any other pseudoscience. He had gone because his shoulder hurt like hell and there was no time to go to the hospital. The healer turned out to be a thick-set Jew by the name of Kramer, the same age as Rubinchik, with a dense tousled head of hair, broad forehead, large sniffly nose, brown eyes, and glasses, and with a Gaulloise-type cigarette gripped in his yellow teeth. To look at him, one might have taken him for a research scientist or a long-term refusenik. But it turned out that Kramer wrote poetry as his main occupation and was a member of the Writers' Union; he had no intention of emigrating; he was studying extrasensory healing at some semisecret biogenetics laboratory attached to a research institute.

As he slowly moved his hands over Rubinchik's body, Kramer began listing all his past and present illnesses.

"There's a weakness in the eyes. You'll soon be wearing glasses. Two metal teeth, and two others filled. But the fillings aren't good. Better get them replaced before you leave, or they could be expensive in the West. There's a dark patch on the right lung. You probably began smoking early in life."

"At the orphanage," Rubinchik said.

"Just a moment . . . there's no shoulder fracture, just a slight sprain, but I can fix that for you. To the right of your shoulder blade there's either a birthmark or some change in the pigment, but it's not malignant. And in general you're in good health. Wait!" He broke off as soon as his hands descended to Rubinchik's groin. "Oh, my God! You didn't get this in a car wreck! Who did it to you? Your blood vessels are a disaster! All shot to hell! Have you been in the hospital with this?"

"Yes," Rubinchik said, amazed at the precision of his diagnosis, "seeing" all this only with his hands, and through Rubinchik's clothing.

"What! They discharged you in this condition? They're savages!" Kramer was outraged and turned to Iosif's father-in-law: "It's good that you brought him. We'll have a look at this. The shoulder is nothing, just a bump. But this . . ." Kramer shook his head. "Of course, you don't have any function? I mean as a male . . . sexually."

"They told me in hospital that it would recover on its own, with time . . ."

"Huh! That's a good one! There's hardly any blood supply, it's stagnating here, starting to thrombose; the whole area's in spasm. 'Recover on its own'! Take your jeans off and lie down. I'm going to try and clean up your inguinal circulatory system. You can keep your underpants on. They aren't in the way. But there's a metal zipper on your jeans."

Kramer walked over to the window, opened it despite the frost, and held his hands up to the sky. He stood like that for about three minutes, breathing deeply and noisily, as though ventilating his smoked-up lungs with clean air and absorbing some cosmic energy through his raised hands. Finally he turned round to face Rubinchik.

"Yes, there is some swelling in the shoulder, but we'll do that later," Kramer said casually, and began moving his hands above Rubinchik's groin. Although Kramer did not touch him and held his hands a few inches away, and although he had just had his hands out in the frosty air, Rubinchik could feel, radiating from those palms, a strange warmth that penetrated through his skin and went deeper and deeper.

"Can you feel the warmth?" Kramer asked.

"Yes, I can," Rubinchik confirmed. By now he could sense how inside him things were getting warmer and relaxing, as though in a sauna. The heat felt so strong that it went through to Rubinchik's back and vertebra, and he felt like sleeping.

But he did not. He felt compelled to keep watching Kramer. After about ten minutes, Kramer began moving his hands over Rubinchik's groin in a downward direction, and after each such passing he would shake his hands as though to free them of some dirt that had stuck to them. Then after about another twenty minutes of this, Kramer began on his left shoulder. Rubinchik meanwhile looked round at the apartment. It was almost bare, only an old writing desk, two chairs, a collapsed couch, and a tall rubber plant. In the corner was a small ikon in a simple frame, and along the wall shelves of books. There were neither curtains nor blinds on the window, and outside he could see snow-covered trees and hear the honking of cars down on Krasnoarmeiskaya Street.

Now Rubinchik began to feel the pain shifting from his shoulder and moving downward, to his arm, then his elbow. Looking down at his shoulder, what he saw made him catch his breath in surprise. As the tousle-headed Jew continued passing his hands, the swelling in his shoulder got smaller and smaller and actually moved down his arm toward the elbow, and this was as easy to see as the neck of a stork as it swallowed a frog and moved it down its gullet. And as the swelling moved, the pain too shifted downward.

After another twenty minutes, it was over. With the same passes of the hand, Kramer gradually forced what was left of the swelling out through the fingers of Rubinchik's hand. Then he shook his hands one last time, and went out to the kitchen to wash them, as though this work had actually involved digging around in blood and filth.

"It's fantastic!" Rubinchik exclaimed to his father-in-law, and he waved his arm in the air, amazed at the absence of pain.

"What did I tell you!" his father-in-law said proudly, almost as if he himself had healed Rubinchik. "And you'll be even more surprised at night, if you get my meaning!"

"How much do we owe him?"

"Nothing. He doesn't take money."

"But he lives like a pauper! Just look at this place!"

But at that point Kramer returned.

"You mustn't lift anything heavy for several days. And with a broken aura like yours, you ought not to be emigrating but going for a vacation.

You know, collecting mushrooms, swimming . . ." As he spoke he began moving his hands over Rubinchik's face and explained: "I'll give your skin some energy, so that the cuts heal quicker. You can't go abroad looking like that."

Rubinchik continued moving his shoulder in disbelief.

"If you can do this sort of thing," he said, "in the West you could become a millionaire."

"Quite probably," Kramer said. "Yesterday I treated a woman for cancer of the cervix; the hospital had given up on her."

"So why are you still sitting here?" Rubinchik exclaimed.

"Someone has to stay," Kramer answered calmly.

"Why?"

"To help these people. They do get sick, after all."

Rubinchik looked into the eyes of this Jew. He appeared neither mad, nor a hippy. He smoked the cheapest Russian cigarettes, and in his fridge he probably had nothing more than two packages of cheap dumplings. But Kramer took no money for healing people and refused to take his wizardry to America.

"We imposed the horrors of Communism on these people, and we have to atone for that and help them to recover," Kramer said. "I was recently baptized."

"That's stupid!" Rubinchik's father-in-law interrupted. "Communism's not Jewish. It's German in its spirit and practice. And don't forget it was the Germans who brought Lenin to Russia. And Marx himself was anti-Semitic. And according to the Bible, the Jews will be saved not when they turn Christian, like you, but when the Messiah appears."

From the fervor of Nelya's father, this evidently was the continuation of an old dispute between them.

"We cannot deny that we Jews had a large hand in the Bolshevik movement," Kramer continued calmly. "Eighty percent of Lenin's government was made up of Jews."

"So you accept the idea of collective guilt?" Nelya's father retorted. "So all the Jews are guilty of crucifying Christ? Or all the Georgians are responsible for Stalin? And are all Jews responsible for what Trotsky did, and for everything else? Because Adam after all was a Jew? Is that it?"

Rubinchik looked with new interest at his father-in-law. He never suspected that this soft-spoken chemical engineer had such ideas or possessed such knowledge.

"I'm not talking about the Jews in general, but about my personal responsibility," Kramer answered. "Over there, in the West, they have the best medical care in the world, superb doctors and hospitals. And that's why it's here I'm needed. So I've stayed."

But Nelya's father was still not satisfied.

"I tell you, Lenin's Jews never dreamt of subjugating this whole country. They were simply madmen who longed to set up a paradise by force in the middle of a barbarian empire! And they themselves paid for it—Stalin killed almost every one of them! Now the whole of Russia is in the hands of local Party secretaries, and there hasn't been a Jew among them for the last forty years."

"Which is something else that needs treatment and healing," said Kramer, and he waved aside the idea of taking any money from Rubinchik.

"I didn't know you knew the Bible," Rubinchik said, when he and his father-in-law were outside. "And what do you make of Kramer? How can your science explain what he does?"

"Science covers everything that is demonstrable and can be reproduced in controlled conditions," Nelya's father said vaguely as he waved down a taxi. "And so far as Kramer is concerned, he's a typical fanatical Jew, even if he is baptized. But he's right about one thing: this country really is sick. Unfortunately."

Rubinchik lay there on the top bunk and felt his left shoulder, which still retained a touch of the pain. He regretted not having gotten to know Kramer and never having had a serious conversation with his father-in-law. But now it was too late. What an awful separation this emigration was!

The children were asleep—Xenia on the bunk opposite, and Borya down below with his mother. Outside the darkened window, small lights drifted past in the distance, and the wheels clattered like horses hooves. The train sped on through the night, snorting every now and then with its whistle. Broken shadows of trees or telegraph poles flashed close by, as though trying to grip the train by the handrails on the doors. The shadows arose like Khazarian horsemen in their chain mail, or like the forgotten phrases of some ancient manuscript. But he was no longer surprised by the Judaic and Khazarian words that wandered through his brain, or by the visions outside the window. His forebears and kinsmen had lived in this country for a thousand years. Now they had all risen from their graves and were galloping alongside the train, traveling with him to yet another exile. As the last of a line about which he knew nothing but which had survived the pogroms of Kievan princes and Russian and Ukrainian cossacks, Rubinchik himself had hung onto life by a miracle in 1941. And now he was taking all of them away with him: the venerable Pesakh, Hashmonai, King Aaron, and Prince Sabriil, the first Jewish chieftain of the Khazars and his wife whose name was Serakh.

Oh God, Rubinchik thought, as he gazed back into the depths of history. Oh God! To think that my own ancestor, who lived before Jesus Christ, fled with his family and the spirits of his ancestors out of the land of Egypt and then from Persia and then from Spain . . . And everywhere we left our books, our houses and our tombs . . . And again we fled, to start all over again with another people, and we learned their ways, and we went along to war with them, and we loved their women, and we sired Einsteins and Freuds and Heines and Pasternaks, and we became their priests, and even their kings. But why? Every century or two, thousands of Jewish souls who were slaughtered by Prince Sviatoslav or Bogdan Khmelnitsky or Stalin rise up from their graves and again follow us into another exile, gripping the handrails of our trains and clattering with the hooves of their galloping steeds.

Rubinchik thought again of Kramer. No, he thought, Kramer wasn't a Jew anymore. The idea of suffering for someone else's guilt was not a Jewish idea. That came from Dostoevsky and even, probably, from Christ. The Jewish idea was not to suffer, but to live with gladness and thank God for the joys of life.

He gazed again into the night. The train raced along and with the shrieks of its whistle tried to chase away the nocturnal wraiths. But once the sound had melted into the darkness, again from the snowy fields and frests emerged the souls of slaughtered Jewish men and women, young and old, coming to flee along with their descendants and escape this beloved, cursed land. Rubinchik tried to catch a glimpse of his own mother and father—he did not doubt it: their souls too would be flying along beside this railway car.

He looked at his wife. Nelya lay across from him on the lower bunk. In the light of a station that flashed by he saw that she was not asleep but weeping.

"Lift Borya up. I want a last look at him!" he remembered his mother-in-law's cry, and he realized why Nelya was weeping. Unlike his forebears, who had all become spirits and could flee with him, Nelya's parents were still alive. Just now she had seen them for the last time.

fifty-six

On the platform at Brest there was chaos. The p.a. system kept announcing the arrival of yet another train from Kiev, Baku, Tbilisi, Kharkov, and Tashkent. And each brought yet another hundred or so emigrants who had been ordered to leave their homes before the Anniversary of the Revolution. And so they poured in—children, parents, suitcases, bundles, babies, perambulators, dogs, canaries in cages—and they joined those who had already come yesterday, the day before yesterday, and the day before that, and who were now beseiging the ticket booths. They all had to get to Vienna—Vienna and the West, as fast as they could! And from there they would journey to a new life in a new world—Israel, the United States, Canada, Australia, and even South Africa. But there was one last obstacle. At the western end of the platform where the engine stopped, soldiers with machine guns were guarding a barrier with the stark announcement:

STATE FRONTIER OF THE USSR

There it was, a stone's throw away! For five centuries, since Ivan the Terrible, these barriers at the border had kept all Russians inside their empire. As Prince Kurbsky once wrote to Tsar Ivan, "You have locked up your Russian realm, which is a free human entity, as though in some hellish fortress. . . . Whosoever would travel from your land into a foreign country, that man you call a traitor, and if they catch that man at the frontier, you execute him in various wise."

One tsar had followed another, with regimes that were lenient or more severe, but from Ivan the Terrible to Leonid Brezhnev, that law of the the sixteenth century had never been rescinded: "If any person—be he prince or boyar, or any other—should send his son or brother on any business whatsoever to a foreign country without our knowledge, that man shall be accused of treason. And his estates and lands and animals shall be seized by the tsar. And if any man should go himself, and if his kin should remain behind, they shall be tortured to see whether they knew of the intent of their kinsman. . . ."

Since then, anyone who left Russia for the West, whether by conveyance or on foot, or even by swimming, "without petitioning, or without the knowledge of the tsar," was guilty of treason. "And so as to maintain them in quiet servitude and fear, none of them shall travel out of the country without leave, nor shall they be informed of the free institutions of other countries"—such was the report on the Russian situation by Adam Oleandrius, a German traveler of the seventeenth century. And even the most pro-Western tsar, Peter the Great, who forced vinegar down the throats of his boyars to inculcate Western tastes into them, held fast to this law and even strengthened it by constructing frontier walls and fortresses, and by creating, in 1711, a special "land militia" to protect those frontiers. And continuing his policies, the Kremlin surrounded its subjects with a wall—from the Great Chinese Wall in the east to the Berlin Wall in the west.

Those Jews now arriving in Brest had indeed "petitioned" Brezhnev and had received the supreme permission of the KGB to leave this hellish fortress, and they had of course left behind all their estates and lands. But even with that, it was still not easy to cross those last three hundred yards to the frontier barrier.

Leaving his wife, children, and suitcases on the platform, Rubinchik ran via the covered crossing to the ticket booths. A notice over one of the windows read TICKETS FOR VIENNA. As he stood in line, Rubinchik wondered at the Jews lurking all about who kept quizzing everyone in a whisper: "You don't know who's on the take here, do you? . . . Who do we have to sweeten, d'you know? . . . They say you have to give the porters something, but there isn't one in sight . . . You haven't seen them here, have you?" But why did one have to slip bribes to a porter if there were tickets on sale? Rubinchik leaned down to the window and proferred his money and the exit visas.

"Two adults and two children to Vienna."

"No tickets to Vienna. Only as far as Warsaw," the girl said.

"Why's that? Your sign says Tickets for Vienna."

"So what if it does! There aren't any tickets to Vienna. Get tickets for Warsaw and change there."

Rubinchik had no choice. He had to get out of here fast, before one o'clock.

"And when's the next train to Warsaw?"

"Tomorrow, nine A.M."

"But I need to leave today!"

"So does everyone else. But there are no more trains in that direction today. So do you want Warsaw?"

"My dear, listen, my dear! I really need to leave today!" Rubinchik put on all the charm he could muster, a quality that had worked wonderfully well for him all over the USSR.

"Huh, come on, we're all 'dear' here! None of us are cheap!" The clerk grinned at her own joke and stared back brazenly.

"Of course, I understand," Rubinchik said. Flustered, he laid a hundred-ruble bill on the counter. "There!"

The woman looked at the money and sighed regretfully.

"Believe me, there are no tickets for today. Take some for tomorrow, or within an hour they'll be sold out too."

"Okay then," Rubinchik said, his heart sinking, bitter that his brilliant plan to get away from Barsky had foundered so stupidly.

"Have you been through the baggage check? What's the name?" The girl pulled open a long list.

"Why?"

"First you have to go through Customs. Go and get yourself signed up."

"My dear! Please!" Desperately Rubinchik fished in his jacket pocket again. But she stopped him.

"No, no! Forget it! No register, no tickets!"

"Oh, come on! Please!"

"Sorry, I can't. That's all there is to it." And she slammed shut her window.

Rubinchik walked away with a chill and a sense of doom in his heart. He was done for. Finished! In five hours Barsky would discover that the Rubinchiks had not turned up at Sheremetyevo. Then he'd need less than an hour to call up the Odintsovo militia and have them check out his apartment, and he'd hear that the family had moved out yesterday. And that would be it! Only two frontier Customs points processed emigrants: Sheremetyevo and Brest. So that by three—or five at the latest—Barsky would call up and have the Rubinchiks frisked from head to toe and given "the works." And he, fool that he was, thought he could outwit the KGB. And he'd come unstuck on the simplest thing of all—the Soviet system of queues! But no, there had to be a way out! There was bound to be some loophole, some side entrance, someone he could bribe! This was Russia after all. And he still had five hours!

"Come on!" he said to Nelya and the children, who were waiting. And picking up the cases he moved off toward the station square, sure that at the rear he'd find some staff entrance, a side door, or one of those porters.

But when they got to the square, his heart sank. Here on this dirty little square was the main emigrant encampment. It was concentrated most thickly around the actual building, blocking the entrance to the waiting room. But the station doors were closed, and new people were let in only when those waiting inside had left the country and freed up the benches, floor, and window ledges for the next contingent. And the greater the distance from the entrance, the thinner the crowd and the more downcast people looked.

Southerners shivering in their light clothing, children wrapped in blankets, old women sitting on suitcases, mothers with babies in their arms pacing and stamping their feet in the frost—a wretched spectacle, like pictures of Napoleon's army in retreat. And looming over all of them stood one standard monument to the leader of the world proletariat, Vladimir Ilyich Lenin, with the inevitable inscription: YOU ARE ON THE RIGHT ROAD, COMRADES! Facing away from the frontier, Lenin stood there like Moses, pointing a hand out straight ahead. But instead of the Commandment tablets, *his* hand was empty. Perhaps that was why all these Jews were heading the opposite way.

When he set eyes on this gypsy encampment, Rubinchik realized that he had lost out. Back there in the East, where Lenin was pointing, Rubinchik was one Jew among ten thousand Russians. And he knew how to get around the queues. Here, though, he was surrounded by Jews and only Jews, a thousand of them. And they doubtless had already tried every possible and impossible way of leaving without delay. And if all this crowd had given up and were obediently sitting and waiting, what chance had he?

fifty-seven

That same day Moscow was hit by a blizzard. In the customs hall at Sheremetyevo, Captain Faskin kept watch, and without taking his eyes off the line of sweaty emigrants, he went over to the staff desk, and dialed a three digit number:

"Comrade Colonel, our love-kike is late. It's already five past two!"

"It's okay. He can't go anywhere. Hang in and wait," Barsky said indolently and hung up.

He was up on the third floor in the office of Major Zolotaryov. In honor of so important a guest, the Chief of Customs had set out some of his trophies: a bottle of ten-year-old Armenian Ararat brandy, black and red caviar and other delicacies confiscated from emigrants who had tried to take out more than the rules allowed. These drinks and foodstuffs were the sort of petty items to be found in almost every Jewish suitcase. But the prizes, which Zolotaryov referred to as his "collector's pieces," were on display in a glass cabinet to the left of his desk. Here was the legendary cast-iron meat grinder from which a vigilant inspector had extracted a twelve-carat diamond. That, along with some Fabergé eggs, had been passed up to higher levels—perhaps to Brezhnev's own daughter—so that nobody now even mentioned it. But the meat grinder itself had remained. The collection also contained a silver pen that had belonged to the poet Nekrasov—this was a prize presented by the scientific community of Akademgorodok to the dissident bard Alexander Galich, and had been confiscated as he left the country. There were also sixteenth-century ikons, antique Tula samovars with medals from the Paris and Milan expositions, and a little stool made from the bone of walrus penises.

Zolotaryov showed all this to Barsky and entertained him with anecdotes like: "Abram-told-Sarah-to-hide-a-golden-ring-and-guess-where?" But all the while, he kept glancing at his watch, and finally he could hold himself in no longer.

"Oleg Dmitryevich, you'll have to excuse me. My guys are sweating their guts out down there. Do you mind my going down to keep an eye on things?"

Barsky dismissed him with a gesture and grinned to himself: the major was afraid of missing out on his share of the lush bribes those Jews offered to get their stuff out.

Left on his own, Barsky drank up his brandy and glanced at the phone, which was ringing again. Most likely it was Faskin—this time reporting that the Rubinchiks now were there. Barsky ignored the phone. To hell with Rubinchik! And anyway, the whole day had been a pain in the neck—both Customs and that servile Zolotaryov with his brandy and ass-kissing. Outside the window he could see the silver, white, and blue airliners of Al Italia, Air France, British Airways, and Lufthansa taxiing on the field and moving out to the take-off runway, all flying toward where Anna had gone last night.

Now as he watched the snow flurries that stitched the distant fir trees with streaks of white, Barsky realized how somber Moscow had become for him without Anna. And he, like an idiot, had wanted her to leave as soon as possible. This "passion" that they wrote about in books, could it really exist? His insatiable longing simply to see the woman, to be next to her, to hold her by the hand and kiss her in a snowstorm—was this what they called love? All this had hit him in the way an adult is sometimes struck down by chicken pox, which he somehow managed to avoid as a child. And when adults are so stricken, they suffer far more than children, racked by high fevers and shivering chills. And this was no illness you could shake off with hard work, swigging brandy, or making it with other women. Last night neither drink nor sex with Bulychev's secretary had consoled him. They'd just made everything seem more vile and made him want to puke. Now, today, he realized that he could not rid himself of this cancer in his soul, that his visions of Rappoport's amours with Anna Sigal would drive him mad. Today she had left Brest and tomorrow, or at the latest in two days' time, Rappoport would be embracing her in Vienna, taking her around to restaurants and the opera, and kissing her on the silk sheets of the Vienna Sheraton. No, no! an inner voice screamed at him. I can't stand it. I'd have done better to kill her!

"Comrade Colonel, they've started boarding, and he's still not here!"

"What?" Barsky tore his eyes from the window and turned. Captain Faskin was standing there.

But before Faskin could repeat himself, the screechy P.A. system announced: "This is a final call for Aeroflot flight two-thirty to Vienna. I repeat: a final call for passengers on flight two-thirty . . ."

Barsky looked hard at Faskin, and the same thing dawned on both of them: Rubinchik had got away! He had left the other way and taken his manuscript with him!

Barsky grabbed the phone and a minute later had Brest on the line. The woman in charge of Brest Customs, a Captain Vasko, reported in a low and smokey voice that passenger Iosif Rubinchik had signed on the waiting list to have his baggage checked that morning. But not only had he not yet left, he had not even been through Customs yet.

"And do you have an Anna Sigal on your list?" Barsky asked with deliberate nonchalance.

"Sigal? One moment and I'll look."

While Captain Vasko rustled through her list and he waited for some supposedly routine information, Barsky was surprised by his agitation as he lit a cigarette and pressed the receiver anxiously to his ear.

At last she came on the line again.

"Sigal, Anna Evgenyevna. I've found her. Traveling with a dog. She's also in line for tomorrow. What do you want me to do? Give them the full treatment, the works?"

Then Barsky had a pleasant brainwave.

"One moment!" he said and then turned to Faskin: "Get down to flight control. Find what they've got to Brest today." Then, in a quite different, jovial voice, to the receiver: "How do I call you, Captain?"

"How do you mean?" she asked in a cautious contralto.

"I mean, what's your name?"

"Elena. Why?"

"Right, Elena, listen," Barsky said with a smile. "I'll be in Brest by this evening. Don't start any inspection of either Rubinchik or Sigal until I arrive."

"But today's flight from Moscow has already arrived, Comrade Colonel," Vasko reported dryly.

"Never mind! I shall be coming. I don't know which flight yet, but I'll be there before the end of the day! And don't process either one of them without me. That's an order. Do you understand, Elena?"

"Orders understood, Comrade Colonel," Vasko continued in her official tone. "We can't do them today anyway. There are no more trains leaving."

"Excellent!" Barsky said and hung up. He walked animatedly up and down the office. So, up yours, Mr. Rubinchik! Thought you'd fool me, did you? Thought you'd get your manuscript out in another meat grinder? Well, I'm coming to Brest and I'm going to settle with you once and for all. And to hell with all this misery and hypochondria! Vengeance tastes better than bread and sweeter than love. How did you put it, Anna Evgenyevna? "Surely my relations with men are not a threat to our national security?" Well, they *are* a threat! They're a threat to *me*!

He stopped short as another idea struck him. Anna was still in Russia! On Soviet territory! While Rappoport was already in Vienna and waiting for her with flowers! Well fuck you, with your three p's! If I can't have her, neither will you. You left a legend behind you about how you fooled the KGB and Colonel Barsky. And I'm going to write a new finale to it. There's ritsine, which takes effect instantly, but our Technical Operations department also has other substances that need a few days.

Faskin reappeared.

"Comrade Colonel," he said, "you can get to Brest by flying from Vnukovo. You change at Minsk and Baranovichi."

fifty-eight

By evening Rubinchik had gone through the whole emigrant routine. First a vain search for any information at all on departure procedures. He'd had to pay a porter called Stakh four hundred rubles merely to get his name on the schedule for Customs inspection tomorrow. "You Jews will all get away," Stakh had announced in a broken mixture of Russian, Ukrainian, and Belorussian. He emerged from somewhere behind the station and reassured the crowd mobbing the locked doors of the Customs office: "You'll all get away . . . if you have cash! If you've got the cash, you leave! If you ain't got it, you stay where you are!"

After paying Stakh, there was another fruitless wait in line for tickets to Vienna. Warsaw turned out to be impossible. There you had to change trains quickly, the anti-Semitic porters ripped passengers off, smashed their suit-cases so that their things fell out, and they had no time to pick them up because the train was leaving.

By five in the evening, as it was growing dark, he made a final unsuc-cessful attempt to try and rent a room in Brest for the night, at least for Nelya and the children. But it was not just that these rooms were horren-dously expensive; other emigrants told stories about their dangers. One man had all his money stolen during the night, and he had no chance to report it because he was in a rush to catch his train for Vienna. Another had all the valuables removed from his baggage, and only at the Customs inspection he discovered that he had been given an iron and a tattered jacket in place of his camera and fur coat. Another family had stayed at a place where the anti-Jewish landlord put either DDT or ground glass in the children's por-ridge, and when they got to Warsaw they could not even get the children admitted to the hospital. Another family had simply disappeared without a trace.

Nobody knew whether these rumors were true or whether they origi-nated from the authorities trying to prevent local people from illegally rent-ing out rooms. Or the rumors could have been spread by communal apartment dwellers jealous of the fat profits made by the owners of private accommodations. But when Nelya heard about the glass in the porridge, she put her foot down.

"We're not going to any lodgings, not even if it's a mansion!"

"But they won't let us into a hotel—we have no passports!"

"So, we'll spend the night here."

"In the frost and cold? You're mad! It's minus five!"

"Other people are," Nelya said and began getting out extra clothing, sheets and blankets—all the warm things which, thank God, she had put into their hand luggage.

"Let's try and rent a room, and I'll stay awake the whole time. I'll be a sentry and watch over you."

"You?" Nelya grinned. "This is Belorussia! They'll hit you over the head with a shovel, and that'll be it! I don't care about you but I'm not risking the children." Then like everyone else on the square, she began making up a bed from their cases.

Rubinchik knew his wife. Once she had dug her heels in, it was pointless to argue. She would stick her hand in flames on a matter of principle. The children were freezing, their noses running, and they looked at their mother in surprise.

"Mommy, I'm not going to sleep here," Borya said. "I want to go home."

"Daddy, what happens if wild animals come?" Xenia asked.

"I'll be right back!" Stepping over a labyrinth of cases and bundles, Rubinchik set off through the crowd and pushed his way through to the locked door of the station and began hammering on it with his fist.

"Another impatient one!" said an irritable woman's voice from the darkness.

"You'll get it in the neck. So you'd better stop," a man's voice advised.

But Rubinchik continued hammering. He still had some of his Moscow journalist's assurance—until recently it had opened doors and even scrambled helicopters! Finally the door did open, and a young militiamen appeared in the entrance. He was the same height as Rubinchik and had a broad pimply face.

"What is it?" he asked. Behind him, in the dark waiting room Rubinchik saw a dense crowd sleeping on benches, on the floor, and on the window ledges. But there was still some free space.

"I'm a journalist," Rubinchik said and produced his ID. "You have no right to keep kids freezing out on the street! I want to see the person in charge here."

He was still speaking when the militiaman began closing the door. Rubinchik, infuriated at being snubbed by this young jerk, jammed his foot in and held on with both hands.

"You're asking for it," the militiaman said amicably.

"Come on then!" Rubinchik defied him.

In a flash, the militiaman dealt him a powerful jab on his nose and sent Rubinchik's head reeling. There was a gasp from the women nearby, and the man's voice said, "I warned you!" But Rubinchik somehow managed to keep his foot in place and clung to the door.

"Better let go," the militiaman said in the same unruffled tone. "Or the next one'll be harder."

Rubinchik felt something warm running from his nose, but kept right on talking.

"You don't have the right! There are kids out here . . ."

Nearby voices came to his support.

"They're gangsters! Worse than fascists! They deliberately put us through all this, just to squeeze the last drop out of us!"

"Are you a Jew?" the militiaman suddenly asked Rubinchik above the murmur of the crowd.

"So what if I am?" Rubinchik snapped back. "You still don't have the right to make these kids shiver!"

"You Jews have got special arrangements with God. He'll keep you warm," the militiaman laughed and landed a haymaker on Rubinchik's cheek that flung him clear of the door. "Now get the hell out!" he said. But he did not close the door, and said to the gasping crowd: "And you all shut up! Anybody that makes noise won't leave here at all! Get it?"

The Jews quieted down. An old lady bent over Rubinchik and began wiping the blood off his unshaven face. A stocky gentleman carefully put down his cello case and dug around in a dirty snowdrift, collected a handful of clean snow from inside and said: "Here, put this on his nose. The cold will seal up the blood vessels." And several others fidgeted around, opening cases and bags, producing bandages, swabs, and iodine.

Rubinchik took a gulp of air through his bloodied mouth and opened his eyes. People he had met on the train and here in Brest stood around him.

"I did tell you not to stir them up," said a bearded man hugging a little blond girl to keep her warm.

"And he's absolutely right about God," said a blue-eyed man with two strapping children. "If God doesn't give up on us, no anti-Semites are going to eat us!"

There was a laugh from the crowd, and more jokes followed.

"It's like in the story where a Jew comes to God and says 'O Lord, please make me a goy!' "

At that point Nelya turned up with the children.

"Daddy!" Xenia cried and rushed to him.

"Watch out! Don't get blood on you!" Rubinchik held out a hand so that Xenia wouldn't get stained. He got to his feet.

"Finished you off, have they?" Nelya said disparagingly. Then she caught the glance of the blue-eyed Levite. She picked up her son in her arm and without a backward glance walked off to their pile of cases where she had rigged up an improvised sleeping bag for the children.

Rubinchik followed, and Xenia held on to his jacket pocket.

"Daddy, I'm frightened here. Let's go home. Please, let's go back!"

Rubinchik put an arm round her.

"Don't worry, honey. Don't be afraid. I'm here with you."

"But why did they hit you?"

He didn't know what to say.

"Daddy, how is that we are Jews? I don't want to be a Jew. Nobody likes Jews, and they keep beating us up."

"Not everybody, honey. There are countries where Jews are more powerful than anyone else."

"Is that where we're going?"

"Of course."

"Is it very far?"

"We're quite near already."

fifty-nine

An hour later the Rubinchiks were like everyone else—a subdued Jewish family, camping out on a dark square on a snowy Belorussian night, and in a hostile country that had closed all its doors and windows on them.

Rubinchik held his son wrapped in a blanket and tried to warm him with his breath. Suddenly he became aware that he was praying to God. "Just save our children! I ask for nothing else. Only save our children! O Lord, save our children!" And he rocked to and fro like the old Jews in the Moscow synagogue and as his ancestors had done. Who knows, perhaps it was thanks to his own father's prayers that his life had been saved in that fatal year of 1941.

Nearby, an elderly man with a wooden stump for a left leg was entertaining his neighbors with a story:

"They think that if they don't allow us to export any old books, we'll forget what Maksim Gorky wrote about us back in 1919! Want to hear it? 'When life is specially bad for a Russian, he blames his wife, or the weather, or God—everyone but himself. That's our Russian nature. We always complain about someone else to justify our own stupidity, laziness, and our inability to live and work. In the Russian soul nowadays, among people who are idlers and layabouts, there is again festering the purulent ulcer of envy and hatred for Jews, who are a lively and active people, who overtake the ponderous Russian on all life's ways because they are able and enthusiastic workers. . . .' "

The snow fell quietly. In the semidarkness, relieved only by the yellow glow of two street lamps lighting up the Lenin monument, the Jews drew closer to the man from Minsk as he rattled off the whole of Maksim Gorky's article "On the Jews," which had never been included in any Soviet edition of his works.

" 'It is the Jews who on this unclean earth nurtured the splendid blossom of Christ, the son of a Jewish carpenter, the God of love and meekness, the God before whom you Jew-haters supposedly bow. And no less magnificent flowers of the spirit were the apostles of Christ, the Jewish fishermen who affirmed the religion of Christianity on this earth. . . .' "

People began dragging their suitcases and bundles nearer, and came carrying their children wrapped in whatever warm things they could find. They also brought food, and thermoses of tea and brandy and vodka, which they had stored for the long journey. They surrounded the man from Minsk and his daughter and sleeping grandson, and Rubinchik and his wife and children. And although they had no campfire, because the militia forbade fires on the square, they sat around that storyteller and felt warmed by the words of one Russian writer who did not hate the Jews.

" 'Of course, not all Jews are righteous men, but I hardly need to tell you about righteousness, honor, and conscience. . . .' "

Nelya began taking out packages of food, and with them she also hauled out a shoe brush wrapped in newspaper.

"What's this?" she asked her husband quietly. "Why did you bring this?"

He took it from her, looked at it, and then at the snow-covered crowd of Jews sleeping on suitcases. He thought about how awful this night was with its freezing children, cruel and violent militiamen, and grim Lenin on his pedestal pointing to the east. Alongside all that, Rubinchik's book struck him as an insignificant trifle. Would God accept it as a sacrifice in return for saving his children? He doubted it, but it was the most valuable thing he had. He stood up, wove his way through the crowd and chucked the brush into the garbage bin with the films he had so carefully hidden. O Lord, he said to his Jewish God, now I understand You. You tempted me with this book, and for its sake I was ready to put even my children at risk. But no book is worth the risk of having to stay on here even for an hour. Forgive me! Forgive me, and save my children! I pray you! Baruch Ataw Adonai Elohainu!

The snow drifted in his face, but he stood with his head lifted to the darkened sky and looked for some sign that his prayer had been heard.

But apart from the drone and light of an airplane coming in to land somewhere outside the city, the heavens were empty.

Near where he stood, the bearded man was embracing the blond girl in the dark, and a young couple were kissing passionately, pressed against one another like two slices of a sandwich. At that moment another gale of laughter went up from the group surrounding the veteran from Minsk, and now another voice joined the conversation and took it on a new course:

"Listen. If we're talking about the Jews and the Russians, I can tell you another incident. And I swear that it's true. I'm from Minsk, too, so our friend here could bear me out. I had a close friend; let's just say his name was Ivan Petrov. He was a Russian, and his father was a colonel in the KGB. And he married a Jewess and was one of the first to leave for Israel. You can imagine what happened to his father. But that's not the point. The thing is that Ivan Petrov went through all the wars and fighting in Israel, and then he cleared off to America. And do you know why? I called him up in New York, and he told me: 'Listen. Whenever I went to a bathhouse in Israel, they all would say, "He's a goy, a goy, a goy! Get yourself circumcised. Go and get your dick cleaned up!" I got sick of it, all the time, whenever I went to the sauna! So I told them: "Look, I speak Hebrew, I've fought for Israel, I love Israel . . . but I'm not going to get myself cut!" What business was it of theirs?' And for that he left Israel! He told me, 'I can't stand it any more. All my friends are Jews, we all drink together, but when we go to the sauna, they all start up: "What, Vanya? Still not had your dick cut? When are you going to get it done?" They simply couldn't understand that I'm Russian! I don't want to be circumcised! I'm fond of Israel, but there's a limit! I have to hold on to something of my roots!' And that, you know, is a sort of Jewish racism. Why should my friend have to get his dick snipped?"

The laughter of the crowd drowned out his last few words, and the square all around shook, and children and dogs stirred in their sleep. People laughed till tears came to their eyes, and some began to hiccup. Maybe, in another place, the story would have raised no more than a smile, but now it was as if a spring had uncoiled. People all found a release from their fears of that cold night and from a sense of oppression that had built up all over the vast expanse of Russia. And here in Belorussia, in the epicenter of Russian anti-Semitism, a few hundred frozen Jews told over and over the story of the Russian Israeli Petrov, and they laughed so loudly that the pimple-faced militiaman stuck his head out of the station door, amazed.

"What's up?" he called.

"Get away! Get back in there!" People waved him away. "Get your dick cleaned up, and then you'll understand! Otherwise get back inside and close your bloody door!"

Stung by this show of Jewish brazenness, the militiaman stepped out.

"I can let in any women with small kids," he called.

Immediately the square came alive, and women carrying sleeping infants ran toward the entrance. Nelya picked Borya up and pulled a sleepy Xenia along by the hand. But the militiaman, taken aback by his own sudden generosity, barred the way.

"I want fifty rubles per person!" he said.

"Of course! Certainly! Thank you!" People thrust their money at him and even thanked him for his kindness.

"Where's that guy? The journalist? You know, the one I whacked?" he asked.

"Hey, you there! Come here, Comrade!" they shouted to Rubinchik.

Rubinchik walked over to the line of women and children.

"Got any kids?" the militiaman asked him.

"Well . . ."

"Where are they?"

Rubinchik said nothing. So the militiaman walked over to where Nelya was standing with Borya in her arms. Xenia stood next to her, half asleep and clinging to her mother.

"Are these yours?" the militiaman asked.

"Yeah . . ." Rubinchik answered reluctantly.

"They can go in free, and first," the militiaman suddenly announced proudly.

There was applause from several men.

"That's all right," the militiaman said, pleased with himself. "We're human after all, aren't we?"

He let Nelya and the children in and began collecting money from the rest in line.

Rubinchik raised his eyes to the dark snow-swept sky and said silently, "Thank you Lord!" and hurried back to where their bags and cases stood. From a suitcase he took out a bottle of export vodka, screwed off the cap, and drank several gulps straight from the bottle. He closed his eyes and felt that wonderful sensation as the icy-cold burning liquid ran down his esophagus into his stomach. As he opened his eyes, he saw in front of him a dagger with something white impaled on the blade.

"Have a bite, dear friend!" said Irakly Katashvili, to whom it belonged. "You deserve our thanks!"

"What is it?" Rubinchik asked.

"It's not lard—not what the Ukrainians eat! Don't be afraid!" Irakly said to an accompaniment of laughter. "Do you know Sulguni? It's Georgian cheese!"

At that moment onto the square from a side street came a Hungarian-built long-distance motor coach. On its side a notice read TASHKENT–MOSCOW–BREST, and lashed to its roof was a mountain of crates and suitcases. After it stopped, about forty Jews emerged wearing Uzbek robes and embroidered skullcaps. The men climbed onto the roof to untie the crates, but one of the people in the crowd stopped them and told them that all freight had to be taken to the station and explained to the driver how to find it. The Uzbek Jews got back in their bus and drove off. But at the bus stop a lovely female figure remained standing, wearing a gray woollen head-scarf, a thick coat, and holding two heavy bags. The woman looked around at the square, bewildered, and rather than anything he actually saw, it was a sudden throbbing of his heart, preempting thought, that told Rubinchik that he knew her. It was Olya. No, no! a voice inside him protested. This isn't possible!

But it was Olya.

He set the bottle down and made his way toward her through the curious and silent throng. On his way he passed a woman sitting on her suitcase with her arm around a shaggy Airedale who looked up and opened her mouth to call to him. But Rubinchik strode past. All he could now see was Olya and the alarm and joy that shone in her eyes as she saw him approaching.

"You must be crazy!" he said as he walked up to her. "Why have you come here?"

"Hello," she said. "I've brought some food for your children. Dr. Yablonskaya asked me to give it to you." Olya handed him two bags still full of the parcels from the Eliseyev food store.

"How is that?" he asked. Then he realized the meaning of this gift. "Didn't she . . . didn't she do the operation?"

"She asked me to say that you shouldn't worry," Olya said. "She's going to help me raise the child. She doesn't have any grandchildren, and she . . . Well, anyway, take all this food."

She went on to tell him something else, in a confused way, as though apologizing for not having had an abortion. But he no longer heard what she was saying. Or rather, he could not make out the words. He gazed into her Scythian eyes, and that Spanish bolero motif struck up again in his blood and in his soul, and everything in him tensed and reared up, even the hair on his chest. This time, however, he mastered himself.

"You have to go back," he said.

"I want to wave good-bye to you."

"You have to leave immediately!" he said more firmly, fighting to supress his hot rush of desire.

But Olya smiled.

"You can't chase me away, Iosif. This is my country. At least, as far as the frontier."

And in her smile and tone of voice there was a new firmness that Rubinchik did not recognize. With a princely gesture, she seemed to have determined the extent of her dominion, up to the barrier at Brest, and she stood there regally, like her namesake Princess Olga, the warrior-princess and ruler of ancient Rus.

Ravel's drums continued to pound in Rubinchik's heart and pulse. And they summoned him forward.

A powerful voice in his mind seemed to prompt him: "And having failed to prevail in the battlefield, the Khazarian Jews made good their losses through love. . . ."

Rubinchik spun round. Not far away, the blue-eyed redheaded Levite was now holding forth.

" 'We are far from Zion,' " he quoted, " 'but rumor has reached us that, through the multitude of our sins, all reckoning is awry.' Exactly a thousand years ago those were the words of the Judaic king of Khazaria, Joseph Togarma, in a letter to the king of Cordoba's Jewish Minister of Finance, Hasdai ibn Shaprut. . . ."

Rubinchik took Olya by the arm. But as he led her away into the darkness of a side street, and as he yielded himself to the engulfing rhythm of Hispanic drums, in the fingers of his right hand he had the sensation of shaping those words written from right to left: "We are far from Zion, but rumor has reached us . . ." Yet he was now certain that no one had ever dictated them to him as an ancient scribe or chronicler. He had written them himself—exactly one thousand years ago.

And his name then had been Joseph Togarma.

sixty

How are murders planned and committed?

Tolstoy maintained that Desdemona's handkerchief was an insufficient reason for the intrigue that followed and that has shattered human hearts ever since the premiere of *Othello* at the Globe. Maybe Shakespeare himself sensed a weak link, and for that reason made Othello a Moor: a savage, even in general's uniform, is closer to nature and might therefore kill for possession of a banana.

Yet Tolstoy and Shakespeare were men of epochs when, no matter how good the motive, few would burden their souls with the sin of murder— because of retribution in the hereafter. But in our enlightened age, men are capable of shooting great artists or randomly killing suburban commuters, simply to be recognized as murderers. Nowadays it is common to shoot at presidents and slit the throat of one's beloved, simply from unrequited love.

The flight from Baranovichi to Brest was a single-engine ten-seater Antonov-2, and it was already dark when the plane touched down at Brest Airport, five miles out of town. The local KGB had sent a car for Barsky, and a luxury suite had been reserved and dinner kept for him at the Brestskaya Hotel. He ordered the driver, however, to take him straight to the railroad station.

In Moscow, seven hours earlier, he had stopped off at KGB headquarters. "I need to destroy a dog," he told the duty officer in Technical Operations. "But there has to be a delay of twenty-four hours, and there must be no trace of how it was killed."

"So long as it's not your mother-in-law," the man joked. "You have to file an application." And Barsky wrote: In view of information concerning the smuggling of valuables in the stomachs of animals being exported by emigrants, I request that I be issued various poisons to check their effects on dogs. I take personal responsibility for the substances issued to me. Head of E Section, Fifth Directorate. Colonel O. Barsky.

After that, Barsky was issued six small colored test tubes from the Technical Operations' safe. He was also given detailed instructions as to which poison should be added to food, which to dissolve in water, and which to sprinkle in the dog's basket or bedding.

"But can a human die from smelling this stuff?" Barsky asked the duty officer.

"Tell me: why should a human being go sniffing at a dog's bedding?"

As he rolled up to the Brest station, Barsky had the six vials in his pocket, wrapped in a Kazbek cigarette packet. He did not yet know how or where he was going to use them. But when the time came, he knew he would have no scruples. And if he didn't manage it in Brest, he also had in his pocket a KGB pass that allowed him to travel as far as Bratislava. And it would be even easier on the train—after leaving the frontier, the emigrants all relaxed and began celebrating in the dining car as they crossed Poland and Czechoslovakia. So let them get a load of this! Anna Sigal and her Yid Rappoport had turned his life upside down, shoved his face in the mud. And to cap it all, they had turned him into a kike! But nothing in this world goes unpunished. Mr. Rappoport would get his Anna back, of course, and might even have time to take her in his arms, but . . . whoever laughs last, laughs longest, remember?

The car pulled up at the edge of the station square. The throng made it impossible to drive up to the building. So Barsky told the chauffeur to wait, and got out and walked to the entrance.

Snow fell from the darkened sky, and all around groups of men sat huddled in blankets, like a soldiers' bivouac, keeping themselves warm with flasks of tea, brandy, vodka, and jokes and yarns. No one paid attention to Barsky, who was in civilian clothes. The thought crossed his mind that Rubinchik might well be here somewhere. But he would deal with that bastard tomorrow morning. Stepping among the suitcases and bundles, he made his way across the square and knocked assertively on the bolted door. It was opened by the sleepy young militiaman.

"What is it now?" he said brazenly.

Barsky said nothing and held up his KGB pass. The militiaman awoke and snapped to attention.

"Comrade Colonel, I have no incidents to report during the period of my duty."

"Stop yelling," Barsky ordered as he walked in. "And button up your tunic if you're on duty!"

"Yessir, Comrade Colonel!" The militiaman began trying to fasten his top buttons.

"Seen a woman with an Airedale terrier?"

"Do you wish for a report, Comrade Colonel?"

"Yes, I do."

"About the dogs here, Comrade Colonel. Both terriers and mongrels have been observed, Colonel. Will any terrier do, Colonel? Or do you need a particular one?"

"I need a particular one. A golden-haired Airedale accompanied by a woman of thirty-two with blond hair and green eyes. She should be well dressed—in a fur coat, shearling, or some good-quality coat. Well?"

"If I may report, Comrade Colonel?"

"Yes. Get on with it."

"If you'll permit me Comrade Colonel, I'll go up to the second floor and look up there, and if you could keep your eye open here. There's more space in here."

"Off you go."

"Yessir, Comrade Colonel!"

Barsky looked about him and meandered toward the far end of the darkened room. He found himself in a strange, unreal world in which the whole space—including the waiting room, ticket hall, buffet, barber shop, and even the corridor in front of the washrooms—was filled with old people, women, and children, asleep on the floor, on benches, window ledges, and lying on their own bundles and suitcases. The air was heavy with the stench of diapers, sweat, disinfectant, and garlic sausage. Occasionally came the wail of a child, but it was quickly silenced by an anxious mother's whisper or the quiet strains of a lullaby.

Stepping over legs, bodies, and cases, Barsky made his way through this encampment, looking hard at the faces of the sleeping figures and feeling that he was in some stuffy and oppressive dream. He saw a child, a little girl, sleeping on a suitcase with her head resting on a miniature violin case, an old woman in a wheelchair, another child, a little boy, clutching a teddy bear with both hands as he slept, another young woman breast-feeding her baby, a silver-bearded Jew with sidelocks in a greasy Bukhara robe rocked at his prayers; his protruding eyes gazed unseeing at the toddler with the teddy bear.

Suddenly—like a stab at the heart—a totally forgotten vision began coming to him. It rocketed up to the surface of Barsky's memory like an old buoy trapped in the depths by a rotten fishing net and now suddenly released. Barsky gazed at the old man, not trusting his memory or the scene that took shape and clarified like the picture on a television screen. Even before it completely solidified, he recognized that old Jew. His blood and memory filled with a thundering of drums interspersed with the shrill of falling bombs, the howl of air-raid sirens, and a hammering at the door. The hammering wrenched him out of his childish slumber, and he saw the door that his mother opened, and in the entrance a fearful, gigantic gray-bearded man with bulging eyes. In a commanding voice that brooked no question, the terrible old man announced: "Stalin has fled. The Germans are already in Khimki. Bring your child and let's go."

His frightened mother made no response, and rushed about gathering food and a bag. But the old man would not wait. He swept up three-year-old Oleg, who was dumbstruck with horror. The boy was in his pajamas and holding on to his teddy bear as the old man picked him up and carried him down the stairs; it was like a nightmare, snatched from your mother and you try to call out but you can't. Only when they were down in the street, and his mother caught up to them and bundled him into his hat, coat, and felt boots, did the boy put his arms round her and burst out sobbing. But she kept on with the repulsive old man and his family. First along city streets where people were dragging everything they could from smashed-up stores, and they kept throwing books from their balconies and burning portraits of Uncle Lenin. Later they joined a long column walking along some roadway. Toward morning, despite the old man's urging, his mother had no more strength either to carry him or even drag him along by the hand. But then, they reached a railroad station.

They sat there for one hour, two, and three, but the only trains were heading in the other direction, military trains crammed with soldiers going toward Moscow. People began freezing on the snow-covered platforms. A babe in arms next to him kept bawling all the time, and a round-faced young mother with pock-marked cheeks—just like the wife of Major Lev Grass in Sonya Grass's album—kept offering the child her breast. But the breast was blue with cold and had run dry, and the child bawled even louder. The old man did not respond to his grandson's cries or the tears of his mother. Sitting on his suitcase with his gaze fixed on little Oleg, who was petrified, the ghastly old man rocked back and forth as he prayed—exactly the same as this silver-bearded Bukhara Jew in front of him rocking on his suitcase.

Holding his breath and with his heart scarcely beating, Barsky became absorbed in this vision of the past. He tried to expand the screen of his memory. On the fringe of his awareness it occurred to him that his mother had always been reluctant to talk about their flight from Moscow: "Well, yes, I had to leave. The neighbors came and said Stalin had fled. I wasn't afraid for myself, but for you. I took you in my arms and left with everyone else. But they allowed only people in authority into the stations, with special reservations. So we had to set off on foot. But the next morning we were bombed, and I went back. And then later, we left for Vyatka by train. That's all there was to it." So Barsky had forgotten that night, as children forget most things from their first few years.

But now, these memories were wrenched from the recesses of his mind. Behind the old gray beard who rocked and prayed, he could see the snow-bound rail platform with its crowds of people, cases, and bags. The baby had bawled all night long in its mother's arms and now, exhausted, had fallen asleep. Barsky's mother leaned over and gave him a candy that miraculously had survived in her pocket. Above her head Oleg could see the sky with its white clouds billowing like images of elephants, whales, and camels. And out from one of those lovely cloudy whales sped two little airplanes with gleaming wings, and he watched captivated as they plunged into a dive and came nearer and nearer. Cheerfully he pointed at them. Then someone—either his mother, or the old man—shouted out and screamed. But by then the first little plane had dropped a bomb that came whistling down onto the platform.

The bomb exploded and wrecked the far end of the station. But the old man and almost everyone else there died not from the explosion nor from the flying debris. Now, thirty-seven years later, Barsky could again see everyone surviving, and again he saw how neatly the second plane followed the first, firing a machine gun and pumping little fountains of scarlet blood from the people on the platform. And he watched as everyone in the path of this bloody stitchwork stood numb with fear and was felled where they stood. The ghastly old man drilled by bullets and his beard all bloody, but still he managed to wrench the infant from beneath its slain mother. With his other hand, he dragged Oleg from the arms of his mother, who stood petrified. Moving crazily, like a lizard in its death throes, the old man crawled and dragged them to the edge of the icy platform and shoved them down beneath the concrete overhang, just an instant before the Messerschmidts made a second run. Recovering herself, Oleg's mother jumped down after them. But the old man had no strength left. At that moment young Oleg heard the shrill of another falling bomb. Then a mighty tremor and shock wave hurled him and his mother somewhere into the bushes in a snow-filled gully.

Now Barsky saw quite clearly that the awful old man who saved his life was his grandfather—the father of the Grass brothers. That was why he had come to Oleg's mother, as the grandfather, on that fateful night and had told her to take the child and follow him. And his mother had obeyed. "I wasn't afraid for myself, but for you." Only now did Barsky realize what lay behind his mother's abbreviated account. She was afraid that neighbors or someone else might report to the victorious Germans that her son was of Jewish origin.

Now, as he stood close to this Jewish grandfather, so like his own, Barsky felt as if two wires severed long ago had been reconnected. On one end, which was buried in the past, there were his own and Sonya Grass's perished relatives—his grandfather, Sonya's mother, and the wife of Lev Grass with a baby who was Barsky's cousin, together with the crowd who were fired on by the Messerschmidts. And at the other end of the wire were these Jews in 1978, with the same array of bundles and fiber suitcases, and probably the same prayers.

"Comrade Colonel, may I report?" came the militiaman's voice from behind.

Barsky turned round.

"You were asking about the woman with the terrier," the militiaman said. 'She's down there, at the other end of the hall. Shall I show you?"

sixty-one

Barsky nodded and followed the obsequious militiaman. something had happened to him, but he was not certain what. It was the sensation that a boxer can have in the fourteenth round, when even a gentle punch can send him reeling.

Yet, there was nothing new in that sudden revelation of his memory. Hadn't his mother already talked about the bombing? And Sonya Grass, too? So why did this recollection and the Bukhara Jew rocking at his prayers stun him so? Barsky could not understand. Inside him a voice was calling "Enough! Stop!" Should he go outside and breathe in a lungful of fresh frosty air?

But without looking back, the militiaman was leading him deeper into the station, and Barsky lacked the strength to turn back. The two of them made their way into the ticket hall, in half-darkness and crammed with sleeping emigrants, huddled together. There, in the farthest corner, Barsky caught sight of Anna. She sat dozing on a low window ledge, the heavy head of her sleeping dog on her lap.

"Here," the militiaman was about to say. But Barsky cut him short with a gesture, and then dismissed him with another wave of his hand. He was left on his own, just paces from Anna. He stood without moving and gazed at her, the woman of his life. Amazed and awed, he realized that he no longer harbored any thirst for revenge. He felt no lust, nor jealousy. His only feeling was one of love—a tired and heavy feeling, with a tinge of tormenting bitterness. It felt scary for a man of his years to be overtaken by such a feeling, but could he avoid it?

Barsky gazed at Anna's tired and relaxed features, her lips parted to breathe the stuffy air, her arms clasping her dog, and her figure curled in an uncomfortable position. But an hour ago he had wanted to poison and destroy this woman. And if now he knelt at her feet and confessed his love, it would alter nothing—nothing whatsoever. It would not delay her leaving even by a day. So what should he do? Go away again? Quietly and with good grace, leaving her here with her dog, her one suitcase, and the path she had chosen? Perhaps that was the most he could ever do for her.

But it was too late. . . .

Alarmed at Barsky's stare, her Airedale jumped up and in an instant hurled itself through the air toward him.

"Hey, Charlie!" Anna called, but too late.

The powerful animal fell with its full weight on Barsky as he shied backward and lost his balance, then it lunged and grabbed him by the throat with its fangs. All this without a growl or bark, swiftly and silently, like a professional killer or a thoroughbred trained by the police.

"Charlie, are you crazy?" Terrified, Anna threw herself at the dog, seized its jaws and only then realized who was lying there. "Oh, it's you! Charlie! Stop it! Let him go, Charlie! Come on, Charlie, you're hurting me!"

His white fangs dribbling, Charlie reluctantly loosened his grip, and with an effort Anna dragged him away by the collar.

"How did you get here?" she asked Barsky. "What are you doing here? Charlie, what's the matter with you?"

"Well, it's like this," Barsky began, annoyed, struggling to his feet and feeling his throat. "There was something I wanted to ask you before you left. . . ."

"What about? Charlie, that's enough! He's gone completely off his rocker!"

"Well, it's not all that important. I didn't realize your dog was so well trained. But you're not comfortable here. Come with me to the VIP lounge. I'd like to invite you."

"Thank you. But I'm okay here. Charlie!" She pulled as hard as she could on the lead, but the dog strained to get at Barsky, showing its fangs. "It would be better if you left," she said. "There's something wrong with him. I've never known him to be like this."

"I'm going," he said. "But isn't there something I can do to help you? Won't you let me?" he repeated in a pained voice.

She looked hard into his eyes.

He felt them piercing into his soul, engulfing him in the darkness of the two fathomless pupils. His stomach went cold, his legs numbed, and his heart seemed to stop.

"Something you can do?" she repeated quietly. Then she smiled. "Probably you can. I wouldn't mind a cup of tea."

"Of course!" he said gladly. "Come with me!"

"No," she said. "I wouldn't mind some tea—but I'd like it here. If that's possible."

"Anna, you've nothing to be afraid of, not with a dog like that! Let's go! I've got a car, and I'll find us a nice restaurant—"

"Oleg Dmitryevich," Anna interrupted with a grin. "I'm not afraid of you anymore, with or without my dog. At first, I'll admit it, I was afraid. Very . . ." She looked around at the sleeping emigrants. "But not now. You can take the last thread of clothing off me or send me for a gynecological examination, but it won't make much difference."

"Anna, don't talk like that."

"Oleg Dmitryevich, just relax. I know where I am—at the Brest Customs. There are legends about this place. They say it's as harrowing as going through the gates of Dachau. But these gates at least are a way *out*. So somehow we'll all get by." She stopped, peering off into the half-darkness of the waiting hall, and looked Barsky in the eye again and smiled gently, almost shyly. "But I would accept a glass of strong tea from you. One for the road, as they say."

A bit later the obliging militiaman produced two aluminum beakers from the duty room and gave them his own Chinese thermos flask full of tea.

"Lord, if only these people knew who you are, Oleg Dmitryevich!" Anna said in wonderment. "That's enough, Charlie! Stop it! No, you know, you'll really have to leave us. Otherwise I can't even pick up my tea."

sixty-two

Adam, as we know, was made in god's image. But whose was the image from which Eve was created? And whence comes that idea of the magical power exercised by female weakness over masculine strength? And O Creator, when You instituted the act of lovemaking, what did You yourself feel just then?

I ask You this as a pupil questions a Great Master.

I ask You this by the right conferred by being in Your image.

What did You experience, as You created this vessel of desire that continues through the ages?

If I, insignificant as I am, laugh when I think I have written something funny, and if I weep when my fictional creatures weep, then what must You have experienced when You introduced the act of lovemaking? Did You faint away and die at that seemingly endless moment, just like the rest of us? Did You soar into a state of bliss, like we men? Or did You swim in ecstasy like a woman? Did You cry out? Moan? Did You call Your own Creator to Your aid?

And if one is allowed to ask, then speak, O Teacher, and admit: Could you have become carried away? Did You not give to woman what You failed to grant in full measure to the man? And then, recovering Yourself and recalling that "the gifts of the Lord are inseparable," You punished her for her excess of pleasure that no man can know, and told her: "Thou shalt give birth in pain and torment."

Rubinchik stood up to his knees in snow and held Olya by her naked buttocks. Then he fell into the snow with her, then raised her up from the snow above his own loins. And all this time he was no longer himself. That sublime vessel created by the Great Master once a century, like the voices of Barbra Streisand or Edith Piaf, turned him into a mere instrument—performing a Hymn to lovemaking. And Olya no longer entwined him with the coils of a python, but with hot and tender fins, like the fingers of a great saxophonist, which ran along his elevated spear.

Beneath the dark sky and amid Russian snows, Olya rose up above Rubinchik in a voluptuous gallop. From somewhere on high, from the cosmos itself, she drew such energy and ardor that the snow beneath them began to melt. Rubinchik again felt a heat that filled his veins and flesh, and he also heard the fervent melody of pursuit, gallop, and attack. Again, again, again! From trot to canter, canter to gallop, thunder of drums, peal of timpani, roar of camel, hot blood and spinning head, and "Kadyma ts'ad! Kadyma-a-a!" The avalanche of his cavalry raced down from the sloping hills, crushing the first summer sprouts of musk beneath their hooves, and surrounded the footbound Russian force that had arrived in his kingdom on a thousand boats from the upper reaches of the great Ityl. The Rus had gathered into an irregular circle, a cluster of spears with the blinding sunlit gleam of shields and an ominous storm cloud of arrows already aimed from their bows.

Behind them, the fruits of their infamous work—the charred ruins of Khanbalyk, where Joseph's own mother had lived with her servants and handmaids, and all the aristocracy of his realm—scholars, rabbis, teachers, priests, astronomers, and builders, all possessed of property, knowledge, and quick intellect. There too there had been synagogues and bathhouses, schools, churches, and palaces of unbaked white brick and wood. There had been much wealth there, mead, wine, delicious food, young dancers, children and youths idling at the bazaars. But now only smoke—nauseating, acrid smoke—and gray ash floating down the Ityl toward the Caspian Sea. The only people left were a few hapless rabbis, mullahs, and priests who had been blinded by their pagan conquerors.

A great sorrow entered Joseph's soul and filled it with bitterness. O Lord, he cried out in his heart, Baruch Ataw Adonai, lend strength to the muscle of my arm! "Kadyma ts'ad!" he cried out to his army. "Strike them until they are dead!"

The kundur-khakan gave a sign to the first line of cavalry to attack in wedge formation, so as to divide the Russian force as with a sword, and then crush them with second and third waves, as the venerable Pesakh had taught them. Daring wins the fight, and wisdom the battle.

But what was this?

Who was this horseman emerging from the circle of the Rus and riding a gray dappled stallion?

Why was he wearing a silver helmet and silvery cloak?

And why was he alone—alone!—and riding madly toward their line, holding before him a flimsy wooden lance?

And why in the space between the Khazarian cavalry and his own warriors on foot, did he suddenly cause his horse to rear? And why did he remain like that, forcing his horse to stand on its hind legs with its front hooves pawing the air?

Lord, this was the ancient pagan summons to him, Joseph, the Scythian and Varangian summons by a prince to meet another prince in combat. This meant the unknown horseman was Sviatoslav himself! Sviatoslav, the prince of the Rus, who had come bringing his murderers and thieves!

The entire Khazarian cavalry halted their snorting horses the distance of an arrow's flight from the young barbarian and looked at their king. One movement of Joseph's finger would have sufficed for them to sweep young Sviatoslav away and hack him to pieces as they avenged the slaughter of their families.

But Joseph made no sign. He would accept the challenge.

"Kadyma," he said quietly to his horse and spurred it gently with his gilded spurs. And he pulled from his scabbard the sword of his ancestors, the sword of Aaron, Hashmonay, and Sabriil.

All was still on the Ityl steppe.

The cavalry fell silent, and the foot soldiers and the camels, and even the blinded rabbis, mullahs, and priests of Khanbalyk fell silent and raised their empty sockets to the heavens and asked why suddenly the world was so still. And the sun shone down, and the great river Ityl lay silent. Only Joseph's steed pounded its hooves on the dry steppe with its growth of bitter wormwood.

Joseph saw only the glowering figure of his foe, waiting there and holding his wooden pike with its sharp iron tip.

Nearer and nearer they drew.

The sword of Sabriil glinted once in the sun and smashed the wooden spearshaft like the harmless quill of an egret. The Russian warriors on foot gasped and reeled back; the Khazarian cavalry roared a triumphant roar, and the white royal stallion carried Joseph past the young barbarian. Joseph then veered round sharply at full gallop so that his opponent had no chance to prepare either attack or defense. Meanwhile, with one jerk Sviatoslav ripped off his cloak without troubling to undo the clasp and revealed his torso— bare and unprotected by even a chainmail vest. With a powerful shake of his head he also threw off his silver helmet, baring his large shaven skull with its one lock of hair at the back. And with his right hand he drew his heavy double-edged sword from its scabbard.

"So that's how it is, Prince Sviatoslav! Who ever said that the Rus are lacking in courage?"

"Kadyma ts'ad!" Joseph ordered his mount, and spurred him forward to impart to his hand not just his own strength but also the momentum of his horse. Now he had a good view of Sviatoslav. Medium height but broad-boned and powerful in the shoulders, with a high forehead and large head. He had an earring in his left ear, and the lock on his head flaxen like the hair of his mother. His narrow waist with its broad leather belt emphasized his broad chest. He had strong hairy legs, like a young bull, and he wore short green leather boots. He braced himself in the stirrups with all the strength of his powerful legs. Indeed, he altogether resembled a young bull.

"Kadyma!" Galloping at full tilt, Joseph stood up in his stirrups and bore down on the enemy with the relentless gleaming sword of Sabriil. He knew his maneuver because Sviatoslav was right-handed and stood his ground waiting. Joseph aimed head on for Sviatoslav's stallion, so the youth could not tell whether he intended to attack from the right or the left. Only at the last moment, when it appeared the horses' heads were bound to smash together and when Sviatoslav had no time to reposition, Joseph with a flip of the reins sent his steed to the *left* of his foe and in a brilliant move shifted his sword from his right to his left hand, to smash through Sviatoslav's bare collarbone.

Joseph's sword glinted in the sun, hardened and tempered as only the Caucasian Alans know how—by galloping into a head wind with the red-hot blade. It crashed down with furious force . . . but it struck not Sviatoslav's bare shoulder, but his powerful cold sword. How, when, and by what lightning movement had the young bull switched the heavy blade to his left hand?

And now, when they came to a dead halt, sword to sword and shoulder to shoulder, Joseph finally met Sviatoslav's gaze. He saw that his eyes were not blue and steely like his mother's, but brown and protruding with black twinkling pupils.

And Joseph saw that this was his own son, and his muscles grew weak and his spirit wavered, for the Jews do not slay their own seed. . . .

"*Ben!*" Joseph breathed the Hebrew word in Sviatoslav's face. "My son!"

But with his free right hand, Sviatoslav drew a short Roman dagger from its sheath strapped to his saddle, and with a lunge embedded it in his father's left shoulder.

Joseph Togarma uttered a gasp, still gazing into the eyes of his son. Then he dropped the holy sword of the Khazarian Kings, the sword of Aaron, Hashmonay, and Sabriil, and fell from his horse.

A wild and joyful cry broke from Sviatoslav's lips. The Rus warriors ran toward the Khazarian cavalry and the fray began. The two wild forces rushed at one another with a snorting of horses and a ringing of swords, showering red-hot blood on every side and uttering shouts of triumph and despair.

But Joseph neither heard nor saw.

Even as the hooves of Sviatoslav's horse trampled his still living body, he saw nothing and felt no pain.

The hair on his chest felt the touch of something gentle and noiseless. Then he fainted away.

In the same way a wild animal halts warily on a woodland path as it hears the wind chase through the treetops.

In the same way any creature faints after a stab to the heart and implores the angels in mute terror and amazement: Surely not now? Is it really time?

The touch of the hand continued—a slow spreading of warm blood across his breast . . . then his stomach . . . then lower . . . And it seemed that angels began singing, drums pealing, and his heart fainted with ecstasy and went limp with a sweet feebleness.

His hand twitched and he felt her fingers—the long, cool, slender fingers of a Russian princess, squeezing his hand in a mute appeal.

He tried to rise, jump up, and soar above this strange princess and angel of death. But her powerful arms with their fine bracelets pinned him down, and he saw her eyes hovering over him—wild eyes, gray-green like hoarfrost, eyes so fathomless that his limbs went weak and his tongue turned dry. It was as though he dove through a hole in a frozen river, and in that frigid depth he became bathed in the hot blood of a pagan sacrifice. And his lips felt the caress of her warm lips. O Lord, hallowed be Thy name! Never had he been touched by such sweet lips! Nowhere had Persian, Greek, Alan, Romanian, or Jewish women ever kissed him like that on the breast, the belly, and the loins! And no one had ever taken his phallus, powerful as that of a Sumerian bull, and plunged it into such a hot, pliant vessel that opened of its own accord and surrounded him with tender and warm coils that drew him in with a python's strength, onward and upward into that magical gallery, forcing him to break the fine membrane of being and nonbeing. And still it continued, further yet—not just his phallus, but his body too, all of him, his entire sinful flesh, and his brain, mind, willpower, and soul. Ever onward! Kadyma! Toward the blinding light where celestial saxophones play, and flutes and violins, and where voices sound of divine sopranos.

"Stop! I'm dying! Wait! Wait!" he shrieked in a noiseless appeal.

She was laughing. Lord, hallowed be Thy name, nobody had ever laughed at such moments as these! But there astride him and preventing any movement, and kissing him both with her lips and with her *fardja*, she laughed as an infant laughs playing with its favorite toy.

"What are you laughing for? Wait!"

"Marry me," she whispered into his ear. "Marry me. Do you hear? I love you, and I want to be your wife! Marry me and take me away from here!"

"But you have a husband, you are the wife of Igor!"

"Kill him! He is your prisoner. Kill him!" She continued whispering and kissing him with hot kisses—everywhere. She played on the stem of his phallus with the tender folds of her bewitching *fardja*. "Kill him and take me away from him! I alone can replace all your other wives, do you hear? Kill him!"

"We never kill our prisoners. You know that."

"But I want to be your wife!" Something had happened to her voice: it had dropped in pitch—turned hoarse and become hard as a blunted blade. "Do you hear, Joseph? I do not want to lose you! I want to be your wife!"

"Impossible!"

The magical fingers went dead, and the heavenly music broke off in midphrase.

He opened his eyes.

Rubinchik was lying amid a boundless field, under a cold night sky, alone. He felt a strange ache in his left shoulder and he was holding two fine bracelets in his right hand. Through the pale night mist—or maybe a flurry of snow—a blurred female silhouette faded into the distance.

AND THE RUSSIAN PRIMARY CHRONICLE, *OR* TALE OF BYGONE YEARS, *TELLS AS FOLLOWS*:

And Sviatoslav did advance upon the Khazars. Hearing of this, the Khazars went forth with their prince and ruler, and they did fight; and in the battle that followed Sviatoslav overcame the Khazars and seized their city.

AND THE ARAB HISTORIAN IBN HAWKAL WRITES OF THE YEARS A.D. 968–9 *AND OF THE CAMPAIGNS OF THE RUS*:

They pillaged the cities of Bulgar, Khazara, Ityl, and Semender, and straightway set out for Rum and Andalus. . . . The Rus laid everything waste and pillaged everything that belonged to the Khazarian, Bulgar, and Bartas peoples on the river Ityl. The Rus took over that country and the residents of Ityl sought refuge on the island of Bag-al-Abvaba, and some in terror settled on the island of Siya-Kukh (Mangyshlak in the Caspian Sea).

AND IN THE YEAR 1834, *THE RUSSIAN HISTORIAN V. GRIGORYEV WROTE AS FOLLOWS*:

The Khazarian people were an unusual phenomenon of the Middle Ages. Surrounded by wild and nomadic tribes, they enjoyed all the advantages of the educated nations: an established system of rule, flourishing and extensive trade, and a regular army. While total anarchy, fanaticism, and darkest ignorance vied for control of Western Europe, the Khazarian state was famed for its justice and tolerance, and people persecuted for their faith fled there from all sides. Like a bright shooting star, Khazaria blazed on the dark horizon of Europe and was then extinguished, leaving no trace of its existence.

Sviatoslav thus annihilated the Khazarian state. With a savagery unknown even to the barbarians of that time, he wiped out all the prisoners of that last battle and left alive not a single witness of his duel with King Joseph. Not even King Joseph's tomb survived, and Sviatoslav renamed the city of Ityl. And he gave the great river the full and sonorous Svensk name of his mother—Volga.

sixty-three

In the morning was the customs inspection. Rubinchik thought he had seen everything Russia had to offer, but this was something new even to him. In the middle of the Customs hall was a ring separated off with ropes. Inside it, behind a row of large flat tables stood the inspectors and the porters. The Jews with their hand luggage were allowed into this area family by family. There they were propelled by a rapidly turning millstone of shouts and orders that whipped and drove them through the relentless machinery.

"Hurry up! Table number five! You old cow, are you deaf? Table five! Move it!"

"Undress the child. Quickly!"

"Put your suitcases up on the table! Whaddya mean, can't lift them? Who's gonna lift it for you? No servants around here! Come on! Get a move on!"

The entire contents were spilled out onto the tables, then sorted and groped by adroit and disdainful hands.

"What's this?"

"School exercise books."

"That's manuscript material. No manuscripts can be exported."

"But these are a student's compositions. Look. *The Image of Natasha Rostova in Tolstoy's* War and Peace . . ."

"Look, just forget it. Give the stuff to the people seeing you off. If you don't have anyone, then toss them over there in the trash. What's this?"

"My mother's necklace."

"Pearls can't be exported. That's contraband."

"What do you mean? Come on, these are just beads!"

"You leave your beads here. And no medicines."

"But they're for my heart! I have a—"

"Just shut up, will you! Now where's your export license for this porcelain? One cup or ten—it makes no difference. Antique porcelain can't be exported without a permit. And what's this?"

The pearls flew across the floor, as if by accident. And china, lacquered wooden boxes, brooches, coral beads, silver, tins of caviar, and bottles of champagne—everything of value was relentlessly swept to one side.

"Hand the brooch to the people seeing you off!"

"We don't have anyone."

"Sorry. Items of national heritage can't be exported. Take those earrings off."

"But personal ornaments are allowed."

"Only to the value of two hundred fifty rubles. Yours are worth more. Take them off! Any other gold items? None, you say? You'll need a gynecological inspection! There, in that booth. Hurry up! And take your daughter too."

"But she's only ten!"

"Doesn't matter. How do we know what you've shoved up between her legs? Think we don't know your tricks? And why are you limping, mister? Take your shoes off! Oh, a wooden leg? We'll have to have a look at that! Take it off! Come on, get moving."

"I'm a war invalid, and a captain of the reserve."

"We've seen you guys before! Probably from Tashkent! Come on, get it off! Looks too heavy to be made of wood. Vanya, give us the saw!"

"What are you going to do? Comrades, how am I going to walk?"

"We're not your Comrades. Your only Comrades are the wolves!"

The saw bit into the wooden leg; screwdrivers dismantled radios and cameras; pliers snapped the levers on a typewriter; an awl pierced accordians' bellows and the heads of dolls; and strong fingers squeezed the paint out of an artist's tubes. It was plain to Rubinchik that here, under the pretense of an official search for contraband, a final act of spiteful vandalism was taking place. Whatever they could not confiscate and acquire for themselves, the Customs officers broke and ruined, creating a pile of scrap and hurling it to the far end of the table along with the torn linings of children's coats, men's jackets, hats, and pillows. All this as if in revenge for the fact that they were forced to stay here while others could leave.

"Don't touch your things! Stand back! The porters will pack everything!"

Hurriedly and carelessly, the porters thrust the jumble back into the suitcases. Half the items would no longer fit in, but the owners were not allowed to touch their own cases, so as to prevent their hiding rings or valuables in them before going through the body search. The gutted suit-cases with the legs of underpants and sleeves of children's dresses sticking out were then carried out onto the platform by porters. These owners then moved along a few yards and stopped at a doorway. Here border guards checked their documents, comparing these with their lists. Every stamp and seal on the exit visa was examined with a magnifying glass and carefully compared with the photographs on the documents. Then two male Customs officers patted down the men and boys, and two female officers gave this treatment to the women and girls.

"Let's see that pacifier! Uncover that child! He won't catch cold, un-cover him and move away! Lay the baby down here, and you go to the gynecologist. That booth over there! You there, turn your pockets out! How many dollars do you have? And what's that pin? Master of sport? No Soviet medals exported. Take it off. And what's that ring? A wedding ring? Precious stones can't be exported. What d'you mean, you can't take it off? If you can't, we'll do it for you!"

People were robbed, undressed, and cleaned out, and then robbed again, down to their last string of beads and their wedding bands—and all this two steps away from the platform where any minute the Vienna train was due. And it was all done quickly, at a set pace, and as if on a conveyor belt. And it was carried out to an accompaniment of barked orders and insults, with such viciousness that who would have imagined these same inspectors, via the porters, had collected four hundred rubles per passenger for performing this charming procedure.

"Baby food cannot be exported!"

"Leave that mink behind. Mink can be exported only if it's an item of clothing."

"But this is a muff."

"No, it's untreated fur. If you don't leave it, you won't get on the train! Quick! Make up your mind!"

People were stunned and in a semitrance gave up their money, furs, necklaces, and rings, letting the officials do whatever they wanted with them, because there, just beyond, just through that door, was a striped barrier marking the frontier.

"Next! Table three! Pick up your cases! Where's the vet's certificate for that dog?"

"Where are your permits for these pictures?"

"Binoculars and optical instruments can't be exported."

"Laundry detergent cannot be exported."

"Measuring instruments cannot be exported."

"Items made of ivory cannot be exported."

As he stood behind the rope awaiting his turn, Rubinchik was constantly watching the clock: yesterday by five Barsky would have discovered he was in Brest, and he'd probably called the Brest Customs. And once he discovered Rubinchik had not yet crossed the frontier, what would Barsky tell them to do? Search and find his goddamned manuscript? But he'd already gotten rid of it, so nothing to fear on that score. On the other hand, Olya had run away and then turned up here, and Barsky at any moment might find out about that. And if he did . . . Oh Lord, what would he do?

As he stood exhausted and sweating in the line to have his hand baggage checked, Rubinchik sensed that his life was hanging by a thread, by a thin nerve end of time. Every ring of the phone at the far end of the Customs Hall could be the fatal summons to repossess his body and soul.

Next to him, across the rope that marked off the ring where suitcases were being gutted, Captain Elena Vasko strode up and down with the gait of an angry bull. Amply built at her breasts and rear, she chain-smoked, her boots clattered on the tile flooring, and through gritted teeth she kept up a grating monologue, "Traitors! Kikes! Fascists! Stand back from the rope! Get back! Filthy Zionists! Back from the rope, you traitors!"

What a bitch, thought Rubinchik. She had collected her share of the bribes from the porters and inspectors first thing in the morning. Now she stalked up and down like a panther swearing at the Jews, so no one would suspect her. Meanwhile the inspectors and porters were all on the rampage, barking and cursing to frighten these Yids and make them dump all their treasures just to get away. It was psychological warfare against helpless victims.

"The Nazis tore off one of my legs with a landmine. And now you've ruined my other one!" the veteran from Minsk called out to Vasko as he sat on the floor strapping on his wooden leg, which had deep saw incisions in two places.

"Go to hell!" she snarled contemptuously.

"Okay, I'm on my way! Even on one leg!" he said. He pressed himself up, stood, and banged on the tiles with his wooden leg. "But neither the blood I shed for you in the war, nor the things you've ripped off us will do you any good. You mark my words, as a captain of the reserve!" And he set off, limping toward the platform.

"Come back here!" Vasko screamed at him, purple with fury. "You're getting a medical inspection!"

The invalid turned and looked straight at her. This new punishment—the anal inspection—would be a ready target for his Jewish wit. He was about to say something to incinerate her or make her a laughingstock, and he had just breathed in to shout it out, when he was gagged by a hysterical cry. "Dad, be quiet! Please!" He looked around at his daughter who had come running up with his two grandchildren.

"Okay, my dear," he said. "Just for you, as a parting gift, I'll go and show them my ass."

"Quiet down! Please, I beg you!" she cut him off again.

Rubinchik looked at the female bison with her captain's shoulder tabs, at the grubby, drink-sodden porters, and at the Customs officers carried away by their frenzy of plundering. Then he looked at the Jews. Like the porters, they too were unshaven, sweating, and frenzied in their stubborn battle for possession of each piece of clothing and every china cup. Good Lord, he thought. To what a bestial state these two nations had reduced one another! Like enraged cattle—both the pillagers, who spared neither old people, women, nor chidren, and the victims, who suffered and fought over every trifle as though their lives depended on it. Yet both were great nations. The Jews were God's chosen people. Yet according to their philosophers, the Russians too were a God-fearing nation. Rubinchik felt like shouting out, "What a fine bunch you are! Just look what you're doing to yourselves!"

But he kept quiet of course. He stood there, filled with a sense of shame and a desire to get drunk. That was a mistake of King Joseph's—such a small mistake—when he offended a young Russian princess by refusing to marry her. And if Pesakh had killed Prince Igor and handed Olga to Joseph as his wife, would all of Russian history have then followed a quite different path?

At that point Rubinchik's thoughts were interrupted as a locomotive drew up outside. The passenger cars were green and had panels on the sides marked MOSCOW–WARSAW–ROME. The queue became agitated. A young Jewess from Baku locked onto the Azerbaijani boyfriend who was seeing her off in a hungry embrace; and a Russian girl from Siberia did the same with a young Jew in horn-rimmed spectacles. It looked almost as if both pairs would get it on with each other right there in public. "I love you! I shall come and find you! I love you!" the temperamental young Azerbaijani shouted after the Jewish girl as she walked off to the Customs examination.

"Shut up!" Captain Vasko yelled at him, then turned to the line: "Next! Table number one!"

The inspectors speeded up their pillaging, and the porters carried suitcases that had been inspected through the control area and onto the platform. There they callously dumped them before returning for a fresh load. Out on the platform, there was nothing left to be gotten from the travelers.

Now, as the train pulled in, the Rubinchiks' turn finally had come.

"Table three! Quickly now! Name?"

"Rubinchik."

Captain Vasko swung round and stared at him.

"Your documents!" she said.

He handed her the exit visas and train tickets.

"Come with me!"

A wave of fear swept through Rubinchik. He grew chilled and his legs turned to cotton-wool as he followed Vasko, with Nelya and the children in his wake.

"All your stuff on the table!" Then, to the inspector, Vasko said, "These people get a category one check!" Then, to Nelya: "You—to the gynecologist!" And again to Rubinchik: "And you for a medical checkup!" Then she grabbed the teddy bear that Borya was hugging and hurled it onto the table with the rest of their things.

Borya began howling.

Two inspectors emptied everything from their suitcases and rapidly began slitting open the linings of jackets, overcoats, children's jackets, packs of fresh women's underwear, packets of tea and coffee. Another inspector began dismantling Rubinchik's camera, a thermos flask, Xenia's doll, and other toys. Thank God, thought Rubinchik, I threw out that brush with the films in it! In a daze, he walked into the small medical examining room. A young red-haired male nurse was waiting; he wore freshly laundered gray overalls and yellow rubber gloves.

"Strip, and put your things down here," he ordered. "Do you have any dental fillings?"

"Yes. Why?" Rubinchik answered.

"Open your mouth! Wider!" The nurse peered into his mouth, and scraped at the fillings with a metal hook. Behind the nurse was a tall door with a mirror set into it. Next to it was a washbasin. A thin stream of water ran from the faucet. "Okay, close your mouth. Right, legs together and bend over with your hands touching the floor! Lower! That's it! Lift your ass! Higher!"

A cold rubber-gloved finger, moist with vaseline, was suddenly rammed up his anus. Rubinchik gasped with pain and tears came to his eyes.

"Ouch, that hurts!"

"Come on, that's nothing!" grinned the male nurse, washing his gloved hands in the stream of water. "Just think what the women put up with! And with no vaseline!"

"Can I get dressed?" Rubinchik asked, looking at his naked self in the mirror. (Why on earth did they need such a big mirror? he wondered. He'd already realized that only Barsky could have detailed that beastly woman to pull him out and give him such a going-over. Anyway, comrade, up yours! Up yours—and with a brass knob! You won't find anything on me! I'm clean! And not in my luggage, either—no manuscript, no gold, no nothing!) "So can I get dressed?"

Rubinchik didn't know that when he almost said "Up yours!," the person he had in mind was a mere two yards away—on the other side of a one-way mirror. Barsky sat there watching every move. On his knee he had a packet of photographs of Rubinchik in action with Natasha Svechkina. He enjoyed seeing his enemy humiliated, and he looked at Rubinchik's thin, bony frame prickled with goose bumps from the cold, the tufts of reddish hair at his groin and under his arms, and his penis dangling lifelessly.

Suddenly, however . . .

Barsky could scarcely believe his eyes! He jumped to his feet and craned his neck forward, almost bumping into the see-through door.

Under Rubinchik's left armpit, close to the shoulder blade was a large birthmark about the size of a string bean.

Exactly like the one Barsky had.

No! he protested, and all his flesh and blood stormed up in revolt. No! Too much! This broke all the rules! Was he living some vulgar melodrama?

Suddenly everything slotted together—the whole guessing game about his own origins and this collision with Rubinchik. So that child—that infant who howled so dreadfully, his own cousin, who had been shoved under the station platform along with Barsky by their grandfather—that child had not been killed, he had survived! By God knows what miracle, he'd ended up in an orphanage, been given a new name, had grown up and become a journalist, and had gone on to seduce his own Olya.

"Okay, get dressed," the male nurse said. Rubinchik quickly put on his clothes, wondering whether this was the end of their travail. If so, it meant Barsky had not learned that Olya was here in Brest. He walked out of the medical booth and saw Xenia and Borya standing by the baggage inspection table looking lost. In one hand Xenia gripped her little violin case, and like a little mother she had her other arm around Borya who stood there, tear-stained and hugging his disemboweled teddy bear. Rubinchik smiled at them from a distance and threw them an encouraging wink. Then he went toward the guards at the platform entrance.

"Turn your pockets out!" they ordered. "Any rings or armbands?"

"No," he answered, and motioned the children to join him.

"No, keep the kids back! How much cash have you got?"

"Three hundred and sixty dollars—the allowance for my wife, me, and the kids."

"Let's see it! And how much in Soviet currency?"

"I don't know. About forty rubles, plus a bit of change . . ."

"Soviet money cannot be exported."

"What do I do with it?"

"None of our business. But it can't be taken out of the country."

Rubinchik raked several crumpled bills and coins from his pocket and looked around for somewhere to put it. He felt like tossing it in the trash bin, but decided against such a show of bravado and simply laid it on the table. The guards pretended not to notice.

"Okay, take the children and go through. The porters will bring your stuff."

"What about my wife?"

"She's on her way. She won't get lost."

Looks like we're through, Rubinchik thought, and at that moment caught sight of Nelya emerging from the gynecological booth. There were tears on her cheeks. Her lips were pale and trembling, and her eyes blazed with more fury than Rubinchik ever thought she had in her.

He prayed that she'd remain quiet and say nothing. She read the message in his eyes and understood.

"Hands out to the side!" said the woman Customs officer and began going over her pockets and clothing.

"I've already been done!" Nelya told her and motioned with her eyes for Rubinchik and the children to go through onto the platform.

Rubinchik picked up Borya and stepped out past the guards towards the platform, when suddenly at the far end of the Customs hall he heard a telephone ring.

One ring ... two ... three ...

A sergeant who was walking along the platform with an Alsatian on a lead, also stopped and listened.

Then someone inside answered the call.

Rubinchik closed his eyes and, despite the frost, felt beads of sweat break out on his forehead. A porter wheeled a hand truck out onto the platform with their three suitcases wide open, their clothing creased and scattered with tea leaves, coffee, and splinters of glass from the broken thermos.

"Here are your things!" he smirked and tipped the whole lot roughly onto the ground at Rubinchik's feet so that the bits of his camera scattered among the dismembered toys.

"Thank you very much!" Rubinchik said, glowering.

"Don't mention it!" the porter retorted and left. Rubinchik knelt down and started repacking their things. Xenia joined in to help. Borya hugged his injured teddy bear.

"That guy was nasty!" the little boy said loudly. "And the lady was too!"

Nelya, finally through passport control, emerged onto the platform. She grabbed Xenia by the hand and picked up Borya and walked down the platform with them, as if to show that the property meant nothing to her.

"Where the hell are you going? Stop!" a guard shouted after her, and the Alsatian growled menacingly. "Emigrants in coaches eleven and twelve only!"

The dog growled again and wrenched at its lead.

Nelya and the children started back in fright.

"Quiet now, Carter!" the guard said. "Sit!"

Further along the platform was a throng of prosperous looking people: well-fed Soviet generals and colonels in astrakhan hats and blue parade-dress overcoats and lower ranking officers, but just as rubicund and in similar dashing jackets, with woven gold belts, gold cockades in their caps, and gleaming epaulettes. There were clean-shaven Soviet diplomats in fur or leather coats, wearing suits from Brooks Brothers and Pierre Cardin; and their wives of varying shapes and sizes, but all in mink capes, sable cloaks, fox coats, or Norwegian shearlings and high-heeled leather boots. The wives of junior officers bought Soviet Eskimo choc ices and Alyonushka chocolates at the kiosk; but the others disdainfully ignored the Soviet-made products and simply walked along the platform, flaunting their stunning coats, gold pendants, and rings ablaze with diamonds. Even the foreign passengers, accustomed to the sight of wealth, looked out of the train windows, surprised. Yesterday evening at the Moscow Belorussky Station, there had been no sables or diamond rings. But here, far from the establishment's ascetic make believe, these people could now demonstrate to one another why they served this Empire, and they showed off the spoils of their castes with the aplomb of aristocrats who ruled half the world.

Only one thing spoiled this fashion parade: the Jews. The changes in them in a single day were amazing. Some forty hours ago, back in Moscow at the station, these same people had seemed prosperous in their Bulgarian shearlings and astrakhan coats. In the train they feasted on caviar, drunk champagne, dreamed boldly of Canada, the States, Australia, and vacations in the Bahamas, and larded their speech with trendy words like "mortgage," "condominium," "bank loan," and "Chevrolet Impala." But after a freezing night on the Brest station square, vicious Customs checks, and painful penetrations of their anal and other apertures, all but gone was the bold self-confidence of God's own people who had once journeyed all the way from Egypt and Spain to Persia and Russia. Where was the famous Jewish wit? Where in those eyes was the wisdom of Spinozas and Einsteins, or the burning passion of Queen Esther? They were now a wretched, tormented, sweaty, and frightened herd, with their snotty and weeping children. Surrounded by guards with dogs, they dragged along the platform suitcases that would not close, with diapers, underpants, and family photographs spilling from them. Just then a gust of snow caught this spillage and swept it off the platform and under the wheels of the train.

"What people!" a young artillery lieutenant commented loudly to his freshly permed wife. "Bloody Jews! They won't even spend two rubles on a porter! Ugh!"

"Like a herd of animals!" his young wife agreed.

"What do you expect from a bunch of traitors?" said a diplomat standing beside them.

"They're like cattle! Nothing but a herd of pigs!" the young lieutenant shared his indignation.

At that point an old, unshaven, lame emigrant in a tattered coat appeared. He had fallen behind the others and was dragging his leatherette case with one hand and a weeping five-year-old grandson with the other. Suddenly his artificial wooden leg gave way, and his face smacked against the frozen concrete. Half his wooden leg flew toward the guard dog-handler with the Alsatian. The animal leapt up and grabbed the scudding piece of wood, and with a playful growl began to chew on it, seemingly daring the old man to come and get it.

"Yuck! Put it down! Leave it!" the soldier yelled. The terrified grandson howled, and the invalid sat there on the ground with his face all bloodied. As the dog smelled blood, it dropped the wooden leg and bristled, no longer playful, and let out a menacing snarl. But the guard shouted again and led the dog away.

"Dreadful! Let's get out of here!" the lieutenant's wife said squeamishly.

The invalid with his face badly cut tried to stand up, but he fell again and only then realized that part of his wooden leg had snapped off. Bleeding and hobbling on one leg, the old man led his sniveling grandson to the train. In his crumpled coat that the Customs had slit open, he looked like a drunk who had staggered out of some second-rate liquor store.

"I don't understand why they let them out," the lieutenant said to the diplomat. "They disgrace us."

Suddenly the bloodied stump of a man addressed him.

"Hey, you in the artillery! If they gave you a mortar, could you hit a stove chimney? Eh?"

"What's he asking?" the lieutenant asked the diplomat.

"He's asking if you can hit a stove chimney with a mortar," the lieutenant's wife said.

"Why on earth should I want to do that?"

"Well, I can!" said the invalid. He leaned on his grandson and stood up. "And I'm going to teach my grandson to do that. So I'll see you on the Golan Heights. Let's go, Menachem."

Leaning on the boy's shoulder, the man hobbled up the platform to the back of the train where the Jews were getting into the eleventh and twelfth cars.

"Hey!" one of the porters shouted after him. "Come back and pick up your leg!"

"I'll take it for him," Rubinchik said. He had already taken two of their

cases to the eleventh car, and with the third one now in tow he picked up
the damaged wooden leg and set off with it. Meanwhile the border guard
with his Alsatian emerged from the eighth car and walked down the platform
toward him, heading for the station. In its teeth the dog held a small black
Grundig dictaphone.

sixty-four

The dog handler walked up to captain vasko, who stood officially at the platform entrance.

"I have something to report, Comrade Captain."

"Let's hear it," she said. "What's your dog got in his teeth?"

"A tape recorder," he said. "Some woman wants it handed to a person
called Barsky."

"Who? Who?" Vasko asked, hardly believing her ears.

The dog handler checked on a scrap of paper.

"That's right, Comrade Captain," he said. "It's for a Colonel Oleg Dmitryevich Barsky. A woman from coach eight, who's emigrating, said it was
to be handed to him personally."

"You're sure it won't explode?"

"If Carter picks it up in his teeth, that means it's clean, Comrade Captain. I can vouch for it."

"Well, okay. Take it to him. He's sitting in my office."

The sergeant and his dog crossed the Customs Hall and went up to
Captain Vasko's office on the second floor. There, two officers were sorting
out a box of items found in nearby garbage bins. Knowing the Jewish emigrants' tendency to panic at the last minute, Vasko had introduced a rule
requiring inspection of all garbage they had ditched before being checked
by Customs. In this trash one could always find things that the bastards had
been too cowardly to show Customs and had not wanted to hand over to
the authorities. Today, for instance, they'd found an unbelievably beautiful
necklace, a small picture of great worth to some museum, several ancient
hand-lettered books in Hebrew, three enamel miniatures, and a shoe brush
from which the experienced inspectors immediately extracted a packet of
photographic negatives. Now, standing by the window with a magnifying
glass, Barsky was examining the negatives and holding them up to the light.

"Excuse me, are you Comrade Barsky?" the guard asked.

"Yes, I am."

The sergeant took the dictaphone from the dog's jaws, wiped off the saliva on his tunic, and then stood to attention.

"Comrade Colonel, I have something to report. A woman in carriage eight asked me to hand over this German tape recorder to you."

Barsky walked over to him, took the recorder and turned it over in his hand, surprised. It was the same little Grundig that Anna had brought with her to the Armenia Restaurant. Had she really decided to present it to him? What a strange gift.

"Will that be all, Comrade Colonel?"

"Yes, you may go." Barsky pressed one of the buttons and the lid popped open, revealing a small cassette. He snapped the lid shut and pressed Play.

He heard Anna's voice.

"You know, Colonel, there's still one thing we didn't finish discussing. . . ."

Barsky immediately pressed the Stop button.

"That's all for the moment," he told the two inspectors. "You can go." With the door closed behind them, he switched it on again.

"I have that sense that women sometimes have," Anna's voice continued, "that something between us was left unsaid. Women always sense these things better than any man, you know that. And I've known for a long time that there's something you want to say to me. So why are you wasting time? Are you afraid? You've got only twenty minutes left before this train leaves. Unless you want to travel with me across Poland, as far as the Austrian frontier. Goodness, Oleg, I can just visualize the surprise on your face. But at our first meeting, remember, you asked me why I have only Jewish men as friends. Well, now you can compete with them on an equal footing, can't you? I'm in coach eight, in the first compartment. Don't ask how much it cost me. But if you come, then I'm sure you can settle my dog up with the conductress while we talk. He seems to have taken a dislike to you. I wonder why? I hope you can tell me. So . . . I'm waiting. This is Anna. Over to you."

At 11:25 A.M the MOSCOW–WARSAW–ROME train slowly pulled out of Brest. A company of young officers, each holding a bottle of Soviet champagne, leapt aboard coach eight when the train was already moving. The conductors with their yellow flags took up positions on the railroad car steps. The locomotive sent a farewell hoot to the motherland and rolled ahead toward the open barrier and the pillar marked

STATE FRONTIER OF THE USSR

The Jews in coaches eleven and twelve impatiently pressed their faces to the windows. And when the striped pillar floated past and disappeared, along with the stern-looking border guards and the Kalishnikovs across their chests, loud sighs of relief broke from a hundred pairs of lungs. People embraced one another, crying with joy and congratulating one another. Someone prayed aloud: "Shema Yisrael! Baruch Ataw, Adonai Elohainu!" Someone else popped a champagne bottle, while another loudly warned them, "Careful, Jews! This is still only Poland!"

"Daddy," Xenia asked, "Are Jews safe from getting beaten up in this country?"

"Oh, they beat them here all right! No doubt about it!" the blue-eyed Levite answered, for some reason quite merrily.

"But is there a place where they won't hit us, Daddy?" Xenia asked.

Rubinchik put his arm round Nelya, who was weeping.

"We're out already!" he said. "You see? We're out!"

Behind the train, beyond the barrier that again was lowered, the border guards with their dogs and the porters walked along the empty platform picking up the bits and pieces that had fallen from the cases of the Yids. Meanwhile, back on the Brest station square, a new encampment was busy settling down with their children, suitcases, dogs, and a cage with a Yiddish-speaking parrot.

And to one side, by the fence that closed off the platform area, three others stood—a youth from Azerbaijan, a girl from Siberia, and Olya Barsky.

Through the swirling wind and snow they all thought they could still hear the sound of the departing train.

But at that moment, the buffers clanged and the train came to a sharp halt.

"This will be another inspection," the war invalid piped up. He now had his face plastered and bandaged. "I guess they still didn't take quite everything!"

Rubinchik froze and closed his eyes.

"Only the Moscow or the Polish secret police can stop a train like this, in the middle of nowhere," the Levite commented.

The door of the car swung open, and two conductors stood there—a tall, solidly built man in his mid-forties and a woman slightly shorter and younger. The man smiled and made an announcement.

"This is a notice to all Jews!" he called. "There are two available coaches on this train going directly to Vienna. Anyone wanting a ticket is welcome. The cost is ninety dollars a person. My advice to you is don't try and save your money, because the porters in Warsaw take thirty for each suitcase!" He kept walking down the corridor, loudly announcing: "Coaches nine and ten go direct to Vienna without changing! The cost is ninety dollars per person!"

The Jews exchanged astonished looks and whispered comments. Ninety dollars was exactly the amount they'd been permitted to take out of the USSR after paying all the Customs duties. Not a cent more. In other words, this was the last money they had.

"I saw it coming!" the war invalid said. "Until they take everything from us, they won't be content. But we're going to have to pay up, my dear," he told his daughter. "Because the Poles could be even worse. At least with this bunch we know who we're dealing with!"

Two hundred Jews hurried to line up in front of the female conductor in the doorway, and she began collecting their money and letting them through into coaches nine and ten. Minutes later she was rejoined by her colleague who'd completed making his announcement. Together they worked at a merry pace and the green dollar bills crackled as they whisked into their hands. While handing his money over, Rubinchik noted the boots worn by the two conductors, identical black leather uniform boots. Rubinchik knew and recognized the style—the militiamen who'd broken into his hotel room at Salekhard had worn exactly this footwear, as had Barsky when he kicked Rubinchik senseless on the shore of that reservoir.

The cold winter air was split by another wail from the train whistle, and the Moscow–Warsaw–Rome express got under way again, heading west. Twelve hours later it reached Bratislava and came to a halt at another border, beyond which lay Austria.

On the far side, Austrian border officials were waiting for the train along with a thick-set, black-haired man with no hat. He wore an expensive leather coat with a fur collar and carried a huge bouquet of red roses.

Earlier, however, the train had stopped just to the east of the border, in Bratislava. There, Czech border guards had carried out their own inspection. As they approached the train, they were met by a Colonel Barsky, who disembarked from coach number eight. He had the illuminated countenance of a man who had just come to know God, via His greatest creation—a Russian woman. Barsky looked down the track toward the border. In the distance he glimpsed the dark man with the bouquet of roses, and his lips curled in a mischievous smile. He stayed lit up by the same smile as he showed the Czech border guards his KGB pass and inquired whether there was any pilsner beer to be had at the station. Hearing that there was, he headed for the buffet.

Meanwhile in the first compartment of coach number eight, a slim oblong had been left lying on the small folding table. Anna opened it curiously and pulled out a wad of photographic negatives. She took the top one off the pile and held it up to the window. By straining her eyes, it was just possible to make out the first lines of a text. It read:

"Do you know what it means to be a Russian woman?" he asked. "That is, what it means to be a real *Russian woman?"*

Lake Mohican, Catskill Mountains, 1991–92;
Alyonushka Camp, Long Island, 1995.

TOPOL Topol, Edward,
    1938-

    The Jewish lover.

$25.95

DATE			

BAKER & TAYLOR